IN THE PRESE
OF MADNESS
BOOK ONE

RAY YARWOOD

This is the first of two
related novels which
are dedicated to my
wonderful family and closest
friends who combined to
help me through the greatest
crisis of my life.
I love you all
Enjoy the journey.

PUBLISHER'S NOTE.
This is a work of fiction. Names, characters, places and incidents are a product of the author's imagination. Locales and public names are sometimes used for atmospheric purposes. Any resemblance to actual people, living or dead, or to businesses, companies, events, institutions or locales is completely coincidental.

Please also note that this novel was written over a decade before the Coronavirus became a pandemic and it therefore should be stated that the author does not intend or never has intended to profit from or make light of the suffering that has been a terrible and almost inescapable consequence.

Cover illustration Mike Kotsch.
Cover design by Mark James Craven

TABLE OF CONTENTS

CHAPTER ONE
SETTING OUT

On a bitterly cold morning on the 12th of December, 2007, an immaculately dressed and exceptionally well groomed old man shuffled along a newly constructed railway station platform on the outskirts of South London and after stopping and resting his battered old leather case on the ground, he drew his right hand to his mouth and began to tremble. He had shown little interest in the cleverly replicated Victorian style station, neither had he considered pausing to admire one or more of the many floor standing vending machines that for one old English penny or a sixpenny bit could, with a little bit of persuasion, dispense a variety of things such as bars of Nestles Five Boys chocolate, packets of Wrigley's Spearmint Gum and sleeves of Bryant and May pocket matchbooks. They were little more than a sideshow as far as he was concerned because he had made his way to that area of London to see and run the rule over one particular thing and one particular thing only-the magnificent Oriental Express locomotive, a modern mechanical and computerised wonder that was an almost perfect replica of the original long distance Luxury Paris to Constantinople passenger train, the Orient Express, which had first entered public service on the 5th June 1883.

The old man's delight and sense of awe had been short lived however because within seconds of settling down on a heavily varnished bench in order to regain his breath, take a pill and admire the hugely impressive engine at closer quarters, he had found his view almost completely obscured by a steadily increasing crowd of rowdy characters many of whom were clearly the worse for strong alcohol and one of which was in the process of vomiting his previous evening's supper into a greasy brown paper bag. Within minutes, the noise level had become such that the aging observer had found himself stooping forward with his frail hands over his ears-a position he might well have chosen to maintain had it not been for the arrival of a tall, powerfully built grey haired individual who had immediately set about the unenviable task of trying to turn chaos into something akin to order.

That particular individual was Tommy Weir, the highly respected and no nonsense Chairman of the Edinburgh Inn Veteran Men's Football Club that was based in Crosby in Merseyside. Weir was an extremely strong willed individual who, within 6 months of being elected into office, had taken the club from the brink of financial ruin to a position of relative economic stability. He was flanked by two stern looking men dressed in club blazers and grey flannels-a beleaguered and harassed looking Jeff Hill who had served as secretary since the club's inception, and Kenny Hulme, the club's recently appointed Vice Chairman who was shivering badly and giving the impression he would rather be somewhere else. Within minutes, those three committee members had found themselves surrounded by a dozen or so highly confused club members, one of which was the enormous former nightclub doorman Paul, Woody, Woodhouse.

How's it hanging girls?" he asked before dropping his tightly packed army surplus holdall onto his toes, peeling back a Velcro strap and removing a parcel containing what looked like the remnants of his breakfast. "You don't mind if I finish this off here do you?"

"Just be quick about it," said the Chairman.

"And make sure you don't take it onto the train with you," said the Club Secretary.

"That's right," said the Chairman.

"Alright," said Woodhouse. "Jesus Christ boys! I thought we were meant to be going away to have a bit of fun."

"We are," said the Chairman.

"You could have fooled me Tommy," said Woodhouse.

"You've got a right gob on you. What's the matter?"

"Your t-shirt, for one thing" said the Chairman.

"This?" said the indignant Woodhouse before taking a step back and picking the shirt off his considerable chest. "What's wrong with it?"

"It's offensive-that's what's wrong with it," said Weir.

"In what way?" said Woodhouse.

"It's offensive to women," said Weir. "And because my late mother just happened to be a woman and my good wife's a woman and my daughter's a woman, it's offensive to me as well."

"Bloody hell Tommy," said Woody. "Just because I wear this thing doesn't mean I think all women should be chained to the kitchen sink in just their underwear. It's just a bit of fun for God's sake."

"Not as far as I'm concerned," said the Chairman. "Get it off."

"Get it off!" said Woodhouse. "Behave yourself will you Tommy. It's got to be minus 10 degrees on this bloody platform. I'll freeze to death."

"Get it off or start making your way back to Crosby," said Weir.

"What if I cover it up with something?" said Woodhouse while trying unsuccessfully to raise the zip on his ill fitting top.

"Take it off," barked the Chairman. "I won't tell you again Woody. Change it or you can forget about boarding this train."

There had been several more problems for the club Chairman to deal with over the next half hour and although all the others had been resolved almost immediately and without too much fuss, there was another that he and his fellow committee members had anticipated for some time.

"Your al fella's not pissed is he?" said Weir after placing an arm around the shoulder of the youngest tourist Anthony Biddo and taking him to one side.

"I don't think so," replied the young man while watching his pale faced father staggering aimlessly through the lines of waiting passengers.

"He's got a fair old stagger on," said the Club Secretary.

"That's what I was thinking," said Weir.

"He's not pissed," said young Anthony. "He's been ill."

"How do you mean, ill?" said Weir.

"Food poisoning," said young Anthony.

"Food poisoning!" said Weir. "That's a good one. I hope you're right Anthony. Because if I find out he's pissed, he can not only say goodbye to our little excursion, he can kiss goodbye to his club membership once and for all."

"Tommy's right Anthony," said the Club Secretary. "This is a brand new, state of the art train. It's cost millions to put together apparently. We can't afford to have him make any mess or do any damage."

"He's alright I tell you," said young Anthony. "He's just a bit under the weather that's all. He'll be alright-I promise you. That's what I'm here for. I'll look after him. He'll be as good as gold, I promise you."

"He better be," said Weir before encouraging the gathering to follow him so that he could give them a tour of the newly constructed Victorian style platform.

For the next fifteen minutes, the Chairman did his utmost to get the group of largely hung over, intoxicated, disinterested or sleep deprived men to appreciate the craftsmanship and attention to detail that had gone into the building and replication of the new station. He had firstly stopped a few yards short of the waiting rooms to point out the intricately carved under eaves and the two stunted brick and mortar stacks supporting a pair of tall crown top salt glazed chimney pots; an aspect of the build that Weir had suggested wouldn't have been out of place in the fine art section of any local antique sale. He had then turned the men's attention to the contextually fitted buffet room with its sturdy oak panelled counter, yellow gingham tablecloths and magnificent Sheffield plated tea urn that because of its numerous spouts and Bakelite handles, looked like something contrived from the imagination of a writer of science fiction. From there, and with ever increasing enthusiasm, he had progressed to one of the two cosy waiting rooms each with their own cast iron wood burning stove and both, despite one or two design differences, as welcoming and authentic as the other. That was when he realised his original 17 man entourage had dwindled to a mere three men and the reason he had chosen to bring the short tour to a premature conclusion.

Thank God for that," said a shivering Woodhouse while trying to dislodge a piece of fried chicken from between his lower back teeth. "I thought I was going to die of boredom in that waiting room. Can we get on board the train now?"

"We're missing a couple of people," said an extremely flustered Jeff Hill while trying unsuccessfully to make an accurate count of those already in attendance.

"Who are they?" said the Chairman.

"Steve Kilgallon and Mark Murphy, if I'm not mistaken," said Hill before puffing out his cheeks and shaking his head. "Why doesn't that surprise me?" said the Chairman. "It beggars belief doesn't it. This happens every time we go away."

"Calm down Tommy," said Woodhouse. "You're going to make yourself ill. I've just spoken to Killer and Murphy. They're on their way as we speak."

"How do you mean, 'on their way'?" said the Chairman.

"They're about twenty minutes away," said Woodhouse. "They're just running a bit late."

"I could have told you they were running late," said the Chairman. "I want to know why."

"Apparently there was six inches of snow on Kilgallon's windscreen," said Woodhouse.

"And don't tell me Woody," said the Club Secretary. "He tried to clear it away with his wipers didn't he?"

"The soft bugger will have blown a fuse," said the

Chairman. "Which is very close to what I'm about to do."

"Do you want me to phone them and see where they are?" said Woodhouse.

"You can phone them if you want," said the Chairman.

"And tell them what?" said Woodhouse.

"Tell them to turn around and go home," said the Chairman.

"What!" said Woodhouse. "Are you having a laugh Tommy?"

"I'm being serious," said Weir. "Tell them to turn their car around and go home. I've had enough of them."

"But they'll be here in a few minutes," said Woodhouse while looking pleadingly to his fellow members for some sort of support. "They're probably just around the corner."

"I couldn't care less," said the Chairman. "It isn't the first time they've let us down. Now ring them and tell them to turn their car around."

"The Chairman's right," said a disdainful club stalwart Brian Matthews after removing a crumpled piece of paper from the inside pocket of his coat and holding it aloft. "It's all here. We were all provided with a schedule. They knew what time they had to be here."

"You keep out of this Matthews," said Woodhouse. "This has nothing to do with you. You're not even on the committee. And despite all your arse licking, you're never likely to be. Watch my lips will you. The lads are on their way. Think about it Matthews-how would you like it if you were forced to miss the trip for the sake of a couple of minutes?"

"It's not a couple of minutes," said Matthews.

"I thought I told you to keep out of this," said Woodhouse.

"Tell them to turn around Woody," said the Chairman.

Had Woodhouse told the truth that Kilgallon and Mark Murphy were actually more than an hour away from the London station at that time, the argument might well have ended right then and there but it was to terminate anyway a few minutes later after a crimson faced Club Secretary had returned from another count of the assembly.

"What do you mean, 'we're going to need to find a mop and bucket'?" said the Chairman while slowly meandering through the tightly knit scrum of confused club members.

"Kenny Biddo's thrown up," said the Club Secretary.

"Oh, for Christ's sake," said the Chairman.

"I warned you Tommy," said the Club Secretary. "Don't say I didn't warn you. He's an absolute disgrace."

"Fuck off Hilly," said Biddo after dabbing his lips. "I'm not very well."

"Not very well!" said the Club Secretary. "I'll tell you what's wrong with you Biddo...You're pissed out of your mind. You can't kid me fella. I know you too well. You've been on the ale."

"I'm ill," said Biddo. "I've been ill all week. I've had food poisoning. I thought I was dying at one time. I thought my end had come. Ask Anthony..Tell him Anthony. Tell him what I've been like. Go on son...tell them."

"I told them before," said Anthony. "I told them you'd been really bad."

"He's pissed," said the Club Secretary.

"I'm not," said Biddo. "Tell them Anthony-tell them what I've been like. They don't believe me. They're going to send me home like the other two poor sods. Make them realise the truth son. Give the bastards some details."

"He's been really ill, I'm telling you," said Anthony. "I've never known him to be so ill. He messed the bed three times last night. There was shite everywhere. His bedroom stunk to high hell. I've never smelled anything like it. Me mum was up all morning washing his sheets. She's even had to throw his Star Wars pyjamas away."

"Oh for crying out loud!" said Biddo. "What are you doing to me son? They don't need to hear all that."

[7]

"I thought you wanted me to give them details," said Anthony.

"I do," said Biddo. "But not that sort of detail. Not personal stuff like that. For God's sake. I'm going to be a laughing stock now."

"What the hell did you want me to say?" said Anthony.

"You could have told them what tablets I'd been on or how high my temperature had been," said Biddo. "You could have told them about the rancid fish I'd ate the Tuesday before. The mackerel that was well past its sell by date. That would have sufficed. You had that fish too, don't forget. You said yourself that it tasted a bit off, didn't you son?"

"I did yes," said Anthony.

"Well I don't think your condition's got anything to do with bad fish," said the Club Secretary. "I still think you're pissed Biddo. And because of that, I don't think you should be allowed to board this train."

"You'd like that wouldn't you Hilly," said Biddo. "You'd love that. That'd suit you down to the ground. The hitman strikes again."

"What's that meant to mean?" said the Club Secretary.

"You know exactly what I mean," said Biddo. "You've blackballed so many people Hilly. There used to be 46 members of this club. Now we're reduced to inviting guests. But I'll tell you what...I'll tell you what should I Hilly.....If it makes you happy, I'll get my things together and make me way home."

"Do you want any help?" said the Club Secretary.

"Piss off," said Biddo.

"It'd certainly make our jobs so much easier if you left," said the Chairman. "But we all know you're not going to do that Biddo."

"And what's that meant to mean Tommy?" said Biddo.

"I'll tell you what it's meant to mean shall I," said the Chairman while pointing towards the restaurant carriage. "There's hundreds of gallons of free ale on that train Biddo. You'd never want to miss out on that would you? It'd break your heart. Now for God's sake, go and get yourself cleaned up. You're a bloody mess. You look like something the cat's just decided not to drag in."

"Does that mean I can still come along?" said Biddo.

"It does yes," said the Chairman. "I'm going to give you the benefit of the doubt on this occasion. But remember this Biddo. And remember it well. You're skating on the thinnest of thin ice lad. And I don't think someone in your delicate condition should be skating at all."

There was no doubt at all that none of the committee members had been entirely convinced by Kenny Biddo's explanation regarding his condition and had it not been for the fact that his son was on the passenger list and would therefore be on hand to keep him out of trouble and restrict the amount of alcohol he consumed, the Chairman would have almost certainly censored him and sent him home at that particular point.

In fact, even when the remorseful looking Biddo had returned from the washroom looking considerably more refreshed, the debate had continued. There was therefore nobody more relieved than the notorious heavy drinker when the focus of the group's attention shifted to another member of the club-a very different individual.

"Are you going to send that privileged waste of space home?" said Woodhouse after suddenly noticing ex public schoolboy Richard Hewlett and his heavily perspiring valet exiting the nearest of the two impressive waiting rooms.

"Hewlett was the first to arrive," said the Chairman. "He's been taking a tour of the station."

"I didn't know it was fancy dress," said Woodhouse.

"Don't be so stupid," said Hewlett before ordering his aide to drop his three antique tan leather Louis Vuitton suitcases at his feet. "Didn't you bother reading the latest club newsletter?"

"What newsletter?" replied Woodhouse.

"The one requesting all members dress appropriate to the great age of steam travel," said Hewlett.

"I didn't receive one of those," said Woodhouse.

[9]

"I can see that," said Hewlett while proceeding to regard the big man from head to toe. "Although you do carry that particular look very impressively."

"What particular look would that be," said Woodhouse.

"The 1970s Scouse benefit scrounger look," said Hewlett.

"It's called a shell suit," said Woodhouse. "It happens to be extremely comfortable. I'll change into something a little more formal later. But listen needle dick-while we're on the subject of clothes-let me ask you something. If we're only going to be away a relatively short length of time, what's with all the fancy luggage?"

"That would be patently obvious to anyone of breeding," said Hewlett.

"Help me out then," said Woodhouse. "I haven't been fed with a silver spoon or afforded the luxury of a public school education."

"Very well, if you insist," said Hewlett while removing his gloves. "I brought along this amount of luggage because we'll be dining at least 8 times and steam travel, people of quality always liked to dress differently for each meal whether it be breakfast, lunch or dinner. I'll be doing exactly that. What have you brought to change into-a pair of pyjama bottoms and a tank top?"

"That's my business," said Woodhouse. "And by the way-whether you like it or not-and whether you think it looks classy or not-I think you look ridiculous."

"You're the one that looks ridiculous," said Hewlett.

"Why's that?" said Woodhouse.

"Because you do," said Hewlett. "You're wearing sports clothes. Look at the shape you're in for goodness sake. Someone as grossly overweight as you can't possibly purport to be a sportsperson. What sport could you possibly indulge in?"

"Golf, for one thing," said Woodhouse.

"Golf!" said Hewlett. "I assume you're talking about the miniature or municipal type."

"It's neither," said Woodhouse. "It's the links type actually. I've just become a member of a prestigious private golf club."

"Would that be the much vaunted Royal Bootle?" said Hewlett.

"It would not," said Woodhouse.

"Aintree Municipal then?" said Hewlett.

"You're getting warmer," said Woodhouse. "I'll give you a clue. It's right next to the coastguard station by Hall Road."

"Right next to the coastguard station!" said Hewlett after placing both his hands on his hips and looking upwards. "Do you mean West Lancs? You don't mean West Lancashire Golf Club do you?"

"That's the baby," said Woodhouse. "It's a bit on the shabby side but it only needs a lick of paint here and there. I was accepted last Monday evening."

"You're a liar," said Hewlett.

"It's the God's honest truth," said Woodhouse.

"Who proposed you?" said Hewlett.

"The chairman of the Crosby branch of the Rotary Club," said Woodhouse. "We go back a long way."

"Rubbish!" said Hewlett.

"It's not rubbish at all," said Woodhouse. "I was welcomed with open arms. My money's as good as the next man's."

"It's not as good as mine," said Hewlett. "I've worked extremely hard for what I own. You've earned your money by punching drunken morons on the nose."

"Only those who deserved it," said Woodhouse.

"Well I don't believe you," said Hewlett. "I can't see a club as prestigious as West Lancs allowing the likes of you to join. You're just not the type. You're a ruffian. You're basically scum. And anyway-look at the state of your clothes...what are you going to go round the course in?"

"Under 80, if my current form is 's anything to go by," said a beaming Woodhouse before breaking off and exchanging a series of elaborate high fives with his nearest neighbours.

For the next few minutes, because he had failed

to get the better of the exchange between himself and a man he felt was vastly intellectually inferior, the infamously aloof Hewlett had done everything in his power to reignite the conversation and he was therefore extremely disappointed when the club Chairman suddenly stepped forward to address the gathering once again.

"Listen lads-I'm hearing a lot of muttering and sensing a certain amount of unrest," he said before folding his arms and taking a step back. "It seems to suggest one or two of you have got issues you'd like to raise. If that's right, I'd like you to speak up now. Does anyone have anything they'd like to get off their chest before we start boarding the train?"

"I've got plenty," came a voice from the rear that was soon recognised as that of Tony Hamill who at best could only be regarded as an occasional member of the club due to his intense dislike of the Club Secretary and his best friend Kenny Hulme, the club vice chairman.

"Fire away when you're ready Tony," said the Chairman. "What's on your mind lad?"

"I'd like to take issue regarding the two members you've just sent home," said Hamill.

"I'm listening," said the Chairman.

"I think you were bang out of order Tommy," said Hamill.

"So do I," said Woodhouse.

"They were late," said the Chairman.

"Considerably late," said the Club Secretary Jeff Hill. And not for the first time, might I add."

"For the umpteenth time," said the Chairman.

"It still seemed a bit heavy handed," said Hamill.

"They've been looking forward to this trip for a long time."

"They have," said Woodhouse.

"That means they've had plenty of time to make preparations for it," said the Chairman.

"They had to be taught a lesson," said the Club Secretary. "Kilgallon's never on time. And Murphy's notorious for sleeping in. Jesus Christ...last year he slept right through the entire Easter holiday period."

"That's a fact," said the Chairman. "Did you know that one of his neighbours felt the need to call the police Hamill?"

"Why's that?" said Hamill.

"The milk bottles were mounting up," said the Chairman. "They thought he'd passed away."

"I couldn't care less what his neighbours thought," said Hamill. "It's what me and the other members think that matters. And I think your punishment was excessive."

"Well I don't," said the Club Secretary.

"Your complaint has been duly noted Hamill," said the Chairman. "And I'll convene an extraordinary club meeting as soon as we get back to Crosby. For now though-those two lads are heading back north and nothing you or anyone else says is going to make me change my stance on the matter."

"That's very democratic of you Tommy," said Hamill before forcing his way through the crowd and returning to his original place at the back of the group.

"It's the way it is," said Weir. "Is there anything else lads?"

"I've got a problem," said Kenny Biddo.

"We're well aware of that," said the Club Secretary.

"You shut your mouth Hilly," said Biddo. "It's alright for you."

"What's alright for me?" said the Club Secretary.

"Your accommodation plans," said Biddo.

"What about my accommodation plans?" said Hill.

"Yes-what about them Biddo?" said the Chairman. "What's your problem?"

"You know damn well what the problem is," said Biddo.

"I'm sorry, I don't," said the highly confused Chairman. "You're going to have to tell me. What's your problem?"

"Who I'm being forced to share a room with is the problem," said Biddo.

[13]

"What are you talking about?" said Weir. "We haven't announced or finalised the room arrangements yet, for God's sake."

"You must have told someone," said Biddo.

"Why's that?" said the Chairman.

"Because someone told me," said Biddo. "I've known the bad news for some time."

"What bad news?" said the Chairman.

"That I'm going to be rooming with one of them," said Biddo.

"One of what?" said the Chairman.

"One of the fudge packers," said Biddo.

"What!" said the Club Secretary.

"What the hell are you talking about?" said the Chairman before turning to the group. "Can somebody please explain what this fella's problem is. Do you know what he's going on about Anthony?"

"The lads have been winding him up Tommy," said Ian, Blackie, Blackhurst, Kenny Biddo's nephew.

"In what way?" said the Chairman.

"They told him he'd be sharing a room with Eddie Meehan," said Blackie.

"Eddie Meehan!" said the Chairman. "Why would that be considered a problem?"

"Because they told him Eddie's an arse bandit," said Blackie.

"Oh nice one," said the Chairman.

"That's what I thought," said Biddo.

"Eddie's a happily married man," said Matthews.

"That's right," said the Chairman. "He's been happily married for nigh on 40 years. Bloody hell lads...who thought that little prank up? Does anyone want to own up?"

"It was just a bit of fun," said Woodhouse.

"Well it was a bit of fun we could have done without," said the Chairman. "You know what he's like regarding homosexuals. He can't get his head around the gay thing. He never has been able to."

"It's not right to be gay," said Biddo. "A man should be

with a woman. It says so in the Bible."
"How would you know?" said Woodhouse. "The only
time you've seen a Bible is when you've been up before
a magistrate. You've never read the bible in your life."
"Maybe not but I've seen the film at least twice," said
Biddo.
"What bloody film?" said Woodhouse.
"The one where John Wayne plays a Roman soldier,"
said Biddo.
"Oh, for the love of God!" said the Chairman.
"I told him not to worry," said Blackie. "Let's be
honest-if there's a gay person on board that train who's
looking for a handsome love interest, he's only going to
be looking one way isn't he?"
"Of course he is," said the Club Secretary. "I
sometimes feel sorry for you Blackie. It must be a hell
of a burden being so damn handsome."
"It's something I've just had to learn to live with," said
Blackie.
"Can we please move on to more serious things now
gentlemen?" said the Chairman.
"Like what?" said Hamill.
"Like a reminder of how to behave," said the Chairman.
"We know how to behave," said Hamill. "We're not
schoolchildren. We're nearly all middle aged family
men for Christ's sake."
"We were nearly all middle aged family men last year
when Tommy McShane kicked a sniffer dog to death for
nuzzling his balls at John Lennon airport," said the
Chairman.
"That wasn't my fault," said McShane. "The thing was
mental. It was more like a wolf than a dog. I thought it
was about to tuck in to me meat and two veg."
"I told you to wear undercrackers," said Woodhouse.
"And what about Alec Morris?" said the Club Secretary.
"What about me?" said the infamously belligerent
Morris after easing his way to the front of the crowd.
"What am I meant to have done?"
"You nearly wiped us all out," said the Club Secretary.

"Don't you remember?"

"I do," said the Chairman.

"When was this?" said Morris.

"On a flight to Benidorm 3 years ago," said the Chairman. "You must remember the incident Alec. The story made headlines in some of the Spanish newspapers."

"You and a few others had been invited to visit the cockpit by one of the stewardesses," said the Club Secretary. "But as usual, you couldn't keep your hands to yourself could you? You had to go poking around, didn't you Alec?"

"I don't remember that," said Morris.

"You wouldn't," said Hill. "You were pissed. You'd had your two and a half pint quota by then,"

"You took the plane off autopilot Alec," said the Chairman.

"Did I?" said Morris.

"You most certainly did," said the Chairman.

"Where was the pilot while all that was going on?" said Woodhouse.

"He was flirting with some tasty young bird at the back of the plane," said Hill. "We plummeted 1000 feet in 6 seconds. It caused pandemonium. It was later reported that 2 people had suffered heart attacks and a fifteen year old schoolgirl from Netherton had given birth to twins 3 months before they were due to arrive."

"I bet she was surprised," said Blackhurst.

"Not as surprised as her parents," said Hill. "They didn't even know the fat cow was pregnant."

"Oh yes...I remember that now," said Morris. "Didn't it rain all that day?"

"I don't know Alec," said the Chairman. "As the Chairman of the club, I was held responsible for your actions. I spent the entire day in a grotty jail cell with a drunk who had the worst bad breath imaginable and someone under the influence of heavy drugs who thought he was Bob Dylan."

"That's just one of the reasons we've asked Eddie

Meehan to come along," said Hill.

"That's right," said the Chairman. "This trip might seem very attractive on the face of it but we're going to be travelling on, dining on and sleeping on millions of pounds worth of train. The club's in no position to pay for damages if something was to go wrong."

"That's right," said the Club Secretary. "Eddie's going to be invaluable to us."

"Why's that?" said Hamill.

"He's a Health and Safety Officer," said the Club Secretary.

"One of the most experienced and respected in the country," said the Chairman.

"That's great," said Hamill. "That's all we bloody well need."

"It's exactly what we need," said the Chairman. "And if anyone doesn't like the idea, now might be a good time to speak up."

"I don't like the idea," said Hamill.

"Your opposition to the matter raised has once again been duly noted," said the Chairman.

"What don't you like Hamill?" said the Club Secretary.

"I don't like any of it," said Hamill. "Why should we be told what to do by someone who isn't even a member of our club?"

"I have to agree," said Woodhouse. "I think the idea's preposterous. I think it's going to cause problems rather than prevent them."

"I think it's going to cause blue murder," said Hamill.

"Then let it cause murder," said the Chairman. "But if you don't like the idea, you could always form an orderly queue in front of Hilly. He'll give you your fares back to Liverpool. I'll sanction that. In the meantime, I suggest those who choose to remain, go and use the men's washroom at the end of the platform."

"Why the platform?" said Hamill. "Are there no toilets on the bloody train?"

"Of course there are," said the Chairman. "But you're not going to be able to use them until we're a few miles

[17]

from the station."

"It states that in the newsletter," said Matthews.

"It does," said Eddie Meehan after striding forward confidently to take up a position at the Chairman's right shoulder. "And that mightn't be a bad place to begin my presentation."

"What mightn't be?" said Woodhouse.

"How to use the train's toilets," said Meehan.

"Oh, for Christ's sake!" said Woodhouse.

"It might surprise you to know that I've actually been potty trained since the age of two," said Hamill.

"It doesn't surprise me at all," said Meehan. "But I very much doubt if you've ever been tutored in the art of using a convenience while a state of the art steam train is in motion."

"It's just common sense isn't it?" said Hamill. "You just have to hang on to something don't you?"

"You'd think so," said a smiling Meehan. "But did you know that last year alone, over 18,000 people suffered minor to serious injuries after slipping off a train's lavatory seat?"

"Did they really?" said Hamill.

"I'm sensing a certain doubt in your tone," said Meehan. "Do you doubt those numbers?"

"I do as it happens," said Hamill.

"Why's that?" said Meehan.

"Because I find it a bit hard to believe so many people would report something like that," said Hamill. "I'd have thought people would have wanted to keep an experience like that to themselves. I know I would."

"Well apparently over 18,000 rail travellers don't think like you," said Meehan. "So might I suggest you pin back your ears and listen very carefully. It might just prevent you from suffering the indignity of being carried off the train semi-conscious with your underpants soiled and your trousers around your ankles."

"It wouldn't be the first time for some of these reprobates," said Woodhouse.

"You shut your mouth Woodhouse," said Biddo. "That

happened only the once."

"Can we cut out the wisecracks for a few minutes lads," said the Chairman who was not only becoming more and more agitated due to the inability of some of the men to take things seriously but because he was becoming increasingly suspicious regarding the presence of the old man who, for some unknown reason, had moved to his rear and seemed to be taking more than a passive interest in what was taking place. Eddie Meehan continued nevertheless.

"What the hell now?" said Hamill after the Health and Safety Officer had produced two laminated diagrams and held them to each side of his body. "I knew it. We're going to be potty trained aren't we?"

"Not exactly," said Meehan. "I want you all to look closely at these diagrams. They show the correct way and the wrong way to sit down on a train's lavatory seat. Take your time. Look at diagram A and then diagram B. What can you tell me about the two diagrams?"

"The fella on the right's reading a Harry Potter book," said Blackie.

"It's actually Harry Potter and the Goblet of Fire," said Woodhouse.

"And what might be the problem with that?" said Meehan.

"Nothing, as far as I'm concerned," said Woodhouse. "I quite like Harry Potter."

"I do too," said Blackhurst. "I like that Hermione. I think me and her could have a future."

"She's a 14 year old child," said Hamill.

"She's not now," said Blackhurst. "She's left Hogwarts now."

"She has yes," said Woodhouse. "Someone said she's working in Home and Bargain at the top of Linacre Road."

"Let's not digress gentlemen," said Meehan. "Look at the diagram again. What might the problem be here?"

"Poor visibility," said Morris. "Me ma always warned me never to read a book in poor visibility. She said I'd end up walking in front of a bus."

"I've got some books you can borrow," said Woodhouse.

"Very funny," said Morris.

"It's nothing to do with poor visibility," said the increasingly flustered Meehan. "I want you to think about the way the man's sitting in the other diagram. Ask yourselves the following question-why might one gentleman have his knees together and the other have them wide apart? Come on lads. This could genuinely prevent accidents or even save lives."

"The one with his legs apart has got a bad case of haemorrhoids," said Woodhouse.

"Or sore plums," said Hamill.

"It's nothing to do with any painful medical condition," said Meehan.

"The man's got his knees apart for purposes of stability," said Matthews.

"Hallelujah!" said Meehan. "At last. Thank you. Thank you very much. What's your name my friend?"

"Matthews," said Woodhouse. "He's our very own Peggy Ollerenshaw from Hi de Hi. He's working feverishly towards his yellow coat. He's the club lick arse."

"Why don't you shut your big fat trap," said Matthews. "I lick nobody's backside. I'm just respectful, that's all. Those committee members work tirelessly for us."

"Can we get back on track please gentlemen," said Meehan.

"I'm sorry Eddie," said Woodhouse. "I couldn't help myself. Me and Matthews have a checkered history. What's your point?"

"My point is this," said Meehan. "The man in the diagram who has his legs together is flirting with danger on two counts. He's not only balanced precariously on his lavatory seat but he's reading a book at the same time."

"So that's wrong is it?" said Woodhouse.

"Very wrong," said Meehan.

[20]

"And why's that?" said Woodhouse.
"Because in this case, the book constitutes a dangerous distraction," said Meehan. "And when you are seated on a lavatory pan while a train's in motion, the last thing you need is a distraction. You need to be concentrating fully on two things-your balance and the eventual release of waste matter. To do that effectively, you will need both hands free and you will need to have your two knees wedged against the partition walls at approximately 45 degrees."
"Why's that?" said Kenny Biddo.
"In case the train brakes suddenly or lurches forward," said Meehan. "As your extremely wise friend Brian just so eloquently said-stability is key. That's why it's very important, while the evacuation process is in progress, that your knees are pressed firmly against the sides of the partition walls as shown in the diagram on my right. Please do not, under any circumstances, follow the example of the gentleman in the other diagram."
"Don't you like him?" said Biddo.
"What do you mean, 'don't I like him'?" said Meehan. "It's nothing to do with whether I like the chap or not. He means nothing to me. He's just a cartoon figure, for goodness sake. He's just a representation of what not to do. Is that clear? Is that clear gentlemen? Has anybody got any questions?"
"Yes just the one," said Hamill. "What happens if you've got bad knees like our notoriously injury prone and nesh vice chairman Mr Kenny Hulme? He's going to need assistance surely."
"Don't start Hamill," said the Vice Chairman.
"That's where Matthews comes in," said Woodhouse. "He can stabilise him. He'll probably wipe and talcum powder his bottom for him too."
"That's very funny that is Woodhouse," said Matthews. "You'll certainly have no trouble wedging yourself against the partition walls. The problem is-we might need to smear you in Vaseline to get you out."
"You'll be smeared in your own blood and guts if you

carry on talking to me like that," said Woodhouse.
"That's enough now lads," said the Chairman. "Our
Health and Safety Officer hasn't finished yet. Carry on
Eddie."

To the dismay of most of the gathering, the
Health and Safety Officer then opened his briefcase and
after returning his toilet-related diagrams, he took out
another sheet of paper upon which were a series of
graphs and a huge amount of statistical information.
"Will there be any homework after all this?" asked
an increasingly puzzled Kenny Biddo. "Because when I
was at school I was always getting into trouble for not
handing me homework in on time."
"You never went to school," said Hamill.
"I did," said Biddo. "I always got an A for P.E. I was
good at games. I was a really fast runner."
"That's because the police were always chasing you,"
said Hamill.
"Behave now boys," said the Chairman. "Let's keep
this serious hey."
"No lads-I assure you, there won't be any homework,"
said a smiling Meehan. "But I suggest you listen
carefully to this next section. This is absolutely crucial."
"Why's that?" said Biddo.
"Because it concerns the amount of alcohol that you're
advised to consume while on board the train," said
Meehan.
"I beg your pardon!" said Biddo. "I'm sorry Can you
repeat that for me please Eddie?"
"Of course I can," said Meehan. "That's not a
problem."
"I think what he's about to tell us is that we're going to
be restricted as to how much alcohol we can drink
during the journey," said Woodhouse.
"Oh dear!" said Hamill. "Is that right?"
"It is yes," said Meehan before thrusting a laminated
sheet in front of the group and pointing to particular
section which had been ringed with a red marker pen.
"Alcohol, excited men and moving vehicles has often

been a recipe for disaster."

"You do realise the danger you've just put yourself in," said Woodhouse.

"I don't understand," said Meehan.

"And neither are most of these lads going to understand," said Woodhouse. "Some of them have been known to drink up to 15 pints a night."

"That's not possible," said Meehan.

"I assure you it is," said Woodhouse.

"It's outrageous," said Meehan. "How are they still alive? How can their livers tolerate such a pounding for goodness sake?"

"I've no idea," said Woodhouse. "I'm not a doctor. But take it from me Eddie-their livers do tolerate it. And you can take this from me too-these men won't tolerate a measure like that. You're going to make yourself extremely unpopular."

"He's going to get himself lynched," said Hamill.

"I'd think again if I was you Eddie. I'd go back to your drawing board."

"I've no intention of thinking again," said Meehan. "My job is to keep you people safe. If it makes me unpopular, then so be it. I know where I stand in the grand scheme of things. I'm hated in factories and warehouses the length and breadth of Great Britain."

"You're going to be hated even more now," said Hamill.

"I don't care," said Meehan. "These figures I have in front of me don't lie. It's a well known fact that an inordinate amount of accidents that have occurred on board a train have been the result of somebody's heavy drinking. Believe me gentlemen-if everyone adheres to my rules, they'll have a lovely accident-free trip."

"I wouldn't thank you for a lovely accident-free trip," said Kenny Biddo. "I like getting drunk and falling over. If I don't arrive home with my head split open or my ankle sprained, my wife begins asking some very searching questions."

"Well if you don't mind-let's use you as an example,"

said Meehan.

"I don't mind at all," said Biddo. "What do you want to know Ernie?"

"How much alcohol you consume would be a start," said Meehan. "Would you say it's more than 25 units a week?"

"I drink more than 25 units before breakfast," replied Biddo.

"Don't be absurd," said Meehan. "That's ridiculous."

"It's true," said Biddo.

"It can't be," said Meehan.

"It is," said Biddo.

"But, for goodness sake man," said Meehan. "Don't you realise that there's a very good chance you're going to end up with cirrhosis of the liver? Does your wife know how much you drink? Does your wife know the drink is likely to kill you?"

"Of course she does," said Biddo. "I think that's why she encourages me to do it."

"The poor woman must be out of her mind with worry," said Meehan. "Has she never tried to help you?"

"Quite often," said Biddo.

"In what way?" asked Meehan.

"She goes the wine stores for me when me gout's giving me gip," said Biddo.

"I can vouch for that," said Blackie.

"Well all I can say is this-if it was up to me, I wouldn't allow you to get on board that train," said Meehan."

"And why's that?" asked Biddo.

"Because apart from the fact you're almost certainly going to injure yourself at some point-you're going to be a liability to all the other passengers," said Meehan while hastily shoving his paperwork back into his briefcase.

"I'll be fine," said Biddo. "You don't have to worry about me Eric. Because, unlike some of the other ignorant bastards you've just been talking to-I've taken in every word you've said. And from now on, I'm going to do exactly what you advised us to do. I'm going to do it to the letter."

"Is that right?" said Meehan after clasping his case shut.

"It is yes," said Biddo. "As soon as I get on that train, I'm going to get myself a couple of bottles of vodka and make my way to one of the toilet cubicles. Then I'm going to lock the door, sit myself down and wedge me knees against the partition walls at 45 degrees. I'll be perfectly safe then because I'll be playing by your rules. And everyone else will be perfectly safe too because I won't come into contact with them. And I promise you this as well Eddie. I won't even read so much as a newspaper while sitting on that lavatory pan. I won't allow myself to get distracted. That's not going to happen. Trust me Eddie-I won't be any trouble at all."

"Well I think you need to take that up with your Chairman," said Meehan before tucking his case under his arm and heading to a less populated part of the platform.

By the time, the utterly perplexed Health and Safety Officer had managed to put a reasonable distance between himself and the main body of the group, he was perspiring heavily and deeply regretting his decision to chaperone the party and at that delicate juncture, it was very much touch and go whether he would remain or start making his way home. That was until he turned around and noticed a rapidly growing circle of agitated passengers that had formed just outside the door to the second carriage.

"What's happened?" he said after quickly forcing his way into the centre of the group and discovering the Chairman and Brian Matthews administering first aid to an old man who was lying motionless.

"The poor old bugger slipped," said Matthews.

"Slipped!" said Meehan while scanning the immediate ground. "Slipped on what exactly?"

"A pool of Kenny Biddo's vomit, if I'm not mistaken," said Matthews.

"Oh for goodness sake," said Meehan. "Did anyone see

him hit the ground?"

"I did," said Matthews.

"Did he hit his head?" said Meehan.

"I think so," said Matthews. "I heard a dull thud."

"Oh for Christ's sake," said the Chairman. "This is all we need. The poor old sod's going to die on us isn't he?"

"I don't think so," said Matthews. "His eyes are flickering. I think he's starting to come around. But I think it might be best if we get him out of the cold."

"I think so too," said Meehan. "Why don't you take him onto the train until he comes to. See if you can find something to put on his forehead. He's probably concussed."

"Yes, you do that," said the Chairman while glaring at a completely oblivious Kenny Biddo who, for some reason and at that particular moment, was trying to insert a brand new one pound coin into the shilling slot of a dummy cigarette machine. "You do that Matthews. I'd really appreciate that."

"Do you think the old boy's going to need his head seeing to?" said an ashen faced Club Secretary while helping the Chairman back to his feet. "I hope not Hilly," said the Chairman. "But I think I'm going to by the time this trip is through. I must have been stark raving bonkers to take this venture on. It would have been easier to organise a troop of baby chimpanzees."

"Are you going to send Biddo home?" said the Club Secretary.

"What for?" said the Chairman.

"He caused the old boy to slip didn't he?" said the Club Secretary.

"That's what I was led to believe too," said the Chairman. "At least until Matthews got the poor sod back to his feet."

"What do you mean?" said the Club Secretary.

"Did you see any sick?" said the Chairman.

"I wasn't really looking to be honest," said the Club Secretary.

"There wasn't any Hilly," said the Chairman.
"And there wasn't any sick on the old boy's clothes
either."
"That's odd," said the Club Secretary.
"It is isn't it," said the Chairman. "Have you made your
final count?"
"17," said the Club Secretary.
"Jesus Christ!" said the Chairman. "Do you fancy
taking over?"
"I don't even fancy coming along," said the Club
Secretary.

CHAPTER TWO
OPULENCE

When the design team initially approached the Department of Transport to put forward their plan to build a new steam train and run it from London to the north of Scotland, they were met with twenty minutes of stony silence. That wasn't because he idea was short on merits or lacked credibility however, it was because of the furore that was expected to erupt when anti-pollution groups such as the Environmental Protection Agency and the Clear Air Association got wind of the proposal. However, that didn't put the resilient team of technically brilliant enthusiasts off for long and within a few months they had come up with a new proposal which they believed would satisfy all. It had meant changing the method of power from steam to hydrogen and although the new Oriental Express engine would ultimately run far slower in comparison to its contemporaries, that had suited the design team perfectly because getting from A to B as fast as possible wasn't high on their list of priorities-getting their passengers from A to B in luxury and absolute comfort was. There were other advantages with the Hydrogen powered version too. The modern engine would run far quieter than the original steam powered and fossil fuel belching locomotive and the train's new fuel source would effectively make it carbon neutral because the hydrogen would have already been created as a waste product by the chemical industry. That didn't mean the train lacked any of those traditional characteristics that are so admired by millions of devotees of railways and steam train travel. It still had team driven pistons that would pump and thump metronomically, there would still be the same hypnotic clickety clack as the huge carriage wheels came into contact with fish plates and rail joints and, arguably most importantly of all from the point of view of those same steam train fanatics, nothing had been done to improve the slow and laborious pick up as

[28]

the engine initially set off and began to encourage it's litter of carriages to follow.

The innovations didn't cease at the method of fuel needed to power the engine though. This was a train that didn't require a driver in the conventional sense. The man at the front of this particular mode of transport was a driver of sorts but in reality was there to operate doors, give start signals, monitor the train's performance and, in case of mechanical or fuel related failure, to take control of the train and bring it back to the depot. That was because the train was designed to be operated from a manned control centre which, as far as the designers were concerned, would make it ultra reliable and ultimately free from human error.

The sleeping carriages were the epitome of elegance and style and therefore a devotee of train travel and person of leisure's dream. In each corner, was an inviting velvet-draped single bed with superbly hand carved headboard and footboards, while at the foot of each was a French red leather armchair and a rosewood wardrobe in the style of Emile Ruhlmann. The walls of the sleeping accommodation were very much in the 'gentleman's private club' style, clad in Peruvian mahogany panels that were interrupted at intervals by four sash sliding windows befit with gleaming brass furnishing and cream leather opening and closing straps. Upon those elevations, framed gleaming chrome and hanging under a multicoloured wall mounted Tiffany lamp were a series of prints by eminent artists such as David Shepherd, Terence Cuneo and David Weston depicting the great age of steam travel. They included an 18 by 36 print of George Stephenson's Locomotion No.1 and a slightly smaller one of the 1T57 'Fifteen Guinea Special' which last saw service running from Liverpool, Lime Street to Manchester, Victoria on the 11th of August 1968.

The dining carriage was coupled to the first carriage and was therefore accessible from the corridor which ran parallel to the first sleeper and the corridor which ran parallel to the second berth. It was spacious and could cater for up to 20 diners at a time and was connected to a small but well stocked bar and an impressive kitchen containing two bright red Chambers C-90 oven ranges that were spaced between three San Cristobal marble worktops and a pair of antique soapstone sinks. However, it was the dining area that the bar and kitchen served that was the most eye catching of all and clearly where most of the architect's imagination had been employed. It was a lavishly furnished room designed to convey the passenger's mindset back to the relatively carefree days of the early 1930s.

That turn back in time had been achieved in two subtle ways. Firstly, through the inclusion of certain classic Art Deco furnishings such as the Harry and Lou Epstein Birds Eye maple dining suites, the six multicoloured Rene Lalique inspired ceiling light fittings and the clever use of four Edgar Brandt style full length steel framed mirrors hung at each compass point. A number of thought provoking pieces of art work by some of the leading lights in commercial art and graphic design such as Cassandre, Jean Carlu and Leonetto Cappiello played a role in the deception too. Each offered possibilities or dreams such as owning a Bugatti Type 41 Royale car, attending the Monaco Grand Prix or travelling to exotic places such as Paris, Venice or Athens. It was a room furnished for many thousands of pounds. A room fit for royalty and people of the highest class and that was almost certainly why the club Chairman Tommy Weir and his Vice Chairman Kenny Hulme had been left scratching their heads and muttering under their breaths after completing their first visit.

One of the things that was deliberated most by the three man committee prior to them leaving Crosby was where to situate themselves in relation to the rest of the passengers in order to best watch over their members. They were to come up with two possible options. They could occupy the carriage at the rear of the train knowing that they would continually have to pass each occupied sleeper while heading to and from the dining carriage, or they could take residence in the foremost compartment next to the dining carriage and make regular patrols of the corridors. In fairness, the first mentioned consideration would have allowed them to supervise and monitor the men so much better but the fact that the dining carriage was where most of the drinking and bawdiness was likely to take place, was ultimately the deciding factor in them selecting sleeper number one as their accommodation for the duration of the trip.

They had also been keen to ensure the Vice Chairman's level headed elder brother Brian Hulme, otherwise known as the Chef, would take the other unoccupied first sleeper bed and because his roommates had been busy answering questions and offering the other confused club members guidance prior to boarding, it was he who had been the first to unpack. "I hope you don't mind but I've taken this bed next to the window our kid," he said before picking up his rolled up newspaper and nestling into a nearby chair. "Good for you," said the Vice Chairman before easing open his wardrobe doors and taking a small step back. "I hope you're comfy?"

"I am thanks," said the Chef. "Did I sense a note of sarcasm there our kid? Is everything alright Hulmey?"

"Not really," said Hulme. "I just thought you might have hung around to help us organise the rabble."

"You should have said," said the Chef. "Is there anything you want me to do now?"

"You can have a look in your bag and see if you've got any Valium," said Hulme.

"Is it that bad?" said the Chef.

"They're like naughty children," said Hulme. "Most of them can't think or act for themselves. You tell them to do one thing and they do the very opposite."

"You're going to have to put your foot down," said the

[31]

Chef. "You're the Vice Chairman now."

"Don't remind me," said Hulme.

"Kenny Biddo's the worst problem," said the Club Secretary. "I still reckon he's off his head. I knew it was a mistake letting him come along."

"He's never been any different," said the Chef.

"He'll settle down in a few minutes," said the Chairman. "He's just excited that's all. It's the first time he's been outside Crosby since the Ribble Buses stopped running."

"He's a complete and utter mess," said Hulme.

"He's a liability," said the Club Secretary.

"He's not a bad lad," said the Chairman. "By all accounts, he used to be a brilliant electrician."

"He used to be," said the Club Secretary. "He's not anymore though. I wouldn't trust him to put the fairy lights on our Christmas tree now. If I recall correctly, the last five companies he worked for all went bust."

"Really?" said the Chef. "Why do you think that was?"

"Because he kept fucking up would be my guess," said Hulme.

"It's the people that hired him that kept fucking up," said the Club Secretary. "They should never have taken the drunken bastard on in the first place."

"Where is he now?" said the Chairman.

"He's in the dining carriage," said Hulme. "He's parked himself next to the bar."

"Oh dear!" said the Chef. "That's likely to get messy. What time does the bar open?"

"I've no idea," said Hulme.

"It opens when I say it opens and not before," said the Chairman. "Who have you got him rooming with Hilly?"

"Let me see now," said the Club Secretary while quickly flicking through several sheets of paper attached to his tired old clipboard. "I seem to recall putting him with Blackie.....That's right, I did...He's with Blackie and Steadman."

"Who've you put Hewlett with?" said the Chairman.

"Eddie Meehan," said Hill. "Our dedicated but highly unpopular Health and Safety Officer. I thought it might be best. Hewlett's one of the few people who know him. I think he's a member of his golf club."

"Who are they with?" said Hulme.

"Nobody now," said the Club Secretary. "They've got a room to themselves."

"Why's that?" said the Chairman.

"Because you sent Murphy and Kilgallon home," said the Club Secretary.

"Of course I did," said the Chairman.

For the next fifteen minutes, while the Chef continued to struggle with the early phase of his junior crossword puzzle, the other three men busied themselves by organising their wardrobes and dressers and dispatching their toiletries and other personal items to the washroom. It would be a rare period of quiet which was eventually disturbed when casual club member Tony Hamill popped his head inside the room and rapped his knuckles against the wall.

"Good morning gentlemen," he said while admiring the room's decor. "I see you've wasted no time in procuring the best room in the house."

"All the rooms are more or less the same," said Hulme.

"That's right," said the Club Secretary. "So don't start letting your persecution complex get the better of you Hamill."

"They're not exactly the same," said Hamill.

"There is one notable difference."

"And what's that?" said Hulme.

"You four aren't going to need to phone a taxi to get to the dining carriage," said Hamill.

"Behave yourself Hamill," said the Chairman. "Nobody's that far away from the bloody dining room."

"It was just an observation, that's all," said Hamill.

"I didn't mean to cause offence."

"Well you can keep your observations to yourself," said the Club Secretary. "Shouldn't you be unpacking?"

"All in good time," said Hamill.

[33]

"And for God's sake Hamill-try to smile and enjoy yourself for once," said Hulme.

"I'm already smiling," said Hamill. "And I'm already enjoying myself."

"Why's that?" said Hulme. "Have you finally got your period?"

"I have yes," said Hamill. "The scares over. I'm too old to have more kids."

"What are you really smiling for?" said the Club Secretary.

"Yes-what are you really smiling for?" said Hulme.

"I've just seen Kenny Biddo," said Hamill.

"What's so funny or unusual about that?" said Hill.

"He's toting a gun," said Hamill.

"He's what?" said the Club Secretary.

"He's carrying a gun," said Hamill before exiting the room.

"Oh Jesus Christ!" said the Club Secretary while watching the highly amused Hamill slowly disappear down the corridor. "Don't tell me that. Where's the daft bastard got a gun from?"

"Take no notice of him Hilly," said Hulme.

"Take no notice of him!" said Hill while proceeding to pace across the room. "For God's sake Hulmey-For God's sake man. We've just been told one of our most irrational and unpredictable members has got his hands on a gun. We need to do something. We need to act now before he shoots someone."

"It's not a gun," said the Chairman. "It's a gas stove lighter in the shape of a pistol. I've got to admit-it's very authentic looking. It took me quite a while before I worked out its function. I saw it before when me and Hulmey went to look at the kitchen. Now get your clipboard and get your ultra efficient secretary head back on. Tell me what room Hewlett's in."

At that particular moment, Hewlett didn't really care what number room he was in. He was celebrating what he considered to be a major stroke of good fortune because, not only had he avoided having to share his sleeping quarters with certain members of the club he considered beneath his status, he had discovered to his delight, that his only room companion was none other than the Health and Safety Officer Eddie Meehan, a popular member of his golf club and someone he respected enormously. "It looks like we've struck gold here Eddie," he said while systematically arranging a large selection of expensive bottles of cosmetics on his dressing table as if they were a toy soldiers.

"What do you mean 'we've struck gold'?" said Meehan.

"Because we have," said Hewlett. "We've got this room all to ourselves Eddie."

"I was wondering about that," said Meehan. "Have you any idea why?"

"I know exactly why," said Hewlett. "The good old Chairman's sent our erstwhile and tardy roommates packing with a proverbial flea in each of their ears."

"I noticed that," said Meehan. "He seems to be a right stickler for discipline your Chairman."

"He is," said Hewlett before squirting a walnut sized dollop of face cream onto his left palm. "He's ruthless. He takes no nonsense from the riff raff. To be honest, I wouldn't be here if it wasn't for him. Without him, the lunatics would soon be in charge of the asylum and the asylum would be no place for the likes of you and me."

"Do you know who we were meant to be sharing with?" said Meehan. "Would I know either of them?"

"I doubt it," said Hewlett. "Steve Kilgallon was one of them."

"Is he bad news?" said Meehan.

"He's not too bad," said Hewlett. "He's employed."

"What does he do?" said Meehan.

"He works for a railway company," said Hewlett.

"Doing what?" said Meehan.

"I've no idea," said Hewlett. "But I know this much-he won't have anything to do with time and motion. He probably just waves a bright coloured flag or blows a whistle. Mark Murphy was the other one."

"Mark Murphy!" said Meehan. "I know that name. "Is

[35]

he a Crosby lad?"

"Oh no, no, no," said Hewlett. "He's from the rough end of Seaforth. He's one of about 12 children. I think they hailed from the Dingle area of Liverpool. Rumour has it none of his brothers and sisters owned a pair of a shoes until they'd left school. They lived one of those, first up, best dressed, life styles. From what I can recall-Peter was the best fighter. And in the Land of the Murphy, that meant he was always the best turned out."

"Was he originally from Lawton Road?" said Meehan.

"He was yes," said Hewlett.

"I do know him then," said Meehan. "I think I met him at one of the Northern Cricket Club's Saturday morning charity functions."

"That wouldn't have been Mark Murphy," said Hewlett. "Mark Murphy doesn't do mornings. Rumour has it, he was 37 years of age before he saw his first milkman and 44 before he realised the postman did a morning delivery as well as a second."

"So neither are what you might call, 'intellectuals' then," said Meehan.

"Certainly not," said Hewlett. "You're not likely to discover Kilgallon reading Kafka or Keats. You're more likely to find him reading the latest abomination from the loathsome Katie Pryce."

"So you think we got lucky then," said Meehan.

"We got extremely lucky," said Hewlett while carefully applying a finger tip of anti wrinkle lotion to his left eye lid. "I had visions of having to coexist with the likes of the revolting barrel of lard Paul Woodhouse or the foul mouthed, vocabulary deficient Tommy McShane. Wait until you meet him Eddie. My word! Everything that man says either begins with an 'f' or ends with an 'off'. They're both as rough and as useful as primate droppings. But never mind that. Look at this place Eddie. Just look at it will you. It's magnificent. People like that shouldn't be here. It's absurd to think they're going to be appointed a personal maid or a waiter. They should be handled by zoo keepers and fed buns on the end of sticks."

"My word!" said Meehan. "Once again, I find myself regretting my decision to come along. Are they all like that? Surely they can't all be rough houses. What about that very tall, slim bloke that was standing outside our room when we arrived. He's got a touch of class about him. I'm sure I've seen him somewhere before. Is his name Spealman something or other?"

"Steadman Hamilton-Swan," said Hewlett. "But that's not his real name."

"What do you mean?" said Meehan.

"Steadman Hamilton-Swan is an alias he likes to use," said Hewlett. "His real name's John Horrocks. He changed his name to a double barrelled title believing it would get him into our golf club. Keep that to yourself by the way Eddie. He's unaware I know that insidious fact. I plan to tell him when the time's right."

"When's that likely to be?" said Meehan.

"If he ever beats me in one of the club knock out championships," said Hewlett. "To be honest, he's one of the more decent members of the mob. Rumour has it, he can actually read and write."

"What about that Kenny Biddo chap," said Meehan. "He's seriously weird. I couldn't believe how much he admitted to drinking. How long's he been doing that?"

"Since he was 13 apparently," said Hewlett.

"13!" said Meehan.

"That's right," said Hewlett. "According to his nephew Blackie, his alcoholism was brought about as result of a traumatic experience."

"What sort of traumatic experience?" said Meehan.

"He got it into his head that his boss wanted to have sex with him," said Hewlett.

"His boss!" said Meehan. "Are you telling me he was working at the age of 13? What was he-a chimney sweep?"

"He was a paper boy," said Hewlett.

"I see," said Meehan.

"By all accounts, the whole thing was blown up out of

proportion," said Hewlett. "The man was harmless. He was just extremely effeminate and camp. The problem was-Kenny Biddo had never come across anyone like that before. He couldn't grasp the concept of a man displaying feminine traits."

"So what happened?" said Meehan.

"The story goes that one Saturday evening, just after he'd returned his bike and bag to the shop, he noticed his boss coming out of the toilet with his trousers by his knees," said Hewlett.

"Really!" said Meehan.

"Apparently so," said Hewlett. "He claimed he was sporting an enormous erection and seemed in no hurry to hide the thing. Biddo thought the moment he had so often feared had arrived. He thought he was about to be buggered senseless. So to avoid being sexually assaulted, he locked himself in the shop's store room."

"Bloody hell!" said Eddie.

"He was there until the following Monday morning," said Hewlett. "By that time he'd got through 6 bottles of Captain Morgan Rum, a litre of Glenfiddich 12 Year Old Malt, 4 half bottles of Smirnoff and a packet of firelighters."

"Firelighters!" said Meehan. "Why firelighters, for goodness sake?"

"He said he'd got hungry," said Hewlett. "He said they were the only things that looked remotely edible."

"How could he do that?" said Eddie. "How could anyone eat firelighters?"

"I've no idea," said Hewlett.

"Bloody hell!" said Eddie. "I'm surprised they didn't find him dead."

"He nearly was dead within minutes of arriving home," said Hewlett. "He almost burnt his house down."

"How did he manage that?" said Meehan.

"He burped," said Hewlett.

"He burped!" said Meehan.

"He settled down in front of the open fire and suddenly burped," said Hewlett. "He turned into a human flame thrower by all accounts."

"Are you sure about this Richard?" said Meehan. "Are you sure people haven't been pulling your leg?"

"I'm positive they haven't," said Hewlett. "I've seen the cutting from the Crosby Herald. His nephew Blackie keeps it in his wallet. He even told the story at one of the club meetings."

"That's awful," said Meehan. "I don't know whether to laugh or feel sorry for the man."

"I know," said Hewlett. "He's drunk like a sailor ever since."

"Well I'm going to have to keep my distance from him," said Meehan. "I can't stand being around drunken people. Their very presence unsettles me."

"I wouldn't concern yourself too much," said Hewlett. "He'll pass out after a while. Anyway-his son Anthony's on board. He's going to try and keep him in order. Anthony's very stable in comparison. My concern is very different in origin. It's in regard to the proximity of the dining carriage. Do you know what Eddie-in all my years, I've never had to travel that far unless wheeled in a perambulator by Nanny Betsy or chauffeured in father's Bentley. I don't know how I'm going to cope. I really don't. One thing's for certain though-I won't be venturing out into that corridor just yet. Have you heard the commotion out there? It's pandemonium. I've not heard that lot so excited since one of them achieved a 5 letter word at Scrabble."

Hewlett's scathingly critical remarks might have been slightly exaggerated for dramatic purpose but he hadn't been far off the mark when describing the scene within the corridors as 'pandemonium' because what was occurring at that particular time was the sort of chaos usually associated with the moment the crew of a Merchant sea going vessel suddenly realises they have been hit by a torpedo. Wherever you looked, there were bewildered men buzzing about like disorientated moths while doors were sliding open and shut as passengers searched frantically for their recently lost property or somebody coherent enough to direct them to their designated rooms. It was a scene that resembled the first day of school for a class of five year olds and just like five year olds, many of those men appeared to be close to tears and ready to abandon all hope.

"Do you know what-those three committee boys couldn't organise a piss up in the Rovers Return," said Tony Hamill after finding himself ejected from yet another room. "I knew this would happen. I knew the trip would be ruined before it got underway. I've told you lot time and time again-that committee's not fit for purpose."

"You're in the third carriage with McShane and Woody," yelled the exasperated Club Secretary who, after hearing the commotion, had left his room to offer the lost and troubled some geographical guidance. "All the details you need are on the yellow 'travelling advice' card I handed to you prior to boarding. And if you've never learnt to read, find someone who has for God's sake."

"Read!" said Hamill. "Have you seen the size of the writing on these cards? The majority of us are middle aged men for God's sake. Our sight started failing ten years ago. I'm within a whisker of being certified blind and being awarded my first Golden Retriever puppy. How the hell do you expect me to read that Hilly?"

"Well, as I've just said Hamill," said the Club Secretary. "You're in carriage 3 with the likes of Woody. And if you can't see big Woody, I'd start looking on EBay for a white stick."

Paul Woody, Woodhouse had actually been the first to find his room and consequently one of the first to get settled in and at that point was lying on his bed reading the tour schedule when the livid and seriously perplexed Hamill entered the room and launched his bags onto the bed next to the window.

"Are you having a bad day?" said the big man without raising his head.

"I'm having a very bad day because of that no good

committee," replied Hamill.

"Why's that?" said Woodhouse.

"Why's that!" said Hamill. "I'll tell you why should I Woody. For the past half hour, I've been traipsing up and down the corridor looking for carriage 33."

"There is no carriage 33," said Woodhouse. "At least I hope there isn't. We're far enough from the dining carriage as it is. What made you think we we'd been allocated room 33?"

"Double vision," said Hamill. "It's a condition I've suffered with for several years."

"That's not the committee's fault," said Woodhouse.

"I beg to differ," said Hamill. "My double vision's nearly always brought on by stress. And, by the way-talking about things that stress me out-why are you lying there buck naked with all your various parts on show?"

"I'm thinking about taking a shower," said Woodhouse.

"A shower!" said Hamill. "Why didn't you take one before you left the house?"

"I did," said Woodhouse. "But for some reason, I still reek of garlic. Have you seen McShane?"

"I have as a matter of fact," said Hamill. "He was outside the 22nd carriage. He had someone pinned to the corridor wall. He shouldn't be long. As you know, very few of his fights tend to go the full distance."

"Have you any idea who's making up our four ball?" said Woodhouse.

"That would be him," said a scornful looking Hamill.

"Who?" said Woodhouse after quickly rolling over and noticing the completely self absorbed Brian Matthews heading towards one of the far beds. "Oh mother of God...Don't tell me that. We haven't got to put up with that snivelling toe rag have we?"

"Go to hell Woodhouse," said Matthews. "I don't like the idea any more than you do. Do you think for one minute I'd have chosen to share digs with someone like you?"

"I reckon he's been sent here to spy on us," said Hamill. "To make sure we don't get up to any mischief."

"Is that right Matthews?" said Woodhouse.

"If you say so," said Matthews.

"I do say so," said Hamill. "You've always been the committee bum boy."

"I'm nobody's bum boy," said Matthews. "I'm as straight as a dart. I've just come along to have a good time. And I'll have that good time provided you two keep out of my face. By the way Woodhouse-is that takeaway food I can smell?"

"There he goes," said Woodhouse. "He wasted no time at all didn't he? You know what's going to happen next don't you Hamill...He's going to blow me up for bringing my own food on the train."

"I'm just repeating what the Chairman said earlier," said Matthews. "You know the thinking behind that rule. This is a very expensive train. The club won't be able to afford the damages if anything gets broken or stained."

"The club-the club-the club-that's all you ever worry about isn't it Matthews?" said Hamill. "Why is that? Why do you think the club's so important Matthews? They've never done anything for you. How many times have you applied for committee membership lad?"

"That's my business," said Matthews.

"Fair enough," said Hamill. "But why don't you face facts lad-they don't want to know you. You'd be better off coming to the dark side with us."

"I wouldn't be seen dead with you lot," said Matthews.

"I wouldn't bet against that," said Woodhouse. "But by the way-if you really want to impress those committee boys-go and tell them Kenny Biddo's got hold of a gun?"

"He's what?" said Matthews before dropping his bag and quickly making his way to the door.

"He's got a gun," said Hamill. "And a list of possible targets."

"Where's he got a gun from?" said the mortified Matthews.

"That would be telling," said Hamill. "Now run along and gain some Brownie points."

[42]

"I'll remain here if it's all the same to you," said Matthews.

By that time, largely through the persuasive abilities of his nephew Blackie, Kenny Biddo was actually unarmed and lying on his bed fluctuating between consciousness and delirium.

"I don't like the look of him," said the tall, angular Steadman, the third occupier of the room.

"To be honest, I've never liked the look of him," said Blackie. "I've offered to pay for him to have plastic surgery but the stubborn bugger won't have any of it."

"You know what I mean," said Steadman. "I think there's a good chance we're going to be carrying him off this train with a sheet over his face."

"He'll be alright," said Blackie. "His lad Anthony's here to look after him."

"His lad Anthony's not here," said Steadman. "His lad Anthony's in the last carriage playing poker with Alty and Larkin. That's where Kenny Biddo should be. I'm telling you lads. We've got trouble here. That free bar's going to be the death of this daft bugger."

"He'll be fine," said Blackie. "I'll go and talk to young Anthony. Just give me a minute to fix me hair."

By the time Blackie had arrived at the last occupied carriage, young Anthony Biddo had already lost a fair portion of his spending money to highly competent gamblers Kenny Alty and Dave Larkin and in all fairness, he would probably have been in even greater debt had it not been for he and his two roommates spending the first part of their stay combing every inch of their sleeper in an effort to discover what practical jokes their cohabitant and notorious prankster Alec Morris might have played before he had left the room wearing a sinister self satisfied grin. Previous pranks, on other trips, included swapping the Chef's heart medication for excessively strong Ecstasy pills. That resulted in the 60 year old becoming so hyperactive, he lost an eighth of his body weight in just under 48 hours. On another occasion, he had replaced the famously self obsessed Ian Blackhurst's hair mousse with rapid acting hair removal cream. That trick resulted in the devastated victim going completely bald and having to undertake a long course of Cognitive behavioural therapy. The occupants of that last carriage had discovered nothing too alarming however and within a few minutes of the search being abandoned, the cards had been dealt and young Anthony was once again losing heavily. That was a pattern and a run of bad luck that would have almost certainly continued had it not been for the train suddenly and violently lurching forward. It meant that only those members of the party that were seated or lying on their beds had been spared the indignity of being catapulted backwards and it gave rise to a period when the air had turned a very deep shade of blue and confusion had become king.

"What the fuck!" said McShane who had only just joined his three roommates in the third carriage. "What the hell's going on?" said a visibly shaken Kenny Alty while slowly scrambling back to his feet. "I thought we weren't scheduled to move off for another hour or so. Bloody hell! That's disappointing that is. I had Larko by the short and curlies there. I had a royal flush to his full house. I was nailed on for that last pot."

"I told you, didn't I," said Hamill after righting an overturned chair. "I told you. I told you but you wouldn't listen. Time and time again I told you. That committee's not fit for purpose. It never has been and never will be. I can't remember a trip going to plan while those three imbeciles have been in charge."

"Shut your face Hamill," said Matthews. "It mightn't be anything to do with the committee. Didn't you watch the news this morning? It could have something to do with the bad weather that's meant to be closing in. Maybe the rail company's decided we should set off earlier to make sure we get through it safely." "You might have a point," said Hamill. "You might have a very good point for that matter. But take my advice Matthews. In order for *you* to make it through

the journey safely with all your bones in one piece, make
sure you don't ever talk to me like that again. Now go
and have a word with that poor excuse for a committee.
Ask them what the hell's going on. And tell them there
are men here suffering the effects of whiplash injuries.
Tell them it's like the first day of the Somme back here.
Tell them that some of these poor buggers are unlikely
to work again."
"Does that include those who are already claiming
Disability Living Allowance?" said Matthews.
"Don't start getting political Matthews," said Hamill.
"I've warned you before. I won't warn you again. Now
get the hell out of my sight, before I do something I
might later regret."

In reality, the committee members were no wiser
than any of the other passengers and by the time Brian
Matthews arrived at the first carriage, the stupefied Club
Secretary was already awash with perspiration and
becoming more desperate by the second.
"I don't get it," he said after emerging from behind a
large fan of paperwork. "We were definitely meant to
depart at 7.30. I'm absolutely certain of it."
"Well I'm sorry Hilly," said the Chairman while
rearranging his chair. "It looks like you've got
something wrong for once. Take a look out of that
window lad. Unless trees have suddenly developed the
ability to move, it must be us that's moving."
"I'm not wrong," said the Club Secretary. "I know I'm
not. I never get things like that wrong."
"I have to agree with him Tommy," said Hulme while
continuing to gather some of his personal effects that
had been thrown from his dresser as the train jerked
forward. "In all my days, I've never known Hilly make
mistakes regarding scheduling."
"Well give me a better explanation, said the Chairman.
"Because I'm lost here."

CHAPTER THREE
CONFUSION

During the chaos and confusion that immediately followed the train moving off unexpectedly, quite a lot of the passengers had filed into the corridors seeking some sort of explanation and because they knew that Kenny Alty had been employed by a private railway company for the past 5 years, he suddenly found himself the centre of attention, the target for some needless and illogical criticism and the recipient of a barrage of questions. "I don't know," he had said upon finding his room besieged by a large number of bewildered passengers. "I'm just a general dogsbody for a small Merseyside Rail Company, for God's sake. How am I supposed to know why the train pulled away early?"

"Did anyone hear a whistle?" said Dave Larkin. "I'd have thought we'd have heard a whistle. Was there a whistle?"

"I was too busy unpacking," said Steadman. "I heard nothing."

"Neither did I," said Blackie. "I haven't even seen a porter, never mind heard a whistle. Has anyone seen a porter?"

"That's a point," said Dave Larkin. "This is meant to be some sort of lavish affair isn't it? I was told this was the train's maiden trip. I'd have thought we'd have been greeted by a brass band and a dignitary holding a huge pair of scissors."

"I'd have thought so too," said Steadman. "I'd have expected a load of razzmatazz and champagne."

"But don't forget-we did arrive here extremely early," said Woodhouse.

"Unnecessarily early, if you ask me," said Hamill. "And not for the first bloody time either. Why on earth does that committee always insist on us arriving at least two hours before we're due to set off?"

"Because we need plenty of time to get you lot

organised," said the arriving Club Secretary.
"Organised!" said Hamill. "Don't make me laugh
Hilly. "You couldn't run a bath. The problem is-you
and your cronies have this annoying habit of continually
overcomplicating things."
"We've overcomplicated nothing," said the Club
Secretary while watching a trembling Kenny Biddo
stagger forward before steadying himself on his son's
arm."
"The train setting off early has nothing to do with the
committee. We're as much in the dark as you lot are.
It's certainly not our fault."
"Well whose fault is it?" asked Woodhouse.
"Mine," said Kenny Biddo while wiping the sleep from
his eyes.
"Why's that?" said the Club Secretary.
"Because it nearly always is," said Biddo. "I always get
the blame when things go plum shaped."
"That's because you're a bloody idiot," said the Club
Secretary. "Look at the state of you Biddo. Why don't
you go and throw yourself under a cold shower. And for
God's sake Woodhouse-put some bloody knickers on.
Where do you think you are-San Tropez?"
"That's right," said the Chairman. "Let's try to
maintain our standards gentlemen."
"What standards are those?" said Hamill.
"The standards I've always set and bloody well
demanded," said the Chairman. "So let's start by getting
Biddo back to his room. Would you mind doing that for
me Anthony? In the meantime, I want everyone to stand
completely still for a few minutes."
"Why's that?" said Hamill.
"Because I want to make another head count," said the
Chairman.
"What the hell for?" said Woodhouse.
"Because it's just possible we've left someone behind,"
said the Chairman.
"What!" said Hamill.
"You heard the Chairman," said the Club Secretary.

"We might have left someone behind."

"How come?" said Hamill.

"Because the committee wouldn't allow us to use the toilets on the train before we set off," said Woodhouse.

"Why's that?" said Hamill.

"You work it out Hamill," said the Chairman.

"And, in the meantime, has anyone thought about going to see the only person qualified to give us an explanation as to what's going on?"

"Who might that be?" said Woodhouse.

"The driver," said the Chairman.

"Brian Matthews has gone," said the Chef.

"Brian Matthews hasn't gone anywhere," said Hamill. "Brian Matthews is standing behind you scratching his head and looking a little bit out of whack."

"Well somebody else go then," said the Chairman. "We need to get to the bottom of this as quick as we can."

"They'd be wasting their time," said a pale faced Matthews while slowly making his way through the confounded gathering. "I've already been and come back."

"What did he say?" said Hill.

"What did who say?" said Matthews.

"The driver," said the Chairman. "Did you talk to the driver?"

"There was no driver," said Matthews.

"What do you mean, 'there was no driver'," said the Chairman.

"There's no driver," said Matthews. "Just how plain can I make that?"

"But that doesn't make any sense," said Woodhouse. "We're moving aren't we? Someone must have started the train. How can there be no driver?"

"I don't know," said Matthews.

"This has got to be a wind up," said Hamill. "It has hasn't it? It's a wind up isn't it lads?"

"It's no wind up," said Matthews.

"If it is, I'm no part of it," said the Chairman.

"Nor me," said the Chef.

"But, as Woody says-it doesn't make any sense," said Hamill. "There's got to be a driver. Are you sure you went to the right end of the train Matthews?"

"Of course I did," said Matthews. "I've even been inside the engine. It was deserted. There was nobody there."

"But that's not possible," said Steadman. "A train can't just take off without a driver."

"I wouldn't have thought so," said the Chairman after pausing alongside the Health and Safety Officer. "Are you able to make any sense of this Eddie?"

"None whatsoever," said Meehan. "Runaway trains aren't really my forte. But as your fellow member Woody just said-I would have thought someone has to be at the front of a train to press buttons and pull levers."

"That's what I'd have thought too," said an increasingly suspicious Chairman while continuing to make a mental count of his members. "Unless the train's been left on some sort of autopilot."

"It's possible," said Meehan.

"I'd have also thought a situation as serious as this, was deserving of every member's presence," said the Chairman.

"What do you mean?" said the Club Secretary.

"It appears there are one or two people missing," said the Chairman.

"Like who?" said Blackie.

"Like Hewlett, for example," said the Chairman.

"I'm here," said Hewlett from the rear of the congregation. "I'm dreadfully sorry. I've been deep in meditation for the past twenty minutes. It's a morning routine I refuse point blank to abandon. Father reckons it's taken years off me. I had no idea there was a problem. What is the problem gentlemen? Pray tell me."

"We've got no driver," said Meehan.

"No driver!" said Hewlett. "Oh dear! That's a bit of filth. Why would that be?"

[49]

"We don't know," said Blackie. "We're trying to work that out. That's why we're all standing in this corridor with puzzled expressions on our faces. And while we're on the subject of faces-do you know you've got sponk around your mouth?"

"I beg your pardon!" said Hewlett.

"You've got sponk around your mouth," said Blackie.

"Sponk!" said Hewlett. "What's sponk?"

"You know very well what sponk is," said Blackie.

"I do not," said Hewlett. "What is it? What's sponk?"

"Man juice," said Woodhouse.

"Man juice!" said the bemused Hewlett.

"Sperm," said Hamill.

"It's all around your gob," said Blackie. "You haven't been partaking in a bit of oral shenanigans with our Health and Safety Officer have you? Although, I wouldn't worry yourself too much Hewlett. I imagine having sex with Eddie is just about the safest form of sex you can have."

"Don't be absurd," said a disgusted Hewlett. "It's La Mer Moisturising Cream. And for your information, it retails at around £1500 a bottle. I was applying it when I was disturbed. You don't doubt me do you Mr Blackhurst?"

"I don't doubt you at all," said Blackie. "I've known for some time that you're disturbed."

"Very droll," said Hewlett. "You want to try using La Mer yourself Blackie. Have you looked in the mirror lately? Have you seen the bags under your eyes?"

"I've just come off a fortnight of 12 hour nights," said Blackie.

"Come off a fortnight of 12 hour nights!" said Hewlett.

"That's right," said Blackie. "It's what a fair proportion of the British population have to do to earn money. Google it if you don't understand what working for a living means. It'll be under the secondary heading, 'shift work'."

"Let's get back to business shall we lads," said the Chairman who was growing more and more impatient by the minute. "Who's still missing?"

"I don't know," said the Club Secretary. "It's difficult to say. We're all bunched up like canned sardines."

"And I'm suffering the further indignity of having Woody's genitals rubbing up against the crack of my arse," said Hamill. "I don't know whether to run for it or brace myself and take one for the club. What do you think Mr Chairman?"

"I think you need to get serious and try to help us establish who's missing," said the Chairman.

"Aye, aye Captain," said Hamill.

"I can't see Kenny Hulme," said Steadman.

"I can't either," said the Chairman. "Where's your brother Chef?"

"He took short," replied the Chef. "I think he's still on the lavatory."

"That doesn't surprise me," said Hamill. "That'll be down to nerves. Your kid's never had the stomach for trouble."

"Have you seen him since the train pulled away?" said Steadman.

"Seen him!" said the Chef. "He fell on top of me when we took off. I think he might have pulled something."

"I suppose there's a first time for everything," said Hamill. "Because he never had any luck pulling anything in the Grafton."

"What about Tommy McShane?" said the Chairman.

"He's here somewhere," said Woodhouse. "I can smell his Brut Aftershave."

"I'm here," said McShane from the very back of the party. "Although I'm seriously wishing I'd gone to work."

"I wish I'd gone to work too," said Kenny Alty. "My nerves are in tatters. We've got Alec Morris to contend with as well as all this. Me and my roommates have spent the last hour trying to avoid being the victim of another of his practical jokes."

At that point, although only one man had appreciated the significance of what Kenny Alty had said, it became clear that the situation had taken a significant turn for the worse. That was because, for the first time since he had been voted into office, the Chairman, at least momentarily, appeared to be completely lost for words and devoid of ideas.

"What's the matter?" whispered the Club Secretary after leading the leaden faced Chairman to a quieter part of the corridor. "What's going on Mr Weir? Speak to me. Tell me what's up. You're beginning to scare me now."

"You're beginning to scare everyone now," whispered the Chef.

"I think we've got a problem lads," whispered the Chairman.

"Another one?" said the Club Secretary.

"A considerable one," said the Chairman.

"Is it likely to be a bigger problem than discovering we haven't got a driver?" said a breathless Kenny Hulme after latching on to the recently formed tight knit huddle. "Because, I'll be honest with you lads-the train taking off without a driver's going to take some beating."

"We're going to need to get everyone sat down," whispered the Chairman.

"Where do you recommend?" whispered the Club Secretary.

"The dining room would be my choice of venue," whispered the Chairman.

"Are you going to explain what's on your mind?" whispered the Club Secretary.

"Let's get them all to the dining room first," whispered the Chairman.

"Alright," said the Club Secretary. "But remember Tommy-there's nothing happened that you're not capable of putting right."

"I wouldn't wager too much money on that," whispered the Chairman.

"Oh dear!" whispered the Club Secretary.

"I've got a feeling this problem's going to finish me off Hilly," whispered the Chairman. "Now let's get these dozy buggers moving."

###

"I reckon I was right all along," said Hamill after
settling into a dining room chair directly opposite the
Chairman and folding his arms. "You soft bastards have
gone and left someone behind haven't you?"
"You haven't have you?" said Steadman. "Is that right
lads?"
"Not exactly," said the Chairman.
"What does that mean?" said Hamill. "Have you or
haven't you?"
"We think there might be someone missing," said the
Chairman.
"Who?" said Steadman.
"That's what we're trying to establish," said the Club
Secretary.
"There's nobody missing," said Woodhouse while
proceeding to circle the room. "Look around you
Tommy We're all here."
"We're not all here," said the Club Secretary.
"Three of the lads have just gone to the washroom."
"Well, maybe the best thing to do is to reel off the
occupants of each room," said Steadman. "Let's be
honest, we only need to know who's checked in to each
room. Therefore, those who haven't checked in must
have missed the train."
"That's a point," said the Chairman. "Take these names
down Hilly."
"Me and Blackie are here," said Steadman. "And
Kenny Biddo's with young Anthony getting freshened
up. There's our lot accounted for."
"That's 3," said the Chairman.
"And me, Hamill, Tommy Mac and the odious Matthews
are present," said Woodhouse. "That's another three
and a half people."
"Shut your face Woodhouse," said Matthews.
"Behave yourself Woody," said the Chairman. "Don't
start getting personal. That's another four members.

[53]

Who else do we definitely know is here?"

"Hewlett and Safety Officer Meehan, to name a couple," said the Club Secretary.

"Which leaves carriage number 5," said the Chairman.

"That's where Alty and Larkin are housed isn't it," said Woodhouse.

"It is indeed," said the Club Secretary. "And neither of them are here."

"They've just gone to get something from their room," said Steadman.

"They're having a sly smoke in the second washroom," said Matthews.

"That figures," said the Club Secretary.

"But they are here," said Woodhouse. "And their two roommates are here as well."

"That's right," said Hamill.

"Their two roommates aren't here," said the Chairman.

"Are you sure?" said Woodhouse. "I thought I just saw them."

"They're not here," said the Chairman.

"Young Anthony's here," said Steadman. "I've just told you-he's taking care of his dad."

"So that's everyone isn't it?" said a far more contented looking Club Secretary while continuing to scan the room. "That's everyone. That's everyone accounted for surely."

"Not everyone," said the Chairman.

"Why not?" said the Club Secretary.

"Because it's not everyone," said the Chairman.

"For the love of God-I'm losing the will to live here," said Hamill.

"So am I," said Woodhouse.

"Hold on a minute," said the Club Secretary. "I know what's happened now. I'm sorry Tommy-you've forgotten about sending Murphy and Kilgallon home?"

"That'll be it," said Woodhouse.

"It's nothing to do with those two," said the Chairman. "I can remember that incident as clear as a bell. I can remember every incident when I've had to censor

members. I'm talking about someone that actually
boarded this train at the same time as the rest of us.
Someone that's rarely been seen since."

"Who?" said the Club Secretary.

"Alec Morris," said the Chairman.

"Alec Morris!" said Blackie. "Alec Morris! Alec
Morris is here. I've just seen him. I swear I've just seen
him."

"And I swear he's missing," said the Chairman before
kicking the dining carriage door shut. "So you know
what that means, don't you lads?"

"I don't," said Hamill. "Please explain if you don't
mind. What does it mean?"

"It means we might have just solved our conundrum,"
said the Chairman.

"Conundrum!" said Hamill. "What do you mean
conundrum? Will you try to talk plain English for a
change."

"I am talking plain English," said the Chairman.

"Not as far as I'm concerned," said Hamill. "Unless
you're suggesting there's a connection between Morris
going missing and the train setting off early."

"I think that's exactly what he's suggesting," said the
Club Secretary before slumping into his chair and
tossing his tour schedule into the air.

"Jesus Christ!" said the Chef.

"Jesus Christ is right," said the Club Secretary. "What a
bloody nightmare. That's it. That's the end of it lads.
The good times are over. You can kiss goodbye to our
club."

"Get a grip of yourself Hilly," said Steadman. "The lad
probably didn't even get on board the train. I think
you're jumping the gun. I don't even remember seeing
him on the platform?"

"I did," said the Chairman. "Me, Hilly and Hulmey had
drawn lots to see who'd be responsible for keeping an
eye on him before we got underway."

"And why didn't you?" said Hamill.

"Because an old man got injured," said the Chairman.

[55]

"Was that the last time you saw him?" said Steadman.
"To be perfectly honest, no," said the Chairman. "I remember seeing him heading towards the platform toilets."

"That's right-he went the same time as me," said Alty. "He looked shattered."

"I thought that when I picked him up," said the Club Secretary.

"So there's a very good chance he's fallen asleep on the pan and missed the train," said Steadman.

"I suppose so," said the Chairman while heading for the dining carriage door.

"There's no supposing about it," said Steadman. "I know he can be a nuisance from time to time but what would he hope to gain from pulling a stunt like that?"

"What would he hope to gain from pulling any of his previous stunts?" said the Chairman. "He just can't help himself."

"He was never given enough good hidings as a child," said the Chef.

"I couldn't agree more," said Matthews.

"I have to agree with Steadman," said Blackie. "I think we're getting carried away. I know he likes to fool around and I know he can be a pain in the butt at times, but this train's a highly sophisticated piece of kit. Someone like Alec Morris wouldn't have a clue how to operate a machine like this. I've never even known him change a spark plug or use a set of jump leads. Has anyone, for that matter?"

"Why don't you ask him yourself?" said the Chairman. "He's coming down the corridor, as we speak. And while you're at it Blackie-ask him what the transmission oil on his face is all about."

CHAPTER FOUR
THE FIRST DIVISION

Tony Hamill's relationship with the Club Vice Chairman Kenny Hulme had not always been so fractious. In fact, for just over 10 years, the two men had been next door neighbours and had often worked side by side for the same Merseyside based civil engineering firm. That had been a decade during which, their children and wives had grown very close and one that had often seen them holidaying together around Britain and some of the less commercialised parts of Northern Spain. However, things changed somewhat dramatically after Hamill had been overlooked for a much coveted promotion that would have brought him financial security until the day he chose to hang up his tools and retire. Furthermore, to confound things further for the bitterly disappointed Hamill, that position had eventually gone to Kenny Hulme, the younger and less experienced technician. It was an indignity compounded the following month when the company announced that 20 workers including the luckless Hamill, were to be made redundant without the agreed redundancy package that had made the job so appealing in the first place. It meant that while Hulme had been able to celebrate and look forward to a bright and secure future, the fifty year old Tony Hamill had been left to dread what the future might hold.

With the country rooted in economic recession, the next few years proved to be extremely difficult for Hamill and his family because despite filling out more than 100 job applications, advertising his credentials in local newspapers and enquiring at over 30 North West industrial estates, the experienced engineer failed to secure a single interview. That meant that he and his family, against all his deeply entrenched principles, had become entirely dependent upon welfare benefits-an income that had been enough for them to survive and get by but one that meant previous luxuries, that for so long had been taken for granted, like running a nice car, improving the home and going on holiday were unrealistic.

That didn't mean Hamill had been short of offers of help however. In fact, several of his former work colleagues including his next door neighbour Kenny Hulme and his recently retired manager had visited him on a number of occasions to offer some financial and moral support. Unfortunately, those acts of kindness had nearly always been met with a derisory comment, a sarcastic remark or even a threat and as a result, the visits became less and less frequent until nobody bothered calling at all.

And that was the way things were until the following Spring, when a cautious and extremely hesitant Kenny Hulme knocked on the Hamill door holding a bottle of Champagne and brandishing a white handkerchief above his head. He had anticipated the door slamming in his face or a torrent of verbal abuse so nobody was more surprised than the Vice Chairman when a smiling Hamill removed the safety latch, drew open the door and invited him inside. That was because news of his cul-de-sac syndicate lottery win had already filtered through earlier that morning via their appropriately named and infamously nosey postman Harry Parker. Of course the warmth that Hamill had initially demonstrated had been a sham because all he had really wanted know was how much they had won, what that figure came to divided by 6 and when the cheque was likely to clear.

However, within days of Hulme calling to Hamill's home, a problem arose. A very serious problem. A problem that had kept Kenny Hulme and his wife awake for much of the previous evening and most of the next day's early hours. That was because the other four members of the syndicate had discovered that Hamill had failed to pay any of his weekly £5.00 lottery dues for the entire period since he had been made redundant. That was a sum that by then amounted to nearly £800. And Hamill's position within the syndicate had become even more precarious when the treasurer quoted a signed and witnessed agreement that stated that if any member fell more than 3 months in arrears, they would be forced to forfeit their place with immediate effect. Most damagingly of all, as far as Hamill was concerned, was the fact that the treasurer had also pointed out that, at that time, their estranged member was not just 3 months in arrears, but a massive and apparently irreconcilable 38.

That hadn't prevented Kenny Hulme from fighting Hamill's corner though. In fact, he had risked his friendship with the other syndicate members and his reputation as an honest man by falsely insisting that Hamill had in fact got every penny of the missing money stashed in a shoe box under his bed and had only failed to pay up because none of the syndicate members had bothered with him since he had lost his job. That had caused each of those members to take a long, hard self-recriminating look at themselves. That had changed things significantly. That was the thing that had swung the argument in Hamill's favour. Therefore, right at the thirteenth hour, and just as the expulsion notice was about to be signed and delivered, Kenny Hulme got reward for his dogged persistence when the members agreed to give Hamill 24 hours to pay the debt in full.

It was a lie that had prevented Hamill's expulsion from the syndicate but Hulme would often argue that it was one that had been contrived in order to save the last remnants of a desperate man's sanity. Nevertheless, it had created yet another dilemma because, with another child on the way and a large unpaid tax demand staring him in the face, Kenny Hulme was in no position to offer any financial assistance at all. It meant that the only way Hamill was going to be able to raise that sort of money within the demanded time constraint was to either get on his knees and beg, do the unthinkable and steal or do what he'd always hated doing and borrow.

IN THE PRESENCE OF MADNESS

In the meantime, while Hamill continued to agonise as to how he was going to raise the missing money, the members of the lottery syndicate, while attempting to verify their claim, had received some very disturbing news. They had learnt that instead of landing a small fortune, there was no money to come because the member of the syndicate that had filled out the tickets at his local newsagents, had failed to tick the box marked, 'Saturday's draw' and because he had unwittingly walked into the shop on a Wednesday afternoon, the syndicate's Lottery money had gone on that particular night's draw rather than the more lucrative Saturday draw which would have netted each one of them an equal share of a tidy £1.250,000.

Ironically, at that very juncture, while the other members of the syndicate were cursing their misfortune, throwing their hands in the air and punching and kicking anything from windows to walls, Hamill was just down the road in a very different, far more contented frame of mind. For once, he wasn't throwing tantrums, swearing or wanting to punch or kick anything or anyone. He was almost purring with immense satisfaction. In fact, he wanted to kiss people, not kick them. He wanted to hug people not hurt them. He wanted to kiss and hug just about everyone. Because, for the first time in a long time, he was back in love with his existence. That was because he had just slipped a bulging brown envelope through the syndicate treasurer's letterbox. A bulging brown envelope, it should be noted, that had contained a sum of money that had been acquired without him having to resort to theft or other foul means. Although, in fairness, he had been forced to pawn his and his wife's gold wedding rings, take out a disturbingly high interest loan with a notorious loan shark and had gone cap in hand with his palms open to his father-in-law. A man who he detested and consequently hadn't spoken to for over 12 years.

For obvious reasons, the unenviable task of explaining the whys and wherefores regarding the lottery debacle had been left to Kenny Hulme but even though the rest of the devastated syndicate members had backed up his account of events, Hamill, who by then was up to his neck in ever worsening debt, would believe none of it and subsequently proceeded with a law suit that failed miserably and only succeeded in putting him deeper into financial meltdown.

As Hamill stood behind his sitting room window considering his own misfortune, (as he had become more and more inclined to do since becoming unemployed), he would have been aware that things had continued to get better and better for his neighbour who, shortly after his firm had merged with a prominent American Elevator Company, had found himself promoted and responsible for managing an entire department with a cohort of 130 men and women. A massive salary rise, appropriate with Hulme's rapidly growing status within the firm, soon followed and in the ensuing months, the mentally shattered and hugely resentful Hamill would watch him oversee the building of a magnificent new conservatory and see him take delivery of a brand new Mercedes-Benz E Class estate. 'They were the rewards for hard work and loyal service', the conscientious Hulme had told his proud family after watching his newly constructed water feature in the shape of a Bottlenose dolphin expel its first squirt of water 30 feet across the newly laid lawn..Hamill had viewed those 'rewards' very differently however. He had seen them as evidence the syndicate, despite all their impassioned denials, had indeed won a large sum of money on the National Lottery, and therefore indisputable proof that he had been the victim of an extremely cruel and elaborate con. That was the reason he had come to hate Kenny Hulme and anybody in any way connected to him so discovering his brother in law Alec Morris had been responsible for the train setting off early had been music to his ears and the highlight of what for everybody else had been a very difficult morning. "I told you didn't I," said Hamill after racing over to the door to see a twitchy and self conscious Morris disappearing into the second carriage washroom. "I knew the problem would have something to do with the committee."

"It's got nothing to do with us," said the Club Secretary.

"It's got everything to do with you," said Hamill. "You lot were meant to be keeping Morris out of trouble."

"Whose responsibility was it to keep an eye on this old boy?" said Steadman after struggling through the far dining carriage door with the victim of the recent platform accident cradled across his arms.

"Bloody hell!" said Blackie after helping lower the old man to the floor. "Where did you find him Steadman?"

"On the floor of the first washroom," said Steadman.

"How the hell did he get there?" said Woodhouse.

"I put him there," said Matthews.

"Why?" said Woodhouse.

"It was cooler in there," said Matthews. "The poor old bugger was burning up."

"Has anyone got any smelling salts?" said the Club Secretary.

"I think I've got some in my room," said the Chef while making his way through the slowly growing circle of concerned and suspicious men. "I'll go and have a look."

"I'd forgotten all about this fella," said the Club Secretary.

"Me too," said the Chairman.

"What happened Matthews?" said the Club Secretary. "How come he's still here?"

"That's what I'd like to know," said Woodhouse.

"I was summoned to an emergency meeting like the rest of you," said Matthews. "The old boy completely slipped my mind."

"He's not the missing train driver is he?" said McShane.

"I wouldn't have thought so," said the Club Secretary. "He's far too old. I reckon he's just an old train spotter. I noticed him hanging around the platform earlier."

"I noticed him too," said Woodhouse. "Just before he slipped in Kenny Biddo's puke."

[62]

'That's nice," said Hamill. "What was it our Chairman said earlier about maintaining standards?"

"Shut your face Hamill," said the Chairman. "This isn't the time for any of your infamous sarcasm. There's an old man in trouble here. Why don't you do something useful for a change. Like see if anyone's sneaked any alcohol on board."

"They shouldn't have," said Matthews. "You told them not to. You made it clear that no alcohol was to be brought on board the train."

"I know I did," said the Chairman. "But I'm not stupid Matthews. I didn't think for one minute everyone would do as they were bloody well told."

"He also told a certain portly person to put some clothes on," said the Club Secretary.

"That's right-I did didn't I," said the Chairman."So run along will you Woody. Go and get dressed lad."

"Yes, get dressed Woody," said Hamill. "I'm expecting guests."

"I will in a minute," said Woodhouse.

"Do it now for God's sake," said a disgusted Kenny Biddo while shielding his eyes. "Grown men shouldn't be seen walking around like that."

"Walking around like what?" said Woodhouse.

"Walking around with all your private parts on show," said Kenny Biddo. "It's disgusting. You're a disgrace. My young son's over there."

"I know very well your son's over there," said Woodhouse before reaching over to attract his good friend McShane's attention. "He hasn't been able to take his eyes off me for the last half hour. I think he wants a piece of my bottom. What do you think Macca?"

"I think you might be right," said McShane while regarding his good friend's rear end with mock admiration. "The question is-what piece of your bottom is he likely to want? There's just so much of it to choose from."

"Don't be hard faced," said Woodhouse.

"And don't be winding Biddo up you two," said the Chairman. "We've just got the bugger straightened out."

Thankfully, the elderly gentleman hadn't suffered serious injury and it therefore wasn't long before he was being helped back to his feet amid a busy mesh of eager fingers, hands and arms. Nevertheless, the incident had left many of the passengers at least mildly shaken and their state of mind wasn't made any better when the old man once again lost the use of his legs momentarily.

"Watch yourself granddad," said Steadman while quickly helping the swooning old man into a chair. "I thought you were going for me throat there when you lunged forward. You're not looking for trouble are you?"

"I'm not, no," said the old man. "I'm just looking to establish my bearings."

"You're aboard a train," said the Chairman.

"A train!" said the stranger. "What sort of train?"

"I don't really know to be honest," said the Chairman.

"It's a runaway train," said Hamill.

"Shut it Hamill," said the Chairman.

"You're in the dining carriage of a train sir," said the Club Secretary.

"Am I really?" said the old man. "The dining carriage of a train hey! How in the name of Zeus has that happened?"

"You slipped and banged your head on the platform," said the Club Secretary. "One of our members brought you on board to look after you."

"I see," said the old man. "Then I'm in his debt. I'm actually in all your debts. I've absolutely no idea how I'm going to thank you."

"You could give me the name of your tailor," said Steadman. "That outfit would look great on me. I'd love to walk into the West Lancs Golf Club bar with that gear on. They'd probably make me Club President on the spot."

The outfit that Steadman had referred to did

indeed have a rare and extraordinary touch of class about it but just like the train and the newly built station, it had clearly been designed for a bygone and very different era. It consisted of a pair of traditional Gibson tan leather brogues, a pair of superbly tailored beige wide leg double pleated trousers and a rear vented burgundy, virgin wool hounds tooth, single breasted blazer with notch lapels and two leather trimmed flap pockets. Even so, it was the bright red, slightly frayed velvet dickey bow that gave the outfit that extra touch of class, particularly in the fashion conscious eyes of the aforementioned Steadman Hamilton-Swan, the notoriously vain Ian Blackhurst and the always immaculately turned out Vice Chairman, Kenny Hulme.

There were other aspects of the old man's appearance that several of the gathering would initially find interesting including the almost aristocratic way he held himself when he stood up and the fact that he was giving off a pleasant, almost intoxicating odour of high quality Cuban tobacco and expensive cologne. There was no doubt he was a man of considerable age though. His almost white beard that came to a point about two inches from his prominent chin, the deeply gouged lines that forked away from his deep set piercing blue eyes and the way he grimaced before he took or rose from a chair were testimony to that fact. And yet, for many, it would be his alertness and intelligence that would impress most of all-something that was first witnessed after one of the least concerned members had uttered some sort of disparaging remark from behind his chair.

"For your information young man," he said with an authority that instantly aroused the attention of those among the gathering that had been otherwise occupied. "I served in the British armed forces for over 30 years. In fact, I've served my country on every continent on our planet. And I assure you this...I wasn't, as you've just tried to infer-one of those toffee nosed officers that stood safely out of the way of the action barking out orders to what you described as 'machine gun fodder'. I was wounded on several occasions while leading my men into battle."

"Take no notice of him," said Blackie. "It's not personal. McShane just has this hatred of authority figures."

"He does yes," said Woodhouse. "Particularly officers of the high ranking sort."

"I hate the bastards," said McShane.

"Why's that?" said the old man.

"That's my business," said McShane.

"He had a bad time of it while he was doing his military training," said Blackie. "He spent most of it staring at the walls of the Glasshouse."

"That's because he hates being told what to do," said Matthews.

"You keep your nose out Matthews," said McShane. "How would you like it if you'd been forced to spend your first 6 months of training, emptying latrines, peeling mountains of spuds and cutting a lazy bastard Colonel's lawn with a pair of nail scissors and a comb?"

"I'd have done what I was ordered to do in the first place," said Matthews.

"Of course you would," said McShane. "That's because you're an arsehole creeper. You're just a yes man Matthews. You always have been. Now get out of my sight while I'm still in a lenient mood."

"Cut it out Tommy," said the Chairman. "I've told you before. Keep your hands and your threats to yourself. In the meantime, do the honours Hilly. I think some formal introductions might be in order."

"I suppose you all must be wondering what the blazes an old fuddy duddy like me was doing on a freezing cold platform at such an unearthly hour," said the old man after the Club Secretary had finally completed his rather laboured and drawn out formalities. "Therefore, let me explain...I'm Professor Seymour

White. And as some of you are already aware, I spend a lot of my leisure time travelling the country looking at and riding upon old trains. Is that why you gentlemen are here? Are you all train enthusiasts too, by any chance?"

"Not really," said the Chairman. "We just like getting away from our humdrum existences from time to time. I think we're guinea pigs to be honest."

"Guinea pigs!" said the old man.

"More like crash test dummies," said the Club Secretary.

"You might be right Hilly," said the Chairman. "We've been invited to take part in a feasibility run so that the railway company can assess things like timings and cost. I haven't got a clue who came up with the idea by the way."

"Or why they chose the likes of us," said the Club Secretary.

"But it's free," said Kenny Biddo. "And because it's free-and because I've escaped the clutches of my long suffering and often difficult wife-I intend getting shit faced."

"Shit faced!" said the old man. "I don't understand. What does 'shit faced' mean?"

"Blotto," said Biddo. "Pissed out of my mind. Drunk as a skunk. Rat arsed stinking drunk. Does that make it any clearer?"

"Much clearer thank you," said the old man.

"Take no notice of him Professor," said the Chairman. "As my secretary just went around the world to explain-we're members of a veteran men's club from Crosby in Merseyside. Right now, most of us are more interested in why the train took off early rather than what it looks like and what sort of horsepower it boasts."

"And more importantly-why it took off without a driver," said Blackie.

"That's right," said Steadman. "That's got me worried sick."

"It's got us all worried sick," said Hamill.

"Why's that?" said the old man.

"Because it has," said Steadman. "Some of us are out of our minds with worry. We want to see our wives and kids again."

"And you will see your wives and kids again," said the old man.

"Not if we collide head on with another big bastard train coming from the opposite direction?" said Steadman.

"Why would we?" asked the old man.

"Because there's nobody to apply the brake," replied Steadman.

"You don't need anyone to apply the brake," said the old man.

"Oh I beg to differ," said Steadman. "Call me old fashioned if you like Professor-but since I started driving at the age of 18, I've been a huge fan of having a brake on my vehicles."

"Maybe so, but you don't really need one right now," said the old man.

"What makes you so sure?" said the Club Secretary.

"Yes, I'd like to know that," said the Chairman. "How can you be so certain Professor?"

"Because, unless I'm mistaken, this is a one way track and a single train service," said the old man. "Think about what you've just told me for goodness sake. It's a test run. Apart from snow, leaves and the odd dead pigeon, there's going to be nothing else on this line."

"I hope you're right Professor," said the Club Secretary. "I pray to God you're right."

"I know I'm right," said the old man. "And if it helps you all rest more easily, I'm prepared to stake my reputation on me being right."

"It's certainly going to help *me* rest more easily," said the Chairman before settling back into his chair and removing his notepad from his breast pocket. "Thank God for that."

"Well don't go thanking the Lord too prematurely," said the approaching Steadman before spreading a badly crumpled piece of paper on the Chairman's table.

"We're going to arrive at our destination sooner or later. Which means sooner or later we're going to hit a set of buffers at a dangerously high speed. It's just a matter of when. That's right isn't it Professor?"

"Ordinarily, it would be," said the old man. "But, according to the literature I've read, this train is scheduled to stop to refuel at least twice before it reaches Selkirk. I am right aren't I gentlemen-you are heading for Selkirk aren't you?"

"We are yes," said the Chairman.

"Well, relax and enjoy the trip then," said the old man.

"Is that what you majored in, back in the day Professor?" said the Club Secretary. "Did you study engineering?"

"I'm an epidemiologist," said the old man.

"A what?" said the Chairman.

"An epidemiologist," said the Professor. "I study diseases. The more serious and more uncommon the better. I'm currently taking a sabbatical from the East African Institute of Tropical Medicine. Me and my colleagues have one goal and one goal alone. To rid the world of disgusting and unwelcome pests and parasites."

"You're going to be a Godsend here then," said the slowly rising Chairman.

"Can you do anything to eradicate the likes of him?" said the Club Secretary while pointing towards Kenny Biddo who for some reason was floundering on the floor like an overturned tortoise.

That incident wasn't the only thing the mightily relieved gathering would find amusing during the short period that followed the Chairman's discreet departure, because within seconds of Biddo succeeding to right himself by means of a table leg and his son's trouser belt, a rather serious looking Richard Hewlett glided into the dining carriage wearing a classic knee length 1930s smoking jacket and matching cobalt blue silk cravat.

"You've got to be kidding me!" said Woodhouse after slapping his enormous right thigh and beckoning the

[69]

other preoccupied men to take notice. "Is it Olivier Award night? It must be mustn't it. Is that who I think it is? Is that the literary giant Noel Coward? I think it is you know. I think it's Noel Coward."

"You think it's Noel Coward!" scoffed Hewlett before settling down gracefully at one of the outer tables. "What would you know about Noel Coward? You're not fit to utter the great man's name. In fairness, you wouldn't be able to discern Noel Coward from Noel Edmunds. By the way-has anybody seen my copy of the Times? I seem to have mislaid it."

"Have you tried looking in the lavatory?" said Hamill.

"Why the lavatory?" said a suspicious Hewlett.

"Because that's where you sometimes find newspapers," said Hamill.

"Is it really?" said Hewlett. "Why?"

"Because a lavatory roll doesn't last forever," said Woodhouse.

"Which means people are sometimes forced to make do," said Hamill.

"Oh dear Lord!" said Hewlett. "That's lovely that is."

"I thought I saw it in the third washroom," said McShane.

"Which means we've got a sneak thief in our midst," said Hewlett.

"It was just a bloody newspaper," said Woodhouse.

"It wasn't just a newspaper," said Hewlett. "It was *my* newspaper. And I demand to know who stole it. What about you Hamill. Can you shed any light on this matter?"

"I'm saying nothing," said Hamill.

"Which probably means you're the culprit," said Hewlett. "Admit it Hamill...You either stole the newspaper or know who did."

"I'm saying nothing," said Hamill.

"It was me," said McShane. "And I'm not prepared to say anymore until my lawyer's present."

"Your lawyer!" scoffed Hewlett. "Who in their right mind would represent the likes of you?"

"Me brother's mate for one," said McShane.

"Your brother's mate!" said Hewlett.

"That's right," said McShane.

"Are you trying to tell me your brother's mate is a qualified lawyer?" said Hewlett.

"I wouldn't go that far," said McShane. "But he's got all his law certificates."

"What do you mean?" said Hewlett.

"He bought a law diploma on EBay last year for £500," said McShane. "There's no stopping him now. He's making one hell of a killing I can tell you. Particularly now drugs are so popular. He's a right clever bastard. He's the smartest person I know by some distance. You'd never win an argument against him. He's got three O levels And one of them was a 'B-'."

"My word!" said Hewlett. "That is impressive. Mensa must be constantly breaking down his door to get him to solve problems for them."

"I wouldn't know about that," said McShane. "I do know this though. He's not soft. He only works cash in hand. He won't have anything to do with cheques or the tax people."

"Why's that?" said Hewlett.

"He doesn't trust them," said McShane.

"Oh for the love of God!" said Hewlett while looking towards the ceiling with his arms reaching skywards. "Please God have mercy and strike me dead right now. I'm ready...I'm ready Father. Into your hands, I commit my spirit. I beseech you Lord-please spare me from any more of this madness. I must be going insane? Did I really just hear all that? Will somebody help me please. Did I just hear that?"

"You did," said McShane with an air of jubilation. "It's hard to believe isn't it Hewlett? £500 for a piece of embossed paper that was marked with a coffee stain and full of basic spelling mistakes. I'm telling you-my missus could have knocked up something more authentic looking on her old Amstrad word processor."

"By the way Hewlett-Hamill's got every right to cite the

fifth," said Woodhouse. "You can't go around accusing people of theft. It's not the done thing this day and age. People have got certain rights."

"Cite the fifth!" said Hewlett. "Cite the fifth Woodhouse! What the hell are you talking about? We're residing in the United Kingdom not the United bloody States. The Fifth Amendment doesn't apply in our country. We haven't even got an equivalent of the Fifth Amendment, for God's sake."

"I'm still not saying anything," said Hamill. "In fact, from this moment on, until that mournful day I depart the earth, I'll never utter another word."

"I don't blame you," said Woodhouse. "You've been wronged Hamill. You're not the guilty party here. You're very much the victim."

"Have you thought of contacting Crime Watch?" said McShane.

"That's an idea," said Woodhouse.

"Why is it?" said Hewlett. "What good would that do?"

"A lot more good than you'd probably think," said McShane. "Those Crime Watch people get results. They caught me twice. They might be prepared to put a crime re-enactment together."

"That's right," said Hamill. "I might even contact Mel Gibson to see if he'd be prepared to double for me during the bottom wiping scenes."

"Why don't you?" said McShane. "In fact, why don't you play yourself Hamill. You don't need Mel Gibson's bottom. You're in superb shape for your age. There's nothing wrong with your backside."

"I'd take part in the crime re-enactment," said Woodhouse. "I'd love to do that. I did a little bit of acting when I was in the Boy Scouts. It was one of those Jamboree things. I was in a very good version of Oliver Twist too. I played Eric Sykes."

"You old dark horse you," said McShane. "You kept that quiet."

"I think you'll find the Dickensian character you've just referred to was called Bill Sykes," said Hewlett while

[72]

shaking his head in utter disdain.

"Well, Bill Sykes then, if you want to nitpick," said Woodhouse. "What does it matter? That's not the point here. We're trying to establish who will play who should the people from Crime Watch come calling. Come to think about it Hewlett-I might suggest I play you."

"Play me!" said Hewlett while easing his cravat. "Play me! How utterly absurd. How could you possibly play me? For the love of all that's holy-you're at least three times the size of me. Your bottom probably weighs more than me. Now where's my newspaper? What have you done with it? What's that on the table next to you McShane?"

"It's mine," said McShane before snatching a nearby copy of a tabloid and clutching it tightly to his chest.

"What is it?" said Hewlett. "Show me. Don't forget-as the victim of the theft, I've got rights too."

"It's mine," said the smiling McShane.

"What is it?" said Hewlett. "Answer me Tommy or I'll make a formal complaint to the committee. I'll make sure your feet don't touch the floor."

"Do your worst," said McShane.

"It's the Sunday Sport if you must know," said the Club Secretary after letting out an exaggerated sigh.

"It's far more than that," said McShane. "It's my Sunday Sport."

"I don't doubt it," said Hewlett. "And I'm certainly not going to contest your claim. I wouldn't be seen using it to wipe dog muck from the sole of my shoes. What's the main article this week Tommy-has some over the hill comedian devoured a live hamster while on stage?"

"It's none of your business," said McShane.

"I was right wasn't I?" said Hewlett. "That's it isn't it? That's the headline isn't it? 'FREDDY STARR ATE MY HAMSTER'."

"You're well short of the mark," said McShane.

"What is it then?" said Hewlett. "Has another London bus been found on the moon?"

[73]

"You're getting warmer," said McShane. "At least you're now in the right part of the galaxy."

"What do you mean?" said Hewlett. "What do you mean Tommy? You're not trying to tell me that the editors of that nonsensical rag of yours are claiming they've found something else on the moon are you?"

"I'm not trying to tell you anything-I'm just stating the facts as I understand them," said McShane.

"What facts?" said Hewlett. "What are those tuppence halfpenny journalists claiming now?"

"A plane's been found," said McShane. "A World War Two bomber to be precise."

"A World War Two bomber!" said Hewlett. "On the moon?"

"That's right," said McShane. "You heard me Hewlett. It's all here. Read it for yourself if you want. It seems that a fully functional Lancaster bomber has been found on the moon during an expedition to collect rock samples."

"Fully functional!" said Hewlett. "That's remarkable. Tell me Tommy. Is it the newspaper people who are claiming the plane's fully functional or are you?"

"I am," said McShane.

"Really!" said Hewlett. "And you can justify that claim can you?"

"Of course I can," said McShane. "The plane's undamaged. There's not a scratch on the thing."

"And that makes it fully functional does it?" said Hewlett.

"I'd say so," said McShane. "Those old planes were built to last."

"They were indeed," said Woodhouse. "They had Rolls Royce engines you know."

"I didn't know that," said McShane. "That's interesting that is. To be honest Woody-unless it was you that had told me that story, I wouldn't have believed it."

"But, for some inexplicable reason, you do believe one of those old bombers could not only fly as far as the moon, but successfully land there," said Hewlett.

[74]

"I wouldn't have done," said McShane while holding up
the newspaper. "I'd have normally laughed the idea out
of town. But take a look at these photographs Hewlett.
Look at them. Look closely. Nothing's been
superimposed. Nothing's been airbrushed. There's no
skulduggery gone on there. That's a genuine photograph
that is. As they say Hewlett-the camera doesn't lie. I'm
telling you-that's definitely a Lancaster bomber."
"It is," said Kenny Biddo. "I once made an Airfix
model of one when I came out of rehab for the fourth
time."
"But it's not necessarily on the moon is it?" said
Hewlett.
"How do you know Hewlett?" said McShane. "Have
you ever been to the moon? Do you know what it looks
like? Anyway, Lord Snooty...I'd rather read my Sunday
Sport than your boring old rag. At least if we crash, I
can say that the last thing I saw was a pair of tits."
"So can I," said a beaming Hamill while pointing
towards the straight faced and unamused committee
pairing of Kenny Hulme and Jeff Hill. "Two very big
tits."
"That was good that was Hamill," said the Club
Secretary. "By the way-I thought you'd decided never
to talk again."
"I had," said Hamill. "But I had to come out of
retirement for that last remark didn't I? I couldn't help
myself. It was too big an opportunity to miss."
"My word-are you people always like this?" said the
Professor while making his unsteady way to Hewlett's
table.
"Like what?" said Hamill.
"Are you always badgering each other?" said the
Professor.
"Only on week days and weekends," said Hewlett.
"They're actually on their best behaviour right now."
"Are they really?" said the old man.
"Very much so," said Hewlett. "For instance, since
your dramatic entrance, Woodhouse appears to have

[75]

gone to extraordinary lengths to avoid breaking wind."
"That's damn decent of him," said the old man.
"It is isn't it," said Hewlett. "And Kenny Biddo, the reason for your unfortunate accident, hasn't thrown up for the last half hour."
"That's a record for an away trip," said Hamill.
"It is indeed," said Hewlett. "It's amazing when you come to think about it. But what's even more amazing is Tommy Mac's newly discovered self control."
"What do you mean?" said the old man.
"Tommy Mac's famous for his vast range of profanities," said Hewlett. "The only thing that usually comes out of his mouth that isn't an expletive is his toothbrush."
"If you're not careful Hewlett, there'll be one or two teeth coming out of yours," said McShane.
"Be nice now Macca," said the Club Secretary.
"Yes-go and lie down," said the Vice Chairman.
"That's the darker side of him Professor," said Hewlett before rising from his chair, and tightening the belt on his housecoat. "When he's behaving like that I always try to give him a wide berth. I've often wondered why he doesn't come with a government health warning."
"I'm beginning to wonder that myself," said the old man discreetly.
"I'm Richard," said Hewlett before straightening his shoulders and thrusting out his right hand. "Richard. T Hewlett. The third son of the Hewletts of Blundelsands. If you've ever stumbled upon a copy of *Horse and Hounds* magazine in a doctor's waiting room, you'll be familiar with the name. The Hewlett family feature regularly. We're historically steeped in equestrianism. We stable several Arabian thoroughbreds near Formby. My brother Kevin looks after the stud aspect of the business. He makes sure things get pregnant, so to speak. I know very little about that sort of thing."
"I wouldn't disagree there," said a beaming Hamill before engaging in a highly complex gangster style handshake with his delighted friend Woodhouse.

[76]

"Take no notice of him," said Hewlett. "He's just a very jealous and malicious man. How are you doing sir? How's that head of yours?"

"I think I'll just about pull through," said the Professor before removing a handkerchief from his breast pocket and wiping his brow. "In fact, as we speak, one or two snippets of recognition are beginning to materialise. I remember seeing you lot heading towards the waiting rooms for some reason. And I recall putting my bag down so that I could get tactile with this superbly crafted engine. But I still don't know why I slipped? Had one of the maintenance chaps spilt oil?"

"You slipped because that man had spewed the entire contents of his gut onto the platform," said Hewlett while gesturing towards Kenny Biddo who, at that very moment, appeared to be remonstrating with some invisible foe. "You must have inadvertently stepped in it Professor. What else can you remember?"

"Not a lot," said the old man. "Although I do recall that rather surly looking gentleman having a remarkably unusual bedside manner."

"Which one?" said Hewlett.

"The one that's engaged in some sort of bizarre ritual with the big naked chap," said the Professor. "The one that just made the disparaging remark regarding your testicles and ability to procreate."

"That's Tony Hamill," said Hewlett. "But if you don't mind me saying so Professor-you use the word 'gentleman' too freely. I assure you-he's no gentleman. Was he a little heavy handed with you?"

"He was extremely heavy handed," said the old man. "He was one of the first on the scene. But instead of tending to my needs, he proceeded to roll me over with the sole of his shoe as if I was a dead frog."

"Oh dear," said Hewlett. "That's not very nice is it."

"Neither is having to look at that enormous character who, for some reason, isn't wearing any clothes," whispered the Professor after pulling Hewlett close. "Why is that? Why is he naked for pity's sake?"

"I'm not sure," whispered Hewlett. "He must have been caught in a state of undress when the train pulled away. As for remaining unclad-I can only assume he likes the sensation."

"He's a strapping big lad isn't he?" whispered the Professor. "Look at the arms on him. I wouldn't like to get on the wrong side of him. What does he do for a living?"

"He's a ballet dancer," said McShane.

"He does a variety of things," whispered Hewlett. "I think he's currently employed as a nightclub doorman somewhere in Liverpool city centre. They say he once wrestled a Ugandan mountain gorilla for money."

"Never!" whispered the old man. "How exhilarating. How did that come about?"

"Demi Roussos organised it," said Woodhouse before cupping his private parts and settling down opposite Hewlett and the old man. "I used to be one of his minders. You must have heard of Demis Roussos Professor."

"I have, as a matter of fact," said the old man. "He was a huge Cypriot with the voice of an Angel, if my memory serves me correctly."

"Greek," said Woodhouse. "He was Greek. It's a little known secret that Prize and novelty fighting were among his passions. He liked to watch karate champions take on boxers and teams of midgets fight grizzly bears. I once escorted him to an abandoned Sydney theatre to see a washed out Rumanian heavyweight box a kangaroo."

"My word!" said the old man. "Who won?"

"The kangaroo," said Woodhouse. "It killed the East European stone dead with one swift kick to the head. Unfortunately, it then jumped the ropes and killed three members of the audience as well. It was carnage. There were police and press everywhere. I had to get Demis out the back door."

"Oh my days!" said the Professor.

"The weirder the arrangement, the more Demis seemed to enjoy it," said Woodhouse.

"And so he set up a fight with you and a gorilla did he?" said the Professor.
"Only after Sly Stallone had bottled out," said Woodhouse.
"Sly Stallone!" said the old man. "Should I know who that is?"
"He's a famous American action film star," said Woodhouse. "He often plays the hard man roles."
"Does he really?" said the old man.
"He's a massive name in Hollywood," said Woodhouse. "And worth a fortune too. That's why the purse didn't mean that much to him. He can earn that sort of money without getting out of bed."
"What was the purse?" said the Professor.
"$30,000," said Woodhouse. "It worked out $1,000 a stone."
"What does that mean?" said the old man.
"The gorilla weighed in at 30 stone," said Woodhouse. "According to his trainer that is. I thought he looked a lot bigger to be honest."
"Holy mackerel!" said the old man. "That's some gorilla. Didn't you find that a bit daunting Mr Woodhouse?"
"Not really," said Woodhouse. "As a Liverpool doorman, I've been known to fight bigger and heavier things than that."
"And some of them were men," remarked the passing Hamill.
"Goodness me!" said the old man. "How did you get on? I mean-how did the fight with the gorilla go?"
"I got disqualified," said Woodhouse.
"For doing what?" said the increasingly fascinated Professor.
"I buried my knee in the gorilla's plums while the referee was still issuing his instructions," said Woodhouse.
"Oh dear!" said the old man. "That wasn't very Marquess of Queensbury was it?"
"He started it," said Woodhouse. "He was a bad

tempered bastard. A right filthy piece of work too."
"Why's that?" said the old man. "Did he go for your
eyes or something?"
"It was nothing like that," said Woodhouse. "I could
have coped with that. I'm no idiot Professor. I was
prepared for that sort of thing. You've got to be
prepared for all kinds of dirty tricks in the back street
fight game."
"Well, what did he do then?" said the old man.
"He did something grossly obscene," said Woodhouse.
"Something that nobody in the history of organised prize
fighting has ever done. At least, not to my knowledge."
"What was that?" said the old man. "Pray tell me Mr
Woodhouse-you've got me intrigued."
"He dropped his shorts, shit in his hand and threw the lot
at me as I was entering the ring," said Woodhouse.
"Never!" said the old man while doing his utmost to
keep a straight face.
"It's absolutely true," said an appalled looking
Woodhouse. "Not even Mike Tyson would have pulled
a stroke like that. He ruined me best trunks and a brand
new silk dressing gown."
"I imagine he did," said the Professor.
"You should have seen the state of me," said
Woodhouse. "I was caked in the filthy stuff. I stank to
high hell. People were backing away from me as if I
was a leper."
"That's because you'd become unclean," said Hamill.
"Don't you start," said Woodhouse.
"And then what happened?" said the old man.
"Another indignity," said Woodhouse. "His punch
drunk trainer threw a clump of bananas at me and called
me a big ape. There's irony for you Professor. That was
when I lost the plot completely."
"What did you do?" said the old man.
"I picked up my stool and beat the gorilla senseless,"
said Woodhouse.
"Dear Lord!" said the old man. "You were an angry
boy weren't you."

[80]

"I was livid," said Woodhouse. "I've never been so angry in my life."

"Would I be correct in assuming you forfeited the right to your share of the purse?" said the old man.

"You would," said Woodhouse. "But Demi compensated me to a certain extent. He said it was the funniest thing he'd ever seen. To be honest, the hassle from the Animal Rights people was far worse than losing the money. I had to flee the country incognito in the end."

"I'm not surprised," said the old man. "You did a bad thing Mr Woodhouse. You'd assaulted one of the world's most endangered and valuable creatures. I'm not surprised you were run out of the country."

"I'm not surprised either," said Woodhouse. "But that wasn't why the bastards were wanting to rip me limb from limb."

"Why was it then?" said the old man.

"They'd lost a hell of a lot of money," said Woodhouse.

"Lost money!" said the old man. "What do you mean?"

"They'd put a small fortune on me being dead or at least being in a vegetative state before the end of the third round," said Woodhouse.

"My word!" spluttered the old man. "How very strange. That seems to reek of double standards to me."

"And me," said Woodhouse before rising from his chair and patting the old man on the shoulder. "That's how mental those do good, politically correct, hippy bastards are. I'll never contribute to their causes. I don't care what happens to the whales and the rain forests. They'll never get a penny from me."

For some time after Woodhouse's almost bafflingly absurd account of his fight with the silverback gorilla, and while the majority of the passengers were heading off in various directions to do a variety of things, the old Professor sat almost stupefied as though he was trying to come to terms with an unfathomable equation. It was therefore some sort of relief when he

felt Hewlett tug on his arm and point towards the door.
"We seem to be the only ones not participating in the
mass exodus Professor," he said after depositing the
rolled up Sunday Sport newspaper into a waste basket.
"Might I suggest you join me and my friend Eddie in our
remote, yet well appointed carriage."
"That's very decent of you Richard," said the Professor.
"Don't mention it old sport," said Hewlett. "Before I
left home I got my manservant Waggers to compile me a
hamper containing, among other things, a variety of high
quality wines, spirits and continental cheeses."
"How intuitive of you," said the old man. "We could
have ourselves a little picnic."
"There's no could about it," said Hewlett. "We shall
indeed have a splendid picnic. And the first thing I'm
going to do when we get to my carriage is introduce you
and Eddie to a recently made friend of mine."
"And who might that be?" said the old man.
"A cheeky little blended Scotch Whiskey I discovered
on an Internet auction site about a fortnight ago," said
Hewlett.
"I'm looking forward to getting acquainted with the very
fellow already," said the old man while rubbing his
hands.
"I've no doubt you are," said Hewlett. "You're going to
warm to him immediately. But listen carefully
Professor. Say absolutely nothing to the heathens. The
Scotch is said to be part of an illicit shipment that was
pulled from a sunken steamer off the coast of Eriskay on
the west coast of Scotland. I think they call them 'booze
cruises' this day and age. It's as rare as hen's teeth. It's
appropriately called, 'King's Ransom'. I say
'appropriately' because the case cost me more than some
of these working class idiots earn in a year. I think
you're going to enjoy it. I think you're going to enjoy it
immensely. And it might just help you forget some of
the nonsense you've just been subjected to."
"Is that what you think it was?" said the old man. "Do

you think that enormous friend of yours was talking stuff
and nonsense?" "It wouldn't be the first time," said
Hewlett. "He's so full of hot air, I'm surprised he
doesn't take off.

CHAPTER FIVE
IMPOSING FIGURE

C lub Chairman Tommy Weir was the classic man mountain but certainly no gentle giant. He stood well over six feet high, was extremely powerfully built and since the age of twenty one had developed a mop of thick grey hair that made him look far older than he actually was. It meant that from a tender working age, he had been handed responsibilities usually set aside for much older and far more experienced individuals. However, nobody was more surprised than he was when, after the unexpected resignation of his predecessor, he was invited to take up the position as Chairman. From that moment on, he had been the mainstay of the club and had guided them through their most difficult period during which they had lost a number of players to retirement and had buried two more. He had a very individualistic way of running things which was not necessarily, his way or no way, but rather his way until one of his members could come up with a better or more effective way. That meant that, during his tenure, it was a rare thing for the club to have an unrealistic motion heard and therefore an even rarer thing to see such a motion passed.

Even before he had taken office, Weir had recognised certain inherent problems which he had been determined to address and iron out as quickly as possible and one of those was the lack of unity between the club members. The need for improved camaraderie and team spirit had therefore been one of the key features of his impressive acceptance speech at the club's annual general meeting. He had hoped to improve things by introducing a series of team building activities such as map reading
exercises in remote parts of the country and assault course challenges against rival clubs but although early

[84]

signs had appeared to be positive, it wasn't long before the old problem resurfaced. That had upset him enormously because he firmly believed that in order to have a successful club, he needed the members to exist in relative harmony rather than do what they had become accustomed to do and separate into a number of bitching factions. That didn't mean they couldn't appear to be close knit however-in fact, there were several occasions when the club members appeared to be as thick as Robin Hood's band of merry men-particularly when the spectre of trouble loomed large. As was the case in the Summer of 2004, when, during their annual trip to the North East of England, the members had been enjoying the delights and hospitality of a notoriously rough and seedy Newcastle nightclub.

It had been around 2am when the committee members were alerted to the news that big Paul Woodhouse, after engaging in a heated argument with a steward, had been set upon by four burly doormen and dragged off to a basement and although most of the members had been intent on storming the room and bringing the big man out, Weir had demanded calm and insisted that he would go and sort the matter out in his own particular way.

According to the Club Secretary, who, at the Chairman's bidding, had unwittingly found himself party to what happened next, that particular way could best be described as extraordinarily heroic. He had stood trembling and awash with perspiration as the smiling Weir entered the room and headed into the circle of curious club and hammer wielding doormen. And to this day, he is able to describe the next incredible sequence of events as if they had happened only seconds ago. How the Chairman, upon noticing a set of keys on the club owner's desk, sprang over and snatched them before quickly retreating and putting his back against the basement door. How one by one the disbelieving and dumb struck doormen had turned to each other for answers and how rapidly the colour on those same men's faces had drained as if some sort of blood pressure related valve had suddenly stopped functioning.

"Now then gentlemen," he had said after locking the door, flinging the keys through an open window and returning to the centre of the circle of disbelieving men. "If you're carrying a mobile phone, I suggest you do this one thing for me. Talk to your wives or partners. Tell them you love them very much. But more importantly-tell them you won't be coming home tonight."

No phone calls or last goodbyes had been necessary however, because within seconds, the club owner had called off his men and requested he and the Chairman go upstairs and sort the whole business out over a couple of drinks. Nevertheless, whether or not any violence flared or whether Weir had been playing an extremely dangerous game of bluff, it was the sort of stuff that creates legends and an example of just how far he would go to fulfil his duty of care regarding his members. That was just one of the reasons Tommy Weir commanded so much respect and why his position as Chairman had never once been questioned or contested.

That duty of care extended to making his members feel as secure as possible and, despite what the old man had said earlier regarding the train being unable to complete the journey to Selkirk without stopping for fuel or water, he knew that he wasn't going to be able to rest until that was confirmed. That was the reason he had sent engineers Kenny Hulme and Jeff Hill to examine the engine-although upon their return to their sleeping carriage less than thirty minutes later, the omens didn't look very promising. "The place is totally deserted," said the Club Secretary while scratching his head. "It's quite spooky really. The wind is howling. The only evidence of anyone having been there is a discarded Snickers wrapper." "We assume it belonged to Morris," said a shivering Hulme before kicking off his shoes and wrapping himself in his quilt.

"That figures," said the Chairman. "Can I also assume you had no luck in finding the brake?"

"You can," said the Club Secretary. "There was nothing resembling a brake. At least, not a brake as we know one."

"I think you'd need to be Einstein to understand the workings of this contraption," said Hulme. "I've never seen so many lights and buttons in my life. It's like something from a Star Trek set."

"We were able to identify the speedometer and pressure gauges," said the Club Secretary.

"What did they tell you?" said the Chairman.

"That we're averaging around 48 kilometres an hour," said Hulme.

"That's not too concerning," said the Chef.

"It is to me," said the Chairman. "I'm a dinosaur. What's that in pounds, shillings and pence?"

"About 30 miles per hour," said the Club Secretary.

"That's encouraging," said the Chairman.

"And the pressure appears to be stable," said Hulme. "Do you want the numbers?"

"Don't bother," said the Chairman.

"And how far are we from Selkirk?" said the Chef.

"About 600 miles now," said the Club Secretary after quickly referring to his notes. "According to the route marked in red on this map, that is."

"Which means what exactly?" said the Chef.

"Take a look for yourself," said Hulme after handing his brother his copy of the trip schedule. "It looks like we're going to be travelling in a gigantic Z shape."

"More importantly, it means that even if we keep running at our current speed, we're not likely to get into Selkirk for another 18 or 19 hours at best," said the Club Secretary.

"That would be about 6.30 to 7.30 tomorrow morning wouldn't it?" said the Chef. "Is that right Hilly?"

"As near as damn it," said the Club Secretary. "If we take into account the miles we've already covered that is."

"Excellent," said the Chairman before flicking the top from his energy drink and taking a large swig. "That gives us plenty of time to sort things out. Now let's get the natives back in the dining carriage and give them an update. I think they deserve to know what we know. Do you want to call them Hilly?"

There had been no need to rally the other passengers however, because when the three committee members, the Chef and the recently apprehended and questioned Alec Morris arrived at the dining carriage, every one of them was already seated and appeared to be unusually attentive.

"What's he had to say for himself?" said Hamill while pointing towards the anxious looking Morris.

"We'll discuss that later," said the Chairman before taking a seat at one of the outside tables. "In the meantime, we've got some good news."

"Have you found the driver?" said Hamill.

"Unfortunately not," said the Chairman.

"Have you found the porters?" said Woodhouse.

"Have you found the key to the bar?" said Biddo.

"Go and lie down," said Blackie.

"We've found the speedometer," said the Chairman. "At least, Hulmey and Hilly have."

"The speedometer!" said Hamill before turning to face the gathering. "They've found the speedometer lads. We're saved. Let's give the committee a huge round of applause."

"Cut it out Hamill, will you," said the Chairman. "It means we know how fast we're going."

"Whoopsy doo!" said Hamill.

"Which in turn means we can calculate whereabouts we are," said Hulme.

"How does that work?" said McShane.

"It's simple," said the Club Secretary before exposing his watch. "The train set off at around 7.30. It's just

[88]

after 11 o'clock now and we've been travelling at around 30 miles per hour. That means we've covered just over 100 miles. Which means we should be about to enter South Wales any time now."

"Am I going to need my passport?" said Biddo.

"You're going to need to go and lie down," said Blackie.

"Why is knowing where we are so important?" said Steadman.

"Because sooner or later this train's going to stop," said the Chairman.

"And that's your good news is it?" said Hamill.

"It's something," said the Club Secretary. "What do you want Hamill? Would you like us to produce a driver like a rabbit from a hat?"

"I'd like Morris to explain himself," said Hamill.

"He will do," said the Chairman. "I'll convene an extraordinary meeting as soon as we get back to Crosby."

"I think we should wait until we're on a severe bend and kick the bastard off the train," said McShane.

"I wouldn't bother waiting for a bend," said Woodhouse.

"Don't be ridiculous," said the Chairman. "This isn't the wild west. We're civilized people for God's sake. We're going to do everything by the book."

"I sincerely hope so," said Hamill. "Because that bastard has put all our lives in jeopardy. And if we go by the book, that's deserving of a really severe punishment."

"Has he admitted what he's done?" said Woodhouse.

"He's taken full responsibility," said the Chairman.

"Full responsibility!" said Hamill.

"That's right," said the Chairman.

"Are you prepared to take any responsibility?" said Hamill.

"Me?" said the Chairman.

"That's right," said Hamill. "You were meant to be keeping an eye on him weren't you? I reckon you fouled up big time Tommy."

"I wouldn't argue there," said the Chairman.

"That's bullshit," said the Club Secretary. "You can't expect our Chairman to keep an eye on everyone. Jesus Christ Hamill-we had people dressed inappropriately, people pissed as farts and an old man cracking his skull after slipping in a member's puke. How many sets of eyes do you think the man's got?"

"He's right Hamill," said the Chef. "There were people trying to sneak all sorts of things onto the bloody train. And don't forget-we wouldn't have a club if it wasn't for Tommy Weir."

"We're not going to have a club anyway if this train picks up speed and goes hurtling off a bridge," said Hamill.

"That's not going to happen," said the Chairman.

"How do you know?" said Hamill. "Have you suddenly become an authority on steam trains?"

"I'm just alluding to what the Professor told me earlier," said the Chairman.

"The tropical disease expert!" said Hamill.

"And a long established authority on steam engines," said the old man.

"Well, with the greatest respect Professor, I think you should stay out of this," said Hamill. "This has got nothing to do with you."

"It's got plenty to do with him," said Hewlett. "He's an interested party."

"Since when?" said Hamill.

"Since he regained consciousness and found himself on board this God forsaken train," said Hewlett.

"And whose fault was that?" said Hamill.

"The individual that puked on the platform," said Hewlett.

"Rubbish!" said Hamill. "The reason the old boy slipped in the first place is because the committee allowed a notorious drunkard to be part of the touring party. Had he not come along, there would have been no puke to slip in. But let's get back to our current predicament shall we. Let's not lose sight of why we're now all hot under the collar and ready to flip out. Let's get back to the subject of Alec Morris. After all-he started the train."

"And he's going to be punished severely for doing so," said the Chairman.

"When exactly?" said Hamill.

"When we get back to Crosby," said the Chairman.

"That's not good enough," said Hamill.

"Why not?" said the Chairman.

"Because I think he should be punished now," said Hamill.

"You're going to have to wait until we get home," said the Chairman while encouraging Morris to get to his rear. "And that's the last I want to hear of the matter. But in the meantime, instead of thinking in terms of doom and gloom and harbouring thoughts of hurtling off bridges, we need to be doing something constructive."

"That's right," said the Club Secretary.

"Like what?" said Hamill.

"Like keeping an eye on the clock and that speedometer," said the Club Secretary.

"What good will that do?" said Hamill.

"Plenty of good," said the Club Secretary. "It'll enable us to know whereabouts we are when the train eventually comes to a halt. Will somebody do that please. Will somebody go and check our speed."

"I'll go," said Larkin. "As long as I'm allowed to light up."

"Go ahead," said the Club Secretary. "You're going to need to wrap up though. You'll be wide open to the elements on that footplate."

"And in the meantime, the rest of you should get your mobiles out," said the Chairman. "I think you should let someone back home know what's happening."

"Good thinking," said the Club Secretary. "Has anyone done that yet?"

"I tried to but I couldn't get a reception," said Steadman.

"Neither could I," said Blackie.

"Can anyone?" said the Chairman.

"I managed to make a call earlier," said Kenny Alty.

"To home?" said the Chairman.

"To my bookmakers," said Alty.

"Your bookmakers!" said the Chairman.

"That's right," said Alty. "I place a Lucky Fifteen with Betfred every morning without fail."

"Jesus Christ!" said the Chairman. "Words fail me Alty! Don't you think your priority should have been to say something to your wife about the predicament you're in?"

"I didn't know we were in a predicament at that particular time," said Alty. "I just thought things would naturally iron out as they so often do."

"Has anyone else managed to talk to somebody back home?" said the Club Secretary.

"I got through," said McShane.

"Who to?" said the Chairman.

"Me missus," said McShane.

"Good," said the Chairman. "It's nice to know at least one of us is on the ball...So she knows now does she Tommy...your missus knows about our dilemma does she?"

"Does she shite," said McShane. "She put the phone down on me. We're not really talking. In fact, she hasn't said more than a couple of words to me for the best part of a month."

"Would I be right to assume the second of those words was 'off'?" said Woodhouse.

"You would," said Tommy.

"Oh for the love of God!" said the exasperated Chairman.

"What about you Woody," said the Club Secretary. "Have you had any luck? Have you been able to talk to your missus?"

"You're joking aren't you," said Woodhouse. "Today's her only sleep in after working ten consecutive 12 hour shifts. If I wake her up, she'll be sticking pins in an effigy of me for the rest of the week."

"Anyone else?" said the Chairman. "Has anyone else managed to contact their loved ones?"

"I think our Anthony did," said Kenny Biddo.

"Is that right?" said the Chairman. "Is your dad right Anthony-have you managed to contact home?"

"I sent a text," said Anthony.

"Saying what exactly?" said the Chairman.

"Nothing really," said Anthony.

"What does 'nothing really' mean Anthony?" said the Chairman.

"It was nothing that's going to help our situation," said Anthony. "I asked me mum to wash me best shirt for when I get back. I'm going to see Green Day."

"Green Day!" said Hamill. "I very much doubt it lad. The way this trip's going, you're unlikely to see fucking Easter Sunday."

"What about the rest of you?" said the Chairman. "What about you Hewlett?"

"I can't help you I'm afraid," said Hewlett. "You see, when you stated in the club newsletter that you wanted all members to dress in accordance with the era, I chose to leave my phone at home. It just wouldn't go with the look would it? To my knowledge, Hedy Lamarr was never seen carrying a Blackberry."

"What about you Matthews," said the Chairman. "Have you got a signal?"

"I've got nothing," said Matthews.

"Are you sure about that Matthews?" said Woodhouse. "Because, unless I'm mistaken, I saw you using your phone not long after we'd taken off."

"You are mistaken," said Matthews. "You might have seen me trying to use it but, as I've just said, my phone's dead."

"For Christ's sake!" said the Chairman after beating his fist on his table. "Are you people telling me that in this great age of rapid technological advancement, nobody can get their bloody phones to work? How about you Morris. Is your phone working? And might I remind you-you might be our last hope-this, therefore, would be a great opportunity for you to repair some of the damage you've caused."

"I'd like nothing more than to help," said Morris. "But I didn't even bring a phone. I accidentally dropped mine down the shitter last night."

"That figures," said the Chairman.

"It does doesn't it," said the Club Secretary. "So what do we do now?"

"We sit tight," said the Chairman.

"Sit tight!" said Hamill. "Is that it? Is that the best you can come up with?"

"It's the only thing we can do for the time being," said the Chairman.

"Or we could entertain ourselves," said the Club Secretary. "That would help pass the time."

"Entertain ourselves!" said Hamill. "What have you got in mind Mr Secretary- Twister or Monopoly?"

"How about a game of Spin the Bottle," said Woodhouse before winking and placing his right hand on young Anthony's bottom. "Maybe me and this good looking young boy can get the game started."

"You keep your dirty stinking hands to yourself," said Kenny Biddo. "I've told you before Woodhouse. Leave my lad alone."

"He's just joking dad," said young Anthony.

"Well, I'm not in the mood to laugh," said Biddo. "I've told you lot before-I don't find that sort of thing funny at all. Touching other men's bottoms is sick and depraved."

"We could play cards," said Alty after producing a brand new deck from his breast pocket.

"No chance," said the Chairman. "Some of these dopey sods are still paying for last year's poker experience. What about a quiz?"

"A quiz!" said Woodhouse. "You've got to be joking. Don't you need a clear head to take part in a quiz? Most of us are still trying to come to terms with being on a runaway train. I'm not sure if I can remember my own name and address right now-never mind where you can find the Taj Mahal."

"The Taj Mahal's located in South Road in Waterloo," said Biddo while scanning the room for approval. "It's right next door to the Old Bank pub."

"That's the Indian restaurant, you daft bat," said Woodhouse.

"I think a quiz is a great idea," said Hamill. "As long as I can be the quizmaster."

"Don't be ridiculous," said the Club Secretary. "We need somebody who's capable of compiling enough questions. And with the greatest respect Hamill, you haven't got the necessary depth of knowledge."

"I'm prepared to give it a go," said Hamill. "I could at least do a section on current affairs."

"I didn't know that was your speciality," said Woodhouse.

"Well, it is," said Hamill. "Anything that's happened recently is of interest to me. I like reading the gossip columns and things like that."

"You just like gossip," said Kenny Biddo.

"I know I do," said Hamill. "I love it. But you be quizmaster if you want Biddo. What's your first question? Let me guess...what time does the bar open? Question 2...what time is Happy Hour? Question 3...what time does the bar close?"

"Leave it out will you Hamill," said young Anthony.

"Yes leave it out," said the Chairman. "The man's got enough problems without you reminding him about them. You be the quiz master if it makes you happy. What's your first question? What's your starter for ten? Is this going to be a team thing?"

"It's going to be an individual thing," said Hamill.

"Oh Christ!" said McShane. "Will I be able to phone a friend?"

"I think we've already covered that problem," said the Club Secretary.

"Don't worry Macca-I'll make it easy for you," said Hamill. "Just slip me a couple of bob when nobody's looking."

"Fire away then if you're ready," said the Chairman. "Who's the first question to?"

"I hope it's not me," said Blackie. "I never read the bloody newspapers. I know nothing about current affairs."

"You know a lot about past affairs though," said Woodhouse.

"What's that meant to mean?" said Blackie while shifting uneasily in his chair. "

You know exactly what I mean," said Woodhouse. "Didn't you once tell me you'd had flings with 3 married former Miss Worlds?"

"And I also told you not to open your big trap about it," said Blackie. "For God's sake Woody Imagine how Barbara would feel if she found that out. Imagine how inadequate she'd feel knowing that."

"Is it true Blackie?" said McShane. "Have you had flings with 3 Miss Worlds?"

"Is it hell," said the Chairman. "He's living in a dreamworld . Now let's get on with the quiz. Who's your first question to Hamill?"

"It's to our club Vice Chairman, Kenny Hulme," said Hamill.

"Really?" said Hulme. "This should be interesting."

"It's going to be very interesting," said Hamill.

"Then let's have it then," said Hulme. "I'm sitting comfortably. Why don't you begin? What do you want to know Hamill?"

"I want to know when you're going to resign?" said Hamill. "And I must remind you at this point-there's to be no conferring."

"That's very funny that is Hamill," said the Chairman. "What's your actual question?"

"That is my actual question," said Hamill. "And question 2 is to your bezzie mate, Jeff Hill. Our hard working and over officious Club Secretary. It's the same question."

"Which means question 3 will be in regard to when I'm

going to resign," said the Chairman. "Is that right Hamill?"

"You've got it in one," said Hamill.

"You're bang out of order Hamill," said Hulme. "I don't mind stepping down. I don't mind at all. I hate being on the committee. It's too much like hard work as far as I'm concerned. But this club wouldn't survive without Tommy Weir and Hilly. They're the heart and soul of our set up."

"This club's on the brink of extinction," said Hamill. "This club's going to the dogs."

"This club's been to the dogs," said Woodhouse.

"This club's already tearing up its betting slips."

"This is your fault this is," said the Chef while pointing towards an extremely edgy Alec Morris.

"Do you see now...do you see what you've done Alec? Do you see the trouble you've caused?"

"I'm sorry," said Morris. "It was just meant to be a bit of fun."

"A bit of fun!" said the Chef. "You've brought down our club Morris. You've destroyed 25 years work. I hope you're proud of yourself. How many times have I told you to keep your hands to yourself?"

"I'll have to hurry you all," said Hamill.

"Piss off Hamill," said the Club Secretary. "You're not in charge here. You're only a mere foot soldier. We don't have to answer any of your stupid questions if we don't want to."

"I'm afraid we do Hilly," said the Chairman. "We've got a lot to answer for. But before I answer my question-I want to make something very clear."

"What's that?" said Hamill while making himself a little more comfortable.

"My Secretary and Vice Chairman must not, in any way, be held responsible for this fiasco we now find ourselves part of," said the Chairman.

"Why's that?" said Hamill.

"Because, at the time Morris was playing silly buggers with buttons and levers in the engine, they were busy trying to revive the old man and organise things," said the Chairman. "I am solely responsible for this mess. The buck stops at me and only me. I'll do as you ask Hamill. I'll resign my position. But I'd rather it not be with immediate effect."

"What do you mean?" said Hamill.

"I want you to allow me to remain in charge until we get back to Crosby," said the Chairman. "And in return for that small favour, I'll do everything in my power to get you all home safely. I'll even look to get you compensated for the damage I've caused. What do you think?"

"I don't know," said Hamill.

"I don't believe this," said the Club Secretary.

"You mind your own business," said Hamill.

"It is my business," said the Club Secretary.

"There is an alternative," said the Chairman.

"What is it?" said Hamill.

"I resign right here and now and allow my understudy Kenny Hulme to take control of the club," said the Chairman.

"I'd rather stick a red hot needle in my left testicle," said Hamill.

"What do you reckon then?" said the Chairman. "Are you going to allow me to stay on until we're safely home?"

"I'm not sure," said Hamill. "What do you think Woody?"

"It can't do any harm," said Woodhouse. "It would save you having to clear up somebody else's mess."

"This is nonsense," said the Club Secretary. "This is utter nonsense."

"It's not," said the Chairman. "I've made some unforgivable errors Hilly. Maybe it's time for someone else to step up to the plate."

"But this club's your life Tommy," said Hill. "You eat, drink and breathe this club. What are you going to do without it?"

"I'll manage," said the Chairman. "I'll find plenty to

do. And if I don't, the wife's certain to find plenty for
me to do. To be honest Hilly, I'm not sure I'm up to
being the Chairman any more. I'm constantly worn out.
To be honest, I've not felt right since I got back from
holiday."

"Where did you go?" said the Professor after noticing
the Chairman wobble before retaking his seat. "Was it a
third world country by any chance?"

"South America," said the Club Secretary.

"Brazil mainly," said the Chairman. "I wanted to see
what's left of the rain forests before they completely
disappear. Why do you ask Professor?"

"I'm just curious, that's all," said the old man before
removing his spectacles from his breast pocket and
settling back down. "I've done a lot of travelling myself
over the years. Travelling's in my family's blood. Tell
me-is it just fatigue you've been experiencing?"

"And the odd chest pain," said the Chairman after
squeezing his secretary's shoulder and pulling him close.
"Which reminds me Hilly-I haven't taken my tablets.
You couldn't go and fetch them for me could you."

"I'll go," said the Chef.

"Thanks," said the Chairman. "They're in the top
drawer of my bedside cabinet."

"They're not the popular blue type of tablet are they?"
said the Chef.

"No, they're white," said the Chairman. "I haven't had
to revert to those blue, sex enhancing rascals yet."

"I didn't even know you were on medication," said the
Club Secretary. "What's the problem big fella? It's
nothing serious is it?"

"I don't think so," said the Chairman. "It's probably
just heartburn. I get a lot of that. You know me Hilly.
I'm always eating the wrong sort of stuff. To be honest,
I'm more worried about the whereabouts of our elusive
Health and Safety Officer. I'd have thought this
situation would have been right up his street."

 The Chairman needn't have worried which street
his Health and Safety Officer was heading down

however, because Meehan was already conducting his own covert investigation of the engine in his familiar, ponderous and very methodical way. He had made his exit while the relentless Hamill was doing his utmost to bring down the current club regime and had successfully maintained his anonymity on his return while the Chairman was being examined by the Professor after he had suffered another brief dizzy spell.

That incident had disturbed the majority of the assembly and brought about a period of relative calm that had enabled the industrious Health and Safety Officer to go to work and begin processing the data that he had gathered from the engine. Within seconds, his computer-like brain had sparked into life and the cogs that were an integral part of that impressive organ were turning and initiating other cogs, and those cogs were engaging other more complex mechanisms until his mind had reached a state of full cognition. He was thinking, questioning, understanding and rationalising and as a consequence, his mind had soon become a maelstrom of numbers and possibilities. Single digits, hundreds, thousands, millions. His brain was now multiplying, dividing, subtracting. Numbers to the power of other numbers, degrees of numbers, fractions of fractions of numbers and numbers concerning time and motion. As Hewlett looked on in fascination, Meehan's eyes began to blink wildly like the lights on a pin ball machine as his brain continued to formulate, convert and calculate. Square roots of numbers began to emerge in his mind. Probability, standard form, equations and fractions. It was thinking that was beyond the scope of most living intellectuals and it therefore wasn't long before he had arrived at the solution to the problem. Seconds later, he closed his eyes, discreetly cleared his throat and slapped both his hands on the table.

"Gentlemen, can I have your attention please," he said after rising from his chair and thrusting what looked like a streamer of white till roll above his head. "I have some information that might just allay some of your worst fears."

"Have you found the key to the bar?" said Kenny Biddo.

"I'm afraid not," said Meehan.

"Shut it Biddo," said the Club Secretary. "Try to be serious for once. Let the man go about his business. What is it you've discovered Eddie?"

"Do you know how to get this bloody contraption to stop?" said Steadman.

"Not as yet," said Meehan.

"Christ!" said Steadman, before proceeding to pace the floor with his hands over his face. "This can't be happening."

"So what do you know?" said Blackie.

"I don't know anything for certain," said Meehan. "But if my calculations are correct, this train's not as out of control as some of you seem to think it is."

"How do you know?" said the Club Secretary.

"It's hard to say," said Eddie. "But let me try to explain
it this way. The readouts I have just studied suggest our speed has been more than reasonably consistent."

"We know that," said Steadman. "Hulmey and Hilly discovered that much."

"I know they did," said Meehan. "But I'm afraid they missed something."

"We missed nothing," said Hulme. "We took those readings over a 40 minute period."

"I don't doubt you," said Meehan. "I don't doubt you for a second gentlemen. But our speed shouldn't have been consistent."

"Why not?" said Hulme.

"Because we've been ascending and descending some seriously steep gradients," said Meehan while holding up his map. "Take a look for yourselves if you don't believe me. The higher parts of the terrain we've covered are shaded dark brown."

"What sort of gradients are we talking about?" said the Club Secretary. "Are we talking Big Dipper type gradients?"

"Nothing quite as severe as that," said Meehan. "But let's say, for arguments sake-one or two have been a quarter of that."

"So what exactly are you saying Eddie?" said Steadman.

"I'm saying that if this train was out of control, we should have accelerated noticeably during any number of those descents," said Meehan. "We should have picked up speed very quickly."

"And you're saying we didn't," said Blackie.

"You tell me," said Meehan. "Have any of you noticed any sudden changes in speed?"

"I haven't," said Steadman. "But then, why would I? I've been out of my mind with worry."

"I don't care how worried you've been," said Meehan. "If our speed had suddenly increased twofold, every one of us would have known about it. As far as I'm concerned, there wouldn't be a thing left standing on these tables. In fact, in all likelihood, we wouldn't be standing. Would you agree with that assessment Mr Hill?"

"I think I'd have to," said the Club Secretary.

"I would too," said Hulme. "Without a shadow of a doubt."

"Thank you," said the Health and Safety Officer.

"Alright," said Woodhouse after taking the floor. "Let's say for instance you're right Eddie. Let's accept that we've been travelling at more or less the same speed since we set off. Why is that significant?"

"Yes, I'm struggling to understand that too," said Blackie. "Why is that such a big thing Eddie?"

"Because it proves the train is being controlled from somewhere other than the footplate," said Meehan.

"What!" said Hamill.

"Someone's controlling this train," said Meehan.

"How's that even possible?" said Blackie. "That's not possible is it?"

"It's more than possible," said Meehan. "Try to

consider a toy train. The Hornby type for instance. Think about how it's operated. You don't have to be on board the thing to set it in motion or bring it to a halt do you? Now magnify that toy train a thousand times."

"Are you trying to tell us that this train's remotely controlled?" said the Club Secretary.

"That's one way of putting it," said Meehan. Think about it gentlemen-how can something that weighs around 170 tons fail to pick up speed on a one in five downward gradient? I'm telling you lads. At that point, whoever's been in control of this train, has been easing off the gas and applying a brake. I'd swear to it."

"But Morris has admitted to starting the train," said Blackie.

"He probably did," said Meehan. "But someone else has been controlling it ever since."

"Well let's hope he's not a lunatic intent upon maiming us all," said Blackie.

"He's not," said the Chairman who, for the last twenty minutes had been staring out of the window.

"What do you mean?" said the Chef upon quickly coming to the Chairman's shoulder. "What's happening?"

"We've stopped," said the Chairman.

"Stopped!" said a suspicious looking Hamill who had suddenly found himself part of a mass surge to the side of the carriage. "What do you mean stopped?"

"We've come to a halt," said the Chairman.

"Bloody hell!" said Steadman. "So we have. I didn't even notice that. Bloody hell! How's that happened?"

"I don't know," said the Chairman. "We must have run out of fuel or broken down. But I want to believe it's a good thing, don't you?"

"It's a very good thing as far as I'm concerned," said Blackie.

"You're not kidding," said Steadman. "We can all start breathing a little easier now."

"And even more importantly, we can get our things together and go home," said Blackie. "That's right isn't it Tommy? We can go home now can't we?"

"I'd like to think so," said the Chairman. "But have you seen it out there. Have you seen how heavy it's snowing? I've never seen a blizzard like that in all my life."

"Nor me," said the Club Secretary. "If you didn't know any better, you'd think we'd just touched down in Siberia. Is everyone equipped to go out in that? Have you lads all brought a heavy coat?"

"I couldn't care less about a heavy coat," said Hamill. "I'll go out there buck naked with an oven mitt wrapped around my todger if I have to. At least we're safe. At least we're not going to go hurtling off a bridge."

"I wouldn't speak too soon if I was you," said the Club Secretary. "Have you seen where we've come to rest?"

"What do you mean?" said Hamill after moving forward and pressing his face against the window.

"Take a look for yourself," said the Club Secretary. "That can't be good can it?"

CHAPTER SIX
A CLUB STALWART

Brian Matthews was very like Jeff Hill, the current Club Secretary, in that, he ate, slept, drank and breathed the veteran men's club and he had done so since he had qualified for membership. Within no time at all, because of his boundless enthusiasm and determination to rise through the ranks, he became a viable candidate for a committee place but had always come up frustratingly short when it was time for the votes to be counted. That was almost certainly because he was an infamous stickler to club protocol and would rarely miss a chance to remind his fellow members when they had been guilty of any rule infringement or were falling short of the etiquette demanded of them. It was a personal trait that had often irritated people, particularly the more dominant, less patient and aggressive members such as Hamill, McShane and Woodhouse who, as a result, had often treated him as if he was an annoying and persistent fly.

Their dislike for Matthews wasn't entirely universal however-in fact there were several club members that held him in reasonably high regard, particularly those whose relationships had been going through a rough patch at some time or another. That wasn't just because he had an inherent caring nature or the ability to keep a secret, it was because he had developed extremely strong people and counselling skills from a very early age while abiding in his little two up and two down terraced house at the bottom of Jubilee Road in Crosby. It was right there, on the middle of that property's bare wooden staircase, where, instead of doing what most other boys of his age were doing at that time and tuning into the radio to hear the next instalment of Biggles or the Goons, the young Matthews would sit for hours listening to his wise old Good Samaritan mother imparting her wisdom and advice to a seemingly endless procession of physically and mentally abused young women. It meant that by the time he had entered his middle teenage years, he knew more about the female mind than people three times his age and knew more about human relationships than the vast majority of highly educated people who were often charging huge sums of money for their clinics.

At that point in his young life, becoming a counsellor of sorts had never entered his head but that had changed after a highly distressed young woman had called one extremely bleak Winter morning only to learn that Mrs Matthews had taken to her bed after coming down with a highly contagious form of influenza. The woman had been so desperate to talk to someone that she had completely ignored the young man's insistence that she should call again when his mother was feeling better. Instead, she had headed straight into the sitting room where she proceeded to explain the reason for her visit. She had stayed until lunch time and had left the house a very different individual from the moist eyed, emotionally shattered and trembling character that had burst in uninvited three and a half hours earlier. By that time, the woman was smiling and looking calm, composed and confident. By then, that young woman had applied lipstick and a touch of rouge and had not felt so good and so ready to face the world for a long, long time. She would call at the Matthews household several more times during the months that followed but on each occasion, she had made it perfectly clear that it wasn't the lady of the house she had called to see.

Young Matthews had been one of a new breed of 'go to people'. Somebody that had recognised that the long established 'you've got to pull yourself together girl', approach to feminine problems was outdated and in need of replacing with a far more empathetic and tailored approach.

He realised that instead of telling those abused women to get on with things and make the best of what they had, they needed to be afforded a sympathetic ear and treated with greater sensitivity. And that's exactly what he did. And he listened and listened and listened. Then he talked for a time while his subjects listened intently and began to take on board his advice.

Within no time at all, he had become a sort of cult figure and was not just the talk of his small town but the subject of many a conversation taking place within a lot of neighbouring towns too. That was because an increasing number of the young women he had been helping were already beginning to reap the benefits of what he had sown. Every day, more and more of those forlorn and badly treated young women he had made a connection with were changing. For the first time in their lives, they were standing up for themselves and refusing to conform to the archetypal, dependent and subservient model that had become something of the norm within so many working class households during that particular era. Many of those women were now refusing to accept what for so many years had been categorised as, 'their lot'. They weren't prepared to accept 'their lot' anymore and as a result, many had changed beyond all recognition. They were the equivalent of a new strain of animal that wanted to prove that they could think and act for themselves and ultimately, go out to work and bring home the 'bread' too. They no longer wanted their partner's cape thrown over a puddle to prevent their delicate little feet from getting muddy-they were now prepared to vault that puddle or walk right through it and take the consequences however unsavoury and regardless of how messy the outcome might be.

During that relatively short period, Matthews had done far more than offer a large number of broken hearted and mistreated women a sympathetic ear and a shoulder to cry on, he had persuaded them to cast off the shackles of conformity and demand more from their current existences. In reality, all he had really done was espouse and promote independent thought but in doing so he had changed women's perceptions as to what a marital relationship was all about and what it should and should not involve. However, the popularity that it had brought him as far as the female of the species were concerned, had come at a considerable cost because, for every woman that had turned their life around, there was an extremely angry partner or ex-partner that now considered Matthews to be nothing more than a meddlesome and loathsome pariah.

Among those were men that were now having to live with an entirely different person from the one they had originally fancied, pursued, courted and wed. They, despite their marriages surviving and continuing to run along the original rails, were full of contempt for young Brian Matthews. Then there were the men that had returned home after a night out to find their suitcases on their doorstep and the Yale lock on their front door gleaming like a newly minted gold sovereign. They now detested Matthews with a smouldering passion that was almost without equal. And then there were those that had been jilted and replaced with, what their previous partners considered to be, a far more dependable, far more caring and far more sensitive partner. They were livid and bursting with rage of the supercharged kind. Many no longer had anything to lose. Nearly all of them now wanted Matthews punished severely. Some even wanted him to die a long, lingering agonising death. They included uncles, cousins and former close friends and as a result it wasn't long before the only man that would have anything to do with him, was his devoted yet deeply concerned father who by then was almost out of his mind with worry.

However, despite his father's desperate and continual pleas to get his son to lie low for a while until some of the anger had subsided, Matthews continued to operate. But not just operate it must be said-to operate in full view of those that had come to despise him so intensely. Three weeks later, he was wishing he had listened to his father because not long after leaving the home of a recently engaged woman who had lately discovered her fiancée in bed with her much younger sister, he was violently set upon and left for dead in an alleyway just 70 yards from his home. It was no coincidence that, prior to the attack, all four of his assailants had been drinking heavily and even less of a coincidence that two of the men had been served their decree absolute that very morning. The beating had resulted in Matthews being rendered comatose for several weeks and placed in cervical traction for a further six months. That had been too much for his parents to take and as a result, three days after the ambulance crew had returned him home to continue his convalescence, they made the decision to withdraw their entire life savings and set about persuading their son to go and live somewhere where he would be safer.

It had never been their intention to allow their son to stray too far from their protective influence however. After all, despite his unique talent as a counsellor and the fact that he was light years ahead of his peers in terms of intelligence, maturity and common sense, he was still only a teenager and therefore in need of constant guidance and reassurance. That is why they had initially wanted him to go and live with his wise old widowed aunt who had a very nice cottage in a secluded part of North Wales or alternatively, with his elderly uncle who had spent the last 10 years restoring an old narrow boat that was now moored on the Norfolk Broads near Coltishall. They believed that by getting their son away from the hustle and bustle of town life, it would enable him to clear his head and help him understand why things had gone so terribly wrong. That wasn't how young Matthews had perceived his situation however. Not for him were thatched cottages, nicely painted long boats or any other traditional aspect of the British countryside. He had already set his heart on places much further afield. Exciting, vibrant places where he could meet and observe other people, embrace and study different cultures and broaden his ever hungry mind.

One of his first considerations had been southern California where it seemed at that particular time, all young Americans were only interested in making love and protesting against social injustice rather than perpetrating hate and committing acts of violence. He had also thought about heading to South Africa to join the fight for women's rights. That was until he turned on the television one Saturday morning and watched a news bulletin which showed scores of policemen violently beating a crowd of women protestors with heavy clubs. 'That would be like jumping out of the frying pan and into the fire," he had told his mightily relieved parents. And he had even thought about journeying to a virtually unexplored part of South America to live with and study one of the many primitive tribes within the Amazon Basin. (An idea he had abandoned shortly after he had read an account of 5 American missionaries that had been speared to death while trying to bring Christianity to the Huaorani people of the rain forest of Ecuador). Nevertheless, the possibilities appeared limitless for a young, unattached individual at that time and because of that he had remained undecided for another 3 months.

That was until he turned on his radio one bright summer morning and listened to a live broadcast from Rishikesh in Northern India where the popular Liverpool band The Beatles had just arrived to attend a Transcendental Meditation course at the ashram of Maharishi Mahesh Yogi. From that moment on, India was world news and, as the new place to be for the young and impressionable, it had usurped California from young Matthews's long list of possible escapes. That is why, less than a fortnight later, the highly excited and starstruck young Matthews found himself part of a large and illustrious throng that included the likes of John Lennon, George Harrison and the famous Hollywood actress Mia Farrow.

However, because of the enormous media circus that had surrounded the famous Liverpool band from day one, the experience had proved to be far less spiritually enlightening and productive than Matthews had hoped for and he would have almost certainly packed his things and headed elsewhere had he not been persuaded to stick around the following morning to attend a peaceful demonstration regarding the appalling rate of female literacy which at that time was at an alarming 8.6%. It was there, during a short break in introduced to two men that would have a profound effect upon his future.

One was a genial, albeit a little eccentric, well-educated middle aged English professor affectionately known to the indigenous natives as 'Fada Dak'. The other was a charismatic young Indian named Chanda Mahesh Yogi who, despite making his reputation as a captain of oppressed Indian women, had often courted controversy within his locality because his teachings had concentrated almost entirely on only one facet of the four goals of Hindu life-the need for sexual fulfilment. However, that didn't mean that Chanda Mahesh Yogi only saw women as objects of his own sexual desire. On the contrary, he adored women. He worshipped them. He considered them to be the most special of all the Earth's creatures. He had often compared women to a priceless vintage car. 'They should be looked after daily and kept in pristine condition. They should be oiled and serviced regularly to ensure they function perfectly and purr contentedly.' That is why he had been so desperate to meet the young Matthews. That is the reason he had immediately welcomed him into the bosom of his large and happy family. He saw Matthews as a sort of mind mechanic. He saw Matthews as someone who could fix and clean up broken women. In no time at all, with the assistance of a brilliant and tireless female interpreter named Akira, Brian Matthews was back doing what he had become extremely good at back on Merseyside-advising and offering a sympathetic ear to a number of downtrodden and abused young women. And he did what he had done in the not too distant past..He listened, and listened and listened some more. Then he talked for

[111]

a time while his fascinated subjects held their collective breaths and listened to him.

They would learn so much in the years that followed. They would learn that there was a far better, much fairer way of life for them if they were prepared to be brave, be more assertive and refuse to be treated like door mats. They would learn that women were just as important as men and should therefore be demanding equal status and at least similar rights. They would also regain their self-worth and rediscover their true identities and long lost personalities. Even more importantly, they would realise that many deeply entrenched norms were not necessarily written in stone but could be challenged, ground away and sculpted in their favour.

It is important to note that Matthews had also learnt something from his time as an amateur counsellor on Merseyside. Something very important that had probably saved his life or prevented him from suffering serious injury. He had learned that it didn't matter what part of the world a man was from, having his wife leave him caused exactly the same kind of pain and perpetuated exactly the same type of anger. That is why, almost ten years after departing Liverpool, and 18 hours after the police had arrested a wild eyed, machete wielding ex-husband who had been making his way to his rented accommodation, Matthews made the decision to pack his things and go home.

The Brian Matthews that descended the gangplank at the Pier Head in Liverpool just over a fortnight later was thus a very different individual from the frightened young puppy-like creature that had stepped onto the busy little jetty in Mumbai almost 12 months to the day. This Matthews had changed almost beyond recognition. This one had matured considerably and was far more self-assured. This one walked with his head up and with a very definite swagger. This one possessed a mind and soul which had been cleansed of all negativity and prejudice. Gone was the need to explain his actions to those he had offended in the past and gone were any previous notions of righting the wrongs of that same painful past. That, as far as he was concerned, would have gone against just about everything he had been taught by his guru, the eccentric Englishman and the multitude of other less prominent luminaries he had come into contact with during the preceding year.

He was still nevertheless aware that he was returning to an environment that was still likely to be extremely hostile. After all, there was a long list of angry and disenchanted men that had lost their wives or partners because of his 'interference'-a continually growing list that included family members, former close friends and two men that had served time in prison for their part in his violent assault. That is why, prior to his return, he had made the conscious decision to keep his head down and have as little to do with his neighbours as was humanly possible.

Word of his return had soon got around however. After all, in some circles, he had come to be revered as some sort of Messiah. He was the man who could bring the metaphorically 'dead' back to life and help the apparently 'blind' to regain their sight. That was why so many young women who had been touched by his ability or had grown familiar with his legend over the past twelve months, saw his return as a more than welcome second coming and very possibly, the last opportunity to benefit from his wisdom before he once again headed out into the 'wilderness'.

They would be bitterly disappointed however, because for the next three months, the determined Matthews did exactly as he had intended. He kept himself to himself and was rarely spotted beyond the threshold of his parent's little house. That hadn't prevented his followers using other means by which to communicate with the young man however. One desperate individual had stood outside his house in torrential rain for five hours broadcasting her problem through a 10 watt loud hailer. Another, after being refused entry at the door for the umpteenth time, had returned with an extension ladder and had attempted to enter the house through the skylight during the early hours of the morning. Many others had tried more orthodox methods such as sweeteners, sob stories and threats. But still Mr and Mrs Matthews remained firm. 'He's not seeing any of you,' the lady of the house had told a small group that had gathered outside her home one bitterly cold morning. "My son was beaten to within an inch of his life for trying to help the likes of you. Go home and sort your own lives out.'

Apart from sighing loudly and politely asking people to go away before closing over her door, it had been one of the few times Mrs Matthews had acknowledged anyone outside her home and for a short while, it looked as if her uncharacteristic show of assertiveness had paid off because from that day forth, unwanted visits to her house became less and less frequent. That didn't mean that those people who were still desperate for the young man's help had given up however. On the contrary-it had just made them more determined.

Less than a week later, the letters began to arrive. Letters addressed specifically for the personal attention of the youngest member of the Matthews household. Letters often marked, 'EXTREMELY URGENT'. Within a fortnight, mail was arriving in such quantity that his parents were sometimes struggling to open their front door. That wasn't their greatest worry at that time however-after all, they had found it no great hardship to gather up the unwanted correspondence and toss it onto the fire. Their greatest worry was that, while either or both of them were out of the house, their good natured son might get curious, open one of the letters and become moved enough to respond.

They did the obvious things nevertheless, such as board over their letterbox and arrange to pick up their mail at the local postal sorting office in Blundelsands, but although that had eased their concerns to a large degree, some of the correspondence still somehow managed to find its way into the house via an air vent or through one of a number of poorly secured windows. Other people had been even more resourceful. Some had bribed a gas meter reader to smuggle their letters to the young man. Others, in an effort to be invited inside the house, had disguised themselves as police women, social workers or doctors. Another, on no less than a dozen occasions, had slipped a Brian Matthews addressed envelope into the back of Mrs Matthews's coat belt while she was standing in the queue of the little corner shop that for so many years had served her little community. However, like so many other ideas that had appeared viable, it had failed miserably, because each time the obedient Matthews had discovered one of the secreted items, he had simply handed it to his mother who, without any fuss or remorse, had duly fed it to the fire.

That was the way of things within that household for the next 12 months, until both the young man's parents had been forced to take to their beds after contracting food poisoning. It had been a day that had passed without incident and had it not been for the newspaper delivery boy calling with Mr Matthews senior's evening edition of the Liverpool Echo, the younger Matthews, who had spent the entire day tending to his sick parents, wouldn't have set his eyes upon another soul. He certainly wouldn't have been afforded the rare opportunity to have the first look at his father's newspaper and therefore wouldn't have discovered a large red envelope that had been slipped inside the centre pages some time during the afternoon. It was a piece of quality scented stationary, beautifully hand written and addressed to himself. On the rear, in red ink and bold capital letters, was written the following highly evocative lines:

IN THE PRESENCE OF MADNESS

MR MATTHEWS JNR. THIS IS A MATTER OF LIFE
AND DEATH. YOU ARE MY VERY LAST HOPE.
FOR GOODNESS SAKE-PLEASE HELP ME.

Despite that impassioned plea, the envelope, like hundreds before it, had immediately been tossed onto the last of the glowing embers of the early evening fire and although there had been a brief moment when he had felt the compulsion to rescue it and examine the contents, Matthews had resisted and had instead returned his attention to a feature within the newspaper regarding a claim by a certain Beatles member that Maharishi Mahesh Yogi's behaviour towards his female Transcendental Meditation students was sometimes inappropriate. What he wasn't to know or couldn't possibly have known at that time was that by dutifully flinging that letter onto the fire, he was ultimately and inadvertently condemning a deeply troubled young woman to an existence that almost defied belief.

That woman was 23 year old Matilda Spendlove who, since she was a toddler, had been affectionately known to all but her hard and notoriously unfeeling mother as Tilly. She was the attractive and quirky wife of 38 year old English teacher Mr Gabriel Spendlove and despite subsequent claims to the contrary, it had been he and not her that had sought out Brian Matthews for help after numerous therapists had failed to improve his partner's peculiar state of mind.

Each of those specialists had at least been able to establish one very important thing however-Mrs Spendlove was suffering from a bizarre delusional disorder which none of them had ever come across before. They had nevertheless treated numerous people who had demonstrated a vast range of delusional behaviour. The grandiose, for example. People who had an over-inflated sense of power, intelligence, talent or identity. They had also treated a great number of people whose problem was persecutory. People for instance, that had come to believe that the whole world had turned against them or someone was out to get them. And they had treated people who, without any reason or justification whatsoever, had become convinced that they were physically or mentally defective in some way. However, regardless of their expertise and experience within their respective fields, they had never been asked to evaluate and treat anybody like the curious Tilly Spendlove, a previously normal individual who, for some reason, had started thinking and behaving like a domestic cat.

A large majority of those mind specialists had been convinced that the root cause of Tilly Spendlove's strange condition could be traced back to her infancy. A childhood which had been almost devoid of love and affection due to her mother's devotion to and obsession with her eight prize winning Burmese cats. It had been a very sad and lonely childhood, the earliest recollection of which, would have likely been looking on with extreme envy as her mother talked to and pampered each of those highly expensive furry show pieces in turn. According to their findings, the often ignored and constantly neglected Tilly had never been afforded anything like that level of love and affection. At least not until her far more caring research scientist father returned home from one of his notoriously long expeditions to the South Pole. Even so, those highlights were infrequent and only occurred until she was 10. After that, for whatever reason, Tilly never saw her father again and was never offered any explanation as to why.

Fortunately for Tilly, her humdrum and often cruel existence wasn't to last forever because just 7 years later, she met her future husband Gabriel Spendlove at a prestigious cat show on the outskirts of Chester. He had been the first on hand to help her back to her feet after she had stumbled while carrying two heavy cat baskets across a badly water logged field. He had also been the first to remonstrate with her mother after she had scolded and humiliated the young girl for being 'useless and utterly incompetent'.

At that time, the well-respected and much loved Mr Spendlove had been employed as head of English at a prestigious private school in Alderley Edge, a village and civil parish in Cheshire, and as a devotee of the Victorian realist novel, he had seen the muddied, exasperated and forlorn Tilly as a living, breathing, modern day version of the Thomas Hardy protagonist, Tess of the D'Urbervilles. That had set his pulse and imagination racing like never before because Tess had been his favourite female literary character since he had first read the novel at the age of fourteen while residing at his first boarding school. In stumbling, wiping herself down, stumbling again and climbing back to her feet without so much as a sigh of dismay, Tilly had exhibited certain personal traits that were peculiar to the Hardy heroine-traits that Gabriel Spendlove in particular had always found irresistible. As a result, and despite Tilly's tender age, he had immediately found himself unashamedly smitten. "It is as it should be," he had remarked after being pressed upon the potential problem of age difference by one of his closest friends.

Problems relating to age difference certainly hadn't crossed young Tilly's mind at that juncture because she had been feeling like the cat that had just been spoon fed the freshest and best part of the cream. She had been too busy revelling in the unexpected attention she had been receiving to consider anything negative regarding her situation. That is why she hadn't even blinked or moved one single muscle when Gabriel Spendlove, (a complete stranger it should be said), stepped forward, took out his silk embroidered handkerchief and began carefully wiping the first of many specks of mud from around her quivering lips. That is the reason she hadn't at any time, felt tempted to withdraw discreetly while he continued to whisper a series of cleverly constructed sentences of reassurance into her ear. It had been a level of care so completely alien to the young woman that she had wanted it

[118]

repeated from the very second it had ceased. From that day on, the unlikely couple were rarely seen apart in public and from that moment hence, neither were ever seen looking anything but utterly content with what fate had provided them with. They were married in a little rustic church in a secluded corner of Dorset on her 18th birthday, a date which coincided with the last time she would see or hear from her mother.

For the best part of the next half decade, Gabriel Spendlove could not have been any happier. He had just booked the function suite at his local golf club to celebrate his and his wife's fifth wedding anniversary and had finished writing the invitations to his chosen guests, many of whom, it should be said, had been utterly convinced his marriage wouldn't last more than a few months. Tilly for her part, had been at the very least, equally as happy during that period and could often be seen whistling quietly to herself while absorbed in a world that she now considered perfect. As a couple, they had just about everything going for them, just about everything they could wish for and just about every possible advantage. That was until something happened just days before their well planned celebration. Something not necessarily too extraordinary, but something that would ultimately lead to Tilly Spendlove's rapid and tragic mental decline.

It occurred during a night very similar to so many that the Spendloves had spent together during their blissfully happy marriage. They had attended a charity fundraising event at a local golf club and had been heading home along a snake-like stretch of road a few miles from their homes known as the Hightown bends, when a cat suddenly sprang out in front of Mr Spendlove's recently renovated Triumph Herald. It had been too late to stop and although the couple had managed to close their eyes to avoid looking upon the gruesome spectacle, the high

pitched screech and the sound of crunching bone had been incredibly disturbing and impossible to erase. For the remainder of the journey and upon arriving home, Tilly Spendlove didn't utter a single word, not even to wish her husband good night or to remind him to set the alarm clock as she always had. She didn't even bother to brush her teeth, slip into her nightdress or climb into their inviting four poster. Instead, she lay across the end of the bed fully
clothed and rolled up into a tightly formed ball.

Many other incidences of odd and eccentric behaviour soon followed including the time when Tilly, upon realising that one of her husband's work colleagues had come to visit, made her way into the living room on all fours, climbed up onto the bewildered and highly embarrassed man's lap and immediately fell asleep. Then there was the time the unfortunate young woman knocked herself out cold after attempting to pounce upon a moving ball of fluff that was on the other side of their newly glazed patio door. The following night, it had been her husband's turn to receive hospital treatment. He had been administered 15 stitches to his neck and left shoulder after his young wife had angrily turned on him for trying to induce her to climb into a steaming hot bath.

It wasn't long before some of his closest friends and family members were urging Gabriel Spendlove to have his wife sectioned for a period and not just because of the extraordinary behaviour they had witnessed but because they had often left his home convinced that his life was in danger. He had perceived the situation very differently however. He had continued to insist that his wife's condition was temporary and an acceptable and natural reaction to what had been an extremely traumatic experience. Nevertheless, his patience finally gave out when he came downstairs one morning to find Tilly curled up asleep on the kitchen floor inside a large cardboard box lined with her favourite shawl. That, as far as Gabriel Spendlove was concerned, had been the very last straw. That had been the ultimate indignity.

The next morning, on the advice of his good friend and long standing neighbour, Gabriel Spendlove paid a visit to a retired psychiatrist who lived no more than a quarter of a mile from his home. He was a man who, during his long and successful career, had seen just about everything. He was also known to be extremely pleasant and approachable and, despite being well into his seventies, somebody that had never lost the will to help people and the desire to increase his already considerable knowledge regarding the human mind.

The opportunity to study somebody like Tilly Spendlove, a previously perfectly rational individual that for some reason had come to believe they had turned into a cat, had therefore intrigued the old man and intrigued him to such an extent that he had even suggested residing with the Spendloves for a fortnight in order to study the woman's behaviour at the closest possible quarters. He did in fact stay for just under a week. By that time, his nerves were shredded, he had developed psoriasis, a rapidly worsening stammer and the last of his grey hair was no longer on his head but upon his pillow and between the bristles of his old tortoiseshell hairbrush.

"I'm sorry Gabriel-I just can't take any more," he had told his hugely disappointed host while struggling to close his hastily packed suitcase. "Your wife spent the small hours of the morning under my bed. I knew she was there because every time I turned over, she would growl menacingly. She is now feral and completely unpredictable. I now appreciate what it's like to be stalked by a predator.'

Upon managing to release the gate latch, he had advised the man of the house to have his wife sectioned, stressing that if he didn't, the attacks on his person might well become more frequent and could very well increase in ferocity. He had also tried his best to explain the root cause of the problem, (Tilly's mother's obsession with cats and her complete lack of affection for her only daughter etc, etc). He had also told Gabriel Spendlove in no uncertain terms that, in pandering to his wife's demands such as only feeding her fresh fish and allowing her to use a cat litter instead of the bathroom toilet, he had been at least partly to blame for her steady and distressing decline. He told him that he had lost control and therefore needed to take control back. He insisted that in order to get the old Tilly back, she should be treated like a normal human being, fed a normal, healthy balanced diet and made to sleep in a proper bed like most other normal human beings.

And that is exactly what Gabriel Spendlove did. He took the old man's advice to the letter and adopted a hard line and far more assertive approach to his predicament. He told his wife, 'enough is enough-the madness has to stop now.' He told her that it was important for her to understand that she was a human being and not an animal. He tore up her cardboard cot in front of her face, disposed of her shawl in full view of the patio windows and from that day on escorted her to the master bedroom at exactly nine thirty every evening.

Those implementations, although improving things slightly, failed to bring things back to full normality however, because despite managing to get his wife to share his bed and despite getting her to use the conventional toilet and despite getting her to take better care of herself, Gabriel Spendlove still couldn't get her to eat the nutritious food he was cooking and serving up on a daily basis.

'Keep your foot firmly down,' his great friend and head of science and technology had urged him.

'You have to keep at it whether it seems harsh or not', Tilly's doctor had insisted.

'She can't possibly defy her hunger pangs forever,' said a respected dietician that the desperate Spendlove had brought in for an obscene sum of money. 'No human being can. She's either carnivore, omnivore or herbivore. One thing's for certain. She'll have to eat at some point or other. Every human being does.'

However, to Mr Spendlove's despair, Tilly continued to resist everything he had put in front of her. The Lancashire hot pot made from his grandmother's much sought after age old recipe. The corned beef hash made with unpeeled King Edwards potatoes, the cottage pie, the full English breakfast, the bangers and mash, the heavily battered cod and home-made chips and the roast beef and Yorkshire pudding. Even the simple bacon sandwich and bowl of piping hot tomato soup had been summarily dismissed and looked at with scorn as though they were last week's leftovers.

It was a pattern that continued for almost a month, until the family doctor, during her weekly check-up, revealed something that had Mr Spendlove scratching his head in disbelief. It seemed that, for some inexplicable reason, and despite refusing food of any kind, and despite being confined to her home for the past 28 days, Tilly had actually been gaining weight. And not just a small amount of weight either. The young woman had been putting on weight steadily at the rate of something like 4 to 5 pounds a week. 'It's truly remarkable,' the bewildered Mr Spendlove had told his closest friend and fellow Samaritan. "How can that possibly happen? How can my Tilly be gaining weight? It doesn't make one ounce of sense. It's a complete and utter mystery.'

A complete and utter mystery wasn't how Gabriel Spendlove's cousin Veronica had appraised the situation however. She had frowned upon the idea of spending vast sums of money on the best psychologists and mind experts. She had personally slated those that believed continuous sessions of therapy would ultimately return the sick woman to normality. She had agreed on one thing however. She agreed that the young woman needed rehabilitating. She agreed that because, for some time, she had been convinced that the source of Tilly's condition lay not in her subconscious but within any number of bottles labelled, 'ALCOHOL'.

'That's the only thing that can explain her bizarre

behaviour and her ability to go without food for a sustained period,' she had told Mr Spendlove during her final visit.

It was a theory that hadn't satisfied Gabriel Spendlove however. After all, he and his wife had always been famously teetotal and had therefore never bought alcohol of any sort, not even to accommodate their many guests. Nevertheless, to his great credit, he had not dismissed the idea entirely and that is why over the days that followed, he tried not to let his wife out of his sight for one moment. That is when he discovered the magnitude of his problem. That is when he realised his wife was indeed a carnivore. That is when he realised Tilly wasn't just behaving like a cat, she possessed all the predatory and opportunistic instincts of a wild one.

Had the garden not been so enormous and so abundant in overgrown shrubs and small trees and had it not been so full of nooks and crannies, he might well have spotted the signs a lot earlier than he did. He would have almost certainly come across the remnants of numerous dead birds, the rotten carcasses of entire families of rabbits and the skeletal remains of other creatures such as squirrels, voles and mice. Each had met a savage and abrupt end. All had been some part of Tilly Spendlove's curious diet since he had changed her eating pattern.

At that time, crumbs of comfort were in short supply for Gabriel Spendlove but at least at that point he hadn't been subjected to the disturbing and previously unimaginable vista of his wife stalking, capturing and devouring any of her live prey. It wasn't long before he had however and to make matters worse, when he did, the quarry was much larger than before. This time the unfortunate creature was something that should have been off limits, even to the depraved Tilly Spendlove. This time the prey was far more than a quick snack. This time the prey was their neighbour's cute little Yorkshire Terrier Sam which had slipped under the fence that divided the two properties after hearing the anguished yelps from a cornered and terrified fox cub. The following morning, the usually whiter than white, famously honest and highly respected teacher did something completely out of character. Something that had made him feel so utterly ashamed, he had immediately headed to the top of his garden and sobbed.

He had done it on his sick wife's behalf of course, but by misleading his distraught and hugely concerned neighbours by calling at their home to inform them that he had just looked out of his bathroom window and watched a seedy looking individual snatch up their beloved pet and head off at some pace on a carrier bicycle, he had not only lied, he had given them false hope at a time when he knew very well there was no hope whatsoever. Furthermore, because he had been the only witness to the apparent 'crime', he had been obliged to visit his local police station to give a statement regarding what he had seen. That meant that he had been left with no alternative but to lie to the police too. Sadly, for Mr Spendlove-it wouldn't be the last time he would feel the need to falsify the truth. It would be far from the last time.

It is probably important to stress that for the past 10 years, Mr Spendlove, together with several of his school colleagues, had been on the panel of a Merseyside domestic violence charity organisation known as !ENUFFIZENUFF!, and although some of those he had been working alongside were highly competent and eminent counsellors and psychologists, he had resisted the temptation to confide in them for fear of his wife's unusual condition becoming common knowledge around his school and he, as a result, becoming a figure of ridicule. That didn't mean he wasn't prepared to listen however. In fact, listening during those meetings, rather than take his familiar active role in proceedings, was pretty much all he had done since his wife had taken ill. That is how he came to hear about an extraordinary young Crosby man who, in the not too distant past, had done remarkable things for a great number of emotionally disturbed young women. A young man that, according to some very reliable sources, could boast results that could put even the most respected and notable psychologist lights in the shade. Gabriel Spendlove wasted no time whatsoever and after informing his deputy head that he was taking a fortnights sick leave, he packed some things and headed for Crosby in Merseyside armed with an optimism he hadn't felt for some considerable time.

Obtaining an audience with the young man who he now firmly believed was his last great hope was to prove far more difficult than expected however. In fact, the nearest he initially got was when he stood close by one Saturday evening and watched the paperboy slip the evening edition of the local newspaper through a tiny gap between the door and the door frame. On that occasion, he had actually heard Brian Matthews talk for the first time. He had enquired as to the health of the paperboy's mother, the delivery boy's newsagent boss and his old form tutor. In fact, he had enquired as to the well-being of so many local people, the young paperboy had eventually been forced to abandon his bicycle for a short time while he relieved himself in a nearby entry. It had been a break in dialogue that had allowed Gabriel the opportunity to move forward and introduce himself but once again, just like on those rare occasions when either of Matthews's parents had responded to his knocks, he found himself staring at the four panelled front door and talking to himself.

At that point, the vast majority of men, regardless of how much they were devoted to their wives, would have almost certainly resigned themselves to failure, climbed into their cars and drove home. After all, by that time, the barrier that had been created to protect the young man, had appeared to be as impregnable as ever. However, that hadn't been how the positive thinking and resourceful Gabriel Spendlove had perceived the situation. He had recognised something

[126]

that he considered to be hugely significant and had actually returned to his car with renewed vigour and a great deal more hope. He had seen Brian Matthews's desire to keep the young paperboy talking as evidence that he might be starting to crave some sort of contact with people beyond his small and tight knit family circle. He had also seen Matthews's enquiries as to the health of so many people as conclusive proof that he was still the caring and sensitive individual he was purported to be. In the context of the situation as a whole, that meant that if he could secure a face to face meeting with him, he would more than likely want to help.

The next evening, Gabriel Spendlove, followed the paperboy home and after watching him close his front door and turn on the hall light, he slipped 5 recently printed twenty pound notes through his letter box, rang the bell and took a few paces back. Within the time it took for the last note to land, he had not only been invited inside but was enjoying a piping hot cup of cocoa with the man of the house. He had wasted no time in explaining why he had come to Crosby. How his wife had been brought up in a house that was more of a cattery than a home in the conventional sense. How she had been deprived of a mother's love for her entire youth. How he had met and immediately fallen in love with her at a prestigious county fair. How he had killed a stray cat on his return home from a fund raising event, how the incident had somehow turned his wife insane and how, despite calling upon the services of some notable and highly esteemed psychologists, she had failed to make any progress. And ultimately, how, despite some extremely generous offers and desperate appeals, the apparently uncaring Mr and Mrs Matthews had continually slammed their door in his face. However, just as he had to the police regarding his neighbour's dog, he had lied very deliberately and very boldly. He had told the boy's father that, early the previous day, Brian Matthews had managed to get a message out to him on the back of a cigarette packet, assuring him that he would gladly help if he could only manage to escape his parent's gaze for a couple of hours. That had been the clincher and after a more than generous sum of money had been agreed, the two men set about formulating their plan.

Over the next two and a half hours, the conspirators put their heads together and concocted the simplest of plans. Gabriel Spendlove would go home and then return to Crosby with his wife the following Saturday afternoon. They would then wait for Mr and Mrs Matthews to leave the house to do their traditional weekly shop. He and his wife would then wait in his vehicle for young Joe the paperboy to arrive and when Brian Matthews opened the front door to receive his father's newspaper, he and Tilly would quickly slip inside. Meanwhile, to ensure that Mr and Mrs Matthews didn't return early and interrupt their son's clinic, Mr Brown would follow the couple and contrive a way to have them detained for as long as he possibly could. 'An hour,' Gabriel Spendlove had said to Mr Brown upon leaving his house. 'Just find me n hour.'

An hour was significant in the context of the situation because his closest and most trusted friend who had done a lot of early groundwork on Gabriel Spendlove's behalf, had told him that one hour under the guidance of young Brian Matthews was said to be the equivalent of a week with an experienced psychologist or a month residing in a National Health psychiatric ward. Unfortunately, it was a claim that was never substantiated because shortly after arriving back in Crosby the following Saturday, he found the road taped off and was informed by one of Matthews's neighbours that the young man had packed a trunk and left the previous day. Just thirty minutes after he had narrowly dodged a petrol bomb that had come hurtling through his parent's sitting room window.

The missile had been thrown by a man with an enormous axe to grind. A man who had become utterly bitter and twisted after his wife, on the advice of

Matthews had left him to bring up his 3 year old son some years before. A man that, until very recently, had been completely unaware that Matthews had returned to Crosby. Mr Brown had also been responsible for daubing-

'BEWARE
HOME BREAKING BASTARD IN
RESIDENCE'

-in big, bold red letters on the Matthews's front door.

In the well balanced eyes of Gabriel Spendlove, and in stark contrast to the belief of so many of his friends and colleagues, there had been only one person to blame for the scheme's failure-his good self. After all, the plan, apart from a few minor details, had been his brainchild and it had been his idea and his idea alone to invite the highly vindictive Mr Samuel Brown to collaborate in it. A man that detested young Matthews to such a degree that he was prepared to do time in prison t to see the area rid of him. 'It constituted poor planning on my behalf,' Spendlove had told his good friend and neighbour on his return home. 'I should have researched Brown before putting so much trust in him.'

In fairness to Gabriel Spendlove, there were lots of things he couldn't possibly have known. For example, he couldn't possibly have known that Sam Brown had been a misogynist, a womaniser and a habitual wife beater for the best part of his married life. He couldn't possibly have known that the same individual's bruised and battered partner had been one of the first people to seek out young Matthews for help. And he therefore couldn't have known that Sam Brown had been one of the first men to suffer rejection as a result of the young man's advice. He had been one of several men that had returned home late from the pub to find a hastily scribbled goodbye note on the kitchen table instead of their much anticipated hot supper.

Due to circumstances beyond the control of the

prosecution, Sam Brown served less than 3 months in prison for carrying out the petrol bomb attack on the Matthews's home but was arrested less than 48 hours after his release for threatening his estranged wife with a carving knife outside her mother's home. He resided at her Majesty's pleasure in Walton Prison for the next 18 months until he was murdered by a fellow inmate during a game of poker. Very few of his Jubilee Road neighbours openly mourned his passing and even less attended his funeral and ensuing cremation ceremony Nobody claimed his ashes. Nobody seemed to care.

Lots of people cared about Gabriel Spendlove though. They cared a great deal about the man. That was because he was known to be a thoroughly decent and respected individual who had never courted trouble or controversy of any kind and had often been the first to support and champion the causes of the impoverished, the most vulnerable and the less capable. The term, 'wouldn't harm a fly,' had apparently been penned with Gabriel Spendlove in mind. That is why so many people had initially poured scorn on a rumour that he might have done away with his much adored but mentally disturbed wife. A rumour that had begun to circulate less than a fortnight after he had returned from his bitterly disappointing visit to Crosby and one that had gathered pace after his abandoned Triumph Herald had been discovered less than a hundred yards from a secluded part of the Leeds-Liverpool Canal. One or two things were undeniable however. Gabriel Spendlove and his sick wife were indeed missing and Gabriel Spendlove was therefore somebody the police were desperately keen to talk to.

It had remained a rumour and little more than a rumour for another month or so until an elderly but keen eyed lollypop man noticed a photograph of the Spendloves that had been pasted on his local police station wall. He had immediately informed the duty sergeant that he had seen the very same man making off at some speed towards a bridge that crosses a section of

the Leeds-Liverpool Canal after snatching something
from outside a local greengrocers. The tabloids had a
field day and were incredibly cruel and insensitive from
that day on. Particularly after the robber had been
identified as the school teacher husband of a remarkable
young woman who had allegedly turned into a cat.
Furthermore, a respected school teacher and husband
who, for some reason, had risked his livelihood and
reputation by stealing nothing more than a dirty old
potato sack! However, despite a nationwide manhunt
and although the area of the canal where the car had
been found had been dredged systematically for over a
week, nothing was ever seen of the Spendloves again. It
was a mystery that spawned a thousand cruel and
amusing quips and an equal amount of theories-one of
the most plausible of which had been put forward by the
old lollypop man himself while he was being
interviewed by a regional outside broadcast news team.
"There's no doubt about it as far as I'm concerned. That
Spendlove fella's done her in hasn't he. He's drowned
the poor cow. That's what a lot of people do you know.
That's what a lot of people have always done with
unwanted cats. They grab them by the scruff of the neck
when they're not looking, put them in a potato sack and
then drown the poor little buggers in the nearest stretch
of water. You mark my words young man-that's where
you'll find that poor Tilly woman. She'll be at the
bottom of the canal keeping the old prams, shopping
trolleys and used Johnnies company."

CHAPTER SEVEN
DELICATE BALANCE

The train had come to a halt in the middle of a century old, 220 metre long bridge much of which had only recently been restored and part of which had lately been reinforced with concrete and steel after several cracks had appeared around the lower seams and abutments. It consisted of 9 semi-elliptical arches made from tens of thousands of red engineering brick and thousands of tons of local quarried limestone. It had been built to span, what had become known to the locals as Dyffryn Yr Enaid A Gollwyd, which roughly translates as the Valley of Lost Souls-a tranquil but often bleak part of the Welsh countryside that had previously contained a large number of graves before it was deliberately flooded by ambitious and insensitive developers. It had not been designed as a stopping off point however because this was a structure built on a north-south axis without any cover or protection from the bitter elements whatsoever. That was the reason nobody had left the train the previous day and why the passengers were still in a state of uncertainty when, at the committee's request, they assembled in the dining carriage the following morning at about 8 o'clock.

"Just take your seats please lads," said a gaunt and tired looking Club Secretary Jeff Hill while rearranging some of the dining room chairs to form a reasonable half circle. "I'm afraid I've got some very bad news to convey."

"More bad news?" said Woodhouse.

"I'm afraid so," said the Club Secretary.

"We already know we're not going to be able to leave the train just yet," said Hamill before sitting down and proceeding to fasten his right bootlace.

"That's right," said Woodhouse. "We don't need to be dragged to assembly like a bunch of schoolchildren to be told that. We know it's nasty out there."

"It's far worse than nasty," said Steadman. "And it's

treacherous too."

"You were told not to go outside," said Matthews.

"You shut your mouth," said Woodhouse.

"I only went to gauge the state of play," said Steadman.
"I was only out there five minutes. I thought I was a
goner. The wind was howling like a bastard. I've never
known anything like it. Only for big Woody thrusting
out his giant left paw, I'd be at the bottom of that
bleeding valley now."

"I'd have let you go if it wasn't for the fact you owe me
a fiver," said Woodhouse.

"I thought you'd forgotten about that," said Steadman.

"An elephant never forgets," said Hamill.

"Up yours Hamill," said Woodhouse.

"Alty and Larkin almost came a cropper too," said
Blackie.

"When was that?" said the Chef.

"About an hour ago." said Blackie.

"Is that why they haven't shown up for parade?" said the
Club Secretary.

"They're getting changed," said Blackie. "They're
soaked right through."

"It doesn't surprise me," said Steadman. "Torvill and
Dean would struggle to stay on their feet out there."

"What were they hoping to achieve?" said the Club
Secretary. "Our Health and Safety Officer Eddie
reckons the wind had been in excess of 75 mph at times.
That's why I'm going to have to insist nobody steps out
onto that bridge until the wind drops considerably. It'd
be shear madness."

"I'm not going to argue there," said Woodhouse.

"It'd be suicide," said Steadman.

"That's right," said Meehan. "This bridge we're on is
too narrow and far too exposed to be walking along.
There are no safety rails. There's nothing to grab onto.
You'll be risking your lives. One freak gust and you'll
take off like a paper aeroplane."

"Even me?" said Woodhouse.

"Even you," said Meehan.

[133]

"When do you think the wind is likely to drop?" said Blackie.

"I don't know," said Meehan. "It's hard to say. I've known storms to last for hours and I've known them to last a week."

"A week!" said Hamill. "Haven't you ever got anything positive to say?"

"I'm just trying to be realistic," said Meehan. "The storm will come and the storm will eventually subside."

"Let's hope so," said Woodhouse.

"You can rest assured it will," said the Club Secretary.

"Can we also rest assured that you won't be dragging us from the warmth and comfort of our beds again just to be given a weather update?" said Hamill.

"That's not the reason we asked you to assemble here," said the Club Secretary.

"What is the reason then?" said Hamill. "Has that idiot Alec Morris been up to no good again?"

"It's got nothing to do with Alec Morris," said the Club Secretary. "He's been as good as gold."

"Then why the hell are we here?" said Hamill. "Why in God's name have we been ordered to assemble here at this ungodly time of the morning? And why isn't our Chairman here? Have you allowed him a nice sleep in have you Hilly."

"That'll be it," said Woodhouse. "There's one rule for the committee and one rule for us plebs."

"I've been saying that for donkey's years," said Hamill.

"Tommy Weir's dead," said the Club Secretary.

"What!" said Steadman.

"Tommy Weir passed away during the early hours of the morning," said the Club Secretary before lowering his head.

"Tommy Weir!" said a highly suspicious looking Woodhouse.

"That's right," said the Club Secretary.

"How?" said Blackie. "What happened?"

"I don't really know," said the Club Secretary.

"The Professor knows more than me. He found his body

on one of the washroom floors."

"Is that right Professor?" said Steadman.

"Not entirely," said the old man while easing through the mumbling ranks of shocked and confused club members. "He wasn't actually dead when I found him. He died a short time after."

"From what?" said Blackie.

"I can't say for certain at this juncture," said the Professor before taking a seat next to Hewlett, removing his spectacles from his breast pocket and proceeding to polish them with one of the provided table serviettes. "At least not without further information."

"Regarding what?" said Woodhouse.

"Regarding his recent health for one thing," said the old man.

"His recent health!" said Steadman. "He was as right as rain wasn't he? He was as fit as a flea wasn't he lads?"

"I'd have thought so too," said Woodhouse.

"He was fine," said Blackie. "There was nothing wrong with the lad."

"He was ill," said the Club Secretary.

"Ill!" said Blackie.

"He'd been ill since returning from his holidays," said the Club Secretary. "He'd been put on medication. I only found out yesterday."

"Medication for what?" said Blackie.

"I don't know," said the Club Secretary. "He said he'd been getting chest pains. He said he'd been feeling exhausted all the time. He told me he wasn't too concerned. I've got to be honest-I'm like you lot. I'm still in a state of shock I don't know what else to tell you."

"Maybe I can help," said the Professor before crossing one leg over the other and smoothing out the creases in his trousers with the palm of his right hand. "But as I've just said-I'm going to need a little more information first."

"What sort of information?" said Blackie.

"Information regarding your friend's state of mind," said

[135]

the old man.

"State of mind!" said Woodhouse.

"That's right," said the old man. "Which one of you knew him best?"

"I'm not sure," said the Club Secretary while scanning the gathering. "I've known him for twenty years or so. But only as a fellow club member. So has Hulmey. But the Chef went to school with him. You were at school with him weren't you Chef?"

"I was yes," said the Chef. "But we lost touch. I didn't socialise with him much. We just had the odd drink after we'd concluded club business."

"I think that's the same for all of us," said the Club Secretary. "We very rarely socialised. He had his own group of close friends."

"What about concerns," said the old man. "Had he recently voiced any concerns? Had he been anxious at all? Did he ever discuss any of his fears with any of you?"

"Fears," said the Club Secretary. "I don't remember anything frightening big Tommy. He feared absolutely nothing."

"What about deeply entrenched fears," said the Professor.

"He feared nothing," said the Club Secretary.

"That's not entirely true now I come to think of it," said Hulme.

"What do you mean?" said the old man.

"He did fear one thing," said Hulme.

"What was it?" said the Professor before leaning forward and tapping the Club Vice Chairman on the knee. "What did he fear Mr Hulme?"

"He feared losing his eyesight," said Hulme.

"Losing his eyesight!" said the Club Secretary.

"That's right," said Hulme. "He was terrified of going blind. I wouldn't have known that myself had it not been for me and him getting together at mine for a few drinks while Ruth and Les were on a hen party in Southport. We ended up watching this film. I can't remember what it was called now. It was about a group of soldiers that get attacked by werewolves in the Highlands of Scotland. There's a scene in it where the men are sitting around a camp fire. One of them, for conversation sake, asked each man in turn what their greatest fear was. That got me and Tommy Weir discussing ours. That's when he told me he'd feared going blind since he was a kid. He'd been counselled because of it apparently."

"Really?" said the old man before leaning back in his chair and folding his arms. "How interesting. How very interesting."

"Why do you say that Professor?" said the Club Secretary.

"I'll tell you shortly," said the old man. "But first of all, I want to establish how his fear might have come about. Does anyone know? Are you able to enlighten me Mr Hulme?"

"I'm not, I'm sorry," said Hulme.

"Can anyone?" said the Professor.

"I might be able to," said the Chef.

"You might?" said the old man after adjusting his position and peering over the top of his slightly misted spectacles. "You know of something that might have perpetuated his fear do you?"

"I might do," said the Chef. "But it was a hell of a long time ago."

"That doesn't really matter," said the Professor. "What was it?"

"He lost the sight in one of his eyes when he was about 14 or 15," said the Chef.

"Did he really?" said the old man.

"He did yes," said the Chef. "Some dickhead 5th former had thought it a good idea to bring a catapult to school. He'd been firing at empty cans at first. But then he got bored and turned his attention to moving targets. Tommy was one of the unlucky ones. A few lads had got hit in their backsides and their legs but Tommy got hit in the eye. He must have been bending down. I remember his

[137]

eyelid being split right across. It was horrible. You could see right through the gash. It was like a piece of torn rag."

"What did you do?" said the Professor.

"I ran to the boy's toilets and threw up," said the Chef. "I hate anything to do with eyes. From what I got told, the school nurse rushed him to the nearby Waterloo Hospital and got him stitched up. She probably saved his sight. I remember him having to wear a patch for the next fortnight or so. He didn't seem to mind at first because he got lots of sympathy and attention. But some of the older kids were cruel. They were calling him Long John Silver and asking him where he'd left his parrot."

"And how did the accident affect him?" said the Professor. "Can you remember?"

"I can't to be honest," said the Chef. "We changed forms and went our separate ways not long after that. I know he recovered his sight. I've never really discussed it until now. I'd forgotten all about it until our kid mentioned the blindness thing. To be honest, I'm not entirely sure where all this is going Professor."

"Me neither," said the Club Secretary.

"Then allow me to explain," said the old man before slapping his thighs and rising to his feet. "Let me tell you all about something called scotomaphobia."

"Scoto what?" said Woodhouse.

"Scotomaphobia," said the old man. "The fear of going blind. It's what I now strongly suspect was a contributory factor in your friend's death."

"I'm afraid you've lost me here," said Steadman. "That's all a bit too technical for me Professor."

"Well, allow me to simplify it for you," said the old man. "Consider this. Imagine losing the sight in one of your eyes. From that critical moment on, you only have one eye. You possess half the vision you were originally allocated at birth. From that moment on, you are one accident or serious eye related illness from being totally blind. That's hard to live with for most people. That's when the fear of going blind can often be at its most intense."

"I'm afraid, I'm with Steadman," said Woodhouse. "You've lost me Professor."

"Alright," said the old man. "Let me explain it this way. Before your friend and club Chairman died, I watched him zig zag across the washroom in a trance-like state bumping into doors and partition walls like a clockwork robot that had got out of control. He was in a state of extreme dread. In all my days, I have rarely seen such a look of intense fear on a person's face. With what you've just told me, I firmly believe he had come to the conclusion that his greatest fear had manifested."

"Gone blind you mean?" said Steadman.

"Absolutely," said the Professor. "He believed he'd gone blind. He believed he would never see again and couldn't cope with that terrible realisation."

"And had he gone blind?" said Woodhouse.

"Not at all," said the old man. "I think it was all in his mind."

"Were you not able to snap him out of the trance?" said the Club Secretary.

"I wasn't unfortunately," said the old man. "To be honest, my first priority was to prevent him from doing himself serious harm. He'd already sustained serious bruising to his nose and forehead. But then he suddenly yelled out in pain, clutched his chest and slumped to the floor. That was it. There was nothing more I could do for the poor man."

"But why now?" said the Chef. "Why did his fear of going blind affect him now?"

"Because he was a very sick man," said the Professor. "He was suffering from a serious disease."

"What sort of disease?" said Woodhouse.

"A very unusual and complex one," said the old man.

"How unusual?" said Woodhouse after leaving his chair and taking a seat opposite the old man. "How unusual Professor?"

"It's extremely rare," said the old man. "For instance,

I've studied medicine and all kinds of diseases for much of my adult life and I've only come across a handful of cases. It's very nasty, to say the least. It somehow plays havoc with people's innermost fears."

"Nice one," said Steadman. "Remind me never to fall foul of it Professor."

"Tommy must have brought it back from Brazil," said the Club Secretary.

"Is it contagious Professor?" said Woodhouse.

"It's been known to be," said the old man.

"What do you mean, 'it's been known to be'?" said the Club Secretary. "Help us here Professor will you. Is it contagious or not? Let's have it Professor. Some of my members are on the brink of filling their trousers."

"Let me put it this way," said the old man. "One of my experiments, consisted of introducing an infected white rat into a large glass tank with 5 other almost identical uninfected white rats."

"And what happened?" said the Club Secretary.

"Nothing at all," said the old man. "Apart from the fact the infected rat stood out like a sore thumb."

"In what way?" said the Chef.

"It was extremely nervous and agitated and appeared determined to maintain a distance from all the others," said the Professor.

"Are you saying, none of the other rats became ill?" said the Chef.

"Not a single one," said the Professor.

"Which surely proves the disease isn't contagious then," said the Club Secretary. "That's right isn't it? That's right isn't it Professor?"

"It would be if we hadn't repeated the experiment," said the old man.

"What happened then?" said the Chef.

"Nothing at first," said the old man. "But after about an hour, two of the uninfected rats began exhibiting the very same symptoms associated with the infected rat."

"Like what?" said Steadman.

"They began twitching nervously," said the old man.

"Then they headed into opposite corners of the tank. A few minutes later, they were shaking violently and recoiling at the sight of their own reflections in the glass."

"What do you mean, 'recoiling'?" said McShane.

"They were terrified," said the Professor.

"Terrified of what?" said McShane.

"Something they'd seen in the glass I presume," said the old man. "Or to put it more accurately-something they believed they'd seen. I can't possibly say what."

"A gigantic cat would be my guess," said Woodhouse. "I'd have thought a gigantic cat would be a rat's worst fear."

"I'd have thought so too," said Hamill.

"Oh Christ!" said Steadman. "This just gets worse and worse. That means the disease *is* contagious."

"And, as I've just said-it's been known to be," said the Professor.

"Nice," said Steadman while raking his fingers through his hair. "That's lovely. That's fucking lovely that is."

"So explain Tommy Weir for me Professor," said Hamill. "He didn't look nervous and agitated. As far as I could tell, he was his usual calm, assured and authoritative self before he left this room. He clearly didn't feel the need to keep a distance between himself and the rest of the rats that had nested in his sleeping carriage."

"I'm sorry!" said the old man. "I don't understand."

"He's being sarcastic Professor," said the Club Secretary. "He tends to do that a lot. He doesn't like us committee members."

"I see," said the Professor.

"He makes a good point though," said the Club Secretary. "Our Chairman didn't look any different than usual before he retired to bed."

"I've no reason to doubt you," said the old man. "And I'm not going to pretend that I have all the answers...because I haven't. What I do know is this-he was extremely and abnormally agitated when I

[141]

encountered him in the washroom in the early hours of this morning."

"And he'd left his room for no apparent reason," said the Club Secretary. "That's not like Tommy Weir. In all the years we've been away, I've never once known him to get up before his alarm goes off."

"That's right," said the Chef. "He's one of the heaviest sleepers I know. He always sleeps right through. Maybe the distancing aspect of the disease had kicked in."

"It's possible," said the old man. "To be honest, I recognised certain signs yesterday."

"When?" said the Club Secretary.

"Around the time when he was being asked for his resignation," replied the Professor. "That's one of the reasons I examined him. That, together with the fact he'd recently toured parts of South America."

"Is that where you believe he came into contact with the disease?" said the Chef.

"Without a doubt," said the old man. "Unless it's reached Western Europe that is."

"He'd been to Manaus to see the rain forest," said the Club Secretary. "He'd been looking forward to it for ages. He was one of the great tourists was Tommy Weir. He wanted to see and experience everything. the world has to offer What a kick in the teeth for the poor bugger."

"So how exactly does this disease work Professor?" said Woodhouse. "You were saying earlier about it doing something to people's inner fears."

"It heightens them," said the old man. "It heightens them appreciably. I don't know if I can put that into numbers, but let's say for instance, if you are scared of spiders, you'll be 100 times more scared of spiders if contracting the disease. Does that make any sense gentlemen?"

"It does for me," said Steadman.

"And me too," said the Chef.

"What about giving us some other numbers Professor,"

said the Club Secretary.

"What sort of numbers?" said the old man.

"The nitty gritty sort of numbers," said the Club Secretary. "Numbers to do with how many of us are likely to become infected. How many? How many is that likely to be Professor?"

"I'm not sure I want to know," said the highly agitated Blackie before rising and heading over to the window.

"I do," said Hamill.

"So do I," said Woodhouse. "How many of us will become affected Professor?"

"It's hard to say," said the old man.

"Well, take a deep breath and have a go," said Woodhouse.

"How many?" said Hamill.

"It could be as many as 1 in 6," said the Professor.

"1 in 6!" said Blackie after coming to a halt and turning to face the group.

"It could be," said the Professor. "That would be my best estimate."

"Which means that 3 or 4 of us are already on the brink of insanity," said Hamill.

"Thanks a lot Hamill," said Blackie. "What a lovely thought to retire to my room on."

"I'm just stating a cold hard fact," said Hamill.

"What if you've never suffered from any fears or phobias?" said McShane.

"That's a point," said Woodhouse. "That's a very good point. What if you haven't got any phobias Professor?"

"I'd pat you on the back and congratulate you profoundly," said the Professor. "I'd be forced to admit that life's been very kind to you. But everyone has some sort of fear. For instance-there must be somebody on board this train who has a fear of heights."

"They've never worried me," said Hamill.

"Nor me," said Woodhouse.

"They terrify me," said Steadman. "I had a three tier wooden ladder collapse under me once while I was 45 feet up. And I'm not ashamed to admit this-I'd already

[143]

kacked me trousers by the time I hit the ground. You'll never see me painting my own gutters and barge boards again."

"Nor me," said the Chef. "But how's vertigo going to affect those on board this train Professor? We're on a solid base no more than a few feet above the ground."

"I think you're forgetting something aren't you Chef," said Blackie. "We've come to rest on a tired old bridge that's about 100 feet up."

"Maybe so, but you're only aware of that if you look outside," said the Chef. "I'm just going to avoid looking out of the window. I'm closing the curtains and keeping them closed. It's mind over matter as far as I'm concerned."

"I'm not sure the concept of mind over matter's going to help in this case," said the old man.

"Why not?" said the Chef.

"Because the disease can be a relentless and cunning adversary," said the old man. "No matter how hard you try, it'll still bring your greatest fear to the surface. For example-for any vertigo sufferers among us. Imagine a scenario when you're lying in your bed and you suddenly become convinced you're 1000 feet above the floor, rather than 18 inches above it. Try to imagine how that would make you feel."

"I'd rather not if you don't mind," said Steadman.

"Well, let me help you then," said the old man. "You'd probably start looking at your single, four foot of bed very differently. You would probably begin to see it as some sort of flimsy, inadequate life raft. You'd probably start to question the stability and integrity of the bed frame. You'd begin to wonder if the joints and glue are strong enough to hold and how long the structure would be able to support your weight."

"Is that all a possibility?" said Steadman.

"A very real one," said the old man. "For instance, one of those handful of sufferers I told you about earlier was an Ecuadorian forestry worker named Pablo, Hernandez, Garcia. He had two extremely beautiful twin daughters

[144]

who were approaching puberty. His friends had been known to tease him from time to time about how the girls would soon be ready to enjoy sexual intercourse with all sorts of well endowed young bucks. And like most fathers, that was something Pablo didn't ever want to face up to, and it consequently became his greatest fear. A fear which intensified when he contracted the awful disease we are now discussing. and very soon going to have to deal with"

"What did he do?" said Woodhouse.

"He took a white hot length of iron and rendered his daughters utterly undesirable," said the Professor. "I'll furnish you with the gory details if you want."

"Don't bother," said Steadman. I think we get it."

"The evil bastard!" said Woodhouse. "He should have been strung up from the nearest tree."

"He needed to be taken care of," said the Professor.

"Taken care of!" said Woodhouse.

"That's right," said the old man. "It wasn't his fault. He was as much a victim himself. He was a very sick man."

"I wouldn't argue there," said the Chef.

"Is the disease terminal?" said Hamill.

"Oh Christ-here we go," said Steadman before covering his ears and heading towards the door. "The nitty gritty's going to come out now. I'm going back to bed. Will someone please wake me up when this bloody nightmare's over."

"Is the disease terminal Professor?" said Hamill.

"I've never known anyone or anything to die from it," said the old man. "Not even one of the lab rats. In the past we've been able to sedate and medicate the afflicted until the illness dissipates."

"So Tommy Weir didn't die from the disease?" said Steadman. "Is that what you're saying?"

"The disease didn't help," said the old man. "But as I said earlier-there was very possibly a contributory factor."

"Like what?" said the Club Secretary.

"I think your Chairman might have had an undiscovered

[145]

heart defect or dangerously high blood pressure," said the Professor. "In fact, I'm now convinced of it."

"What about the contagious aspect of the disease Professor," said Hamill. "Can we assume that those who have recently been in closest contact with our Chairman are the most likely to be at risk?"

"Do you mean those that have shared accommodation with your Chairman?" said the Professor.

"That's exactly what he means," said the Club Secretary.

"I wouldn't have thought that would matter," said the old man. "You've all been in close enough proximity to your Chairman at some time or other since the train set off."

"Bloody hell!" said Steadman.

"So let me try to put our situation into perspective," said Woodhouse. "We're on a train with no driver and no staff, there's the mother of all hurricanes coming and there's a possibility that a deadly virus is going to drive a quarter of us insane."

"1 in 6," said the Professor.

"1 in 6 then," said Woodhouse. "I feel so much better now."

"But don't forget this Woody-this trip of a lifetime and all it entails is free," said Hamill. "I've read the club newsletter."

"We seem to be somewhat in your hands Professor," said the Club Secretary. "What do you suggest we do next?"

"Get rid of the corpse for one thing," said the old man.

"What do you mean, get rid of it?" said the Club Secretary.

"Discard it," said the old man. "And do it quickly. There's a very real danger of infection from it."

"Do you mean dump it?" said the Chef.

"Just get rid of it," said the Professor. "Use your nous."

"We could dump him over the side of the bridge," said Hamill.

"We'll do no such thing," said the Club Secretary. "He's our friend. He deserves a proper Christian burial.

And I'm going to see to it he gets one."
"We could store the body in one of the vacant carriages at the end of the train," said the Chef. "What do you think Professor?"
"If you insist," said the old man. "Although I'd prefer it if the body was out of here altogether. But before you do, you might want to get one of your engineers to disengage the heating to that carriage."
"I'll do that," said the Club Secretary. "Me and my mate Hulmey will sort that out. Are there any precautions you think we should take?"
"Like what?" said the Professor.
"Like wearing protective masks or gloves?" said the Club Secretary.
"I don't think it'll make any difference," said the old man. "But if wearing a mask and gloves makes you feel any safer, by all means go ahead. The problem is-the virus has been airborne for some hours. Your Chairman's been very much at the hub of things since your party arrived at the station."
"So what you're saying Professor, is that nobody's safe?" said the Club Secretary.
"I'm afraid not," said the old man.
"But what if we were able to leave the train," said Steadman. "What if the storm passes and we were able to get to a hospital."
"That's right," said Woodhouse. "If we could all get to a hospital, we could get jabs or something."
"There are no effective jabs," said the Professor.
"The disease isn't curable. It's manageable. But it has to complete its cycle."
"And how long is that cycle likely to be?" said Woodhouse.
"About a week to ten days in most cases," said the old man.
"Oh dear Christ!" said McShane. "Fuck, fuck, fuck, fuck, fuck."
"I'd have saved one or two of those expletives for when you hear the Professor's next statement," said the

[147]

Health and Safety Officer after moving across and taking a seat next to the Professor.

"What do you mean?" said McShane.

"Yes-what are you talking about Eddie?" said Woodhouse.

"I'm going to let the Professor explain," said Meehan.

"What's going on Professor?" said Woodhouse.

"Is there more to all this?" said Hamill.

"I'm afraid so," said the old man.

"Can't you work it out for yourself Hamill?" said the Club Secretary.

"Apparently not," replied Hamill. "Why don't you explain, mastermind.

"We're not going to be able to leave the train," said the Club Secretary.

"Why the hell not?" said Hamill.

"For obvious reasons," said the old man. "The disease is highly contagious. Think about the numbers I gave you earlier gentlemen. 1 in 6. Think about that. 1 in 6 of you will fall victim to the disease. Do you really think it would be wise for almost 20 potential carriers to walk into a highly populated town? I certainly don't. I wouldn't sanction it."

"Nor would I," said the Health and Safety Officer. "It would be reckless in the extreme."

"It would be catastrophic," said the Professor. "In no time at all, there'd be something like 150 raving lunatics to every 1000 normal, unaffected human being. It would be a logistical nightmare."

"That's nice," said Hamill. "That's got to be a worse ratio than New York."

"So in the meantime we just have to wait," said the Chef. "We have to wait until one of us starts exhibiting the symptoms. It's like a bloody lottery."

"It's very much like a lottery I'm afraid," said the old man. "Because even as we speak, the disease is in the air looking for a suitable host."

"Well at least that's a little bit more encouraging," said Hamill.

[148]

"Why's that?" said the Professor.

"Because nobody has ever accused me of being a suitable host," said Hamill.

"I'll second that," said Woodhouse.

"Can I ask you what the symptoms are?" said the Club Secretary.

"Of course you can," said the old man. "I think you can expect gritty eyes, headache, fever, hot flushes and perspiration."

"It sounds a lot like flu symptoms," said Woodhouse.

"It's not too dissimilar," said the old man before removing his glasses and rising to his feet. "But unlike flu, the sufferer will also start to see things."

"See things!" said the Chef.

"Like what?" said Steadman.

"Things associated with their greatest fears," said the Professor. "For instance-if the sufferer is scared of rats, he might start seeing gigantic, menacing looking rats at the end of his bed. He might find himself locked in a small and inescapable room with thousands of the creatures. Now then-if you'll excuse me. I believe I might just have some helpful information on the disease in one of my old diaries. I'll retire to my room and see what my little grey cells can come up with. Don't despair gentlemen. I could be wrong. It wouldn't be the first time."

For about fifteen minutes after the Professor had exited the dining carriage, the only noise that had been heard was the tick of the large wall clock, the howl of the increasingly ferocious wind and what sounded like the occasional boom of a bass drum as a particularly violent blast thudded against the outer skin of the dining carriage. That was until the forward carriage door suddenly burst open and in strode an extremely determined looking Kenny Biddo carrying a monkey wrench the size of a small child.

"What's that you've got there Biddo?" said an anxious and suspicious Club Secretary while trying unsuccessfully to make his way through the dense line of

[149]

seated men.

"It's the key to the bar," said Biddo before reducing the elaborately carved bar door into a pile of splinters. "I've been looking for it everywhere. I knew I'd put it somewhere. I'm always the same with keys."

"Jesus Christ!" said the Club Secretary. "Jesus H Christ! Are you out of your tiny, beer saturated bloody mind? Have you any idea how much a door like that will cost to replace?"

"I haven't actually," said a wheezing and coughing Kenny Biddo while wafting away a small cloud of dust. "I haven't the faintest idea Hilly. Will it be more than my monthly state pension? I hope to Christ I'm not going to have to apply for another Crisis Loan. I've not paid the last one off yet."

"Crisis Loan!" said the incandescent Club Secretary. "Crisis fucking loan! You'll need 50 bloody Crisis Loans to pay for a door like that. I've read about that door."

"You've read about a door!" said Biddo. "Bloody hell Hilly. You need to get a life lad. Why don't you read Treasure Island or something like that?"

"I don't want to read adventure stories," said the Club Secretary. "I like non-fiction. I'm a technician. I want to learn things. I want to read things that stimulate my mind. I want to read about things to do with engineering and design. That's why, for the past few months, I've been learning about this train and its many fabulous fixtures and fittings."

"Did you not think to learn how to get the thing running?" said Biddo.

"It never once entered my head," said the Club Secretary. "But I did learn this. That beautiful door you've just turned into firewood, was hand-made by a 75 year old master craftsman somewhere in the Black Forest region of Bavaria. There isn't another door like it in Western Europe."

"There certainly isn't now," said Biddo.

"Very funny," said the Club Secretary. "But you won't

be making wise cracks when you get the bill. You won't
be joking at all. You and the rest of your family will be
eating chips and egg for the next 10 bloody years.
Because Crisis Loan or not Biddo-you certainly won't be
able to afford to replace it."

"I will," said Biddo. "You can take it out of the money
I already owe the club."

"How does that work?" said the Chef.

"Take no notice of him," said the Club Secretary while
righting an overturned chair. "He thinks he's a
comedian. I'm wiping my hands of him. He's a bloody
disgrace. He's never been any different."

"Does that mean you won't be joining me for a drinkie
poo?" said a breathless Kenny Biddo after emerging
from the cloud of dust with a jingling case of bottled
lager balanced precariously across one arm.

"I won't be joining you for anything," said the Club
Secretary. "And neither will any other member of this
club if they know what's good for them."

"I'll join you for a drink," said Hamill before tearing
open the case, picking out three bottles and handing one
each to his good friends Woodhouse and McShane. "In
fact, I might just join you for a session now it's happy
hour."

"I'll take a bottle too," said the Health and Safety
Officer.

"You will!" said Biddo. "I thought you were against
drinking on board the train. I thought you said it was
dangerous."

"It can be," said the Health and Safety Officer before
carefully placing the bottle horizontally on a nearby
table and watching it roll quickly away before falling to
the floor.

"What was that?" said a highly suspicious looking Club
Secretary. "What did you just do Eddie?"

"I conducted a basic experiment," said the Health and
Safety Officer.

"To establish what?" said the wary Steadman.

"To establish if we've remained level since we came to a

stop," said Meehan.

"And have we?" said Steadman. "Have we remained level Eddie?"

"We've tilted a fair bit," said the Health and Safety Officer before picking up the bottle and handing it to a confused but nevertheless appreciative Kenny Biddo.

"Which means what?" said Woodhouse. "What exactly does 'tilted a fair bit' mean Eddie?"

"It means we're in trouble," said Steadman.

"It means no such bloody thing," said Hamill. "It just means the table's not level."

"That's what I'd have thought too," said Woodhouse.

"And me," said the Health and Safety Officer. "But I discreetly carried out the same experiment with my fountain pen a couple of hours ago."

"And what happened?" said the Club Secretary.

"Nothing," said Meehan. "My pen didn't move a millimetre. And before you ask-it remained completely still on every other table within this room."

"Which proves what exactly?" said the Chef.

"It proves the train has tilted," said Steadman. "Have you not been listening to the man?"

"It doesn't prove that at all," said the Health and Safety Officer.

"What's it proved then?" said Steadman.

"It's proved the bridge isn't as sound as the company directors suggested it was," said Meehan.

"When did you speak to them?" said the Club Secretary.

"I've never spoken to them," said Meehan. "I read about the bridge renovation on line. The repairs were only completed a month ago."

"Bloody hell!" said Steadman. "Is that enough time for the concrete to go off?"

"In normal conditions, yes," said Meehan.

"What would you say were normal conditions?" said Steadman.

"No rain, frost or snow," said Meehan.

"Oh Christ!" said Steadman while turning to face the snow shrouded window. "Has anyone got a parachute they're prepared to lend me?"

"Behave yourself Steadman," said Hamill. "There wasn't any snow or rain about a month ago. In fact, the weather was extremely mild a month ago. I was in Bristol city centre a month ago and was walking around in shorts and a vest."

"Which means the concrete would have been fine," said the Club Secretary.

"I couldn't agree more," said Meehan. "But what if the directors lied about the restoration completion date."

"Do you think they'd do that?" said the Chef.

"It wouldn't be the first time," said Meehan.

"Are you telling us that this bridge we're on is unstable?" said the Chef.

"I wouldn't go as far as that at this point," said Meehan. "But there's a fair chance it might be becoming unstable."

"For fucks sake!" said Woodhouse.

"But why?" said the Chef. "This bridge must have been standing for hundreds of years. Julius Caesar and his legions probably crossed this bridge at some time or other. Why in God's name would it start to collapse now?"

"Because, apart from the structural problem I've already told you about, it's having to bear the entire static weight of the train and stand up to winds that are almost unprecedented." said Meehan.

"How unprecedented?" said the Chef.

"They could reach in excess of 175 miles per hour," said Meehan before removing a small rectangular box from his pocket and holding it at arm's length. "That's about 90 miles per hour stronger than what we were hit by last night during a forty five minute barrage.

"Jesus Christ!" said the Club Secretary while rubbing his eyelids. "That's bad. That's very bad. I imagine that's some kind of record?"

"It beats the previous British record by just over 2 miles an hour," said Meehan.

"And for an extra bonus point, you're probably able to

tell us where and when it happened aren't you?" said
Hamill.

"It was recorded at Cairn Gorm in the Scottish
Highlands in 1986," said Meehan. "Would you like me
to furnish you with any more details Mr Hamill?"

"That won't be necessary," said Hamill. "Although, you
could do one small thing for me if you wouldn't mind."

"What's that?" said Meehan.

"You could shove that little box where the sun's unlikely
to shine," said Hamill. "If I remember right, that thing
cost me a lot of time, money and inconvenience."

"You had men working on your attic conversion in
temperatures in excess of 120 degrees," said Meehan.
"One of them had to be carried out of your house on a
stretcher and given oxygen."

"And that's how you're likely to end up if you don't
keep out of my way," said Hamill.

"Is that right?" said Meehan.

"You better believe it," said Hamill.

"Leave it out will you lads," said the Club Secretary.
"We should be putting our heads together at this point,
not going three rounds with the nearest contender."

"It's a miracle we're not at the bottom of that bloody
valley already," said the Chef.

"It is indeed," said Meehan. "We're in trouble
gentlemen. Big trouble. Don't forget-this train wasn't
meant to stop here and this bridge wasn't built to bear
enormous static loads."

"That's why you should all be having a drink," said
Biddo. "If we all get stuck into the ale, and piss over the
side of the bridge, we can have the load reduced in no
time at all. And, in the meantime, big Woody could be
doing his part by emptying all the fridges and freezers."

"Go to bed Biddo," said Woodhouse.

"Is there any way we can get the train to move on?" said
Blackie.

"Me and Hulmey have tried," said the Club Secretary.
"The console's computerised. I've never seen anything
like it. It's like a spaceship. I think we'd need to key in

a code of some sort."

"Which means we need to get our things together and leave," said the Club Secretary.

"And go where?" said the Chef.

"We could try to make some sort of tented camp at the foot of the bridge until the storm peters out," said the Club Secretary.

"That would suit me," said Woodhouse. "That would suit me right down to the ground, if you'll pardon the pun."

"And me," said Blackie.

"It would suit me too," said Meehan. "But there lies our next dilemma. We can't leave. As someone said earlier, it'd be suicide to go out on that bridge right now. That's the quandary that now exists. That's the catch-22. We're damned if we do and we're damned if we don't. I don't envy you and your fellow committee members right now Mr Hill."

"Neither do I," said the Chef.

"I don't envy me," said Blackie while slowly traipsing over to the window.

"So let me try to put our situation into perspective again," said Woodhouse.

"Don't bother," said the Club Secretary while watching the party, almost as a man, pick up their chairs and various personal belongings and very slowly and cautiously head over to the other side of the room.

CHAPTER EIGHT
MISSING!

Owing to their nagging concern that the bridge might collapse at any moment, very few of the men had managed to get any worthwhile sleep the previous evening and that had been despite the Club Secretary lifting the drinking ban he had imposed earlier after Kenny Biddo had forced his way into the bar. Some members *had* abstained from the use of alcohol however and it was probably no coincidence that three of those had been the first to rise the next morning just after 7.00 am. Within an hour, they had established two vitally important things-the approximate position of the stranded train and the fact that it was amply stocked with all manner of provisions. Both of those discoveries had provided them with a little more hope and more importantly, given them something positive to tell their increasingly anxious members when they eventually rose. By 8.25am, the Chef, at the request of his brother the Vice Chairman, had three pots of strong coffee simmering nicely on the stove and had built two small towers of thick buttered toast and it therefore wasn't long before the attractive mixture of aromas had penetrated deep into each of the occupied carriages.

"What's cooking lads?" said Woodhouse before taking a table next to the two remaining committee men and burying his tired and heavily lined face in his hands.

"It's just toast I'm afraid," said the Club Secretary. "The Chef's got some coffee on the go if you want some. Why don't you help yourself."

"I don't mind if I do," said Woodhouse before sliding back his chair and heading to the kitchen.

"Are your roomies up?" said the Vice Chairman.

"Matthews is," said Woodhouse while testing the warmth of the nearest coffee pot. "I haven't seen anything of Hamill or Tommy Mac since late last night. By the way-while we're on the subject of Matthews-tell me this Hilly. Why the hell was he put with us?"

[156]

"In case any of you are in need of counselling," said the Chef after popping his head out of the serving hatch. "We need counselling because we're having to share a room with him," said Woodhouse. "Jesus Christ-he never stops tidying up or making beds. He's like an old mother hen. He changed Tommy Mac's sheets earlier this morning while the poor bugger was still in his pit. It's a good job he was too drunk to protest. Did you manage to do anything with Tommy Weir's body, by the way?"

"We've put him in the last carriage," said the Club Secretary. "We could have done with you Woody. He was one hell of a weight."

"I'd have been no good to you," said Woodhouse. "I couldn't hold myself up by the end of the night. Kenny Biddo had me on the Jagerbombs. 18 he dropped before his bowels eventually succumbed to the inevitable."

"Where is he?" said the Club Secretary.

"He's here," said Blackie while holding the door to allow his groggy roommates Steadman and Kenny Biddo to enter. "He's not in bad fettle either. You're not are you Biddo?"

"I'm in the form of my life," said Biddo before reaching upwards and yawning loudly.

"That's because we've got a free bar with no door," said Steadman. "Have you any idea where we are Hilly?"

"North Wales, I think," said the Club Secretary while referring to a rail map he had discovered on the mail room wall. "Not too far from the coast."

"That means we can't be too far away from a town doesn't it?" said Dave Larkin after taking a seat next to young Anthony and Kenny Alty.

"We've travelled exactly 171miles according to the engine's milometer," said the Club Secretary while once again referring to his map. "By my estimation, that puts us somewhere near Cardigan Bay. I'm just waiting for Eddie Meehan to arrive to confirm it. Has anyone seen him this morning?"

"I just assumed he'd be here," said a concerned looking

Hewlett upon arriving with the Professor. "Although, I'm beginning to wonder now."

"Beginning to wonder what?" said the Club Secretary.

"If something's happened to him," replied Hewlett.

"Why would you think something might have happened to him?" said the Chef.

"Because his bed's not been slept in," said Hewlett.

"What!" said the Chef.

"Have you checked your washroom?" said the Club Secretary.

"I've checked everywhere," said Hewlett. "Me and the Professor have searched high and low for him. That's why we're the last to arrive."

"You're not," said a panting Tommy McShane before joining Hamill and big Woody at their chosen table. "But I have got a perfectly good excuse for being late."

"What is it?" said the Club Secretary.

"I couldn't get out of bed," said McShane. "Some bastard tucked me sheets in during the night. I couldn't bloody well move. I literally couldn't move. It was like being in a straightjacket. Did nobody hear me shouting for help?"

"I heard you," said Woodhouse.

"I did too," said Hamill.

"Well why didn't you help?" said McShane.

"Because I thought you were having a nightmare, "said Hamill.

"Can we get back to the matter in hand please gentlemen,," said the Club Secretary.

"What matter in hand?" said McShane.

"Eddie Meehan's missing," said the Club Secretary.

"Is that such a bad thing?" said McShane.

"Since when?" said Woodhouse.

"I don't know," said the Club Secretary. "When was the last time he was seen? Can anyone remember?"

"The last time I remember seeing him was around the time we learned that we weren't going to be able to leave the train," said the Chef. "Did anyone see him after that?"

"He passed our sleeping carriage at about 8.30," said Steadman.

"That's right, he did yes," said Blackie. "But I'd have thought it was a little later than that."

"I saw him about then." said Larkin.

"That would be about right then," said Blackie.

"Did any of you speak to him?" said the Chef.

"No," said Larkin. "I don't really know the fella."

"He didn't stop," said Alty. "He was in a world of his own."

"I saw him at about 10.30 last evening," said the Professor.

"You did!" said the Club Secretary.

"He was leaving one of the washrooms," said the Professor.

"And how was he?" said the Club Secretary.

"Not very good to be honest," said the old man.

"What do you mean, not very good?" said the Chef.

"He looked extremely distressed," said the Professor.

"Distressed!" said the Chef.

"Why the hell didn't you come and tell us?" said the Club Secretary.

"Because a lot of people were distressed at that particular time," said the old man. "Forgive me if I'm wrong Mr Hill, but I imagine a lot of your members have never been so distressed. For goodness sake, they'd just learned that the bridge they were on might be on the brink of collapse and there was a hurricane on its way."

"Of course," said the Club Secretary. "I'm sorry Professor. That was stupid of me."

"Don't mention it old chap," said the Professor. "You've just lost your rudder. You're under enormous stress."

"Did anybody see him after 10.30?" said the Chef.

"I very much doubt it," said Hamill. "Most of us were rat arsed stinking drunk by then."

"I can vouch for that," said Biddo. "I couldn't see anybody or anything after 10.30. In fact, I think I'd lost the use of most of my vital organs."

"That figures," said the Chef.

"And you definitely didn't see or hear him Hewlett?" said the Club Secretary.

"I didn't see anyone but the Professor," said Hewlett. "I didn't read anything into his absence until earlier this morning. You know what he's like. You've seen him operate. He's like a whirlwind. He's constantly assessing and evaluating things. His mind's never at rest."

"Which means he's a clever boy who can make rational decisions and take care of himself," said Hamill. "So why the hell don't we concentrate on the important people."

"And who might they be?" said the Club Secretary.

"The people who've bothered to show up," said Hamill.

"Are you suggesting Eddie simply hasn't bothered to show up?" said the Club Secretary.

"I'm not suggesting that at all," said Hamill. "But he's not a member of the club is he? He doesn't have to jump to attention at the committee's bidding."

"That's a point," said Woodhouse.

"It is actually," said the Club Secretary. "But it doesn't explain why he never slept in his bed. I've got a duty of care here. I can't just allow people to disappear willy nilly."

"Well why don't we conduct a search for him after we've had breakfast," said Steadman.

"That makes sense," said Blackie.

"That makes sense to me too," said Woodhouse before folding a toasted crust and jamming it into his gaping mouth.

"Very well," said the Club Secretary. "But I'd still like to know who was the last person to talk to the man. Come on lads-who was talking to him before he left this room?"

"I've got a feeling that might have been me," said Biddo while scanning the room for other possible candidates.

"You!" said the Chef.

"That's right," said Biddo.

"What would you be talking to Eddie Meehan about?" said the Chef.

"My heavy drinking at first," said Biddo. "He wanted to help me stop. And then we moved on to men things."

"What do you mean, 'men things'?" said the Chef.

"You know-men things. Personal things," said Biddo.

"To do with what?" said the Club Secretary.

"I'm not prepared to say," said Biddo.

"Why not?" said the Chef.

"Because it wouldn't be right," said Biddo. "It's personal."

"How personal?" said the Club Secretary. "Was the man alright?"

"That's our business," said Biddo.

"I disagree," said the Chef. "I think it's our business too, under the circumstances. We're a man down Biddo. It's important we establish his state of mind prior to him going missing."

"What did you talk about dad?" said young Anthony. "Tell them for God's sake and we might be able to move on."

"I've told you," said Biddo. "We talked about very personal things. I don't want to divulge anymore. As I've just said-it wouldn't be right."

"Well, what if we locked you up and cut off your drink supply?" said the Club Secretary.

"You wouldn't," said Biddo while squirming in his chair. "You wouldn't do that. You wouldn't do that would you Hilly?"

"Oh I would," said the Club Secretary.

"And we intend to," said the Chef.

"Tell us what you and Eddie were talking about Biddo," said Blackie.

"Tell us Biddo," said the Club Secretary. "Because I'm not going to let this matter drop until you do."

"Do it dad," said young Anthony. "Do it for me. Do it for your favourite son. Then you can have a drink."

"Then you can have a few," said the Chef.

"Do it dad," said Anthony. "Please tell them."

[161]

"Alright son," said Biddo after clearing his throat and taking a deep breath. "Just for you, I'll tell them. But this isn't going to be easy."

"Just get on with it," said Hamill.

"What were you and Eddie talking about Biddo?" said the Chef.

"His love life," said Biddo.

"What about his love life?" said the Club Secretary.

"He'd been having an affair," said Biddo.

"The dirty ram!" said Steadman.

"With who?" said the Club Secretary.

"I'd rather not say," said Biddo.

"With who Biddo?" said the Chef.

"With who Biddo?" said Steadman.

"Brian Matthews's wife," said Biddo before lowering his head and clearing his throat.

"What!" said Blackie.

"Brian Matthews's wife?" said the dumbfounded Club Secretary. "Are you talking about Rose?"

"That's right," said Biddo.

"Eddie's been seeing her on the sly," said Biddo.

"Bloody hell!" said Blackie.

"I warned you about Meehan, didn't I lads?" said Hamill.

"Eddie was telling me that he'd bought Rose this sexy French maid outfit from an adult mail order catalogue," said Biddo. "He said he was looking forward to getting back to Crosby so she could wear it for him."

"That was me you were talking to, you drunken, bloody imbecile," said Matthews. "It was me that bought the sexy outfit for Rose."

"Was it?" said Biddo. "Was it really? Oh God-so it was. Bloody hell! What am I like? I told you my sight was failing. I told you that didn't I? I need to start wearing my glasses more often."

"You need to start cutting the bloody ale down," said the Chef. "You almost had Eddie lynched."

"And by the way Biddo-I told you all that in the strictest confidence," said Matthews.

"I know you did," said Biddo while yanking at Matthews's sleeve. "But you heard them. They broke me Brian. They were cruel. They were going to cut off my alcohol supply."

"Whatever!" said the stupefied Brian Matthews before heading to the kitchen with a pile of rattling plates, cups and saucers. "I hope you realise that in the eyes of some of these men, I'm now going to be a laughing stock."

"That's not entirely true," said Woodhouse. "In my eyes, you've always been a laughing stock."

The absurdity of what had just occurred had in some way eased a lot of tension and for the next thirty minutes the men, after splitting into small groups to take breakfast, had talked light-heartedly for the first time since the train had prematurely pulled out of the London Station. However, it wasn't long before they were back discussing the more serious aspects of their situation such as the untimely and curious death of their highly respected Chairman Tommy Weir, the prospects of getting home and what they were going to do if one or more of their roommates contracted the disease. Nobody, it should be said, had discussed the whereabouts of Alec Morris, another of the party that, for some reason, had failed to show for the morning assembly.

"Can I have your attention again please gentlemen," said the Club Secretary after he had watched the Chef and Brian Matthews take their seats after returning from putting the kitchen into some sort of order. "I have something I want to discuss with you all before I tell you the state of play."

"I'll tell you the state of play," said Hamill while dabbing his open mouth with a serviette. "We've dropped too many catches. We're 3 goals behind with a minute to play. We've fallen at the first fence. That's the state of bloody play."

"I'd say the game's afoot," said Hewlett before resting his book against his empty teapot and folding his arms.

"I'd say the game's very much afoot," said the

Professor.

"What do you mean, 'the game's afoot?'" said Blackie. "What does that even mean?"

"It's a much used Sir Arthur Conan Doyle expression," said Hewlett. "His most famous creation Sherlock Holmes often used it when he sensed foul play had taken place."

"Foul play!" said Steadman.

"Indeed," said Hewlett before gesturing to the Chef for more tea.

"Is that what you think it is?" said Blackie. "Do you think someone's done away with Eddie Meehan?"

"It's possible," said Hewlett.

"It's not possible at all," said the Chef. "Jesus Christ. We might have our fights and disagreements, but nobody's ever resorted to doing somebody in."

"I'd have agreed with you ordinarily," said Hewlett. "But on this occasion, I don't think I'm too far from the truth."

"You've been reading too many crime novels," said Woodhouse before reaching across and snatching Hewlett's book. "What is this? What are you reading lad?"

"It'll be one of his self-help books," said Hamill. "*How to be more tolerant of the underclasses.*"

"It's an Agatha Christie classic, if you must know," said Hewlett. "It's called *Ten Little Indians.*"

"And don't tell me," said Woodhouse. "It's a murder mystery isn't it?"

"It's a brilliant murder mystery," said Hewlett. "As the great Oscar Wilde once said-one should always have something sensational to read while travelling by train."

"And one should also do one's utmost to avoid letting their imagination run away," said Woodhouse before tossing the book back into the disgusted Hewlett's lap.

"Is that what you think's going on Woody?" said the Club Secretary. "Do you think we might be getting carried away?"

"I do yes," said Woodhouse.

"I do too," said Hamill.

"I hope you're right," said the Club Secretary. "In fact, nothing would delight me more than to see Eddie walk through one of those two doors in the next few minutes. But until he does, I'm going to adopt an open mind. Particularly in light of what I've just discovered."

"What was that?" said Blackie.

"I was told that a commotion took place late last night," said the Club Secretary.

"A commotion!" said Blackie. "What sort of commotion?"

"A heated and serious sounding one, according to the account I was given" said the Club Secretary.

"Where and when did this take place?" said the Chef.

"In the corridor adjacent to the third carriage at about midnight," said the Club Secretary.

"The third carriage.....that's...that's your carriage isn't it Alty?" said Steadman. "Isn't that where you, Larko and a couple of other mean desperados are berthed?"

"It's where I'm berthed," said Matthews before heading to the kitchen.

"With who?" said Steadman.

"Woody, Tommy Mac and Hamill," said Matthews.

"Is that right Hilly?" said the Chef.

"It is yes," said the Club Secretary after quickly referring to his rooming plan.

"I'll tell you what it is," said Woodhouse. "It's bullshit. It's absolute codswallop. Somebody's mischief making. There was no commotion outside our carriage. And certainly not at that time of the night. Who the hell's claiming this by the way?"

"I am," said the Professor. "Richard and I are just one carriage up."

"Did you hear the commotion Hewlett?" said the Club Secretary.

"I can't say I did," said Hewlett. "I always like to sleep with quality ear muffs on. I wouldn't hear a 30 piece brass band if they were marching around my bed."

"What about anyone else?" said the Club Secretary.

"Did anybody else hear the commotion?"

"I'm more interested to know who was meant to be involved in the commotion," said McShane. "Do you know? Do you know who they were Professor?"

"I think I know who one of them was," said the old man.

"Who?" said Woodhouse.

"Your missing Health and Safety Officer," said the Professor.

"The plot thickens," said Hewlett.

"Are you absolutely sure about that?" said the Chef.

"As sure as I could be," said the old man. "Unless there's someone else aboard the train who can recite the Health and Safety manual verbatim."

"What do you mean?" said McShane.

"The individual I'm referring to was employing highly technical language," said the old man. "He was reeling off all sorts of complicated figures and statistics."

"What about the other one," said the Chef.

"I'm afraid I couldn't make that voice out," said the old man. "What I can tell you is this. He was extremely aggressive and used an awful lot of profanities. He was clearly worked up."

"I think at this point in the investigation, you might want to ask the men if they came across any signs of a struggle," said Hewlett before dunking the remains of a chocolate digestive biscuit into his tea. "And ask them if they came across any signs of a struggle. That would be my next step Mr Secretary."

"That's what I was just about to do," said the Club Secretary.

"There was no sign of any struggle along our corridor," said McShane. "Our corridor floor was spotless."

"Spotless!" said the Club Secretary.

"You could have eaten your dinner off it," said McShane.

"How come?" said the Club Secretary. "Why would your corridor be spotless when all the other corridors were a sight for sore eyes and resembled the Cresta Run on medal Sunday?"

"That's right," said the Chef. "Men had been out on that bridge earlier. They would have trodden in dirty snow, oil and all sorts of unpleasant things."

"I'm going to ask you again Tommy," said the Club Secretary. "Why was your corridor so clean?"

"Because I'd mopped it," said Matthews.

"You'd mopped it!" said the Club Secretary.

"That's right," said Matthews.

"Why?" said the Club Secretary.

"Because it was a mess," said Matthews.

"I wouldn't read anything into that," said Steadman. "Matthews is always cleaning up. I think he's got one of those compulsive disorders. Don't ever go to his house. You're afraid to breathe. It's absolutely immaculate. You're scared to spill your tea or drop a breadcrumb."

"That's right," said Blackie. "There's nothing untoward in Matthews mopping up."

"I'd be forced to agree," said the Club Secretary. "But I'm just wondering how mopping that part of the train suddenly became a priority when most people were hanging onto their butts waiting for the bridge to collapse under us."

"I made it a priority," said Hamill.

"What!" said the Chef.

"He mopped the floor at my request," said Hamill.

"And why was that?" said the Club Secretary.

"Good question," said Hewlett.

"And I've got a perfectly good answer," said Hamill.

"What is it?" said the Club Secretary.

"I didn't want to slip," said Hamill. "My left knee wouldn't take another bad knock. And you might want to bear this small thing in mind Sherlock. If I was trying to hide any blood or guts, I'd have mopped the floor myself. I wouldn't have asked someone else to do it would I? Particularly not Matthews."

"You didn't ask," said Matthews. "You ordered me to do it."

"Well, I've got another order for you," said the Club

Secretary. "And everyone else for that matter. I want this train searched from back to front. And I want it done now."

"What about outside?" said the Chef.

"Forget about outside for now," said the Club Secretary. "We'll have to wait for the blizzard to stop. Just search the carriages, the engine and the mail room. Maybe Eddie's had the sort of fall Hamill was trying to avoid. Perhaps he's lying unconscious somewhere."

"Well let's hope if the poor lad *has* taken a fall, he kept his knees and ankles together when he landed," said Hamill. "After all, that's the safe and recommended way to fall."

"That's low that is Hamill," said the Chef. "You've excelled yourself. That's low even for someone like you."

CHAPTER NINE
ANSWERS WANTED

Before the men had departed the dining carriage to begin their search of the train for the missing Health and Safety Officer, another important issue had been raised by experienced motor mechanic Dave Larkin. An issue just as critical as any of the others that had been brought up or drawn to the attention of the committee during the last, often frenetic hour. It was regarding the heating and lighting and in particular how long the system was likely to function while the train was standing still and therefore unable to generate its own energy. That, for obvious reasons, and despite their concern for Eddie Meehan, had usurped the missing passenger situation as the group's most pressing concern, particularly after the Professor had explained that without any form of heating, certain members of the party were likely to survive no more than a few days should the temperature continue to drop. Three technicians, Jeff Hill, Kenny Hulme and the aforementioned Dave Larkin, had been designated the task of assessing the train's battery capacity and each were looking reasonably upbeat when they arrived back at the dining carriage about three quarters of an hour later.

"So what's the scores on the doors lads?" said the Chef after handing each of the returning men a mug of piping hot tea. "How long have we got before we all turn into Frosty the snowman?"

"It's impossible to say for certain," said Larkin. "But I'd say the signs are quite encouraging. Wouldn't you Hulmey?"

"The batteries are massive," said the Vice Chairman Kenny Hulme. "To be fair, they're like the things you'd find on a modern passenger aircraft."

"Is there any way of telling how much battery life's left?" said the Chef. "Would that be asking too much?"

"There's a gauge," said Hulme.

"That's very much up to the max," said the Club Secretary.

"If we've read it right, we've used next to nothing up until now," said Hulme.

"That's good," said the Chef.

"It's very good," said Steadman.

"I don't think we've got a problem regarding the heating," said Larkin. "Although I think to be safe, we should cut off the supply to the other vacant carriage."

"Is that something you're going to be able to do?" said the Chef.

"I'll see to it as soon as I've finished this tea," said Larkin.

It was then that certain other members began traipsing back into the carriage but it was immediately clear from their blank expressions that their report was going to be far less encouraging.

"There's no sign of the bloke," said Alty while slowly peeling off his gloves. "He's nowhere to be found."

"What about the washrooms?" said the Club Secretary. "Did you check them?"

"Every single one," said young Anthony. And every single cubicle. Some of them haven't been used yet. There is a problem with the toilets opposite Hamill's sleeping carriage though."

"What sort of problem?" said the Club Secretary before dropping his pen and leaning back in his chair.

"One of the lavatory pans is blocked," said Alty.

"With what?" said the Club Secretary.

"My guess would be a boa constrictor," said Alty. "The place reeks to high hell."

"Why hasn't it been flushed?" said the Club Secretary.

"You don't flush something like that," said Hamill. "You bring a team of zoologists in to examine it."

"Who's responsible?" said the Club Secretary.

"Woody," replied Hamill. "He's filled the entire pan. I'm convinced he'd have filled a second one if I hadn't broken his concentration by calling him to get the last sandwich. Only God knows what the greedy bugger had eaten. Where is Woody, by the way?"

"He's in the kitchen making toast," said McShane.

"That figures," said Hamill. "Anyway-whether you like it or not, I'm going to be using one of the other unoccupied carriage toilets from now on."

"Well I'd make it quick if I was you," said the Club Secretary.

"Why's that?" said Hamill.

"Because Davie Larko's going to be turning off the power to those rooms soon," said the Club Secretary.

"What for?" said McShane.

"To preserve as much battery life as we can," said Larkin.

"Are things that bad?" said McShane.

"Not at all," said the Club Secretary. "We'd just rather be safe than frozen."

"Have you any idea how long the batteries are likely to hold out?" said Steadman.

"In a word-'no'," said Larkin. "I'm not even prepared to speculate at this stage. We can only keep our fingers crossed and hope."

"And have plenty of extra blankets on standby," said the Chef.

"Do you think it'll come to that?" said Blackie. "Do you think we'll reach the point when we're having to rely on blankets and coats to stay warm?"

"I don't know," said the Club Secretary before rising to allow the pensive looking Professor and his roommate Hewlett access to their table. "I suppose it depends how long we're going to be here."

"I reckon we should get our things and leave right away," said Blackie.

"I'd agree," said McShane while pointing to an empty beer bottle that was lying horizontally on Hewlett's table. "But I'd want someone to explain that to me first."

"Bloody hell!" said Steadman. "It's not rolling. Why isn't that bottle rolling?"

"I've no idea," said McShane.

"That's amazing," said the beaming Club Secretary. "It doesn't make any sense."

"It makes perfect sense if the same thing that happened to the foundations on one side of the bridge, has happened to the opposite side," said the Professor.

"Do you think that's what's happened Professor?" said the Club Secretary.

"It looks like," said the old man.

"So all my prayers were for nothing?" said Steadman.

"Maybe they've been answered," said the Club Secretary.

"My hopes certainly have," said the Professor.

"What do you mean Professor?" said the Club Secretary.

"It's my fervent wish that you all remain here until those infected with the disease have fully recovered," said the old man.

"And how long do you think that might be?" said Steadman.

"I told you earlier," said the Professor. "A week to 10 days. No more than that."

"A week to 10 bloody days!" said Steadman.

"Oh Christ!" said Blackie. "What's my hair going to be like by then?"

"But that doesn't make sense to me," said Woodhouse. "Surely we'd be better off in a hospital surrounded by doctors and trained staff."

"Trained in what?" said the Professor. "None of those doctors will have come across the disease that contributed to the death of your Chairman. They'll be shooting in the dark. It's one of the rarest diseases ever identified. There isn't even a name for it yet. They wouldn't have a clue where to start."

"Do you know where to start Professor?" said the Club Secretary.

"I do as it happens," said the old man while pointing to an old beaten up leather medical bag that was resting against his left leg. "There's a very effective sedative I can mix. Me and two former colleagues developed it in a laboratory in Lima about 15 years ago. I'm not going to lie to you though. It doesn't cure the disease. That's not possible at this stage. But it's been known to calm the sufferer considerably until the disease eventually dissipates. In lay man's terms, it reduces the infected person's suffering by as much as 97 percent. In most trials, the infected individuals have taken to their beds and slept through the very worst. I assure you gentlemen, if you remain here for the relatively short period I've suggested, the two of you that are now infected will be in the safest possible hands."

"What if none of us become infected?" said Woodhouse. "What happens then?"

"Yes, what happens then?" said the Club Secretary. "Do we still have to wait?"

"I think you've missed something," said Hamill.

"Missed what?" said the Club Secretary.

"What the old boy just said," said Hamill.

"As far as I'm concerned, I haven't missed anything," said the Club Secretary. "The man's just told us that he's got the means to reduce the suffering should somebody become infected. What exactly did I miss Hamill?"

"The part where he told us that two of us are now infected," said Hamill.

"What!" said Steadman.

"I don't remember that," said the Club Secretary.

"Neither do I," said Steadman.

"I'm afraid he's right," said the Professor.

"He's right?" said the Club Secretary.

"He is yes," said the old man. "Two of you are already demonstrating certain familiar symptoms."

"Who?" said Woodhouse while scanning the room. "Which two? Who are they? Is one of them me?"

"I don't feel at liberty to say right now," said the Professor.

"Why not?" said Steadman. "Why not for God's sake? Some of us are sharing sleeping quarters with those infected people. One or two of us are even using the same towels and bars of soap."

"Tell us who's infected," said Woodhouse after advancing on the old man's table with more than a degree of menace. "Who's got the fucking disease Professor? We could be sitting next to them for God's sake. We've got every right to know."

"I'm afraid I can't divulge that information at this time," said the old man after carefully lifting the tea pot lid to check the contents.

"Why the hell not?" said Steadman.

"Yes, why not?" said Blackie.

"Because those that are infected are going to need treating by me," said the old man. "They are therefore my patients and I am therefore obligated through doctor-patient confidentiality to discuss the matter with them and only them. I am prepared to talk in general terms however."

"That's very nice of you," said McShane. "Remind me to send you a Christmas card Professor. By the way-has anyone got any good news?"

"I think I might have," said Hewlett who for some time after returning to the dining carriage had been looking extremely anxious and perspiring heavily. "At least it's likely to be good news for the majority of our gathering."

"What is it Hewlett?" said Woodhouse. "You haven't had a pregnancy scare have you? Have you finally started your period?"

"No I haven't," said Hewlett. "But I often feel as if I have whenever you're around. Funny that isn't it? Now why don't you go away and do something productive like break wind or light a fart. You're becoming a little tiresome."

"I'd have to agree there," said the Club Secretary.

"What is it Hewlett? What's on your mind lad?"

"Yes, what is it Richard?" said the Professor.

"It's regarding the disease," said Hewlett.

"What about the disease?" said the Professor.

"I think I might be one of the two people infected," said

Hewlett.

"You what!" said Blackie after easing his chair back a few feet.

"I think I've become the first victim of the disease," said Hewlett.

"But why?" said the Chef. "Why would you think that Hewlett?"

"Because I've got all the associated symptoms," said Hewlett. "I've been feverish, I've been perspiring heavily and the rest of it."

"What do you mean, 'the rest of it'?" said the Professor while pouring his sleeping carriage companion a glass of water. "Have you been hallucinating?"

"I have yes," said Hewlett.

"I see," said the Professor. "Do you want to talk about it? Or would you prefer to discuss the matter in private?"

"I think I'd prefer privacy," said Hewlett.

"And I think you should get it off your chest right here and right now," said Woodhouse after driving his huge right fist down onto his table. "Because if you are one of those infected, every one of us here has got a right to know."

"You're not wrong there Woody," said Hamill.

"He's right Hewlett," said the Club Secretary. "Your fellow members are worried. They need to know what's going on."

"I have to agree with them on this occasion Richard," said the old man. "These people do have every right to know. Why don't you finish your water, calm yourself down and when you're ready, tell us what you've been seeing."

Hewlett puffed out his cheeks and after watching McShane and Woodhouse head over and place themselves in front of each of the exits, he wiped his brow and dropped the soggy remnants of his serviette into a bin. Then, after taking a long slow drink of water, he sat down, took a deep breath and flicked his matted fringe from his soaking wet brow.

[175]

"Very well then-if you insist," he said. "But I've got to be honest Professor. I'm feeling a little bit confused right now. I don't really know where to start."

"Why don't you start by explaining what your greatest fear is," said the old man.

"I reckon living in a high rise flat in a Liverpool suburb would be right up there," said Woodhouse.

What about being stranded on a train with a load of working class ruffians," said McShane.

"That's enough now lads," said the Club Secretary. "Let's get serious again. What's this fear of yours Hewlett?"

"Monkeys," said Hewlett.

"Sorry!" said Steadman.

"It's monkeys," said Hewlett. "I've been terrified of monkeys since I was 10."

"Is there any reason for that?" said the old man.

"I was attacked by one," said Hewlett. "I was attacked by a Barbary macaque while on holiday in North Africa."

"Bloody hell!" said the Club Secretary.

"Did the attack take place while you were on safari or something?" said the old man.

"It was while my parents and I were looking around a market in Marrakesh," said Hewlett. "An Arab approached us with a monkey on his shoulder. I remember him having one of those old Brownie cameras. The type that looks like a concertina. In hindsight, I doubt if there was any film in the bloody thing. He plagued my mum and dad for what seemed like an age. He wore them down in the end but I remember them insisting the monkey stayed out of the shot."

"Why was that?" said the Professor.

"Because it was a vicious little thing," said Hewlett.

"I can testify to that," said Steadman. "They can be nasty little buggers, those things."

"So what happened?" said the old man.

"The Arab tied the monkey next to what looked like a

small rucksack and went to work taking his photos," said Hewlett. "He took ages and I remember being bored stiff."

"You did something to the poor little thing, didn't you Hewlett?"

"I just threw a few salted peanuts at it," said Hewlett.

"Why? would you do that" said the Chef.

"Because the thing was impertinent," said Hewlett.

"What do you mean?" said the Chef.

"It kept pulling faces at me," said Hewlett.

"Did you hurt it?" said the Chef.

"Not at first," said Hewlett. "It was really agile. It was catching all the nuts initially. It was like a little goalkeeper. But then one got through its defences and hit the intolerable thing in the left eye."

"What did it do?" said the Chef.

"It started whimpering like a new born baby," said Hewlett. "I think it was the salt."

"You wicked bastard," said Larkin.

"I was just playing," said Hewlett. "I love animals."

"How did hurting the creature make you feel?" said the Professor.

"Quite satisfied to be honest," said Hewlett. "I was actually quite pleased with myself."

"Did you suspect you were in any danger at that point?" said the Professor.

"Not at all," said Hewlett. "I thought the damn creature was securely tethered."

"And then what happened?" said the Professor.

"I bombarded it until I eventually hit it in the other eye," said Hewlett. "That's when it went berserk. That's when it got loose of its lead and leapt on me like something possessed."

"What did you do?" said the Professor.

"Nothing," said Hewlett. "I just froze on the spot. I couldn't do anything. I couldn't move. I couldn't get the horrible thing off me. It stank like rotten cabbage. I didn't want to touch it."

"What did your parents do?" said the Professor.

[177]

"They laughed," said Hewlett.

"They laughed!" said the old man before quickly jamming a knuckle between his teeth.

"They were laughing uncontrollably," said Hewlett.

"The story goes that my father laughed so much he wet his favourite beige flannels. That's certainly how he recounts the tale around our dining table. They did absolutely nothing to help me."

"That's because they were able to see the funny side of the situation," said Woodhouse.

"There was no funny side," said Hewlett. "I was being violently assaulted by a primate in broad daylight. It wouldn't let go of my ears. It was ragging my head as if it was a sort of football trophy. Where's the humour in that?"

"I wouldn't know where to start," said Woodhouse.

"It must have been awful," said the Professor. "And not necessarily because of the violent nature of the attack but because those who should have been protecting you were delighting in your misery."

"Absolutely," said Hewlett. "I've been terrified of monkeys ever since."

"I don't blame you," said the old man.

"I don't blame the monkey," said McShane. "I'm just sorry I wasn't there to see the incident."

"I bet you are," said Hewlett. "But you wouldn't know what it was like McShane. When I returned home, I was so traumatised, I refused to leave my room for three months. I even ended up missing our annual family croquet mixed pairs at Aunt Veronica's."

"Bloody hell!" said Woodhouse. "You should have given me a ring. I'd have stood in for you."

"You're hilarious," said Hewlett.

"I've got no sympathy for you," said McShane.

"I've got nothing but sympathy," said the old man.

"Thank you Professor," said Hewlett.

"However, I think your fear of monkeys is something you should have dealt with a long time ago," said the Professor. "But that said-your fear is entirely justifiable. Had you been scared of monkeys prior to your holiday in Morocco?"

"That was very much the catalyst," said Hewlett while pouring himself a glass of water. "I'd only ever seen monkeys in books or on wildlife documentaries prior to that."

"Has anything happened to you since?" said the Professor. "Have you had any other disturbing experiences regarding monkeys?"

"None at all," said Hewlett. "At least not until the early hours of this morning."

"What happened?" said the Club Secretary.

"I somehow became convinced that I wasn't alone in my room," said Hewlett.

"You weren't alone," said the Club Secretary.

"You're sharing a room with the Professor aren't you?" said the Chef.

"I'd moved," said Hewlett. "The Professor had been working late. He had his bedside light on. I can't sleep with any light on whatsoever. I need pitch darkness and complete quiet. So I took my top bedding and headed to one of the vacant carriages."

"And then what happened?" said the Club Secretary.

"A couple of hours after managing to nod off, I became aware of a suspicious presence and what sounded like heavy breathing emanating from the far side of the room," said Hewlett. "I became so scared that I pulled the covers over my face, jammed my eyes tight shut and began to pray."

"And then what?" said the Club Secretary.

"I heard the two far beds creaking," said Hewlett. "Then I heard the sound of heavy footsteps coming towards me. It was terrifying. I held my breath for what seemed like an eternity. Then the door opened and light began to filter in. That's when I plucked up the courage to peel back the sheet and open my eyes a tiny bit. That's when I saw the back of the horrible things."

"What horrible things?" said Steadman.

"Two apes," said Hewlett.

[179]

"Two apes!" said the Club Secretary. "Did you say 'apes'?"

"I did," said Hewlett. "I saw a massive one which must have stood at least 8 feet tall and one just over half that size."

"How real did all that feel?" said the Professor.

"Very real," said Hewlett. "Terrifyingly real."

"Couldn't you have just been pissed?" said Steadman. "Let's be honest Hewlett, it's no secret you like to hammer the red stuff."

"That's because I'm a renowned authority on wines and spirits," said Hewlett. "But I was as sober as a judge."

"Do you still believe what you saw was real?" said the Professor.

"Of course not," said Hewlett. "I'd been hallucinating. Let's be absolutely honest-why on Earth would a couple of monkeys be on board our train?"

"Which means, you're very possibly a very sick boy," said the Club Secretary.

"Why does it?" said Steadman.

"Because it looks like he's started seeing things just like Tommy Weir did before he died," said the Club Secretary. "You heard what the Professor said earlier-if you're scared of rats, you're likely to see a gigantic one. Hewlett's scared stiff of monkeys."

"And he's consequently seen an enormous one," said the Chef. "Am I right Professor?"

"It's possible," said the old man. "I'm going to need time to think about this. Would anyone mind if I smoked?"

"I don't see why not," said the Club Secretary. "I think getting cancer or being burnt alive is well down our list of worries right now."

The Professor then picked up a half smoked cigarette from his ashtray and after placing it between his lips, he patted his jacket pockets and sighed. "Why is it that I can never find my bloody lighter?" he said as he watched Dave Larkin approach his table and flick open his well-used but ever reliable Zippo. "I must be getting

[180]

old."

"I know the feeling Professor," whispered the Club Secretary after joining the two men. "Are you able to confirm that Hewlett is now your newest patient?"

"He has issues, that's for sure," said the old man. "But I'm not prepared to stick my neck out just yet. I'll keep a close eye on the boy. The next few hours are going to reveal much."

"Will you keep us informed?" said the Club Secretary.

"I will indeed," said the old man.

"Thanks Professor," said the Club Secretary. "I think everyone would appreciate that. In the meantime, we might as well return our attention to the whereabouts of our missing Health and Safety Officer."

"Well here's something that might just help," said a breathless and shivering Brian Matthews after making his way to the back of the room and placing a heavy, soaking wet trench coat on the Club Secretary's table. "I found that on the floor of the engine."

"Whose is it?" said the Club Secretary.

"I've no idea," said Matthews.

"Does anyone recognise it?" said the Club Secretary.

"It's not mine," said Steadman while proceeding to rearrange the almost completely rigid garment to something resembling its former shape.

"Nor mine," said the Chef.

"Could it belong to the missing driver?" said Steadman.

"I sincerely hope not," said the Club Secretary. "I don't want to be having to solve another bloody missing person mystery."

"It's mine," said Hamill.

"Yours!" said the Club Secretary.

"That's right," said Hamill. "It's an old going out coat of mine. Unlike most of you, I anticipated bad weather. I noticed it was missing some time last night."

"Did you not think to say something?" said the Club Secretary.

"Say what?" said Hamill. "That my coats gone missing. Don't you think there were far more important things to discuss last night?"

"I still think you should have said something," said the Club Secretary.

"To be honest, I thought Woody had borrowed it to go outside for some fresh air," said Hamill. "It couldn't have been easy sitting in that God forsaken lavatory."

"I didn't take it," said Woodhouse. "We've been told not to venture outside, haven't we?"

"Does anyone know who owns this little gadget?" said the Chef after removing a small box from the inside pocket. "What is it?" said Steadman.

"That's Eddie Meehan's," said Hewlett after stepping forward to examine the item at closer quarters. "That's his so-called magic box."

"And, unless I'm mistaken, that's blood on the lapel," said Matthews before heading over to the window and clearing a small viewing patch. "That can't be good can it?"

"I wouldn't have thought so," said the Club Secretary.

"Meehan must have borrowed your coat Hamill," said Woodhouse.

"We can't say that for sure," said the Club Secretary.

"What can we say?" said Hamill.

"We can say the person who last wore the coat has very possibly been hurt in some way," said the Club Secretary. "Take a closer look at the thing. There's more blood on one of the sleeves."

"Can anyone shed any light on this lads?" said the Chef.

"I might be able to," said Matthews. "Although you're all probably going to think I'm stark raving mad."

"What is it?" said the Chef.

"Just take a punt Matthews," said the Club Secretary. "Because the rest of us have got nothing at all to offer these proceedings."

"What do you know Matthews?" said Hamill.

"It's what I thought I saw, rather than what I know," said Matthews.

"What do you think you saw then?" said Hamill.

"Animals," said Matthews.

"Animals!" said the Chef. "What sort of animals?"
"Bears or something like that," said Matthews. "There
were two or three of them."
"When and where was this?" said the Club Secretary.
"When we were searching for Eddie," said Matthews.
"I was in the mailroom when I suddenly got this feeling
I was being watched. I turned around and looked out the
window and saw what appeared to be a group of bears
heading away from the train."
"What makes you think they were bears?" said the Chef.
"Because they looked like bears," said Matthews.
"Did they walk on all fours?" said the Professor.
"Sometimes," said Matthews. "And sometimes they
walked upright like us."
"Could they have been apes?" said Hewlett.
"Apes!" said Matthews.
"Is it possible that what you saw were two apes?" said
Hewlett. "Could they have been what I saw in my
room?"
"I've no idea what you're talking about," said
Matthews.
"Matthews didn't hear your story Hewlett," said the
Club Secretary. "He's been on one of his walkabouts."
"Hewlett thought he might have seen two apes in one of
the far carriages," said the Chef. "Is it possible that's
what you saw?"
"I don't know," said Matthews. "I never considered
that possibility to be honest. I suppose they could have
been apes. The snow was falling really heavily.
Visibility was really poor. They were mere shadows
most of the time."
"Could they have been men in fur coats?" said the Club
Secretary.
"I doubt it," said Matthews.
"Why's that?" said the Chef.
"Because one of them must have been nine feet tall,"
said Matthews.
"Bloody hell!" said Hewlett.
"Well, if they *were* apes, it proves one thing," said the

[183]

Professor after taking his seat and folding his arms contentedly.

"What's that?" said Blackie.

"It proves that my newly acquired friend and roommate Richard wasn't hallucinating after all," said the old man.

"That's a point," said the Chef.

"A very good point," said Steadman.

"Which means, if he wasn't hallucinating, he isn't necessarily one of the two people suffering from the disease," said the Club Secretary.

"Tre bien Monsieur Secretaire," said the Professor.

"Which means the odds on one of the rest of us having the disease have just shortened," said Alty.

"To what?" said Blackie.

"You work it out," said Alty.

"I don't think the disease is our most immediate and greatest concern right now," said the Club Secretary.

"I don't either," said the Chef. "Those two wild creatures are. Because, if we are to believe Hewlett's account, they're not just a menace-they're reasonably intelligent too."

"What makes you say that?" said Steadman.

"They can open and close doors," said the Chef.

"And they're as bold as brass too," said the Club Secretary. "They weren't deterred by the lights from the train and our advantage in numbers."

"They certainly weren't scared," said Blackie.

"I wouldn't be scared if I was that big and strong either," said McShane. "Don't forget lads-they must have made it up and onto that bridge when the wind was at its strongest. Bloody hell! I can bench press 280kgs and I've completed 75 deep squats in a minute. Yet despite that, I struggled to walk 10 paces out there yesterday before being forced back onto my rear end. I might as well have been tied to a lamppost."

"Well, I personally hope they're human," said Blackie.

"Why's that?" said the Chef.

"Because you can often reason with humans," said Blackie.

[184]

"And most self respecting villains can be bought off for
a price," said Hewlett.

"We're going to have to secure all the doors," said the
Club Secretary. "We're going to have to lock this place
down as tight as a drum. Are we all here?"

"I think so," said Steadman while quickly scanning the
room.

"All except Alec Morris," said Hamill.

"Why doesn't that surprise me," said Blackie.

"Where is the little shit?" said Steadman.

"I've confined him to our carriage," said the Club
Secretary.

"That's cosy," said Hamill.

"It's for the best," said the Club Secretary. "The very
sight of him was making men angry. Now let's turn our
attention to these outer doors."

CHAPTER TEN
MAGIC BOX

While the men continued to be divided as to what their two fellow members had seen, they all nevertheless agreed that they had seen something that posed a threat of some sorts and that was illustrated by the fact that over an hour after Brian Matthews had recounted his version of events, nobody had left the dining carriage, not even to use one of the washrooms.

The period hadn't been unproductive though because the Club Secretary had been able to explain to those that didn't already know that any fears relating to the heating system were unfounded at that point. He had also, with the aid of Eddie Meehan's so-called 'magic box', been able to convince the party that, although the blizzard still remained impenetrable, the wind had not gained any strength over the last eight hours and if anything, might just be beginning to drop. Both announcements had been warmly received but a third, regarding the immediate appointment of Kenny Hulme as the new Chairman, had caused a number of eyebrows to rise and had brought about one or two noticeable murmurs of discontent. However, reminding the party that there were a couple of suspicious characters in the vicinity of the train that might just have designs on making off with their valuables, had soon realigned the men's thoughts and within a few seconds, the dining carriage was empty apart from the Chef who, upon the Club Secretary's request, had agreed to stay behind to prepare a light afternoon meal.

The Professor and Hewlett had deliberately held back during the unseemly exodus that had ensued and had therefore been the last to arrive at their sleeping carriage. Both had been public school educated and were therefore very different to the other men who had attended a variety of state and comprehensive schools, a number of now defunct polytechnics and a few correctional institutes. The ambience of their room therefore reflected their loftier status because whereas most of the other carriages were already reeking of cheap deodorant, body odour and stale beer, their room was emanating far more pleasant aromas such as expensive cologne, sweet tobacco and quality Cognac. Hewlett had turned his side of the room into a miniature version of his own bedroom back in Blundelsands with his suits tagged and arranged along his wardrobe rail to coincide with each particular stage of the journey. He had been one of the few members intending to conform fully with the committee's request that each member should embrace the great age of steam and dress appropriately to that period. He had therefore been at pains to include in his wardrobe only clothing compatible with the late 1930s and early 1940s such as tweed suits, hand knitted waistcoats, a black and yellow ribbon trimmed straw boater and several pairs of Italian made two tone brogues. However, despite the considerable cost of putting such an impressive collection together, none of that was what he had raced back to his sleeping carriage to rescue because none of that was worth one hundredth of what his jewellery and personal accessories were worth. Items which included a French Art Deco 1920s enamel and lacquered cigarette case, a collection of Eisenberg Original Austrian gold and crystal encrusted tie clips and half a dozen pairs of solid silver Givenchy cuff links.

"Do you think it was wise to bring so many valuables along with you?" said the Professor after handing his sleeping carriage companion a diamond tie pin that had inadvertently slipped between Hewlett's fingers and come to rest against the heel of his left shoe. "I feel they're essential," said Hewlett after placing the last item, an Omega De Ville gold watch into a small bag and tugging the string. "They reflect my superior intellectual and financial status."

"They're likely to reflect somebody else's status if you're not careful," said the old man. "Have you nothing safer than that little bag to put them in?"

"I assumed there'd be a strong box on board," said Hewlett before heading to the dresser to rearrange some of his toiletries which had been disturbed during the height of the storm. "Mind you-I rather foolishly expected we'd have a driver too."

"I would have expected that too," said the old man. "Do you mind me asking why you're here Richard?"

"What do you mean?" said Hewlett.

"Why are you here?" said the Professor. "You clearly don't fit in. You're nothing like the others. And it's certainly not because the trip is a freebie because it seems to me, you possess the financial clout to buy this train, never mind book a short excursion on it. Why would you want to be among people who clearly don't like you?"

"They fascinate me," said Hewlett.

"Fascinate you! said the old man.

"That's right," said Hewlett. "Don't they fascinate you Professor? Don't you ever stop to wonder how they are able to function effectively on a daily basis when they've got brains the size of garden peas."

"I'm not sure that's entirely fair, if you don't mind me saying so," said the Professor. "Quite a few of the men aboard this train are reasonably intelligent. Many of them are holding down very responsible jobs."

"I know," said Hewlett. "But who makes the everyday key decisions for them Professor? Who does their planning and forward thinking?"

"Their partners, I imagine," said the old man.

"Trust me Professor-their partners are little better," said Hewlett. "And might I remind you, their partners aren't currently here to think and decide for them."

"Maybe that's why everything appears to have gone considerably awry," said the old man.

"And it might be about to get worse," said Hewlett while applying a tiny dab of hair gel to his unruly fringe.

"Why would you say that?" said the Professor.

"Because of the recently announced change," said

Hewlett. "You must have heard the murmurings of discontent when the Club Secretary announced Tommy Weir's successor."

"I did yes," said the old man. "What was that all about?"

"It's common knowledge the new Chairman Kenny Hulme is not universally respected," said Hewlett.

"Really!" said the Professor. "That does surprise me. Compared to some of the others, he appears to be completely sound and rational."

"He is," said Hewlett. "But there's a small but powerful minority that resent him. It's something to do with Hamill and a lottery ticket."

"Do *you* like him?" said the old man before removing a silver cigarette case from his waist jacket pocket and taking out a recently smoked half stub. "Or are you with that minority?"

"I don't mind him," said Hewlett. "But whether he's up to stepping into the previous Chairman's shoes is highly questionable. By the way Professor-what camp do you find yourself in regarding our two mysterious intruders? Do you think they're men or beasts?"

"I'm probably in the beast's camp," said the old man while fumbling around his badly cluttered bedside cabinet for a lighter. "As one of your members quite rightly said earlier-no man could remain on his feet in that weather-never mind survive in such extreme cold."

"But you're not a hundred per cent convinced are you Professor?" said Hewlett.

"Why would you say that?" said the old man a little indignantly.

"Because I couldn't help noticing that you're gathering your valuables like me," said Hewlett. "I wouldn't have thought wild animals would be interested in gold and jewellery."

"I'm doing nothing of the sort," said the Professor. "I'm just checking to see if my medical bag's in order. I don't want the bottles containing the sedative components to get broken. Let's be honest-if someone

[189]

or something does manage to get back on board this train again, they might ransack our room in their pursuit of money and the like. In that event, we would almost certainly have to kiss goodbye to the medication and thereby shatter the hopes of two or three unfortunate club members in the process."

"Well let's hope that doesn't happen," said Hewlett. "The fact that you've got some sort of a sedative that can significantly reduce the effects of the disease is the only good news we've had since the train left London. It's just about the only thing giving our members hope. By the way Professor, if they are animals, where do you think they might have originated?"

"It's hard to say," said the old man. "My guess would be a circus or a discontinued zoo that had fallen upon hard times. I must be honest Richard-your guess would be every bit as worthy as mine."

In the third carriage, the occupants had already finished packing their valuables and after a short discussion regarding who or what had managed to gain entrance to the train, had moved on to discuss a matter that was already eating away at the fiery and resentful Hamill-the appointment of the new Chairman.

"It just doesn't make sense," he said before snatching up his pillow and volleying it to the far side of the room. "For Christ's sake, we've never been under so much pressure since the club was formed and now we've got a complete and utter wuss in charge. That bastard's not capable of making vital decisions. He's going to get us all killed."

"Why don't we just refuse to acknowledge him?" said Woodhouse.

"I already have," said Hamill.

"Why don't we ask everyone to put it to a vote?" said McShane.

"That's not going to happen," said Matthews.

"Why not?" said Woodhouse.

"Because that would go against club protocol," said Matthews. "And whether you like it or not, the right and proper thing's been done."

"What right and proper thing?" said Hamill.

"The appointment of Kenny Hulme as the new Chairman," said Matthews. "He was the Vice Chairman at the time of Tommy Weir's death. He therefore steps into the vacant role of Chairman. The king is dead, long live the king, as they say. It's as simple as that whether you like it or not."

"I don't like it at all," said Hamill. "And I'll never like it. That spineless bastard's not fit for office and I intend making that plain."

"You can make it as plain as you want," said Matthews. "They're not going to change their minds. Rules are rules."

"I disagree," said Hamill. "I've always believed rules are there to be rejigged, broken or ignored."

"Rules are put in place to make things run as smoothly as possible," said Matthews.

"As smoothly as possible!" said Hamill. "As smoothly as possible. Don't make me laugh Matthews. Have you been on Mars or somewhere during the last 36 bleeding hours? Have you no idea what's been going on here?"

"He's not interested in what's been going on," said Woodhouse. "In fact, he's actually one of the few people who've profited from Tommy Weir's death."

"What's that meant to mean?" said the indignant Matthews after zipping his holdall and kicking it under his bed.

"You know exactly what I mean," said Woodhouse.

"You've moved up the pecking order," said Hamill.

"What pecking order?" said Matthews.

"The committee pecking order," said Hamill.

"Your big chance has arrived," said Woodhouse. "Your boat's finally come in. There's a vacancy now. And don't try to pretend you're not aware of that fact."

"It had never crossed my mind," said Matthews.

"Bollocks!" said Hamill.

"It's not bollocks," said Matthews. "Getting on that committee has never been further from my thoughts."

"You're a liar," said Hamill. "You're obsessed with getting on that committee. It's what you've lived and breathed for, for nigh on twenty years."

"That's not true," said Matthews.

"It bloody well is," said Woodhouse. "You'd lick a sick donkey's dick to secure a place on our committee."

"I wouldn't," said Matthews. "I'm no longer interested."

"In licking sick donkeys dicks?" said Woodhouse.

"In getting on the committee," said Matthews. "I've told them. I've told them in no uncertain terms."

"Of course you have," said Hamill before approaching Matthews and tapping him on the shoulder. "Of course you have. Now scurry along and talk to someone who's far more likely to believe your bullshit."

Next door, in carriage two, the conversation had centred almost entirely upon the two mysterious intruders and as a result the atmosphere was extremely tense with questions being reeled off like gun fire during a wild west shoot out.

"I'm sleeping in the dining carriage tonight," said Steadman after peeling the topmost blankets from his bed and tossing them over his shoulder. "I'm not staying here to be molested."

"Molested!" said Biddo.

"That's right-molested," said Steadman. "What if the motive of those two dodgy fuckers that Hewlett saw is sexual?"

"Sexual!" said Biddo. "I thought somebody said they were bears."

"They said they might have been bears," said Steadman. "But one or two people are convinced they were men in fur coats."

"And very big and powerful men at that," said Blackie.

"They could be runaways," said Steadman.

"Runaways!" said Biddo.

"They might have escaped from a nearby prison?" said Steadman.

"What nearby prison?" said Biddo before quickly

[192]

heading over to the window.

"I don't know," said Steadman. "But it's more than possible. The authorities often used to build prisons in the middle of nowhere. It makes escapes less likely."

"What if they're lifers," said Blackie.

"What difference would that make?" said Biddo while trying desperately to peer through the relentless blizzard.

"A hell of a lot of difference," said Blackie. "If they're lifers, they've probably been deprived of certain things."

"What sort of things?" said Biddo.

"Sex, for one thing," said Blackie. "They won't have had their leg over for ages."

"They'll more than likely be gagging for it," said Steadman.

"For Christ's sake, don't say that," said Biddo before crossing his arms and placing his hands around both shoulders. "I don't want to hear that. I don't want to hear any of that."

"They've probably got ball sacks on them the size of baby pumpkins," said Steadman.

"Stop it," said Biddo. "That's enough of that talk."

"You never know-they might fancy spit roasting one or two of us," said Steadman.

"Pack it in Steadman," said Biddo. "It's not funny. You know I hate that sort of talk. What does that even mean, by the way?"

"Spit roast?" said Steadman. "I don't really think you want to know."

"I do want to know," said Biddo. "Tell me. I'm a grown man for God's sake. I've raised children. I can take it. What does it mean?"

"I'm not telling you," said Steadman. "It'll worry you too much.

"Tell me," said Biddo.

"It's a way of performing a sexual act," said Blackie.

"What sort of sexual act?" said Biddo before returning to his bed and drawing his knees to his chest.

"A very rude one," said Blackie. "That's all you need to know."

[193]

"It's not all I need to know," said Biddo. "If it's going to happen to me, I want to know exactly what it is. I'd like to be prepared for the experience."

"Just drop it Biddo," said Blackie. "You're going to make yourself sick."

"I won't drop it," said Biddo. "Tell me what spit roasting means? Just tell me. I'm going nowhere until one of you tells me."

"Alright then," said Steadman. "I'll tell you. But don't blame me if you spew your guts or struggle to get to sleep when you turn in later tonight."

"I won't," said Biddo. "Honest, I won't. Is it something to do with being buggered?"

"Something like that," said Steadman. "But there's a bit more to it than that."

"How much more?" said Biddo.

"About four inches on average," said Blackie before exchanging a quick high five with the highly amused Steadman. "It depends on the individual."

"Stop messing around, you two," said Biddo. "Just tell me. Or at least tell me the first part."

"Alright," said Steadman. "If you insist. I'll tell you. You'll be asked to remove your clothes."

"Really!" said Biddo. "What if I refuse? What if I just tell them to go to hell?"

"Then they'll more than likely beat you and strip you themselves," said Steadman. "You'll then be forced onto all fours."

"And then what?" said Biddo. "Will they take it in turns to bugger me?"

"Sort of," said Steadman.

"What do you mean?" said Biddo after reaching for his pillow and placing it over his mid section. "What do you mean, 'sort of'?"

"One of the attackers will then enter you from behind while the other forces you to suck his cock," said Blackie.

"Oh, for the love of all that's holy!" said an utterly disgusted Biddo while slowly shaking his head. "The

filthy, depraved bastards. The dirty rotten pigs."
"I know," said Blackie. "Don't say you weren't
warned. I told you it'd disgust you."
"It's certainly done that," said Biddo. "It's more than
disgusted me. It's got me all queasy. I think I'm about
to throw up. But why do they call it 'spit roasting'?"
"Isn't that obvious?" said Blackie.
"Not to me it's not," said Biddo.
"Well, maybe you should get out more," said Blackie.
"I get out plenty," said Biddo. "I get out more than any
man I know.
"I wouldn't argue there," said Blackie.
"It's because from a certain angle, it looks as if the one
that's getting entered is on a roasting spit," said
Steadman.
"Does it really?" said the mortified Biddo.
"And they sometimes spin their victim round," said
Blackie. "By all accounts, it makes the spit roasting
procedure look more authentic."
"It adds a certain realism to the routine," said Steadman.
"I can appreciate that," said Biddo.
"But only people who are experienced regarding the
procedure tend to do that," said Blackie.
"Why's that?" said Biddo.
"Because it's not uncommon for either of the
perpetrators to suffer groin damage or a hernia if they try
to spin the heavy roast around too quickly," said
Blackie.
"Is that right?" said Biddo through the tightest of pursed
lips. "That'd be awful for them wouldn't it. Groin
damage or a hernia! I wouldn't want that. The last thing
I'd want is for one of the filthy, inbred degenerates to get
hurt in some way."
"That's extremely unlikely," said Blackie before
heading over to the wardrobe mirror to rearrange his
hair. "The people who engage in that sort of activity are
extremely safety conscious. And it's always done in the
best possible taste."
"Really!" said Biddo. "You've actually witnessed this

[195]

disgusting thing have you?"

"I'm not prepared to admit anything until my lawyer's present," said Blackie. "But anyway-what are you getting all hot and bothered for Biddo? I'm the one that should be worried. I'm the devilishly good looking one here. I'm the one with the comely cherry-like lips and pert little bottom. If anyone's going to find themselves on the spit being pumped full of man fat, it's likely to be me. That's right isn't it Steadman?"

"Very much so," said Steadman while slipping on his right shoe. "I'm not afraid to admit it. But I've told you time and time again Blackie-you've only got yourself to blame."

"Why's that?" said Biddo.

"Because he's always flaunting his body like some cheap dock road hussy," said Steadman. "And he's forever wearing unfeasibly tight trousers and going without knickers."

"I know," said Blackie. "That's the commando in me. That's my adventurous nature I suppose. I'm a fool to myself. I always have been."

"You're disgusting, that's what you are," said Biddo. "You're a disgrace to our bloody family."

"Why am I?" said Blackie.

"You know why," said Biddo. "Leaving the house without briefs! It's disgusting. Admit it Blackie. That's a disgusting thing for a grown man to do."

"And once again, I'm not prepared to admit anything until my lawyer's present," said Blackie.

"I couldn't agree more," said Steadman. "It's your legal right to remain silent."

"You don't need a lawyer present to admit something like that," said Biddo. "You're not under oath in the dock at Bootle Magistrates Court. This is between me and you. This is a family matter. This is between uncle and nephew. Just admit it lad. A grown man going without underpants is disgusting."

"There's nothing wrong with it," said Blackie. "Loads of fellas I know do it. I think it's nice to have a little bit of breeze circulating the ball sack. It gives a man a sense of freedom."

"It's wrong," said Biddo. "It's unhygienic and it sends out the wrong sort of messages to the wrong sort of people."

"It's not wrong at all," said Steadman. "There's nothing more irritating than sweaty plums on a swelteringly hot day in July. You want to try it some time."

"I'll give it a miss, if it's all the same to you," said Biddo through the tightest of clenched teeth.

"And the spit roasting?" said Steadman. "Might I tempt you to participate in that in the foreseeable future? Is that something you'd consider? Should we say next Saturday evening?"

"I'll give that a miss too, thank you very much," said Biddo before snatching up his bedding and belongings, blowing out his cheeks and heading out of the door.

It was just after 5 0'clock when the last of the passengers returned to the dining carriage and it was interesting that while most of them had found Hewlett's tale regarding apes highly amusing and Brian Matthews's account of wild bears, bordering on the ridiculous, very few of them had been prepared to risk sleeping in their allotted carriages until either or both of those potential threats had proved to be unfounded. Those were fears that the new Chairman had been quick to allay by informing the gathering that all the train doors had now been tightly secured with rope and the entrance to the train engine, which had previously been a point of obvious vulnerability, had been blocked off with a large number of heavy crates and boxes. There had also been good news for those who had been concerned about their valuables because, on his return from making another quick search of the forward carriages, the Club Secretary had discovered a number of safe deposit boxes near to the mail room and within touching distance of his own sleeping carriage. The Chef had been equally as industrious-he had prepared a large vat of vegetable soup and a selection of well filled sandwiches and as a result, had been one of the last to settle down at his respective table. That constituted tea time for the men and gave rise to a rare period of calm and quiet where the only sounds to be heard were spoons rattling against porcelain and the occasional polite request for salt, pepper or fresh tea. It wasn't until about 5.45 that the noise level began to increase and it was no surprise that much of it was emanating from Hamill's table where owing to the application of strong alcohol, all three occupants were becoming more and more animated and vociferous by the second.

"To be perfectly honest, I don't understand what all the fuss has been about," said Woodhouse after easing back his chair and placing his hands on the back of his neck. "If what the lads saw, were in fact large wild animals, we've already got the upper hand."
"In what way?" said Tommy Mac.
"Superior intelligence, for one thing," said Woodhouse. "We can plan. We can strategise. And we can adapt tools and use weapons. We just have to make sure we're always one step ahead of the enemy."
"What if they're men?" said Alty.
"Bring them on," said Woodhouse.
"Yes, bring the bastards on," said McShane. "Look at our numbers. Surely there are enough of us on board this train to handle a couple of chancers."
"I agree," said Hamill.
"I do too," said the new Chairman. "But I don't think we should get complacent. It might be an idea to go everywhere in twos until we know exactly who or what we're up against."
"I like that idea," said Alty before grabbing his best friend Larkin by the hand and pulling him onto his lap. "I like the idea of twosomes. I like that a lot."
"I do too," said Larkin before planting a kiss on his

[198]

friend's cheek. "Two has always been my favourite number."

"Oh, for the love of God," said the disgusted Biddo. "What is it with you two freaks? Will you take a long, hard look at yourselves. You've both got beautiful wives at home."

"And very understanding wives at that," said Alty while patting his close friend's backside.

"They need to be understanding," said Biddo. "By God, they need to be."

"They're joking dad," said young Anthony. "They're just messing around. Just try to ignore them."

"I can't ignore them," said Biddo. "They're doing it right in everybody's faces."

"They're playing with you dad," said young Anthony. "They're straight."

"They're not," said Biddo. " I know them. I've watched them. They're bent. They're a couple of Nancy boys. I've seen them playing strip poker. And two mature men don't play strip poker unless they're a pair of Pansy Potters. They make me want to puke."

"Well, go and puke then," said the new Chairman. "Go to the washroom and have a good old puke. Have one for me while you're there. In the meantime, we'll be right here looking forward to your safe return."

"That's right," said the Club Secretary. "We'll be discussing a number of very real concerns. By the way- have you all made sure your sleeping carriage windows are securely bolted?"

"Jesus!" said Hamill. "The windows! The bloody windows! I never thought of that. I've gone and left mine wide open."

"Why?" said the Club Secretary. "Bloody hell Hamill. Why in God's name would you do something like that?"

"I'm joking with you," said Hamill. "Loosen up Hilly. You're going to make yourself ill."

"I'll loosen up when I know everything's in order," said the Club Secretary.

"And everything's going to be in order," said the

Chairman. "We just have to sit this out until help arrives."

"And when might that be?" said Steadman.

"Soon," said the Chairman. "Think about it lads. Back at the station there'll be all sorts of embarrassed stewards and porters running around like blue arsed flies wondering where the hell their train has gone. A rescue party is probably on its way or being organised as we speak."

"A rescue party!" said Hamill. "A fucking rescue party. Do you really think so? Have you forgotten about the weather? Has that escaped your notice has it Hulmey? I seem to remember Eddie Meehan telling us the weather was breaking all British meteorological records. I know those rescue people are very good at what they do, but they're not superhuman you know."

"And they won't be in any hurry either," said Larkin.

"Why not?" said the Chairman.

"Because they know we're well off for food and we've got cover, light and heat," said Larkin.

"They'll know that will they?" said Steadman.

"Of course they will," said the Chef. "The company's catering staff will have stocked the kitchen. They'll have a manifest."

"And their engineers fitted the heating and lighting system throughout the train," said Blackie. "They'll know exactly how long the batteries are going to last."

"Do you think they might attempt an airlift?" said Alty.

"That's a point," said Steadman. "Maybe they'll try to get a chopper out to us."

"In this weather?" said Hamill. "How the hell are they going to find us?"

"By following the tracks from the station," said the Chairman.

"What bloody tracks?" said Hamill. "Have you taken a look outside? Have you been outside since we stopped?"

"Not yet," said the Chairman.

"Oh, I forgot," said Hamill. "You don't like the cold

do you Hulmey? You're the last one who's likely to
venture out there aren't you? Well let me describe the
scene for you. Everything's completely white. There
aren't any visible tracks. The track disappeared God
knows how many hours ago. And, what's even worse,
the train's as good as disappeared too."
"What do you mean 'the train's disappeared'?" said the
Chairman.
"It's as good as disappeared," said Hamill. "It's
cocooned in hundreds of tons of pure white snow."
"I think you're underestimating modern technology
aren't you," said the Chairman.
"What sort of technology?" said Hamill.
"Heat seeking stuff and things like that," said the
Chairman.
"Heat seeking stuff!" said Hamill. "Bloody hell! I very
much doubt if there's a heat seeking system in the world
that would function in weather like we're experiencing
now."
"I'm afraid he's right Hulmey," said the Club Secretary.
"I know I'm right," said Hamill. "You can forget about
an airlift. We've already been absorbed into the
landscape. We're now beyond the scope of radar,
satellite navigation and things like that."
"Well maybe we should turn our attention to finding
Eddie Meehan," said the new Chairman. "At least that
would occupy some of our dead time and prevent
negativity and depression setting in."
"I agree," said the Club Secretary. "I think we need a
bit of structure."
"Structure!" said Hamill. "Fuck structure. And fuck
Eddie Meehan for that matter. Who the hell was he
anyway?"
"He was a thoroughly decent man," said Hewlett.
"He was an interfering, meddlesome, power crazy twat,"
said Hamill.
"He was a good man," said the Chairman. "And as the
new Chairman, it's my sworn duty to keep looking for
him until I find his body or at least evidence that he

[201]

deliberately left this train of his own free will. And I'll tell you this much Hamill-I'll turn over every stone until I do find him."

"Get turning then," said Hamill. "Be my guest. Enjoy yourself. But don't expect me to help you. And don't expect any of these boys to help you either. You'll just be putting more bloody lives at risk."

"In what way?" said the Chairman.

"For fucks sake Hulmey," said Hamill. "Where have you been hiding? Haven't you been paying attention? You must have heard what Matthews and Hewlett said. There might be wild and desperate creatures roaming close by. It's therefore not beyond the realm of possibility for one or two of our unsuspecting lads to be picked off. You'll have blood on your hands then. And if that does happen, I'll see you do time for it. I'll make it my life's mission to see that you're locked up."

"I think it's more likely to be you doing the time," said the Chairman.

"What do you mean by that?" said Hamill after flinging back his chair and approaching the Chairman's position. "Explain what you mean by that or I'll..."

"You'll what Hamill?" said the Chairman after taking a step back. "You'll do the same to me as you did to Eddie. Is that what you'll do?"

"I haven't touched Eddie," said Hamill while being encouraged to return to his chair by his close friend Woodhouse. "Although I somehow wish I had."

"Why's that?" said the Chairman.

"Because the man was a constant pain in the arse," said Hamill. He got under just about everybody's skin at one time or another. Take Kenny Biddo for instance. Like many of us, he's in his early sixties. Did you know that he was scolded yesterday for not using the corridor handrail in the correct manner? Believe it or not, he was told to go back to the end of the corridor and do it properly."

"That's right that," said Woodhouse.

"Then he was sent to his room for not wearing shoes and

socks in the kitchen," said Hamill.

"I can confirm that too," said Woodhouse.

"He could have got himself scalded," said the Chef.

"Let him get badly scalded," said Hamill. "Let him burn his feet to a crisp. Let him run stark naked through the kitchen if he wants to. Let him end up looking like a pork scratching. He's a middle aged man for goodness sake. He's capable of making his own decisions and learning by his own mistakes. He certainly didn't deserve to be treated as if he was a naughty child. But let's get back to your earlier inference Hulmey. Do you want to accuse me of something?"

"Not just yet," said the Chairman. "But I do suspect you were the one who was arguing with Eddie in the corridor late last night."

"Do you Sherlock?" said Hamill. "Why's that?"

"Because you're the one that hated him most," said the Chairman. "You've hated him ever since he shut down the work on your loft extension."

"That's ancient history now," said Hamill. "I've had my say on that matter."

"Have you had your very last say?" said the Chairman.

"I'd like to think so," said Hamill.

"I think you have," said the Chairman. "In fact, I'm convinced you have. Make no mistake Hamill-I don't think for one minute you've killed Eddie. I think you've just intimidated him. I think he'd reached the point when he'd had enough."

"You're way off the mark," said a smirking Hamill.

"On the contrary-I think I'm not too far away," said the Chairman.

"You're miles away our kid," said the Chef after discreetly nudging his brother.

"What?" said the Chairman.

"It wasn't Hamill," said the Chef. "It was Alec Morris who'd been rowing with Eddie last night."

"Alec!" said the Chairman.

"He'd gone to use one of the washrooms," said the Chef. "And in case of reprisals, I'd gone along with him, just as you'd asked. We just happened to bump into our Health and Safety Officer while we were making our way back to our carriage."

"What happened?" said the Club Secretary.

"Eddie immediately turned crimson," said the Chef. "He was shaking violently. He gave Alec what for. He read him the riot act. He told him what a reckless piece of work he was. He told him he'd endangered the lives of every man on board the train. Alec gave a load of shit back as well. You know what a defiant little fucker he can be. He wouldn't admit anything. But there was definitely no fighting. There were no blows exchanged. I can assure you of that. I then escorted Morris back to our room after watching Eddie head off in the opposite direction."

"Hallelujah!" said Hamill before thrusting his hands towards the ceiling. "I rest my case. Justice has been served. Do you mind if I take a few moments to pay tribute to my brilliant defence team?"

"Go to hell," said the Chairman. "It was a mistake anyone could have made."

"Are you going to apologise for your mistake?" said Hamill.

"If you insist," said the Chairman.

"I most certainly do," said Hamill.

"I'm sorry," said the Chairman.

"Is that it?" said Hamill.

"What more do you want?" said the Chairman.

"A lot more," said Hamill. "I want you to find out what really happened to Eddie Meehan. I want you to interrogate the rest of these men now. And I want you to do it in the same prejudiced and hardnosed manner you adopted while questioning me."

"But none of these men had an axe to grind with Eddie," said the Chairman.

"How do you know?" said Hamill.

"Because I know them and I trust them," said the Chairman.

"Biddo wasn't happy with him," said Hamill. "Don't

forget, Meehan had threatened to ration the amount of alcohol everyone could consume."

"Kenny Biddo wouldn't harm a fly," said the Chairman.

"What about the others," said Hamill. "What about Davie Larkin for instance."

"What about me?" said Larkin.

"I know for a fact you'd had serious words with Eddie this summer gone," said Hamill. "I saw the two of you arguing outside the Bug."

"That was nothing," said Larkin. "That was just a misunderstanding."

"What happened Larko?" said the Chairman.

"I did a mini service on Eddie's Mercedes," said Larkin. "But I wasn't in the garage when he dropped his car off. My new apprentice ticked the wrong box on the to do sheet."

"Eddie had wanted a full service," said Hamill. "He accused Larko of only doing half a job."

"That's all been well sorted out now," said Larkin. "I hadn't even charged him for a full service. I've never ripped anybody off. Go to my garage any time you want. You'll see a long queue of cars stretching the entire length of Manor Road on any given day of the week. That's not just evidence of my ability as a mechanic, that's evidence of my integrity."

"That's right," said the Chef. "No mechanic's got a better reputation than Larko."

"I wasn't accusing you of any underhanded dirty dealing, Larko," said Hamill. "Calm down lad. There's no need to go throwing your toys out of your pram."

"I'll throw more than my fucking toys if you carry on in that vein," said Larkin.

"What was the point you were trying to make Hamill?" said the Chairman.

"The point I was trying to make was this," said Hamill. "I'm not the only person on board this train that didn't like Eddie Meehan."

"You're the only one *I* wouldn't trust," said the Chairman.

[205]

"Really?" said Hamill. "What about Blackie?"

"What about me?" said a startled Blackie who, at the time had been leaning back on the rear two legs of his chair.

"Are you whiter than white?" said Hamill. "Or have you got the odd skeleton in your cupboard too?"

"I've got no skeletons," said Blackie after successfully returning to four legs. "I've just got quality designer clothing in *my* cupboard. I'm as honest as they come. It's the way I've been brought up."

"Is that so?" said Hamill.

"Absolutely so," said Blackie.

"Would you say you've always played fair?" said Hamill.

"Without exception," said Blackie.

"Which means you've never cheated at golf then," said Hamill.

"Never in my life," said Blackie.

"Are you sure about that?" said Hamill.

"I'm positive," said Blackie.

"What about last year's prestigious West Lancs Annual Match play Trophy," said Hamill. "The trophy every West Lancs member would give an arm or a leg to win."

"What about it?" said Blackie. "I won that fair and square. I beat Steadman in the final by just the one shot. It's a game that's gone down in West Lancs folklore. I was one down and chipped in for a birdie on the final hole. It was a great game. It was epic. It was one of the best I've ever been involved in."

"But you definitely didn't cheat," said Hamill. "Is that what you're saying?"

"It's exactly what I'm saying," said Blackie.

"You're out of order Hamill," said the Chef.

"Am I?" said Hamill. "Well why don't you ask him how he got on in the relatively minor competition that took place just a week before?" said Hamill.

"The week before!" said Blackie.

"That's right," said Hamill.

"I can't remember," said Blackie.

[206]

"You should do," said Hamill. "You recorded one of the best scores that day. I know that because you were paired with my son Christopher. He said you played like an established tour professional. You were creaming the ball off the tee and your short game was brilliant apparently. You went round in five under par on a tough track in extremely difficult conditions."

"And as I just said, I don't remember," said Blackie.

"That's convenient isn't it," said Hamill.

"What do you mean by that?" said Blackie.

"You failed to hand your scorecard in after the game didn't you?" said Hamill.

"Did I?" said Blackie.

"You did," said Hamill. "I know that for a fact."

"Is it true Blackie?" said Steadman. "Did you fail to put a card in the week before our big final?"

"He did yes," said Hamill. "He very deliberately failed to hand it in. Because if he had have done, the handicapper would have come down hard on him. He'd have chopped him a couple of shots at least. And if he'd have come down a couple of shots, he wouldn't have won the following weeks competition. That's right isn't it Blackie?"

"It is yes," said a clearly unsettled Blackie after clearing his throat and lowering his head. "I'm sorry Steadman. I don't know what to say fella. It was an unforgivable thing to do."

"That's alright Blackie," said Steadman. "Don't worry about it. I didn't put my card in the previous week either. And I went around in six under."

"Bloody hell," said the Chef. "Who have I been playing with? No wonder I lose money every week."

"You see Hulmey," said Hamill. "I bet you thought those two hard working lads were cleaner than whistles didn't you?"

"I did yes," said the Chairman. "But neither of them would have attacked Eddie."

"Maybe not," said Hamill. "But they're still capable of deceit. Like a lot of your members. What about you

Kenny Alty? Have you anything in the cupboard you want to tell us about?"

"I'm not going to be claiming I'm whiter than white, if that's what you mean," said Alty after quickly downing the last of his tea.

"I know you're not," said Hamill. "Because you're far from whiter than white aren't you? Why don't you tell the lads where your brother Chris is at this moment in time."

"Fuck you Hamill," said Alty.

"Yes do one Hamill," said Larkin. "This is nonsense. You're no saint. In fact, you've got a worse track record than the rest of us put together."

"I'm just making a point," said Hamill. "I just want to prove to our new Chairman that, when it comes to knowing his members, very little is likely to be as it seems. I want him to know that his members aren't necessarily the decent and upstanding citizens he might have imagined. Go on Alty. Tell the lads where your brother Chris is.'""He doesn't have to tell us anything if he doesn't want to," said Larkin.

"That's right," said Blackie. "This is just a mass character assassination. It's not necessary. It's only going to cause more bad feeling."

"That's right," said the Chairman. "Let's change the subject shall we."

"I couldn't agree more," said the Chef.

"And I couldn't agree less," said Hamill. "I want my question answered."

"Say nothing Ken," said Larkin. "Just say nothing lad."

"Where's your brother Alty?" said Hamill.

"Ignore him," said Larkin.

"Just drop it Hamill," said the Chef.

"He's in Guantanamo Bay," said Alty.

"What!" said Blackie after stopping dead in his tracks while on his way to the kitchen. "He's where?"

"He's been detained at Guantanamo Bay for just under 3 years," said Alty.

"Bloody hell!" said Larkin. "I didn't know that."

"I've tried to keep it quiet," said Alty.

"Do you want to explain how and why he ended up there?" said Hamill.

"Through my recklessness and stupidity," said Alty. "And a despicable and deceitful work colleague."

"Who did what?" said Hamill.

"He swindled me out of a hell of a lot of money," said Alty.

"How did he manage that?" said the Club Secretary.

"It's complicated," said Alty.

"Well, take your time," said Hamill. "Why don't you start by telling the lads about the position you held. If I remember right, it was with a Merseyside rail company wasn't it?"

"It was yes," said Alty. "You used to work for them, didn't you Hamill?"

"I did yes," said Hamill. "I'm still in regular contact with the man who fired you."

"What did the job entail?" said the Club Secretary.

"It was menial work," said Alty. "You could have trained a chimpanzee to do it. But I'd been out of work for a while so I was prepared to take anything. I was one of two general workers that had been taken on just before Christmas. The other fella was this little streak of piss called Cyril. We'd been assigned to the main communications room. The job was a doddle to be honest. We just had to keep the place tidy and run errands for the technical staff. The main problem was boredom. The hours seemed to drag. But then we found a way of making the days more interesting."

"How did you manage that while on the brush?" said Blackie.

"By betting on the trains," said Alty.

"Betting on the trains!" said Blackie. "How did you do that?"

"It was easy," said Alty. "The main wall of the communications room was a huge screen with loads of different coloured lights. It was like a motor racing circuit. We soon learnt that the lights represented the

[209]

different trains that were heading towards Lime Street Station. That excited the two of us. And that's when money started changing hands."

"I don't get you," said the Chef. "Are you saying that you and this Cyril were betting on which train arrived at Lime Street Station first?"

"That's right," said Alty.

"But those trains will have had very definite schedules," said the Chef. "They'd have been arriving at pretty much the same time every day."

"I know," said Alty. "That's why we implemented a sort of handicap system. The difference being, instead of giving weight like they do in horse racing, we would add on time. So, for instance, if we knew the train from London was scheduled to arrive at Lime Street 30 minutes before the train from Nuneaton, we'd adjust the times by 30 minutes. In theory, that would result in a dead heat-which, as most punters know, is the racing handicapper's Holy Grail."

"Bloody hell!" said the Chef. "Trust you Alty. "What sort of money were you and this Cyril forking out?"

"About £100 a month at first," said Alty. "But then, just like many mug punters often do, we decided to up the ante. That's when things started to spiral out of control."

"How badly out of control?" said Larkin.

"Before long, we were sometimes betting our entire wages," said Alty. "That's also when I began to lose far more often than not."

"That's when you should have got out," said the Chef.

"I wanted to," said Alty. "You've no idea how much I wanted to. But by that time I was down hundreds of pounds and constantly having to get sly subs off my dad to pay the missus her housekeeping. At one point, things were that bad I was having to walk to and from work."

"That would have been some walk," said the Chef.

"It was," said Alty. "Especially in the Winter."

"As the Chef just said, you should have cut your losses and run," said Steadman.

"I wanted to," said Alty. "But I was watching my workmate having a ball. I desperately wanted to have my day in the sun. He was constantly wafting huge wads of money in my face. He bought his first second hand car out of what I'd lost. It was a jet black Mark two Ford Escort, if I remember right."

"He sounds like a right arrogant twat," said Larkin.

"He was that and a lot more," said Alty. "Then, one day, I got offered a lift to work by a new neighbour. He'd just landed a job as manager in one of the shops on the station concourse. The only problem was, his hours were slightly different from mine. It meant that I was having to get up an hour earlier and arrive at work an hour early too. But I didn't mind because he wouldn't take any money off me for petrol. That meant that even on those occasions when I was completely skint, I was still able to get to work. And that earlier start was the reason I caught the bastard."

"Caught him!" said the Chef. "What do you mean,

"I used to sit in a little nearby cafe at first," said Alty while making himself more comfortable. "I think the owner had taken pity on me."

"Why's that?" said the Chef.

"I think it was because I used to count my copper before paying him," said Alty. "I was more than often a few pence short. We used to talk a lot of football. He was a staunch Evertonian like me. He'd played semi pro for Burscough and a few other half decent teams. Many a time he'd give me a mug of coffee and a couple of rounds of toast on the house. But then one day his area manager arrived at the same time as us. It meant that there was no freebie. No coffee and no toast. I had no alternative but to go straight to the office and read my paper. That was the first time I became suspicious."

"Suspicious of what?" said Steadman.

"Of my work colleague doing something underhanded," said Alty. "We were meant to be working the same shift you see. And as far as I was concerned, there was no reason at all why he should be in work an hour early.

Don't forget-he had a car by that time."

"Did you confront him about it?" said the Chef.

"He hadn't noticed I'd arrived," said Alty. "And to be honest, I would have let on to him had he not been on the internal phone to someone. And even then, I wouldn't have known what he was up to had he not been called away by one of the bosses. I certainly wouldn't have found his notes."

"What notes?" said Blackie.

"It was a list of the day's expected delays," said Alty.

"The scheming little toe rag," said Larkin.

"That's exactly what I thought," said Alty.

"I'd have filled the bastard in right there and then," said Steadman.

"I would have done," said Alty. "But that wouldn't have got me my money back would it?"

"What did you do?" said Larkin.

"I did the sensible thing," said Alty. "I used my brain instead of my fists. I sat down and devised a way to get my cash back. The problem was I didn't have any money to bet with by then. And trust me-nobody on this planet was more aware of that than my workmate Cyril."

"Get to the nitty gritty," said the Chef. "What did you do?"

"I pretended I'd won £5,000 on a £1 Lucky Fifteen over the weekend," said Alty.

"Did he swallow it?" said Steadman.

"Not one bit of it," said Alty. "Not until I produced a huge wad of twenty pound notes."

"How huge?" said the Chef.

"£1,000," said Alty.

"Bloody hell!" said Larkin. "What did you pawn to raise that sort of cash?"

"I didn't pawn anything," said Alty. "My neighbour loaned me it."

"Your neighbour!" said Larkin. "Your new neighbour? The cafe man?"

"That's right," said Alty. "I'd broken down and poured my heart out to him on the journey home the previous

Friday."

"And that was it was it?" said Larkin. "You just poured your heart out to a man you hardly knew and he agreed to lend you a thousand pounds. Who was this fella?- Who was this living saint? Ghandi's nephew? Mother Theresa's better natured son?"

"He was just a great bloke with a kind heart," said Alty. "But it wasn't really a loan. The money was just a prop. It was just for show. It was just to lure Cyril into my trap. The money was back in my neighbour's wallet within fifteen minutes of me showing it to the other fiddling bastard."

"And then what did you do?" said the Chef.

"I made my first selection of the week," said Alty. "I think it was the train from York, if I remember right. He'd picked the train that was arriving from Newcastle. I actually won that bet."

"How much?" said Steadman.

"£20," said Alty. "Cyril would often allow me to win small amounts to draw me in and keep me interested."

"How were you able to place your bets?" said the Chef. "I thought you were on the bones of your arse."

"I was," said Alty. "I'd never been so skint. Our betting was all done on credit. No money ever changed hands until Friday. And we always settled up at 5 o'clock on the dot without fail. We were weekly paid in those days. Friday was our pay day back then."

"Why do you think he allowed you to win at all?" said Blackie. "Why didn't he just take you to the cleaners and wipe you out?"

"Because he knew I'd have packed the game in for good," said Alty. "And he wouldn't have had his regular meal ticket then would he?"

"So what happened?" said the Chef. "What happened that particular week?"

"It was pretty much the same as every other week," said Alty. "He was familiar with my betting pattern by then. I'd lose a little, win a bit and then I'd lose some more. And then, to get back what I'd lost, I'd inevitably up my stakes. I'd lost about £1,000 by Thursday afternoon that week."

"Jesus Christ!" said Larkin. "You did have it bad didn't you. You should have come and talked to me."

"It wouldn't have done any good Larko," said Alty. By that time, I was in too deep."

"What did you do?" said the Chef.

"I went chasing the big one," said Alty. "I went all in with the remaining £4,000 on the Friday."

"What do you mean 'all in'?" said Steadman.

"I put the last £4,000 of my fictitious Lucky Fifteen winnings on a train that, according to his revised schedule, was going to be delayed by at least half an hour," said Alty.

"Wow!" said the Chef.

"I don't get it," said Steadman. "I know he left the revised schedule behind initially, but surely he wasn't foolish enough to make the same mistake twice."

"He wasn't," said Alty. "But I watched him like a hawk. I watched him when he came off the phone each morning. He always put the schedule in the same place. He always hid it in the wallet side of his mobile phone case-between his two cash cards. Don't forget-he had no idea I was on to his scam. All I had to do was borrow his phone and pretend mine had run out of credit. That was certainly no lie. That was nearly always the case anyway. To this day, I can still remember the look on his face when I suggested we should have one final mammoth bet and then call it quits for good."

"What did he say?" said the Chef.

"He said very little," said Alty. "He headed straight for his coat and made out he needed to leave the office to make a quick call home."

"Who do you think he was calling?" said Steadman.

"I don't think he was calling anyone," said Alty.

"He'd have been checking his schedule," said the Chef.

"Had you already seen it?" said Larkin.

"I'd seen it earlier that morning," said Alty. "I'd made a copy of it."

[214]

"Good lad," said Larkin.

"He must have been creaming his kecks when he returned," said the Chef.

"He was," said Alty. "He even looked a bit embarrassed. He was actually shaking. Even his lips were quivering and within seconds there were little balls of saliva forming on each side of his horrible mouth. I'm still convinced to this day he had a hard on."

"I bet he did," said the Chef. "I'd have had a hard on myself."

"Can you imagine his mindset?" said Alty. "Can you imagine being in his position at that very moment? Can you imagine what it would have been like for him betting £4,000 on an even money shot, knowing that he couldn't possibly lose?"

"I don't get you," said Steadman. "It still doesn't make any sense to me. Unless you were actually gambling on his train being delayed a lot longer than yours? Is that what you were doing?"

"I wasn't gambling at all," said Alty. "I knew his train was going to be delayed for much longer than mine."

"How?" said Steadman. "Had you managed to get your own inside information?"

"I didn't need inside information," said Alty. "On that particular Friday, I'd arranged for my brother Chris to be travelling on Cyril's train."

"For what purpose?" said the Chef. "To pull the emergency cord?"

"To pretend he was a terrorist," said Alty.

"What!" said Steadman.

"To pretend he was a terrorist," said Alty.

"How exactly does somebody do that?" said the Chef.

"It's not hard, to be fair," said Alty. "He donned a false beard, waited until the train was about half an hour from Lime Street Station and, after lifting his top to expose a dummy bomb made from a load of tin cans, batteries and wire, he shouted something that sounded Arabic. The next minute, all hell let loose. Then somebody alerted the driver and the train came to a shuddering halt."

[215]

"Bloody hell," said the Chef. "Bloody hell Alty!"

"That's brilliant that is," said Steadman. "But how did your Chris manage to get away?"

"That's the thing," said Alty. "He couldn't get away. The train driver wouldn't open the doors."

"Why was that?" said Steadman.

"I can't say for sure," said Alty.

"Maybe it was to do with new anti-terrorist protocol," said the Chef.

"That would be my guess too," said Steadman.

"It's the best explanation I've ever been able to come up with," said Alty.

"But how would the driver know the problem was terrorist related?" said Blackie.

"I'd have thought that would have funnelled through to him very quickly," said Alty. "People would have been screaming and running amok. I'm sure somebody would have uttered the words 'bomb' or 'terrorist' at some point during the commotion. It was chaos apparently. The only passenger that wasn't running was our poor Chris."

"Because he was the only one who knew the bomb was fake," said the Chef.

"That's right," said Alty.

"How long was the train held up?" said Steadman.

"I'm not sure," said Alty. "But I imagine it was hours rather than minutes, don't you?"

"Bloody hell!" said the Chef. "Your brother must have been in a right state."

"You're not wrong there," said Alty. "He told me he'd never been so scared in his life."

"I don't doubt it," said the Chef. "He must have been cursing you."

"I don't doubt that either," said Alty.

"I hope he stayed in character," said Hamill.

"What do you mean?" said Alty.

"I hope he cursed you in Arabic," said Hamill. "Otherwise he'd have spoilt the whole effect."

"Behave yourself Hamill," said the Club Secretary.

[216]

"You can see the lad's upset."

"He's alright," said Hamill. "He'd won thousands of pounds hadn't he. His train had won the race. He'd had the result of his life."

"I'd had the worst result of my life," said Alty.

"Why's that?" said Steadman.

"Because things then turned sour," said Alty. "Within minutes, an armed response team arrived and after sending in a bomb disposal robot to investigate, they dragged our kid off and bundled him into the back of an unmarked van. Within 48 hours, he was on the other side of the world blindfolded and dressed from neck to foot in a bright orange overall."

"Where about on the other side of the world?" said Steadman.

"I thought I told you before," said Alty. "Guantanamo Bay."

"Bloody hell!" said the Club Secretary. "What did your mum and dad say?"

"They don't know," said Alty.

"They don't know!" said the Club Secretary.

"I've told them he's touring the West Indies with his old band," said Alty. "I've told them he's on a remote Caribbean island where it's impossible to send or receive calls or mail. Up to now, they're buying it. God help me if they ever find out the truth."

"God help you is right," said Biddo. "I've seen the size of your father."

"It's not my father I'm worried about," said Alty. "Our Chris has always been my mother's favourite."

"Have you spoken to your local MP?" said the Club Secretary.

"You're joking aren't you," said Alty. "What good would that do? Think about it Hilly. I was an accomplice to what had gone on. I'd planned the operation. I'd probably be wearing an orange boiler suit myself if I'd owned up to my part in the plan."

"Why didn't he just pull the emergency cord?" said Blackie.

"Because that wouldn't have provided enough of a delay," said Alty. "The train would have been back up and running within ten minutes and I'd have lost my £4,000."

"Maybe your kid should think about getting the bus next time," said Hamill.

"And maybe you should stop badgering the lads," said the Chairman.

"Alright," said Hamill. "But I just thought it was important for you to know the type of people you're travelling with. As I said before-none of them are angels. None of them could be described as choir boy material. So in future, whenever you're tempted to call someone 'low' or something equally insulting, take a deep breath and count to ten."

"That was me that called you low," said the Chef.

"Was it?" said Hamill. "Oh yes it was wasn't it. The very man that was caught up in that rather distasteful business in an Aintree Hospital when 20 elderly patients died from the effects of food poisoning."

"That had nothing to do with food preparation," said the Chef. "Those poor buggers had been poisoned by a rogue nurse who'd suffered a complete mental breakdown."

"If you say so," said Hamill.

"I do say so," said the Chef. "I say so because it's true. The story made national headlines. The nurse was jailed for life."

"It's just a pity Brian Matthews wasn't a patient at that time," said Hamill.

"Why's that?" said Matthews.

"Because we'd all be rid of a right bad egg by now," said Hamill.

"What's he done?" said the Club Secretary. "Have you got something on him?"

"Not as yet," said Hamill. "But I've got a feeling I'll find something."

"Why's that?" said Matthews.

"I'm not sure," said Hamill. "I'm not sure yet. I've just

[218]

got this feeling you're up to something. And when I get those feelings, I'm rarely wrong."

"I'm up to nothing," said the agitated Matthews. "I just came on this trip to have a good time. And I certainly had nothing to do with Eddie Meehan's disappearance, if that's where this is going."

"Did you know him prior to this trip?" said Hamill.

"I'd come across him once or twice before," said Matthews. "He made quite a first impression on me to be honest. And an even bigger one on our trade union rep."

"Where was this?" said the Club Secretary.

"Vauxhall Motors on the Wirral," said Matthews. "Eddie had arrived at around 8 o'clock in the morning to do a general inspection of the shop floor and by 10 o'clock, he'd shut the place down for the day."

"Why was that?" said Hamill.

"Because of a faulty conveyor belt," said Matthews. "The operatives had been complaining about it for months. One of them had almost lost his thumb. I remember that day well because we were all allowed to go home on full pay. By mid afternoon, I was walking down the 18th fairway at Kirkby Golf Course after breaking a ton for the first time."

"Did you not think of asking Eddie to go along with you?" said Hamill.

"It never entered my head," said Matthews. "Why would I?"

"Because you were going to be hitting any number of golf balls," said Hamill. "And for the life of me, if Eddie Meehan thought that a conveyor belt was a danger to those around, he's clearly never seen you swing a 5 iron ."

"Ha ha ha," said Matthews ironically. "You're not funny Hamill. You're not funny at all."

"I'm afraid I'm going to have to disagree with you on this occasion," said Steadman. "I thought that line was hilarious."

"Me too," said Blackie.

"He's not funny at all," said Matthews. "So don't encourage him."

"Have you finished?" said the Chairman.

"Finished!" said Hamill.

"Is there anyone else you want to have a go at?" said the Chairman. "Is there anybody else that you suspect of being implicated in the disappearance of Eddie Meehan?"

"What about me?" said Biddo.

"He's already had a go at you," said the Chef.

"That's right," said Hamill. "You need to pay attention Biddo. You needn't worry now. I've had second thoughts about you."

"Why's that?" said Biddo.

"Because you wouldn't be able to hold a weapon steady for long enough to murder anyone," said Hamill. "You'd be seeing three of your potential target. Just relax and think of vodka. Your son Anthony interests me though."

"Why's that?" said Biddo.

"Just leave the lad out of this," said the Chairman. "He's only here to look after his father."

"So what," said Hamill. "That doesn't necessarily place him above suspicion."

"He's a good lad," said Biddo. "Don't you dare have a go at him."

"He's a heartbreaker," said Hamill.

"What do you mean by that?" said the Chairman.

"I know what he means," said Biddo. "I know exactly what he means. Our Anthony once stood your eldest daughter up didn't he Hamill? He left her standing on the corner of College Road in the rain didn't he?"

"I don't know," said Hamill. "Did he really? I didn't know that. I really didn't know that."

"Thanks a lot dad," said a mortified young Anthony.

"To be honest, that's not what I was referring to," said Hamill. "I was referring to something that happened some time ago. Quite a number of Christmases ago, to be more precise."

"What was that?" said Biddo.

[220]

"When your son messed up the Nativity display in Crosby Village," said Hamill.

"Messed it up in what way?" said Biddo.

"He replaced the baby Jesus with a Teletubby," said Hamill.

"He did what?" said the Chairman.

"He replaced the baby Jesus with one of the Teletubbies," said Hamill.

"Oh for crying out loud," scoffed Biddo. "It would have only been a bit of fun. It would have only been a teenage prank."

"I imagine it was," said Hamill. "It probably was just a teenage prank. But it seriously confused my youngest daughter. She became absolutely convinced the son of God was in fact the blue Teletubby commonly known to 3 million television viewers as Tinky Winky. It took me and the missus years to convince her otherwise."

"She's not the only one confused," said Woodhouse while scratching his head. "I thought Tinky Winky was a deep shade of purple?"

"No, he was definitely blue," said McShane.

"Are you sure about that?" said Steadman. "I could have sworn he was yellow. Or am I thinking of Po?"

"Po was red," said Blackie.

"Was he?" said Steadman. "Well what colour was Dipsy?"

"Oh, for the love of God!" said Hamill. "I don't give a shite if Dipsy was yellow and black stripes or liked to appear in the Queen's racing silks from time to time. You're all missing the fucking point."

"What point?" said Biddo. "Is there any point to all this? Because, try as hard as I can, I'm struggling like crazy to see one. This is a load of nonsense Hamill. Is that the sum total of the dirt you've got to dish on my son? Is that the full extent of it?"

"For now it is," said Hamill while proceeding to eye the young man up and down with an air of curiosity. "At least until I've made up my mind about his sexuality."

"I beg your pardon," said Biddo. "What are you

[221]

inferring Hamill?"

"I'm not inferring anything yet," said Hamill. "But I am prepared to admit this-I've often looked at your lad and wondered whether the name Antonia would have been more suitable."

"You bad minded bastard," said a trembling Biddo. "You insipid pig. My lad's straight. He's as straight as an arrow. All the male Biddlestones are straight. You can trace our ancestry back thousands of years. We've never once had a shirt lifter in our family."

"What if I told you differently," said Hamill. "What if I told you your son was a self-confessed fudge packer?"

"I'd say you were lying," said Biddo. "My son likes girls. He always has done. Bloody hell-the lad's been married twice and engaged three times and he's yet to celebrate his 40th birthday. I've still got a brand new Goblin Teasmade and a 36 piece dinner service in our loft to prove it. What does that tell you Hamill?"

"Apart from the fact you don't like tea parties, it tells me he's had enough of women," said Hamill. "He's been hurt and now wants to try the penis."

"You ought to be ashamed of yourself," said Biddo after slamming his dishes down on the serving hatch. "Just go to hell will you Hamill. I'm sick and tired of your nastiness. I'm not going to listen to any more of it."

"Quite right too," said the Chef. "I think we need to get things back on track. I think we need to stop the infighting. As far as I'm concerned, the danger's not within this room. The danger's very much outside."

For several minutes after the Chef's eloquent attempt to bring some common sense to a situation that at times had teetered on the brink of farce, nobody said a word but instead stared at the window and beyond as though to do anything else would further inflame the existing toxic atmosphere. Two people hadn't been staring in the direction of the window however. They had fixed their eyes on each other and for some time neither had so much as blinked. That was until Hamill slowly leant forward, pulled up his collar and pretended to shiver violently.

"Why don't we get onto what this is really all about Hamill?" said the Chairman after rising and taking the floor. "Why don't we discuss the leadership situation? What is it about me being in charge of this club you don't like Hamill?"

"Just about everything," said Hamill. "You're not fit to be in charge."

"Would you care to say why?" said the Chairman.

"It'd be my pleasure," said Hamill. "The problem is, I wouldn't really know where to start. You're not strong enough for one thing."

"What do you mean, 'not strong enough'?" said the Chairman.

"You're not assertive enough," said Hamill. "Make no mistake, you might be capable of running the club in a domestic capacity when we're home-but the fact is-we're not home. We're away. And if Matthews is right about intruders, we're about to go to war. And if we do go to war, we need strong leadership and you're not capable of providing that."

"How do you know?" said the Chef. "You haven't given him a chance. He's only been in the job five minutes."

"I know," said Hamill. "And look at the state of us. We're arguing constantly. We're at each other's throats for little or no reason at all. We should all be pulling together. We should be unified."

"For the love of God!" said the Chef while forming a tower of used cups. "Have I finally gone insane? Did I really hear all that?"

"You did," whispered the Club Secretary.

"I'm afraid Hamill's right," said Woodhouse. "If my history lessons have taught me anything, it's this. At times of crisis, a country has to form the best possible government."

"Hear, hear!" said McShane.

"A government made up of the strongest and most

capable men," said Hamill. "It's what's commonly known as a coalition."

"And let me guess Hamill," said the Chairman. "That coalition would have you as its figurehead."

"It would yes," said Hamill.

"I disagree," said the Chef. "I say the sensible and most rational should lead."

"Do you?" said Hamill. "And are the so-called sensible and most rational going to be on the front line when the fighting begins?"

"We'll be right to the fore," said the Chairman.

"Bollocks!" said Hamill. "You'll be the first to turn and run when it all goes off. You're a shithouse Hulmey. You always have been. Tell me something. Why haven't you conducted a search of the outside?"

"Because of the weather," said the Chairman. "It's horrendous. You heard your mate Tommy Mac. He's as strong as a bull and he could hardly move out there."

"You don't have to be able to move to see if there's a body stretched out on the ground," said Hamill. "Why don't you be honest for once in your lily livered life Hulmey. You didn't want any of us to go out there because you wouldn't have been able to join us. That would have exposed one of your many weaknesses. I know you Hulmey. You despise the cold. You can't handle it. It's well documented. That's why you never completed a full football season."

"He suffered with bad knees," said the Chef.

"Well if that's the case, he better hope he's over the worst," said Hamill. "Because, when the fighting starts, he's going to be spending an awful lot of time on them begging me, Tommy Mac and Woody for help."

"We'll get by without your help if we have to," said the Club Secretary.

"Is that right?" said Hamill before leaving his chair to circle the seated ranks. "Is that right boys? Do you want this wuss to lead you, or do you want to remain relatively safe? You don't mind me putting that to them do you Hulmey?"

[224]

"I don't mind at all," said the Chairman. "As long as they're aware that if they side with you, they'll be forfeiting their right to be members of our club. If they can accept that, then good luck to them."

"Good luck to us all," said Hamill before encouraging his two close friends to follow him to the exit. "You never know lads. Before this night's through, you might all need treatment for your poorly knees. Because you're all going to be doing a hell of a lot of praying."

"Who will you be praying to Hamill?" said the Chef. "The son of God or Tinky Winky?"

"That's a good one that is Chef," said Hamill. "That's nearly as good as my 'five iron' remark. Let's hope your sense of humour's still intact in the morning."

"Does that mean you won't be sleeping in the dining carriage with the rest of us?" said Steadman.

"I wouldn't think of it," said Hamill. "I'll be staying where I was originally billeted. I'll be with my loyal and honest band of followers. I might even do some butt munching. I will be thinking of you all though. I'll pop in and see if any of you are still alive later."

"Will you check on me too?" said the Chairman.

"Where will you be?" said Hamill.

"I'll be in my own carriage with my own little band of loyal and honest followers," said the Chairman. "The one I was originally billeted."

"Really!" said Hamill. "That does surprise me. I thought you'd have stayed here with your members to help keep their morale up."

"I'd have thought so too, if you don't mind me saying so" said Steadman.

"I'll be no more than spitting distance away," said the Chairman. "I want to keep my eye on Alec Morris and everybody's valuables."

"Do you want me to keep an eye on Morris?" said Hamill.

"Certainly not," said the Chairman. "I'd like him to survive the night in one piece. By the way-I noticed you paid him a visit earlier on. What was that all about?"

[225]

"I'm concerned for the lad," said Hamill.

"He was taunting him," said the Chef.

"I was just having a bit of fun with the lad," said Hamill. "And I wanted to have another look at the best and most luxurious carriage on this train."

"It's exactly the same as yours," said the Club Secretary.

"That's right," said the Chairman. "But if you ever fancy a swap, just let us know. Trust me-moving will be no bother at all to any of my roommates."

"I'll pass on that thank you very much," said Hamill. "And I'll bid you all a good night. Try your best to have the sweetest of sweet dreams. And let's just hope the big bad wolves don't come huffing and puffing and blow you all away."

CHAPTER ELEVEN
DRESS CODE

The Chairman knew only too well that Hamill's attempt to wrestle the club leadership from him wasn't likely to be his last and that was why the first thing he had decided to do upon rising the following morning, was to ask the Chef to cook a special full English breakfast for every member of the party. 'That might just help raise morale and get the day off to a positive start', he had told his elder brother shortly after they had woken simultaneously just after 7 o'clock when the first evidence of daylight had begun to brighten their room. However, inwardly his own morale was wavering fast and not just because of the various life threatening problems that were prevalent such as a serious infectious disease, animal attack and an unstable bridge that could give way at any moment, but because he was now beset with a feeling that he had let his members down by not being there for them during the previous evening and the subsequent early hours. Nobody was therefore more relieved than him when, just after 7.30, he opened the dining carriage door to discover every member had not only survived the night unscathed but each was in remarkably good spirits.

"Hewlett seems to think it's fancy dress," said Blackie upon noticing the Chef and the new Chairman making their discreet morning entrance. "Have you ever seen anything like him?"

"I think he looks good," said the Chairman while easing back his chair. "What is it exactly Hewlett?"

"It's called a smoking robe," replied Hewlett. "It's Mulberry silk. Father brought it back for me from London."

"What colour would you say that is?" said the Chairman.

"Lilac," replied Hewlett.

"It's very striking," said the Chairman.

"I know," said Hewlett. "My great Aunt Margareta

often used to say, 'a man wearing lilac is a man worthy of interest'."

"You've certainly gained my interest," said Blackie.

"What's with the eye glass thingamajig?" said the Chef.

"It's what's known as a monocle," said Hewlett.

"It looks like half a pair of glasses to me," said Blackie. "What's it for?"

"It's just a gimmick," said Alty.

"It's not a gimmick at all," said Hewlett after taking a seat next to the slowly rousing Professor. "I need it. I've got a lazy eye."

"A lazy eye!" said Larkin.

"It's what is commonly known as amblyopia," said the old man. "It's a disorder of sight due to the eye and the brain not functioning together. It's quite common actually. I must say though Richard-I've never known a monocle improve the condition."

"I know that Professor," said Hewlett while continuing to do his utmost to attract the Chef's attention. "But try not to say it out loud. Alty was partly right. It is a gimmick of sorts. It's a fashion accessory actually. I'm determined to dress in context with the great age of steam travel. I'm determined to stand out from the proles. But I do have a lazy eye though."

"Is there any part of you that isn't lazy?" said Alty.

"What's that meant to mean?" said Hewlett after turning his head almost a full circle.

"You know exactly what it's meant to mean," said Alty. "You've never done a hard day's graft in your life."

"How dare you!" said Hewlett.

"It's true," said Alty. "You have butlers and man servants to do your work."

"He probably doesn't even have to wipe his own backside," said Larkin.

"I do, as a matter of fact" said Hewlett. "I've been wiping my own bottom since I was ten."

"Ten!" said Larkin.

"That's right," said Hewlett. "So don't you dare

suggest otherwise. And regarding work-I've worked.
I've worked damn hard. I used to fag for Ginger
Morston while residing at the prestigious Tinkerhorn
Boarding School. He was one tough taskmaster was old
Ginger. If the fags didn't get his tucker to him on time,
he'd drop their shorts and cane their bottoms without a
by your leave."
"And did this Ginger Morston bugger you senseless on
occasions when you stepped out of line?" said
Woodhouse immediately upon entering the dining
carriage, closely followed by Tommy Mac and a
noticeably suspicious looking Hamill.
"No he did not," said Hewlett. "Buggering was
administered very rarely. Ginger was hard but fair. You
might be surprised to know, he's now a well respected
Conservative party front bencher?"
"It doesn't surprise me one bit," said Woodhouse. "By
the way-what's with the purple maxi dress?"
"I was wondering that," said Hamill.
"It's not a dress," said Hewlett. "It's a Sulka and Co
smoking jacket robe. And it's lilac not purple. It
probably cost more than you three earn in a month."
"It probably did," said Woodhouse. "But it's not a look
I'd choose to adopt."
"Is that because you consider yourself something of a
style icon?" said Hewlett.
"I suppose it is," said Woodhouse before turning to
view himself in one of the full length wall mirrors.
"Would you like to explain that particular look to me,"
said "Hewlett. "Because, for the life of me, I'm at a loss
to make sense of it."
"I like to call it 'the first morning of my holiday look',"
said Woodhouse.
"I'd prefer to call it a fashion project gone badly wrong,"
said Hewlett.
"Why's that?" said Woodhouse while proceeding to
suck his enormous stomach in and then out.
"I'd have thought that was obvious," said Hewlett. "For
goodness sake...take a look at yourself man. That t shirt

is far too tight for you. I'm surprised you're still able to breathe. And I don't even want to start on your briefs."

"What's wrong with me briefs?" said Woodhouse.

"What's wrong with them!" said Hewlett. "Maybe you need to see them from our perspective."

"What the hell's wrong with them?" said Woodhouse before raising his shirt to reveal an enormous buttock cleavage.

"Everything," said Hewlett. "They're wholly inadequate. They're far too tight for a man of your immense proportion. They hardly cover your bottom."

"That's today's style," said Woodhouse. "Everyone's wearing things with holes and rips in. These days, you're encouraged to show a bit of flesh."

"A bit of flesh!" said Hewlett. "For pity's sake. My family own a chain of quality high street butchers. And there's more flesh on view here than I've seen for the last 12 bloody months."

"Just hold on there Hewlett!" said Woodhouse after taking his seat. "If you're not careful, you're going to offend me. The problem with you is-you're not up with the times lad. You're a prude. You're a dinosaur. Nobody else seems to be complaining about my outfit."

"That's because everybody's either speechless or they've run to the toilet to throw up," said Biddo. "I actually think you look a mess too. And I've never been accused of being a prude. And, to be honest, I don't think you should be allowed in the dining room looking like that."

"Why the hell not?" said Woodhouse.

"Because you shouldn't," said Biddo. "This is where people come to eat. You're going to put them off their food."

"That's alright," said Woodhouse. "That means there'll be more for me. I don't know what all the fuss is about. I really don't."

"I'm not making a fuss," said Biddo. "I'm making a point. I just don't think it's right for a grown man to show his bare bottom in public. Especially a bare

[230]

bottom that's as enormous as yours. Bloody hell! People could fall into that and never be seen again. Right now, I'm considering dropping a penny into it and making a wish. Where's your dignity Woodhouse?"

"I lost that somewhere between my fifth and sixth divorces," said Woodhouse before raising his right butt cheek and breaking wind loudly. "Now leave me alone-I'm about to do what I do best. Where's that bone idle Chef? I hope he doesn't burn the toast again."

"He's cooking you all a full English breakfast," said the Chairman.

"What!" said Woodhouse. "Was that positive news I've just heard?"

"I wouldn't get your hopes up Woody," said Hamill. "We were the last to arrive. It'll probably be Easter before we get served."

"You can have yours first if you want," said the Chef after popping his head through the serving hatch. "Will it be the vegetarian version for you Woody?"

"Don't be bloody stupid," said Woodhouse. "Just load my plate up until it's on the verge of cracking under the weight of calories."

"Very well," said the Chef. "Yours will be ready in about five minutes. By the way lads-there are three pots of tea ready here."

"And three pots of tea that aren't going to pour themselves," said Hamill.

"I'll do the honours," said Matthews.

"I should think so too," said Woodhouse. "By the way-what was going on in the fourth corridor earlier?"

"There'd been an accident," said Steadman.

"Involving who?" said Woodhouse.

"The old boy," said Steadman.

"It was nothing," said the Professor while returning from the kitchen with a glass of iced water. "I just stumbled, that's all."

"You stumbled!" said the Club Secretary.

"That's not entirely true Hilly," said Steadman. "Our poor old buddy fainted."

[231]

"Oh dear!" said the Chairman.

"I'm fine," replied the old man. "It was just another of my episodes. I'm an old man. To use golfing parlance-it's probably par for the course for a man of my advanced years."

"Do you feel alright now?" said Steadman.

"I'm a little better thank you," said the old man. "And I really do appreciate your concern."

"Don't mention it," said Steadman. "But for God's sake, don't go making a habit of blacking out. My heart won't take it."

"Why's that?" said Hamill. "Have you and the old boy got something going?"

"Don't be ridiculous," said Steadman.

"He's concerned I might snuff it," said the Professor. "And if I die before you and your friends are rescued, there'll be nobody to administer the sedative. That's right isn't it Mr Swann?"

"It is yes," said a sheepish looking Steadman.

"What's to stop one of us administering the stuff?" said Larkin.

"You wouldn't know how," said the old man.

"Why not?" said Larkin.

"It has to be mixed in a very particular way," said the Professor.

"Well, that's alright," said Blackie. "Just show us how to mix it."

"And then what?" said the old man.

"We'll all sleep a lot easier for one thing," said Steadman.

"But I won't sleep any easier," said the Professor.

"Why not?" said Larkin.

"Because you won't need me then," said the old man. "And once you don't need me, there's every possibility you'll start treating me very differently."

"What makes you think that?" said Larkin.

"Let's call it intuition," said the Professor.

"You can call it what you like," said Larkin. "But I think you're wrong Professor. Regardless what happens,

we're still going to need you. You're the one with all
the background knowledge regarding the disease. You're
the only one that's seen the effects of the disease at close
quarters."

"That's right," said Alty. "You're our go to man
Professor. Our only go to man for that matter. You're
the only one capable of talking the next sufferer through
the various stages of the illness."

"Nobody's going to turn on you," said the Club
Secretary. "I can guarantee it. We already owe you a
huge debt of gratitude for what you've done for us so
far."

"That's right," said Steadman. "You've already gained
our lifelong respect Professor. Trust me for God's sake-
you're the last person aboard this train that's going to
find themselves surplus to requirements."

"That's very nice of you to say so," said the old man.
"And very succinctly put too. I really appreciate it. But
I'm afraid I can't divulge the formula. That'd be stupid
of me. I'd be leaving myself wide open. I could end up
going the same ominous way as your Health and Safety
Officer."

"But that won't happen," said Steadman. "We didn't
harm Eddie. Many of us liked and respected the man.
You seem to have got us all wrong Professor. We're
good people. We're decent upstanding people."

"Are you?" said the Professor.

"We like to think so," said Steadman.

"Well answer me this then," said the old man. "Do
decent upstanding people turn on each other at the first
sign of trouble?"

"We haven't turned on each other," said Steadman.
"We've had some minor disagreements, that's all."

"For goodness sake-you've got a long standing member
of your club locked up in one of the sleeping carriages
for his own safety," said the Professor. "Now he can't
go anywhere without an escort. What does that tell you?
And furthermore, you've even got people questioning
your new Chairman's ability to lead. Just try to imagine

[233]

what it'll be like on this train if things continue to deteriorate over the next few days. You lot are already close to full blown anarchy. But even so, you still have and will continue to have, one significant advantage over me."

"What's that?" said Steadman.

"You have a certain numerical security," said the old man.

"Security!" said Alty. "I've never felt so insecure in my life."

"Me neither," said Blackie.

"You've already broken into very definite factions," said the Professor. "You might want to call them gangs. It doesn't really matter what you call them. What does matter is this-from now on, you will look to protect each of your fellow gang members. Little old me, on the other hand-I'm a part of no faction or gang. I'm a virtual outsider, so to speak. I've got nobody to watch my back."

"You're also a very old man Professor," said Steadman.

"And you've quickly gained the respect of all and sundry," said the Club Secretary.

"I think you'll find that's not entirely true," said the Professor. "I passed one of the sleeping carriages early last evening and heard myself being referred to as a 'senile old fool who should have been put down 10 years ago'."

"That's bang out or order," said Steadman.

"Do you know who said it?" said the Club Secretary.

"That's not important," said the old man. "What is important is this-I'm going to hang on to my little secret for at least the time being. It'd be madness not to, under the circumstances."

"I don't know what you're worrying about Steadman," said Tommy Mac. "If it comes to the crunch, I'll just confiscate the old boy's bag. There's bound to be one clever dick amongst us who'll be able to come up with something close to the formula."

"You're welcome to try by all means," said the

Professor. "I'll even tell you where I've hidden my bag so you don't feel it necessary to break the lock. But you're going to need a human guinea pig. And he's going to have to be a complete idiot, an audacious gambler or a very brave man."

"Why's that?" said Tommy Mac.

"Because if you get the mixture wrong, your chosen guinea pig will end up either in a permanent vegetative state, clinically insane or as dead as the proverbial dodo," said the old man.

"That's nice!" said Steadman.

"It's not nice at all, I can assure you," said the old man. "It's anything but nice. I recall a situation when I was stationed in a poverty stricken town called Lurin on the outskirts of Lima. I'd been treating an extremely pleasant thirty two year old shepherd called Basilio who'd recently been diagnosed with the very same disease that so cruelly took your previous Chairman's life. The disease that by now, you are all quite familiar with."

"Only too familiar with," said Blackie.

"Anyway," said the Professor. "I'd been called out to deal with an emergency which had taken place about 30 miles from where I'd been practising. There'd been an explosion in an old copper mine and a large number of native workers had been overcome by poisonous gases. The journey was through dense, almost impenetrable forest and the roads were often unidentifiable. Then, to confound our miserable situation further, the rain came bucketing down. And by Jove gentlemen, when it rains in that particular part of Peru, it really rains. We ended up getting stuck and had to spend an extremely uncomfortable night in our little makeshift ambulance. That's the reason the tragedy occurred."

"What tragedy?" said Alty.

"The tragedy that befell poor Basilio," said the old man. "You see-I'd expected to be back at the hospital the same evening. That would have given me plenty of time to mix another batch of the formula."

[235]

"Wasn't there anybody else capable of mixing the stuff?" said Blackie.

"Only one other person knew how," said the Professor. "My number two Eduardo. He knew the formula like the back of his hand. But unfortunately, I'd taken him with me without thinking."

"Oh dear!" said Blackie.

"What happened?" said Steadman.

"The story goes that, as the evening went on, Basilio's condition got worse and worse," said the old man. "He was almost climbing the walls apparently."

"But there must have been somebody back at the hospital with a bit of nous?" said Blackie.

"There was yes," said the old man. "My trainee Lorenzo. But he was just an 18 year old kid. He was less than three months into his internship."

"That's not good," said Blackie.

"So what happened?" said Steadman.

"He did the only thing he could do under the circumstances," said the Professor.

"What was that?" said Steadman.

"He tried to mix the sedative from memory," said the old man.

"What happened?" said Steadman.

"Something I can only describe as calamitous," said the old man while shifting uneasily in his chair.

"How calamitous exactly?" said Blackie.

"He mixed the sedative spectacularly wrong," said the Professor. "He actually ended up exacerbating Basilio's condition."

"Did he end up going insane like our old Chairman?" said Blackie.

"He went irrevocably insane," said the old man. "About as insane as any individual can become. In the early hours of the morning, while the aforementioned Lorenzo and the night duty nurse were on the other side of the building attending to another patient who'd suffered a seizure, he tore off his shirt, ripped the flesh from his chest with his fingernails and broke into his thoracic cage."

"His what?" said Larkin.

"His thoracic cage," said the old man. "His rib cage."

"Bloody hell!" said Larkin.

"Hold on Professor," said Blackie. "Let me get this straight. Are you saying the man tore open his own chest with his bare hands?"

"That's exactly what I'm saying," said the old man.

"And then he proceeded to break his own ribs one by one?"

"My God!" said Steadman.

"But why?" said Blackie. "Why would he do that?"

"Because he was ornithophobic," said the old man.

"He was what?" said Larkin.

"Ornithophobic," said the Professor while making himself a little more comfortable. "He'd suffered from an irrational fear of birds since early childhood."

"Birds!" said Steadman. "You mean the type that fly?"

"Do you know of any other type?" said the old man.

"I suppose not," said Steadman.

"Are we talking about bald eagles and hawks and angry birds like that?" said Larkin.

"I'm talking about any type of bird," said the Professor. "Big ones and small ones. Birds of prey or harmless, brightly coloured budgerigars."

"But what have birds got to do with the man mutilating himself in such a terrible way?" said Alty. "Had one flown in through the hospital window or something? Did he think one was in the room?"

"He thought one was residing within his rib cage," said the old man.

"What!" said Alty.

"He'd become convinced there was a bird living in his rib cage," said the old man. "He'd earlier told the night nurse he could hear it chirping."

"Jesus Christ!" said Blackie.

"How bizarre is that?" said Larkin.

"It's sick," said Tommy Mac.

"Is that the sort of thing that could happen to one of us

Professor?" said the Club Secretary.

"Indubitably," said the old man.

"Nice!" said Alty.

"That's why I strongly recommend you don't waste any of the ingredients," said the Professor. "Right now, it's more valuable to you people than gold dust or diamonds. You're likely to need every last drop of the stuff."

"Can we take it you're immune to the disease Professor?" said Steadman.

"I am as a matter of fact," said the old man while staring intently at his cup. "I discovered that deeply satisfying fact some time ago. It was a massive relief, I can tell you."

"I bet it was," said Steadman.

"I think you're a bit out of order Professor," said Alty.

"Why would you say that young man?" said the Professor.

"Because you've just made our existence about a thousand times worse."

"He hasn't said he's not going to help," said the Club Secretary.

"With the greatest respect Hilly-he's not going to be able to help anyone if he has another one of his episodes and fails to recover," said Alty.

"He's alright," said the Club Secretary. "You heard the man. It was a just a fainting fit. He'd probably just rose from the toilet too quickly."

"I want my hands bandaged and tied," said Woodhouse.

"You want what?" said the Chairman.

"In the event of me displaying any symptoms of the disease, I want to be tied to my bed," said Woodhouse. "I don't want to go the same way as that poor bugger Basilio. I've always had a terrible fear of rats. I cornered a big fat one in the entry at the top of Jubilee Road once. It was as big as most domesticated cats. The bastard eyeballed me for about five minutes before it went for my throat. I only just managed to get out of its way. I've been terrified of the things ever since. I hate to think what it would be like to suddenly believe there's one inside my body."

"My father hates snakes," said Hewlett.

"Is that why he hates you?" said Hamill.

"My father worships the ground I hover above," said Hewlett.

"He told me you were the runt of the litter," said Hamill. "He said that when you were a toddler, he constantly anguished over taking you to the top of the garden and putting a spade over your head."

"Very funny," said Hewlett while once again trying to attract the attention of the beaver like Chef.

"I wasn't joking," said Hamill. "Your father's still got the old Spear and Jackson spade I lent him."

"Would you like to learn how to mix the sedative Richard?" said the Professor.

"Who me?" said Hewlett.

"That's correct," said the old man. "I think these men are right. They've already suffered far too much as it is. They need some sort of insurance."

"I'll gladly help," said Hewlett while topping up the old man's tea. "I think I'd make an excellent sorcerer's apprentice."

"Let's drink to it then," said the Professor.

"Oh shit!" said Tommy Mac.

"That's what I was about to say," said Woodhouse. "This isn't happening. This surely can't be happening. I'm now a dead man if I get that disease. I'm going to have rats running riot throughout my mid section. Goodbye gentlemen. It's been nice knowing you all."

"Why do you say that?" said the old man.

"Because your roommate and soon to be apprentice Hewlett hates me with a passion," said Woodhouse while proceeding to pace the floor. "Which means, if I go down with the disease, I'm just going to be left to suffer like that poor bloody sheep herder."

"Richard wouldn't do that," said the old man. "He's too well balanced and, as far as I'm concerned, is not only capable of being taught a concept, but more than capable of keeping what I divulge to him a secret. I think he'd have been Bletchley Park material had he been born a decade before the Second World War started. He'd make a marvellous spy."

"He'd make a better archery target," said Woodhouse.

"My word!" said the Professor. "You really do hate the chap don't you? Why is that?"

"Because he thinks he's so superior to everybody else," said Woodhouse.

"That's invariably because I am superior," said Hewlett.

"I think you might be making a big mistake Professor," said the Chef while serving Hamill's table.

"Why's that?" said the old man.

"Because Hewlett can't look after himself," said the Chef. "What if somebody tries to beat the secret out of him?"

"They can try all they like," said Hewlett. "Ginger Morston once had me roasted in front of the common room fire for two and a half hours to find out where my dorm mate Toby Lofthouse had hidden his almond muffins. It was sheer hell. Pure, unadulterated hell. But I didn't squeal. I didn't tell old Ginger anything. I ended up in the school infirmary for a month wrapped up like Tutankhamun, the boy king. I'll tell you this-people looked at me very differently from that day forward."

"Was that because from the rear you resembled some sort of scaly lizard?" said McShane.

"It was because I'd gained a massive amount of respect," said Hewlett.

"Well you'll never gain my respect," said Woodhouse. "You're a jumped up, privileged arsehole and you always will be. You'll never gain my respect if you live to be a thousand."

"And here's someone who'll never gain mine," said Hamill after watching an unusually self-satisfied looking Club Chairman enter the dining carriage and very deliberately drape his coat and scarf across the back of his chair.

For the next fifteen minutes or so, the Chairman did his utmost to look the epitome of efficiency. He

[240]

made a point of visiting each different faction to discuss things such as the need to maintain a high level of personal hygiene. He asked each of them in turn if they had slept well and whether they had been happy with what the Chef had provided. He gave them the latest weather update, reassurances regarding their valuables and advice as to how best to pass the time in order to relieve boredom and prevent fretting. He had also informed his members that, in order to keep an eye on them more effectively, he had decided to bring everybody as close to the dining carriage as possible. That meant that from then on in, only two of the sleeping carriages, the first and the second, the ones directly connected to the dining carriage, were to be occupied. It had not escaped his notice however, that for the first time since he had been handed the leadership position, nothing of what he had suggested had been challenged. At least not until the subject of safety had once again been raised.

"What's the situation with the outer doors?" said Woodhouse.

"Excellent," said the Chairman while slowly peeling off his gloves. "Everything's watertight. Every one of the ropes has held strong."

"That's good," said Larkin. "At least that's one less thing to worry about. Nice one Hulmey."

"I wouldn't sit back on your laurels just yet," said Hamill.

"Why's that?" said Larkin.

"Because I happen to know differently," said Hamill.

"What do you mean?" said Alty.

"You've just been lied to," said Hamill while gesturing towards the Chairman.

"What!" said Larkin.

"You've just been bare faced lied to," said Hamill.

"What are you talking about Hamill?" said the Chairman before taking a cup of tea from his brother and settling down on his familiar chair.

"I'm talking about you misleading your men," said

Hamill.

"I'd never do that," said the Chairman.

"That's right," said the Chef.

"Your brother's a liar," said Hamill. "He's a dirty rotten liar."

"Behave yourself Hamill," said the Club Secretary. "You've got no right to be accusing the man of something like that. At least not without justification."

"I've got plenty of justification," said Hamill.

"Let's have it then," said the Club Secretary. "But if you're wrong Hamill, you're almost certainly going to find yourself looking for a new club. I'll personally see to it. What's he meant to have lied about?"

"The ropes," said Hamill.

"The ropes!" said the Club Secretary. "What about the ropes?"

"They haven't been as effective as our Chairman's tried to make out," said Hamill.

"What do you mean?" said Larkin.

"Yes-what do you mean?" said the Club Secretary.

"I found one of the doors wide open," said Hamill.

"What!" said the Club Secretary. "What door? Where?"

"The third carriage door," said Hamill.

"The third!" said the Club Secretary. "Do you mean yours?"

"That's the one," said Hamill. "The outer door. The one you have to open to get on and off the train."

"You can't have done," said the Club Secretary. "When did you discover this?"

"Earlier this morning," said Hamill. "Before your mate did his so-called rigorous check on things. You see-I prefer to do my own safety checks. I think it's because I lack trust."

"You can trust me and Hulmey," said the Club Secretary. "We checked every single door."

"Every one?" said Hamill.

"Every last one," said the Club Secretary. "I started at the engine and Hulmey started at the rear. We met in the middle. That's right isn't it Hulmey?"

[242]

"It is yes," said the Chairman after a brief hesitation.
"It's not right at all," said Hamill while shaking his head
and approaching the Chairman. "You missed one. You
missed a very important one. You missed the third one
to be precise. Could that have been because it was my
door? Is that how much you hate me Hulmey? Didn't
the integrity of my door matter? Wasn't my safety of
any interest to you?"
"Behave yourself," said the Chef.
"You behave yourself," said Hamill. "I'm right."
"Is he Hulmey?" said the Club Secretary. "Is Hamill
right?"
"He could be," said the Chairman. "He could be right.
I'm not going to deny it. But it had nothing to do with
any bad blood between the two of us. I got distracted
momentarily."
"Distracted, my arse," said Hamill.
"It's true," said the Chairman.
"Distracted by what Hulmey?" said the Club Secretary.
"By some sort of commotion," said the Chairman.
"You're a liar," said Hamill.
"What sort of commotion?" said the Club Secretary.
"I heard a high pitched scream," said the Chairman.
"Bullshit!" said Hamill.
"What sort of high pitched scream?" said the Chef.
"Like a young woman in distress," said the Chairman.
"I felt I had no choice but to go and investigate."
"What a load of horse shit," said Hamill. "There are no
young women on board this train and you know it. There
might be one or two men on board who could easily pass
as women-but there are no actual women. You're lying.
Just admit it."
"He might not be," said an apologetic young Anthony.
"That's what I'm beginning to think," said Larkin.
"Why?" said Blackie.
"Because what our Chairman heard, might just have
been me," said young Anthony.
"Why you?" said a highly suspicious Kenny Biddo.
"Because we'd been arsing about in the showers," said

young Anthony.

"What do you mean 'arsing about'?" said an extremely stern looking Biddo before leaving his seat to confront his son.

"We'd been messing about," said Alty. "It's what's commonly known as having fun. Some of you want to try it some time."

"What form, did this fun take?" said the Chairman.

"Me and Larko filled a mop bucket with snow and freezing cold water and waited for Anthony to come out of the shower," replied Alty.

"Then we let him have it," said Larkin.

"The high pitched scream the Chairman heard was probably me," said Anthony. "Trust me-I would have liked to have sounded masculine. But it just came out that way."

"I bet it did," said Biddo. "I bet it did. And let me guess Anthony-you were stark naked when all those shenanigans were going on, weren't you?"

"Of course not," said Larkin. "He was wearing a white tuxedo and a Panama hat."

"I'd been taking a shower dad," said Anthony. "Wearing clothes isn't recommended."

"But showering in complete privacy is," said Biddo.

"Whatever," said Anthony.

"Thanks," said the Club Secretary. "Thanks a lot Anthony. That's cleared things up nicely. Are you satisfied now Hamill?"

"I'm not satisfied at all," said Hamill after returning to his chair.

"But you've just heard Hulmey's reasoning," said the Club Secretary.

"I couldn't care less about his reasoning," said Hamill. "He was still lying. He's just told his members that all the doors had been checked thoroughly. He said everything was 'watertight'..He's just put all these men's lives at risk by only doing half a fucking job. And if he'd have done his job properly, he'd have probably discovered something even more disturbing?"

[244]

"What's that?" said Blackie.

"The rope hadn't just come loose as I'd first suspected," said Hamill.

"What do you mean?" said Blackie.

"Someone had cut it," said Hamill.

"Cut it!" said the Club Secretary. "What do you mean 'cut it'?"

"It had been cut," said Hamill. "As with a sharp instrument. As with a knife or something similar."

"Are you sure?" said Alty.

"I'm absolutely positive," said Hamill.

"Nice," said Larkin. "How nice. That means those bastard creatures are somewhere on board the train again."

"And they can use tools," said Woodhouse.

"Oh, for fuck's sake," said Steadman before heading over to the door and placing his face against the lightly frosted panel.

"If that's the case, we're going to have to organise another full search of the train," said the Club Secretary.

"And we're going to have to do it sooner rather than later," said Blackie.

"Not necessarily," said Woodhouse. "Just reign in those horses lads. Let's just think about this for a moment."

"Think about what?" said Blackie.

"Think about how the ropes were tied," said Woodhouse.

"They were tied more than adequately," said the Club Secretary.

"I don't doubt it," said Woodhouse. "They probably were. But don't forget-they were tied inside the train."

"Which means what?" said Steadman.

"Which means, whoever cut that rope was already on board," said Woodhouse.

"Of course it does," said Blackie.

"Jesus Christ!" said Alty. "This is going from bad to worse."

"But we searched the train from top to bottom," said the

Club Secretary. "We searched every wardrobe, every nook and cranny and looked under every bed. Nothing could have evaded us. There was definitely nobody on board."

"Are you sure the rope had been cut Hamill?" said Blackie. Are you sure it hadn't just snapped under the strain? Who tied it? Who tied that door? Can anyone remember?"

"I did," said McShane.

"Well, there you are then," said the Club Secretary. "Charles Atlas tied the bloody thing. I'm surprised he didn't pull the door off its bloody hinges."

"That doesn't explain this," said Hamill after producing a small bread knife from his rear trouser pocket.

"Where did you find that?" said the Club Secretary.

"It was in the washroom adjacent to the third carriage," said Hamill.

"That's one of the kitchen knives isn't it?" said Steadman. "What do you think Chef? Is it one of the kitchen knives?"

"I don't know," said the Chef.

"You do fucking know," said Hamill.

"I don't," said the Chef. "Let me have a closer look."

"You don't need a closer look," said Hamill. "It's part of a set. It's from the kitchen isn't it?"

"It is yes," said the Chef with an obvious sense of reluctance.

"What's this all about Hamill?" said the Club Secretary. "You're not suggesting the Chef had anything to do with the rope being cut are you?"

"I'm not suggesting that at all," said Hamill. "But I'm certainly not going to rule the possibility out."

"It's preposterous," said the Chairman. "There's no logic in what you're saying. It just doesn't make any sense. I'm telling you Hamill-none of these men would have cut that rope. What would they have hoped to gain from it?"

"Satisfaction," said Hamill. "Or possibly a bit of pay back."

[246]

"Pay back!" said the Chairman. "Who exactly would be looking for pay back?"

"Alec Morris for one," said Hamill.

"Alec Morris!" said the Chairman.

"That's right," said Hamill. "He'd love nothing more than to see the likes of me or Woody shit our trousers."

"It's ridiculous," said the Chairman.

"He might have a point Hulmey," said the Club Secretary.

"He might," said the Chef.

"Maybe so but.....I don't know.....I'll go and talk to him," said the Chairman.

"You won't," said Hamill.

"I beg your pardon," said the Chairman.

"You're going to stay right where you are while me and the rest of your members conduct the next stage of this investigation," said Hamill. "You're going to sit right there on the naughty chair. You've been a bad boy Hulmey. You've lied to your members. You've put them at risk. That's unforgivable as far as I'm concerned. And *you* can take the seat next to him Hilly."

"I'll do nothing of the sort," said the Club Secretary. "You've got no jurisdiction here Hamill. I take my orders off the Chairman of this club and nobody else."

"The Chairman's going to be taking a short sabbatical," said Hamill before grabbing the Club Secretary by the throat and forcing him into his chair. "Now be nice while Woody goes and fetches the accused."

Woodhouse's exit had coincided with a ferocious blast of wind that had thundered without warning into the window side of the badly exposed train. A gust so powerful that, for just over a minute, the train had rocked like a baby's cradle and nobody had dared to move a muscle or utter a single word for fear of being the one that shattered the equilibrium. The big man's return was to change that dynamic however and not just because the rocking had ceased and the men had begun to regain some of their lost composure-it was because of the retched condition of his unfortunate prisoner.

[247]

"What the hell's been going on Woody?" said the Chairman. "What happened to him?"

"He fell," said Woodhouse after slamming the barely conscious Morris into a chair near the centre of the room.

"Rubbish!" said the Club Secretary. "Look at the state of him. He's been given a good hiding."

"Don't be so bad minded," said Woodhouse. "He fell, I'm telling you. Didn't you hear the wind? Didn't you feel that shudder? I thought we were about to plummet to our deaths. I just about managed to stay on my feet myself. Poor Morris got the worst of it. He flew from one end of the room to the other like a trapeze artist. I've never seen anything like it. He even landed on his two feet. That's right isn't it mate?"

"Fuck you," spluttered Morris without raising his head.

"This is an outrage," said the Club Secretary. "That man requires immediate first aid."

"And he'll get immediate first aid," said Hamill. "Just as soon as his trial's over."

"That's not what I'd consider immediate," said the Chef.

"It's immediate enough for me," said Hamill. "So the sooner you and your buddies stop fussing, the better."

"This isn't a trial, it's a lynching," said the Club Secretary. "You've already made up your mind he's guilty."

"That's because he is guilty," said Hamill. "Just about every man and his dog knows he's guilty."

"And I do too," said the Chairman. "So why don't we discuss what we're going to do with him when we get home? Let's talk about it again when we're all a bit less pumped up. Most importantly-let's do it the civilized and lawful way. For goodness sake Hamill. He's history as far as his club membership's concerned. He's pulled his very last stunt. What more do you want?"

"I want to be sure he fully appreciates the gravity of our situation," said Hamill before drawing over his chair to sit opposite the accused. "I want him to realise the

damage he's caused. Fucking hell Hulmey. I heard
grown men sobbing into their pillows like frightened
children last night. Men who are renowned hard cases, I
might add. I've watched atheists get on their knees and
pray to a God they've always denied the existence of.
I've never known lavatory pans to be used so much in
my life. The men are shitting themselves 24 hours a
day. Their systems can't cope. They are fucking
terrified. But they're not just terrified of monsters.
They'll deal with monsters if they have to. They're not
just terrified of falling foul of that horrendous disease
that makes birds appear in your rib cage either. They'll
somehow cope with that eventuality if the need arises.
They're terrified because they're starting to believe
they'll never see their loved ones again. And there's
only one person to blame for that. One mindless idiot.
The one that started the fucking train in the first place.".
"Well said," said Woodhouse.
"Well said indeed," said McShane.
"I'm afraid he's right Hulmey," said Blackie after
taking a seat next to the Chairman.
"I know he is," said the Chairman. "Nobody knows that
better than me. Jesus Christ Blackie-Morris has made
my job a thousand times harder than it ever should have
been. But I can't abandon him. I can't just hang him out
to dry."
"I'm not suggesting you hang him out to dry," said
Blackie. "Let's just see what Hamill's got in mind by
way of a suitable punishment. Let's be honest, he's not
going to hang, draw and quarter him is he?"
"Blackie's right," said the Club Secretary. "Let's open
the floor to Hamill. Let's give him his fifteen minutes of
fame. This business has dragged on far too long
already."
"That's right," said Blackie. "Let's get it over with and
set about getting through the rest of the bloody day."
"Do I get a say?" said Morris after raising his head to
reveal the gruesome extent of his recent beating.
"Of course you do," said the Club Secretary.

"As long as it's in the form of an apology," said Woodhouse.

"It's not actually," said Morris. "Saying sorry is the last thing I'm going to do."

"Then I'd shut the fuck up if I was you," said Blackie.

"What do you want?" said the Club Secretary.

"I want to tell a few people some home truths," said Morris.

"I strongly recommend you don't do that," said the Chef.

"And I for one, forbid you to," said the Chairman.

"Let him," said Woodhouse while settling down in his chair. "Let the lad have his say. This is the age when free speech should be encouraged. I'd certainly be interested to hear what he's got to say-I don't know about anyone else. What is it Morris? What's on your mind lad?"

"A lot of things," said Morris. "My club membership for one thing."

"What club membership would that be?" said Woodhouse. "You've no longer got club membership. You've forfeited the right to membership."

"That's fine," said Morris. "I couldn't be more pleased, to tell you the truth. I'd have resigned anyway. This club's been going to the dogs for years. It's been going to the dogs since we started allowing thugs and reprobates to become members."

"Just drop this will you Morris," said the increasingly wary Chef. "Think for once in your life Alec. You're in no position to be firing bullets at people."

"I agree," said the Club Secretary.

"Leave him alone," said Hamill. "He's not a child-let him express himself."

"That's right," said Woodhouse. "The boy's started, so let him finish."

"For God's sake, call it quits while you're still breathing Morris," said the Club Secretary.

"Never mind, call it quits," said Hamill. "I want to know who these thugs and reprobates he was referring to are. Come on Morris-don't be shy. Nobody's going to bite. Name names."

"Do you think I'm stupid?" said Morris. "Do you think I'm out of my mind? What I am prepared to say is this. This isn't the club that I originally joined. That was a great club. That was the best club ever."

"Until what?" said Woodhouse.

"Until me, you and Tommy Mac arrived," said Hamill after taking Morris by the right ear. "I think that's what he's trying to say. That's right isn't it Morris?"

"I've said all I'm saying," said a grimacing Morris while slowly being lowered to his knees.

"He's said enough," said the Chef. "This is madness lads. This is sheer madness."

"Madness!" said Hamill. "You're one to talk about madness aren't you Chef. Don't forget, you're still the number one suspect in a serious crime yourself."

"Why am I?" said the Chef.

"It was your knife that was found in the third carriage washroom," said Hamill.

"It was one of the kitchen knives," said the Club Secretary. "One of a set of twenty four if I've got my sums right. We've all had access to the kitchen since the train pulled out. Any one of us could have taken that knife.".

"Maybe so," said Hamill. "But I saw the Chef's face when he was examining it. There was guilt written all over it. He turned the colour of boiled shite and was visibly shaking."

"I noticed that too," said Woodhouse.

"Everyone must have noticed it," said Hamill.

"Everyone except me," said Morris.

"You weren't there," said Woodhouse.

"I was there when the rope was cut," said Morris.

"You were under arrest," said the Chairman.

"I was there," said Morris.

"Who did it?" said Hamill.

"Wouldn't you like to know?" said Morris.

"Who cut the rope Morris?" said Hamill.

[251]

"What if I told you it was Woodhouse?" said Morris.
"I'd punch you in the face," said Hamill.
"What if I told you it was McShane?" said Morris.
"I'd punch you harder in the face," said Hamill.
"What if I told you it was me?" said Morris.
"I'd shake your hand firmly and tell you that you're a very brave boy," said Hamill.
"Is it true?" said the Club Secretary. "Is it true Morris? Did you cut the rope?"
"I most certainly did," said Morris.
"Jesus Christ!" said the Club Secretary.
"What the hell for?" said the Chairman.
"Because I wanted to give Hamill and his cronies an uncomfortable night," said Morris. "Something similar to the terrifying nights they'd been giving me."
"Oh Christ!" said the Chairman.
"Is that right?" said a smiling Hamill after placing the sole of his shoe upon Morris's neck. "Are you going to tell us how you managed to get hold of the knife?"
"Never," said the grimacing Morris.
"I've already explained that," said the Club Secretary. "He must have taken it from the kitchen. We've all had access to the kitchen at some time or other."
"Morris hasn't" said Hamill. "Morris hasn't been allowed in here."
"Who gave you the knife Morris?" said Woodhouse.
"Is it that important?" said the Club Secretary.
"You shut your mouth," said Hamill. "Who was it Morris? Was it my mate Hulmey?"
"Don't be ridiculous," said the Club Secretary.
"I'm not being ridiculous," said Hamill.
"And I say you are," said the Club Secretary. "Kenny Hulme wouldn't knowingly arm somebody."
"I wouldn't have thought so either," said Steadman.
"Nor me," said Blackie.
"It was me," said the Chef.
"You?" said Blackie.
"I felt I had to," said the Chef. "Hamill and his crew had been persecuting the poor bugger. They'd been

[252]

threatening to strip him naked and throw him off the bridge. He'd been out of his mind with worry. I knew he was never going to use the knife as a weapon. He's not the type. He's a 36 carat nuisance but he'd never stab anyone. It was just to wave at his tormentors in the hope they'd back off and leave him alone."

"I can't believe it," said the Chairman. "I just can't believe it. I thought we had Morris under constant watch."

"It appears you were wrong," said Hamill.

"I wouldn't go blaming yourself Hulmey," said the Club Secretary. "I don't think it's possible to control Morris. It's like trying to hold on to a soaking wet bar of soap during a monsoon. But at least his last revelation's brought a welcome end to the inquisition."

"Not for me it hasn't," said Hamill. "I've got at least one more question I want answering. A very important one too."

"Fire away," said the Club Secretary. "Who's the question to?"

"The occupants of carriage one," said Hamill before rising to his feet and clasping his hands behind his back. "Minus the disgraced Alec Morris, that is."

What is it you want to know? know?" said the Chef.

"I want to know if Morris was aware of the existence of the two creatures that were seen in the vicinity of the train," said Hamill.

"Why do you want to know that?" said the Chairman.

"You'll find out shortly," said Hamill. "Just answer the question. Take your time. It's a simple enough question. Was Morris aware of those two dangerous creatures?"

"I'm not sure," said the Chairman. "I would have thought so."

"Think hard Mr Chairman," said Hamill. "This is very important. Did he know about those creatures?"

"I can't say for certain," said the Chairman. "I know I didn't tell him."

"I didn't either," said the Chef.

[253]

"What about you Hilly," said Hamill. "Did you tell him about the creatures?"

"Not as far as I remember," said the Club Secretary. "I was very sceptical about the entire business. I still am to be honest."

"Could anyone else have told him?" said Hamill.

"I don't think so," said the Chairman. "What difference does it make anyway?"

"A hell of a lot of difference," said Hamill. "Because if Morris knew there were dangerous creatures lurking around the train, it makes his crime all the worse."

"Why does it?" said Steadman.

"Because, in cutting that rope, he's as good as invited those creatures on board," said Hamill. "He's as good as said, "there you go nasty monkey men-have a free pop at the helpless occupants of carriage three'."

"Oh Christ yes!" said Steadman.

"Jesus!" said the Club Secretary.

"Did you know about the creatures Morris?" said Woodhouse.

"Of course not," said the Chef.

"He's not talking to you," said Hamill before lashing out with his right arm and sending the Chef hurtling into the full length mirror.

"You bastard," said the Chairman after quickly racing to his injured brother's side. "You fucking horrible bastard."

"Sticks and stones," said Hamill. "Sticks and stones will break my bones, but names will never hurt me. It's remarkable this. I can count on the fingers of my right hand the number of people who'd stick their necks out for me if I was in trouble. So why in God's name, do so many people want to protect an idiot who has caused them so much distress?"

"Because I'm a decent man," said Morris. "And to prove it, I'll tell you the truth. But you've got to promise you'll stop hurting my friends."

"I'll make no bargains with you," said Hamill.

"Then I won't disclose what I know," said Morris.

[254]

"Alright," said Hamill after some thought. "It's a deal."

"What is it you know Morris?" said Woodhouse.

"I knew about the existence of the hairy creatures," said Morris. "I've known for some time. But nobody told me. I overheard someone talking about them when I was having a dump. Don't forget-those washroom walls are paper thin."

"Do you realise you could have got me and my mates killed?" said Hamill.

"I do now," said Morris.

"If you had the chance to do it again, would you?" said Woodhouse.

"Don't answer that Alec," said the Club Secretary upon returning from the kitchen with a cold compress. "You've already told them what they wanted to know."

"I can't tell you how disappointed I am Alec," said the Chairman. "You've excelled yourself this time. .I'm almost lost for words. You do realise your club days are over for good?"

"I couldn't give a fuck about my club days," said Morris.

"Is that you being remorseful?" said Woodhouse.

"Go to hell," said Morris.

"You need to get back to our room pronto," said the Chairman.

"I'll take him," said the Club Secretary.

"I don't think so," said Hamill before taking the still semiconscious Morris by the scruff of the neck and dangling him like a puppet. "That would represent easy time. He's coming for a little walk with me and my friends."

"What are you going to do to him?" said Steadman. "You're not going to throw him off the bridge are you?"

"I'm going to educate him," said Hamill before handing his prisoner to the eager McShane. "I'm going to educate him in the same primitive and tried and tested way you educate a naughty dog."

"We could be rescued tomorrow Hamill," said the Chairman. "And if we are, you're going to have to explain that man's cuts and bruises to the authorities."

"That's fine," said Hamill while heading to the door. "I'll just tell the police that he sustained his injuries while trying to make good his escape."

"But they're going to want to know why he was trying to escape in the first place," said the Chairman.

"I know," said Hamill. "And I intend telling them the truth, the whole truth and nothing but the truth."

"Which is what?" said the Chairman.

"That the man's a notorious thief," said Hamill.

"But he's not a thief," said the Chairman.

"Not a thief!" scoffed Hamill. "Bloody hell Hulmey- A few days ago, he stole a brand new £5,000,000 state of the art steam train from a newly built London station. How is that not theft?"

CHAPTER TWELVE
REPERCUSSIONS

Because Hamill had threatened to hand out more of the same to any passengers who tried to intervene as he and his men dragged the terrified and hysterical Morris off to one of the far carriages, nobody had been close enough to witness the beating. They *had* heard the prisoner's impassioned screams and frantic appeals for mercy however. They had heard those heart rending cries echoing through the empty corridors for just over thirty haunting minutes. It had left many of the remaining occupants of the dining carriage feeling a terrible sense of guilt and others harbouring enormous shame and it therefore wasn't long before fingers were being pointed, voices were becoming raised and accusations were being meted out almost indiscriminately.

"There wasn't a thing we could have done," said the Chef after slamming his pile of dirty dishes onto the sink drainer and tearing off his apron.

"The Chef's right," said the Club Secretary. "Hamill was determined to carry out the punishment. And nothing was going to stop him."

"And some might say his action was fully justified," said Alty.

"What do you mean?" said the Chairman.

"Alec put those three men's lives in danger," said Alty. "If he'd have done that to me, I'd have wanted him punished too."

"I have to agree," said Larkin.

"But that's not the way the club does things," said the Chairman. "We can't allow an unruly mob to make important decisions like that."

"I'm going to see to it he's prosecuted," said Steadman.

"For what?" said the Chairman.

"For assault," said Steadman. "For grievous bodily harm. For actual bodily harm. For wounding with intent. Any one of those. Any two of them if necessary."

"Hamill won't have taken part in the beating," said the Chairman. "He's far too clever and calculating to do something like that."

"He'll have just stood by and watched the show," said the Chef.

"I've never heard screams like that in my life," said Blackie. "That's going to haunt me. That's going to haunt me for a very long time."

"What if they've killed him," said young Anthony.

"They won't have done that," said Steadman.

"Why did his screams and pleas for help suddenly stop then?" said young Anthony.

"Because the beating must have stopped," said the Chef.

"Or he could have lost consciousness," said the Club Secretary.

"Or he might have reached his pain threshold," said the Professor.

"What does that mean?" said young Anthony.

"It means he'd reached the maximum amount of pain he could tolerate," said the old man. "At that point, people have been known to black out."

"Well let's hope that was the case," said the Chairman.

"Amen," said Steadman.

"Do *you* think he's dead Hulmey?" said Anthony.

"I'm not going to rule the possibly out until I see him sitting up and hurling abuse," said the Chairman.

"Do you think they'll let us see him?" said Larkin.

"I don't know," said the Chairman. "I suppose it depends what state he's in."

"I suggest we keep our heads down until we're rescued," said the Chef.

"I do too," said Blackie. "I think we should do everything in our power to avoid antagonising them."

"Well in the meantime, I'm going to do everything in my power to make us all a nice cup of tea," said the Chef "Would anybody like a drop of Scotch in theirs?"

"We all would," said the Chairman before settling back down and opening his ledger. "And make them large measures Chef."

[258]

In the meantime, Hamill, Woodhouse and Tommy Mac were just returning to their room and it was immediately clear each was beginning to appreciate the seriousness and magnitude of what had recently taken place

"Bloody hell!" said Woodhouse after thrusting out his trembling arms. "Look at the state of me. I can't stop shaking. I thought he was dead. I thought we'd killed him."

"I think he was dead at one point," said McShane.

"Keep your voices down," said Hamill. "And get a fucking grip. He's breathing. isn't he."

"I know he is," said Woody. "But for how long Hamill?"

"He'll be fine," said Hamill. "Morris is a fit lad. He cycles a thousand miles a week."

"He's going to die Hamill," said Woodhouse. "I felt his cheekbone shatter under my fist."

"The bastard got what he deserved as far as I'm concerned," said Hamill. "Bloody hell Woody. If we'd have been murdered by those creatures, your nine kids would be fatherless. They might have had to be taken into care."

"No they wouldn't," said Woodhouse. "Me missus would have looked after them. There isn't a better mother in the world than that woman."

"What if she was to suffer a nervous breakdown due to her loss," said Hamill. "She wouldn't necessarily cope then. You did nothing wrong Woody."

"I've left a man hanging onto life by the merest thread," said Woodhouse.

"Rubbish!" said Hamill. "You responded angrily because an idiot deliberately left you vulnerable to a ferocious attack. You were well within your rights to lash out Woody. You could be minus a leg, an arm or even an eye today. Even the most placid of individuals would have snapped under those circumstances."

"Hulmey's going to demand I hand myself into the police," said Woodhouse.

"Fuck Hulmey!" said Hamill. "Hulmey's got his own troubles to worry about. Don't forget-he was the one that failed to report the severed rope."

"He's going to have me prosecuted," said Woodhouse. "I know it. I just know it."

"I could have a quiet word in his ear if you'd like," said McShane.

"And say what exactly?" said Hamill.

"I'll threaten to blow him away unless he keeps quiet," said Tommy Mac,

"Blow him away!" said Hamill. "What do you mean, 'blow him away'?"

"He's got a gun," said Woodhouse.

"A gun!" said Hamill.

"He's got an old Colt 45," said Woodhouse.

"A what?" said the bewildered Hamill.

"I've got an old Colt 45," said Tommy while pointing towards his holdall.

"How come?" said Hamill. "How come Tommy? How the hell have you got a gun? You're not a gangster. You're not a fucking drug dealer. You're a master builder. What are you doing with a gun?"

"I needed one," said McShane.

"What for?" said Hamill. "Have you got yourself into a spot of bother?"

"It's nothing like that," said Tommy. "I got asked to start the races at my granddaughter's sports day. I'd done it the year before but I didn't like it.

"Why's that?" said Hamill.

"The bastard kids were so noisy," said Tommy. "They couldn't hear my instructions. It was a nightmare. Every race bar one was a false start and, as a result, the last race ended up taking place in pitch fucking darkness. I think it was the one mile dash. One of the kids nearly drowned if I remember right."

"Why was that?" said Hamill.

"He took a wrong turn down Edge Lane and ended up in the canal," said Tommy. "I did try to buy a proper starting pistol but none of the sports shops were stocking

them because of new gun legislation. So I put the word
out on the street and ended up buying an old Colt 45 and
half a dozen boxes of ammunition for £50."
"Not for the first time, words fail me," said Hamill.
"Words fucking well fail me. But why you Tommy?
Why would they want you to officiate? You've no
celebrity status. You're not the Mayor of Crosby or Mo
Farah."
"He's a celebrity at that school," said Woodhouse. "At
least a sort of one."
"Why is he?" said Hamill.
"I'd been taken on by Bolton Wanderers when I was
15," said McShane. "They'd offered me schoolboy
terms. The school made a big thing of it. It was in all the
local papers. I was hailed as the next Nat Lofthouse. I
actually made 8 appearances as a substitute for the
reserve side. I once partnered Frank Worthington in
attack when he was coming back from injury. I was the
nearest thing to a celebrity our shit hole of a school ever
had. The only well known people from our school until
then had been an armed robber and a one armed boxer."
"He was a brilliant player," said Woodhouse. "He used
to run rings around me."
"He must have had some stamina then," said Hamill. "Is
this true Tommy? Did you really start your old school
sports day races with a Colt 45?"
"I did yes," said McShane.
"With a Colt 45, loaded with live ammunition?" said
Hamill.
"It's all I could get hold of," said McShane. "It was
either that or use our Frank's AK-47."
"What's your Frank doing with an AK-47?" said
Hamill.
"He's in the army," said McShane. "He sometimes
brings his rifle home to get extra practice. He's risen
through the ranks in no time at all. He's a corporal now."
"God give me strength!" said Hamill.
"I only had to fire the gun into the air for fuck's sake,"
said McShane. "Although I do admit, I was tempted to

[261]

blow this particular little red headed fucker's brains out."
"What little red headed fucker?" said Hamill.
"This Year 10 kid I caught cheating during the egg and spoon race," said McShane. "He was one hard faced little fucker. I caught him using Superglue. He cheated in the sack race too. He tested my patience to the limit that day, I can tell you."
"But you didn't kill him did you Tommy?" said Hamill. "Please tell me you didn't kill him."
"Of course I didn't kill him," said McShane. "I just knocked the little cunt out when nobody was looking. I can't stand cheats."
"Oh for Christ's sake!" said Hamill. "That must have taken some explaining."
"I told his teacher he'd had an asthma attack," said McShane. "The kid was as tough as old boots. He came round after a while and couldn't remember a thing. But I reckon he'll think twice before he cheats again. And I'll do a job on the new Chairman if you want me to. Just give me the word and I'll make sure he keeps his big mouth shut regarding the Morris incident."
"I don't think so," said Hamill while trying to gauge his friend's level of seriousness. "Listen to me Tommy-and listen to me very carefully-Hulmey must never find out you've got a gun. If he finds out you've got a gun, we're always going to be considered the bad guys. Have I made myself clear?"
"As clear as daylight," said McShane.
"But you have given me an idea though," said Hamill.
"Are you going to share it with us?" said Woody.
"I don't think I'm going to need to," said Hamill. "Just follow my lead. Improvise if necessary. The name of the game is 'deflection'. We're going to have to try to win people over. And by the way lads-get those blood drenched clothes off and dump them over the side of the bridge.""They're sopping wet," said Woodhouse.
"They're beginning to stink," said McShane.
"They're incriminating evidence," said Hamill.

###

By late afternoon, Kenny Biddo had been added to the small but growing list of people who had been found lying on the floor of a washroom in a less than conscious state. This time however, there had been a distinct lack of fuss and a noticeable absence of sympathy or concern.

"Here we go again," said Larkin as he watched Steadman and Blackie struggle through the doorway before dropping the heavily inebriated individual into his chair.

"This is getting beyond a joke," said the appalled Alty. "Haven't we got enough to contend with without having to look after that drunken old get?"

"I'd have thought so too," said Larkin.

"How much has he had?" said the Club Secretary.

"It's impossible to say," said Blackie. "Quite a lot would be my guess."

"Where's young Anthony?" said the Chef.

"I've no idea," said Steadman. "Probably having some sort of nervous breakdown."

"He's no doubt trying to steal a bit of well needed kip," said Larkin. "He's shattered. The poor lad's close to the end of his tether. He had to pin his father to the floor earlier."

"Why's that?" said the Club Secretary.

"Because he was wanting to strangle Steadman," said Larkin.

"He was wanting to do what?" said the Club Secretary.

"He was wanting to strangle Steadman," said Larkin. "They'd had some sort of altercation earlier."

"Is that right Steadman?" said the Chef.

"He was on one of his paranoid trips," said Steadman. "He accused me of being an arse bandit."

"Why would he do that?" said the Chef.

"He saw me rubbing antiseptic cream onto a cut on Blackie's posterior," said Steadman.

"Oh dear!" said the Chef.

"How did you manage to get yourself cut Blackie?" said the Club Secretary.

"I'd been trying to avoid the melee when Hamill's

henchmen dragged Morris off," said Blackie. "I fell and landed on a piece of broken ashtray."

"Does your wound need stitching?" said the Professor.

"It's just a scratch Professor," said Steadman. "It just needed cleaning up and dressing. Although to hear the screams coming from the wuss, you'd have thought he was giving birth to a baby hippo."

"It stung like hell," said Blackie. "Wait until you get a cut and I'm the one rubbing the stuff onto your wounds. You'll see what it's like. You'll be the one sounding like you're giving birth then."

"So it looks like Biddo's got the wrong end of the stick again," said the Chef.

"He must have thought Steadman was getting ready to give me one," said Blackie. "It's comical, when you come to think of it. I was bent over a chair with me trousers and boxers down by my knees."

"And having your arse massaged," said the Chef.

"That's brilliant that is," said Larkin.

"And you were groaning too," said Alty.

"He was groaning like a well trodden wooden staircase," said Steadman.

"It wasn't a groan of pleasure, I assure you," said Blackie.

"Are you sure about that?" said Steadman.

"I'm perfectly sure," said the indignant Blackie. "I love women and only women. I've been fascinated with the heavenly creatures since the day the lovely Lottie Spungen stole a kiss off me during our junior school production of *Annie*. I didn't sleep for a week after that. But listen lads-on a more serious note. Biddo's on the edge. He's as bad as I've ever known him. He can't differentiate between a joke and reality. You're going to have to do me a favour and cut the pranks out for a while."

"I have to agree," said the Chef. "We could do with finding Anthony."

"I'll have a look for him," said the Club Chairman.

"He might be packing his bags," said Alty.

"Packing his bags!" said the Chef.

"He wants to go home," said Alty. "He's had enough. He's actually been talking about going for help."

"Has he?" said the Chef.

"He has yes," said Alty.

"Would anyone have a problem with that?" said Steadman.

"I would," said the Chairman.

"Why's that?" said Steadman.

"He's just a young kid," said the Chairman. "He wouldn't last five minutes out there in that climate and over that terrain."

"He would if we got him kitted out in all the best gear," said Steadman.

"What best gear's that?" said the Chairman.

"I don't know off the top of me head," said Steadman. "I've got a pair of decent boots and some fur lined leather gloves."

"And I've got some good thermal underwear and a pair of waterproof kecks," said Blackie. "What more is he going to need?"

"A decent full length coat," said the Chef. "That's going to be the biggest problem."

"Hasn't Hamill got one?" said Steadman.

"He did have," said Blackie.

"It's still saturated?" said the Chef.

"And it may be needed for evidence," said the Chairman.

"Well someone must have a decent coat," said Steadman. "It's Winter for God's sake. Somebody must have anticipated bad weather. What about you Hewlett?"

"What about me?" said Hewlett without averting his eyes from his half completed Times crossword.

"Have you got a heavy coat," said Steadman.

"I've got two heavy coats," said Hewlett before placing his pencil behind his left ear and sitting upright. "One of them's a vintage Ted Lapidus I bought while in Paris last April."

"Would you consider lending it to us?" said Steadman.

"Lending it to you!" said Hewlett.

"We're thinking of kitting one of the lads out and sending him for help," said Steadman. "He's going to need the best possible gear in order to survive the journey."

"He's going to need more than a Ted Lapidus," said Hewlett while pointing to the window. "He's going to need to be superhuman. Have you seen it out there?"

"Of course we've seen it out there," said Steadman. "It's impossible not to see out there. The view's staring us right in the face 24 hours a day."

"Who've you got in mind for this expedition?" said Hewlett.

"Young Anthony," said Steadman.

"Anthony!" said Hewlett. "Oh dear!"

"What do you mean?" said Steadman.

"Well he's not exactly Ernest Shackleton material is he?" said Hewlett.

"He doesn't have to be Shackleton," said Steadman. "He's not going to have to find the North Pole. He's just going to have to find a nearby town or settlement. We're somewhere in Wales, not in the middle of the Sahara Desert. There's got to be one."

"Does his father know what you're proposing?" said Hewlett.

"His father's arguing with an invisible enemy right at this moment," said the Chef.

"And his father's the main reason he wants to go," said Steadman. "The lad's had just about enough of him."

"Come on Hewlett," said Steadman. "The boy can do it-I know he can. He's a lot younger and much fitter than the rest of us. If we can just find a way to get him safely off the bridge and on to level ground, I think he'll be home and hosed."

"It's not going to happen," said the Chairman.

"Why not?" said Steadman.

"Because it's too much of a risk," said the Chairman. "And I'm not prepared to lose another soul."

[266]

"With the greatest respect Hulmey-I don't think the call's yours to make," said Steadman.

"Why not?" said the Chef.

"Because, unless I'm mistaken, Hamill's in charge now," said Steadman. "Hamill's the one who's going to be making the big calls from now on."

"Over my dead body," said the returning Club Secretary just as the door flew open and a breathless Hamill and his two man cohort entered in a state of utter consternation.

"What's going on?" said Blackie before rising and quickly adding his own weight to the back of the door. "Speak to me lads. What exactly are we trying to keep out?"

"We're not sure," said Hamill. "We think they might be hunters."

"Hunters!" said the Chef.

"Why would you think that?" said the Chairman,.

"We found these three rifle cartridges," said Hamill.

"Bloody hell!" said the Chef.

"Where was this?" said the Chairman.

"In one of the far carriages," said Hamill. "We also found a poorly drawn map, some cigarette butts and the remains of a meal."

"What's the map of?" said the Chairman.

"It's impossible to say," said Hamill. "The ink's run."

"They must have been what Matthews saw," said Blackie.

"Why haven't they introduced themselves?" said the Chef.

"I don't know," said Hamill. "But the fact that they haven't suggests they're not wanting to make friends."

"That's what I reckon too," said Woodhouse.

"It's possible," said the Chairman.

"They must have climbed on board while the third exit door was open," said the Chef.

"Thanks for reminding everyone of that our kid," said the Chairman.

"Well there doesn't seem to be anything nasty and

[267]

menacing out there now," said Blackie while peering out along the corridor through the upper glass panel. "Maybe they've lost interest."

"Maybe they've found something else to hunt," said Steadman.

"Don't you believe it," said Hamill before snatching a glass of water from the Chef's tray and consuming it in one continuous gulp. "I think they're here to rob us. And they're probably waiting for the weather to break before they do."

"Why would they need the weather to break?" said Blackie.

"They'll be able to make their escape then," said Hamill.

"Jesus Christ!" said Steadman.

"How have they managed to get up on the bridge?" said Larkin.

"You tell me," said Hamill.

"This is bad," said Steadman.

"What do we do?" said the Chef. "Shall we barricade ourselves in?"

"That would be what I'd advise," said Hamill. "But not before you've let me and my lads out."

"What!" said the Club Secretary.

"Are you abandoning us?" said the Chef.

"We're going to look for the bastards," said Hamill.

"Look for them!" said the Chef. "Are you mad Hamill? They're likely to be armed to the teeth."

"We'll take our chances," said Hamill. "I think it's the least we can do under the circumstances."

"What do you mean?" said the Chairman.

"I'm not going to apologise Hulmey but I am prepared to admit, I'm more than a tad ashamed regarding the treatment of Morris," said Hamill.

"Really!" said the Chairman.

"Is he alright?" said the Club Secretary.

"He's sitting up and firing off all sorts of abuse," said Hamill.

"Thank God for that," said the Chef.

"We lost the plot," said Hamill. "I'm not going to try to pretend otherwise. We let things get out of hand. Tommy and Woody have been in a terrible state over the whole unpleasant business."

"I don't know what to say lads," said Woodhouse. "I just kept reliving that moment when the train pulled away. I saw Morris as the person responsible for me never seeing my wife and kids again."

"You'll see them again Woody," said the Chairman.

"Is he definitely alright?" said the Club Secretary.

"He's expressing himself perfectly well," said Woodhouse.

"Can we see him?" said the Chef.

"He's in custody lads," said Hamill. "I'm not going to lie to you all. He's black and blue and several shades of yellow."

"How black and blue?" said the Chairman.

"He'll become less black and blue with each passing hour," said Hamill. "If you open this door from time to time, you'll hear him yelling. He likes to use the 'C' word while making references to Woody's weight. Oh, and he's had plenty of water and a packet of chocolate biscuits too."

"That's good," sighed the Chef.

"It is," said Steadman.

"Do you mind me asking what the current situation with the leadership is?" said the Club Secretary.

"What do you mean?" said Hamill.

"You took over the leadership not that long ago," said the Club Secretary.

"I did nothing of the sort," said Hamill. "I took charge of a rapidly deteriorating situation. I don't want to run this club. How would I ever get a motion passed? I've got too many enemies."

"You might have one less if you manage to chase off those bastard intruders," said Steadman.

"Make that two," said Blackie.

"Are you hungry?" said the Chef.

"I could eat a bowl of parrot droppings," replied Hamill.

[269]

"I'll make the three of you a bacon sandwich," said the Chef.

"Is everyone accounted for?" said the Chairman.

"I think so," said the Club Secretary .

"The Professor's not here," said Hewlett.

"And Matthews is missing too," said Blackie.

"They're probably still having their handbag fight," said Woodhouse.

"What do you mean?" said the Chairman.

"They were having a right old ding dong when we passed the second carriage washroom earlier on," said Woodhouse.

"The Professor and Matthews were?" said the bemused Chairman. "How come? What have they got to argue about?"

"I've no idea," said Woodhouse after jamming a chair under the door knob and making his way to his seat. "But they were definitely arguing. I'm sure I heard the term 'ungrateful bounder' being hurled at one point."

"Are you being serious Woody?" said the Chairman.

"Absolutely serious," said Woodhouse. "They were going at it like a pair of Tom cats in a jigger."

"Well that does surprise me," said the Chairman.

It was at that particular moment when a tired and slightly dishevelled looking Professor made his way into the room and, after wiping his deeply furrowed brow and stifling a cough, he headed to the kitchen without uttering a single word.

"Are you alright Professor?" asked Steadman after trying unsuccessfully to bar the old man's way.

"You haven't had another one of your funny turns have you?" said the Club Secretary while following the old man to his chair. "Talk to me sir. You're scaring me now."

"He's scaring me too," said Steadman.

"He's scaring everyone," said the Chef. "What's happened old fella?"

"I'm afraid there's been another development," said the trembling old man while pouring himself a glass of

[270]

water.

"What sort of development?" said the Club Secretary.

"A very serious one," said the Professor. "It's regarding your friend."

"Which one?" said the Chef.

"Mr Matthews," said the old man.

"What's happened to him?" said the Chairman.

"I'm afraid he's fallen foul of the disease," said the old man.

"What!" said the Club Secretary.

"He's our first confirmed victim of the disease," said the old man.

"Oh dear!" said the Chef. "The poor sod."

"When did you discover this Professor?" said Blackie.

"Shortly after he'd accosted me in one of the washrooms," said the old man.

"Accosted you!" said Steadman. "That's not like Brian Matthews."

"Not at all," said the Club Secretary.

"Matthews is a pacifist," said the Chef.

"It didn't seem like that to me," said the Professor. "He was ranting and raving and threatening to tear me limb from limb."

"Bloody hell!" said Blackie.

"Did he give you any reason for his attack?" said the Club Secretary.

"It was something to do with his wife," said the old man. "Is her name Rose by any chance?"

"It is, yes," said the Club Secretary. "What about Rose?"

"He'd got it into his head I'd been sleeping with her," said the Professor.

"You!" said Woodhouse.

"That's right," said the Professor.

"That doesn't make any sense," said Woodhouse.

"I know," said the old man. "It's the disease.

"Discovering his wife's having an affair with an older man must be your friend Matthews's greatest fear."

"It's quite high on my list too," said the Chairman.

"And mine," said Blackie.

"Where is he now?" said the Chairman.

"In one of the beds in the second carriage," said the old man. "I was eventually able to distract him and sedate him before he got any worse."

"Good for you Professor," said the Club Secretary. "Is there anything I can get you?"

"A stiff brandy would be most welcome thank you," said the old man. "I'm still all of a dither. I've never known a sufferer turn aggressive so quickly before."

"To be honest Professor, I'm more worried about that man there," said Blackie while gesturing towards the snoring Biddo. "He wanted to assault my best friend earlier. I reckon he's got some very serious issues himself."

"Do you really?" said the old man. "What sort of issues?"

"He's seriously homophobic for one thing," said Blackie. "And as a result, he's got it into his head that our friends Larko and Alty are determined to have their wicked way with his young son."

"Can there be any justification in his fear?" said the Professor.

"None at all," said Blackie. "They're both happily married men."

"But they love nothing more than to wind Biddo up Professor," said Steadman.

"That's because it's so fabulously easy," said Alty.

"And so much fun," said Larkin.

"Well that sort of fun's going to have to stop from now on," said the Chairman. "You heard what the Professor told us earlier. He could get extremely violent if he ended up getting the disease."

"Do you reckon?" said Larkin.

"He could do far worse than get violent," said the Professor. "He could end up wiping the lot of us out."

"Do you really think so Professor?" said Larkin.

"I know so," said the old man.

"Do you think he should be restrained as a precaution?"

[272]

said the Club Secretary.

"Certainly not," said the Professor. "Would *you* like to be restrained simply because someone suspects you're sick?"

"I suppose not," said the Club Secretary before guiding the sleeping Biddo's dangling arm back onto his lap. "But if *I* start becoming too much of a nuisance, like this drunken sot here, feel free to put the bracelets on me Professor."

"Feel free to restrain me too," said Alty. "Feel free to drop me kecks, plunge your needle into me backside and put me to sleep for the remainder of this catastrophe of a trip."

"And that goes for me too," said Larkin.

"And me," said Steadman. "You can be my guest Professor. Particularly if Hamill and his boys fail and those bastard intruders try to break in here."

"What intruders?" said the Professor.

"We don't know for certain," said the Club Secretary after emerging from behind the bar with a new bottle of brandy. "Hamill found some spent rifle cartridges in one of the carriages. We suspect they belong to members of a hunting party."

"May I see the cartridges?" said the old man.

"I'd rather keep hold of them if it's all the same to you," said Hamill. "If I can get my hands on one of the hunter's rifles, those little cartridges are going to come in handy."

"Do you intend confronting them?" said the old man.

"I intend doing a lot more than confronting them," said Hamill.

"My word!" said the Professor. "Do you think that's wise?"

"It's better than the alternative," said Hamill.

"Which is what?" said the Professor.

"Wait around until they confront us at gunpoint," said Hamill.

"Do you think they're after money?" said the old man.

"That's the best explanation we can come up with,"

said Hamill.

"Have you got any advice for the rest of us regarding what to do if confronted by someone with the disease?" said Blackie.

"I don't know what you mean," said the Professor.

"It's not that hard Professor," said Blackie. "What do we do if we have an experience like you've just had with Matthews? Do we try to keep the sufferer calm? Do we avoid eye contact? Do we behave submissively? Do we tell them to sit and be nice? What do you recommend?"

"I recommend you run for your lives, and keep running until you've outrun your pursuer, found somewhere safe to hide or have stopped breathing ," said the old man.

"But you didn't run," said the Chef.

"That's because I'm not capable of running," said the old man. "And I was fortunately in possession of the sedative. That's the only reason I'm here, about to drink neat brandy and not already beginning to solidify in one of the unoccupied carriages like your previous Chairman. Cheers gentlemen! And the very best of luck regarding your adventure Mr Hamill."

CHAPTER THIRTEEN
FROM DUTY TO BEAST

Due massively to Hamill's announcement that the hunters had fled, the late evening had passed by without any further upheaval and that had resulted in the occupants of the first carriage enjoying their best and least interrupted sleep since the train had come to its unscheduled halt. That didn't mean the weather had improved however. In fact, if anything, the wind had been even stronger and the snow that had fallen far heavier than before, had turned the train into something resembling a long greyish white caterpillar. It meant that seeing out of any of the windows had become impossible and because of that, there would be a general prevailing sense among the party that there was nothing at all beyond the glass and therefore nowhere to aspire to be.

"Are we to believe Hamill regarding the hunters?" said the Club Secretary who had been the first to rise and get dressed just after 7 the following morning.

"I think we have to until we discover otherwise," said the Chairman. "The cartridges certainly looked authentic. Why Hilly? Are you suggesting he's been a little economical with the truth?"

"Not at all," replied the Club Secretary. "I just can't understand why people, after making it to the top of the bridge, wouldn't introduce themselves in some way."

"It proves they were almost certainly up to no good," said the Chef after flinging his blankets to one side and stretching upwards . "They probably expected the train to be empty and were going to loot it. I reckon we've seen the last of them."

"I hope you're right," said the Club Secretary after handing the Chairman his shirt. "By the way Hulmey-congratulations on finding a new best friend?"

"What do you mean?" said the Chairman.

[275]

"You were all over Hamill like a rash last night," said the Club Secretary.

"I noticed that," said the Chef. "What was that all about?"

"I want to keep on the right side of him," said the Chairman.

"Why?" said the Club Secretary.

"To see if I can get him to release Morris," said the Chairman. "I'm surprised you can remember anything."

"Why's that?" said the Club Secretary.

"You were well on," said the Chairman. "You were talking to yourself at one point."

"I needed a blow out," said the Club Secretary. "I've been itching to have a good drink since we stopped."

"What time did you get up?" said the Chef.

"I've been up for over an hour," said the Club Secretary.

"Have you had time to look in on Matthews?" said the Chairman.

"I have as a matter of fact," said the Club Secretary.

"And I'm sorry to report, I've already got the first bit of bad news of the day."

"What's that?" said the Chairman. "He's not got worse has he?"

"He's changed form," said the Club Secretary.

"He's done what?" said the Chairman.

"He's changed form," said the Club Secretary. "He's gone through a dramatic overnight transformation."

"What sort of transformation?" said the Chairman.

"He's turned into a weasel," said the Club Secretary.

"A weasel!" said the Chairman.

"That's right," said the Club Secretary. "At least I think he's a weasel. I suppose he could be a stoat. Or even a chipmunk. To be honest-all those little animals look the same to me."

"What the hell are you talking about Hilly?" said the Chairman after breaking off from massaging his eyelids. "You're not suggesting...you're not are you?.....they haven't have they?"

"I'm afraid they have," said the Club Secretary before

settling down on the end of his bed and opening his club register. "And a bloody good job they've made of it too. I doubt if a Walt Disney illustrator could have done a more effective job. They've even given the poor bugger a set of long grey whiskers."

"The bastards," said the Chairman before snatching his trousers from the back of his bedside chair. "Wait until I get my hands on them. Just wait until I get my bloody hands on them. I warned them Hilly. You heard me warn them. I told them, no more arsing around. I told them. I told them countless times. I told them till I was nearly blue in the face. I want them here. I want them here right now Hilly. Will you go and get them for me please."

It was at that very moment however, while the Chairman was continuing to work himself into a frenzy and gearing himself up for a major confrontation with the two notorious pranksters, when the first carriage door slowly opened and a rather apologetic looking Steadman popped his head inside.

"Sorry to interrupt you guys-but I think you might want to follow me," he said. "We've got a problem."

"I know we have," said the infuriated Chairman while struggling to get his right leg into his trousers. "Hilly's just told me."

"Told you about what?" said Steadman.

"About Matthews's face being painted," said the Chairman.

"This has got nothing to do with Matthews's face," said Steadman.

"What's it got to do with then?" said the Chairman.

"We've got a fire," said Steadman.

"A fire!" said the Chef.

"Oh, for crying out loud?" said the Chairman while proceeding to stumble backwards into his startled brother's arms. "Where? Where about?"

"Is it in the kitchen?" said the Chef. "It's not in the kitchen is it? Don't tell me I've gone and left something cooking."

"It's in the second carriage," said Steadman.

"What!" said the Club Secretary. "Bloody hell! That carriage is full to bursting with our members isn't it?"

"It was at one time," said Steadman.

"What do you mean, it was at one time?" said the Chairman while struggling to put his foot into his left shoe. "No one's dead are they? No one's been killed have they Steadman?"

"Not up to now," said Steadman.

It had taken the shoeless and livid Chairman less than a minute to make his way through the dining carriage and in and out of those who had gathered in the corridor to see what all the commotion was about, and although he had mentally prepared himself to see something extremely distressing, Davie Larkin covered from head to toe in a suit of pure white foam wasn't exactly it.

"It's out now," said Alty before placing a small fire extinguisher at the Chairman's feet. "The fire's out. I've managed to put it out."

"Well done," said a breathless Club Secretary before dropping to his haunches and nodding approvingly. "Well done Mr Alty."

"What the hell's been going on?" said the spluttering Chairman while trying to survey the smoke shrouded scene. "Talk to me gentlemen. What's been going on?"

"What's been going on!" said Larkin before bursting through a trio of bystanders and taking an extremely inebriated Biddo by the throat. "I'll tell you what's been going on shall I. This drunken, neurotic, fucking lunatic has finally lost all touch with reality."

"In what way?" said the Chairman after quickly stepping between the two men and urging the infuriated Larkin to step back. "What's he done?"

"He's just tried to set me alight," said Larkin.

"He did what?" said the Chairman.

"He's just put a match to my bed," said Larkin. "The crazy bastard's tried to kill me."

"It's true," said Alty. "As ridiculous as it might sound

[278]

Hulmey-it's absolutely true."

"Oh shit," said the Club Secretary while examining Larkin's badly scorched bedding.

"Is it true Biddo?" said the late arriving Blackie.

"It's a load of bollocks," said Biddo.

"It's not a load of bollocks at all," said Alty. "I lay right there in my pit and watched you do it."

"You're talking shite," said Biddo. "It was an accident."

"It wasn't an accident at all," said Larkin. "How could it be an accident?"

"What's going on Biddo?" said the Chairman. "What the hell's been going on?"

"I've just told you," said Biddo. "There's been a little accident. I accidentally spilt some of my vodka on one of the beds."

"On my bed," said Larkin. "You spilt it on my bed. That's the important part of this. It wasn't the Chairman's bed. It wasn't our Club Secretary's bed. It wasn't the Professor's bed. The vodka was spilt on my fucking bed. And you might want to examine the bottle Hulmey. That's his own vodka. He must have smuggled it on board while you and your mates weren't looking. Take a look at the label. It's 200 percent proof."

"What difference does that make?" said the Chairman.

"It's highly flammable," said Larkin. "It might as well have been paraffin."

"And then he just happened to strike a match and drop it," said Alty. "Ever so conveniently, I might add."

"That was an accident too," said Biddo. "I've got the shakes. I'm always dropping things."

"Don't talk shite," said Alty.

"That's the only language the mental bastard knows," said Larkin.

"Alright lads, let's try to keep a lid on this," said the Chairman.

"I agree," said Blackie.

"It's too late," said Larkin while continuing to lunge at the accused. "The lid's been blown off. The damage is done Hulmey."

"We can sort this," said the Chairman. "We can deal with this lads. For God's sake, please don't let this go the way the Morris situation went. Don't let that happen gentlemen. Take plenty of long, slow, deep breaths."

"Deep breaths!" said Alty. "And breathe in what exactly Hulmey? Toxic fumes?"

"Well, get some air in here," said the Chairman. "Open some windows for pity's sake."

"We've tried," said Alty. "They're all frozen shut."

"Well let's get the hell out of here then," said Blackie. "Wedge that door ajar and let's get one of the main exits open."

"Good idea," said the Chef. "We need to flood this place with clean air."

"That bastard doesn't deserve to breathe clean air," said Larkin. "We should just lock him in here and throw away the key."

"I couldn't agree more," said Alty.

"And I couldn't disagree more," said the Chairman. "Can't you see lads. That's exactly what I'm trying to avoid. That would just be a repeat of the Alec Morris fiasco."

"But, for the love of God Hulmey," said Larkin. "The mental bastard shouldn't have been here in the first place. This isn't even his room."

"It's my son's room," said Biddo. "Can't a father visit his son, for crying out loud?"

"Of course he can," said Larkin. "As long as he's not a potential Norman Bates like you."

"Alright Larko, that's enough," said Blackie. "Have a little respect will you. That's my uncle you're talking to."

"I know that Blackie," said Larkin. "And the last thing I want to do is fall out with you. We've been good friends too long. But he's a very sick and depraved individual. Do you realise that? Do you realise how sick your uncle is?"

"I realise he's got a number of issues, yes," said

Blackie.

"He's got more than a number of issues," said Alty.

"He's got issues by the container load."

"What exactly were you doing here Biddo?" said the Chairman.

"He's just told you," said Blackie. "He was visiting Anthony."

"But what for?" said the Chairman.

"He was spying on him," said Larkin. "He's done nothing else since we got stuck here."

"I wanted to say 'good night'," said Biddo.

"Goodnight!" said the Chef. "What do you mean, 'good night', Biddo? It's early morning, for goodness sake."

"It is now," said Biddo.

"And it *was* half an hour ago when you set fire to my fucking bed," said Larkin. "And his boy Anthony's not even here," said Woodhouse.

"He's not now," said Biddo while pointing to the corner of the room. "But he was here. That should have been his bed."

"What do you mean, 'should have been his bed'?" said the Club Secretary.

"Take a good look at it Hilly," said Biddo.

"What for?" said the Club Secretary.

"It's not been slept in," said Biddo.

"So what?" said the Club Secretary. "Maybe he slept in the dining carriage with the rest of the lads."

"He didn't," said Biddo before pointing at Larkin's bed. "He slept right there with Larry Grayson."

"Larry Grayson!" said the Club Secretary.

"He means me," said Larkin. "Anthony slept with me."

"There you are," said Biddo. "There you have it. Now you know the ugly truth."

"Ugly truth about what?" said the Chairman.

"About what's been going on," said Biddo.

"And what's that?" said the Chairman.

"Larkin's finally done what he's been intent on doing for some time," said Biddo.

"What's that?" said the Chairman.

[281]

"He's sodomised my son," said Biddo.

"Oh, for fuck's sake!" said Larkin. "Has anybody got a gun? Is there anybody outside in that corridor who would be kind enough to provide me with a gun and one bullet?"

"Are you serious?" said McShane.

"Of course he's not serious," said the mortified Hamill. "He's just joking."

"I'm not," said a lunging Larkin while being restrained by a rapidly formed spider's web of hands and fingers. "I'd like nothing more but to shoot him. I'd like nothing more but to take that lunatic outside and blow what's left of his brains out. He's a disgrace."

"You're the disgrace," said Biddo. "At least I'm straight. At least I'm no bum bandit."

"And neither am I," said Larkin. "Anthony shared my bed because his own bed was soaking wet."

"Are you accusing my thirty year old son of bed wetting?" said Biddo.

"I spilt a jug of water over it when we were hit by one of those sudden blasts," said Larkin.

"Of course you did," said Biddo. "That was convenient wasn't it?"

"It's the God's honest truth," said Alty. "The entire bed was saturated."

"You're a liar," said Biddo.

"It's the truth," said Larkin.

"It sounds reasonable enough to me," said the Chairman.

"Does it Hulmey?" said Biddo.

"It does yes," said the Chairman. "I think you're overreacting Biddo. You've been given a perfectly acceptable explanation as to the sleeping arrangements. What more do you want?"

"I want Alty and Larkin exposed as the faggots they are," said Biddo. "I want them kept away from the straight men among us. And furthermore, I want them to explain why my Anthony walked out of this room in the early hours of the morning caked in makeup looking like

[282]

some cheap Lime Street hussy. Why don't you ask those two depraved fudge packers to explain that Hulmey?"

"I'll explain it gladly," said Alty. "We'd been playing cards like we always do. We often make the loser pay a forfeit."

"What does that entail?" said the Chairman.

"One of us might have to streak naked or wear a dress," said Alty. "On the most recent occasion, Anthony had to put on a bit of makeup, wear a blonde wig and lap dance for me and Larko. He'd have probably made a few bob if he'd have been wearing knickers."

"What difference would knickers have made?" said the Chef.

"We'd have had somewhere to slip the five pound notes," said Alty.

"There you are," said Biddo. "I rest my case your honour."

"It was just a bit of fun," said Larkin. "Arsing about and winding people up is probably the only thing that's kept us sane for the last few days. We get up to all sorts of things together."

"I know you do," said the Chairman while wagging an accusing finger. "And don't for one minute think you're going to get away with what you did to Matthews."

"Did they shag him too?" said Biddo.

"We'll discuss that matter later," said the Chairman. "Now's not the time."

"Why not?" said Woodhouse.

"Because we've got more important things to discuss," said the Chairman.

"I disagree," said Woodhouse. "If I'd have done something wrong, it'd be discussed immediately."

"And you'd have been punished immediately too," said McShane.

"There's no doubt about that," said Woodhouse. "What did you do Alty?"

"We painted Matthews's face?" said Alty.

"Is that all?" said Woodhouse.

"It's outrageous," said the Club Secretary.

[283]

"The man's seriously ill," said the Chairman. "How would you like it Woody? How would you like it if you were lying in bed suffering all manner of terrifying hallucinations, and someone comes along and paints you to look like a badger?"

"I think he'd make a great looking badger," said McShane.

"Why don't you tell them about the depraved sex act you performed on me while I was sleeping," said Biddo.

"What depraved sex act?" said Larkin.

"You know exactly what I mean," said Biddo. "We were in the Hotel Helios in Benidorm. You two cretins had the room next door to me. Larkin ejaculated all over my face."

"Oh Christ!" said the Club Secretary.

"It was Ambrosia semolina," said Alty. "Had you not been so rat arsed stinking drunk, you'd have worked that out."

"How would I?" said Biddo.

"We left the half empty tin on your bedside cabinet," said Larkin.

"Maybe you did," said Biddo. "But you still stood over me with a raging hard on."

"It was a 12 inch strap on rubber dildo," said Larkin.

"And once again Biddo-had you been remotely sober, you'd have noticed it was black," said Alty.

"Did you bring that thing through customs Larko?" said the Club Secretary.

"I found it under a table in the hotel lobby," said Alty.

"It's just a shame you found a fire extinguisher in time," said Biddo. "Because if you hadn't have done, Larkin would be where he should be now-burning in the hobs of hell with all the other perverts and sexual deviates."

"I rest my case," said Larkin before shoulder charging Biddo into his nephew's arms, snatching his towel and heading for the washroom.

"That's as good an admission of guilt you're likely to hear Hulmey," said Hamill. " I think you need to don your black cap and get prepared for sentencing."

###

It was another 45 minutes before an extremely self conscious and fresh faced Anthony emerged from the second carriage washroom to begin the short journey to the Chairman's room, and although he had refused to respond to those passengers who were still hovering in the corridors, it was still clear he had reached a very definite catharsis.

"I've had enough," he said after settling down on the end of the Chairman's bed. "I want out of here Hulmey. I want out of here before I'm the next one needing psychiatric treatment."

"That's perfectly understandable," said the Club Secretary. "But what we've got to establish first and foremost is whether you're up to the challenge?"

"I'm prepared to give it my best shot," said Anthony. "I've done plenty of walking and cycling over the last few months."

"Have you ever walked in weather like that?" said the Chairman while pointing towards the window.

"Of course he hasn't," said Hamill who was in attendance at the request of the committee. "None of us have ever walked in weather like that. You heard Eddie Meehan. This is the worst winter for 500 years."

"Are you aware of that Anthony?" said the Chef.

"Of course I am," said Anthony. "And I'm also aware that several mysterious hunters have been seen in the vicinity of the train. Which means, if *they* can survive, I've got a good chance of surviving too."

"Good point," said the Club Secretary.

"It's an excellent point," said Hamill.

"What do you think Hulmey?" said the Chef.

"I don't like the idea," said the Chairman.

"Why the hell not?" said Hamill.

"Because there's a huge difference between an office worker like Anthony and one of those gnarly old mountain man types," said the Chairman. "Those people are fully acclimatised to seriously bad weather and

[285]

hostile terrains."

"And Anthony will be after a few hours," said Hamill.
"We've just got to kit him out in the right gear."

"And there's loads of plastic sheeting in the mailroom,"
said the Club Secretary. "He'll be able to rig up some
sort of tent."

"And even more importantly, he's going to have the
advantage of Eddie Meehan's magic box," said the Club
Secretary.

"I've heard you talking about that thing," said Anthony.
"How do you think it's going to help?"

"It'll help in a variety of ways," said the Club Secretary.
"For one thing, it'll show you where the worst of the
weather is. You'll then know when to move on or stay
put until the worst of the storm has passed. They use
pretty much the same system to warn tower crane
operators of impending high winds and the like."

"Take a look for yourself," said the Chef before handing
Anthony the device. "Have a feel of the thing. Get
familiar with all the buttons and features. It's just like a
minicomputer. You young people are normally great
with things like that."

"What are these numbers in the left top corner?" said
Anthony.

"That's the current wind speed," said the Club
Secretary. "If you press the right arrow, you'll see what
the wind speed is likely to be at this very time
tomorrow."

"And that's highly significant," said the Chef.

"Why is it?" said Anthony.

"Because it shows there's a window of opportunity
tomorrow," said the Chef.

"When?" said Anthony while shifting nervously in his
seat.

"Between 7 and 10.30 in the morning," said the Club
Secretary. "According to our calculations, the wind's
going to be at its weakest during that period. And there's
going to be another three hour lull just after midday."

"And more importantly, according to that little box, that

pattern's going to continue for the next three or four days," said the Chef.

"Just three or four days!" said Anthony.

"How long do you think you'll need?" said Hamill.

"I've no idea," said Anthony.

"Three or four days should be well enough time to reach the nearest settlement," said the Club Secretary.

"Even when you take into account the hurricane force wind and the lousy underfoot conditions," said the Chef.

"You make it sound so simple lads," said Anthony. "I'm beginning to wonder why one of you isn't going."

"Our kid's going to be needed here," said the Chef.

"And neither of these two are physically up to it," said the Chairman.

"I was considered too old," said the Chef.

"You are too old," said the Chairman. "And Hilly's still recovering from a nasty virus. You two wouldn't last five minutes out there."

"And neither will I if I end up getting lost," said Anthony.

"You won't get lost," said the Club Secretary. "That box won't allow you get lost. That box is going to be as useful as a Himalayan mountain guide. It's going to show you the best and most economical way and prompt you when you're going off course."

"How's it going to manage that?" said a suspicious looking Anthony.

"Like this," said the Club Secretary after taking the device from the Chef and making his way to the centre of the room. "Watch this Anthony. Watch and learn young man......I'm looking out of the window. Which means I'm facing due east."

"Why does it?" said Anthony.

"Because, according to my calculations, the train was heading due north when it came to a halt," said the Club Secretary. "That's a fact I've been able to establish with the device, by the way. It's not negotiable. It might as well be written in stone."

"Alright," said Anthony.

"Which means, what we see directly beyond that window is due east," said the Club Secretary. "Would you agree?"

"I would yes," said Anthony. "Provided your calculations are right, that is."

"They are," said the Club Secretary. "I promise you they are...I'm now going to walk forward a few short steps. And when I do, you'll notice nothing at all happens......One, two, three. What do you think?"

"You were right," said the unimpressed young observer. "Nothing at all happened."

"That's right," said the Club Secretary before turning to his left almost robotically. "But watch what happens when I turn and walk towards Hulmey's bed.....One, two, three."

"Bloody hell!" said a startled Anthony after quickly placing his hands over his ears. "What the hell's that?"

"That's the magic box informing me I've just strayed off my intended course," said the Club Secretary.

"I punched in the coordinates for due east while you were in the shower. Impressive that, isn't it?"

"It's very impressive," said Anthony. "Wow! You were right Hilly. That thing really does talk. Although...."

"Although what Anthony?" said the Club Secretary. "What's the problem?"

"He's probably wondering why you want him to head due east," said the Chef.

"I am, as a matter of fact" said Anthony. "You must be a mind reader Chef. Is there a reason?"

"Of course there's a reason," said the Club Secretary after settling back down on his bed and reaching for his notepad and pen. "Let me explain it this way shall I. It's a commonly known fact among geographers that wind speed is slower over land than across seas and oceans. It's due to undulations and mountains and things like that."

"And the fact that seas and oceans are relatively flat and contain no trees," said the Chef.

[288]

"That's right," said the Club Secretary. "Now if you press the square button on that magic box, you'll find what looks like a weather map. The sort you often see on the television after the local news."

"I think I've got that," said Anthony. "Is it the one with loads of squiggly lines and fluctuating numbers?"

"That's the one," said the Club Secretary after arriving at the young man's shoulder. "We're pretty certain that those numbers correspond to temperature in degrees Celsius and wind speed in kilometres per hour."

"I actually pointed that out," said Hamill.

"He did yes," said the Club Secretary. "And we're also pretty certain that the yellow flashing star in the centre of the screen is our current location."

"It's where we are at this precise time," said the Chef.

"That's right," said the Club Secretary. "Are you still with us Anthony?"

"I think so," said Anthony. "But there's nothing on that screen that appears to prove the existence of any towns or villages. I thought you had a map Hilly. I thought I was going to be following a map. Didn't you have a map? Didn't you have a map when you were trying to work out where we'd stopped?"

"I did yes," said the Club Secretary. "I had a half decent one. But it's vanished. I've searched high and low for the thing. I can't find it anywhere."

"Woodhouse has probably wiped his fat arse on the thing," said Hamill.

"It wouldn't surprise me," said the Chairman.

"But you're not going to need a map," said the Chef. "You'll have the magic box."

"Which shows something significant," said the Club Secretary.

"What's that?" said Anthony.

"Look at the top section of the screen," said the Club Secretary. "Look at the horseshoe shaped area. Now look at the numbers within that horseshoe shaped area. What do you notice about them?"

"I don't know," said Anthony. "There's so many of

[289]

them."

"What do you notice about them in relation to the numbers immediately outside the horseshoe?" said the Club Secretary.

"I don't know," said Anthony. "They're bigger than the numbers outside, I suppose."

"That's right," said the Club Secretary. "Go to the top of the class Anthony. They're considerably bigger than the rest actually. And I believe I know the reason why. I think those numbers are much bigger than the others because that horseshoe shaped area is a bay."

"A bay that's less than 15 miles from here," said the Chef.

"14.721 miles, to be precise," said the Club Secretary.

"Which means what?" said Anthony.

"If it's a bay, there could very well be fishing boats on it," said the Chef.

"In this weather?" said Anthony.

"Maybe not in this weather no," said the Club Secretary. "The boats will be moored up right now. But there'll almost certainly be a community surrounding it."

"What if your calculations are wrong and it's not a bay?" said the Chairman.

"Oh Christ!" said Hamill. "Negative Man's arrived on the scene. Everybody, hold on tight to all positive thoughts. Why don't you do one Hulmey? You're going to be putting the poor lad off."

"But what if it's not a bay," said Anthony. "What if you've got it wrong. What if you've got me heading into the middle of nowhere. Let's be fair and honest about this-none of you are geography teachers or weathermen."

"There you go," said Hamill. "Well done Hulmey. Your seed of doubt is already sprouting buds."

"I'm just trying to prevent a tragedy from occurring," said the Chairman. "Hilly could be wrong. That horseshoe shaped area might not be a bay."

"I think you'll find it is," said the Professor who had slipped into the room unnoticed several minutes earlier.

"How can you be so sure?" said the Chairman.

"Because I've just come across a map of Wales at the back of one of my old scouting diaries," said the old man while easing himself between the Club Secretary and young Anthony. "It's not in the greatest condition but I should think it'll more than suffice for your purpose. There used to be maps of parts of Britain at the back of every quality diary in my day. I used to study them for hours when I was a boy. They fascinated me. I don't understand why publishers stopped doing it. Perhaps it has something to do with the advent of the Internet."

"It probably has," said the Chef. "Are there any towns marked on this map of yours Professor?"

"Unfortunately not," said the old man. "At least none that are legible. I'm afraid that particular part of the map has been obliterated by a rather large and unsightly tea stain."

"Why doesn't that surprise me?" said the Chairman.

"But there is a bay that's clearly defined," said the old man.

"Where exactly?" said the Club Secretary.

"About 15 miles due east of here," said the Professor while pointing towards the window. "14.7 miles, as the eponymous crow flies."

"14.7 miles?" said the Club Secretary.

"14.721 miles, to be absolutely precise," said the old man.

"Bloody hell!" said the Club Secretary.

"That's got to be it hasn't it Hilly?" said the Chef. "That's got to be the bay you identified with the magic box hasn't it?"

"I'd have thought so," said the Club Secretary. "And 14.7 miles is achievable."

"I know it is," said the Chef. "Even for a virtual novice like Anthony."

"It's only achievable provided the box remains functional," said the Chairman.

"Fuck me with a 12 inch length of cucumber," said

Hamill. "There he goes again. Can't you ever see the glass as half full Hulmey?"

"I'm just trying to be realistic," said the Chairman.

"Let's be honest Hamill. If that box malfunctions or fails to hold out for some reason, Anthony could find himself walking around in circles."

"Why wouldn't the box hold out?" said Hamill.

"Because there's every chance it'll need charging at some point," said the Chairman. "As far as I'm aware, that thing hasn't been plugged into a power source since we left London."

"So what," said Hamill. "It's almost certainly state of the art. It probably won't need charging for another six months. It hasn't really been used has it? You all heard that siren. It nearly deafened the lot of us. My ears are still ringing . That thing must still have plenty of power left in it. I swear it must."

"It's got exactly 33 minutes of power," said the Club Secretary.

"What!" said the Chef.

"It's got 33 minutes of power left.....hang on.....hang on.....make that 32," said the Club Secretary before sighing heavily and handing the object to the Chairman. "You were right Hulmey. You must have a sixth sense lad."

"Either that or he's a jinx," said Hamill upon snatching the device. "For God's sake! We were doing so well. Are you sure you've read the data right Hilly?"

"I'm positive," said the Club Secretary. "The thing's fading fast."

"Just like our hopes and dreams," said the Chairman.

"Is there no charger?" said Anthony.

"That's a point," said Hamill before easing the Club Secretary aside and quickly making his way to the door. "I'll go and search Eddie's things. He was in the third carriage wasn't he?"

"The fourth," said the Club Secretary.

"His personal effects are on top of my wardrobe," said the Chairman. "I put them there for safe keeping after

Matthews had spotted the two imposters. I thought the police might want to examine them. You're welcome to go through them if you want. Be my guest. I've already looked. I don't remember coming across any charger."
"Which means our best laid plans are scuppered," said the Club Secretary.
"Not necessarily," said the old man before removing a small circular leather case from his trouser pocket and handing it to the Chairman. "You could always use this old thing."
"What is it?" said the Club Secretary.
"It's a Mk V Short & Mason pocket compass," said the Professor. "That little device has saved my bacon on numerous occasions. It's said to have belonged to Percy Fawcett at one time."
"Who's Percy Fawcett?" said the Chairman.
"He was one of Britain's most celebrated explorers, said the old man. "He went missing around Mato Grosso in Brazil in 1925 while searching for a fabled lost city."
"Which doesn't say much for the accuracy and durability of the compass," said the Chairman.
"It'll show you where due east is, if you ask it nicely," said the Professor.
"Oh I'll ask it nicely," said the Chef.
"So will I," said the Club Secretary. "I'll even buy it a few drinks."
"Now we just need to find a nearby nautical college where young Anthony can learn to use the thing," said the Chairman.
"There he goes again," said Hamill after stopping in his tracks right opposite the Chairman. "No wonder we're still here scratching our heads after a week. No wonder we never seem to get anywhere."
"I'm just trying to keep everyone grounded," said the Chairman. "Let's be honest, Anthony's probably never seen a compass before, never mind use one."
"I could teach your young friend how to use that gadget competently in less than an hour," said the Professor.

[293]

"Could you really?" said the Club Secretary.

"Of course I could," said the old man. "After all-you've already established your point B."

"What do you mean point B?" said the Chairman.

"The bay," said the old man. "I assume that's where you're hoping to get to."

"It is yes," said the Club Secretary. "We don't know what bay it is though. I reckon it could be any one of three."

"I don't really think that's important," said the Professor. "As long as there are English speaking people living around it. Do you mind me asking how you've been able to establish its existence without a map? I'm afraid I arrived late and missed much of the early part of your discussion."

"Not at all," said the Club Secretary. "We'd been fiddling around with our missing Health and Safety Officer's magic box."

"Magic box!" said the old man. "Do you mean that thing that's just caused you and your companions a minor breakdown?"

"That's it," said the Club Secretary. "It shows wind velocity and things like that. We identified a horseshoe shaped patch where the wind speeds were significantly stronger than the other neighbouring areas. I came to the conclusion that....."

"That it's a bay," said the Professor while putting on his spectacles. "I wholeheartedly concur. What an amazing gadget. It's a pity these ingenious fellows weren't around during my exploration days. I might have a few more friends to call on from time to time. I once lost three in the jungles of Borneo after our light aircraft crash landed. Good chaps, they were too. All in their prime."

"You didn't lend them your compass did you Professor?" said the Chairman.

"I don't think so," said the old man. "I certainly couldn't have lent them that one could I? Why do you ask?"

"Take no notice of him Professor," said Hamill. "He's trying to be funny. He's having a bad day. He's not been the centre of attention for once."

"I see," said the old man. "Anyway-well done gentlemen. Good work. I think we've got everything we need now. Well, maybe not everything. I'm going to need a quiet and secluded spot where I can begin my young adventurer's education."

"I wish you the very best of British luck Professor," said the Chef. "I think you're more likely to find Percy Fawcett than a quiet and secluded spot on board this bastard train. By the way-how are your patients doing?"

"My patients!" said the old man after rising slowly, grimacing and placing his two hands on the base of his spine. "Oh, you mean the unfortunate Mr Matthews."

"That's right," said the Chef. "How is he?"

"Well, apart from turning into something resembling a large water rat over night-he's doing reasonably well," said the old man.

"What do you mean 'doing reasonably well'?" said the Chairman. "I thought he was meant to be suffering from a serious disease."

"He most certainly is," said the old man. "But he's blissfully unaware of his affliction. Which means that, while he's under sedation, he's oblivious to the constant mayhem and madness that's going on all around him."

"That's true that is," said Hamill. "Matthews is actually better off than any of us at this moment in time. He's likely to be the last one to go insane. You couldn't score me a little drop of that sedative, could you Professor? I'd be prepared to make it worth your while."

"I'm sorry-I'm afraid that would be unethical," said the old man.

"It was a nice try though Hamill," said the Club Secretary. "By the way Professor-how's Davie Larkin doing?"

"Who?" said the old man.

"Our mechanic friend," said the Club Secretary. "The

[295]

one who almost got cremated."

"The fire victim," said the Chef.

"The smoke affected, homosexual deviate," said Hamill.

"Take no notice of him Professor," said the Club Secretary. "That was just Hamill being Hamill. Is he alright? Is Davie Larkin alright?"

"He's doing absolutely fine too," said the old man. "I've given him a couple of cough drops to suck on and told him to drink plenty of fluids. I'll go and check up on him when our meeting's concluded."

"We'd appreciate that Professor," said the Chef. "And when you've finished your rounds, I'll have a nice pot of tea waiting for you in the dining carriage."

"Have we got any tea left?" said the Chairman.

"Gordon fucking Bennett!" said Hamill. "There's no end to it is there. There's just no end to this man's negative thinking."

"I'm just trying to be realistic," said the Chairman.

"You're just trying my patience," said Hamill.

It was just after what had become the designated lunchtime when the last of the passengers trundled into the dining carriage and although several of them had been keen to get stuck into what the tireless Chef had provided, most of the others were even more determined to put certain questions to the Chairman.

"Is it true you've managed to persuade Anthony to go and look for help?" asked Steadman.

"Shush!" whispered an extremely edgy Chairman while watching the main entrance for latecomers.

"Never mind shush," said Steadman. "Is it true?"

"It is yes," said the Chairman. "But if it's all the same to you Steadman, I'd rather discuss that matter a little later."

"Why's that?" said Steadman.

"Because I said so," said the Chairman just as a short buzz signalled the end of the magic box's battery life.

"Because you said so!" said Steadman. "What sort of answer's that Hulmey? For God's sake. Somebody going for help is the best news we've had for days.

[296]

Come to think of it, it's probably the only good news we've had. What's wrong with discussing the matter here and now?"

"Because I want to run the idea by Kenny Biddo first," said the Chairman while continuing to watch the door.

"Why's that?" said Steadman.

"Because it's the decent thing to do in the circumstances," said the Chairman.

"And the fact that we're pretty damn sure he's not going to like the idea," said the Club Secretary.

"And you'd be absolutely right," said Biddo while slowly emerging from a window facing chair in the far corner of the room. "I think the idea stinks."

"Why does it?" said Woodhouse.

"Because it involves a young lad who's not physically up to the task," said Biddo. "Anthony's not Action Man material. He's gutless. He's just a child."

"Anthony's thirty years of age Biddo," said the Chairman. "He's an adult."

"Not as far as I'm concerned," said Biddo. "Not in the real sense of the word. He's just a wimpy kid. And he's far too slow to think for himself if the going gets tough."

"He's not slow at all," said the Chairman. "He's highly intelligent."

"He's got a degree," said the Club Secretary.

"He might have," said Biddo. "But it's not been achieved in outdoor pursuits. He's slow witted. He's not in the least bit street wise. I'm sorry. If you've got hopes of me agreeing to his participation, you've got another thing coming."

"He can make it Biddo," said the Club Secretary.

"He won't," said Biddo. "It's too dangerous. Even Tommy Mac said so. As far as I'm concerned, the idea needs scrapping. It's nigh impossible. It can't be done."

"It can if it's planned correctly," said the Chef.

"Which it has been," said the Club Secretary. "It's been planned meticulously. Everything's been thought out and considered to the last detail."

"We've made provision for every possible eventuality,"

said the Chef.

"And we're going to get him all the best gear," said the Club Secretary. "And provide him with a big plastic sheet for him to make a tent."

"We've got everything he's likely to need," said the Chef.

"But most importantly, thanks to Eddie's magic box, we've been able to provide him with a very definite route," said the Club Secretary. "He can't go wrong."

"Is that the same magic box I just heard peter out like a wet fart?" said Biddo.

"It is yes," said the Club Secretary. "But we don't need it now. We've already got all the information we need from it."

"And what information might that be?" said Biddo.

"We know the weather patterns for the next 5 days," said the Chef. "That means Anthony will know when to move on and when to make shelter and stay put. He'll be as right as rain.""

I beg to differ," said Biddo. "He's going to die out there. He's going to die horribly and alone. Bloody hell- the daft little bugger sometimes gets lost when he goes to our local wine store for me Vodka."

"He'll be alright," said the Club Secretary.

"He's going to die," said Biddo. "And if he does, those of you that have organised the expedition are going to be held to account. I'll see to it. I'll see that you bastards go to jail for a very long time."

"That's your prerogative," said the Chairman. "But I want to assure you this Biddo-Anthony didn't need any persuading."

"And, once again, I choose to differ," said Biddo.

"It's true," said the Chairman. "He volunteered to go. He's right up for it."

"He wasn't up for it early last evening," said Biddo. "In fact, I heard him telling the faggots the idea was ridiculous. He was refusing to have any part of it."

"That was until you added the straw that broke the camel's back," said Larkin.

"What are you talking about?" said Biddo.

"I'm talking about the fire incident," said Larkin. "Or were you hoping we'd very conveniently sweep that under the carpet?"

"Let's discuss that matter later," said the Chairman.

"Why not discuss it now?" said Alty.

"I said, we'll discuss it later," said the Chairman.

"Leave it Alty," said the Club Secretary.

"You need to face facts Biddo," said Larkin. "Anthony wants away from here because you've become too much of a liability. He feels let down."

"He feels more than let down," said Alty. "He's come to the conclusion that, as a father, you're a walking, talking disgrace."

"Me a disgrace!" said Biddo. "Me a disgrace as a father! You hard faced bastard. At least my son can hold his head up when he leaves the house."

"What's that meant to mean?" said Alty.

"You know exactly what I mean," said Biddo. "I've seen your Daniel. He's just like you. A long haired namby-pamby fucker. Do you know what Alty-I saw him skipping along your road last week with a pink ribbon in his hair."

"Did you really!" said Alty.

"I did," said Biddo. "He was skipping along and singing nursery rhymes like a little girl. I felt like removing my belt and tanning his arse good and proper. That's what they used to do with homos years ago. They used to beat the queerness out of them."

"I might just try that," said Alty.

"You want to," said Biddo. "I'll even hold him for you. He should be playing football with the other lads. If you're not careful, he's going to turn out to be a bum bandit like you and Larko."

"I very much doubt it," said Alty.

"I don't," said Biddo. "I don't doubt it at all. It's what's commonly referred to as, 'like father like son'."

"My so-called boy's a little girl actually," said Alty.

"He's what?" said Biddo.

[299]

"Her name's Danielle. She's 8. And she loves skipping. She actually likes playing football too. But that doesn't make her any less feminine."

"And she loves and respects her straight as a dye father too," said Larkin.

"That must be because he's like a second mother to her," said Biddo.

"It's because I work very hard at being a good father," said Alty.

"So do I," said Biddo.

"Don't talk wet," said Alty. "You're a bloody disgrace and a bigot. You should have been sterilised once you'd reached puberty."

"And you should have been put down like a mad dog the first time you started taking an interest in men's private parts," said Biddo while proceeding to circle the gathering. "Jesus Christ-look at the way this lot are looking at me. You'd think they were all candidates for Father of the Year. You lot are no better than me. I know you lot. I know you far better than you might think. You've all let your kids down at some time or other. Admit it-there's not one of you that can call himself the perfect father."

"Maybe not, but we're not pissed 24 hours a day," said Larkin.

"And we don't go around trying to set people on fire," said Alty.

"For God's sake!" said the Chairman. "Let's discuss the fire matter later."

"No Hulmey-let's discuss it now," said Larkin.

"That's the reason Anthony finally snapped and decided to go for help," said Alty. "Not because me and Larko persuaded him. But because he'd had enough of his father's lunacy."

"That's not the reason at all," said the Chairman. "He's volunteered to go because he appreciates he's the youngest and fittest. He knows he's the only one that could survive the rigors of the journey."

"That's bullshit!" said Larkin. "That's absolute bullshit.

He's volunteered to go because he wants to get away from his nutcase of a dad. And you know it Hulmey. What's going on here? Why are you protecting the drunken bastard all of a sudden?"

"I'm not protecting him at all," said the Chairman before excusing himself and heading over to the door to talk to an extremely anxious looking Professor.

"This is wrong this is Hilly," said Alty while approaching the Club Secretary. "Larko was viciously assaulted this morning and nothing at all has been done about it."

"It'll be sorted, I promise you," said the Club Secretary. "Let's just deal with one thing at a time."

"There you go," said Alty upon taking the floor. "He's no better than his mate. They've closed ranks on us."

"I know they have," said Larkin. "And I think I know why. They're trying to avoid offending Biddo. That's right isn't it Hilly?"

"Not at all," said the Club Secretary.

"Bollocks!" said Alty. "You're pussyfooting around the bastard. You're concerned he'll pull Anthony out of his expedition. You want his blessing don't you Hilly?"

"There's only one person in need of a blessing right now," said the Chairman after returning to his place and taking a deep breath.

"What do you mean?" said the Club Secretary. "What's happened now?"

"Brian Matthews has just suffered some sort of seizure," said the Chairman.

"A seizure!" said Steadman. "What do you mean? Is he alright?"

"He is now," said the Chairman. "Although it had apparently been touch and go at one time."

"How do you mean?" said Blackie.

"He'd stopped breathing twice," said the Chairman. "The Professor had to revive him."

"My God!" said Blackie.

"That's awful," said the Club Secretary.

"It is," said Steadman. "A seizure hey. Another

[301]

charming thing to look forward to if we take ill. Although, I can't remember being told seizures were an aspect of the disease."

"I can't either," said Blackie.

"The seizure had nothing to do with the disease," said the Chairman while glaring accusingly at Larkin and Alty. "At least, not according to the Professor. He reckons it was caused by a reaction to a foreign substance."

"What foreign substance?" said Steadman.

"Paint," said the Chairman.

"Paint!" said Hewlett. "What paint?"

"The paint on his face," said the Chairman. "He suspects there might have been lead in it. He thinks some of it might have trickled into Matthews's mouth and eyes overnight."

"Oh Christ!" said Steadman. "The poor bastard. He must have been in mortal agony."

"He's lucky not to have lost his sight," said Blackie.

"That's precisely what the Professor said," said the Chairman.

"How is he now?" said Hewlett.

"Reasonably stable," said the Chairman.

"What do you mean, 'reasonably stable'?" said Blackie. "Is he out of the woods?"

"Apparently so," said the Chairman. "But he's got the mother of all sore throats."

"Maybe we should adjourn this meeting and come back later," said the Club Secretary.

"You're probably right," said the Chairman.

"I think you need to do some house cleaning first," said Biddo.

"What do you mean 'house cleaning'?" said the Club Secretary.

"You need to clean house," said Biddo. "You need to get certain affairs in order. A thoroughly decent man's been poisoned and taken to the brink of death. And it's not as though it's a mystery who was responsible. I don't think any of us should be going anywhere just now. I think the matter needs to be dealt with, as of this minute."

"And I think you should keep your drunken mouth shut," said Larkin. "Me and Alty know we've messed up. We know what we've done. We don't need the likes of you reminding us."

"But you do need the likes of me to remind you," said the Chairman after pounding his two fists against his table. "You've almost killed one of our members. What were you thinking? What the hell were you both thinking?"

"We weren't thinking," said Alty. "It was just meant to be a bit of fun. Painting someone's face while they're asleep is something we've done hundreds of times."

"As far as I'm aware, we used the same sort of paint we always use," said Larkin. "How were we to know the makers have started putting lead in it?"

"What sort of paint was it?" said Steadman.

"I don't know," said the Club Secretary. "But I do know this much. It's the sort that's almost impossible to remove from skin."

"What!" said the Chairman.

"It must be an oil based substance," said the Club Secretary. "It certainly isn't water based. I don't think it's going to come off."

"How do you know?" said the Chairman.

"Because I've tried," said the Club Secretary. "I tried earlier this morning."

"What with?" said the Chairman.

"A sponge and some soapy water," said the Club Secretary.

"You're not going to get it off with soap and water," said the Chairman. "You're going to need a solvent such as Turpentine or Methylated Spirits."

"And you're not likely to find any of that lying around," said the Chef.

"Especially while Kenny Biddo's around," said Woodhouse.

"Go to hell, fat boy," said Biddo.

[303]

"Let's cut the smart arse remarks out for the time being," said the Chairman. "There's a man lying extremely ill in that next carriage. Try to keep the tone appropriate to his situation."

"Did you try using washing up liquid?" said the Chef.

"I tried just about everything," said the Club Secretary. "Apart from a blow lamp, that is."

"I don't know what you're worried about," said Hamill. "It'll come off eventually."

"Eventually!" said the Chairman. "Eventually! Bloody hell Hamill! I don't want eventually. I want right now. I want the paint off immediately in case a rescue team arrives. For God's sake-what are they going to think of us?"

"What are his family going to think?" said the Chef.

They'll probably think he's never looked better," said Hamill. "I've certainly never seen him looking better. You never know-they might build a nice little hutch for him in the garden."

"Sod off Hamill," said the Chairman. "I know you've never liked the man, but there's no call for that sort of tasteless remark."

"What happens if he dies and his family demand an open casket?" said Woodhouse. "His grandchildren are going to be awfully confused. Let's be honest, there's nothing in the bible to suggest people turn into rats or squirrels once they pop their clogs."

"And you can sod off too Woody," said the Chairman.

"Is that what they painted him as?" said Steadman.

"Yes," said the Club Secretary. "I think that's what he is."

"What is he Larkin?" said the Chairman. "Would you care to enlighten us?"

"A weasel," said Larkin while twitching nervously. "At least that's what it said on the stencil packaging."

"A weasel!" snarled the Chairman through the tightest of clenched teeth. "That's nice. That's lovely. That really is lovely. A fucking weasel."

"What's wrong with a weasel?" said Woodhouse.

"What's wrong with a weasel!" said the Chairman. "What's wrong with a weasel Woody! I'll tell you what's wrong with a weasel shall I...Weasels are infamously sneaky. Weasels are sly and deceitful creatures. They're thieves."

"Thieves!" said Woodhouse.

"They steal anything," said the Chairman. "They've been known to steal baby rabbits and bird's eggs and things like that. Jesus Christ! I know Matthews isn't everybody's cup of tea, but he doesn't deserve to be remembered as a weasel."

"Is a weasel a rodent?" said Hamill.

"I don't know and I don't fucking care," said the Chairman.

"I think it's a mammal," said McShane. "I think it's a mammal Hulmey."

"It's a mammal then," said the beleaguered Chairman while shaking his head in utter disdain.

"I thought all rodents were mammals," said Woodhouse. "What's a raccoon then?"

"I think it's a sort of monkey," said McShane.

"It's not a monkey," said Hamill. "A raccoon's a baby bear. I think it's like a small panda."

"It's not," said Woodhouse. "It's a marsupial."

"A marsupial!" said Hamill. "What's a marsupial?"

"A small bear," said Woodhouse. "They carry their young in pouches. And I think they eat eucalyptus leaves."

"That's a koala," said McShane. "I've actually looked after one of them."

"When was this?" said a highly suspicious Woodhouse.

"A couple of years ago," said McShane. "It was a lovely little thing. Our Frank pinched it."

"Your Frank did what?" said Woodhouse.

"He stole it from Chester Zoo," said McShane.

"What the hell for?" said Steadman.

"He didn't have the money for a decent birthday present for his step daughter," said McShane. "He'd just been laid off by the Corpy."

[305]

"He should be laid 6 feet under the ground," said the Chairman. "I think those beautiful things are on the endangered species list."

"They are," said Steadman. "As far as I recall, there are only six of them left in captivity."

"I think you'll find that's five now," said McShane.

"Why?" said Steadman. "The poor little thing didn't die did it?"

"No," said McShane. "It's still very much alive. Our Chantelle refused to give it up when the R.S.P.C.A called to collect it. She can be a defiant little fucker when she wants to be. It's probably up in the loft with all the Christmas decorations and all that sort of stuff."

"Oh God give me strength!" said the Chairman. "Where's the Professor? We're going to need stronger sedatives. I think our members have all come down with the disease. I think they've all gone stark raving bonkers."

"What's a ferret?" said McShane. "Is a ferret the same as a polecat?"

"Oh Christ!" said the Chairman while looking to the ceiling.

"I've often wondered that," said Woodhouse. "That's actually a very good question that is Tommy."

"Does anyone know?" said McShane. "Do you know the difference Hewlett? You spend a lot of time in the British countryside hunting and shooting defenceless animals."

"My family owns most of the English countryside," said a vacant and perturbed looking Hewlett before turning to face the window. "Now leave me alone-this is my meditative hour."

"I'm sorry to have troubled you sir," said a sheepish looking McShane while tiptoeing back to his chair. "Try and remind me not to bother you again. Particularly if you're choking to death on a chicken bone or something. What about you Hulmey. Do you know the difference?"

"Know the difference between what?" said the Chairman.

[306]

"The difference between a ferret and a polecat," said McShane.

"I don't actually," said the Chairman before slumping into his chair. "And, to be honest, I don't really care. I think I've lost the will to live. I couldn't care less if a ferret has just been sworn in as the new President of the United States. And I couldn't give a damn if a polecat has just become Manchester United's record signing centre forward. I do know the difference between right and wrong though. And I therefore know that what happened to Matthews was wrong. It was wrong on every conceivable level. It was a grave insult to a thoroughly decent man. And for that matter, in order to prevent the same thing happening again, I'm going to suspend Larkin and Alty with immediate effect."

"And I should think so too," said Biddo.

"You shut your drunken mouth," said Alty.

"For how long?" said the Club Secretary after opening his ledger and raising his right hand to urge for some quiet. "For how long Hulmey?"

"Twelve months," said the Chairman.

"Twelve months!" said Alty. "Fucking hell! Twelve bloody months! The Yorkshire Ripper got less than that for murdering numerous prostitutes? That's a bit stiff isn't it?"

"I'd have thought so too," said Hamill.

"That means we'll miss the entire Cheltenham Festival trip," said Alty.

"If it was up to me, you'd miss the next 10 festivals," said Biddo.

"And if it was up to me, you'd already be doing time for arson," said Larkin. "What about it Hulmey? What are you going to do about this mental bastard?"

"We're going to have to deal with that matter some other time," said the Chairman.

"Why some other time?" said Alty.

"Because I want to get Anthony suited, booted and away first," said the Chairman. "That's what everyone wants isn't it?"

[307]

"It is," said Hamill. "But Anthony's not going anywhere until tomorrow morning. Don't forget-I was there when we established that. What are you stalling for Hulmey? What's going on lad?"

"I've already told you that," said Larkin. "He's afraid that if he punishes Biddo, he'll order his son to pull out of the expedition."

"Is that right?" said Hamill. "Is that right Hulmey? Has drunken arse got you by the short and curlies?"

"Not at all," said the Chairman. "I intend punishing Biddo. Make no mistake about it. But it's going to be done in my own good time."

"I don't think so," said Hamill. "I'd prefer it done in my own good time. And don't worry about Biddo. If he attempts to pull his son out of the expedition, I'll take him to one side and have a word in his shell like."

"Like you did with Morris?" said Biddo.

"I never laid a hand on Morris," said Hamill.

"Alright lads," said the Chairman. "Let's not go back there. This situation's volatile enough as it is."

"That's because it's not being handled properly," said Hamill.

"Then why don't you handle it," said the Chairman. "Why don't you take control Hamill. That's what you've always wanted isn't it? Do your worst fella. Go ahead-take control of the madhouse."

"I would do," said Hamill. "But my very astute and wonderful dad once advised me never to clean up anyone else's mess. He told me that if I cleaned up someone else's mess once, I'd end up cleaning up their mess again and again and again. And this is your mess Hulmey. This is your unholy mess. You've caused much of this through your lack of assertiveness. Make no mistake-I'm going to continue to have my say like any member's entitled to-but you're the one that's ultimately going to have to decide Biddo's fate. You're the one who's going to have to suffer the wrath of the self righteous this time."

"What do you mean?" said the Chairman.

"You know very well what I mean," said Hamill. "I saw the filthy looks some of your whiter than white members gave me, Woody and Tommy when we came back after locking Morris up. You'd have thought we'd returned with the plague."

"And I've heard a rumour the same people want the police involved when we get home," said Woodhouse.

"I've heard that too," said McShane."

"So what exactly will satisfy you Hamill?" said the Chairman. "Will punishing Biddo satisfy you?"

"It will yes," said Hamill. "But bear this in mind Hulmey. Biddo's punishment is going to have to be a lot harsher than the one you've just handed out to Alty and Larko."

"Why's that?" said the Chairman.

"Because his was a far worse crime," said Hamill.

"Why was it?" said the Chairman.

"Because what Biddo did wasn't a childish prank that went wrong," said Hamill. "It was premeditated and wicked in the extreme."

"That's right," said Larkin. "And I've got several eye witnesses to prove it."

"Like who?" said the Chairman.

"Like me," said Alty. "I saw everything. I watched Biddo creep into the room and look around. He must have been making sure everyone was asleep. I then watched him very slowly and carefully unscrew the top off his vodka bottle and proceed to sprinkle the entire contents over Larko's bed."

"And then he very deliberately dropped his cigarette," said Larkin.

"There you go," said Hamill. "What more do you want Hulmey?"

"Another witness would be nice," said the Chairman. "And preferably, one that's likely to be impartial."

"Would you like to know the truth?" said Anthony who had just quietly entered the room unnoticed and was making his way to the kitchen. "Would you like to know what really happened lads?"

[309]

"I'd like nothing more than to know what really happened," said the Chairman while adjusting his position. "As long as it's the truth that is."

"It is the truth," said Anthony. "It's the God's honest truth. So I'll start by exposing a lie."

"What lie is that?" said the Chairman.

"Larko's account wasn't entirely honest," said Anthony.

"What do you mean?" said Larkin.

"I'm afraid you got part of your account wrong Larko," said Anthony.

"In what way?" said the Chairman.

"My dad hadn't been smoking," said Anthony.

"What!" said Alty.

"He hadn't been smoking," said Anthony. "I'd hidden his cigarettes from him the previous evening to prevent him setting fire to his bed. It's a habit I got into when living under his roof while my new flat was being decorated. You wouldn't believe the amount of fires he's started through smoking."

"Bloody hell!" said the Club Secretary.

"Bloody hell, is right," said the Chef. "That's left a lot of people with egg on their faces hasn't it."

"It certainly has," said Blackie. "Maybe people will stop to think before they pass judgement in the future."

"Thank you Anthony," said a smiling Biddo after opening out his arms as if to receive acclaim. "Thank you son-I knew I could depend on you."

"Well, that's a turn up for the books," said Steadman.

"It is isn't it," said the Chairman. "Perhaps we can get on with the rest of the club business now."

"Hear, hear," said Blackie.

"I'm not sure we can just yet," said the Club Secretary.

"Why not?" said the Chairman.

"Because someone caused that fire," said the Club Secretary. "Somebody set fire to Larko's bed."

"That's a point," said the Chef.

"But who?" said the Chairman.

"Don't look at me," said Hamill.

"Nor me," said Woodhouse.

"What if I was to tell you, it was your number one suspect," said Anthony after popping his head through the serving hatch.

"Which number one suspect?" said the Chairman.

"My old fella," said Anthony.

"Your old fella!" said the Chairman. "But I thought you'd just exonerated him."

"I did nothing of the sort," said Anthony. "My dad mightn't have had any cigarettes but he did have a box of matches on him. A half full box of Swan Vesta, if I remember right. I've no idea where he got them. The first two matches he struck failed to light. That was probably because his hands were shaking so much. But the third match worked. The third match landed lit and set Larko's bedspread alight."

"Bloody hell!" said Steadman.

"Why didn't you stop him?" said the Chef.

"Because I thought he'd struck the matches to see where he was going in the dark," said Anthony.

"Jesus Christ!" said the Chairman. "Jesus H Christ! What's this club coming to? I don't know what to say. I'm sorry I asked for the truth now. I've got to be honest here lads-I wanted to believe it was an accident. I really don't know what to say."

"I do" said Larkin. "Thank you Anthony. Thank you very much. That couldn't have been easy for you."

"And I'm going to say, 'what the fuck!' and continue to scratch my badly confused head for a while," said the Club Secretary.

'What the fuck', doesn't do justice as to what we've just heard," said Steadman. "I can't believe it. Kenny Biddo an arsonist. I'm gobsmacked. It's incredible."

"And what's also incredible is the fact that nobody tried to stop him," said Blackie.

"That's what I was thinking," said Woodhouse.

"I was still half cut and shattered," said Alty. "I didn't get to sleep until about 5 o'clock. Everything was a blur. It was almost surreal. I was struggling to comprehend what he was up to at first. I thought he was

just going to swig the vodka, not pour it all over the bed.
And even when he started to pour it, I thought he was
having a piss. Let's be honest, it wouldn't have been the
first time he's pissed on someone else's bed."
"What about when he lit the match," said Blackie.
"Didn't that arouse your suspicions?"
"I just thought he was going to light a ciggie," said Alty.
"Isn't that what you'd have thought Blackie?"
"I suppose so," said Blackie.
"When did you finally realise what was actually going
on Anthony?" said the Chairman.
"When the quilt finally caught fire," replied Anthony.
"Did you help put it out?" said the Club Secretary.
"I ran," said Anthony. "I just took off like a scalded cat.
I can't explain why."
"You were traumatised," said the Chef. "You'd just
witnessed your father commit an unspeakable crime.
That must have been hard to process."
"It must have been," said the Club Secretary.
"It's because I'm gutless just like my dad said, "said a
head bowed Anthony while making his way to the exit.
"I never said you were gutless," said Biddo after
stiffening up in his chair and rapping his fingers against
the arm.
"I'm afraid you did," said Anthony. "Don't forget dad-
these walls are wafer thin. You also called me a wimpy
kid and said that I was too slow to think for myself under
pressure. What the hell dad! Have you any idea how
many times I've bailed you out over the years? Have
you any idea how many times I've pleaded with mum
not to throw you out after you've come home shit faced?
And you repay me by calling me all those names. I'm
sorry dad. I've had enough."
"It's alright son," said Biddo. "I understand. The long
knives have been out for me for some time. I know
what's going on here. I've known for a long time."
"What's going on here is you've just been exposed as an
arsonist and a menace to society," said Alty.
"Congratulations Biddo. You are now what you'd

[312]

hoped Larko would become once you'd set him on fire.
You're toast."

"Are you satisfied now Hulmey?" said Hamill.

"I wouldn't necessarily call it satisfied," said the
Chairman.

"Why not?" said Hamill.

"Because I wouldn't," said the Chairman. "Why the
hell would I Hamill? I've just found out one of my
members and closest friends has committed an act that
can only be described as pure evil. It's unbelievable.
I'm struggling to come to terms with it to be honest."

"So am I," said the Chef.

"What are you going to do with him Hulmey?" said
Hamill. "How are you going to punish him?"

"I don't know yet," said the Chairman. "I just don't
know. Would you mind if I slept on it?"

"I would, as it happens" said Hamill. "I want the matter
dealt with now."

"So do I," said Woodhouse. "You dealt with Larko and
Alty quick enough."

"But why can't it wait?" said the Chairman.

"Because I've been offended," said Hamill. "And I
therefore want swift retribution. Now answer my
question Hulmey. What are you going to do with
Biddo?"

"What *should* I do with him?" said the Chairman while
scanning the room. "Have you any suggestions lads?
Don't forget, I'm brand new to this job."

"Why don't you lock him in one of the carriages with his
arson victim Larko and a monkey wrench and let nature
take its course," said Woodhouse.

"Behave yourself Woody," said Blackie. "We're not
barbarians."

"I actually like that idea," said Hamill. "It has a nice
ring to it. It would be like a scene from the film
Gladiator. Larko would be the people's champion."

"Why would he?" said Blackie.

"Because that fire could have spread and killed the lot of
us," said Hamill. "That's right isn't it Hulmey?"

[313]

"I suppose so," said the exhausted looking Chairman. "But I'd rather the matter be dealt with in a much more civilised way."

"Would you?" said Hamill before turning to the group. "What does everyone else think? What do you think lads. Should we put it to a vote? Should I start tearing up strips of paper?"

"I wouldn't waste your time," said the Chairman.

"Why not?" said Hamill.

"Because I'm not a big fan of the voting procedure," said the Chairman. "And because what you're proposing is cruel and barbaric."

"Don't let them do that Hulmey," said Blackie while approaching the Chairman with his hands clasped as if in prayer. "Don't let them hurt him. Let the proper authorities deal with the matter. Let's wait until we're rescued and then hand him over to the police."

"The police!" said the Chairman.

"That's right," said Blackie. "Let's hand him over to the police."

"Do you realise the ramifications of that?" said the Chairman.

"I do yes," said Blackie. "But I'd rather see him arrested than see his skull turned to mush."

"So would I, to be honest," said Steadman.

"You're growing soft in your old age Steadman," said Hamill.

"I'm just trying to be reasonable," said Steadman. "To be fair-I wasn't too enamoured by the terrible hiding Alec Morris received. I thought the police should have been allowed to handle that too."

"Well, it's been handled now," said Woodhouse.

"You do realise he's likely to serve up to 5 years in prison?" said the Club Secretary.

"I do yes," said Blackie. "And so be it. He's committed a very bad crime. But he'll also get treatment for his alcoholism while inside. By the time he's released, he'll be well and truly dried out. He'll be like a new man. He'll be like the old loveable and highly popular Biddo again."

"That actually makes sense," said Steadman.

"It does doesn't it," said the Chairman. "It makes very good sense. What do you think lads?"

"I couldn't agree more," said Larkin. "But what are you going to do in the meantime Hulmey? Are you going to allow a potential arsonist to move around as he pleases?"

"Now there's a point," said Hamill.

"I'll watch him," said Blackie. "I'll watch him like a hawk. You just put your feet up Hulmey. Just transfer all responsibility for him over to me. I'll make sure he behaves himself. I'll have the bugger under 24 hour watch."

"That's not going to be good enough," said Alty. "Not nearly good enough," said Larkin.

"It's not a bad idea as it happens," said the Chairman.

"Only because it allows you to pass the buck onto someone else," said Hamill.

"It's called diplomacy," said the Chairman.

"It's called burying your head in the sand," said Alty.

"You can call it what you like Alty," said the Chairman. "Right now, this has got nothing at all to do with you. You're serving a suspension, don't forget. It wasn't that long ago, you almost blinded one of my members. Now do yourself a massive favour and back the fuck off."

"Back the fuck off!" said Alty after turning to face the group. "He's going to do it isn't he? He's going to let the bastard get off with it."

"I'm not going to let him get off with anything," said the Chairman. "He'll get his punishment in good time. But in the meantime, Blackie's suggestion regarding the proper authorities appears to be the most sensible option."

"Thanks Hulmey," said Blackie. "I won't forget you for this."

"Well make sure you don't make me live to regret it," said the Chairman.

"You won't," said Blackie. "I won't let him out of my sight for a second. I promise I won't. And you know

[315]

my word Hulmey. You know how good my word is."

"Very well," said the Chairman. "As long as you understand what you're taking on."

"I understand exactly what I'm taking on," said Blackie.

"I don't believe this," said Larkin.

"I couldn't care less what you don't believe," said the Chairman. "I'm going to go with Blackie's idea. I'm going to entrust Biddo into his care until we get rescued. And that's the last I want to hear of the matter. It's done. It's over. It's settled."

"Settled!" said Alty. "It's not settled as far as me and Larko are concerned. There's a man on board this train who's gone completely and utterly insane."

"And he's still in denial, by the way," said Larkin.

"I've made my decision," said the Chairman.

"Made your decision!" said Alty. "Are you blind Hulmey? Have you got your head so far up your arse you're unable to see the big picture? Less than a couple of hours ago, that lunatic tried to kill one of your members. How long's it going to be before he tries to kill another?"

"He won't," said Blackie. "I'm going to have him on such a short reign, we'll be sharing the same lavatory pan and sliver of toilet paper."

"That's not good enough Blackie," said Alty. "He needs locking up. Don't you understand? He tried to murder someone earlier. Alec Morris was mutilated and almost left for dead for doing far less. We need to feel safe in our beds at night."

"Everyone does," said Woodhouse.

"I couldn't agree more," said Hamill.

"Which is why he should be locked up," said Larkin.

"And he will be," said Blackie. "Haven't you been listening to me? He's going to do time. He's going to do proper time. He's going to do a lot of it. I'm going to see to it."

"I'd like to believe that was true," said Alty. "I really would. But I think you're playing a blinder here Blackie. I think you're stalling for time. I think you're hoping Biddo's catalogue of crimes will be forgotten once we're rescued."

"What do you mean, 'catalogue of crimes'?" said Blackie. "He's only committed one misdemeanour."

"He's done more than that," said Woodhouse. "He mightn't have succeeded in killing Larko but he still managed to set fire to a very expensive quilt set. That's going to have to be replaced".

"Then I'll replace it," said Blackie. "As soon as we get home, I'll go on Amazon and find a similar one."

"And are you going to pay for the carriage to be cleaned from top to bottom?" said Woodhouse.

"I will yes," replied Blackie. "I'll do that as well Woody. I'll even clean the carriage myself if I have to."

"What about the bar door," said Tommy Mac. "How are you going to replace that? Do you think you're going to find one of them on Amazon?"

"Probably not," said Blackie.

"That's going to cost you thousands to replace," said Alty.

"It's not," said Hamill. "It's going to cost the club members thousands to replace. That's right isn't it Hilly?"

"I don't know off the top of my head," said the Club Secretary.

"You do fucking well know," said Hamill. "You told me that door had been hand made in Bavaria. You told me it was a one off. Very much like Biddo. Who-if it was up to me, would be under lock and key right now."

"That actually wouldn't be the worst idea in the world right now Hulmey," said the Club Secretary after suddenly becoming aware that the entire gathering had broken into two obvious and unevenly divided factions. "I'm sorry mate, but you're going to have to come up with something better than put Biddo into his nephew's custody. The natives have donned their war paint and are massing on the top of the ridge. Regardless of your decision, I don't think they're going to be satisfied with you handing him to a sympathetic chaperone to mind."

"You couldn't be more right," said Alty.

"I have to agree with Hilly our kid," said the Chef.

"You're going to have to watch yourself. You're going to have to play this very carefully. You're standing slap bang in the middle of a minefield. World War Three's about to break out here any minute."

"And as usual, our troops are badly outnumbered," said the Club Secretary.

"You've got me on your side," said Blackie after placing his right arm around the Chairman's shoulder. "I'm with you mate. I'm with you all the way as long as you don't lock him up. Biddo will be as good as gold. I'll even keep him off the sauce until we're rescued. I'll stay with him while he goes cold turkey. Just say the word and we'll go and gather some provisions. I promise, you won't see sight nor sound of the pair of us until we're rescued."

"And what happens when you fall asleep Blackie?" said Alty. "What happens then?"

"I won't fall asleep," said Blackie. "I'll ask the Professor to give me something to keep me awake. He's bound to have something in that little bag of tricks of his. And anyway Hulmey-I thought you'd made your mind up. I thought you'd agreed to put Biddo in my care. I thought the matter was done and dusted."

"It *was* done and dusted," said the Chairman. "But there was an awful lot I'd failed to consider."

"Like what?" said Blackie.

"Loads of things," said the Chairman. "The fact that Biddo was only allowed to come along if his son was here to keep an eye on him."

"Which hasn't really worked out has it?" said the Club Secretary.

"And then there was his appearance when he arrived in London," said the Chairman. "Bloody hell Blackie-when was the last time he had a proper shave?"

"And how long has he had those same clothes on?" said the Club Secretary.

"I've no idea," said Blackie.

[318]

"He spewed up his guts on that new platform Blackie," said the Chairman.

"So what," said Blackie. "We've probably all done that some time or other."

"It caused a frail old man to slip and suffer a concussion." said the Chairman.

"And only for some quick thinking by one of our members, that nice old man could well have died where he lay." said the Chef.

"In his defence, Biddo hadn't been well Hulmey," said Blackie. "He'd had some sort of stomach bug prior to leaving Liverpool. He doesn't throw up when he's been drinking. I've certainly never known it to happen."

"Neither have I to be honest," said the Chairman. "And I've never known him to be aggressive in drink before. What's all that about?"

"I don't know," said Blackie. "Maybe it's the new tablets he's been on."

"It probably is," said the Chairman. "But the chances are, they're in his system now. They seem to have sent him doolally. And it's anyone's guess for how long."

"Which means you're going to lock him up doesn't it Hulmey?" said Blackie.

"I've been left with no alternative," said the Chairman.

"Is right," said Alty.

"It's wrong," said Blackie.

"I think you'll find it's not negotiable," said Hamill before poking Blackie in the ribs and encouraging him to sit down.

"We could lock him in the fourth carriage with Alec Morris," said the Club Secretary. "That would keep him out of trouble."

"And out of danger," said the Chef.

"And he'd have company," said the Chairman.

"I actually don't agree with the shared cell idea," said Woodhouse. "I personally think he should be placed in solitary confinement. If it was up to me, I'd lock him in the mail room on his own."

"And I'd personally throw away the key," said Larkin.

"He's not going to be locked up in any mail room," said the Chairman. "We're going to do this the just and civilized way. I'm going to go with Hilly's suggestion. I'm going to put him with Alec Morris. And by the way lads-while I've got your undivided attention-I want you all to consider this. Biddo's a lot older than Morris. I don't want him hurt."

"Not even a teeny weenie bit?" said Woodhouse.

"Not in the slightest," said the Chairman.

"That's a pity," said Alty. "But at least we'll be able to sleep a little easier now."

"You don't deserve to sleep any easier," said Biddo. "The wicked shouldn't be allowed to rest easy. They should be shovelling coal in Hell."

"Would that be with all the other alleged gays?" said Alty.

"It's nothing to do with your sexuality," said Biddo. "It's to do with that hair brained expedition. You were the one that persuaded my Anthony to go. I won't forget that Alty. I'll never forget that. He's going to die you know. My boy's going to die cold and alone, calling for his mother. Do you think you're going to be able to live with that?"

"Anthony volunteered to go," said the Chairman.

"Anthony was coerced," said Biddo before snatching a glass ashtray and hurling it Frisbee-like in the direction of the Chairman. "Anthony's always been a soft touch. That's why Alty and Larkin like playing silly games with him. He's got a worse losing record than Eddie the Eagle. You're a spineless bastard Hulmey. You're a worthless, excuse for a human being. It seems Hamill was right about you all along."

"And it seems, people were right about you," said the Chairman while carefully picking up the larger fragments of the tray. "You're out of control Biddo. You're a loose cannon. And whether you like it or not, that's the main reason Anthony wants to get away."

"Where is he now?" said Biddo.

"Why?" said the Chairman.

[320]

"That's my business," said Biddo.

"Fine," said the Chairman before folding his arms and leaning back in his chair. "Let it remain your business."

"I'd like to talk to him in private before he sets off towards his certain death," said Biddo.

"About what?" said Hamill.

"That's my business," said Biddo.

"And mine too if that talk's likely to affect his decision to go for help," said Hamill while slowly inching forward.

"Where is he?" said Biddo.

"He's with the Professor," said the Chairman.

"He's having a full internal examination before he embarks on his journey," said Woodhouse. "It's obligatory. All explorers have to have one apparently. You know the procedure by now Biddo.. The latex glove.....the knees raised to the chest. The index finger up the arsehole. That sort of business. It can be quite harrowing to be fair."

"It's never worried me," said Alty.

"Nor me," said Larkin. "I've always found it quite pleasant."

"You would," said Biddo. "You probably ask for the full fist treatment. What's Anthony really doing?"

"He's learning basic navigation," said the Club Secretary.

"And he's making extremely good progress, by all accounts," said the Chairman.

"Is he really?" said Biddo. "Do you mind me asking when his lesson began?"

"Not at all," said the Chairman. "I'd say it was about an hour after the fire had been extinguished. What do you reckon Hilly?"

"I'd say it was just less than that," said the Club Secretary. "Perhaps half that."

"Why do you ask Biddo?" said the Chairman.

"Because I wanted confirmation that you're the two faced conniving twat I suspected you are," said Biddo while finding his sudden lunge towards the Chairman halted by Woodhouse's powerful left arm. "You said you were going to run the idea by me first. If I remember right, you said it was the decent thing to do." "It was the decent thing to do," said the Chairman. "But you'd already decided Anthony was going on the expedition," said Biddo. "You'd already got him equipped. You'd already lined up navigation lessons for him."

"I know," said the Chairman. "That was really naughty of me. Just like you were naughty when you claimed you'd gone to the second carriage to kiss your son goodnight. You were just looking for trouble. Running the idea by you *was* the decent thing to do Biddo. But in fairness, I was never going to wait for your permission. You're a disgrace. As one or two of the lads have already said-you're not fit to call yourself a father."

"And while we're on that particular subject Biddo," said Hamill. "Don't you ever accuse me of being anything less than the perfect father. And don't you ever try to suggest I've ever let my kids down. I might have far more enemies than friends and I might be as unpopular as a fart in a two man sleeping bag, but I pride myself on being the best father on this planet. In fact, I believe I'm the Real Madrid of fucking fathers."

"I wasn't referring to you," said Biddo.

"Oh you were," said the Chairman. "You were talking about all of us. Now, why don't you run along with Woody and collect a few things. And by the way Biddo-a few things means, soap, a couple of blankets, a toothbrush, a razor and some reading material. It doesn't include highly flammable alcoholic spirits, matches and cigarettes. I don't want that carriage fire-damaged like the other one. The club's in enough trouble as it is."

"And there's only so much Blackie's going to be able to order from Amazon," said the Club Secretary. "He certainly won't be able to order you a taxi to get you to the fourth carriage."

"Morris isn't in the fourth carriage," said Woodhouse

[322]

while ushering the snarling and unrepentant Biddo towards the exit.

"Well, put him in the next carriage up then," said the Chairman. "He isn't in that one either," said Hamill.

"I beg your pardon," said the Chairman.

"Morris isn't in that carriage," said Hamill.

"Where is he then?" said the Chairman.

"He's in the very last one," said Hamill.

"The very last one?" said the Chairman.

"That's right," said Hamill while watching a grey faced Chairman slowly pick his way through an arc of confused club members. "He's in the last one along. What's the problem?"

"What's the matter Hulmey?" said Woodhouse.

"There's no heating!" said the Chairman.

"What!" said Steadman.

"There's no heating in that carriage," said the Club Secretary.

"Why not?" said Hamill after taking evasive action to allow the Chairman to get by. "Why would there be no heating?"

"Because I told Larko to shut the heating off in that carriage to conserve battery life," said the Chairman before opening the dining carriage door, pinching his collar closed and drawing as deep a breath as was humanly possible.

CHAPTER FOURTEEN
JUST VISITING

For reasons known only to the club's devastated top brass, it had been left to the gaunt and badly shaken Chef to inform those who had remained in the dining room that the frozen body of Alec Morris had been discovered on the floor of the last carriage; an announcement which had sent the recently boosted spirit of the entire group plummeting several tiers beneath its more familiar depth. Confirmation, which those stupefied members had almost immediately demanded, had been provided by the Professor less than an hour later and not just because he was the person best qualified to pronounce the unfortunate Morris dead, but because the devastated Chairman had refused to raise his head in response to his club member's enquiries as he made his short, ponderous journey through the dining carriage on his way back to his appointed sleeping berth.

The rest of the men were still determined to get answers however and it therefore wasn't long before the Professor found himself at the centre of a large rolling maul that was to come to rest to the left of the serving hatch. For instance, Hewlett, who had immediately suspected foul play, had been desperate to know what condition the body was in because he was convinced the two creatures he had seen days earlier, were still at large and therefore, very possibly, Morris's killer. The question as to whether Morris had died from malnutrition or dehydration had also been raised, albeit extremely tentatively-but that hypothesis had been quashed in its infancy after a self satisfied Hamill had returned from the scene of the tragedy with several dirty dishes and a large assortment of torn chocolate bar wrappers. Blackie, while clearly concerned, was by some way the least interested in the whys and wherefores regarding Morris's death because his mind was still very much on what was going to happen to Kenny Biddo, his recently condemned and disgraced uncle.

"I think there's a lesson to be learnt here lads," he had said during a rare and brief period of silence and contemplation. "Locking someone in those remote carriages is wrong. You might as well be condemning them to death."

Paul Woodhouse and Tommy Mac had responded to the news very differently from everyone else. They had asked for no clarity at all and had made no comment on the tragedy whatsoever. Instead, after exchanging a few private words, they had quietly picked up their things and taken up residence at a table in the far corner of the room; a vantage point that would enable them to watch and listen to the subsequent enquiry unfold in its entirety. As a result, none of the other members had felt safe enough or confident enough to ask one of the most pertinent questions of all-'had Alec Morris died from the injuries sustained during his violent arrest and vicious beating?'

Hamill had reacted to the situation in a most unexpected way because, unlike the majority of the other near frantic passengers who were clearly wanting to attach culpability to someone, something or anything, he had been the epitome of calmness and diplomacy. There had been none of his familiar ranting, raving or threatening behaviour. There had been no accusations fired or any scathing criticism apportioned and even when one of the highly strung passengers complained about the weakness of the tea, he had simply, without any fuss at all, donned the Chef's apron, gathered up a stack of dirty cups and saucers and headed out into the kitchen to make a fresh and more palatable brew. So out of character had Hamill's behaviour been, very few of the passengers had noticed the solemn and moist eyed Chairman enter the dining carriage and hand his brother a neatly folded white cotton sheet.

"Would you do me a massive favour our kid- will you go and lay Morris's body out on his bed and cover him with this please," he said before taking his seat, removing his pen from his breast pocket and very deliberately opening his register.

"Why me?" whispered the clearly agitated Chef from behind the partition of his right hand.

"Because you're one of the very few people qualified to do it," said the Chairman.

"Why am I?" said the Chef.

"Because you worked in a hospital for 30 or so years," said the Chairman.

"Only as a cook," said the Chef. "I wasn't a porter. I wasn't a mortician's assistant. I was never asked to do anything like that. To be honest, I never saw anything worse than s a badly sprained ankle during my time at the hospital."

"Just do as you're told our kid," said the Chairman.

"I'm sorry, I'm not sure I can," said the Chef. "I don't think I've got the stomach to do something like that."

"Oh, for Christ's sake," said the Chairman.

"I'll do it," said Steadman. "I've handled a dead body before. "But I want you to tell me what the hell's been going on first. What do you think happened Hulmey?"

"I'd rather not discuss that right now," said the Chairman after adding Morris's name to the list of deceased and missing. "In fact, I don't really want to talk about anything right now. I want to put this register in order, make myself a sandwich and a drink and then retire to my room. I suggest the rest of you do the same and we'll talk some more when we've been rescued. You're on your own now lads. I've had enough. I'm finished with this club."

"What the hell!" said Steadman. "What do you mean, 'finished'? We're your subscription paying members. Don't you think we've got a right to some sort of explanation?"

"What sort of explanation?" said the Chairman.

"Like what happened," said Steadman.

"Like the condition of the body," said Hewlett.

"Go and see the body if you want to," said the Chairman. "Go and see it for yourself Hewlett. It's in

the 7th carriage. You can't miss it. It's the one that's
under the far bed."
"Under the bed!" said Larkin.
"That's right," said the Chairman.
"What was he doing under the bed?" said Larkin.
"I don't know," said the Chairman. "That's how I
found him. He was rolled up in a tightly formed ball
under his bed with one hand pointing towards the
window. It was horrifying. His eyes were wide open.
You'd swear he was still alive. To be honest-forget
about what I've just said about going to see the body.
That was really insensitive of me. It'd probably be best
if you all keep well away."
"That's right," said the Chef. "There's nothing to be
gained by looking at something as affecting as that.
You're likely to be haunted forever."
"Have you any idea how long he's been dead?" said
Blackie.
"None at all," said the Chairman. "Why would I? I'm
an engineer not a bloody pathologist. You'd probably be
best asking Woody or Tommy."
"Why's that?" said Blackie.
"Because they were meant to be feeding him weren't
they?" said the Chairman.
"We did fucking well feed him," said Woodhouse. "We
fed him three meals a day. He didn't starve to death if
that's what you're insinuating."
"What does the Professor think?" said Steadman.
"I don't know as yet," said the Chairman.
"You must know," said Steadman. "The old boy
pronounced him dead. He must have made some sort of
comment."
"He didn't," said the Chairman. "He just shook his
head and went to his room. We haven't seen him since,
have we our kid?"
"No," said the Chef.
"Had his body been mutilated in any way?" said
Hewlett.
"Not as far as I could tell," said the Chef. "He was

[327]

badly bruised, but we already know why that was. He looked as if he'd been frozen in time."

"Like us," said Larkin.

"So have you drawn the same conclusion as me?" said Hamill while heading to the Chairman's table with a fully laden tray.

"That would depend what your conclusion is," said the Chairman.

"Mine would be accidental death," said Hamill while proceeding to stir the pot.

"That would be my conclusion too," said Woodhouse.

"That's fine," said the Chairman.

"Is it?" said Hamill. "Does that mean you're agreeing with me for once Hulmey?"

"I wouldn't say that," said the Chairman.

"What would you say then?" said Hamill.

"I'm saying nothing at all right now," said the Chairman. "I'm saying nothing more until I know all the facts."

"Why?" said Hamill after taking his chair and folding his arms.

"Because without all the facts, I'd only be speculating," said the Chairman.

"I reckon you're already speculating," said Hamill. "You don't believe Morris's death was an accident do you?"

"That's for me to know," said the Chairman.

"With the greatest respect Hulmey-I think that's for your members to know as well," said Steadman. "You've got me wondering now. What's going on fella? Do you know something we don't?"

"Not at all," said the Chairman.

"But you clearly don't believe Morris's death was a tragic accident," said Steadman.

"He wants someone to blame," said Woodhouse.

"I'm not going to blame anyone as yet," said the Chairman. "It's not my position to apportion blame."

"Whose position is it then?" said Hamill.

"The proper authorities," said the Chairman.

"Why the authorities?" said Hamill.

"Because this matter's far too big for me to deal with," said the Chairman. "This is no longer a club matter. It's a matter for the police and the law courts to sort out."

"But why?" said Hamill. "Everyone but you seems to agree Morris's death was an accident."

"That's fine," said the Chairman. "They're all adults. They're all entitled to their opinions. But it's still up to the police and the authorities to get to the bottom of the matter. Let's just put it to bed for now and come back to it when we've been rescued."

"I'd rather not," said Hamill. "I want to know what's on your mind Hulmey. I've got a funny feeling you believe Morris died from the injuries he sustained during his fight with Woody. That's right isn't it?"

"It's got to be possible," said the Chairman.

"And it's also got to be possible he died from the effects of the extreme cold hasn't it?" said Hamill.

"I suppose so," said the Chairman.

"You suppose so," said Hamill. "How was it your kid described Morris when you first found him? 'Frozen! Or frozen stiff! It was one or the other. That's right isn't it?"

"If you say so," said the Chairman.

"Well for God's sake Hulmey-give your head a shake will you lad. I'm trying to help you here," said Hamill.

"Help me?" said the Chairman. "Help me in what way?"

"Help you avoid being charged with manslaughter," said Hamill.

"What!" said the Chairman. "What the hell are you talking about?"

"You were the one responsible for Morris's death," said Hamill. "You as good as killed him."

"How have you worked that out?" said the Chairman.

"You told Larko to turn the heating off in that carriage," said Hamill. "That was your decision. Yours and yours alone. You did that off your own bat. Nobody else but you. If you hadn't have done that, Morris would still be alive"

"Maybe so, but it was you that decided to put him in an unheated carriage," said the Chairman. "I didn't drag him there."

"Did Morris freeze to death?" said Hamill.

"I'm not qualified to say," said the Chairman.

"You are," said Hamill before rising and approaching the Chairman's table. "You've just told us you found him frozen stiff. Now I'm going to ask you again. And this time, I want you to think very carefully before you answer me. Is it possible Morris froze to death in that carriage?"

"It's possible yes," said the Chairman.

"And was it you that made the decision to have that carriage's heating switched off?" said Hamill.

"It was yes," said the Chairman.

"That's better," said Hamill.

"But it was you that put him there," said the Chairman. "You did that Hamill. And it was probably you that ordered him to be....."

"I know," said Hamill after raising his hands as if to submit. "I know I'm partly to blame. In fact, we're all partly to blame when you come to think of it."

"I'm not to blame," said Steadman.

"Nor am I," said Larkin.

"Aren't you Larko?" said Hamill. "I wouldn't be too sure of that if I was you."

"Why's that?" said Larkin.

"Because this could turn very unpleasant for you," said Hamill. "Don't forget-you were the one that physically turned the heating off."

"Only because I was told to," said Larkin.

"I know," said Hamill. "And you wanted Morris punished didn't you?"

"I did yes," said Larkin. "I was livid with him for what he'd done. But I didn't want him dead."

"I know that too," said Hamill. "But try to imagine how that would sound in court. You wanted the lad punished and you were the one that turned off the heating to the

room he'd been occupying. That wouldn't sound too
good would it Larko?"

"I suppose not," said Larkin.

"And you Steadman," said Hamill. "You've got some
nerve haven't you?"

"Why have I?" said Steadman.

"Because you've just had the audacity to suggest you're
not to blame in the slightest," said Hamill.

"I'm not to blame in the slightest," said Steadman.

"I disagree," said Hamill. "Isn't it possible you could
have done more?"

"In what way?" said Steadman.

"Like challenge my decision to have Morris locked up in
that aforementioned unheated carriage?" said Hamill.

"I didn't know the heating had been turned off," said
Steadman.

"Oh yes you did," said Hamill. "You were standing
right next to our Chairman when he gave Larko the order
to unplug."

"I don't remember that," said a highly confused
Steadman while looking to the group for support. "I
don't remember any of that."

"But I do," said Hamill. "I remember that clearly. And
Woody probably does too. Don't you Woody?"

"I remember it as if it happened a nanosecond ago," said
Woodhouse.

"What about you Blackie?" said Hamill. "Do you
consider yourself blameless too?"

"I do yes," said Blackie. "I don't think I could have
done anything to help."

"Did you not consider jumping in when Morris was
getting beaten?" said Hamill.

"I considered it yes," said Blackie. "But there were
fists, legs and boots flying everywhere. It would have
been like jumping into a giant threshing machine. I
didn't know what to say or do to be perfectly honest."

"You could have spoken out," said Alty. "We both
could have spoken out. We could have appealed on
Morris's behalf. Instead, we took the coward's way out

and said absolutely nothing."

"You could have all spoken out or done more," said Hamill. "That's why I'm going to stick by what I said earlier. We're all pretty much to blame in some way."

"We're not all to blame for his death though," said the Chairman. "You are Hamill. "And the charge of manslaughter's not going to be laid against me or any of these lads-it's going to be laid against you and your two heavy handed cronies."

"It's going to be laid against you," said the enraged Hamill before sending the tea tray and its entire contents hurtling across the room. "I know the law every bit as well as you do."

"It's going to be laid against you, Woody and Tommy," said the Chairman. "Because you didn't just lock Morris up. You did what you'd been threatening to do when Morris was under my protection in carriage one."

"What do you mean?" said Hamill.

"Morris was stark naked when we found him," said the Chairman while politely making way for the Professor to take his customary chair.

"He was what?" said Steadman.

"He was stark naked," said the Chairman. "The poor bugger had been stripped naked. What happened to the other part of your plan Hamill?"

"What the fuck are you talking about?" said Hamill.

"You know exactly what I'm talking about," said the Chairman. "You and your mates had threatened to strip him naked and throw him off the bridge. And don't try to deny it Hamill. I've got several witnesses to prove it."

"I've no doubt you have," said Hamill. "And I'm not going to try to deny it. But they were just playful threats. That was just to put the willies up him and make him feel uncomfortable. I wasn't really going to do anything bad to him. I'm not that way inclined. Do you know anything about this Woody?"

"I've no idea what he's talking about," said Woodhouse.

[332]

"What about you Tommy," said Hamill.

"I'm just as ignorant as you," said McShane.

"When was the last time you saw him?" said the Chef.

"Yesterday evening about 7 o'clock," said McShane. "But I didn't actually see him."

"What do you mean?" said the Chef.

"I just saw his outstretched arm as he reached for his supper," said McShane.

"That's all we ever saw of him," said Woodhouse.

"Why?" said the Chef.

"Because he never opened the door wide enough to see any more," said Woodhouse.

"But you must have been able to see him through the glass panel in the door," said the Chef.

"We couldn't," said McShane. "He'd pulled the blind down."

"But come to think of it-he must have had some clothes on," said Woodhouse.

"What do you mean?" said the Chef.

"His arm was covered by a sleeve of some sort," said Woodhouse. "I think he must have been wearing a coat. He was definitely wearing something. He certainly wasn't naked at that point."

"When was the last time anyone had a conversation with him?" said the Chef.

"On the day of his arrest," said Woodhouse. "I tried to talk to him a few days later after he'd regained consciousness, but my attempts were met with a torrent of abuse. He did talk to Tommy Mac though."

"Only the once," said McShane.

"What did he talk about?" said the Chef.

"He asked me if I'd bring him a bucket," said McShane.

"A bucket!" said Larkin.

"That's right," said McShane. "He wanted to relieve himself."

"That's sick," said Alty.

"It's disgusting," said Larkin.

"Why is it?" said McShane.

"Because it's wrong," said Larkin. "You should have

allowed him to use the washroom."

"We did allow him to use the washroom," said Woodhouse. "But he didn't want to leave the carriage."

"Who could blame him?" said Alty. "He'd have probably been expecting another good hiding."

"It sounds to me as if he'd given up," said Steadman.

"What do you mean given up?" said the Chairman.

"You're not suggesting he killed himself are you?" said the Chef.

"It's possible," said Steadman. "Particularly as he'd had time to consider the damage he'd caused by setting the train in motion."

"But he wouldn't have known about the overall chaos he'd caused?" said the Chairman.

"Oh he would," said Woodhouse. "He undoubtedly would. I'm not afraid to admit it. I reminded him of how much mess he'd caused on the hour and every hour."

"There is another possibility worth considering," said the old man while checking the contents of the nearest teapot.

"What's that?" said the Chairman.

"It's something often referred to as known as paradoxical undressing," said the old man.

"Could we have that in English please Professor," said Steadman.

"Of course you can," said the old man. "Paradoxical undressing takes place during the first stage of hypothermia when a paralysis of the vasomotor centre occurs, creating the sensation the body temperature is higher than it actually is. As a result, the sufferer has been known to remove clothes rather than put clothes on. That's the paradox. In effect, the sufferer's senses have been tricked. That would also explain why your friend was found under his bed."

"Why would it?" said the Chef.

"Because it's just possible your friend Morris was exhibiting classic burrowing behaviour," said the old man.

"Burrowing behaviour! said the Chef. "Do you mean like a hedgehog or a badger?"

"That's exactly what I mean," said the Professor. "It's one of the more peculiar aspects of the paradoxical undressing phenomenon."

"That's weird that is," said the Chef.

"It is isn't it," said the old man.

"You learn something new every day don't you Professor," said Hamill.

"Some members of the populace do," said the old man. "Keeping an open mind is the key to learning as far as I'm concerned. And avoiding making hasty assumptions helps too."

"You should have a word with our new Chairman," said Hamill.

"Why's that?" said the Professor.

"He's convinced Morris was murdered," said Hamill.

"Really," said the old man. "I'd be more inclined to assume accidental death."

"Why's that Professor?" said the Chairman.

"Because nobody consciously set out to kill the poor man," said the Professor. "He was just the victim of cruel circumstance."

"But what about the horrific beating he'd received," said the Chairman. "Isn't it possible he died from internal bleeding or something similar?"

"It's possible," said the old man. "Would you like me to examine his last stool?"

"How are you going to do that?" said Hamill. "His stools are probably making their way down the Welsh coast right now."

"Why are they?" said the Chairman.

"Because I dumped the bucket and its vile contents when I went back to gather proof that Morris had eaten," said Hamill.

"Why did you do that?" said the Chairman.

"For health and sanitary purposes," said Hamill. "The carriage stank to high hell."

"It did actually," said the Professor. "Did you think to

[335]

leave a window open?"

"I didn't," said Hamill. "I just got in and out before I puked."

"I'll sort the window," said Steadman before picking up the white cotton sheet and folding it over his arm. "Is there anything you want me to do while I'm there Professor?"

"I don't think so," said the old man.

"You could try to straighten him out and lay him on one of the beds," said the Chairman.

"I actually had something far less gruesome in mind," said Steadman.

"Do you think you could straighten Biddo out while you're at it?" said Larkin.

"That's not funny," said Blackie.

"I thought it was a great line," said Woodhouse.

"You would," said Blackie. "That's because you're a cynic Woody. As I tried to tell you and the others before-there's a lesson to be learnt here."

"What lesson's that?" said Woodhouse.

"Those vacant carriages are death traps," said Blackie. "They should never be used as holding cells again."

"Oh yes they should," said Alty.

"Too damn right they should," said Larkin.

"Blackie makes a good point actually," said the Chairman. "In fact, he makes a very good point."

"Thank you Mr Chairman," said Blackie.

"Oh Christ!" said Alty. "Here we go. It's amnesty time."

"Does that mean you're going to do the decent thing and allow me to take Biddo into my care?" said Blackie after arriving at the Chairman's shoulder.

"It does yes," said the Chairman.

"What the hell!" said Alty.

"This is nonsense," said Larkin.

"It's called a result!" said a fist pumping Blackie. "And then you can take him along to the mail room where, with any luck, he won't get into any more trouble," said the Chairman.

[336]

"What!" said Blackie. "What was that?"

"That's what's called an even better result," said a more animated fist pumping Alty.

"Can I do the honours and turn the key?" said Larkin.

"Can I do the honours and swallow the key?" said Alty.

"It might be best if someone like Woody plays warder," said the Chairman. "You never know-our prisoner might make one last desperate bid for freedom."

"I'm on it," said Woodhouse.

"What about yourself Hulmey," said Hamill. "Are you still going to retire to your room and wipe your hands of the matter?"

"I don't know," said the Chairman. "What does everyone else think?"

"I couldn't care less what you do," said McShane. "As long as you don't take an age to decide."

"We need somebody level headed at the helm," said the Chef.

"We need someone in charge who's not going to blow a gasket every time something goes pear shaped," said Steadman. "I think you should stay on Hulmey. At least until we're rescued."

"So do I," said Hamill.

"You do?" said the Chairman.

"Very much so," said Hamill. "But only as long as you record everything that's gone on over the past hour without exception."

"I've already done that," said the Club Secretary while holding up his ledger.

"Does your report include the switching off of the heating decision?" said Hamill.

"It includes everything," said the Club Secretary. "Nobody keeps more immaculate books than me. It includes everything from the train setting off prematurely, Morris's subsequent arrest, his kangaroo court trial, his incarceration, his subsequent beating and his eventual transformation to life size ice sculpture."

"That's good," said Hamill before dropping to his knees to begin scooping up the first of hundreds of pieces of

[337]

shattered crockery. "It's at times like these I miss old Brian Matthews."

"Why's that?" said the Chef.

"Because he'd have been the first to don his yellow marigolds and reach for the dust pan and brush," said Hamill. "How is he, by the way?"

"He's much the same," said the Professor.

"Still a weasel then," said Hamill.

"Behave yourself Hamill," said the Chef.

CHAPTER FIFTEEN
PUSH START

The Chairman's return to his sleeping quarters had been to the accompaniment of three progressively louder cracks of thunder and a violent and colourful barrage of verbal abuse from the unrepentant mail room bound Kenny Biddo. It had been his intention to escape for a while to try to make sense of the events which had taken place just prior to and including the past 12 hours; events which had included an unprovoked arson attack on a club member and the discovery of a long standing club member's frozen corpse. To his immense consternation however, that much desired period of isolation had been short lived because less than 10 minutes after he had wrapped himself in his quilt and curled up on his bed, an oil spattered and extremely excited Club Secretary had called to demand his presence in the engine.

Meanwhile, Woodhouse and Tommy Mac and several other passengers were heading back to join the main party after locking Biddo in the mail room. They had been spat at, clawed, kicked and had been on the wrong end of some terribly scathing personal abuse and yet, despite such relentless provocation, each had been as good as their word to the recently appointed Chairman; never once had any of them returned the vile abuse and at no time had they lashed out in retaliation. That might or might not have been because the watchful and wary Blackie had been among the interested observers but it wasn't long before even his renowned patience was beginning to wear thin.

"I hope you're satisfied now," he said while approaching the wooden barred cell where his indignant and bile spouting uncle was prowling from one side to the other like a newly caged beast.

"What do you mean, 'satisfied'?" said Biddo after coming to a sudden halt and placing his face between the two centre bars.

[339]

"I hope you've finally learnt your lesson," said Blackie.
"What lesson's that?" said Biddo.
"You can't just go shooting your mouth off and making unfounded accusations," said Blackie.
"They weren't unfounded," said Biddo. "I've had Alty and Larkin's card marked for a long time. They're a pair of faggots."
"They're a pair of extremely happily married men," said Blackie.
"They're not," said Biddo. "They're hiding a dark secret. The marriage certificate is just a ruse. It's to put queer hunters like me off their scent."
"Queer hunters!" said Blackie.
"That's right," said Biddo. "There's an army of us back in Crosby. We've even got our own website. We're dedicated to exposing them."
"How big is this army?" said Blackie.
"It's big," said Biddo. "And our numbers are growing by the day."
"What are your numbers?" said Blackie.
"I can't say for sure," said Biddo.
"Why not?" said Blackie.
"Because I haven't got me lap top with me," said Biddo. "All that information's on spreadsheets and things."
"Just give me a ball park figure," said Blackie. "What are your numbers?"
"8," mumbled Biddo.
"800?" said Blackie.
"Just 8," said Biddo. "As at last week's count."
"Oh, for the love of God!" said Blackie while looking to the ceiling. "What an army. The gay community must be shitting themselves. They must be boarding up their homes and stocking up on provisions as we speak. You need treatment Biddo."
"It's you that needs treatment," said Biddo. "You seem to be blind to the problem. Faggotism is at epidemic proportions. I read an article in a magazine recently. It stated that 10% of men under 60 are now homosexual."
"Why under 60?" said Blackie.

[340]

"I don't know," said Biddo. "I didn't conduct the survey. Maybe it's because men over 60 often struggle to bend over to touch their toes."

"Oh, for the love of God!" said Blackie. "Will you listen to yourself. What was this magazine?"

"I can't remember," said Biddo. "A very close friend lent it to me."

"What very close friend?" said Blackie. "A boyfriend?"

"Fuck off!" said Biddo. "Don't you dare imply such a disgusting thing."

"I'm sorry," said Blackie. "What friend are you talking about?"

"Ian Jasper," said Biddo.

"Ian Jasper!" said Blackie. "That explains it then."

"Explains what?" said Biddo.

"Explains why he was in possession of a gay magazine," said Blackie.

"Why does it?" said Biddo.

"Because Jasper went to sea for many years," said Blackie. "He was a sailor. And you know what they say about sailor boys."

"How dare you insinuate such a dreadful thing!" said Biddo. "Ian Jasper's as straight as a dart. He's sired about ten healthy and stunningly attractive kids. As far as women are concerned, he'd give Warren Beattie a run for his money. And by the way Blackie-allow me to remind you of something while we're on the subject of familiar sailor-related clichés-it's also said, sailors have a woman in every port."

"That'll be the sailors in the lesbian branch of the navy," said Blackie.

"Go to hell," said Biddo. "And while you're on your way there-think long and hard about those statistics I've just given you. 10 per cent. 10 fucking per cent! Think about that Blackie. 1 in 10 men is now as bent as a nine bob bit 1 in 10 men is now a fudge packing Pansy Potter. Doesn't that worry you?"

"Not at all," said Blackie. "It just means there's more women for good looking hombres like me."

[341]

"It doesn't," said Biddo. "It means the fag population is increasing rapidly."

"Do you think they might be breeding?" said Blackie.

"I wouldn't put it past them," said Biddo. "I don't know what they're doing. I know this though. You wouldn't have seen statistics like that just after the Second World War."

"Why not?" said Blackie.

"Because there were no such thing as homos then," said Biddo. "Things were different then. Men were men. Those boys knew what side to flick their tie and button up their shirts. You couldn't be a soldier and a Nancy boy at the same time."

"Why not?" said Blackie. "Is it because you've got to take your hand off your hip to fire a rifle?"

"Very funny," said Biddo. "You won't find it so funny when you get approached by one."

"I've been approached by plenty of gays," said Blackie. "I've even had my arse felt by one."

"I sincerely hope you put him straight with a swift right hook," said Biddo.

"I took it as a compliment," said Blackie.

"A compliment!" said Biddo. "Are you for real? That dirty bastard had no right to touch your bottom. It was a violation of your personal space. You should have kicked the filthy creature in the dick."

"I couldn't," said Blackie.

"Why not?" said Biddo.

"Because I was sucking it at the time," said Blackie.

"You're sick," said Biddo.

"You're the one that's sick," said Blackie. "Do you want me to get the Professor to take a look at you?"

"What the hell for?" said Biddo.

"Because you don't look right to me," said Blackie.

"What do you mean, 'don't look right'?" said Biddo.

"You're sweating like a pig, you're shivering and your eyes are bloodshot," said Blackie. "You look a mess to be honest."

"I'm just stressed over our Anthony," said Biddo before

exhaling loudly.

"He'll be fine," said Blackie.

"He's not going to make it off the bridge," said Biddo while pointing to the loading hatch. "Can you hear that Blackie? Listen to it. It's howling out there. The poor bugger's going to be blown away like a piece of discarded tissue paper."

"He won't," said Blackie. "He's going to be secured to the track at intervals until he's down on ground level. It's the lads who are going to have to feed him the rope that need to worry most."

"If I slip you a couple of bob, can you arrange for them to be Alty and Larkin?" said Biddo.

"No I can't," said Blackie. "Is there anything I can get you?"

"A sleeve of cigarettes and a couple of bottles of Smirnoff would be nice," said Biddo. "You needn't bother fetching any mixers. I like my vodka straight. The same way I like my male friends."

"You're not getting any vodka," said Blackie.

"Why not?" said Biddo.

"Because you need to dry out for a while," said Blackie. "You need to get your head right for when you go before the magistrate."

"I won't be going before any magistrate," said Biddo.

"I'm afraid you've got no choice," said Blackie.

"I have got a choice," said Biddo. "I'm getting out of here. And what's more-you're going to help me."

"I don't think so," said Blackie.

"You are," said Biddo. "Because if you don't, you're going to lose one of the best friends you've ever had."

"What do you mean?" said Blackie.

"I'm going to tell the Chef about the time you failed to tell him his tee off time had been changed," said Biddo.

"It wasn't up to me to tell him," said Blackie. "I didn't organise the event."

"Maybe not but it would have been the decent thing to do," said Biddo. "You cost the Chef a possible trophy that day. If I remember right, he was, the leading points

earner by some distance going into that final round."
"You swore on your life you'd never say a word about
that," said Blackie.
"That was way back when," said Biddo. "That was
when I had a life worth living."
"He won't believe you," said Blackie while slowly
approaching the mail room bars. "He'll just think you're
trying to discredit me because I allowed you to be locked
up."
"That's the chance you're going to have to take," said
Biddo. "You owe me Blackie. You owe me big time
lad."
"I owe you nothing," said Blackie. "I've been good to
you over the years Biddo."
"Be good to me one last time," said Biddo.
"How exactly?" said a suspicious looking Blackie.
"Bring me a screwdriver," said Biddo.
"The orange and vodka type?" said Blackie.
"The slotted or the Phillips type," replied Biddo.
"What's it for?" said Blackie.
"Never you mind," said Biddo.
"You're not going to stab someone are you?" said
Blackie.
"Of course not," replied Biddo.
"Alright," said Blackie. "I'll try to slip you one later."
"And tell Larko and Alty I want to have a word with
them," said Biddo.
"Now you're pushing it," said Blackie. "You need to
keep well away from those two bloody nuisances.
They're out of bounds as far as you're concerned."
"I want to bury the hatchet," said Biddo.
"Rubbish," said Blackie. "You want more trouble."
"I don't," said Biddo. "I want to try to persuade one of
them to accompany our Anthony."
"No you don't," said Blackie.
"I do," said Biddo. "You know as well as I do, he's got
no chance of making it on his own. He's not cut out for
something like that. Will you do it please? Will you
have a word with them? Will you ask them to come to

[344]

see me?"

"I'll think about it," said Blackie. "But you're going to have to promise not to say anything to the Chef about that end of season golf tournament."

"I promise with all my heart," said Biddo.

"How do I know I can believe you?" said Blackie.

"Because that event took place about 10 years ago," said Biddo. "And to this day, only two people on this planet know what you did. Or, to put it another way-what you failed to do."

"Who might they be?" said Blackie.

"I'm one of them," said Biddo.

"Fair enough," said Blackie after a short delay. "I'll see what I can do. In the meantime, I suggest you get a little shut eye. I think we're in for another wild and rocky night.

When the somewhat self conscious Blackie arrived back at the dining carriage, he was surprised to find his fellow passengers in markedly improved spirits. That didn't mean champagne corks were popping or people were dancing on tables however, after all, by that time, two members of the club had been confirmed dead, another had mysteriously vanished and a fourth had very recently been locked up for carrying out a violent attack on a long standing and well liked and respected club member.

"Are you all having a good time are you lads?" asked Blackie while scanning the serving hatch for a sandwich of his fancy. "Are you all happy now? Are you feeling more secure now? Has big, bad Biddo the bogeyman been locked up has he?"

"The improved atmosphere's got nothing to do with your uncle's imprisonment," said the Chairman.

"Of course it hasn't," said Blackie. "It won't be long before the party poppers are going off and the singing starts."

[345]

"Nobody's going to be singing," said the Chairman. "We've just lost Alec Morris, for Christ's sake. I don't think any of these lads are going to want to sing and dance again."

"We've finally had some welcome good news," said Woodhouse.

"What's that?" asked Blackie.

"Larko and Hilly have found a way to get the train moving," said Woodhouse.

"Then why isn't it moving?" said Blackie while pointing towards the window.

"It's not as simple as that," said the Club Secretary.

"Why not?" said Blackie before helping himself to a bottle of beer and settling onto a chair a good distance from the main body of the group.

"Because we're going to have to clear a hell of a lot of snow from the track first," said the Club Secretary.

"And we're not going to be able to do anything until it's light," said the Chairman.

"What's wrong with letting the engine smash through it?" said Blackie.

"We can't," said the Club Secretary.

"Why not?" said Blackie.

"We can't get it running," said the Club Secretary.

"You what!" said Blackie.

"We're going to try and hand crank it forward yard by yard," said Larkin.

"Hand crank it!" said Blackie. "Do you mean like they used to do with old cars?"

"That's right," said Larkin.

"Like they did in the old John Mills movie, *Ice Cold in Alex*," said Woodhouse. "They put the ambulance in gear and cranked the engine over."

"But this thing isn't an ambulance lads," said Blackie. "This thing we're on must weigh the equivalent of a thousand ambulances."

"It might well do," said Larkin. "But I still managed to get it moving."

"He did Blackie," said the Club Secretary. "I watched it

move. I swear to God it did. I've got to be honest-I
nearly wet myself with excitement."
"How far did it move?" said Blackie.
"A few feet," said the Club Secretary.
"A few feet!" said Blackie. "A few fucking feet! How
long did that take you?"
"About twenty minutes," said Larkin.
"Jesus wept!" said Blackie.
"But that was Larko working all on his own," said the
Club Secretary.
"And having to propel the wheels through thick snow,"
said Larkin.
"Which we intend clearing as soon as it's light," said the
Chairman.
"And we're going to unhitch the last three carriages to
lighten the load," said the Chef.
"I already have," said Larkin.
"It did move," said the Club Secretary.
"I don't doubt you," said Blackie. "But where would 3
feet every 20 minutes get us? That's only 9 feet an hour.
That's slower than some of our players"
"It'll be 18 to 20 feet an hour with two strong men
cranking the engine over," said Larkin.
"Alright 18 to 20 feet an hour," said Blackie. "You'll all
be in need of breathing apparatus or dead from
exhaustion by the time you reach the nearest town."
"That's not our initial aim," said the Club Secretary.
"We just want to get to where the bridge starts
dropping."
"That's right," said the Club Secretary.
"And as long as we work nonstop in sensibly allocated
shifts, we reckon we can achieve that in about 24 hours,"
said the Chairman.
"And then what?" said Blackie.
"We allow gravity to take over and freewheel down,"
said Larkin.
"And we ultimately end up on flat ground," said the
Club Secretary.
"Which means we'll be out of danger from the high

winds," said the Chairman.

"Which also means we'll have no more sleepless nights wondering if the bridge is going to give way under us," said the Club Secretary.

"And, by the time we stop, we're likely to be nearer civilization," said Larkin.

"That's if we stop," said Blackie. "Have you thought of that Larko? Are you going to be able to stop the thing?"

"I don't know," said Larkin. "I haven't had time to think about that yet."

"Well might I suggest, now might be a good time," said Blackie.

"Why would we want to stop?" said the Chairman.

"In case we fucking well crash," said Blackie.

"We're not going to crash," said the Club Secretary.

"There shouldn't be anything else on the line to crash into," said the Chairman.

"What about snow drifts?" said Blackie.

"I suppose there's always that possibility," said the Chairman.

"It's more than a possibility," said Blackie. "You can guarantee it. The snow's been falling heavily all week. And there's every chance it's now turned to ice."

"And there's every chance we're going to be able to plough right through it once we've gained enough momentum," said Larkin.

"Well, let's hope you're right," said Blackie. "Because I've got to be honest-I think we're better off staying where we are. I think it's a ridiculous idea."

"That's fine," said the Club Secretary while holding up his ledger. "And your comments are duly noted."

"We weren't waiting for you to give us your blessing Blackie," said the Chairman. "We just thought the news might give you a lift after what happened to Biddo. How is he, by the way? Has he calmed down at all?"

"Not in the slightest," said the entering Professor while holding up his bloodied and bandaged left thumb. "If anything, he's got considerably worse."

"What happened?" said the Chairman.

[348]

"He bit me," said the old man.

"Bit you!" said the Club Secretary.

"He nearly took off the end of my thumb," said the Professor.

"When did this happen?" said the Chairman.

"About ten minutes ago," said the old man after removing his pocket watch and holding it up to the light. "He accused me of trying to sexually molest him.""It doesn't surprise me," said Larkin. "And that's without any alcohol down him."

"You're going to have to put a danger sign up Hulmey," said Alty.

"Or tie the bastard up," said Larkin.

"It's your own faults as far as I'm concerned," said Blackie. "If you treat a man as though he's an animal, he's more than likely going to behave like one."

"That's the irony," said the old man. "I was trying to be kind. I was in the process of helping the man."

"Helping him in what way?" said Blackie.

"I was trying to administer his first dose of the sedative," said the Professor. "And as long as a couple of you can hold him down for me, I still intend doing so."

"I want nothing to do with the bastard," said Larkin. "He can suffer in agony as far as I'm concerned."

"That's very compassionate of you Larko," said Blackie.

"Don't mention it," said Larkin.

"I'll hold him for you Professor," said Woodhouse. "But I'm not going to put up with any nonsense. If he bites me, he'll be on a liquid diet for the rest of his life."

"So it's true then is it Professor," said the Chairman.

"Is what true?" said the old man.

"That Biddo's fallen foul of the disease," said the Chairman.

"I'd have thought that was obvious by now," said Larkin.

"I'd have thought that had been obvious for some time," said Alty.

"He hadn't been exhibiting the whole range of

symptoms," said the old man.

"He'd certainly been angry enough," said Larkin.

"Is it true Professor?" said Blackie. "Is my uncle the latest disease victim?"

"It certainly looks that way," said the old man.

"Which means he's exactly where he should be," said Alty.

"I tend to disagree there," said the old man.

"Why's that?" said Alty.

"Because those bars he's currently behind are only made of relatively light wood," said the old man. "And that individual behind them's got so much pent up anger inside him, it's frightening. That enclosure's only going to be able to hold him for so long. I'd much prefer him to be tethered in some way, as somebody just suggested."

"So would I," said Larkin.

"How was he with you Blackie?" said Steadman.

"He was alright," said Blackie. "I wouldn't say he was full of remorse-but he seemed resigned to his immediate fate. Although....."

"Although what?" said Steadman.

"It was probably nothing," said Blackie.

"What was probably nothing," said Steadman.

"Let's just say, it might be best if the Chef stays out of his way for a while," said Blackie.

"Why's that?" said the Chairman.

"He's very angry with him for some reason," said Blackie.

"Angry with me?" said the Chef.

"He mentioned something about your son Mark making a play for Anthony," said Blackie.

"That's ridiculous," said the Chef. "Our Mark's not gay. He's girl mad."

"He's been engaged about 15 times hasn't he?" said Steadman.

"23," said the Chef. "It'll probably be 24 by the time we get home. I don't believe that. Did Biddo really say that about our Mark?"

"It's the disease," said the Club Secretary. "Don't take it to heart Chef.

"Just keep away from him our kid," said the Chairman.

"Did he make any threats towards me?" said the Chef.

"Not threats as such," said Blackie.

"What does 'not threats as such', mean?" said the Chef.

"He never made any direct threats," said Blackie. "But he didn't have to, to be fair."

"What do you mean?" said Steadman.

"He just had this manic look about him when he mentioned the Chef's name," said Blackie.

"What sort of look?" said the Chef.

"A look of extreme menace," said Blackie. "A look of intense hatred. It was as if he was concocting something. My advice is to keep well away from him until he's been sedated."

"I couldn't agree more," said the Professor.

"Has Anthony been to see him?" said the Club Secretary.

"I don't know," said Blackie.

"Does Anthony know about our plan to crank the train?" said the Chairman.

"I don't know that either," said Blackie ."What difference would that make?"

"Because if we can get down onto flat ground, we can make our way to the nearest town as an entire group," said the Chairman. "There'll be no need for Anthony to go it alone."

"That's a point," said the Club Secretary.

"He knows about the train," said Larkin.

"And he's still intent upon going for help," said Alty.

"I'll talk to him," said the Chairman.

"Why bother?" said Hamill. "Let him go if he wants to. We need as many irons in the fire as possible."

"That's right," said Woodhouse.

"I hope you realise I won't be leaving the train," said the old man.

"Why not?" said the Chairman.

"I think I've already made that perfectly clear," said the

[351]

Professor. "I'm going to stay here with my two patients until they've fully recovered. I'm not taking infected people into a densely populated area."

"I understand," said the Chairman. "How is Matthews by the way?"

"He's heavily sedated" said the old man.

"How long do you think he's likely to need to be out?" said the Club Secretary.

"About a week," said the Professor.

"Bloody hell!" said the Club Secretary.

"Which means, with any luck, we won't be here to celebrate his reawakening," said Woodhouse.

"I'm going to touch wood to that," said Hamill before placing his right hand on top of the Chairman's head.

"And I'm going to keep everything crossed that's crossable," said Steadman.

"So am I," said McShane.

"I didn't know people still subscribed to that sort of thing," said the Professor.

"What sort of thing?" said Steadman.

"Keeping fingers crossed and touching wood and the like," said the old man.

"Hamill does," said Woodhouse. "He's the most superstitious bloke I've ever met. His mother was a sort of witch apparently."

"Don't be at it you," said Hamill. "She wasn't a witch. She was what is now commonly referred to as a 'wise woman'."

"What's the difference?" said Woodhouse.

"Where do you want me to start?" said Hamill. "For instance-witches ride around on broom sticks and cause mischief. My mother rode an old Raleigh sit up and beg bike and tended to the sick and needy. Do you know what-I never had an ounce of bad luck while that wonderful woman was alive. Now, if it wasn't for bad luck, I wouldn't know what luck was. Just about everything I've tried to do since she passed away has turned to mush. And it's been no different on this bloody train. Every time things have begun to look up, our hopes have gone crashing down."

"Well the omens were good this morning," said Woodhouse.

"Why's that?" said Hamill.

"A bumble bee found its way into our sleeping carriage," said Woodhouse.

"A bee!" said Steadman. "That's odd. I thought bees died off during the Winter months."

"So did I," said McShane.

"On the contrary," said the old man. "Certain members of the Apis species have been known to be freeze tolerant."

"Is it still there Woody?" said McShane. "Is it still in our room?"

"In a manner of speaking, it is," said Woodhouse.

"What do you mean?" said Hamill. "You didn't swat the thing did you?"

"I had to," said Woodhouse. "It wouldn't leave me alone. It was like one of me ex wives. It did everything but ask me for more maintenance."

"You bloody imbecile," said Hamill.

"Sod off Hamill," said Woodhouse "The bastard would have stung me. It might have stung you or Tommy while you were sleeping. You ought to be thanking me, not having a go at me."

"I ought to be kicking your fat arse from here to Knotty Ash," said Hamill before slamming his right hand down on his table, causing a tall pillar of cups and saucers to rock unsteadily for several seconds. "For fuck's sake Woody. You don't kill a bee that enters your home. You help it back out of the window and send it on its merry way. Did you really kill the thing?"

"I'm afraid so," said Woodhouse. "And I'm going to make no apologies for doing it either. I've been stung by a bee once and know exactly how it feels. Did you know this Hamill-did you know that in this country, more people die from bee stings than as a result of terrorist attacks?"

"That's a pity," said Hamill. "But it's more of a pity

your name hasn't had to be added to the list of recently deceased passengers. You're a moron Woody. An absolute moron. What were you thinking?"

"I was thinking about avoiding excruciating pain," said Woodhouse.

"What's the problem?" said the Professor.

"We're in trouble-that's the problem," said Hamill.

"Why are we?" said the old man.

"Because we are," said Hamill.

"Because, according to folklore, if you kill a bee that's just entered your home, you've as good as invited an evil spirit to come calling," said McShane. "That's right isn't it Hamill?"

"Not quite," said Hamill while proceeding to right some of the precariously balanced crockery. "In killing the bee, you've actually invited an unpleasant stranger to visit you. And it happens. Believe me lads, it happens."

"It happens without fail," said McShane.

"You seem to be well versed in this superstition business Tommy," said the Professor. "Why would that be?"

"Hamill's mum and my old girl were best friends," said McShane. "I used to watch them casting spells and doing incantations together when I was a kid. It was spooky. But I like spooky. I love haunted house stuff and things like that. But that doesn't mean I believed any of it. To be honest, I used to think it was a load of baloney."

"That was before the gypsy paid him a visit," said Hamill.

"What gypsy was this?" said the Professor.

"She was just an old gypsy," said McShane. "She and about 30 of her fellow travellers had set up camp on a field not far from where I lived."

"What did she want?" said the old man.

"She was selling shite in the guise of shiny plastic trinkets," said McShane.

"And, of course, Tommy duly sent her packing without so much as a 'thank you anyway'," said Woodhouse.

"Is that right?" said the old man.

[354]

"I'd never liked gypsies," said McShane. "Don't get me wrong-they'd never done me any harm. I'd just never trusted them. And I was right too."

"What happened?" said the fascinated old man.

"She put a curse on him," said Woodhouse.

"She did what?" said the Professor.

"She put a curse on me," said McShane. "Just after I'd frog marched the evil bitch down our path and out of our gate, she turned around and muttered something in some foreign language or other. I couldn't make it out at the time. I made out the rest of what she said though. That was in plain English."

"What was it?" said the old man.

"She told me, because I'd shown her no warmth, I'd never know warmth again," said McShane.

"How interesting," said the Professor. "How did you interpret that Tommy? Do you think she meant it in a metaphorical sense?"

"She meant it literally," said McShane. "From that day on, my home was never warm again."

"What do you mean, 'never warm again'?" said Steadman after drawing his seat forward.

"The house was never warm again," said McShane. "At times, it was like we were living in Siberia."

"When was this?" said the Club Secretary. "I mean-what time of the year was this?"

"It wasn't Winter, if that's what you're thinking," said McShane. "It was the middle of July. The sun had been threatening to crack the flags, the barbecue had been checked over and the duvets had all been rounded up and stored away."

"Bloody hell!" said the Club Secretary.

"How long did the problem persist?" said the Professor.

"Until we'd sold up and moved out about 15 months later," said McShane. "That was after we'd had the best central heating system fitted. And that was after we'd had the entire house rendered, the roof fully retiled and new pvc double glazing installed."

"Christ!" said Steadman.

[355]

"Do you happen to know if the new owners had any trouble getting the place warm?" said the Club Secretary.

"That's a very good question Hilly," said McShane.

"And one I kept asking myself at the time. That's why I decided to pay them a visit."

"Really!" said the Club Secretary.

"I'd be feeling so terribly guilty, " said McShane. "I hadn't been able to sleep a wink."

"Why's that?" said the Chef.

"They had three little children under the age of five," said McShane. "I'd been waking up in a lather of sweat thinking of the poor little things lying dead in their cots."

"And did they freeze to death in their cots?" said Steadman.

"They were fine," said McShane. "Stepping over their parent's front door step had been like stepping onto a runway in the Bahamas in mid Summer. Stepping into the living room was very different however."

"What happened then?" said the Club Secretary.

"I suddenly felt a freezing cold chill on the back of my neck," said McShane. "It was as if I'd opened a door and invited Antarctica inside. And then my nose started running, goose bumps started appearing on my arms and little clouds of icy vapour began billowing from my mouth."

"What did the new owners say?" said Steadman.

"Had they noticed the dramatic change in temperature?"

"Not at all," said McShane. "Nothing had changed as far as they were concerned. They were still as warm as toast. They'd noticed the change in me though. They must have thought I'd taken ill."

"Did you tell them about the gypsy curse?" said the Club Secretary.

"I just quietly excused myself and got off," said McShane. "I was so cold, I was on the point of collapse. They rang me later that afternoon to see if I was alright."

"Did you tell them about the gypsy then?" said the Club Secretary.

"I didn't think there was any need to," said McShane.

"There wasn't," said Hamill.

"What did you tell them?" said Steadman.

"I told them I'd suffered an allergic reaction to something I'd eaten in the morning," said McShane. I've never been back since. And I'll never step foot in that house again."

"What's the heating situation like within your current home?" said Steadman.

"We haven't had any problems," said McShane. "But before I leave for work, I always make sure there's a little bit of cash in an ashtray by the front door."

"Why?" said Steadman.

"In case another old gypsy pedlar comes calling while I'm out," said McShane.

"Quite wise too," said the Professor.

"Really Professor," said Woodhouse. "I thought you'd scoff at all that 'double, double, toil and trouble' stuff. I thought you were meant to be a man of science."

"I am a man of science," said the old man. "But I've learnt not to be too hasty in dismissing the apparently absurd and illogical."

"Are you admitting to be superstitious Professor?" said Steadman.

"I wouldn't go as far as that," said the old man. "But over the years, I have seen and been privy to certain things that have left me scratching my head."

"What sort of things?" said Steadman.

"Where would you like me to begin?" said the Professor while pouring himself more tea.

"Why don't you start with the strangest thing you've ever seen or been privy to," said Hewlett upon closing his book. "The thing that shook you most. The thing you found the hardest to fathom."

"The thing I found hardest to fathom," said the old man while stroking his chin. "That's easy. That would be something that happened to an Ecuadorian Indian I came across when I was helping out at a small hospital near a place called Guiyero."

"When was this?" said Steadman.

"Around the mid 1950s," said the Professor. "He was a tribal elder called Isandro. He was like an enforcer of the laws."

"Like a magistrate?" said Steadman.

"I suppose so," said the old man. "Anyway-the morning after he'd been operated on, I entered his ward to find every other patient huddled in a corner in a state of abject terror and an enormous male jaguar sprawled across his chest."

"Bloody hell!" said the Club Secretary. "You don't see things like that in any of our Merseyside hospitals."

"I don't know about that," said Woodhouse. "You want to go to the Accident and Emergency Department of Fazakerley Hospital on any given Saturday night. There are more animal attacks there than on the Maasai Mara Game Reserve."

"Do you think the jaguar had been attracted by the smell of blood?" said Steadman.

"It's very possible," said the Professor.

"Was this Isandro fella dead?" said Steadman.

"He was very much alive," said the old man. "The big cat was definitely dead though."

"How come?" said Steadman.

"Who knows?" said the old man. "I suppose it could have been dying. It could have reached the end of its life. I just don't know. I do know that nobody had killed it. Nobody at that hospital had the means. My patient certainly hadn't. He hadn't been well enough to blow his own nose."

"So what did happen?" said the Club Secretary.

"I still don't know for sure," said the Professor. "But superstition soon abounded that the animal had sought out Isandro to deliver its soul and strength as its final gesture on Earth."

"Meaning what?" said Woodhouse.

"Once again, I don't know," said the old man. "What I do know is this. An hour later, after the orderlies had dispatched the dead beast to the kitchen cold room, a

smiling Isandro threw off his bedclothes, sprang out of
bed like a monkey and began his long 25 mile journey
home. I couldn't believe it. He'd only been operated on
the day before. I was dumbfounded."

"I bet you were," said Alty.

"What had been the problem?" said Steadman.

"A ruptured appendix," said the Professor.

"Bloody hell!" said Steadman. "That's pretty serious
isn't it?"

"It's very serious," said Larkin. "It happened to me on
my 21st birthday. I thought I was dying."

"I've no doubt you did," said the old man.

"What about his wound?" said the Club Secretary.
"Wouldn't it still have been open and prone to
infection?"

"His wound had healed," said the Professor.

"What!" said Larkin.

"His wound had completely healed," said the old man.

"But that doesn't make sense," said Larkin. "I was in
hospital for over two months. I thought my wound was
never going to close up."

"I don't doubt you," said the old man. "But you only
had doctors and nurses in your camp. Isandro had the
healing power of the mighty and fabled jaguar."

"I don't get you," said Larkin. "Are you suggesting the
animal healed the man's wound in some way?"

"It's not beyond the realm of possibility," said the
Professor. "That's what a lot of animals do in the wild.
They can't call into a veterinary practice can they? They
just lick their own wounds until they're better. But the
wound healing business wasn't what bewildered me
most."

"What did?" said an increasingly enthralled Steadman.

"Isandro had been a virtual cripple since the age of 17,"
said the old man. "He'd been unable to walk unaided
since being savaged by a wild boar during a hunting
expedition. But he strode out of that hospital with the
posture of an Olympic athlete. He didn't even consider
using his crutches or asking for assistance."

[359]

"That's freaky," said the Chairman.

"It's amazing," said Larkin.

"Did you ever see him again?" said Steadman.

"Never," said the old man. "But I did come across a distant relative of his. He was a Laron native by the name of Bernardo. It could be argued, I killed the chap."

"Killed him!" said the Club Secretary. "How did you manage that Professor?"

"I meddled with native affairs when I should have been minding my own bloody business," said the Professor. "I shouldn't have even been there to be honest. I should have moved on after helping set up the new wing of the hospital."

"Why hadn't you moved on?" said the Club Secretary.

"I wanted to study the nearby Laron population," said the Professor. "To be honest, every pathologist and epidemiologist worth their salt wanted to study them at that particular time."

"Why was that?" said the Club Secretary.

"Because the Larons appear to be immune to cancer, diabetes and other such diseases," said the old man. "To be honest, they'd be considered perfect human beings if it wasn't for the fact they never grow more than four feet tall. It's said that they're descended from Sephardic Jews from Spain and Portugal. That's almost certainly the reason they knew all about the Angel of Death."

"What Angel of Death?" said the Club Secretary.

"The Angel of Death that passed over the children of Israel the night before they were to leave Egypt," said the Professor. "Have you never heard that story?"

"I have," said Alty. "Didn't the Israelites have to smear blood above their doors to protect themselves?"

"Very good," said the old man.

"And those houses that had been marked with blood, were spared," said Alty.

"Spared what?" said Steadman.

"Spared losing their first born child," said the Professor. "The Angel of Death passed over them. God had tipped them the wink, so to speak."

"So what's this got to do with your friend Bernardo?" said Woodhouse.

"Quite a lot," said the old man. "But let me first of all put you right on one small matter-Bernardo was no friend. He was corrupt, arrogant and a constant thorn in the proverbial backside."

"Why was that?" said Woodhouse.

"He made things very difficult for our medical team," said the Professor. "He believed entirely in witchcraft and therefore had no respect for modern methods. And no matter how hard you tried, you couldn't persuade him otherwise. He was without doubt, the most difficult and stubborn human being I've ever come across."

"Is that why you killed him?" said Steadman.

"It's why some people suspected I killed him," said the old man.

"What did you mean when you said you'd meddled with native affairs?" said the Club Secretary.

"I'll come to that soon," said the Professor. "What you need to consider first, is that Bernardo's tribe had suffered an inordinate amount of fatalities over a relatively short period of time."

"How exactly?" said Steadman.

"Animal attacks during hunting expeditions," said the old man. "They'd actually lost 9 men on 9 consecutive days with Bernardo leading every hunt."

"Would that be considered a lot?" said Steadman.

"It was unprecedented," said the Professor. "Up until that time, it had been a very rare occurrence to lose anybody while on a hunt. In fact, according to the Chief, only 2 hunters had been lost during the previous decade. Those natives were super efficient scavengers and knew the forest like the back of their hands. They could escape up a tree as fast as any fully grown monkey."

"So what was going on?" said the Club Secretary.

"Evil spirits were at work," said the old man. "Evil spirits that had followed the Europeans into the village. At least that's what the poisonous and vitriol spouting Bernardo was telling his tribe."

[361]

"But you thought differently?" said the Club Secretary.
"Of course I did," said the Professor. "I'm a man of
science. But even so-one thing kept nagging away at
me. One thing that was almost impossible to
comprehend and ignore."
"What was that?" said the Club Secretary.
"The victims," said the old man. "Every one of the
victims had been the first born son of an elder."
"All nine of them?" said Steadman.
"Every one without exception," said the old man.
"That's uncanny," said Alty.
"There's no doubt about that," said the Professor.
"That's why Bernardo decided to do what the
Israelites had done about 3500 years before."
"The smearing of the blood above the door thing?" said
Steadman.
"That's right," said the old man while making himself a
little more comfortable. "The night before their next
hunt, he slaughtered a goat and daubed all the hunter's
huts with its blood."
"What happened?" said the fascinated Club Secretary.
"Every member of the hunting party returned home
safely after the next hunt," said the Professor. "And not
one of them had suffered so much as a scratch."
"Bloody hell!" said Steadman.
"It was probably just a coincidence," said the Chairman.
"To this day, I've still no doubt it was," said the old
man. "But Bernardo wasn't having any of it. He basked
in his glory and constantly laughed in my face. He had
risen to cult status overnight. He saw it as an
opportunity to mock and scoff at our modern methods.
He demanded a return to the traditional witch doctor
ways. Particularly after the 6th hunting expedition in
succession returned unscathed with 26 wild boar and 12
tapir-their biggest hunting haul in living memory. That's
when he started a campaign to get the Europeans to
leave. And within no time at all, he had the backing of
half the tribe. The more volatile and unpredictable side,
I might add. I was convinced things were going to get

ugly. Things had already got ugly a bit further afield."

"In what way?" said Steadman.

"A respected American missionary called Jim Elliot and his four friends had been butchered at the hands of the Huaoranis not far from the Curaray River," said the Professor.

"That would have been enough for me," said Woodhouse. "I'd have just packed up and left right then and there."

"Many European doctors and nurses already had," said the Professor. "But Bernardo had got under my skin to such an extent, I was determined to prove him a charlatan. I wanted to wipe his eye. I wanted to belittle him the same way he'd belittled me. and so many of my esteemed colleagues "

"And did you?" said Steadman.

"I more than belittled him," said the old man after leaning forward in his chair and tapping the enthralled Steadman on the left knee . "The night before the next hunt, I snook out with a damp sponge and removed the blood from above all the tribesmen's huts and replaced it with tomato juice."

"What for?" said Steadman.

"I wanted to prove the blood over the door had nothing to do with the hunter's recent success," said the Professor. "I wanted to prove the ritual was a complete and utter fallacy. And then I fired up my old Meerschaum pipe, sat back on the hospital veranda and waited for the party to return. And I waited.....and I continued to wait..... and I waited some more."

"What do you mean?" said the Club Secretary.

"None of the hunters were ever seen again," said the Professor."

"None of them?" said the Club Secretary.

"Not a single soul," said the old man. "

"Jesus Christ!" said Steadman.

"How did you feel about that?" said the Club Secretary.

"I chose to evaluate the situation as a man of science would," said the old man. "I'd done nothing wrong in theory. And nothing supernatural could have occurred, because I don't believe in the supernatural."

"But you must have wondered what had happened to them," said the Club Secretary.

"I did indeed," said the Professor. "I agonised over that for a long time. It tormented the life out of me to be honest. Some of those young tribesmen were good friends of mine."

"What conclusions were you able to draw?" said the Club Secretary.

"I could draw just the one," said the old man.

"What was that?" said Steadman.

"The hunting party had been wiped out by a hostile neighbouring tribe they had inadvertently stumbled across," said the old man.

"But I thought you said those tribesmen knew those forests like the back of their hands," said the Club Secretary.

"They most certainly did," said the Professor. "But they might have got disorientated during the hunt. It's probably impossible not to. Think about the mindset of what they were chasing. Those wild boar and tapirs wouldn't have been aware of any territorial restrictions or boundaries would they?"

"Of course not," said the Club Secretary.

"They would have just kept running for their lives," said the old man.

"And the hunters would have just kept chasing," said the Club Secretary.

"And before they knew it, they'd have found themselves on rival ground," said the Professor. "And that's a massive faux pas in those parts of the world."

"So it seems," said the Club Secretary.

"But what about the bodies?" said Steadman.

"They'd have possibly become meals for a variety of forest dwelling carnivores," said the old man.

"And the bones?" said Steadman.

"Tools, ornaments and jewellery for the victors," said the old man. "Spoils of war, I believe they're often called."

"Do you harbour any guilt regarding what you did?" said the Club Secretary.

"None at all," said the Professor. "I didn't kill those men."

"I suppose not," said Steadman.

"Do you think this blood over the door thing would work for us?" said Hamill.

"I've just told you-I'm a man of science," said the old man. "But if it makes you feel more secure and helps you sleep any better-don't let me put you off."

"It's not going to do any harm," said McShane.

"I think it's utter nonsense," said Hewlett.

"Nobody cares what you think," said McShane.

"What are you going to do for blood?" said Steadman.

"I'm going to get it from Hewlett's nose," said McShane.

"Why me?" said the indignant Hewlett.

"Because you're the least likely to punch me back," said McShane.

"I wouldn't be too sure of that," said Hewlett. "When I was at Eaton, I once punched Buster Murdoch in the ear and made him cry. I dropped him good style, to coin a well used Scouse expression."

"Well while we're on the subject of dropping things, has anybody dropped a wallet?" said Hamill.

"A wallet?" said Steadman.

"If it's bursting with twenty and fifty pound notes, it'll be mine," said McShane.

"It's mine," said the pan faced Hewlett.

"Is it really?" said Hamill before unclipping the item, removing two small colour photographs and holding them up to the light. "Are you sure about that Hewlett?"

"I'm positive," said Hewlett. "Give it here Hamill. Give it here right. away. You've no business going through my things.""Where were these taken?" said Hamill.

"Where those photographs were taken, has nothing at all to do with you," said Hewlett.

"Where were they taken?" pressed Hamill. "That's not your home is it? Was this photo taken at your house?"

"That's none of your business," said Hewlett. "They're my personal things. Give them here."

"I will do," said Hamill while fending the agitated Hewlett off. "Just tell me where they were taken first. Trust me-you can stamp your feet and complain all you like, but you're not going to get them back until you tell me where they were taken."

"Very well," said the heavily perspiring Hewlett. "The one on the left was taken at the Forbes-Brown Stud Farm near Lambourn. The other one was taken in my parent's drawing room last Easter."

"Who's the girl with the big tits?" said Hamill.

"Don't be so vulgar," said Hewlett.

"Who is she?" said Hamill.

"Prunella Forbes-Brown," said Hewlett. "The stud farm owner's youngest daughter. And my current girlfriend, as it happens."

"Girlfriend!" said Woodhouse. "I didn't know you were into girls."

"Well you know now," said Hewlett.

"Is she the one with the big nose and long straggly grey hair?" said Hamill.

"Very droll," said Hewlett. "That's her Irish Wolfhound Max. And that's her ten year old bay mare Palmerston in the background being shod."

"Being shot!" said Woodhouse.

"Shod," said Hewlett.

"She's not a bad looker for a poor farm lass," said Hamill before handing the photograph to the eager Woodhouse. "What do you think Woody."

"She's got one hell of a pair of three penny bits on her," said Woodhouse. "What's she doing with you Hewlett?"

"She's with me for a variety of reasons," said Hewlett. "None of which have anything to do with your sexual prowess," said McShane.

"My God!" said Hewlett through the most pursed of

[366]

pursed lips. "Prunella's not like that. She likes cultural things like opera, quality theatre and ballet."

"Bollocks!" said Hamill. "Posh birds love the cock. They can't get enough of it."

"Have you tried your hand yet?" said Woodhouse.

"What does that mean?" said Hewlett.

"Have you copped a feel of the goods?" said Woodhouse.

"Have you had it bent over the back of the old leather Chesterfield settee yet?" said McShane.

"No I have not, and don't you dare suggest such a disgusting thing," said Hewlett.

"Alright Hewlett," said McShane. "Keep your hair on lad. I was only asking."

"You were being intrusive and extremely rude," said Hewlett. "And in future, will you please refrain from referring to Prunella as an 'it'. She's not an object. She's got a heart and a soul. She's a very caring and sensitive human being."

"You do know that people associated with stud farms are often sex mad don't you Hewlett?" said Hamill.

"Why are they?" said Hewlett.

"Because they see nothing but sex every day of their lives," said Hamill. "The smell of stallion semen is all around them. It's in the air. It's in their nostrils. It's on their clothes.

"You're filthy," said Hewlett. "She's just been awarded her cap and gown. She's a right brain box. And a real go getter too. She's one of those people who's going to get anything she sets her heart on."

"Well, let's hope for her sake, one of those things isn't a good stiff shag from you," said Hamill. "Because if it is, I've got a feeling, she's going to be very disappointed."

"I wouldn't concern yourself if I was you," said Hewlett. "When the right and proper time presents itself, Prunella will be more than adequately fulfilled. And it'll be done extremely tastefully as well-It'll be done under silk sheets on a four poster bed. Not the apparent favoured way of the working class lethario-in the rear of an old Ford Escort."

"I think the lad deserves a lot of praise," said McShane. "I didn't think he had it in him. I didn't think he was capable of pulling a bit of minge of that calibre."

"A bit of minge!" said the mortified Hewlett before snatching up his book and shoving back his seat. "A bit of minge! In the name of all that's holy! What an appalling and demeaning expression. You need your filthy mouth washing out Tommy."

"He does, doesn't he," said Hamill. "And I could do with mine having a good swill around too. So why doesn't somebody get behind that bar and pour some bloody drinks."

"What are you having?" said Woodhouse.

"Whatever it is, make the measures small," said the Chairman.

"Why's that?" said Hamill.

"Because we're up early tomorrow," said the Chairman.

"We're not," said Hamill.

"What do you mean?" said the Chairman.

"Me and my mates are having a well earned sleep in," said Hamill.

"Really?" said the Chairman.

"Yes, really," said Hamill. "Playing at prison warders and running off intruders is damn hard work."

"But I thought with you three being the strongest, you might have wanted to take the first shift to get us off to a good start," said the Chairman.

"You thought wrong," said Hamill. "We're going to arrive late in the day like the Seventh Cavalry."

"Who, by the way, we're all massacred," said the Club Secretary.

"Shut your face," said Hamill.

"Do you want *me* to take the first shift?" said Steadman.

"If you don't mind," said the Chairman.

"We'll do it Hulmey," said the Club Secretary. "As long as the Angel of Death hasn't paid us a visit during the early hours."

"I'd forgot about her," said Hamill.

"What makes you think the Angel's a woman?" said Woodhouse.

"Call it 'instinct'," said Hamill. "Added to the fact she's vindictive, malicious and intent upon taking her anger out on the male of the species. No man could be that wicked Woody. Now then-do you want to help me and Tommy carry out a final search of the corridors before we settle down for the evening?"

"I thought we were going to have a nice drink," said Woodhouse.

"That can wait," said Hamill. "Let's go and check those outside doors before our all action hero Hulmey tells us he's already done it."

"I have already done it," said the Chairman.

"You see Woody," said Hamill. "I'm so far ahead of the field I sometimes wonder why I'm not running the country."

CHAPTER SIXTEEN
LOCK DOWN

The drinking bout had lasted far longer than the Chairman had hoped and recommended but those that had assembled in the dining carriage earliest the next morning were still nevertheless looking reasonably alert and enthusiastic by the time the Chef emerged from the kitchen with the first two cooked breakfasts and a dubiously stacked tower of thick buttered toast.

"I suggest the two men who are taking the first shift in the engine, eat first," he said while wiping his greasy hands on his apron.

"That would be me and Tommy then," said Hamill while violently shaking a new bottle of tomato ketchup across his chest.

"Sod off Hamill," said the Club Secretary. "I'm afraid you're going to have to wait."

"Why am I?" said Hamill.

"Because you said you were going to do one of the later shifts," said the Chairman.

"I've had time to reconsider since," said Hamill.

"We want to get the team off to a good start," said McShane. "We reckon we can more than double the distance Larko estimated yesterday."

"Let's hope you're right," said the Club Secretary. "Because we might be home for supper if you are."

"Don't forget, Biddo will need feeding," said Blackie. "Unless starving the poor old bugger to death is part of his punishment."

"He should be getting nothing but porridge like all the other old lags," said McShane.

"He'll get what everyone else is having," said the Chef. "I'm not prejudice against offenders. Have you been to see him this morning Blackie?"

"I haven't had a chance yet," replied Blackie. "I've been waiting for one of the showers to become available."

"Has anyone seen Larko?" said the Chairman.

"At this time of the morning?" said Hamill. "You'll be lucky won't you."

"He should be well up by now," said the Club Secretary. "He was meant to be helping Alty guide Anthony down off the bridge at 6.30."

"How did you manage to talk the buggers into that unsavoury chore?" said Hamill.

"I reduced their suspension so they could go to Cheltenham," said the Chairman.

"Nice thinking for once," said Hamill.

"Was it your idea for Woody to help them on the rope?" said the Chairman.

"He volunteered," said Hamill.

"What was the weather like for them?" said the Chef.

"Better than it's been for some time," said the Chairman.

"As I forecasted, I might add," said the Club Secretary.

"Did anyone hear a commotion earlier on?" said a yawning Steadman while holding the forward door to allow the heavily perspiring Chef to manoeuvre through with his tray of piping hot food."

"What sort of commotion? said the Club Secretary.

"Raised voices mainly," replied Steadman.

"What time was this?" said Blackie.

"Around five o'clock," said Steadman. "I'd just come out of the washroom."

"Did you check outside?" said Hewlett after hurrying over to the window.

"What for?" said Steadman.

"Because the voices could have been a rescue party calling out to us," said Hewlett.

"I never thought of that," said Steadman.

"I doubt if it was a rescue party," said the Club Secretary.

"Why's that?" said Hewlett.

"Because, if it was, they'd be here having breakfast with us by now," said the Club Secretary.

"Not if they'd failed to see us," said Hewlett while

[371]

returning to his seat.

"They'd have seen us," said the Club Secretary. "They couldn't miss us. They'd have seen the bridge."

"They'd have seen at least one of our carriage lights," said Steadman.

"I suppose so," said Hewlett.

"By the way-did anyone else apart from us do the blood over the door ritual thing last night?" said the Club Secretary.

"We did," said Hamill. "We weren't going to take any chances. Especially after what Woody did to that poor bumble bee."

"What did you do for blood?" said Hewlett.

"I drained ours from the meat cooler," said the Chef.

"And I pricked my thumb several times," said McShane.

"That was brave of you," said Steadman.

"Well I couldn't wait for Hewlett to start his period could I?" said McShane. "The Angel of Death might have done her dirty deed and been gone by then. I daubed some over the dining carriage doors as well."

"That was very thoughtful of you," said Steadman. "What do I owe you Tommy?"

"Just your life, if the legend turns out to be true," said Hamill.

"I can't give you that Tommy," said Steadman. "But I will stand you a few bevies when we get back to Crosby."

"I'll hold you to that," said McShane.

"No, seriously Tommy-I really am grateful," said Steadman. "I'm not normally that superstitious, but after all those stories of Jaguars, scars that heal mysteriously and vanishing tribesmen, I didn't sleep a wink last night. I kept having these visions of that Angel of Death character swooping down on me."

"That's because you're on edge," said the Chef.

"You're not wrong there," said the Chairman. "For God's sake-where are the lads?"

"They've probably gone back to bed," said Hamill.

[372]

"That's where Woody will be. Would that be a problem?"

"It would yes," said the Chairman. "I want their report. I want to know if young Anthony got away alright. By the way lads-which bloody idiot left a trail of suitcases strewn along the first corridor floor?"

"I've no idea," said McShane.

"Neither have I," said Steadman. "I rarely venture along there unless I'm reporting instances of arson."

"It was me," said the Club Secretary after dropping his knife and fork and folding his arms.

"You!" said the Chairman.

"I was going to leave them by the first carriage exit but I got distracted," said the Club Secretary.

"Distracted by what?" said the Chairman.

"By your brother calling me to get my breakfast," said the Club Secretary.

"But why bring your cases now?" said the Chairman. "What was the hurry?"

"I don't know," said the Club Secretary. "I suppose I just liked the idea we were finally going home. Don't you ever do that Hulmey? Don't you ever pack early when you're excited about going home?"

"I do yes," said the Chairman. "And I don't blame you for being excited. But we've got at least one full day's hard work ahead of us before we can even think about home. For God's sake Hilly. You know that better than anyone-you were the one that did the maths."

"Steady on now," said Steadman. "Hilly's only done what a lot of us have done. We're all as high as kites because of the news regarding the train moving."

"Well I'm not," said the Chairman while wiping his brow. "I'm dreading getting home."

"Why's that?" said Steadman.

"Because when we get home, my problems will just be starting," said the Chairman. "Think about it lads. When you get back, you'll be able to disappear behind the doors of your cosy three ups and two downs. I probably won't see you again until the January monthly meeting.

[373]

You haven't got the responsibility I've got."

"You're not the only one who'll be expected to answer questions," said Hamill. "At some point in the future, every one of us is going to be taken in for questioning."

"But none of you are going to be questioned the way I am," said the Chairman. "It's going to be like the Spanish Inquisition for me. I'm going to have to explain the deaths of Tommy Weir and Alec Morris and the disappearance of Eddie Meehan. To be perfectly honest, that's not going to be the worst of it. Looking Alec Morris's wife and kids in the face is going to be a nightmare. What the hell am I going to tell them?"

"You're going to tell them Alec died as a result of a tragic accident," said Hamill. "That's what you're going to tell them. Don't forget-and I'm not going to tell you this again Hulmey-if Morris hadn't started the train when he did, we'd probably still have a full fucking crew now."

"I'm afraid he's right on that count Hulmey," said Steadman.

"That's the thing Steadman," said the Chairman. "I know he's right. But that doesn't make my situation any easier."

"Why don't you sit yourself down and I'll get you a nice cup of tea laced with strong brandy," said Steadman. "And try to concentrate more on what you're going to miss when we've left here."

"Like what?" said the Chairman.

"Like Woody parading round like one of the Chippendales in his ill fitting tanga briefs," said Steadman. "And Hewlett doing his impression of Noel Coward in his dressing gowns and silk cravats."

"It's called dressing contextually," said the sneering Hewlett. "And might I remind you again-it's what we were all meant to be doing."

"I'll tell you what I'm not going to miss," said Blackie.

"What's that?" said Steadman.

"I'm not going to miss lying in my bed, squeezing my butt cheeks together while waiting for that one final almighty blast of wind to send us all to hell," said Blackie.

"I'm going to miss my verbal jousts with Hewlett," said McShane.

"Verbal jousts!" said Hewlett. "You presumptuous oath! You don't possess anywhere near the sort of intellect to verbally joust with me."

"Then, why don't you help me?" said McShane.

"Help you in what way?" said Hewlett.

"Why don't you take me into your lovely home?" said McShane. "You could do it as part of a care in the community project. You could school me like that Professor so and so did with the lovely flower girl Audrey Hepburn. What was his name now?"

"Higgins," said Hewlett. "Professor Higgins. He was a George Bernard Shaw creation. And for your information, the lovely flower girl was Eliza Doolittle, not the absurdly miscast Belgian, Audrey Hepburn."

"Was she really?" said McShane. "Anyway-let's get back to business. Do it Hewlett. Take me into your home for a spell. Make a proper gentleman out of me. I'll wash me hands and face before I come. You could learn me to talk proper."

"You'd be well advised to stay away from my home," said Hewlett. "I wouldn't have you in our home as a wall mounted hunting trophy."

"I might just pay you a visit whether you like it or not," said McShane. "I've always wanted to see the inside of a rundown stately home."

"Rundown stately home!" said an indignant Hewlett while adjusting his position. "How dare you suggest such a thing. My parent's house is not in the least bit run down. We have 26 domestic staff to ensure the place is immaculately kept. The very idea! You could eat your meals off our stable floor."

"Is that what the servants have to do?" said McShane.

"The servants have got their own well appointed dining room in the basement," said Hewlett. "They're more than adequately provided for."

"That's a relief," said McShane. "Because I'm a shop steward. I'd hate to think of them being treated unkindly. When do you think it would be convenient to call?"

"How about never?" said a finger wagging Hewlett. "You stay away. You keep to your own bloody kind. You keep to your run down and rat infested Council estates."

"But I want to meet your parents," said McShane. "In fact, as soon as we get back, I'm going to call round and have a spot of tiffin with them."

"You most certainly are not," said Hewlett.

"I am," said McShane. "They actually owe me money for a little gutter repair job I did for them about a month ago."

"I know nothing of that," said Hewlett.

"It's true," said McShane. "It's not your old dad's fault though. I told him I'd come back to check the repair, but I haven't had the time."

"How much do they owe you?" said a determined looking Hewlett after quickly removing his wallet and sending some of the contents floating to the floor.

"That's nothing to do with you," said McShane.

"It's got everything to do with me," said Hewlett. "You've just told me my father's in your debt. And you told me that, in front of a considerable audience. How much is it exactly? How much does he owe you?"

"I'm only going to deal with the man of the house," said McShane. "With any luck, I'll get round before Christmas. Tell him to have the Mull wine on the go. And I wonder if you could arrange for that tasty bit of strumpet Prunella to be round. I think I could do a bit of damage there."

"I've no doubt you could," said Hewlett. "She'd probably end up in a nunnery or on a psychiatric ward after meeting you."

"Why's that?" said McShane.

"Because you're almost another species compared to her," said Hewlett. "In fact, you're more like a

[376]

subspecies. Prunella's in a totally different class to
you."
"Class has nothing to do with it," said McShane. "Have
you never heard of Lady Shatterley?"
"I've heard of Lady Chatterley," said Hewlett. "What do
you understand of her character?"
"I know she shagged her gamekeeper behind her
husband's back," said McShane.
"Nicely phrased," said Hewlett. "Do you happen to
know why?"
"Because she was gagging for it," said McShane. "She
was no different to a lot of posh birds."
"Have you ever read the novel?" said Hewlett.
"No but I've seen the film twice," said McShane.
"Can you read?" said Hewlett.
"I can read as well as anybody," said McShane. "How
do you think I gained my advanced City and Guilds
Certificates? And here's something else that might
surprise you...I can play a reasonable piano."
"Play a reasonable piano!" scoffed Hewlett. "Don't
make me laugh. I doubt if you've ever seen a piano-let
alone played one."
"I've played plenty of pianos," said McShane.
"How come?" said Hewlett.
"I was brought up above a city centre pub," said
McShane. "There used to be a piano in every pub until
jukeboxes were introduced."
"Who taught you to play?" said Hewlett.
"Me old girl," said McShane. "We had our own cheap
upright. She played entirely by ear. She could play
anything. She'd only have to hear a tune once and that
was it."
"Do you think she could play Chopin's *b-flat minor
scherzo*?" said Hewlett.
"Who was that by?" said McShane.
"Frederic Chopin," said the unamused Hewlett. "The
clue was in the question."
"I've never heard of her," said McShane. "She could
play Roll Out the Barrel, the Lambeth Walk and Knees

up Mother Brown, to name a few. She used to regularly lift the roof off the Hare and Hounds on Great George Street. And she had all the great pianists' albums."

"Like who?" said the keen eyed Hewlett while edging forward.

"I can't remember now," said McShane.

"Why not?" said Hewlett.

"Because I can't," said McShane. "It's not one of those things that's important to me."

"Not important to you!" said Hewlett. "All the great pianists I was introduced to are now etched into my soul. Surely you remember one."

"I do, as it happens," said McShane.

"Who is he?" said Hewlett. "Les Dawson?"

"Bobby Crush," replied McShane after a short pause.

"Bobby Crush!" said a confused looking Hewlett.

"That's right," said McShane.

"He was excellent," said Steadman. "My Aunty Lona saw him live."

"Where was this? said Hewlett. "The Royal Albert Hall?"

"Allinsons in Litherland," said Steadman. "He brought the house down apparently. You must have heard of Bobbie Crush Hewlett. He was brilliant. He rarely played a bum note. I thought he was better than Russ Conway."

"I thought so too," said McShane. "But he didn't have Conway's enigmatic smile. Didn't he win Opportunity Knocks?"

"He won it a few times," said Steadman.

"Did he really," said Hewlett. "He must have been good then. Who did he beat-some husband and wife knife throwing act?"

"He beat a lot of very good talent," said McShane. "Me mum had his *Piano Party* album. Do you play Hewlett? Do you play the piano?"

"I'm a grade 8," said Hewlett. "I'm classically trained. I attended the Royal Academy of Music for 8 years."

"Was it any good?" said McShane.

[378]

"Any good!" sneered Hewlett. "It was the Royal
Academy of Music for goodness sake. Of course it was
good. It's one of the best music academies in the world.
Simon Rattle, Arthur Sullivan and Alan Bush attended
it."

"Alan Bush hey!" said McShane. "Which reminds
me.....While we're on the subject of 'bush'-try to make
sure the lovely Prunella's had a good pubic trim before I
see her next."

"You're disgusting," said Hewlett. "And you're a bare
faced liar too. You can't play the piano."

"I can," said McShane. "I've got my own. Have you?
Have you got your own piano?"

"Not as such," said Hewlett. "But I do have
unrestricted access to one of the 'grand' variety."

"Would that be the Steinway?" said McShane.

"I beg your pardon!" said Hewlett in a very definite tone
of suspicion.

"Would that be the Steinway?" said McShane.

"How do you know about our Steinway?" said Hewlett.

"I just do," said McShane.

"He's been having private tuition at yours," said
Woodhouse. "He's been seeing your mother behind
your father's back."

"He wouldn't be seeing anything if he'd made a pass at
my mother," said Hewlett. "He'd have been dragged
into the garden by his ear and thrashed to within an inch
of his miserable life. Now answer my question Tommy-
how do you know about our Steinway?"

"I don't just know about it," said McShane. "I've
actually played it. "And do you know what Hewlett-I
think it's in need of a good tuning."

"It's tuned regularly by the Myerscough brothers," said
Hewlett. "It's superbly maintained. Mitsuko Uchida
played that piano less than three months ago."

"Did he really?" said McShane.

"Mitsuko's a woman," said Hewlett. "A very talented
woman at that. You're a rogue Tommy. I bet you were
the mindless idiot that ran your wheelbarrow across our

[379]

croquet lawn."

"I wasn't going to go around," said McShane. "Have you seen the size of that lawn?"

"I've seen the massive great groove running through the centre of it," said Hewlett. "You were lucky you weren't shot Tommy. Of all the impertinence. You've not heard the last of that business. I've a good mind to have you prosecuted."

"For pushing a wheelbarrow across a croquet lawn?" said McShane.

"For unlawful intrusion," said Hewlett. "My father gave strict instructions, no builders were to be allowed in the main house. Bloody hell-that considerate old man gave you a perfectly good shed to have your breaks in. What more did you want?"

"A roof and a window would have been nice," said McShane.

"A roof and a window!" scoffed Hewlett. "You ungrateful pig. It just goes to show, if you give the under classes an inch, they'll start expecting a couple of miles."

"And it also goes to show how quick the toffee nosed upper classes are to judge their so-called inferiors," said McShane upon handing Hewlett his photograph of Prunella ."

"Where did you get this?" said Hewlett.

"You dropped it when you were putting your wallet back in your pocket," said McShane. "That picture was taken in your living room wasn't it Hewlett."

"The drawing room," said Hewlett.

"And what's the lovely Prunella leaning over?" asked McShane.

"I don't know, and I don't care," said the scowling Hewlett before turning to face the window.

"You do know," said McShane. "What's she leaning over?"

"I don't know-some sort of sideboard, I suppose," said Hewlett.

"What's she leaning over?" said McShane after

spinning Hewlett around to address him face to face. "Answer the lad Hewlett," said Hamill. "What's the girl leaning over?"

"Our piano," muttered a blushing and enormously self conscious Hewlett.

"I couldn't quite hear that," said McShane. "What's she leaning over Hewlett?"

"Our piano," yelled Hewlett. "Our piano! Our piano! Our piano! There, I said it three times for you. Are you satisfied now Tommy?"

"She's leaning over your Steinway, to be more precise," said McShane. "Which goes to show Hewlett, that regardless of your so-called superior intellect and my apparent lack of it, when it comes to verbal jousting, you're not in my league."

"Nice one Tommy," said Hamill.

"He's still an unseemly vagabond," said Hewlett.

"Why is he?" said Hamill.

"Because only a vagabond of the opportunistic kind would have spotted the sort of details he saw in that photograph," said Hewlett. "What else did you recognise Tommy? Was it father's much coveted Roman coin collection? Was it mother's rare and priceless Chinese Ormolu Clock? Was it the gleaming silver cabinet? You didn't happen to establish where father hides the safe did you?"

"I didn't notice any of that to be honest," said McShane. "I was more interested in the size of your bird's tits. I'll tell you what-she's in remarkable shape for a horsey type. I bet that girl doesn't need much of a saddle."

"What do you mean?" said Hewlett.

"Look at the size of the backside on her," said McShane. "Her arse roasted or grilled could sustain a small African community for a month."

"You are utterly deplorable," said Hewlett. "How would you like it if someone insulted your daughter?"

"I'd leave it up to my daughter to sort out," said McShane.

"Is she one of those hard knock Scouse girls is she?"

[381]

said Hewlett.

"She's currently serving three years in a young offenders institution," said McShane.

"She's what?" said Hewlett.

"She's been detained at her Majesty's pleasure," said McShane.

"For doing what?" said Hewlett.

"Beating the shit out of three lads," said McShane.

"My God!" said Hewlett. "Where was this?"

"Outside the Plaza Cinema on Crosby Road," said McShane. "She'd been to see the director's cut of Reservoir Dogs. The lads had pushed her over and trampled on her on the way out apparently. She caught up with them and beat them to a pulp."

"Do you think that had anything to do with what she'd seen?" said Hewlett.

"What do you mean?" said McShane.

"Reservoir Dogs is commonly regarded as one of the most violent films ever made," said Hewlett. "If I remember right, a man gets his ears cut off."

"I don't think it was anything to do with that," said McShane. "I think it was more to do with her failing her SATS."

"Her SATs!" said Hewlett. "Failed her.....How old is this daughter of yours? Oh for goodness sake Tommy. You've done me again haven't you?"

"I most certainly have," said McShane. "My other daughter really is a nut job though. She's an evil little fucker. To this day, I'm convinced it was her who cut the brake pipes on my Rover 2000."

"Rubbish!" said Hewlett. "I'm not listening anymore."

"It's not rubbish," said McShane.

"I'm not listening," said Hewlett. "You're trying to play me for a fool. It's utter nonsense."

"It's the God's honest truth," said McShane. "She cut the brake pipes on my Rover 2000. I've even got the receipt for new brake pipes in my coat pocket. Do you want to see it?"

"It won't be necessary," said Hewlett. "But why? Why

would she cut your brake pipes?"
"Because I'd confiscated her Game Boy the previous
evening," said McShane. "She loves that Game Boy.
She went berserk. You should have heard the things she
was calling me."
"But why cut your brake pipes?" said Hewlett. "I've
heard of kids having tantrums and lashing out, but I've
never known one to damage a car in order to exact
revenge on a parent."
"Have you ever heard of a young girl changing a clutch
at the age of 11?" said McShane.
"Never," replied Hewlett.
"Well, my daughter did," said McShane. "She's a
brilliant little mechanic. She changed the clutch on my
old Honda Civic. She's got her own full set of tools
now. They're all Dewalt. She's got top quality welding
gear too. That's all she wanted for Christmas. She's
always loved fixing things. She's rigged our gas and
electric meters so we don't have to pay any bills."
"And you encouraged her to do that did you?" said
Hewlett.
"We get three holidays a year from the money she saves
us on domestic bills," said McShane.
"I think it's outrageous," said Hewlett. "I've a good
mind to report you to your energy provider Tommy."
"He's pulling your plonker," said Steadman.
"He's doing what?" said Hewlett.
"He's been taking the Mickey again," said Hamill.
"The swine," said Hewlett. "You time wasting swine
Tommy."
"I was just trying to lighten the mood in the camp," said
McShane.
"Well, you haven't lightened my mood," said Hewlett.
"The only way you could lighten my mood is to promise
to stay away from my home. I want you to keep away
from us Tommy. I don't want to see you anywhere near
the old place. That's not to say you'd ever get further
than our boundary wall."
"Why wouldn't I?" said McShane.

[383]

"Because of Waggers," said Hewlett. "Once he gets his teeth into your backside, your days of sitting comfortably are numbered."

"Is Waggers your butler?" said Tommy.

"Don't be funny," said Hewlett. "Waggers is our 6 year old Doberman Pinscher. He is almost human though. Do you know-he wakes me up every morning at exactly the same time. It's uncanny. You could set your alarm clock by him."

"We could do with him here," said the Chairman before sighing loudly. "He could go and wake Larkin up. Where the hell is the lazy sod?"

"Relax Hulmey," said the Club Secretary. "He'll be here soon."

"Steadman's just gone to give him a shake," said Blackie.

"He'll be wasting his time," said an anaemic looking Chef who had just returned almost unnoticed and was making his slow and very deliberate way to the bar.

"Why's that?" said Blackie.

"Because I don't think Larko's in his room," said the Chef.

"Well where the hell is he then?" said the Chairman. "Is he getting a shower? Has anyone checked the washroom?"

"I just have," said the returning Steadman. "There's no sign of him. There's no sign of the other two buggers either."

"Have their beds been slept in?" said the Chairman.

"I think so," said Steadman.

"Did you notice if any of their clothes had gone?" said the Club Secretary.

"I didn't," said Steadman. "I was looking for missing people to be honest."

"Why would you ask that Hilly? said Blackie. "You don't think they've gone with Anthony do you?"

"I don't know," said the Club Secretary. "It'd be a lousy trick if they had though. That would leave us two men light regarding manpower."

"Has anyone thought of checking the engine?" said Woodhouse.

"There's a thing," said Hamill. "Maybe they've already started work."

"They can't have done," said the Club Secretary.

"Why not?" said Hamill.

"Because the track needs clearing first," said the Club Secretary.

"Maybe that's what they're doing," said Hamill.

"I'll go and have a look," said Steadman.

"I wouldn't bother," said a visibly shaking and pale looking Chef while heading towards his chair with a half empty bottle of whiskey and a heavily stained pint glass.

"Just go and search the engine please Steadman," said Hamill. "The Chef might have missed them for some reason or other."

"I missed nobody," said the Chef.

"Well, check the mailroom then," said Hamill.

"That's an idea," said Steadman. "They might be tormenting the life out of Biddo as we speak."

"They're not tormenting anyone," said the Chef.

"How do you know?" said Steadman.

"Because they're not," said the Chef.

"What's the matter our kid?" said the Chairman after kneeling at his brother's feet and gently raising his chin. "What's going on fella? Look at you-you're sweating cobs and shaking like a leaf. Just take a deep breath and tell us what's wrong. What's happened mate?"

"People are dead our kid," said the Chef.

"Dead!" said Steadman.

"Which people?" said the Chairman. "Who's dead, Chef?"

"All of them," said the Chef.

"But who?" said the Chairman after taking his brother by the upper arms. "Who the hell are you talking about our kid? Are you talking about our club members?"

"I'm not entirely sure," said the Chef.

"Why's that?" said the Chairman.

"Because it's impossible to say," said the Chef.

[385]

"Why is it?" said the Chairman before releasing his grip and slowly climbing to his feet.

"Because it is," said the Chef. "There are bits of body parts strewn all over the mailroom floor. It's a bloodbath our kid. I'm telling you-I'm telling you all-Hamill must have been right about the myth. The bumble bee should have been released. In killing that innocent little creature, Woody's unknowingly invited someone or something very nasty on board this train."

CHAPTER SEVENTEEN
DECISIONS

The half dozen dumbfounded passengers that had remained in the dining carriage while the Chairman, his Club Secretary and Tommy McShane were seeking confirmation as to what had taken place in the mailroom, had assembled in an almost perfectly shaped arc just inside the forward door but despite their urges and desperation to learn the truth as quickly as possible, that truth hadn't been divulged by any one of the returning investigative party for another thirty agonising minutes. At that point, the arc immediately but ever so slowly disassembled and the first murmurs of anguish, incredulity and despair had been heard. What they had learned through what ultimately consisted of a series of mumbled responses and a number of sporadic grunts, nods and other mimed gestures, was that four of their members, including the recently incarcerated Kenny Biddo and nightclub doorman Paul Woodhouse had been brutally murdered and another two, experienced motor mechanic Dave Larkin and transport worker Kenny Alty, had been so horribly dismembered, their identification had only been established by their tattoos, wedding rings and what was inside their blood spattered wallets.

"I don't get it," said a badly shaken Steadman upon handing the equally pallid looking Club Secretary an overfilled glass of brandy. "I thought we had this place nicely locked down."

"The place *is* nicely locked down," said the Chairman. "Those outer doors are checked at least 6 or 7 times a day."

"I can reluctantly vouch for that," said Hamill.

"Maybe Alty or Larko left a door open after seeing young Anthony off," said the Chef.

"That's a point," said Hewlett.

"They didn't," said Hamill. "I checked every one of those doors earlier this morning."

"What about the barricade we built to stop anyone entering the train via the engine?" said the Chef. "Did you happen to notice if that was still in one piece?"

"That's still intact too," said the Club Secretary. "It's as sturdy as it ever was. The ice has bonded it all together. Nothing's got through there."

"Well they got on board the train somehow," said Hewlett.

"Isn't there a delivery hatch in that mailroom?" said Steadman.

"There is yes," said the Chairman. "But it's locked. Me and Tommy tried to open it to let some fresh air circulate. There was just no budging it."

"This is insane," said the Chef.

"It's beyond insane," said the Chairman. "Remind me again please Hewlett-what was it you saw in that vacant carriage?" said the Club Secretary.

"I'm still not entirely sure," said Hewlett. "As I told you before, it was really dark. My instincts told me they were animals. They certainly had the putrid scent of animals."

"I'm not having that," said the Club Secretary.

"Why not?" said Hamill.

"Because animals don't behave like that," said the Club Secretary. "Animals don't rip people to pieces for the sake of it. Animals only tear up their prey to make it easier to chew and digest."

"And animals don't smash heads to a pulp," said the Chairman.

"That's right," said the Chef. "Only a deranged human being would do something like that."

"Can anyone shed any light as to what they were all doing there?" said the Chairman.

"Big Woody would have been checking on Biddo," said Hamill. "Me, him and Tommy had been taking it in turns."

"And knowing Alty and Larkin, they were probably tormenting the life out of Biddo again," said Blackie.

"And therefore, in the wrong place at the wrong time,"

said the Club Secretary. "By the way lads-while we're on the subject of being in the wrong place at the wrong time-didn't we implement some sort of, going everywhere in pairs rule?"

"Alty and Larkin *were* in a pair," said Hamill.

"Those two were almost joined at the hip," said Steadman.

"I'm not talking about them," said the Club Secretary. "I'm talking about you Tommy."

"What the hell have I done?" said McShane.

"You've just been to check the ropes again haven't you?" said the Club Secretary.

"I have yes," said McShane.

"And despite the going everywhere in pairs rule, you went on your own," said the Club Secretary. "What did you do that for?"

"Because I asked him to," said Hamill.

"And because I can look after myself," said McShane.

"And so could big Woody," said the Club Secretary. "Jesus Christ Tommy. I once saw him take three Wigan rugby second eleven players down with one swish of his right arm."

"I saw that too," said Hamill. "They were built like brick shithouses."

"I wish he was here now," said the Club Secretary. "Because there's every chance, whoever or whatever killed those four poor lads, is still on board this train."

"Oh Christ yes," said Steadman before racing over to put his shoulder against the rear door. "I never thought of that. We're going to need to make this room safe. Is everyone here?"

"I think so," said the Club Secretary.

"Where's the Professor?" said the Chairman.

"He's gone to examine the bodies," said Hewlett.

"Why?" said the Chairman.

"I don't know," said Hewlett. "But I'm sure he had his reasons."

"But why now?" said the Chairman. "Couldn't it wait? Couldn't that have waited until we've got our heads together and know exactly what we're up against?"

"I suppose so," said Hewlett.

"Would someone go after him please?" said the Chairman.

"What for?" said Hamill. "I would have thought the old boy can look after himself. If he can survive the Amazon Jungle amongst lions, poisonous snakes and tigers, he can survive here."

"That was donkey's years ago," said the Chairman. "He's a frail old man now."

"A frail old man who's had a pretty good innings by all accounts," said Hamill.

"And we're going to need him to keep batting on," said the Chairman. "Aren't you forgetting something Hamill?"

"Forgetting what?" said Hamill.

"The sedative," said the Chairman. "We need that old man. Matthews and maybe one or two others will go insane or die without that old man's medicine and expertise."

"Go after him then," said Hamill while pointing to the door. "Go on. Don't let me stop you Hulmey."

"I can't," said the Chairman.

"Why not?" said Hamill.

"Because I'm needed here," said the Chairman.

"No you're not," said Hamill. "I can keep an eye on things here. Go on. Run along and make sure the Professor's alright."

"He's needed here," said the Chef. "This is a critical time."

"He's got decisions to make," said the Club Secretary.

"What sort of decisions?" said Hamill.

"Like what were going to do next," said the Club Secretary.

"That's not hard," said Hamill. "I can do that. Let me see now...We're all going to have to keep an eye out for monsters and things like that. We're all going to have to camp in here until the danger passes or we're rescued. We're going to have to make a temporary toilet...and

[390]

both dining room doors are going to have to be nailed shut. That's about it isn't it? That's right, isn't it lads? Is there anything else you need to know?"

"There's something I need to know," said McShane.

"What's that?" said Hamill.

"I want to know who provided Biddo's refreshments," said McShane.

"What refreshments?" said Hamill.

"There were two empty vodka bottles on the floor of the mailroom," said McShane.

"Really!" said Hamill.

"Two empty litre bottles to be more accurate," said McShane.

"Are you sure it was vodka?" said the Chef.

"I'm positive it was vodka," said McShane while settling down opposite Blackie and folding his arms. "The labels said, 'Smirnoff'. That's vodka isn't it?"

"It is where I come from," said Hamill.

"Could that be why Alty and Larkin were there?" said the Club Secretary. "Could the vodka have been a peacemaking token of some sort?"

"I wouldn't have thought so," said McShane. "Not after the way Biddo had treated them. Why would they want to make peace?"

"That's true," said the Club Secretary.

"So who was it?" said Hamill. "Who was it lads? Who gave him the drink?"

"I think I might be staring at the culprit right now," said McShane.

"Don't look at me," said Steadman.

"I'm not talking about you," said McShane. "I'm talking about your mate next door to you."

"It wasn't me," said Blackie. "Although I will admit this-I had thought about taking him a drink."

"Why?" said McShane.

"Because he asked me," said Blackie. "And the fact that I knew he was going to go through hell."

"In what way?" said Hamill.

"You'd have to be a recovering alcoholic to appreciate

that," said Blackie.

"He'd have been climbing the walls and seeing pink elephants without a drink," said the Club Secretary.

"Well who did it then?" said Hamill.

"My guess would be nobody," said the Chef. "There are bottles of spirits lying around everywhere. This train's a heavy drinker's paradise. He might have snaffled a couple of bottles while on his way to the mailroom."

"It's possible, I suppose," said Hamill.

"It's not possible," said McShane. "Woody and I hardly allowed him enough room to breathe."

"Well how did he get it?" said Hamill.

"I gave it to him," said the Chairman.

"You!" said Hamill.

"He'd driven me half out of my mind," said the Chairman. "I couldn't listen to his ranting and raving any longer. It was alright for you lot. You were well out of hearing range."

"Did you know about this Hilly?" said McShane.

"I knew Biddo had been making one hell of a commotion," said the Club Secretary.

"He'd promised to shut his trap if I brought him a drink," said the Chairman. "It seemed like an attractive proposition at the time. It was either that or go insane."

"It was pure stupidity," said McShane. "The daft bastard was already half mad."

"It was probably a Godsend when you consider what happened to him," said the Chef.

"What do you mean?" said Hamill.

"It probably helped him," said the Chef. "With any luck, Biddo was completely pissed off his face by the time he was attacked. And if he was, there's every chance he didn't feel a thing."

"Well, let's hope the other three poor bastards were pissed off their faces too," said Steadman before backing away from the door to allow the Professor to enter. "And as for you Hulmey-couldn't you have just put your fingers in your ears?"

"I tried that," said the Chairman. "I even considered

taking my bedding and climbing inside the wardrobe at one point."

"For what purpose?" said the old man while taking his seat.

"To get a bit of peace and quiet," said the Chairman.

"We're talking about Biddo Professor," said the Chef.

"And how he'd been a nuisance," said the Club Secretary.

"That's putting it mildly," said the old man.

"We've just found out he'd been given alcohol," said Blackie.

"Had he really?" said the old man after removing his handkerchief from his trouser pocket and wiping his brow. "My word! That wasn't very clever was it. What blithering idiot thought that was a good idea?"

"I did," said the Chairman. "He was going off his head. He was showing no signs of calming down. It was a like a Chinese torture."

"Is that why you let him out of his cage?" said the Professor.

"I did no such thing," said the Chairman. "I didn't need to let him out. The bottles slipped through the bars."

"What did *you* make of that horror set Professor?" said the Club Secretary.

"It's hideous," said the old man. "It's like no crime scene I've ever been privy to before. I've certainly never seen human heads flattened like that before."

"Were they definitely all dead?" said Steadman.

"I'm afraid so," said the Professor.

"Does that include Biddo?" said Blackie.

"Biddo?" said the old man.

"My uncle," said Blackie.

"The man who'd recently been locked up for setting fire to one of our member's bed," said the Chairman.

"Oh, that deplorable character," said the Professor. "He's actually nowhere to be seen."

"He's what?" said Blackie.

"He's scarpered," said the Professor.

"Scarpered!" said Blackie. "What are you talking about

Professor-I've just been told he's one of the four dead."
"Not by me you haven't," said the old man. "Who told you that?"
"I did," said the Chairman. "I saw him as clear as daylight. You saw him too didn't you Tommy?"
"I did yes," said McShane.
"What's going on Professor?" said Blackie. "What's happening Hulmey? Is my uncle dead or isn't he?"
"He was dead," said the Chairman. "As far as I'm concerned, he was very definitely dead."
"I'm afraid you're very much mistaken," said the old man. "He wasn't part of the horrific crime scene I've just surveyed."
"Are you sure Professor?" said the Club Secretary.
"I'm certain," said the old man.
"Nice one Hulmey," said Hamill. "Take my advice lad-make sure you're never tempted to go for a career in the police. And in future, might I recommend you apply this general rule of thumb when examining what appears to be a dead body...if the assumed dead person is capable of breathing and walking, that person is almost certainly alive."
"Go to hell Hamill," said the Chairman.
"There's no need to take that tone," said Hamill. "I'm just trying to ensure you don't make the same ridiculous mistake twice. Particularly if that assumed dead person just happens to be me."
"Could Biddo have been dragged off by something or other?" said Steadman.
"Now there's a possibility," said Hamill.
"What do you think Professor?" said Steadman.
"It's possible," said the Professor. "But dragged off where? I didn't see any trails of blood or paw prints. And if there were any doors left open-I can assure you this-with my sciatica the way it is, I'd have felt any draught first."
"This is beyond belief," said the Club Secretary.
"It doesn't make sense," said the Chairman. "I definitely saw what appeared to be four dead bodies."

"I did too," said McShane. "There were four. There were definitely four."

"What you probably saw was a mish mash of intertwined body parts," said the Professor. "Did any of you men examine the bodies, by any chance?"

"I didn't feel it necessary," said the Chairman.

"And I didn't have the stomach to do it," said the Club Secretary. "But Biddo did look very, very dead to me."

"Why was that?" said the old man.

"For a variety of reasons," said the Club Secretary. "It looked as if rigor mortis had set in."

"He was like something out of Madame Tussauds," said McShane.

"And his body was contorted," said the Chairman.

"What do you mean contorted?" said the Professor.

"His jaw was locked open and his arms and legs were in unnatural positions," said the Chairman.

"And you couldn't see his heart pounding, could you Hulmey?" said the Club Secretary.

"Definitely not," said the Chairman.

"Can you see my heart pounding?" said the Professor.

"I suppose not," said the Chairman. "But you've got your shirt and jacket on Professor. Biddo was nearly naked."

"Nearly naked!" said Steadman.

"Almost," said the Chairman. "He was stripped down to his boxer shorts."

"What's going on Professor?" said Blackie. "Why would he be naked?"

"I don't know as yet," said the old man. "But I wouldn't think there was anything sinister in that. That mailroom's like a sauna. It's designed to keep parcels and people's personal belongings dry. I imagine if you spent any length of time there, any one of us would feel the urge to peel off a few layers."

"Fair comment," said Blackie. "But where the hell is he Professor. Where's my uncle? Where the hell's he gone? Do you think he's been abducted? Do we need to go searching for him?"

"You need to avoid him at all costs," said the old man.

"Why's that?" said Blackie.

"Because he's a very dangerous individual," said the old man.

"Why is he?" said Blackie.

"Isn't that obvious?" said the Professor.

"Not to me it's not," said Blackie.

"For goodness sake-the man lost his mind and brutally murdered three of your friends," said the Professor.

"That's nonsense," said Blackie.

"Have it your own way then," said the old man.

"I hope you're right Blackie," said Steadman.

"How can you be so sure Kenny Biddo was the killer Professor?" said the Chef.

"Because it couldn't possibly have been anyone else," said the old man. "Who else hated those two men with such passion and intensity? Who else, apart from your heavily sedated friend in carriage two has been found to have that atrocious disease?"

"That's a point," said the Chef.

"How did Woody die Professor?" said Hamill. "Have you any idea?"

"Among other things, massive head trauma," said the old man.

"That's rubbish!" said McShane.

"It's not rubbish at all," said the Professor.

"He'd been blinded," said McShane.

"My God!" said Hamill.

"Which, in turn, resulted in massive head trauma," said the old man.

"How come Professor?" said the Chairman.

"Do you really want to know?" said the Professor.

"I consider it vital I know," said the Chairman. "I'm going to be having to make a detailed report."

"Very well," said the old man. "Have it your way. His eyes had been forced through his brain and out of the back of his skull."

"Jesus Christ!" said Steadman.

"This is unreal," said Hewlett. "This is pure Poe. This

can't be happening."

"Where exactly was he found?" said Hamill.

"That's another thing I'm struggling to get my head around," said McShane.

"Where was he found Tommy?" said Hamill.

"Inside one of the mail room storage cupboards," said the Professor.

"What!" said Hamill.

"He was inside one of the mailroom cupboards," said the old man. "I can only assume he'd tried to take refuge there."

"Take refuge!" said Hamill. "Don't talk shite. Woody's never hidden from anything or anyone in his life."

"He was inside the cupboard with his knees drawn to his chest," said the Professor. "He'd defecated heavily too."

"He'd done what?" said McShane.

"He'd shit himself," said the Club Secretary.

"Oh Christ!" said Hamill.

"The poor bastard," said Steadman.

"The lads didn't need to hear that particular detail Professor," said McShane.

"I'd have preferred not to have heard that particular detail too," said Hewlett while making his way to the kitchen. "'Too much information', I think they call it."

"I'm just trying to give you all an honest and accurate appraisal," said the old man.

"Well, try to make the next instalment a little less graphic will you," said McShane. "At least until we've started to come to terms with what we already know."

"I don't think I'll ever come to terms with this," said the Club Secretary. "Especially the fact that two of the lads had been torn to shreds. How could Biddo have done that? What would he have used?"

"His hands, his fingernails or his teeth," said the old man.

"What!" said Steadman.

"He'd have used the same weapons a wild animal is equipped with," said the Professor. "I've actually witnessed such a frenzied attack. It's one of those deeply unpleasant things that lingers long in the memory."

"I'm not having that," said Hamill.

"What *are* you having?" said the Chef. "What do *you* think happened Hamill?"

"I think they were all victims of an animal attack," said Hamill. "And I think the drink and the presence of Alty and Larko are the clues as to why it happened."

"What do you mean?" said the Chairman.

"I believe some sort of daft, irresponsible drinking game had taken place," said Hamill.

"That's interesting," said the Professor.

"And because it involved the consumption of alcohol, there was only ever going to be one winner," said Hamill. "It would have literally been 'last man standing'."

"And that man would have been Kenny Biddo," said McShane.

"Of course it would," said Hamill. "And by the time the 2 bottles of vodka had been consumed, Woody and the other two unfortunates would have been completely out of the game."

"And at the mercy of the diseased and crazed Biddo," said the Professor.

"Or something that would soon home in on the scent of the men's remains," said Hamill.

"They'd have been easy pickings," said the Chef.

"They would," said Hamill. "They'd have been completely helpless. And the one that was still capable of moving, would have, in all likelihood, been the first attacked."

"Why's that?" said Steadman.

"Because predators respond to movement," said Hamill. "You only have to watch a cat stalking a mouse."

"How would you explain the flattened heads?" said the Professor.

"I can't," said Hamill. "I'm not even going to try."

"That would explain why Biddo was there when Hulmey and the others visited the crime scene," said Steadman.

"And why he was absent when the Professor arrived there," said Hamill.

"It would yes," said the Chairman.

"Your friend Biddo wasn't there when I arrived at the mailroom, because he'd come round, realised what he'd done and absconded," said the Professor.

"He's been taken," said Hamill. "Don't forget-food's in short supply at this time of the year. He's probably been taken somewhere more secluded so the animal can feast without fear of losing its meal."

"I think the whole idea's ridiculous," said Hewlett. "An animal couldn't possibly carry off a fully grown man. Especially an under nourished one."

"An animal could," said Steadman. "I was once on safari in Kenya with the family and saw a leopard drag a Giant Eland up a tree."

"What's a Giant Eland?" said McShane.

"A huge antelope," said Steadman. "Those things can weigh over 2000lbs."

"Are you trying to suggest a leopard was responsible for that carnage?" said McShane.

"Not at all," said Steadman. "I'm saying there could be something mighty powerful out there."

"What I can't understand is this," said the Club Secretary. "If Hamill's right and a starving animal has somehow managed to get on board the train, why didn't it just mop up the scattered remains while it had the chance?"

"I can't understand that either," said Steadman.

"It might have been disturbed by something it heard," said the Chef.

"Like what?" said Steadman.

"Like a flushing toilet, a slammed door or a lot of raised voices," said the Chef.

"And there's been plenty of that over the last few days," said the Club Secretary.

"It might have had young to feed," said Hamill.

"Young!" said Steadman.

"That's right," said Hamill.

"I don't get you," said Steadman.

"Animals don't carry shopping bags or trolleys," said Hamill.

"So it would have taken the biggest and most convenient thing it could carry," said the Club Secretary.

"Which was Kenny Biddo," said Hamill.

"For fuck's sake!" said Steadman. "That's sick. You don't think...."

"Don't think what?" said Hamill.

"Nothing," said Steadman. "Just ignore me gentlemen. My imagination's beginning to run wild."

"Don't think what, Steadman?" said Hamill.

"He's probably wondering if Biddo was still alive when he was he was being fed to the animal's young," said McShane. "I know that, because I've been wondering the same thing myself."

"So have I," said the Chef.

"Let's not go there," said the Chairman. "The situation's bad enough without something as gruesome as that playing havoc with our minds for the next few bastard days."

"Well, whatever it was, it's likely to come back now that it's got the taste for human flesh," said McShane.

"I'd go even further than that," said Hewlett before moving away from the window and taking a seat closer to the main group. "I suggest it's had the taste for human flesh for about a week."

"What are you talking about?" said the Chairman.

"I'm talking about Eddie Meehan," said Hewlett.

"Eddie Meehan!" said the Chairman.

"That's right," said Hewlett. "Wouldn't Hamill's animal attack theory explain his disappearance?"

"Oh Christ yes," said the Club Secretary. "It would wouldn't it."

"It's probably the only thing that can explain his disappearance," said the Chairman.

"And what worries me most-the creature wasn't put off by the noise we continually make and our advantage in numbers," said McShane.

"It wasn't put off in the slightest," said the Club Secretary.

"That's because the creature doesn't exist," said the Professor after slapping his bony right hand on his table. "As someone so rightly suggested earlier. A starving animal would have gorged on those bloody remains without hesitation. It wouldn't have been able to resist them. No hungry animal would. For goodness sake gentlemen-I beseech you. Will you please listen to me. There is only one culprit responsible for those murders and he's a human being. He may no longer resemble the human being formerly known to you as Biddo, but he is very much the human being that now represents your greatest danger."

"I'm not having it," said Blackie.

"Why not?" said the Club Secretary.

"Because I'm not," said Blackie. "My uncle wasn't strong enough to overpower those three men."

"I'd have to agree with that," said the Chairman after pulling up a chair next to Blackie and tapping him on the knee. "But your uncle hadn't been himself for days. He'd been a very sick man. He'd changed beyond all recognition."

"And consider those who are dead Blackie," said the Chef. "Two of them are the very same men he's been threatening to kill for the best part of a week."

"One of which he'd already tried to murder," said the Chef.

"I'd take heed of your Chairman if I was you," said the old man. "If I'm proved right and your uncle is alive, he'll be no better than a wild beast at this moment in time. He'll more than likely treat you with enormous mistrust. I promise you-he won't see you for what you really are. He won't see you as somebody who's trying to help him. He'll perceive you as an enemy. He might even see you as his next meal."

"He won't," said Blackie. "And I'll prove it."

"How?" said the Chairman.

"I'll go and find him and talk to him," said Blackie.

[401]

"Not on my watch, you won't," said the Chairman.

"Why's that?" said Blackie.

"Because I'm responsible for your safety," said the Chairman.

"And for Biddo's too," said Blackie.

"For God's sake-listen to him Blackie," said the Chef. "Don't be a bloody fool. He's trying to save your life."

"I'll be fine, I'm telling you," said Blackie. "I can look after myself."

"Not against someone as potentially violent and unpredictable as that," said the Professor. "For goodness sake, will you listen to your friends."

"I'm sorry Blackie-I can't let you go out there," said the Chairman.

"You can't stop me," said Blackie.

"I can and I will if I have to," said the Chairman.

"What do you think Hamill?" said Blackie. "Don't you think I should at least be given the chance to talk to my uncle?"

"I might do if I thought he was still alive," said Hamill.

"He is still alive," said Blackie. "I can feel it. There's no evidence to suggest otherwise."

"Don't do it Hamill," said the Chairman. "For God's sake, don't authorise his harebrained idea. You'll be condemning the lad to death."

"I've no intention of authorising his idea," said Hamill. "But I'm not going to go out of my way to stop him either. On his own head be it, I say. To be honest, I couldn't give a damn what happens to him. He's one of your mob. He's one of those who originally blackballed me."

"Nearly everyone blackballed you, if I remember right," said Blackie.

"I'm well aware of that," said Hamill.

"Don't do it Blackie," said the Chef. "You heard the Professor. Biddo won't know you anymore."

"For crying out loud Chef-it's not Biddo he's going to have to worry about," said Hamill. "It's the thing that dragged him off he's going to have to avoid."

"What if I got tooled up and took one or two of the lads with me," said Blackie

"Oh Jesus!" said the Club Secretary.

"Like who?" said the Chairman.

"Like my old mate Steadman," said Blackie.

"That won't be happening," said Steadman.

"Why not?" said Blackie.

"Because what you're proposing is sheer madness," said Steadman.

"No it's not," said Blackie. "What I'm proposing is a rescue mission. To put it another way-it's a mission to rescue my uncle and one of your closest friends."

"Who is almost certainly dead or a threat to our lives," said Steadman. "Why can't you get that into your thick skull? You know me Blackie. You know how loyal a friend I've been to you over the years. If I thought the man was still alive and in any way approachable, I wouldn't be standing here talking now-I'd already be out there searching high and low for the bugger."

"He is alive," said Blackie. "And he will be approachable. And I intend proving it."

"Fair play to you," said Steadman before thrusting out his right hand. "And the very best of British luck to you. But I'm afraid you'll be searching for him alone or with someone other than me."

"Why don't you go with him Hulmey," said Hamill.

"Don't start Hamill," said the Chef.

"I'm going to stay here, thank you very much," said the Chairman.

"Why's that?" said Hamill.

"Because I want to see Ruth and the kids again," said the Chairman.

"You're not a scaredy cat are you?" said Hamill.

"I am, as it happens," said the Chairman. "I'm scared shitless. Jesus Christ Hamill-Larko could unscrew wheel nuts without a brace. I've even seen him lift a Volvo estate engine out of a car without a winch. And as for big Woody-well we all know what monumental feats of strength he was capable of. You can call me all

[403]

the scaredy cats you like Hamill-I don't really care. But whether it's an insane and ridiculously strong Biddo or a starving wild beast out there-I for one, don't ever want to come face to face with it."

"Why don't you go Hamill?" said the Club Secretary.

"I'm needed here," said Hamill. "Tommy might go though. He loves a good scrap."

"I'm going nowhere," said McShane.

"Why's that?" said Hamill.

"For the same reason Hulmey refused," said McShane. "I want to see my lovely wife Cathy and the kids again."

"You do surprise me," said Hamill. "I never thought I'd see the day to be honest."

"See what fucking day?" said McShane.

"The day you bottled out of a challenge," said Hamill.

"Well, put the flags out Hamill," said McShane.

"Because that day's finally arrived. And as hard as I am, I'm not ashamed to admit it. Why don't you get yourself along to the mailroom. Go on.....Take a good look for yourself. See what's been done to the old place. Pay particular attention to the new colour scheme. You'll find the ceiling's undergone the most radical change. It used to be a bland shade of magnolia. Now it's an unusual combination of brain grey and blood red. Get yourself along there Hamill. I reckon once you've feasted your eyes on all that blood and guts, you'll begin to understand my reluctance to meet the decorator."

"You can't blame him Hamill," said the Club Secretary.

"I've no intention of blaming him," said Hamill before turning his attention to another of the members. "Why were they there Blackie?"

"Who?" said Blackie, who for the last few minutes had stationed himself at the centre of the window.

"You know damn well who," said Hamill. "Why were Alty and Larkin in that mail room?"

"I don't know," said Blackie.

"I don't believe you," said Hamill before bursting forward and taking the startled Blackie by the throat.

"It's the truth, I tell you," said Blackie.

"You're a liar," said Hamill. "I think you do know. In fact, I'm certain you know. Why were they there Blackie?"

"I promise you Hamill-I don't know," said Blackie. "All I know is Biddo wanted to ask them something."

"Ask them what?" said Hamill.

"Nothing of any relevance to all this," said Blackie.

"Ask them what?" roared Hamill.

"If one of them would accompany Anthony on his journey," said Blackie.

"Accompany Anthony!" said a confused Hamill.

"That's right," said Blackie.

"That makes good sense to be honest," said McShane.

"It makes perfect sense," said the Chef.

"It does doesn't it," said Hamill before releasing his grip.

"I spent the rest of the evening with you lot in this room," said Blackie while readjusting his collar. "I'm going to be honest with you all-I did think about confronting those two lads. I thought about it long and hard."

"Why didn't you then?" said Hamill.

"I couldn't get their attention," said Blackie. "They were both buzzing from the excitement of finally getting away from here. And I suppose, because of my close relationship with Kenny Biddo, they'd decided to give me a wide berth. I hardly moved from my chair all night."

"I can vouch for that," said Steadman.

"Not even to go to bed?" said Hamill.

"I slept there on the very chair I'm just about to park my backside on," said Blackie.

"Did Alty and Larkin sleep here?" said the Chairman.

"They eventually grabbed some things and headed back to their carriage to play cards," said Steadman.

"They did, come to think of it," said the Club Secretary. "Larko had actually asked me to lend him some cash out of club funds. Alty had cleaned him out apparently."

"Did you give him any?" said the Chairman.

"Of course not," said the Club Secretary. "It's not club policy to lend a member money to gamble with."

"Which means they would have been playing for other things," said Steadman.

"Like what?" said Hewlett.

"Like forfeits and dares," said the Chef. "That's what probably happened. I think somebody alluded to it earlier. They must have gone to the mailroom to torment Biddo. It's nobody's fault but their own."

"Nobody's fault but their own!" said McShane. "Jesus Christ Chef. When did you become a fully fledged member of the Nazi Party? Those lads didn't do anything especially wrong. They were just playing games. They didn't ask to be butchered."

"I didn't mean it like that," said the Chef. "I just mean-there's nobody else to blame for them being there."

"What about Biddo's mental state at the actual time of the attack," said the Chairman.

"What do you mean?" said the Professor?

"Would he have known who Alty and Larkin were?" said the Chairman.

"I would have thought so," said the Professor.

"Well why did you say he wouldn't recognise me?" said Blackie.

"Because from the very moment he made his first kill, he became a very different individual," said the old man. "He'd crossed an invisible but very significant line. He'd become Mr Hyde, so to speak. That's pretty much his current incarnation now. And that's how he's likely to remain until the disease dissipates. Why do you ask Mr Hulme?"

"Because I'm wondering if his lust for blood has now been satisfied," said the Chairman. "Let's be honest-he's killed the two main objects of his hatred. Maybe that's it. Maybe he's done now. What do you think Professor?"

"I suppose it's possible," said the Professor. "But I wouldn't build your hopes too high."

"Why not?" said Blackie.

"Because he could already have new targets for his smouldering rage," said the old man.

"Like who?" said Blackie.

"You tell me," said the old man. "I'm a virtual stranger, don't forget. I don't really know you people. What about yourself?"

"He worships me," said Blackie. "I've always been his favourite nephew. I've been very good to him over the years. Why would he want to harm me?"

"Have you ever quarrelled with him?" said the Professor.

"Not really," said Blackie. "Not seriously."

"What does that mean?" said the old man.

"We've had the odd disagreement over each other's golf handicaps and clothes," said Blackie.

"Clothes!" said the old man.

"He tends to be a bit of a tramp," said Blackie.

"He's not a tramp at all," said Steadman. "He dresses quite smartly to be honest. It's just that Blackie refuses to wear anything but expensive designer clothes like Armani or Hugo Boss."

"Why's that?" said the old man.

"I like to be noticed," said Blackie. "In fact, I think it's my duty to be noticed."

"By who?" said the Professor. "Just women?"

"Behave yourself Professor!" said Blackie. "I'm a happily married heterosexual.

"I'm sorry," said the old man. "That was discourteous of me. Please forgive me. Do you mind me asking you one more thing?"

"Not at all," said Blackie. "Providing it is only one more thing. What do you want to know?"

"I want to know if your uncle has ever questioned your sexuality?" said the Professor after clearing his throat.

"Not as far as I can recall," said Blackie.

"Ahem!" said Steadman.

"What's that meant to mean?" said an indignant looking Blackie. "What the hell's that meant to mean Steadman?"

[407]

"Biddo had a pot at you only a few days ago," said Steadman.

"Did he?" said Blackie. "I don't remember that. What about?"

"About the time the gay fella made a pass at you," said Steadman.

"What gay fella?" said Blackie.

"The one that tried to throw the lips on you," said Steadman.

"Throw the lips on me!" said Blackie.

"That's right," said Steadman. "You were in the Lisbon Bar in Liverpool city centre. I think you told me he was a mail order catalogue model."

"That's right," laughed Blackie. "He was yes. Littlewoods, I think he worked for. I remember that now. I think that was my thirtieth birthday. That boy really took a shine to me. Conrad I think his name was. Every other good looking fella in the place was swooning over him."

"But he only had eyes for you," said Hewlett.

"He was only human," said Blackie. "He was alright, to be fair. He even bought me a bottle of Champagne. Premier Cru Non, if I remember right. Beautiful stuff it was."

"Premier Cru Non!" scoffed Hewlett.

"That's right," said Blackie. "What's the sour puss look of disgust for?"

"It's cheap muck," said Hewlett. "You can't describe Premier Cru Non as 'beautiful stuff'. Beautiful stuff! It's about one step up from cat urine. I wouldn't use it to scrub our back door step."

"Scrub your back door step!" said Blackie. "Bloody hell Hewlett...Do you know what a yard brush is?"

"Of course I do," said Hewlett. "I've seen our green keeper Bywaters using one."

"That figures," said Blackie. "Anyway-I don't care what you say. I thoroughly enjoyed the Premier Cru Non. And I thought it was a really nice gesture."

"I do too," said Steadman. "But I'd have stopped short

of telling Biddo you'd been flattered by your newly acquired gay friend's attention."

"Did I do that?" said Blackie.

"You most certainly did," said Steadman. "You said you saw his attraction towards you as a compliment. I saw the look on his face when you said it. It was one of those, 'if looks could kill', moments. He was thoroughly disgusted with you."

"I've no doubt he was," said Blackie. "But he won't remember any of that. He must have downed about 12 litres of vodka since then. He's not going to remember that. He's not going to remember that is he Professor?"

"He could be festering on that recollection as we speak," said the old man.

"Really?" said Blackie.

"Very much so," said the old man.

"Well I've done nothing to offend him," said the Club Secretary.

"Are you absolutely sure about that?" said the Professor.

"I'm positive," said the Club Secretary.

"Did you back the man up when he was having a go at two of the recently deceased for allegedly being gay?" said the old man.

"Of course not," said the Club Secretary. "His claim was preposterous."

"I've no doubt it was," said the Professor. "But it wasn't preposterous as far as the deeply troubled Biddo was concerned. By all accounts, he was convinced those boys were going to take advantage of his son. And by not backing him up, he probably assumed you were in the enemy camp."

"Nobody was going to back him up on that issue," said Hewlett.

"Which means we are all potential targets for his wrath?" said the Chef.

"It does, I'm afraid," said the old man.

"What about me," said the Chairman. "If Biddo is on a killing spree, would I be a potential target?"

[409]

"You could well be his number one target," said the Professor.

"Why for Christ's sake?" said the Chairman. "I spoke up for that mental bastard. You heard me Professor. I fought his corner for quite some time. I took a lot of risks for that man."

"But you ultimately had him locked up," said the Professor. "And in locking him up, you left his son Anthony at the mercy of what he saw as a degenerative gay faction. That's probably made you public enemy number one Mr Hulme."

"That's nice," said the Chairman. "That's lovely that is. That's another bastard reason not to feel safe in my cot tonight."

"None of us are safe," said Steadman.

"Which means he needs to be restrained and sedated before he does any more damage," said Blackie.

"It means we need to avoid him at all costs," said the Club Secretary.

"We don't need to avoid him at all," said Hamill while pointing towards the window. "If he was the lunatic the Professor suspects he is, we'd have seen him by now. He wouldn't be trying to hide, that's for sure. He'd be pounding on these doors hell bent on killing the rest of us. He's dead, I'm telling you. He's now some delighted creature's main course."

"Go to hell Hamill," said Blackie.

"It's true," said Hamill. "As far as I'm concerned, he's no longer our main concern. The creature that carried him off is. And mark my words lads-that thing's going to return when it's ready for its next feed. Now then-remind me again Tommy-how secure were those outer carriage doors?"

"Very secure," replied McShane.

"As secure as a constipated duck's rear end," said the Club Secretary.

"What about the barricade by the engine," said Hamill.

"That's fine as well," said the Club Secretary.

"It's iced over," said the Chairman.

"It's as good as rendered," said the Club Secretary.

"Check it again," said Hamill.

"There's no need to," said the Club Secretary.

"Check the fucking thing again," said Hamill. "In fact, take a couple of the lads and strengthen it further."

"I'm on it," said the Club Secretary while heading to the kitchen. "Just let me grab a glass of water."

"Do it now," said Hamill. "Sod your glass of water for the time being. It's not like you're on your hands and knees in the middle of the Sahara. Desert. There'll be plenty of time for you to rehydrate later. Just get that barricade sorted. Let's turn this place into something resembling Fort fucking Knox. And might I suggest you take another look at that mailroom delivery hatch. As far as I'm concerned, that's the only possible entry and exit point for any animals or intruders."

"It won't budge," said the Club Secretary.

"It's jammed tight shut," said the Chairman.

"Take a look at it from the outside then," said Hamill.

"In this weather?" said the Club Secretary while pointing to the window that had become one long ribbon of white. "Have you seen it out there?"

"Just man up Hilly," said Hamill. "You're getting like your wimpy mate Hulmey. Wear a couple of coats or something like that."

"A couple of coats aren't going to stop me being blown off the bridge," said the Club Secretary. "Have you seen how much the wind's picked up?"

"Just get on with it Hilly," said Hamill. "And in the meantime, the rest of you need to be looking for things to use as weapons."

"Like what?" said the Chef.

"Like knives," said Hamill before turning over his table, kicking off one of the legs and tossing it to Steadman. "You do know how to use a knife don't you Chef."

"Of course I do," said the Chef.

"What do you want me to do?" said McShane.

"I want you to go and get your little friend," said Hamill.

"You want me to do what?" said McShane.

"I want you to go and get your gun," whispered Hamill after discreetly pulling his friend to one side.

"Why?" whispered McShane.

"Because the chances are, we're going to need it," whispered Hamill.

"Not if we barricade ourselves in here and sit it out we won't," whispered McShane.

"Go and get the fucking gun Tommy," whispered Hamill.

"I will in a minute," whispered McShane.

"Go and get it now," whispered Hamill.

"I'll get it later," whispered McShane.

"Why later?" whispered Hamill. "What's going on Tommy?"

"Nothing's going on," whispered the agitated McShane. "I just don't want anything to do with that bloody gun. It was stupid of me to bring it along in the first place."

"It was a masterstroke when you consider how things have panned out," whispered Hamill.

"It wasn't," whispered McShane. "It was the most reckless thing I've ever done in my life. It was pure stupidity. I don't know what I was thinking. I think I've been watching too much crap television. I don't mind a good fight on a Saturday night, but I couldn't knowingly shoot anyone. I haven't got it in me to kill another human being."

"You're not going to be killing another human being," whispered Hamill. "You're going to be killing a vicious monster that's intent upon killing you and your friends."

"But what if that vicious monster turns out to be Kenny Biddo?" whispered McShane.

"Haven't you been listening to a word I've said?" whispered Hamill. "Kenny Biddo's dead. Kenny Biddo's long stopped breathing."

"But what if you're wrong?" whispered McShane.

"Then shoot him," whispered Hamill. "Don't hesitate for one second. Shoot him between the eyes before he

[412]

tears you limb from limb."

"I couldn't," whispered McShane.

"Why not?" whispered Hamill.

"Because I couldn't," whispered McShane. "I've shared digs with that man. We've split our last five pound note. As a work colleague, I've got nothing but praise and respect for him."

"But you'll be putting him out of his misery," whispered Hamill.

"That's not entirely true is it," whispered McShane.

"It is," whispered Hamill. "You heard the Professor. Biddo's gone crazy. He's the abominable Mr Hyde now. He's lost the plot completely. For pity's sake Tommy-he'd probably ask you to shoot him if he could return to coherence for a few minutes. Right now, he's going through a living hell."

"But according to the Professor, that living hell will eventually come to an end and he'll begin to get better," whispered McShane.

"And according to certain highly regarded and well meaning psychologists, Ian Brady and Myra Hindley were going to get better too," whispered Hamill.

"I won't do it," whispered McShane. "I'm not shooting Kenny Biddo. I don't care if it is in our best interest. I'm not going to do it. How could I ever look any of his family members in the face again? I'm sorry Hamill-you can ask me to do anything else. I'll even polish your shoes, do your ironing and wipe your fat arse if you want. But I'm definitely not going to shoot anyone on your behalf."

"Very well Tommy," whispered Hamill. "I understand. I'll do it myself if he's confirmed as the killer. Where is it? Where's this bleeding gun of yours? And don't try telling me you can't remember."

"It's inside a plastic bag in one of the cisterns in the third washroom," whispered McShane. "But be careful Hamill-it's got three bullets in the chamber and one bitch of a sensitive trigger. Don't go shooting yourself."

"I won't," said Hamill before turning his gaze onto a

vacant looking Chairman. "Now go and supervise the work on those barricades at the front of the train. I don't trust Blackie and some of the other hippy do gooders. If they suspect Biddo's still alive, they might just leave him a big enough gap to enable him to sneak back on board. Try to make that barrier so tight, not even the anorexic grandchild of the bee Woody killed can slip in."

"Which reminds me Hamill," said the approaching Chairman. "Your blood over the door ritual wasn't very effective was it?"

"It was a ridiculous idea in hindsight," said Hewlett.

"It kept you alive didn't it?" said Hamill.

"Providence and the proximity of my carriage kept me alive," said Hewlett.

"It certainly didn't help Alty, Larko and Woody," said the Chairman.

"It would have done had they been good boys and stayed in their rooms," said Hamill.

"What do you mean?" said the Chairman.

"Those men were murdered in the mailroom," said Hamill.

"Of course they were," said McShane. "Bloody hell! Of course they were."

"And you hadn't thought to protect the occupants of the mailroom, had you Hamill?" said Blackie.

"Not for one second," said Hamill.

"That figures," said Blackie.

"What's that meant to mean?" said Hamill.

"Nothing," said Blackie before latching onto the small group of hesitant and uncertain men that were milling by the forward door.

"Is there anything you want me to do?" said the Chairman.

"There is, as it happens," said Hamill. "I want you to get a sheet of paper from our Club Secretary and start writing your letter of resignation."

"What!" said the Chairman.

"You heard me," said Hamill. "Start writing your

[414]

resignation letter."

"Behave yourself Hamill," said the Club Secretary.
"I've told you before-that's not the way this club does
things."

"It's how the new Sheriff in town does things," said
Hamill. "Come on Hulmey. I want that letter, and I
want it within the next 10 minutes."

"But why now?" said the Chairman. "It wasn't that
long ago, you were urging me to remain in office."

"I know that," said Hamill. "But you've fucked up big
time since then."

"Why have I?" said the Chairman.

"Because you provided the drink that knocked all those
men out," said Hamill.

"I didn't force them to drink the stuff," said the
Chairman.

"I know that," said Hamill. "But they did and that left
them extremely vulnerable. You've got a hell of a lot to
answer for Hulmey. Particular if my predator theory's
wrong and Kenny Biddo does turn out to be the
murderer. Am I right Professor?"

"Right about what?" said the slightly startled old man.

"Would I be right in saying that supplying vodka to
those three dead men in the mail room made them
extremely vulnerable?" said Hamill.

"I don't know," said the old man before quickly burying
his head in his bag.

"I'm talking to you Professor," said Hamill. "Don't
make me come over there and force a reply out of you.
Answer my fucking question. Did the vodka make
things worse?"

"That would depend upon the individual constitution of
the consumers," said the increasingly befuddled
Professor. "So, if you don't mind, I'd prefer to remain
uncommitted at this juncture."

"I do mind," said Hamill before approaching the old
man and clasping his bag shut on his long and bony
fingers. "I mind very much. Why won't you commit
yourself Professor?"

"Because I don't want to make waves," said the Professor.

"Make waves!" said Hamill. "You're having a laugh aren't you. The waves have already been made. 30 foot monumental waves are now a common feature of our day. Now climb down off your fence and answer my question-did the vodka provided by our outgoing Chairman, make Biddo's condition worse?"

"It could have done," said the Professor.

"That's not good enough," said Hamill. "I want something more concrete. Now listen Professor. I'm going to ask you again and I'm going to ask you for the last fucking time-did the vodka make the diseased and mentally ill Biddo's condition worse?"

"It probably did yes," mumbled the Professor before lowering his head.

"How much worse?" said Hamill.

"Oh, for goodness sake!" said the old man upon snapping his bag shut.

"He's just answered your question Hamill," said the Chef.

"You shut your fucking mouth," said Hamill. "How much worse Professor? How much worse did that vodka make Kenny Biddo?"

"Substantially worse," barked the old man. "Are you satisfied now?"

"I'm encouraged rather than satisfied," said Hamill before placing his right arm around the trembling old man's shoulders. "Now listen very carefully to my next question Professor-because this is where it gets a little complicated.....Could the vodka have sent the diseased victim Biddo over the edge?"

"You can't expect the man to be able to answer something like that," said the Club Secretary.

"Oh I can," said Hamill. "It's not quantum physics. It's his field. It's within his area of expertise. What do you reckon Professor-could the vodka have been the difference between Biddo murdering those two boys or just feeling a massive resentment towards them?"

[416]

"Possibly," said the old man.

"How possibly?" said Hamill.

"Very possibly," said the Professor almost inaudibly.

"Thank you Professor," said Hamill. "No further questions. Is that resignation letter written yet Hulmey?"

"Not yet no," said the Chairman.

"I suggest you get on with it then," said Hamill. "And while you're at it, I want you to think about the three lovely lads you recently helped kill. Because, whether it was Biddo or a wild creature that slaughtered them, it was you that provided the means to zonk them out. It was you that left them at the mercy of something extremely vicious. And then I want you to think about Alec Morris and the times you pointed the finger of blame at me and my two good friends."

"I think we've already established the fact that Morris's death was a tragic accident," said the Chef.

"That's right," said the Club Secretary. "Why don't we leave it at that Hamill?"

"Yes-why don't we," said Hamill before plucking the middle of three biros from the Club Secretary's breast pocket.

"So what are we going to do about Biddo?" said Blackie.

"Biddo's dead," said Hamill.

"Well, let's say for argument's sake he isn't," said Blackie. "What are we going to do about him?"

"We'll make sure he doesn't murder anyone else," said Hamill.

"How exactly?" said Blackie.

"By making sure he doesn't get back on this train, for one thing," said Hamill.

"He's going to die out there," said Blackie.

"He needs to die if he's murdered those poor lads," said Hamill.

"He needs to be handed over to the proper authorities," said Blackie.

"He's right Hamill," said the Club Secretary. "Two

[417]

rights don't make a wrong."

"What does that mean?" said Hamill while looking to the rest of the group. "Has anyone ever worked out what that stupid bloody expression means?"

"It means we've got no right to take the law into our own hands, " said the Club Secretary.

"That's right," said the Chairman. "If Biddo dies out there, we're all in a shit load of trouble."

"Can't he sleep in the engine?" said Steadman.

"That's an idea," said the Chef.

"Have you stood in that engine for any length of time Chef?" said Blackie.

"I haven't actually," said the Chef. "But it's got to be better than being outside in the freezing cold."

"It is," said Blackie. "But only slightly. There are no doors to that engine. And there's no heating. And when the wind's at its most ferocious, it's like being on the Big Dipper at Blackpool during a force 10 gale. And don't forget-if Hamill's right about a starving animal being on the prowl, Biddo's going to have nothing to protect himself with."

"That's a point," said the Chairman.

"He can do what the rest of us would do if we were in his shoes," said Hamill.

"What's that?" said the Chairman.

"Run like hell and hide," said Hamill.

"From a starving predator?" said the Chairman.

"I thought he was meant to have turned into some sort of monster with superhuman strength," said Hamill.

"He's not a monster," said Blackie. "He's just a very sick and confused man."

"It's the engine or the outside," said Hamill. "You make your mind up Blackie. The one thing he's not going to get is a welcome back into the fold and a warm carriage."

"Would you mind if I took him a few things?" said Blackie.

"Like what?" said Hamill.

"Like food and blankets," said Blackie. "And maybe

some warmer clothes."

"I think I can allow that," said Hamill. "But if I find you've sneaked him any alcohol or anything that resembles a weapon, you'll be the next one sleeping rough. By the way-has anybody covered up what's left of those mutilated bodies?"

"I have," said the Professor.

"Thank God for that," said the Chairman. "For one minute, I thought that nasty and unenviable chore was going to be left for little old me."

"You've got a letter to compose," said Hamill before handing the Chairman the well chewed pen and heading over to the rear door. "And I want it written in your very bestest handwriting."

"Who do I address it to?" said the Chairman.

"To your fellow members'," said Hamill. "And date it too. I want the date to coincide with the very moment things on board this train took a considerable turn for the better."

CHAPTER EIGHTEEN
RESCUE

The men who had been designated barricade reinforcing duty had returned to the dining carriage with some extremely interesting and encouraging news because not only had they managed to complete their allotted task without sustaining injury or falling foul of a diseased madman or ferocious wild beast, they had also found something of huge significance in the context of future security-they had discovered the mail room delivery hatch could in fact be opened from the outside by means of a heavy but easy to operate sprung latch. It meant that the mystery relating to how someone or something had seemingly been able to board the train at will, had at last been solved. Within minutes of that news breaking, McShane had rendered the latch redundant and just under half an hour later, Hamill had put a strict hourly patrol system into place that was scheduled to commence just after tea. That was the reason the Chairman was alone in the fourth carriage just after 8 o'clock that evening, when he noticed what looked like a long, thin slither of light about 10 feet to the right of the heavily frosted window. Seeing lights and shadows beyond the carriage windows had been nothing unusual however but they had always been dismissed as reflections from any one of the many internal wall light fixtures or fancy, multicoloured art deco bedside lamps. Nevertheless, seeing a light that moved ever so slowly from south to north while pointing diagonally downwards was something very different and in the wary and observant eyes of the Chairman, something worthy of investigation. In fact, it had been of such interest, it's appearance had caused the increasingly excited Chairman to follow it the length of the carriage until there was no longer any window left to view it from. There was the next carriage however and within seconds, despite having stumbled a number of times and although the jammed sleeper door had seemingly tried to deny his exit for what seemed like an eternity, he was next door with the palms of his hands spread and his nose pressed flat against the freezing cold pane.

However, because of the relentless blizzard and the fact that most of the window had become heavily glazed in a thick white cream, the answer as to what was out there beyond the window continued to elude the fascinated and vigilant Chairman. In fact, for the next thirty minutes, all he had been able to confirm was that it was a slow moving light peculiar because of its propensity to appear and then disappear at irregular intervals. Nevertheless, it was something very different from the norm and something that had him intrigued. That intrigue was to intensify after he had heard what sounded like three progressively louder cracks of thunder in quick succession .

For the next few uncertain minutes, his mind remained in conflict. He wondered if, through his desperation to see something promising, or see something that would offer hope, he was beginning to see things he wanted to see in the same extraordinary way a desperately thirsty man sees an oasis in the middle of a scorching hot desert. He certainly knew what he wanted the strange light to be. He wanted to believe the beam of light was emanating from a resilient rescuer's flashlight. He wanted to believe that badly. And yet, the other part of his mind, the rational rather than optimistic, hopeful and romantic aspect of his mind, was continually urging caution. That part was preventing him from getting too carried away. That part was reminding him of so many anticlimaxes he had been forced to endure since the train had set off prematurely. And yet, he still nevertheless, couldn't help getting a little excited and he still nonetheless couldn't stop the goose bumps forming on his lower arms or the hairs on the back of his neck standing to attention. He couldn't prevent himself thinking that whatever was happening outside at that particular moment was a good thing, a positive thing and something that was almost certainly in his and the rest of his party's favour. That wasn't how another keen eyed observer had been viewing things however. He had been tracking the same shadowy figure for much longer than the Chairman. He had been tracking the shadowy figure in the manner of a hunter.

"I nailed the bastard," said an almost breathless Hamill after joining the Chairman at the window no more than a couple of minutes later. "I told you didn't I. I told you it was a bear."

"What was a bear?" said the Chairman.

"That wild and woolly thing that's lying on its belly out there," said Hamill while carefully removing the two remaining bullets from his pistol. "I assume that's what you've had your eyes on too."

"It was.....yes," said the highly confused Chairman. "At least I think it was. Bloody hell....Bloody hell Hamill. How long have you been toting a gun?"

"It's a long story," said Hamill.

"What's a long story?" said the equally confused Club Secretary after joining his two fellow club members at the window. "What's going on lads?"

"Hamill thinks he's killed a bear," said the Chairman.

"A bear!" said the Club Secretary.

"That's right," said Hamill. "Take my torch, open that top window and take a look for yourself."

"I'll take your word for it," said the Club Secretary while rubbing his freezing cold hands. "By the way Hamill-how long have you been carrying a gun?"

"It's a long story apparently," said the Chairman.

"It belongs to Tommy Mac," said Hamill. "He calls it his 'little friend'. I took it off him for safe keeping."

"Good for you," said the Chairman. "Now will you put the bloody thing away before somebody or something else gets hurt."

"Not a problem," said Hamill before very cautiously slipping the weapon into the waistband of his trousers. "Now can we go and celebrate?"

"Celebrate what?" said the Club Secretary.

[422]

"Celebrate the end of our biggest concern," said Hamill. "That thing out there tore Woody, Alty and Larko apart. That's got to be seen as something of a result, hasn't it?" "I suppose it has yes," said the Club Secretary. "A real result. The result of the season actually. Are you coming Hulmey?"

"I'll follow you on," said the Chairman.

"Why follow us on?" said the Club Secretary. "Come on Hulmey. Our shift's as good as over. We're off the clock in thirty seconds. Let's go and tell the lads the news and have a bloody good drink."

"I'll be with you shortly," said the Chairman. "You two go ahead. I've had a belly full of false dawns. I'm celebrating nothing until I've had definite confirmation."

"Confirmation about what?" said Hamill.

"Confirmation as to what exactly is lying dead out there," said the Chairman.

"For fuck's sake!" said Hamill. "I've just told you what's lying dead out there."

"I know that," said the Chairman. "But I still want definite confirmation."

"Definite confirmation!" said Hamill before taking the Chairman by his lapels and leading him back to the window. "Take a look Hulmey. Open that top fucking window and take a look for yourself. It's a dead fucking bear. I followed it the length of the train. It's a bear I'm telling you. And more importantly, it's almost certainly the bear that killed our mates. It's no longer a danger to us. Can't you see that?"

"I can yes," said the Chairman.

"It is a bear Hulmey," said the Secretary after sliding the top window shut and immediately slipping his freezing cold fingers under his armpits. "It's a big bastard too."

"You know what the trouble is, don't you Hilly?" said Hamill.

"What's that?" said the Club Secretary.

"Your mate doesn't want me to get any credit," said Hamill.

[423]

"It's not about credit or any bad feeling towards you," said the Chairman.

"Then what is it about?" said Hamill.

"It's about being certain," said the Chairman. "For all we know, that thing out there might be a large man in a thick fur coat."

"Oh do me a favour!" said Hamill.

"It might be," said the Chairman.

"Bollocks!" said Hamill. "I watched that thing crawl on all fours the entire length of this fucking train. What normal human being does something like that?"

"A human being who'd been battling against the elements for a while," said the Chairman. "A human being, who was very possibly on his last legs."

"Rubbish!" said Hamill.

"It's not rubbish," said the Chairman. "Listen to me Hamill-it might well have been a bear...it probably was a bear. But it could also have been a huge man."

"God give me strength," said Hamill.

"But what man?" said the Club Secretary.

"That's right," said Hamill. "What sort of idiot would be outside in weather like that?"

"I don't know," said the Chairman. "A traveller. Somebody who'd got lost in the blizzard. Somebody with mental health issues. I don't know."

"It was a bear," said Hamill. "I'm telling you, as I live and breathe. I watched the thing crawl the length of three carriages. And, as I said before-human beings don't tend to move like that."

"They do if they're exhausted," said the Chairman.

"And by the way-bears don't carry flashlights."

"Flashlights!" said the Club Secretary. "What do you mean Hulmey?"

"He's talking more shite," said Hamill.

"I'm not," said the Chairman. "Whatever I saw out there was carrying a flashlight of some sort.-I swear to God it was. I saw the beam pointing down and moving forwards."

"Rubbish!" said Hamill. "What you saw were the

carriage lights reflecting in the animal's eyes. And the reason you can't see any reflection now is because I've just put the fucker's lights out."

"I hate to say it but I think he's right Hulmey," said the Club Secretary. "We've all said it at some time or other...no sensible human being would be out there in weather like that."

"It was a dangerous wild animal," said Hamill.

"It might well have been," said the Chairman. "But it's not necessarily a dead one."

"What do you mean?" said Hamill.

"Have you ever known a dead animal to move?" said the Chairman.

"Of course not," said the Club Secretary. "Why do you ask Hulmey?"

"Because whatever's lying out there just moved," said the Chairman. "Now it's ever so slowly getting to its feet. Now it's.....Now it's.....Oh dear!"

"Rubbish!" said Hamill. "I put at least three bullets into that thing."

"You might have done," said the Chairman while urging Hamill to join him at the window. "But it hasn't stopped whatever you hit from making off."

"Making off!" said Hamill before prising the Chairman away from the window. "What are you talking about?"

"He's right Hamill," said the Club Secretary after rejoining his close friend at the window. "It's gone. It's vanished."

"Which proves conclusively that the thing I shot was a bear," said Hamill.

"Why does it?" said the Club Secretary.

"Because no human being could take three bullets and walk away," said Hamill.

"He could if you'd glanced him or missed with a couple of shots," said the Chairman.

"I didn't miss," said Hamill. "The bastard thing was a sitting duck."

"You must have missed," said the Club Secretary.

"And that 'thing' was a man Hamill," said the

Chairman. "I know that because, before he staggered away, he looked me straight in the face and mouthed a few intelligible words."

"What words?" said the Club Secretary.

"I couldn't quite make the first couple out," said the Chairman. "But the last word was very definitely a swear word."

"Oh, for crying out loud!" said the Club Secretary. "Oh, for Christ's sake! You don't think it was one of the lads do you Hulmey? It couldn't have been Kenny Biddo wearing someone's fur coat, could it?"

"I don't know," said the Chairman. "Your guess is as good as mine Hilly."

"Where did he go?" said Hamill.

"Towards the train," said the Chairman. "The only way he could go to be fair. He must be under it."

"What do you want to do?" said the Club Secretary.

"I want to go back to the dining carriage and see who's missing," said the Chairman.

"What do we tell the others?" said the Club Secretary.

"As little as possible at this stage," said the Chairman. "And, as soon as it's light and the weather's a bit better, the three of us will make a search of the track and the surrounding area."

"Would there be anything to be gained by telling the lads the truth?" said the Club Secretary.

"I wouldn't have thought so," said the Chairman. "But there's plenty to be gained from getting rid of that bloody gun."

"I couldn't agree more," said Hamill. "I'll ditch it as soon as the weather breaks."

"I think you should get rid of it now," said the Chairman. "Or alternatively, you could lock it away in my holdall for safe keeping."

"I'll do just that," said Hamill while heading for the door.

"You'll need this key," said the Chairman. "And for God's sake Hamill-don't let anyone see you."

"I won't," said Hamill. "I'll just be glad to see the back

[426]

of the bloody thing."

###

The three men returned to the dining carriage in far less celebratory mood than Hamill had anticipated just over an hour earlier and for some time after, despite numerous enquiries from the other inquisitive occupants of the room, they had each sat separate, motionless and completely unresponsive.

"I'm going to try again," said Steadman while cupping his hands around his mouth tannoy fashion. "Is-there-anything-you-gentlemen-want-to-report?"

"Not at this point," said the Chairman.

"What do you mean, 'not at this point'?" said Steadman. "Have you anything to report or haven't you?"

"Just leave it for now Steadman," said the Club Secretary before heading to the kitchen with a disorganised tray of dirty dishes.

"I won't leave it," said Steadman. "I think I'm entitled to an answer. It's a simple enough question. What the hell's happened?"

"Yes-what's been going on lads?" said the Chef. "You all look completely drained."

"We're just struggling to make sense out of something," said Hamill.

"Sense out of what?" said Steadman. "Help us here, will you lads. What the hell happened while you were away?"

"Have those creatures come back?" said the Chef.

"Have they?" said Hewlett while heading to the central window. "Are they back?"

"We can't say for certain," said the Chairman.

"Why not?" said the Chef.

"Because I want a certain amount of confirmation first," said the Chairman.

"Confirmation regarding what?" said Steadman.

"A few things," said the Chairman.

"Like what?" said the Chef.

[427]

"I don't know yet," said the Chairman.

"What do you want confirmed our kid?" said the Chef. "For Christ's sake-just give us a snippet of something will you."

"It's not as simple as that," said the Club Secretary.

"Why the hell not?" said Steadman.

"Because it's not," said the Club Secretary.

"Why not?" said McShane. "I don't get this. I don't know about anyone else, but I get the distinct impression these three are hiding something from us."

"So do I," said Hewlett.

"And me too," said Steadman.

"Alright then," said the Chairman. "But before I commit myself, let me ask you all something...Did any of you lads bring a long fur coat with you?"

"A what!" said Steadman.

"A long fur coat," said the Chairman

"What's that got to do with anything?" said McShane.

"You'll find out shortly," said the Chairman. "Did anyone pack a long fur coat?"

"This is ridiculous," said Steadman.

"Just answer the man's question will you lads," said the Club Secretary. "Does anybody own a long fur coat? What about you Tommy?"

"I wouldn't be seen dead in one," said McShane. "It wouldn't be me would it? I have brought a heavy Winter coat with me though-but it's a genuine North Face, not a fur."

"I own quite a few furs as it happens," said Hewlett.

"Why doesn't that surprise me?," said McShane.

"Did you bring any of them with you?" said the Club Secretary.

"I can't say for certain," said Hewlett.

"Why not?" said the Chairman.

"Because I never do my own packing," said Hewlett. "I've never needed to. I simply explain to Waggers the length of time I'm likely to be away and what sort of journey I'm going to undertake and he packs the appropriate wardrobe for me."

[428]

"Do you think he'd have packed you a fur coat?" said the Chairman.

"I would assume so yes," said Hewlett. "It is Winter after all."

"Assume so!" said the Club Secretary. "Why don't you know Hewlett? Are you telling us you haven't unpacked yet?"

"Not completely no," said Hewlett. "I don't think anyone has. Which is due entirely to the enormous upheaval that's been caused. Now could you please explain what this is all about."

"I need you to go and check your luggage," said the Chairman.

"I don't need to," said Hewlett. "I have every faith in old Waggers. He would have definitely packed at least one of my furs. Don't forget-it was starting to snow the night before we set off from Crosby. It would have been negligent of him to deny me a fur, wouldn't it?"

"Would you do me a massive favour and go and check please Hewlett," said the Chairman.

"I don't need to," said Hewlett.

"Just do it will you Hewlett," said the Club Secretary. "Just to give us all a bit of peace of mind."

"Very well," said Hewlett while heading for the door .

"And then I want some answers. And they better be satisfactory answers too."

"Yes, I want answers too," said Steadman. "And I'm going nowhere until I get some."

"We'll explain everything when Hewlett returns," said the Club Secretary. "Things should be a lot clearer then."

"I think you should tell us now," said Steadman.

"So do I," said McShane. "I think we've got every right to know now. Or at least tell us this much-are we in more danger?"

"I don't think so," said the Club Secretary.

"That's not really eased our concern Hilly," said Steadman.

"It's not helped at all," said McShane. "What the hell's

[429]

going on lads?"

"Just be patient will you Tommy," said Hamill.

"I don't see why I should," said McShane.

"I don't either," said Steadman. What's this all about lads? Just tell us will you. We can take it. We've taken everything else that's been thrown at us."

"Very well," said the Chairman after exhaling loudly. "We have reason to believe Kenny Biddo's been shot."

"You what!" said the Chef.

"We think someone might have shot Kenny Biddo," said the Chairman.

"Why?" said Steadman. "Why would you think that?"

"Because he's the only one of us who's unaccounted for," said the Club Secretary.

"We heard, what we assumed was gunfire while we were carrying out our patrol," said the Chairman.

"Gunfire!" said the Chef. "How do you know it was gunfire?"

"We just know," said the Chairman.

"Bollocks," said the Chef. "I'm sorry our kid, but you wouldn't know the sound of gunfire if you'd been shot in the arse at close range."

"I would actually," said the Chairman. "Me and Ruth fired guns at the back of a convenience store the last time we visited the States. She even wanted to bring a gun home as a souvenir."

"I didn't know that," said the Chef. "Why have you never mentioned that to me?"

"I don't think that's important right now," said Steadman. "I want to know why someone would want to shoot Kenny Biddo."

"We think the gunman might have mistaken him for a bear," said the Club Secretary.

"A bear!" said Steadman. "A fucking bear! Why would he think that?"

"Because he was wearing a thick fur coat," said the Club Secretary.

"He did look like a bear," said Hamill. "Didn't he Hilly?"

"He did yes," said the Club Secretary.

"It was the sort of mistake any one of us could have made, to be honest," said Hamill.

"Did you not think to get confirmation?" said the Chef.

"Would you?" said Hamill. "Would you have sought confirmation Chef? Would you have gone outside after hearing several rounds go off?"

"I suppose not," said the Chef.

"And, strange as it might seem, confirmation wasn't possible because the gunshot victim had moved off within a few minutes," said the Club Secretary.

"Moved off!" said Steadman. "So he wasn't dead then?"

"Not at that point," said the Chairman. "But there's a good possibility he is now."

"Why's that?" said the Chef.

"Because we heard three shots before whoever it was went down," said Hamill.

"Three shots!" said the Chef. "Jesus Christ. They weren't taking any chances were they."

"Neither would I if I'd been stalking a starving hungry grizzly bear," said Hamill.

"Did you see the gunman by any chance?" said Steadman.

"No," said the Chairman.

"Neither hide nor hair," said the Club Secretary.

"But that's not that important in the grand scheme of things," said the Chairman. "The most important thing is to establish whether Hewlett's fur coat is missing."

"And whether Kenny Biddo was wearing it," said the Club Secretary.

"Bloody hell lads," said Steadman.

"It is missing," said the returning and extremely breathless Hewlett. "At least I think it's missing."

"What do you mean?" said the Club Secretary.

"My largest suitcase that would normally contain my coats has been very clumsily prised open," said Hewlett. "It's now empty."

"Oh God!" said the Chef. "So it must have been Biddo

[431]

then."

"Not necessarily," said Steadman while heading over to the window.

"What do you mean?" said the Chef.

"It could have been Blackie," said Steadman.

"Blackie!" said the Chairman while attempting to make a rapid count of those present. "He's here isn't he? I just saw him. I thought I just saw him. Is he in the kitchen?"

"He went looking for Biddo a few hours ago," said Steadman. "I couldn't persuade him otherwise. He asked me if I had a warm coat to lend him. I told him Hewlett would be his best bet."

"That was very accommodating of you," said Hewlett. "I trust you provided him with fresh briefs, suspenders and socks too?"

"Shut up Hewlett," said Steadman.

"So much for club rules and going everywhere in pairs," said the Club Secretary.

"Why don't you shove your club rules up your arse Hilly," said Steadman.

"Alright Steadman, calm down," said the Chairman.

"That'd be far easier if people stopped talking shite," said Steadman.

"We're going to have to find him our kid," said the Chef. "Whoever it is, we're going to have to find him. If he's still alive, he's almost certainly going to need emergency treatment."

"That's right," said Steadman.

It was right then, at that precise moment, to the enormous surprise of the majority, that the forward door suddenly burst open to reveal a shivering, fur clad and snow encrusted Blackie.

"Who's going to need emergency treatment?" he asked while proceeding to kick the snow from his left shoe.

"I thought you were told to stay here," said the Chairman.

"And I thought I told you I had every intention of going looking for my uncle," said Blackie.

[432]

"You're bang out of order," said the Chairman. "If you'd have got hurt or gone missing, we'd all be having to go outside to help or look for you now."

"Ground me then," said Blackie. "Or confiscate my Play Station for a week."

"I'll do more than that," said the Chairman. "I'll give you your marching orders."

"Marching orders!" said Blackie. "I wasn't aware you were still the bloke in charge."

"We've come to a temporary agreement," said Hamill.

"Have you really," said Blackie. "I wonder why that is."

"It's our business," said Hamill.

"Are you alright Blackie?" said Steadman. "Are you alright lad?"

"I've had far better days," replied Blackie.

"Were you hit?" said Steadman.

"What do you mean, 'hit'?" said Blackie.

"There's a strong rumour going round, you've been shot," said the Chef.

"Up to three times actually," said the Professor while slowly circling the thoroughly confused focus of everybody's attention. "Is it true, young man?"

"I've absolutely no idea what you're talking about," said Blackie.

"For the love of God-will somebody please explain what's going on," said Steadman while watching the forlorn but apparently uninjured Blackie remove the sopping wet fur coat and sling it on top of a nearby waste bin. "Has that man been shot or hasn't he?"

"Evidently not," said the Professor before removing his spectacles, tucking them into his breast pocket and returning to his chair. "There's no evidence of any crime at all."

"I beg to differ most profoundly," said the disgusted Hewlett. "That was my coat that's just been discarded like somebody's recently soiled undergarments. And that coat was stolen from my room. That's a crime as far as I'm concerned. Where I come from, that

[433]

constitutes theft."

"I only borrowed it," said Blackie.

"You had no right to," said Hewlett. "You're now going to have to pay for the item to be cleaned."

"Whatever!" said Blackie while heading to the kitchen.

"Never mind 'whatever'," said Hewlett before retrieving the saturated garment and placing it lovingly on one of the outside tables with the sort of care and affection usually set aside for a much loved, recently deceased family pet. "That coat was handed down to me by my great uncle Topper. It was his favourite outdoor garment. He used to wear it for the annual Cross Country Meet."

"Which means it was second hand goods when it eventually came into your possession," said Blackie.

"Maybe so but it's still probably worth ten times more than any coat you own," said Hewlett. "And don't get me started regarding my suitcase."

"What about your suitcase?" said Blackie.

"You've ruined the clasp," said Hewlett. "What did you do that for?"

"I couldn't find your key," said Blackie.

"You're a complete and utter bounder Blackhurst, said Hewlett. "You had no right to be anywhere near my things. You had no right be in my room for that matter. I hope you know the name of a proficient quality luggage repairer.

"I'll fix it for you," said McShane. "Stop worrying Hewlett. I'll wrap a bit of duct tape around it. That stuff sorts anything out."

"You stay away from it," said Hewlett. "I've heard all about your emergency repairs."

"The club will foot the bill," said the Chairman.

"The club, won't," said the Club Secretary. "Have you any idea what one of those cases costs Hulmey? They're about a grand a piece you know."

"£6000 a piece actually," said the smug looking Hewlett before settling back down and folding his arms.

"Bloody hell!" said the Chairman. "And how much is

[434]

duct tape?"

"About £3.00 a roll." said McShane.

"We'll take Tommy's option then," said the Chairman.

"I can get my hands on some new Louis Vuitton suitcases, if you want any," said McShane.

"Where from?" said the Chairman.

"Great Homer Street Market," said McShane. "I can get you a full set for less than a hundred quid, if you're prepared to pay cash and wave the receipt."

"That's remarkable," said the exasperated Hewlett.

"Real, bona fide Louis Vuitton luggage hey. I'll have to tell mother."

"I'll tell you what is remarkable," said Steadman. "It's remarkable we're here discussing something as trivial as a broken suitcase when a man might be bleeding to death within a few yards of where we're all sitting."

"What man's this?" said Blackie.

"We don't know for sure," said the Chairman.

"Is it one of our lot?" said Blackie.

"Nothing's been confirmed as yet," said the Club Secretary.

"Who is it?" said Blackie. "Or, at least tell me who you think it is."

"We're not sure," said the Chairman.

"They think it might have been Kenny Biddo," said Steadman.

"Biddo!" said Blackie.

"As I just said, it's not been confirmed yet," said the Club Secretary.

"Why not?" said Blackie.

"Because there's no body," said Hamill.

"I don't understand," said Blackie. "What's been going on?"

"We think Biddo's been shot," said the Chairman.

"Really!" said Blackie.

"We think whoever did it must have mistaken him for a bear," said the Chef.

"A bear!" said Blackie. "Why a bear?"

"Because we think he was wearing one of Hewlett's fur

coats," said the Club Secretary.

"What do you mean, one of his coats?" said Blackie. "As far as I'm concerned, Hewlett only had the one fur coat with him."

"How do you know?" said the Club Secretary.

"Because I was the one who broke into his case," said Blackie. "I promise you-there was only one fur coat. And I took that for myself. I've been wearing that. How long ago did this happen?"

"About an hour ago," said the Club Secretary.

"An hour!" said Blackie.

"About that yes," said the Chairman. "Me and Hulmey had been making our patrol of the corridors and sleeping carriages. We heard three shots ring out and then saw someone go down."

"It wasn't Biddo," said Blackie.

"We actually think it was," said the Chairman.

"It could have only been Biddo," said the Club Secretary.

"It wasn't Kenny Biddo," said Blackie.

"How do you know?" asked the Chairman.

"Because Kenny Biddo died about 3 hours ago," said Blackie.

"What!" said the Chairman.

"Kenny Biddo passed away about 3 hours ago," said Blackie.

"I don't understand," said the Club Secretary.

"What's there to understand?" said Blackie. "It's about minus 20 degrees outside. And you all know as well as I do, the poor bugger was ill equipped for that sort of climate. I can only assume he died as a result of the extreme cold. He certainly hadn't been shot."

"Oh for pity's sake," said the Club Secretary.

"I'm sorry to hear that Blackie."

"You can stick your sympathy up your backside," said the trembling Blackie. "I worshipped that man. That man was like a second father to me."

"We know that Blackie," said Steadman.

"I held him in my arms as he passed away," said

Blackie. "And I've nursed him like a baby since he gurgled and drew his last breath. I couldn't bring myself to leave him."

"Of course you couldn't," said Steadman.

"How was he up to the moment he passed away?" said the old man.

"He was extremely poorly," said Blackie. "How do you think he fucking well was Professor?"

"I'm sorry," said the old man. "Please forgive me. That was a ridiculous and poorly considered thing to ask. I was referring to when you first discovered him. How did he respond to you? Was there any aggression?"

"None at all," said Blackie. "He hadn't gone crazy if that's what you're getting at."

"Where is he now?" said the Chairman.

"In the engine under my bedspread," said Blackie. "That was his last resting place. Jesus Christ-it's bitterly cold up there."

"Would you mind if we go and pay our respects?" said the Club Secretary.

"I would, as it happens," said Blackie. "You can all just leave him in peace."

"Very well," said the Club Secretary.

"I think we're going to need to see him," said the Chairman.

"What the hell for?" said Blackie.

"We're just going to need to see him," said the Chairman.

"But why?" said Blackie. "Tell me why Hulmey."

"Because I don't think they believe your story," said McShane.

"What!" said Blackie.

"They don't believe you," said McShane. "They probably think Biddo's still alive. They probably think you're trying to protect him."

"Is that right?" said Blackie. "Is that true Hulmey?"

"We just need to be sure," said the Chairman.

"You hard faced bastards," said Blackie after rising and kicking away his chair. He's dead I tell you. And what's more, just about every one of you had a hand in his death."

"Why's that?" said the Club Secretary.

"Because you drove him from this train as if he was a leper," said Blackie.

"We did nothing of the sort," said the Chairman. "As far as I recall, he just ran away. That's right isn't it lads?"

"It is yes," said the Club Secretary. "He vanished not long after we discovered the remains of Larko and the others."

"Maybe so but you all made sure he could never return," said Blackie. "Jesus, Mary and Joseph! So did I, come to think of it. You had me securing barricades to make sure he didn't try to break back in. You denied him something as basic as warmth. You as good as killed him. You're all going to have to live with that. And you're going to have to live with something else too. Something that's quite poetic when you consider our desperate and increasingly dire situation."

"What's that?" said the Chef.

"I came across a body while on my way back here," said Blackie.

"What!" said the Chef.

"I found a dead body," said Blackie.

"Where was this?" said the Chef.

"Between the tracks under the second carriage," said Blackie.

"Who was it?" said the Chef. "Do you know who it was?"

"Was it Eddie Meehan?" said the Chairman.

"It wasn't young Anthony was it?" said Steadman.

"Oh Christ!" said the Club Secretary. "Don't tell me that."

"That would explain why he was carrying a flashlight," said the Chairman.

"That would also explain why he was crawling on his hands and knees too," said the Club Secretary. "The poor bugger must have been physically spent."

"It wasn't young Anthony," said Blackie. "It was a

complete stranger actually."

"And that complete stranger's death can be considered poetic can it?" said Hamill.

"It can be considered incredibly poetic if it turns out somebody on board this train killed him," said Blackie before removing a tightly folded bundle of papers from his rear trouser pocket and dropping them onto the Chairman's lap. "Because if somebody on board this train did indeed kill the poor chap, they've almost certainly made sure none of us will live to see our loved ones again."

"Why's that?" said the Club Secretary.

"What are these?" said the Chairman.

"Take a shufti," said Blackie. "Read them and weep, as they say in Vegas."

"What are they?" said the Chef.

"They're a variety of personal effects belonging to the late Mr J.B. Standish," said Blackie.

"J.B who?" said the Club Secretary.

"J.B. Standish," said Blackie. "Take a good look through them. I think you'll find them interesting. There's a roughly sketched map of what I assume is this region, some identification and a list of instructions."

"Regarding what?" said the Chef.

"Regarding our rescue," said Blackie.

"What!" said the Chef.

"Our rescue?" said Hewlett.

"That's right," said Blackie. "The recently deceased, six foot eight, brown eyed, father of three, J.B Standish was the leader of a rescue team sent out to bring us all home. That's whose body I found under the train. He's been travelling overland for the best part of 3 days."

"How could you possibly know that?" said the Chef.

"There's a pocket diary among those items," said Blackie. "Almost every step of his journey has been documented. On one of the pages, he mentions finding the frozen body of a young man near an abandoned sheep farm."

"What young man?" said the Club Secretary.

[439]

"I don't know," said Blackie. "I know who I don't want it to be though."

"Fucking hell!" said Steadman.

"They were my very sentiments too," said Blackie.

"I don't believe it," said Hewlett. "Are we jinxed or something? I just can't believe our run of luck."

"I can't believe someone managed to reach us in such foul weather," said McShane.

"I can't either," said Hamill. "Especially someone unsupported."

"He wasn't alone," said the Chairman before handing the wad of papers to the Club Secretary.

"What!" said Hewlett.

"Our J B Standish wasn't alone," said the Chairman. "There were originally three of them."

"Three of them!" said McShane.

"There was another mountain rescuer and erm...." said the Chairman.

"And what?" said Steadman. "And what Hulmey?"

"And what Hulmey?" said the Chef.

"A driver," said the Chairman.

"A driver!" said Hewlett. "Do you mean a train driver?"

"No-he means a fork lift driver," said McShane. "That's what mountain rescue companies do. When people need rescuing, they send a fork lift driver out. It's a tried and tested method apparently."

"Go to hell Tommy," said Hewlett.

"No, you go to hell," said McShane.

"I don't believe this," said Steadman. "I just don't believe it."

"Have you any idea how he died?" said the Chef.

"I think you'll find he was shot," said the Chairman. "I can only assume from ground level. Me, Hilly and Hamill watched the incident unfold from behind the second carriage window."

"That's right," said the Club Secretary.

"And might I just add-from that vantage point, our powerfully built would be rescuer J.B Standish did look remarkably like a huge bear," said Hamill. "As I said earlier, it was a mistake anyone could have made."

"Bloody hell!" said Steadman. "This cannot be happening. It's beyond belief. By rights, we should all be on our way home now."

"And we still might be if we can find the missing train driver," said the Chef.

"Of course," said the Club Secretary before springing to his feet. "I never thought of that. He's probably somewhere nearby looking for the train as we speak. What are we going to do?"

"We're going to sit here and wait for the engine driver to find us," said the Chairman.

"Why's that?" said Club Secretary.

"Because it'd be too dangerous to do anything else," said the Chairman. "The weather's horrendous and there's at least one wild animal on the prowl."

"And somebody armed with a high powered rifle," said Hewlett.

"That's right," said Hamill.

"Well let's hope that rifleman's only hunting wild animals," said the Chef.

"I'll drink to that," said Hamill.

"What if our J B Standish was the only surviving member of the rescue party," said Steadman.

"That doesn't bear thinking about," said the Chairman.

"I can't help thinking about it," said Steadman.

"Fucking hell Hulmey. I'm on the brink of a full blown breakdown here."

"You're going to have to get a grip Steadman," said the Chairman. "You're beginning to fall apart fella."

"Fall apart!" said Steadman. "You hard faced bastard. You cheeky fucker. Is it any wonder? Is it any wonder I'm falling apart Hulmey? What have we got to cling on to? Until you read that log or whatever it is, I felt we had some sort of hope. We knew that Anthony was out there somewhere. That was a possibility. We knew that a rescue team would eventually get to us. That was another possibility. Now we've got nothing. I'll tell

you this much Hulmey...And listen to me very
carefully...I've had it up to my eye teeth with you and
your dithering and your lack of strong leadership. If we
do get out of this-if we do manage to make it back to
Crosby, I want you to promise me you'll never so much
as darken my doorstep again. What a ridiculous idea
this trip was. 20 scousers, nobody to keep them in check
and a train full of free fucking ale. That's a recipe for
disaster If I've ever heard of one. You've got us all dead
in the water lad."
"We're not dead in the water," said the Chairman. "I've
already made contingency for Anthony failing to return
and nobody reaching us."
"Really!" said Hamill.
"Yes really," said the Chairman.
"And what exactly is that contingency?" said Steadman.
"I'm going to go looking for help myself," said the
Chairman.
"You're what?" said the Chef.
"I'm going to go for help," said the Chairman.
"You're not," said the Chef. "You're cryophobic for
God's sake. You can't cope with the cold. You won't
last 5 minutes out there."
"I will if I'm wrapped up and equipped right," said the
Chairman. "And by the way our kid-this idea isn't open
to negotiation. As the legitimate Chairman of this club,
it's my duty to go. It's my duty to look after these
remaining men. To be honest, I should have made the
decision days ago. There might be so many more of us
alive if I had done."
"I'm afraid you've lost the plot our kid," said the Chef.
"He's not lost the plot at all," said Hamill. "He's just
discovered the contents of his ball sack."
"I'll go with you Hulmey," said the Club Secretary.
"And by the way-that's not negotiable either."
"I'll go too," said the Chef before sighing heavily.
"That's good to hear," said the Chairman.
"Not to me it isn't," said Hamill.
"Why's that?" said the Chef.

[442]

"Because I think at least one of you three good comrades should remain here," said Hamill.

"Why, for God's sake?" said the Chef.

"I have my reasons," said Hamill.

"What reasons are they?" said Steadman. "Surely the bigger the party, the better the chance of them succeeding."

"I'd have thought that too," said Hewlett.

"So would I," said McShane. "What's the problem Hamill?"

"I've got abandonment issues," said Hamill.

"Abandonment issues!" said McShane. "I don't understand."

"I know what he means," said the Chairman. "I know exactly what he means. He thinks we're going to leave you all stranded here. He thinks we're not going to come back for you. That's right isn't it Hamill? I'm right aren't I?"

"You are, as it happens," said Hamill. "Let's be honest. What incentive will you have for sending us help if all your nearest and dearest are already safe? The chances are, when you find a settlement of any sort, you'll be taken to the nearest hospital and taken care of. You'll be treated like long lost heroes. You'll have jelly and ice cream and a tasty nurse to give you each a bath. You won't be thinking about us. You'll be thinking about getting back to your families. We'll be a million miles from your thoughts."

"Bloody hell Hamill!" said the Club Secretary. "You've just slumped to an all time low there. In the long history of your notorious bad mindedness, that's about the most bad minded thing I've ever heard you say. Do you really think we'd leave you stranded? Is that what you think?"

"I wouldn't put it past you," said Hamill.

"It's ridiculous," said the Chairman. "These are my friends."

"Who are?" scoffed a wide mouthed, open armed and beaming Hamill before taking to the floor like a circus ringmaster. "Tell me Hulmey. Who are your friends?

[443]

Name them. Go on, point them out to me. Which of these are your friends?"

"They all are," said the Chairman.

"Rubbish!" said Hamill. "I think you're deluded lad. The Professor's not your friend. Hewlett's certainly not your friend. He wouldn't piss on you if you were on fire. You're way beneath his status. And you've just heard what Steadman thinks of you. He now considers you a complete waste of space. He no longer wants anything to do with you. He doesn't want you to darken his doorstep again. Then there's Blackie. He's not going to forget what you did to him. Not for a long, long time."

"I've done nothing to Blackie," said the Chairman. "We've always been close."

"Close!" said Hamill. "I very much doubt if you're close now. Think about the way you treated his recently departed uncle. Think about the way that, despite all his protestations, you still had the poor bastard locked up in the mail room. A mail room, I might add, that was like some sort of vortex where the wicked and criminally insane could enter, murder at will and then leave without so much as a 'thank you for having us'. It's no wonder Biddo went crazy after what he witnessed. And then there's my last remaining mate Tommy Mac. You can't call him your friend. You've never had any time for old Tommy. You were one of those who kept him out of this club for years. You kept blackballing him for no apparent reason. You considered him an undesirable, if some of the accounts I've heard are true."

"They're not true," said the Chairman. "It's just another example of your devious mind at work. And anyway- what about Brian Matthews."

"What about him?" said Hamill. "You're not suggesting he's your friend are you?"

"He's been a very good friend of mine for many years," said the Chairman. "We go back a long way. Do you think I'd leave him swinging?"

"I think there's a possibility," said Hamill. "Matthews

isn't your friend. Matthews is not remotely your friend. He might pretend to be your friend. He might lick your arse from time to time. But that's only because you're on the committee. A committee he's always craved to be on, I might add. Did you know he bears you a very serious and deeply entrenched grudge?"

"I didn't," said the Chairman.

"Well it's true," said Hamill. "I'll be honest with you-he's never said exactly what the nature of that grudge is, but he definitely harbours one. And then of course, there's little old me. You know what I think of you. You certainly won't be rushing back on my behalf will you Hulmey?"

"I'll come back for every one of you," said the Chairman. "And that's whether you or any of the others like me or not."

"You will now," said Hamill. "Because the Chef's not going anywhere. He's staying here with us. He's going to be our insurance."

"Don't you mean hostage?" said the Chairman.

"If you like," said Hamill.

"What if I point blank refuse to stay?" said the Chef.

"I won't hesitate to break one of your legs," said Hamill. "And another thing lads. There still remains a very real possibility the man who shot our poor would be rescuer J B Standish is one of us."

"What!" said the stupefied Chairman.

"That's nonsense," said Steadman.

"You're probably right," said Hamill. "But would it do any harm if we conducted a quick search of everyone's belongings? What do you think Hulmey? Should we start with your bags?"

"I think you're being your bad minded self again," said the severely shaken Chairman. "There's no gun on board this train. Nobody here shot that man."

"Are you absolutely sure about that?" said Hamill.

"I'm positive," said the Chairman.

"What about you Hilly," said Hamill. "Have you got the same faith in your fellow club members?"

"I've got complete and utter faith in every one of them," said the Club Secretary.

"That's good," said Hamill. "That's good to hear. And just for the record Hilly-how much faith have you got in your own ability to discharge your duties as Club Secretary?"

"Every faith," said the Club Secretary.

"Nobody could do the job better," said the Chairman.

"Really?" said Hamill. "Then tell me this Hulmey-was it Hilly's job to search the men before they boarded the train?"

"It was yes," replied the Club Secretary. "Why do you ask?"

"Because I was wondering how the already mortal drunk Kenny Biddo managed to smuggle so many of his own bottles of vodka on board?" said Hamill. "And how, for that matter, did Woody manage to sneak a veritable banquet on board?"

"I was distracted when the Professor slipped over and hurt himself," said the Club Secretary.

"Did you search my mate Tommy Mac?" said Hamill.

"I made a point of doing so," replied the Club Secretary.

"Did you really?" said Hamill. "Then, what if I told you he'd brought a loaded Colt 45 on board?"

"What!" said McShane.

"He did what?" said Steadman.

"Take no notice of him," said the Chairman. "He's making mischief again. He'll be telling you the gun was once owned by John Wayne next. Now, will you excuse us please Hamill. Me and Hilly have got plans to make for tomorrow's journey."

"Do you want to borrow Uncle Topper's fur coat?" said Hamill.

"Excuse me!" said Hewlett.

"Hulmey's going to be needing a heavy coat," said Hamill. "Let's be honest Hewlett-I can't see that old thing making another Royal Ascot appearance."

"Take the damn thing," said Hewlett dismissively.

"That was always going to be my intention," said

Hamill. "And might I suggest the late J B Standish
provides your coat Hilly?"
"I'm not wearing that thing," said the Club Secretary. "I
couldn't wear a dead man's coat."
"I'm afraid you're going to have to bite the bullet Hilly,"
said the Chairman.
"Go and get it Hewlett," said Hamill.
"I beg your pardon!" said Hewlett.
"Go and fetch Mr Standish's coat," said Hamill.
"Why me, for goodness sake?" said Hewlett.
"Because I've appointed you expedition dresser," said
Hamill. "You're going to get our two brave adventurers
kitted out for their journey."
"Of all the cheek," said the rising Hewlett.
"Go and get it," said Hamill. "Go and get the coat
before some thieving rambler finds it. And watch out for
nasty creatures while you're out there. Oh, and by the
way Hulmey-the Chef sleeps in my room tonight.
Comprende?"

CHAPTER NINETEEN
VISITOR

The disenchanted, enormously resentful and bitterly cold Hewlett arrived at his previously designated sleeping quarters just as another tremendously powerful blast of wind had left the train vibrating like a cheap spin dryer and although he had been desperate to return to the dining carriage to inform his many doubters that he had been up to the unenviable and highly dangerous task allotted him, he had almost immediately found himself drawn to an unusual odour that seemed to be emanating from the far, dimly lit corner of the room.

"Who's there?" he asked before quickly snatching an empty wine bottle from the top of his bedside cabinet and thrusting it before him at arm's length.

"Is there somebody there?"

"Please don't be alarmed my young friend," came a deep gravelly voice from the vicinity of the diagonally opposite corner bed. "I mean you no harm. I'm just an ageing traveller who happened upon your train by sheer good fortune."

"A traveller!" said Hewlett while trying desperately to establish whether the stranger was alone. "Do you mean a gypsy?"

"That's right," said a small, shabbily dressed old man after stepping out of the dark triangular shadow and taking a bow. "But don't worry son, you've nothing to fear from me."

"I know damn well I've nothing to fear from you," said Hewlett, who, despite his apparent boldness was still nevertheless retreating inch by increasing inch. "It's you who should be fearful. You're the one that's trespassing. And, by the way-does it look as if I'm in fear of you?"

"It does to be perfectly honest," said the stranger. "In fact, it looks as if you've pissed your pants."

"I've done nothing of the sort," said Hewlett. "I spilt a drop of wine when I snatched up the bottle. Now tell me...and be quick about it-what the hell do you think you're doing in my room?"

"I saw the lights from the train and thought I'd pop up and see what was happening," said the old man. "I thought I was seeing things at first, to be honest. There hasn't been a train along this stretch of track for many a long year."

"It's a brand new service," said Hewlett as he watched the old man turn very deliberately, reverse onto the far corner bed and begin testing the springs. "And you can pack that in right away. That bed belongs to a thoroughly decent fare paying passenger."

"Does it really," said the old man.

"It most certainly does," said Hewlett.

"Well he's welcome to it," said the old man after one more disappointing bounce. "I couldn't sleep on that. It isn't half as comfortable as it looks."

"That's because it wasn't designed for the likes of you," said Hewlett. "You should be sleeping on a bale of hay in some nearby barn. What are you really doing here?"

"I've just told you," said the old man while examining his few remaining teeth in the Professor's portable shaving mirror. "I'm just a tired old traveller who's looking for somewhere to shelter for the night."

"Why don't you shelter under the train like any other self respecting tramp would?" said Hewlett.

"Because it's far warmer and cosier in here," said the old man. "And it's going to get dark soon. And when it gets dark around here, nasty things abound."

"You're up to no good, aren't you?" said Hewlett. "You're a vagabond aren't you?"

"Vagabond!" laughed the old man. "Goodness me! That's a term I haven't heard for a long time. Where did you pick that up?"

"Where my considerable command of the English language evolved has nothing at all to do with you," said Hewlett. "Now will you leave or do I have to come

[449]

over there and box your ears?"

"Box my ears!" laughed the old man. "You are a strange one aren't you. You remind me of someone. Someone very famous. Someone from an old film it was. It'll come to me in a few minutes."

"You haven't got a few minutes, you filthy old trout," said Hewlett. "Now, get out of my room. Go on-scram. Shoo! Crawl back to your rat's nest before I call one of the stewards and have you forcefully removed."

"There's no need to take that attitude," said the old man while examining Hewlett's large array of perfectly arranged toiletries. "I've done you no disservice."

"I couldn't disagree any more emphatically," said Hewlett. "And you can keep your filthy hands off those. That collection of cosmetics probably cost more money than you've earned in your entire life."

"I don't doubt it son," said the old man. "David something or other.....David Niven...David Niven, the chap's name was."

"What about David Niven?" said Hewlett.

"He was the character from the film I was telling you about," said the old man. "You're the spitting image of a young version of him."

"And you're the spitting image of an elderly and typically dishevelled Charlie Chaplin," said Hewlett. "You're a no good tramp on the lookout for what you can pilfer from honest, decent people."

"Are you honest and decent?" said the old man.

"I'm the very epitome of honesty and decency," said Hewlett. "In the long and distinguished history of my much respected family, no ancestor of mine has ever stood in the dock as the accused."

"That's the advantage of being moneyed," said the old man.

"It's nothing to do with money," said Hewlett. "It's to do with genes, education, moral standards and proper, structured upbringing."

"Of course it is," said the old man. "*Thank you Jeeves*, was the name of that film."

"Excuse me!" said a confused Hewlett.

"That was the name of the David Niven film I was telling you about earlier," said the old man. "I saw it at the Coliseum in East Finchley in 1938. That was one of my first ever dates. I was a bit disappointed to be honest."

"Why's that?" said Hewlett. "Did your date insist on you paying for the tickets and the popcorn?"

"It wasn't that," said the old man. "It was the way the central characters were portrayed."

"What do you mean?" said Hewlett before yanking open one of the windows and proceeding to waft a few handfuls of fresh air inside. "Were they using too many syllables? Was the language too rich for you to process?"

"Not at all," said the old man. "The use of language was quite impressive. It was just that it wasn't how I imagined the character Jeeves to be."

"Why's that?" said Hewlett.

"Because it wasn't," said the old man while unbuttoning his coat. "Wodehouse even said so himself."

"What!" said Hewlett.

"Wodehouse was aware of that flaw," said the old man.

"How would you know that?" said Hewlett.

"I knew him," said the old man.

"I beg your pardon!" scoffed Hewlett.

"I knew the man," said the gypsy. "I knew P G Wodehouse very well."

"Don't be absurd," said the sneering Hewlett.

"I did," said the gypsy. "Me and old Plum were on very good terms for many years."

"Plum," said Hewlett. "His name was Pelham. Pelham Granville actually."

"Pelham Grenville," said the old man. "He liked his friends to call him 'Plum'."

"Friends! Don't make me laugh," said the continually suspicious Hewlett before folding his arms and settling onto his own bed. "How could you two be friends? You'd be like substandard chalk and a slab of Beaufort

D'Ete. Wodehouse was a true gentleman. Oh no, no, no...there's no way your paths will have ever crossed. You're deluded."

"I hate to disappoint you but our paths crossed on a number of occasions," said the old man. "We became very good friends actually."

"Rubbish!" said Hewlett. "How could that possibly happen? P.G. Wodehouse was a master of language and characterisation. He was a gentleman and a scholar. I doubt if you can string a coherent sentence together. You only have to look at you to see how disgustingly low you are. I mean-you're just a bundle of rags. I imagine just about everything you're wearing is some sort of hand me down."

"Well I've always believed good manners maketh the man, not the clothes on his back," said the gypsy.

"Is that so?" said Hewlett. "I personally believe in positive first impressions."

"I do too," said the old man. "And to be honest-at this particular moment in time, you're a bit of a disappointment."

"Me a disappointment!" said Hewlett before heading over to the door. "You impudent little guttersnipe. The very nerve of you. Get out. Be gone with you. And if you try to board this train again, I'll have a friend of mine break one of your legs."

"Break one of my legs!" said the old man. "That seems a bit extreme in the circumstances. Why would you want him to do that?"

"Because you're an undesirable swank and a liar," said Hewlett after drawing open the door and cocking his head to one side. "Now, do as you're told and get out."

"I'm going nowhere," said the old man. "At least, not this evening I'm not. There's a nasty storm brewing."

"There's no storm brewing," said Hewlett. "The weather has actually improved a little over the last hour."

"Take it from me son," said the old man. "Take it from one who knows British weather patterns as well as any

man. There's a storm brewing. A storm, the likes of
which you've probably never witnessed before."
"Well, hurry along and you might just avoid it," said
Hewlett. "I'll even provide you with a few cheese
biscuits and a nice bottle of red for your journey."
"That's very decent of you," said the old man. "They'll
do me for breakfast."
"They'll do you for an early evening supper," said
Hewlett. "So I suggest you leave now if you know
what's good for you."
"I'll leave first thing in the morning," said the old man.
"By the way-you couldn't spare me a bit of fresh meat
could you? I haven't had any fresh meat for weeks.
Could you do that for me? Is there any way you could
do that for me please?"
"I could," said Hewlett. "But only provided you leave
right away. Trust me-there are men here who won't
hesitate to hurt you if they find out you've been going
through their things."
"I imagine there are," said the old man. "And by the
way-it wasn't me that jemmied open the lock on that
tatty old suitcase."
"Tatty old suitcase!" said Hewlett. "Tatty old suitcase!
You insufferable rogue. It's not just a tatty old
suitcase.....it's....."
"It's an original Louis Vuitton," said the old man. "Old
Plum had a half decent set of three if I remember right.
They were the genuine article though."
"And so are mine," said an indignant Hewlett. "Mine
are very much the genuine article. They were handed
down to me by my great Uncle Septimus."
"A hand me down hey!" said the old man. "You do
surprise me."
"I'll do more than surprise you if you don't start making
tracks," said Hewlett.
"Will at least one aspect of that surprise, be the
employment of civility?" said the old man.
"It's likely to be the employment of a swift kick to your
bony backside," said Hewlett. "Now, for the last time-

[453]

get out of my room before I call a steward and have you removed."

"Your capacity for deceit knows no bounds, does it young fellow?" said the old man.

"What do you mean?"said Hewlett.

"There *are* no stewards on board this train," said the old man.

"There are," said Hewlett. "There are dozens of them. You can't move for stewards at times."

"You're telling fibs," said the old man. "There are no stewards. There are no staff at all. You haven't even got an engine driver."

"We have," said Hewlett. "At least, we will have shortly. A replacement driver is on his way here, as we speak."

"I wouldn't put too much trust in that rumour son," said the gypsy.

"Why not?" said Hewlett.

"Because it's just possible, I met your so-called replacement train driver a couple of days ago," said the gypsy. "He was with another chap. A stout chap he was. They were both in a seriously bad way. I wrapped their feet and directed them towards an old barn which would give them a little shelter. But I've got to be honest with you, mine host-I don't think either of them were going to survive the night."

"Why not?"said Hewlett.

"Both were badly frostbitten," said the gypsy. "It was pitiful. They were in so much pain, they were crying like hungry babies. They even gave me some of their personal effects to send to their families."

"Oh mother of God!" said Hewlett. "That's awful. That really is awful. What else do you know about our predicament?"

"I know certain members of your party like a bloody good argument," said the gypsy.

"I wouldn't disagree with that," said Hewlett. "What else?"

"I know you've got a distinctly bad egg among you,"

[454]

said the old man.

"Why would you say that?" said Hewlett.

"Let's just call it instinct shall we," said the old man. "And I'll thank you kindly not to press me any more on that matter, if you don't mind."

"Very well," said Hewlett. "You've been watching us for some time haven't you."

"From when the first light of the morning broke," said the old man. "By the way-are you aware the mail room door isn't particularly secure?"

"We discovered that only recently," said Hewlett. "I think it's been sorted now."

"Have you any idea why your train left the station unstaffed and without a driver?" said the old man. "Because that seems very strange to me."

"One of our members set it in motion," said Hewlett.

"My word!" said the gypsy. "For what reason?"

"He's a notorious prankster," said Hewlett.

"Well that mindless idiot has put all your lives in mortal danger," said the old gypsy. "You couldn't have stopped in a worse place. The only thing going for you and your party is the bridge. There are very few people that could make it up to the top of this bridge in the sort of weather we're currently experiencing."

"You managed it," said Hewlett. "And you've got to be touching 90 years of age."

"I can climb like a mountain goat," said the old man. "I've been climbing hills and mountains all my life. And I know when to climb and when not to climb. And I know exactly when to stop and I know when to bivouac for the night. How many are you, by the way?"

"About 30 or 40," said Hewlett. "Most of them are ex army lads. Royal Marines and Special Air Servicemen."

"That's some army," said the gypsy. "But alas, you're forgetting what I've just told you. I've been watching you and your mates for quite some time. There's nowhere near 30 or 40 of you. And as regards ex army personnel-most of your travelling companions look as if they'd struggle to be accepted into the Salvation Army.

[455]

How many are you? And tell the truth this time. I might be of some help to you all."

"There were about 18 or19 of us originally," said Hewlett after a moment's hesitation during which, to the obvious delight of the old man, he had produced a bottle of red wine from under his bed. "We're all members of a veteran men's club from Merseyside. We were heading up to Scotland and back via Wales and the Lake District. It was the train's maiden voyage so to speak."

"What did you mean when you said there were 18 or 19 of you originally?" said the gypsy.

"We've lost quite a few," said Hewlett.

"Lost them!" said the old man.

"Our Chairman died of a heart attack the very night we set off," said Hewlett.

"Oh dear!" said the old man. "That's unfortunate."

"And a couple of people have mysteriously vanished and a few have been murdered by someone or something," said Hewlett.

"What someone or something?" said the old man.

"We don't know for certain," said Hewlett. "Some of the lads suspect it to be the work of a wild animal."

"Why's that?" said the old man.

"Because of the condition of the victim's bodies," said Hewlett. "They were torn to shreds and barely recognisable. Some even suspect a bear did it. Do you think it could have been a bear?"

"It's hard to say," said the old man. "I wouldn't have thought so."

"Why's that?" said Hewlett.

"Because something as big as a bear would stand out like a sore thumb in this landscape," said the old man. "And I'd have heard something through the grapevine by now. But I wouldn't dismiss the idea completely. It might have been a bear for all I know. It wouldn't surprise me. We often hear reports of large wild animals roaming these parts."

"Like what?" said Hewlett.

"Like jaguars and other big cats mainly," said the old

[456]

man. "I've been interviewed by scores of roving television and radio reporters over the years. And I've told them all sorts of fantastic tales for the price of a nice square meal and a bottle of stout."

"What's the biggest and angriest thing you've ever seen?" said Hewlett.

"My cousin's 18 stone wife seconds after she caught him cheating on her," said the old man without any hesitation whatsoever. "I've never seen anything as big and as angry as that in my life."

"I'm talking about wild animals," said Hewlett.

"Trust me son-so am I," said the pan faced gypsy while prompting his host to hand him the uncorked bottle of wine.

The old man was relatively short and painfully thin and had long almost white hair that had been combed back to form a thin pony tail which was held together by a short strip of faded reddish brown ribbon that was peppered with tiny holes. He was wearing a heavy grey trench coat with a length of old rope for a belt and which, because of his lack of height, almost reached down to touch the floor. The mud encased old boots that the coat was almost hiding, were of the heavy military hobnail type and had clearly been discarded or donated by somebody much bigger. Each had been crudely, yet very effectively adapted for the arduous rural British winter. In other words, both had been wrapped in blue and white plastic supermarket carrier bags and secured to the gypsy's lower legs with short lengths of orange string and a number of brown rubber bands. However, it hadn't necessarily been the old man's ragged appearance that had brought the ex public school boy's renowned class prejudice to the surface-it had been his lack of appreciation that he was somewhere uninvited and therefore somewhere he shouldn't really be.

"Have you ever considered doing something about your disgusting fingers?" he said while trying unsuccessfully to open another window.

[457]

"It's Rheumatoid Arthritis son," said the old man. "Some mornings I can't even open my hands."

"I'm talking about the unsightly dark brown stains," said Hewlett. "You had those filthy things in your mouth when you were examining your teeth. Aren't you scared of getting some sort of poisoning?"

"It's not dirt son," said the gypsy. "It's nicotine. Those stains have been there for many years. I've been smoking since the age of six. I was smoking thirty Capstan Full Strength a day by the time I was nine. Those stains are a part of me now."

"Well what about your fingernails," said Hewlett. "Might I suggest there's enough soil and dirt under them to create a small vegetable garden. What's your excuse for not looking after them?"

"I do now and then," said the gypsy. "But then again I sometimes leave them for a while. It adds to my performance in the sack, so to speak. Most women love having their back clawed. I think it evokes the cavewoman in them."

"Are you telling me you're still sexually active?" said Hewlett.

"Very much so," said the gypsy. "I can't get enough. What about yourself?"

"That's got nothing to do with you," said Hewlett.

"You started it," said the gypsy.

"I'm entitled to start it," said Hewlett. "This is my allotted room. I'm not the one trespassing. Do you mind me asking you something?"

"You can ask me whatever you want," said the gypsy before swallowing the last of the wine, patting his chest and handing the empty bottle to his host. "As long as it's not too personal. What is it? What do you want to know?"

"I want to know where you got that unsightly scar," said Hewlett while pointing to a deep groove running down from the old man's right eyebrow to the side of his mouth.

"Oh that," said the gypsy. "I don't really like talking

about that. Let's just say that it was an unfortunate consequence of my unchecked youth."

"So it wasn't an accident then," said Hewlett. "Can I at least assume that?"

"You can," said the gypsy.

"Well how did you get it?" said Hewlett.

"I told you I don't want to talk about it," said the gypsy.

"Tell me," said Hewlett after retrieving another bottle of wine from under his bed. "Go on, tell me."

"Alright," said the gypsy. "But I want another good swig first."

"You can have the whole bottle if it's a story worth hearing," said Hewlett.

"Very well," said the gypsy while making himself more comfortable. "It was a punishment meted out by my clan elders."

"Really!" said Hewlett. "For doing what exactly?"

"For being a bad boy," said the old man. "I violated an old established gypsy code."

"By doing what?" said Hewlett.

"I was cruel to an animal," said the gypsy. "A nanny goat to be more exact."

"Oh dear!" said Hewlett. "What happened? Did you fail to return her calls? Did you stop writing all of a sudden?"

"I kicked it," said the gypsy.

"You kicked it," said Hewlett.

"I kicked it in the belly," said the gypsy. "It was pestering me for food. It wouldn't leave me alone. I was in a twat of a mood after an argument with me girlfriend. I just lashed out in frustration."

"And the elders scarred you for life for that did they?" said Hewlett.

"It was a milker," said the gypsy. "It was extremely valuable."

"Did you not feel the punishment was a bit harsh? said Hewlett. "After all-you only kicked the flea ridden thing. It's not as though you killed it."

"I did kill it," said the gypsy while holding out his hand

[459]

to receive his reward. "I'd shattered the poor things ribs.
It died a terrible death. I can sometimes still hear the
poor thing bleating in pain. The incident haunts me
terribly. The next morning, I was dragged from my
caravan and pinned to the ground by 3 burly men. The
result is the scar you were so curious to learn about."
"Is this true?" said Hewlett.
"I told you-I violated a gypsy code," said the old man. "I
got what I deserved. I harmed an innocent creature.
They're very sensitive people gypsies. They might like
nothing more than to knock several kinds of shite out of
each other on a Saturday night, but they won't tolerate
cruelty to their animals. Do you have any animals?"
"Me and my family own plenty," said Hewlett.
"Pedigree dogs and horses mainly. We have several
Arabian thoroughbreds. One of them's standing at stud
as we speak."
"Do you ride?" said the gypsy.
"I've been riding since I was 5," said Hewlett. "I won
the Pony Derby at Hickstead when I was 10."
"Do you still ride?" said the gypsy.
"I ride most Sunday mornings, weather permitting," said
Hewlett.
"Do you use a crop and spurs?" said the old man.
"Of course," said Hewlett. "What respectable
equestrian gentleman doesn't? How else do you expect
me to control half a ton of highly strung horse flesh?"
"With practice and patience," said the gypsy. "There's
never any need to strike a horse. You can get a horse to
do what you want through patience, kindness and
reward. Crops and spurs hey! The likes of you make
me sick."
"Make you sick!" said Hewlett. "You've got some
nerve haven't you. I've just watched you put your dirty,
nicotine stained fingers in your mouth. I bet you don't
even wash after you've been to the toilet. I mean.....take
a look at yourself. Look at the state of you. Look at the
bloody state of you. How often do you have to check
yourself for fleas?"

"I dress for a specific purpose son," said the old man.

"Dress for a specific purpose!" scoffed Hewlett.

"Don't make me laugh. Whether you dress for a specific purpose or not, you could dress better than that. Can't you see-you're sending out all the wrong messages."

"What do you mean?" said the gypsy. "This is winter. The message I want to send out is clear. I'm keeping warm and to hell with vanity and what other people think."

"But you look like the classic vagrant," said Hewlett. "People see you and know instinctively that you have nowhere to live and no possessions. That's their first impression. And because of that-they instinctively look down on you and become suspicious and defensive."

"I don't understand what you're getting at," said the old man. "Are you trying to imply I'm disadvantaged in some way? Is that what you're saying?"

"It's exactly what I'm saying," said Hewlett. "You are disadvantaged. You're a complete and utter failure. Your rags are the emblems of that failure. You've achieved nothing in your life. You've got absolutely nothing to show for all your years on this planet."

"I haven't failed at all son," said the gypsy. "I've never craved anything but good health. I have everything I need. My home is anywhere under the stars and God provided me with a sturdy pair of legs to get around on. What more could I possibly want?"

"But surely you crave certain luxuries," said Hewlett. "Even if it's as simple as hot water and a bar of soap."

"Not really," said the gypsy. "Look what having the finer things in life has done to you."

"What do you mean by that?" said Hewlett.

"You're a pompous spoilt brat with no respect at all for your elders," said the gypsy.

"I have plenty of respect for the elderly," said Hewlett.

"Well I certainly haven't witnessed any respect," said the gypsy. "You've never met me before in your life but from the moment you laid eyes on me you've done nothing but insult me. I'd have thought you'd have been brought up better. You clearly weren't thrashed enough when you were a child."

"You impertinent fop," said Hewlett. "Don't you dare say that. I was brought up properly and chastised in an appropriate manner whenever necessary. My father was a noted disciplinarian. He was hard but fair. Do you know, he once withdrew my riding privileges."

"He once withdrew what?" said the gypsy.

"My riding privileges," said Hewlett. "He wouldn't let me mount Hugo for a week."

"Was Hugo one of your servants?" said the gypsy.

"Don't be ridiculous," said Hewlett. "Hugo was my first pony. I got him for my fifth birthday."

"What exactly were you punished for?" said the gypsy.

"I'd kicked my manservant in the shins," said Hewlett. "And by the way-it's lucky for you Waggers isn't here to witness that last remark. He'd have knocked your block off and no mistake. He boxed for the R.A.F during the war. He actually beat a promising London fighter who was 10 years his senior to take the middleweight title."

"Shouldn't he have been fighting Germans?" said the gypsy.

"Very funny," said Hewlett. "It's just a pity you haven't got any fixed abode. I'd get Waggers to pay you a visit."

"I'd welcome that," said the gypsy after standing up and adopting the classic south paw stance. "Because I'm no mug at the old boxing game myself. I once floored old Plum with a peach of a left hook."

"You did what?" said Hewlett.

"I knocked old Plum out," said the gypsy. "You know-Wodehouse."

"Did I just hear you right?" said a scowling Hewlett. "Did you just say, you once assaulted the great P.G. Wodehouse?"

"It wasn't assault," said the old man. "We were sparring partners. He loved his boxing did old Plum. He was quite handy, if the truth be told. He was a very good judge of an up and coming boxer too."

"But very clearly, an extremely poor judge of character," said Hewlett.

"What do you mean?" said the gypsy.

"I just find it hard to believe he could befriend the likes of you," said Hewlett.

"What do you mean, 'the likes of me'?" said the old man.

"Someone with nothing at all going for them," said Hewlett.

"Well he did," said the gypsy. "We were friends. And very good friends at that. I did odd jobs for him from time to time. I was there the day he was taken away by the Germans. That's the last time I ever saw him in the flesh."

"Where was this?" said Hewlett.

"At his home in northern France," said the old man. "A place called Le Touquet. Do you know it?"

"Of course I know it," said Hewlett. "Le Touquet. It's in the Oise Department."

"It's a department of Pas-de-Calais," said the gypsy. "But don't worry son. It's a mistake any greenhorn geographer could make."

"Might I assume you took full advantage of his absence," said Hewlett.

"I minded his home, if that's what you're getting at," said the gypsy.

"Which probably translates as 'squatted there'," said Hewlett.

"You can translate it how you like," said the old man. "But somebody had to look after the old place."

"What about the great man's possessions," said Hewlett. "What happened to them?"

"He didn't seem to have many," said the gypsy. "There were a lot of books, manuscripts and a few paintings. But I burnt most of those when all the timber ran out."

"You did what?" said the incandescent Hewlett while appearing to freeze momentarily.

"I burnt them," said the gypsy. "I used them to make

[463]

fires."

"You burned some of P.G Wodehouse's masterpieces?" said Hewlett.

"Well Plum used to do it," said the old man. "There was often a shortage of wood. We had to keep warm somehow."

"You're nothing but a Philistine," said Hewlett.

"I'm a Roman Catholic actually," said the gypsy. "At least I used to be."

"What do you mean?" said Hewlett.

"I received the old bell, book and candle," said the gypsy.

"You received what?" said Hewlett.

"I got barred," said the gypsy.

"You got barred!" said Hewlett. "You got barred from the Catholic Church! What the hell for? You didn't get caught stealing collection boxes did you?"

"It was nothing like that," said the gypsy.

"What did you do then?" said Hewlett. "Did you assault a priest?"

"I did something far worse than that," said the gypsy.

"Something worse than assaulting a priest?" said Hewlett.

"I'd say so," said the gypsy. "It's certainly something I've never been able to forgive myself for. The old priest at Sainte-Jeanne d'Arc certainly never forgave me."

"What did you do?" said Hewlett while slowly moving to the edge of his bed.

"I'd rather not say if you don't mind," said the gypsy.

"Why not?" said Hewlett.

"Because I'm ashamed," said the old man. "What I did still gives me sleepless nights. And to this day, I've never confided the whole story to anyone. Apart from that hypocritical, self righteous bastard priest that is."

"Well maybe it's time you did confide in someone," said Hewlett. "Maybe it's time you got your heinous sin off your chest. What did you do?"

"Something I deeply regret," said the gypsy.

"How deeply?" said Hewlett. "Just tell me. Open up. Let

[464]

it go. You'll be surprised how much better you'll feel. What did you do?"

"I sold Wodehouse's dog," said the gypsy.

"Sold his dog!" said Hewlett.

"That's right," said the old man.

"Bloody hell!" said Hewlett. "Did he know?"

"He was in Berlin at the time," said the gypsy.

"Berlin!" said Hewlett. "That's right...he'd been arrested and taken there hadn't he. You inscrutable miscreant. By all the accounts I've read, Wodehouse worshipped that little dog."

"I know he did," said the teary eyed gypsy upon lowering his head. "And I loved it too."

"Rubbish!" said Hewlett. "If you loved the thing, you'd have looked after it. You'd have kept it safe until his master returned."

"I did look after it," said the gypsy. "And I did keep it safe. I shared every meal with it. But then the food ran out. I had nothing to feed it on. It became emaciated. The poor thing would have starved."

"So you sold it," said Hewlett.

"I sold it to two high ranking German officers," said the gypsy. "For a small pittance really. I assumed they wanted it as a pet or even a regimental mascot. I used to watch them playing with it in a nearby park. They were friendly and very reasonable. Quite the gentlemen really. They used to invite me over to their billet from time to time to have drinks. We fell out shortly after."

"Why's that?" said Hewlett.

"They began to suspect I'd stolen something from them," said the gypsy.

"Now there's a surprise," said Hewlett. "And had you stolen something? Had you stolen the dog back? You had, hadn't you?"

"I'd stolen food," said the gypsy. "I was passing their home one Sunday afternoon when I smelt something divine emanating from their open kitchen window. It was freshly baked bread and a roast of some sort . It was incredible. I couldn't resist it. I was starving. I was on

[465]

the brink of collapse. It brought out the opportunist in me. I had to have it."

"So you stole their Sunday lunch," said Hewlett.

"I did indeed," said the gypsy. "And I ate the lot without cutlery, trimmings and without any remorse at all."

"You're lucky you weren't taken out and shot," said Hewlett. "I imagine beef, lamb and pork were in short supply at that time."

"They were," said the gypsy. "But that's not what I'd eaten."

"What had you eaten?" said Hewlett.

"The dog," said the gypsy before once again lowering his head.

"The dog!" said Hewlett.

"I'd eaten Wonder-Wodehouse's dog," said the gypsy.

"Oh dear Lord in Heaven!" said Hewlett. "Oh, Lord have mercy on your soul. That's awful. That's the most hideous and revolting thing I've ever heard. I don't know what to say. You have me almost lost for words."

"I didn't know it was his dog," said the gypsy. "I really didn't . It smelt like any other roasted meat."

"How did you find out?" said Hewlett.

"The German officer's housekeeper told me," said the gypsy. "She told me how she'd begged for the poor creature's life."

"Did she know you'd eaten the dog?" said Hewlett.

"You're joking aren't you," said the gypsy. "I was sleeping with her at the time. She'd have probably slit my throat if she'd have found out."

"I can't believe it," said Hewlett. "I have it on good authority, Wodehouse worshipped that animal as if it was his child. Unless I'm mistaken, he even used to allow the little thing to sit at the dinner table with him."

"You're not mistaken," said the gypsy. "I shared that same old dinner table on numerous occasions."

"Did Wodehouse ever find out about all that?" said Hewlett.

"Not as far as I'm aware," said the gypsy. "I sincerely

hope not. I made sure I wasn't around when he returned."

"What about the rest of his things?" said Hewlett.

"What things?" said the gypsy. "There was nothing left apart from things like old furniture and pots and pans. Just about everything else had been thrown on the fire."

"Jesus Christ!" said Hewlett. "Have you any idea what you've done?"

"I know exactly what I've done," said the gypsy.

"I'm talking about his works of art now," said Hewlett.

"What about those? I studied Wodehouse for 3 years while at college. Every member of my class, hero-worshipped the man. To even touch one of those first editions would have been beyond my wildest dreams. And you set fire to them. You destroyed them. And in doing so, you denied the world them. You probably changed literary history. It's tantamount to sacrilege. I am absolutely mortified. I feel sick to my stomach. Why did you have to tell me all that?"

"Because you insisted," said the gypsy. "And there was a strong possibility you were going to call your friends."

"There still is," said Hewlett. "Unless you vacate this carriage right away."

"I will," said the gypsy. "I'll do that right away sir. And I'm not even going to hold you to that promise of fresh meat."

"Just get out," said an obviously dismayed Hewlett.

"I'm going," said the gypsy while fumbling with his upper coat buttons. "But I want you to know this. I'm not a wicked man. I'd have never sold Plum's dog if I'd known those German officers were going to kill it and cook it. I loved that dog as if it was my own. I love all animals. I've just acquired myself a little puppy that looks a lot like Wonder. It's only a cross breed. But it's a smashing little thing. I've left him sitting under the engine wrapped in a blanket. He's as snug as a bug. I'll fetch him if you want."

"Just leave," said Hewlett.

"As you wish," said the gypsy before heading to the

door, turning around and making an over elaborate salute. "I bid you good day sir."

"What was that meant to be?" said Hewlett.

"What was what meant to be?" said the gypsy.

"Was that meant to be some sort of military salute?" said Hewlett.

"It was yes," said the gypsy. "I was saluting a scholar and a gentleman. I want to thank you for your kindness and excellent hospitality sir."

"You should have just said, 'thank you' and toddled off," said Hewlett. "By the way-what are they? What are those things pinned to your tatty waist jacket?"

"These?" said the gypsy while fumbling nervously. "They're just me medals son. To be honest-they've seen better days. I'm ashamed to say, I've neglected them. They need a right good polish. And the ribbons have seen better days. I keep meaning to have them replaced. I've just never got round to it."

"They're British service medals aren't they?" said Hewlett.

"They are indeed sir," said the old man.

"I thought as much," said Hewlett while smiling wryly. "But they're not yours. They're not your medals are they?"

"They are mine," said the indignant gypsy after taking a short step back.

"They're not," said Hewlett. "I happen to know for a fact they're not."

"Why aren't they?" said the old man.

"Because you told me you'd been a gypsy all your life," said Hewlett. "And if that's the case, you've never had any permanent address. Apart from when you squatted illegally at the Wodehouse property that is. That was during the war wasn't it?"

"It was," said the gypsy before hurriedly removing the medals and slipping them into his right hand coat pocket.

"Which proves you didn't see active service," said Hewlett.

"It does yes," mumbled the gypsy after a short delay.

[468]

"I thought as much," said Hewlett. "You avoided the draft like so many of your clan members, didn't you?"
"I most certainly did not," said the old man. "How dare you accuse me of that."
"I dare to accuse you, because you're a liar," said Hewlett. "You're nothing but a dirty stinking liar. You're a scoundrel. How could you have possibly been called up? You'd have had no fixed abode. Therefore, you'd have had no contact address. Where would the Ministry of Defence send your call up papers-to a particular tree or something?"
"I enlisted," said the gypsy.
"You enlisted!" scoffed Hewlett. "Don't make me laugh."
"I did," said the gypsy. "I enrolled with my three brothers. I swear to God I did."
"I wouldn't bother swearing to God," said Hewlett. "I thought you told me you'd been excommunicated. God won't have anything to do with you now. God knows you for the coward and charlatan you are. I reckon you stole those medals. Let's be honest-nobody earns and receives the same four identical medals. You're a liar. You're a liar aren't you?"
"I'm not a liar," said the gypsy. "I enrolled with my four older brothers, 3 months after Chamberlain announced our country was at war. December 1939, it was. And I'm going to be honest with you son-killing Germans wasn't the attraction. The main reason we enlisted was because we'd been promised a bit of money, 3 square meals a day and a brand new pair of boots each. That seemed to be an attractive deal to us back in those poverty stricken days. After all, the recruitment officer insisted the war would be over in a few months."
"Did you see any action?" said Hewlett.
"None at all, I'm ashamed to say," said the gypsy.
"Why not?" said Hewlett.
"I fell off a transport ship in the middle of the English Channel a couple of hours after we'd set sail for France."

[469]

"That was convenient," said Hewlett.

"It was terrifying," said the gypsy. "It was just fortunate I was wearing a lifejacket. To this day, I blame me brothers."

"Why's that?" said Hewlett.

"Because they got me rat arsed stinking drunk the previous night," said the gypsy.

"Why would they do that when you were going to need every ounce of your wits about you on the front line?" said Hewlett. "Were they imbeciles?"

"They wanted me arrested by the Military Police," said the gypsy. "I was the baby of the family you see. I wasn't quite 16. They wanted me to serve out the war peeling spuds and emptying latrines. They were protecting me. They wanted me out of the way and out of the line of fire."

"How did you end up in Le Touquet?" said Hewlett.

"To this day, I have absolutely no idea," said the gypsy. "I just remember waking up in this really comfortable bed and seeing this smiling man holding a yapping dog that seemed intent on doing me injury."

"Would that be Wodehouse?" said Hewlett.

"It would indeed young man," said the gypsy. "It was Plum. He nursed me back to full health. He told me I'd been knocking at Death's door quite relentlessly. He was an absolute gent."

"Did you not think about making your way to the front line when you recovered?" said Hewlett. "You could have helped your brothers out. Or at least, blasted them for getting you in such a state."

"I wanted nothing more," said the old man. "But I was ill for a hell of a long time. I'd contracted some sort of debilitating disease which had left me unable to walk more than a few yards unaided. The local doctor couldn't fathom it."

"I'd have fathomed it in no time at all," said Hewlett. "It was almost certainly a case of Yellow Belly Fever."

"It wasn't cowardice son," said the gypsy. "I really envied my four brothers. I didn't want to miss out. I

[470]

imagined them fighting side by side and becoming the talk of our little community after the war was over."

"And did they?" said Hewlett.

"They fought side by side," said the gypsy. "But that's about it."

"What do you mean?" said Hewlett.

"The four of them were killed within an hour of their first military engagement," said the gypsy. "And they were never the talk of our little community because people were far too upset to raise the subject of them."

"Oh dear Lord!" said Hewlett. "How awful. How awful. Did you ever find out how they died?"

"According to their war records, they'd volunteered to take out a heavily guarded machine gun post," said the old man. "Which doesn't really surprise me, because they all loved nothing more than a good scrap."

"My God!" said Hewlett after clearing his throat.

"I know I didn't win those old medals son, but I'm still entitled to wear them with pride." said the old man. "And I intend donning them again as soon as I'm out of your way. Do you know what they are by any chance?"

"They're the Distinguished Conduct Medal, unless my eyes deceive me," said Hewlett.

"Very good," said the more than surprised old man.

"My father fought in that same war," said Hewlett. "He was decorated too on a number of occasions. Although getting him to talk about it is almost impossible. He was at Arnhem."

"Was he really!" said the gypsy. "That was no picnic was it son?"

"No picnic at all," said Hewlett.

"What was it Montgomery said about Arnhem?" said the old man. "What was it he said now? Oh bloody hell! My memory's getting worse the older I get."

"He said, 'In years to come, it would be a great thing for a man to be able to say, 'I fought at Arnhem'", said Hewlett.

"That's it," said the gypsy. "That's the one. That's brilliant isn't it. And your father is one of the few who

[471]

can justifiably say that."

"I know," said Hewlett. "One of only a few remaining now. Why don't you put the medals back on. And why don't I try to find you a little bit of polish and a cloth."

"That would be most kind of you," said the gypsy. "Are you sure you don't mind?"

"I don't mind at all," said Hewlett. "And when you've finished doing that, me and you are going to have a good drink. We'll raise our glasses to all medal winning servicemen. How does that sound?"

"It has a nice ring to it," said the beaming gypsy. "My name's Arthur, by the way."

"It's an unexpected pleasure to meet you Arthur," said Hewlett.

The old man had subverted all of Hewlett's preconceptions because despite his shabby appearance and despite his propensity for telling the odd tall story, he had proved to be extremely intelligent, surprisingly articulate and as interesting and enthralling as most bestselling thriller writers. For the next hour, Hewlett was to sit back and gorge upon fascinating anecdote after fascinating anecdote like a captivated child at bedtime. And just like that captivated child, he continued to want to hear more. That was until he stopped to question something that from time had caught the light and had caused him to shield his eyes.

"What's that Arthur?" he asked while pointing to an unusual piece of jewellery that was hanging around the old man's neck.

"This?" replied the gypsy. "It's just an old pendant. I was given it by a Rumanian Count for setting his leg in a splint after he'd taken a nasty fall on Tryfan."

"They're not diamonds are they?" said Hewlett.

"I wish they were," said the gypsy. "If they were diamonds, I wouldn't be dressed like this and asking for fresh meat. They're paste. That's a sort of glass to you and me. It's a nice thing. It's said to give the wearer certain special powers."

"You don't believe that do you?" said Hewlett.

"I keep an open mind Richard," said the gypsy. "Do you not believe in things of the supernatural bent?"

"Not really," said a puzzled looking Hewlett while stroking his chin. "But that's not to say I'm not just a little bit intrigued by the concept."

"What's the matter?" said the gypsy. "You've gone all suspicious and accusing looking again. Have I offended you in some way?"

"You haven't offended me at all," said Hewlett. "My demeanour's changed because you've just addressed me by my Christian name for the first time."

"Is that a problem?" said the gypsy. "Have I been over familiar?"

"Not at all," said Hewlett. "It's just that.....I don't remember telling you my name. In fact-I know I haven't told you my name. How do you know Arthur? How do you know my name?"

"I don't know to be honest," said the gypsy. "It just came to me when I was handling the pendant. Once again, I'm sorry if I've caused you offence."

"You haven't caused me any offence," said Hewlett. "It's just creepy that's all. Would you do me a favour please. Would you do something for me?"

"What's that?" said the gypsy.

"Would you take hold of the pendant again and see what you come up with," said Hewlett.

"Come up with!" said the old man. "What do you mean, 'come up with'?"

"I'm referring to what you said about the pendant having supernatural qualities," said Hewlett.

"I don't understand," said the gypsy.

"You called me by my first name," said Hewlett. "And there's no way in the world you could have known my first name. Even my so-called friends refer to me by my surname. They have done since I first attended school."

"Which is Hewlett," said the gypsy.

"Whooooo!" said a spooked but fascinated looking Hewlett before rising and heading to the far side of the room. "What's going on here Arthur? Bloody hell!

[473]

How's that even possible?"

"I don't know," said the gypsy. "I suppose I could have overheard somebody address you while I was keeping a watchful eye on your goings on."

"I doubt it," said Hewlett. "Not with the way the wind's been howling. This is strange this is. This is very, very strange. Are you a Romany gypsy by any chance."

"I am yes," said the gypsy. "I've got pure Romany blood. Why do you ask?"

"Because I've heard the Romany gypsies are the real deal."

"Real deal!" said the gypsy.

"They're apparently endowed with special gifts," said Hewlett. "My mother told me that. She was a massive believer in the supernatural and the occult. What about yourself Arthur. Do you boast any special powers?"

"Some," said the gypsy after a moment's contemplation.

"Like what?" said Hewlett.

"I can tell when someone's behind me without them making a sound or saying a word," said the gypsy.

"I can do that," said Hewlett. "In fact, most people can. That's just another of our untapped senses as far as I'm concerned."

"I agree," said the old man. "But I can tell who they are. In theory, I could create a photo fit of them."

"Do they have to be in the room?" said Hewlett. "For instance, if I gave you something to hold that belonged to a member of my family, could you tell me something about them?"

"Almost certainly," replied the old man. "I don't even need anything to hold. Just give me your right hand and close your eyes. And don't worry Richard-your watch will still be on your wrist when I've finished."

"My watch is in a safe deposit box at the back of the mailroom," said Hewlett before immediately finding his hand released as if it was scorching hot "What the hell! What's the matter Arthur?"

"Nothing," said the gypsy before lowering his head and making his way to the door. "I really should be on my way."

"Why's that?" said Hewlett while discreetly barring the old man's exit. "What's the matter Arthur?"

"Nothing's the matter," said the twitching gypsy while easing up his collar. "I just need to leave."

"You saw something didn't you Arthur?" said Hewlett. "You had some sort of vision when you were holding my wrist didn't you?"

"I don't know," said the gypsy.

"You do know," said Hewlett. "What did you see Arthur? Please don't leave me wondering like this. I wouldn't do it to you. What did you see?"

"I saw a tall, dark handsome man with a huge grin on his face," said the gypsy.

"That could be a lot of people I know," said Hewlett.

"He's closely related to you," said the gypsy. "I saw you under the same roof. I saw you riding ponies together."

"That's likely to be my brother," said Hewlett.

"It was your brother," said the gypsy while entering a sort of trance. "It was very definitely your brother. He's in trouble Richard. He's in a great deal of trouble."

"Why's that?" said Hewlett. "Why's that Arthur?"

"I see him holding a knife," said the gypsy. "The image doesn't seem right. It's ironic. It doesn't seem to fit together. He's holding a knife while grinning manically. I'm going to give you his name now. Could it be Calvin? No, not Calvin. Kelvin. No.....Kevin. That's right Kevin."

"What about our Kevin?" said Hewlett. "What's happening Arthur? Tell me. For goodness sake, tell me."

"He's been hiding something from you," said the gypsy.

"Hiding what?" said Hewlett.

"Something that would appear to be sinister," said the gypsy.

"What do you mean?" said Hewlett.

"He's got a lot of blood on his hands," said the gypsy.

"Blood on his hands!" said Hewlett.

"That's right," said the gypsy. "Is your brother Kevin the aggressive type? Has he got a violent temper?"

"Not at all," said Hewlett. "He's extremely placid. He's well known for being placid. Our Kev wouldn't harm a fly."

"Well I see him with blood on his hands," said the gypsy. "A hell of a lot of blood. Try to think. Has somebody offended him lately?"

"I don't think so," said Hewlett. "Kev's very popular. Although...."

"Although what?" said the gypsy.

"He told me something quite recently," said Hewlett.

"Told you what?" said the gypsy.

"He told me that his wife Michelle had got a new area boss," said Hewlett. "He's a really good looking bloke by all accounts. Smartly dressed, highly amusing, well perfumed and all that. He's the talk of the office apparently. All the young girls fancy the pants off him."

"Do you think Michelle's fallen under his spell?" said the gypsy.

"She wouldn't allow that to happen," said Hewlett. "She'd never do that. She worships our Kev. But he did tell me quite recently how the smarmy bastard had made a play for her during a weekend convention in a Chester hotel. That's right. He was livid. To be honest-I've never seen our Kev so angry. I actually urged him to confront the bloke. Oh God! Oh dear Lord in Heaven! He hasn't has he? He hasn't gone and hurt somebody has he?"

"I couldn't possibly say," said the gypsy. "I suppose any reasonable man can snap at some point or other. All I know is that I can picture him with lots of blood on his hands. He's not a surgeon is he?"

"No," said Hewlett. "It would be great if he was. That would explain it. That would explain everything. That would be fantastic. That would explain the knife and all the blood you saw."

"What does he do?" said the gypsy.

"He's a butcher," said Hewlett while continuing to pace

the floor. "He's a Master butcher like me."

"Really!" said the old man.

"It's true," said Hewlett.

"Would that explain my vision of him with blood on his hands?" said the old man."

"What!" said Hewlett after coming to a sudden halt.

"Do you think that might explain the blood I envisaged?" said the gypsy before handing Hewlett an old leather bound wallet.

"I suppose it would yes?" said Hewlett. "What's this? What's this Arthur? Is this mine? What are you doing with my wallet?"

"It was on the floor by your bed," said the gypsy.

"On the floor!" said Hewlett before peeling the item open and immediately letting it drop to the floor as if it was electrified. "Bloody hell!"

"What's the matter?" said the old man.

"I've been robbed-that's what's the matter," said Hewlett. "There was about £500 in that wallet. £500! Wait a minute.....wait a bloody minute.....Oh no Arthur. Oh don't tell me that Arthur. You haven't have you? You haven't taken my money have you?"

"Finders keepers," said the old man.

"Never mind 'finders keepers'," said Hewlett. "There's no such legitimate law. You hand back every penny of that money or you'll find yourself before a local magistrate first thing in the morning. Or would you prefer me to call my friends? That might actually be the better option. That would resolve the matter so much quicker. Is that what you'd like me to do Arthur?"

"I'd like you to calm down and get a grip," said the old man. "And just accept the well established concept of finders keepers, losers weepers."

"I will not," said the livid Hewlett. "And I never will. I don't believe in it. It's theft as far as I'm concerned. Give me my money Arthur? Give it back right this very minute."

"I haven't got it," said the gypsy.

"What do you mean?" said Hewlett. "What do you

mean, you haven't got it? Give it back or there's going to be hell to pay."

"It's under your pillow," said the old man.

"It's what?" said Hewlett before racing over to his bed and tossing aside his pillow. "It's not...it's not here. Give it back I tell you. Don't play games with me Arthur. I'm not one to be trifled with."

"It's under that pillow," said the old man while pointing to the adjacent bed."

"But that's not my bed," said Hewlett before very slowly peeling back the second pillow to reveal a bulging old sock. "That's the Professor's bed."

"How was I to know?" said the old man. "Is the money there?"

"I assume so," said Hewlett.

"Take a look," said the old man. "Count it. You'll find it's all there."

"I'm going to do the gentlemanly thing and take your word for it," said Hewlett before discarding the dirty old sock into a waste bin and quickly stuffing the wad of notes into his left trouser pocket.

"That's very decent of you," said the gypsy. "And very trusting too. Who's Julie, by the way?"

"Never you mind," said Hewlett.

"I'm sorry," said the old man. "Is she a sore point?"

"That's none of your business," said Hewlett.

"Who are the people on the photographs?" said the old man.

"That's nothing to do with you either," said Hewlett.

"I don't mean any harm by it son," said the old man. "I'm just trying to make polite conversation. I often find it helps pass the day."

"Which photograph were you referring to?" said Hewlett.

"The one outside the butcher's shop," said the old man. "I recognise a younger version of you. Is that your shop?"

"It's the family business," said Hewlett. "That's me, my aforementioned knife wielding maniac brother Kev and my father."

"The hero of Arnhem," said the gypsy. "Your father Tom."

"How could you possibly know that?" said Hewlett. "I didn't tell you my father's name. Is that more evidence of your special Romany gypsy powers?"

"The names of those posing for the photograph are scrawled on the back," said the old man.

"Of course they are," said a blushing Hewlett after a short delay. "Of course they are. How infantile of me. Bloody hell! Special Romany powers! You crafty old rascal. You old rapscallion. I feel a bloody fool now. You knew all along didn't you? You knew me and my brother were butchers all along. 'Blood on his hands' you claimed.. That's a good one that is Arthur. You knew our Kev's hands would often be stained with blood. Why didn't I see that coming? Damn it! Damn it! You had me thinking he'd murdered his wife's boss. You've done me up like a kipper haven't you Arthur? I've a good mind to throw you to the wolves."

"You know about the wolves do you?" said the gypsy.

"I was referring to some of our less civilized club members," said Hewlett. "Why Arthur? Are there wolves roaming this area?"

"I told you before-there are all sorts of wild creatures roaming these parts," said the old man. "Although I'm not sure they're wolves. I think they're just a large pack of stray dogs.

"They'll still represent a formidable menace," said Hewlett.

"You'll be fine as long as you remain on board the train and wait for help to arrive," said the old man.

"That's just it," said Hewlett. "Help's not going arrive. At least, not for some considerable time."

"What makes you think that?" said the old man.

"Our initial rescue party failed miserably," said Hewlett. "That's why two of the lads have decided to head out tomorrow morning."

"Head out where?" said the gypsy.

"I don't know exactly," said Hewlett. "I wasn't in on
the planning. Towards the coast I imagine. I think
somebody had a map of some sort. I believe they were
able to identify a small bay "
"They need to travel inland," said the gypsy while
heading over to the window.
"Why's that?" said Hewlett.
"Just take my word for it," said the old man. "In fact,
they want to head in any direction but the way I'm
facing now."
"But why?" said Hewlett. "They reckon that bay will
have a community around it."
"It does," said the gypsy. "But their chances of
reaching it are remote."
"Why's that?" said Hewlett.
"Because of the nature of the terrain," said the old man.
"There are hundreds of ponds, potholes and small lakes
between here and the coast. They're unlikely to see
some of them until it's too late. But that's not the worst
thing your friends are going to have to contend with."
"What do you mean?" said Hewlett. "Are you talking
about the wild animals?"
"I'm talking about two crazy, murderous old bastards,"
said the gypsy.
"What two crazy old bastards?" said Hamill after
slipping into the carriage unannounced. "He's not
talking about Hulmey and Hilly is he? Who's your new
boyfriend Hewlett?"
"His name's Arthur," said Hewlett.
"Arthur hey!" said Hamill before taking a couple of
steps back to consider the old man's bedraggled
appearance. "And what exactly are you doing here
Arthur? Do you represent a bespoke tailors in Savile
Row? Have you come to measure us all up for new
suits?"
"He got caught in the storm," said Hewlett. "I've told
him he can shelter here until it blows over."
"You had no right to tell him that," said Hamill.
"I had every right to," said Hewlett. "I'm humane and

[480]

he's a fellow human being."

"He's a human being that stinks to high hell," said Hamill. "And to be honest-I don't like the look of him. He looks a bit shifty to me. Have you thought of asking him how he managed to get on board our train?"

"I invited him on board," said Hewlett. "He can be of help to us. He knows this area like the back of his hand. All he asks in return is a bit of fresh meat and something strong to drink. That's right isn't it Arthur?"

"It is son yes," said the gypsy. "It's the weather you see."

"Has the weather affected your hearing?" said Hamill.

"My hearing!" said the old man. "No son. I can hear perfectly well as it happens."

"Then answer my initial question," said Hamill. "What two crazy old bastards were you referring to a minute or so ago?"

"They're a couple of gnarly, bitter and twisted old soldiers," said the gypsy. "They own a big old house directly due east of here. It was used as a hospital during the second world war. And then, for some reason, it became a nuthouse. It's a bad place. A very bad place."

"Is that very bad place likely to have a telephone?" said Hamill.

"I don't know," said the gypsy.

"What *do* you know?" said Hamill.

"I know it's only about 9 miles from here as the crow flies," said the gypsy.

"Could you draw us a map?" said Hamill.

"I wouldn't think of it," said the old man. "You don't want to go there son. No reasonable man should go there. You're not planning to go there are you son?"

"I wouldn't think of it," said Hamill. "But two of my closest friends are. They're making plans and getting kitted out as we speak."

"But that's madness," said the gypsy while making his way back to his seat.

"Why is it?" said Hamill.

[481]

"Because it's well known as a place to be avoided at all costs," said the gypsy. "You should tell them to stay well away from it."
"And they will," said Hewlett. "I'll tell them about it. I'll tell them to give it a wide berth."
"That won't be as easy as you might think," said the gypsy.
"Why not?" said Hamill.
"Because of the way the land sweeps," said the gypsy.
"I don't get you," said Hewlett.
"The area surrounding the old house is like a huge lavatory pan," said the old man. "Anyone who gets lost around here, ends up getting flushed there. It's uncanny. It just happens naturally. It's almost impossible to avoid landing on the crazy old bastard's doorstep. Unless you know where you're going that is."
"You know where you're going," said Hamill. "You could lead them. We might even be able to scrape some decent money together and pay you for your trouble."
"That's right," said Hewlett. "You'll be able to buy as much fresh meat as you want then."
"You've got no chance," said the gypsy. "I'd rather starve. I wouldn't do it for all the money in the world. I'd be leading those lads to their certain deaths."
"Why's that?" said Hamill. "What's wrong with the place? Is it meant to be haunted or something?"
"I wouldn't know about that," said the gypsy. "It wouldn't surprise me if it was haunted though. It's certainly got a reputation as a house of horrors. The place should have been demolished years ago."
"Why's that?" said Hamill.
"Because too many people who call there, are never seen again," said the old man.
"Well maybe they liked the place and decided to stay," said Hamill.
"I suppose it's possible," said the gypsy.
"It's more than possible," said Hamill. "And anyway-how would you know who comes and goes there? You're constantly on the move aren't you? I'd have

[482]

thought you'd never be in one place long enough to
know what goes on."
"That hasn't stopped me hearing stories about the place,"
said the gypsy.
"Well that's what they probably are," said Hamill.
"Stories. Stories made up by backward people like
yourself. People who've got nothing better to do but
gossip."
"Or stories put about by the owners to keep hawkers and
other undesirables away," said Hewlett.
"That's a good point that is Hewlett," said Hamill.
"That's actually an age old ploy that is."
"You can believe what you want," said the gypsy. "Just
don't say you weren't warned."
"We won't," said Hamill. "We'll take everything you've
said on board. But I'm going to believe what I want to
believe. And I believe there's a house somewhere out
there, not too far away, that might just have a telephone
or some means of transport."
"That's your prerogative son," said the old man. "But if
it was up to me, I'd tell your friends to take a chance and
head in the opposite direction."
"Is that where the nearest community is?" said Hewlett.
"Not really," said the gypsy. "But it takes the dangerous
old house out of the equation."
"How much longer would the other route take ?" said
Hamill.
"That's hard to say," said the old man.
"Well give us a ball park figure," said Hamill.
"A what!" said the gypsy.
"Give us an estimate," said Hamill. "Give us a rough
idea. How much longer would it take our lads to find a
settlement if they headed west instead of east?"
"A couple of days," said the old man.
"A couple of days!" said Hamill. "A couple of fucking
days! Are you sure you're not the one that's crazy. For
Christ's sake-there's a house out there that can be
reached in a matter of hours. It doesn't make any sense
to go another way."

"It makes perfect sense if you want your friends to stay alive," said the gypsy. "You must listen to me. Please listen to me. I'm begging you both to listen to me. That house should be avoided. Too many people who have called there have never resurfaced. A local bobby with almost 40 years experience on the beat told me that."

"Have you ever been inside the place?" said Hewlett.

"Not on your Nelly," said the gypsy. "The very thought of it has me awash with sweat. The locals often talk about weird creatures that abide in the surrounding trees and a seven foot giant that patrols the grounds."

"Oh for crying out loud," said Hamill.

"That's what the locals say," said the old man.

"But don't you think that's likely to be superstitious nonsense?" said Hewlett. "With the greatest respect Arthur-you know what country folk can be like. They're full of strange tales."

"What happened to the son of a friend of mine wasn't superstitious nonsense," said the gypsy. "I can assure you of that."

"Is he one of those who went missing after visiting the place?" said Hewlett.

"Yes and no," said the gypsy. "He was one of the few that managed to make it out of there. But he was never the same again."

"What do you mean 'never the same'?" said Hewlett.

"He'd changed beyond all recognition," said the gypsy. "It was as if he'd been broken in some way. All his spirit had been sucked out of him. He never spoke another word to anyone. He was a big strapping lad was young Malcolm. He'd boxed all over the country at scores of gypsy fairs. I only ever saw him knocked down the once. Every other fight went the full distance."

"What distance would that be?" said Hamill.

"A whole day," replied the gypsy.

"Which means he was almost certainly punch drunk," said Hamill.

"It's possible," said the gypsy.

"How long had he been missing?" said Hewlett.

[484]

"About three days according to his father," said the old man. "He was discovered cowering almost naked under a dead gorse bush. The wood cutter who found him said he'd been whimpering like an abandoned kitten while pointing in the direction of the old house."

"Had he been abused at all?" said Hewlett.

"He had bruises where no young man should have bruises, if you know what I mean," said the old man.

"That's awful!" said Hewlett.

"It's not that awful," said Hamill. "That sort of thing goes on in prisons and borstals all the time. As the old boy said-he's as tough as old boots. I bet he's fine now. I bet he's over it all now."

"He's completely over it," said the gypsy. "He blew his head off with a shotgun a few months later. He's buried in a corner of a little cemetery not too far from here."

"Oh dear!" said Hewlett. "That's sad. That's very sad that is Arthur. What did the police have to say?"

"The police did nothing," said the gypsy. "What could they do? They had nothing to go on. The lad couldn't speak. So he couldn't explain what had happened to him. To be honest-I think the police were too scared."

"Too scared to do what?" said Hamill.

"Too scared to approach the owner," said the gypsy.

"Rubbish!" said Hamill.

"I think it's dreadful," said Hewlett. "But, once again-with the greatest respect Arthur-our friends are only going to ask if they can use the telephone. They don't even have to step inside the place. What harm could that do? How could that possibly incite someone to use violence against them?"

"In normal circumstances, it wouldn't," said the gypsy before rising from his chair, dropping to his knees and taking Hewlett firmly by both wrists. "But look at it this way-my friend's son was a gentle giant. He was inoffensive. Everyone loved him. He'd never been known to upset anyone in his life."

"So why did he call there?" said Hamill. "Was he an idiot? Was he one of those straw munching country bumpkins? He must have heard the rumours regarding the house."

"I'd have thought so too," said the gypsy. "But he might have been desperate. He might have got lost in the dark. He might even have been injured. And, for all anyone knows, he mightn't have even called there."

"What do you mean?" said Hewlett.

"He might have been abducted," said the gypsy.

"Nonsense!" said Hamill. "Two old men couldn't possibly abduct anyone."

"Their manservant could," said the gypsy. "He's the biggest man I've ever seen. He's capable of anything. Some say he's deranged too. Listen to me.....please listen to me and listen to me good."

"We will when you stop talking shite," said Hamill.

"I'm talking perfect sense," said the gypsy. "The people that live in that house aren't reasonable human beings like us. They don't abide by the same rules as us. They've been a law unto themselves for a very long time and they're unlikely to change. I'm imploring you now- for God's sake, tell your two friends to abandon their plan to go east. Tell them they'd be better off going the opposite way inland or following the track the way the train's facing. That's it...bloody hell!.....what was I thinking? They should just follow the track north."

"Until they come to what?" said Hewlett.

"A smallholding," said the old man.

"How far away is this smallholding?" said Hamill.

"About 60 miles," said the gypsy.

"Jesus Christ!" said Hamill.

"That's not a long way in the grand scheme of things," said the gypsy. "They can make it. The people are very accommodating. They've given me many a hot meal and a dry place to kip over the years. And what's more, they've got a good and dependable truck as well. It's one of those Land Rover jeep type of things. Are you hearing me son? Did you hear me? Or should I spell it out for you?...I know somebody who's got a truck."

"But it's 60 bloody miles away, across snow covered,

treacherous terrain," said Hamill.

"I know it is," said the gypsy upon taking Hewlett by the upper arms. "But it's doable Richard. And at least your mates will know exactly which way they're going. They certainly won't have any dangerous frozen ponds and lakes to contend with. What do you think son?"

"I can't help agreeing with you," said Hewlett. "Although I think it's ultimately going to be up to our Chairman and his Club Secretary. They're the ones who have most to lose. I'll go and explain the pros and cons and let them decide."

"You're going nowhere," said Hamill after shoving Hewlett back onto his bed and putting his back against the door. "And you're not saying one fucking word about all this. Do you hear me Hewlett?"

"I hear you loud and clear," said Hewlett. "But I don't like it. I don't like it one little bit. Bloody hell Hamill. You've just heard what this man said-the house should be avoided. Nobody should go near it. We have an obligation to warn Hilly and Hulmey. For goodness sake-we can't let them risk their lives."

"They're not going to be risking their lives," said Hamill. "This senile old bleeder's been talking a load of tripe. You're still wet behind the ears Hewlett. But I can see right through him. He's probably got traps laid around that house. I'll bet you my pound to your penny, he's a poacher. He doesn't want his traps discovered. You're a poacher aren't you Arthur?"

"I'd much prefer the term 'hunter'," said the old man.

"You're a no good poacher," said Hamill. "And the snow's come down and covered your traps. That's why you haven't had any fresh meat for a while."

"Alright-I'll admit this much...I'm not averse to the odd bit of poaching," said the gypsy while shifting his feet nervously. "I do lay the occasional trap. But that's not the reason I wanted to warn you about the old house."

"It is," said Hamill. "It's the only reason you want to steer us clear of the house. And I reckon you're not just a poacher. I reckon you're a sneak thief too?"

[487]

"Now that's something I won't hesitate to deny," said the gypsy.

"Really!" said Hamill. "Then explain what you're doing here again."

"I've already told you-I invited him," said Hewlett.

"You didn't invite him," said Hamill? "Liar, liar, pants on fire Hewlett. What are you doing here old man?"

"I found one of the outside carriage doors open," said the gypsy.

"That's better," said Hamill. "That's much better. You found a carriage door open."

"That's the God's honest truth, so strike me dead" said the gypsy.

"And you took that as an invitation to board our train did you?" said Hamill. "Even though you haven't got a ticket."

"Neither have we," said Hewlett.

"You shut your mouth," said Hamill. "This poor old bugger can't get a word in edgeways."

"I just needed shelter from the gathering storm," said the old man. "You wouldn't begrudge me that would you?"

"I would, as it happens," said Hamill. "And I also begrudge you anything you've managed to pilfer during your time on board."

"I've pilfered nothing son," said the gypsy.

"He's stolen nothing," said Hewlett.

"He's managed to break into one of your suitcases," said Hamill.

"That wasn't me," said the gypsy.

"That wasn't Arthur and you know it," said Hewlett.

"For God's sake Hamill-stop being so bloody belligerent. He's a decent old man."

"He's a tramp who's likely been on the make," said Hamill.

"He's not been on the make at all," said Hewlett. "He found and returned my wallet, if you must know."

"Did he really?" said Hamill. "Where did he find it?"

"On the floor by my bed," said Hewlett.

"Is that right?" said Hamill.

"It is yes," said Hewlett.

"Had you misplaced it?" said Hamill.

"Not really," said Hewlett. "I hadn't had time to misplace it. I'd been too busy recovering fur coats and boots from dead mountain rescue men."

"That's interesting," said Hamill. "So what you're saying is this-and correct me if I'm wrong-your gypsy beggar friend found a wallet that you hadn't even lost. A wallet that you'd have found anyway had you got to the carriage before him."

"I don't understand," said Hewlett.

"Never mind," said Hamill. "Was it all there-by the way?"

"Was what all there?" said Hewlett.

"The money," said Hamill. "Did you count it?"

"I don't need to count it," said Hewlett while patting his bulging trouser pocket. "I trust the man."

"Count it," said Hamill.

"I don't need to," said Hewlett.

"Count the fucking money!" said Hamill. "Take the money out of your arse pocket and count every last note."

Over the next few minutes, and undeniably because the imposing Hamill had perched himself only inches from his left shoulder, Hewlett found himself fumbling with and losing count of the money and only when he had taken a pace back to give himself some extra space was he able to succeed with, what should have been, under normal circumstances, a relatively simple task.

"Well!" said Hamill after once again putting his powerful back to the carriage door.

"Well what?" said Hewlett.

"Is it all there?" said Hamill.

"Of course it is," said the gypsy.

"I'm not talking to you," said Hamill. "Is it all there Hewlett?"

"I think so," said Hewlett before quickly stuffing the notes back in his pocket. "It's all here yes. It's all

[489]

accounted for."

"I told you," said the gypsy. "I took nothing."

"You're lying," said Hamill. "And you're lying too Hewlett. I can tell by your face. You've gone the colour of boiled shite."

"It's you," said Hewlett. "You've been cramping me. I can hardly breathe."

"It's nothing to do with me cramping you," said Hamill. "You've changed colour because you've just suffered a serious shock to your system. Admit it Hewlett-that money's wrong isn't it? Some of it's missing isn't it?"

"None of it's missing," said the gypsy.

"You keep your fucking mouth shut," said Hamill. "What's wrong Hewlett? What are you suddenly sweating for?"

"I don't know," said Hewlett.

"It's all there isn't it?" said the gypsy.

"It's not Arthur-no," said a despondent Hewlett.

"There you are," said Hamill.

"But that can't be," said the gypsy. "I put every last penny in that old sock."

"How much Hewlett?" said Hamill. "How much of it has that thieving bastard taken?"

"I can't say for certain right now," said Hewlett.

"You can and you will," said Hamill. "Don't make me force it out of you Hewlett. How much is missing?"

"£50," said Hewlett before lowering his head.

"Nice one!" said Hamill.

"But it's not possible," said the gypsy. "I took all the money out of your wallet and transferred it to my old sock. Have you checked the wallet Richard? Have you checked all the compartments thoroughly?"

"There's nothing left in the wallet," said Hewlett. "Apart from some photos and several bank cards."

"Turn your pockets out," said Hamill.

"I'll do no such thing," said the gypsy. "My word has always been my bond."

"Turn your fucking pockets out," said Hamill. "What are you worried about? If there's no money in your pockets, you're in the clear."

"But there is money in my pockets," said the old man.

"How much?" said Hewlett.

"I'm not sure," said the gypsy. "There's some loose change and a few notes."

"How many notes?" said Hamill.

"Five," replied the old man.

"In what denominations?" said Hamill.

"What do you mean?" said the gypsy.

"What notes are they?" said Hamill. "Are they fives, are they tens, are they twenties?"

"They're tens," muttered the gypsy.

"There you are," said Hamill while simultaneously clapping his hands. "I told you Hewlett. I told you didn't I? I told you his sort couldn't be trusted. He probably thought you wouldn't count it until he was well on his way."

"Oh Arthur," said a massively disappointed Hewlett. "What on Earth did you do that for? If you needed money, you only had to ask me for some."

"But I don't need money," said the gypsy before reaching into his trouser pocket and producing 5 crumpled ten pound notes. "This is just money I've been given to buy some chickens on behalf of my clan. That's where I was going when the storm suddenly started closing in."

"Give it here," said Hamill.

"But it's not my money to give," said the gypsy.

"I know it's not," said Hamill before taking the old man by the scruff of the neck and leading him to the door. "I want you out of here. I want you a hundred miles from here within the hour. I don't like you. I don't like you one little bit. You're nothing but a liar and a worthless thief. Adolf Hitler was right about you lot. There's no place for the likes of you in a modern, law abiding society. And the only reason I'm not going to beat you to a pulp is because I want you fully conscious while you listen to my warning. Do you understand me Arthur?"

[491]

"I do sir yes," replied the old man.

"And are you listening to me Arthur?" said Hamill while urging the agitated old man down the steps of the train.

"Yes sir," said the gypsy.

"I didn't hear you," said Hamill. "Are you listening to me?"

"I'm listening sir, yes," said the old man.

"That's good," said Hamill while prompting the old man forward. "Because it's very important you understand my next set of instructions. Is that clear?"

"Perfectly clear," said the old man. "What are they?"

"I want you to vanish and never be seen again," said Hamill.

"That's not a problem sir," said the gypsy. "I promise, you'll never see me from this day forward."

"That's good," said Hamill. "And furthermore, and this is the most important aspect of my warning. You must promise me you'll never interfere in any of our forthcoming plans. Do you understand what I mean by that Arthur?"

"I think so sir," said the old man.

"What do I mean?" said Hamill.

"You don't want me to approach your two friends after they've left the train," said the gypsy.

"You're not as daft as you look," said Hamill. "Do you know why you mustn't approach them?"

"I do yes," said the gypsy. "It's because....."

"It's because the consequences will be grave if you do," whispered Hamill while scanning right and left for any sign of Hewlett or any of the other passengers. "I've already killed one man during this excuse for a jolly boy's outing. And I won't hesitate to add your scum bag name to my growing list of victims. Is that understood Arthur?"

"Perfectly," said the old man while adjusting his collar which, for several minutes, had been used by his tormentor as a leash. "I'll just get this little fella here and

I'll be away."

"What little fella where?" said Hamill while watching the old gypsy stoop down and remove a small bundle of fur from beneath the engine. "That's not a fucking rat is it?"

"It's Nipper," said the gypsy. "It's me puppy. His mum died about six week ago. I think she had distemper. He's a smashing little thing."

"He is isn't he," said Hamill. "He's fantastic. You conniving old bugger. You crafty old sod. You've done this deliberately haven't you Arthur?"

"Done what deliberately son?" said the gypsy.

"Produced a bloody puppy to melt my dark heart," said Hamill. "You'll be kissing babies next like the American Presidential candidates do. Did Hewlett tell you?"

"Tell me what sir?" said the gypsy.

"About my love for dogs?" said Hamill.

"Do you know what-I think he might have done," said the gypsy. "Do you own a dog yourself?"

"I've got two Golden Receivers," said Hamill.

"Golden Receivers!" said the gypsy. "That's nice. What have you called them?"

"Erm....do you know what....their names escape me right now," said Hamill. "The wife named them. I never get involved in things like that. I love them. And I envy them too."

"Why's that?" said the gypsy.

"They've got so much vitality compared to me," said Hamill. "I've never been able to resist a puppy. Can I have him? If I promise to always love, protect and cherish him, would you give him to me Albert?"

"I'd rather keep him if it's all the same to you," said the increasingly perplexed gypsy while allowing the excited pup to lick his face. "I'm very fond of him. He's my very good boy."

"I understand," said Hamill. "And by the way-I want to apologise for my previous overzealous behaviour. It's just that I wanted a reason to warn you off. I wanted

[493]

you out of the way. I didn't want you interfering with
our plan. But don't worry yourself Arthur-our two
intrepid adventurers graduated from the Merseyside
school of hard knocks. They're both ex Royal Marines.
They can look after themselves. They'll be fine.
Although I do fully appreciate your warnings and
concerns."

"And I fully appreciate your apology," said the gypsy
before thrusting out his right hand. "My father always
said, 'it takes a real man to admit his mistakes'."

"Thank you," said Hamill. "Is he trained? Is the little
rascal trained at all?"

"He's very clean for one of such a tender age," said the
gypsy.

"Have you allowed him off the lead yet?" said Hamill.

"I'm a bit scared to-to be honest," said the gypsy.

"Scared of what?" said Hamill.

"Scared of him running off," said the old man. "He's a
bit frisky."

"Nonsense," said Hamill before gently taking the
puppy, placing it on the ground and kissing it on the
nose. "He won't run off. You've just got to be firm
with the little fella. I'll show you."

"If it's all the same to you, I'd still prefer it if you gave
him back," said the gypsy. "It's dangerous out here. He
could bolt after a rabbit and slip over the side of the
bridge. Please, give him here. He's easily spooked. You
don't know him like I do."

"How long have *you* known him?" asked Hamill.

"Since the moment he was born," said the gypsy. "He
was very weak. He was the runt of the litter. I nursed
him day and night. I had to bottle feed him for 6 weeks.
He was just skin and bone. It didn't look as if he was
going to make it."

"Has he had his jabs?" said Hamill.

"What jabs?" said the gypsy.

"His injections," said Hamill. "Surely you've heard
about puppy inoculating."

"I haven't actually," said the gypsy. "None of my other

[494]

puppies have ever needed injections."

"They all will have done," said Hamill before slapping the cowering animal's nose, taking him by the neck and heavy handedly shoving him into his coat pocket. "Injections are essential in order to prevent disease spreading. What you are, is an inconsiderate dog owner Arthur. That's why I'm going to have to do the sensible thing and confiscate him."

"Don't do that son," said the gypsy. "He's very often the only company I've got."

"What was that yelp?" said the groggy Hewlett while making his very deliberate descent from the train ladder. "What's going on Arthur?"

"He's taken me puppy," said the bitterly distressed gypsy. "He's been a bit rough with him to tell you the truth. I think he might have hurt his little neck. He doesn't seem to be moving."

"He's not moving because I've got him under control," said Hamill. "I've managed to relax him. I think they call it dog whispering."

"Give the puppy back Hamill," said Hewlett.

"I will in time," said Hamill. "Or I might keep the pathetic thing as part payment for the money his master stole from you."

"He didn't steal any money," said Hewlett. "It suddenly dawned on me when I was putting the cash back in my wallet...I gave Waggers £50 to top up the petrol tank."

"Rubbish!" said Hamill.

"It's true Hamill," said Hewlett. "I'm not just saying it. It's absolutely true."

"It might very well be true," said Hamill. "But I'm still going to hang on to the pup for the time being."

"Why for goodness sake?" said Hewlett.

"I'll tell you why," said the gypsy. "He's worried I'll tell your friends what I know about the old house. He's concerned I'll tell them to avoid it."

"Is that right?" said Hewlett.

"The thought had crossed my mind," said Hamill.

"Well you don't have to worry about that now," said

Hewlett. "You get on your way Arthur. I'm going to tell them myself. And I'm also going to tell them about that little dog he's stolen. Let's see how much authority you have then Hamill."

"You're going to have to be fully conscious to do that," said Hamill before suddenly lunging at the retreating Hewlett and pinning him to the ground.

"Get off me," spluttered Hewlett while struggling desperately to break free from Hamill's powerful grasp. "I'm warning you Hamill. I'll have you up in court for this."

"You're going to have to be alive to do that," said Hamill before delivering two vicious punches to either side of Hewlett's nose. "It's make your mind up time Richard. How many blows do you want to take?"

"Leave the lad alone," said the gypsy. "You're going to kill him. Look at him. He's going to slip off the bridge if you're not careful."

"Is he really?" said Hamill. "Well, there's a thing. Wouldn't that be awful? And the interesting thing is-nobody's going to know that it wasn't an accident. Do you realise that Hewlett?"

"I'd know," said the gypsy. "I'd testify to that effect."

"Yes, but you don't count," said Hamill. "You're just a shit stain on the landscape. You'd be about as welcome in a court of law as an outbreak of Anthrax."

"He's more of a man than you'll ever be," said the struggling Hewlett.

"Is that right?" said Hamill. "Then why's he crying."

"He's upset," said Hewlett. "You've taken his puppy. You've taken his companion and best friend."

"Only for tonight," said Hamill. "He can have the scrawny thing back tomorrow as long as he heads west."

"He's just a baby," said the gypsy. "He'll never find me in weather like this."

"He's not much of a dog then, is he," said Hamill. "I thought dogs were meant to be excellent trackers. Now then Hewlett-let's get back to you-how strong is your desire to maintain your good looks?"

[496]

"Very strong," said Hewlett while doing his utmost to wedge his left foot under the nearest rail.

"Well let's come to some sort of gentleman's agreement shall we," said Hamill.

"And if I refuse?" said Hewlett.

"You might find yourself at the bottom of this bridge," said Hamill. "Or alternatively, I could always leave it to the other passengers to punish you."

"Why would they want to punish me?" said Hewlett.

"For any number of reasons," said Hamill. "You've been a naughty boy Richard."

"In what way?" said Hewlett.

"You've been hiding certain facts from your fellow travellers," said Hamill.

"What facts are they?" said Hewlett.

"Facts about the Professor's medication for one thing," said Hamill.

"How would you know about that?" said Hewlett.

"I'm naturally inquisitive," said Hamill. "I make it my business to know about things that have a direct bearing on my health and well being."

"Did the old boy tell you?" said Hewlett.

"In a manner of speaking," said Hamill.

"Why haven't you told the others?" said Hewlett.

"Leverage," said Hamill. "I always like to keep a few cards up my sleeve. It's a policy that's always served me well in the past."

"So if I've read this right, you want me to say nothing about the dangers associated with the old house in return for you saying nothing about the lack of medication-is that right?" said Hewlett.

"Clever girl," said Hamill. "Or we can both come clean. I'll admit my misdemeanours and you can tell them how you allowed them to wrongly believe their fellow club members were receiving or would eventually receive the treatment that would ease their suffering. Or we could just draw a line under this whole unsavoury business and say nothing at all. Think about it Hewlett. The men are going to hate me for what I've done, but let's be honest-

[497]

most of them already do. I can live with that. I've lived with being unpopular most of my adult life. Your position's very different. They're going to want to string you up for what you've withheld from them. What do you think?"

"I don't think you've left me much choice," said Hewlett.

"So shall we draw that line?" said Hamill.

"Alright," said Hewlett after wiping a snake shaped trickle of blood from the side of his mouth. "The only thing is-how am I going to explain all my cuts and bruises?"

"That's simple," said Hamill. "Tell them you were attacked by a gang of thieving gypsies. Tell them you found them going through your belongings. There's at least some element of truth in that."

"I suppose there is," said Hewlett resignedly.

By the time the still unsteady and badly dazed Hewlett had been helped back to his feet, the gypsy had stopped protesting and his previous demeanour had been replaced by a look of utter contempt. That is when the wind dropped and two purplish black clouds the size of Japanese oil tankers suddenly appeared directly above the train.

"Here's that storm I was telling you about Richard," said the gypsy.

"Are you still here?" said Hamill before scooping up a handful of snow and shaping it into a tight and perfectly formed ball. "I thought I'd made myself abundantly clear Arthur. You're not welcome. You have to leave. You have to go west young man."

"I'm going," said the gypsy while backing away cautiously between the treacherously slippy tracks. "But hear me well young man. For you, life as you've previously known it, is a thing of the past."

"Is it really?" said the smiling Hamill after feigning to hurl the snowball.

"It most certainly is," said the old man. "Something very sinister is going to come your way in the not too

[498]

distant future."

"You don't scare me," said Hamill. "You can send whoever you want. You can send your punch drunk mate if you want. Oh I'm sorry-he blew his mushed up brains out didn't he."

"He did yes," said the gypsy. "He escaped his tortuous existence. But there'll be no such escape for you. You're going to have to live through every miserable second of yours. Your life will never be the same."

"Ooh, I'm scared," said Hamill while ever so slowly and surreptitiously reducing the gap between himself and the retreating gypsy.

"Just let the man go Hamill," said Hewlett while brushing the snow from his arms and shoulders. "You've had your fun. Let him go."

"Why for God's sake?" said Hamill. "The fun's just starting as far as I'm concerned. Didn't you hear what that cheeky bastard just said? I think he's put some sort of gypsy curse on me. And anyway-I'm more than a little bit curious now."

"Curious about what?" said Hewlett.

"I want that cheeky fucker to tell me why he thinks my life will never be the same," said Hamill.

"Wouldn't you want to know that Hewlett?"

"It's because you've stepped over a very significant mark," said the gypsy. "You've done something completely and utterly unacceptable. You've violated a long held gypsy code. You've been extremely cruel to an innocent."

"What's an innocent?" said Hamill.

"An innocent is an animal or person that, for any number of reasons, can't stand up for themselves," said the gypsy.

"Don't talk shite," said Hamill. "I've been good to the thing. I'm going to give it a better life. You couldn't have looked after it properly. You can't even look after yourself properly."

"You've been cruel to an innocent," said the gypsy. "And in doing so, you've brought eternal misery upon

[499]

yourself and your family."

"What does that mean," said Hamill. "Am I going to be persecuted with boils or a plague of locusts or something?"

"No...you're going to be visited by the Pig Men," said the gypsy.

"Pig men!" laughed Hamill.

"That's right," said the gypsy while continuing to reverse inch by inch. "They have a very unique way of dealing with wicked people like you."

"Do they really?" said Hamill. "I'm intrigued. Why don't you stick around and tell me about it?"

"That would spoil the surprise," said the gypsy. "You'll see. You mind what I say young man. You'll see."

"And my family?" said Hamill. "What'll happen to them? Do they get a visit from these pig men?"

"They won't suffer like you," said the gypsy. "They'll just get colder and colder and colder and colder. From this day forward, no matter what they do and no matter how hard they try, they'll never feel warmth as they've known it ever again."

"What!" said Hamill.

"You heard me," said the gypsy.

"What did you say?" said Hamill. "What did you just say about the cold Arthur?"

"You heard me," said the gypsy before disappearing into an eerie and menacing looking mist which had slowly been descending since the puppy had let out its last anguished and pitiful yelp.

"Don't you toy with me old man," shouted Hamill who, through his increased urgency to bridge the gap between himself and the surprisingly fleet of foot gypsy, had found himself floundering on his back. "Don't you toy with me Arthur. Come back. Come back this bloody minute. You can have your dog back."

"The little dog's dead," said the gypsy.

"What!" said Hamill.

"My dog died several minutes ago," said the gypsy.

"Oh Christ!" said Hamill after carefully removing the

limp and lifeless puppy from his coat pocket and hastily
placing it on the ground.

"Oh Jesus!" said Hewlett.

"Are you satisfied now?" shouted the gypsy.

"Of course I'm not satisfied," said Hamill. "I'm sorry
I'm so very sorry."

"You're going to be," shouted the gypsy.

"Come back Arthur," said Hamill.

"Bye bye," came a low and mournful voice from
beyond the mist.

"Let him go Hamill," said Hewlett.

"I won't let him go," said a quivering and distressed
looking Hamill before reaching out and bringing Hewlett
down on top of him. "Did you hear what that little fucker
said about the cold?"

"He's just upset that's all," said Hewlett. "He didn't
mean anything by it."

"Oh he did," said Hamill. "Oh he most certainly did.
You don't understand Hewlett. Can't you see?"

"Can't I see what?" said Hewlett.

"It's happening all over again," said Hamill.

"What's happening all over again?" said Hewlett.

"Don't you remember?" pleaded a trembling Hamill.
"Don't you remember what Tommy Mac told us about
the old trinket pedlar he upset some years ago?"

"Vaguely," said Hewlett. "An old gypsy woman wasn't
she?"

"That's right," said Hamill. "A nasty, bad minded old
hag. She cursed him for chasing her away. She was the
reason he had to move house. He loved that house. Now
it's going to happen to my family. "

"Nonsense," said Hewlett.

"It's not nonsense at all," said Hamill. "You heard what
that old bastard said. He's going to make sure my house
never gets warm again. I'm telling you Hewlett. Call
him for me. For God's sake-tell him to come back. Tell
him I didn't mean to kill his dog. Tell him I'll get him
another one. Oh dear God! My missus hates the cold.
She'll never survive. Please call him Hewlett. He might

come back for you. He likes you. You were able to strike up a friendship. Call him Hewlett. Tell him I won't harm him. Tell him I'll give him his money back. For pity's sake Hewlett-do something. Bring him back."

"It's too late," said the unimpressed Hewlett while carefully easing Hamill's fingers from his right arm. "He's gone. I'm afraid he's gone Hamill!"

CHAPTER TWENTY
ONE DOLLAR COIN

B ecause of his agreement with Hamill and the possibility that there was still someone or something menacing on the prowl, Hewlett had barricaded himself in his room the previous evening and had it not been for his intense hunger, that's where he might have chosen to remain until a rescuer arrived at the scene or things had changed for the better in some way. Hamill had also distanced himself from the main body of the group but unlike his co conspirator, he had been extremely restless and had spent much of the evening and the first few hours of the morning pacing the corridors, particularly the one adjacent to Hewlett's sleeping carriage. Everybody else had chosen to remain in the dining carriage where, because of Blackie's continuing resentment regarding the treatment of his uncle prior to his tragic death, the atmosphere had been as terse as ever and quarrels had been breaking out frequently. That is probably the reason Hewlett's entrance had been met with unusual fuss and warmth.

"How are you lad?" said Steadman while politely making way for Hewlett to take his usual seat. "We hear you've had a nasty experience."

"You could put it like that," sighed Hewlett.

"Are you alright now?" said the Chef after handing the new arrival a mug of freshly made tea.

"I'll live," said Hewlett. "I've just got a belter of a headache."

"I bet you have," said the Chef. "That's one hell of a shiner."

"You need to hold a lump of steak against it," said Steadman.

"That's right," said the Chef.

"You need to do no such thing," said the Professor.

"Why's that?" said Steadman. "I've always been led to believe that was the best remedy for a black eye. A piece of raw steak draws the bruise out doesn't it?"

"It's a myth," said the Professor. "It's utter nonsense. It's a very stupid thing to do in reality."

"Why's that?" said Steadman.

"Because there's likely to be bacteria like E. coli in meat," said the Professor. "And that could cause a very nasty infection."

"What should he do then?" said the Chef.

"Ice it," said the Professor. "Wrap some ice in a clean tea towel and hold it against the affected region for short periods."

"Well how did the 'steak on the eye', myth come about?" said Steadman.

"That's what I'd like to know," said the Chef.

"It's because meat was always kept very cold," said the Professor. "Don't forget-having ice at one's disposal is a relatively modern concept."

"That's true," said Steadman. "My mum didn't get her first fridge until the early seventies."

"Neither did mine, come to think of it" said the Chef. "That's incredible that, isn't it? What did we do to keep food fresh until then?"

"We had salt, cold pantries and cellars," said the Professor. "And we bought most of our food on a daily or twice weekly basis."

"Of course we did," said Steadman. "I'd forgotten about that. There were no big supermarkets in those days were there?"

"None at all," said the Professor.

"Lucky for you, Hamill was close at hand," said the Chef while continuing to serve drinks.

"It was wasn't it," said Hewlett.

"Did the thieving bastards get away with anything?" said Steadman.

"Nothing of any value or importance," said Hewlett. "Just a couple of bottles of wine, I think."

"Does anyone know how they managed to get on board?" said the Professor.

"I've no idea," said Steadman.

"Me neither," said the Chef.

"Hamill reckons they got in through one of the outer carriage doors," said the Chef.

"Which should have been secured, if certain people would have done as they were told," said Blackie.

"I know," said Steadman. "I thought we had those doors soundly blocked off. This place is starting to leak like a bloody sieve."

"Well at least we know they won't try that again in a hurry," said the Chef.

"Why not?" said Hewlett.

"Because Hamill kicked the shit out of them," said the Chef. "Didn't you know that?"

"I didn't," said Hewlett. "I must have been out for the count at that juncture."

"You must have been," said the Chef.

"He knocked seven bells out of them," said Steadman. "He still had some of their blood on his clothes when he got back here."

"I hope you all realise you're never going to hear the last of it," said the Chef.

"I don't doubt it," said Hewlett.

"Did he say how many of them there were?" said the Professor.

"Three in all," said the Chef. "And big strapping lads they were too."

"And one of them had an enormous, ferocious dog the size of a Shetland pony," said Steadman. "Which might just explain one or two things."

"It might," said the Chef.

"What's the status of the carriage door now-has it been secured?" said Hewlett.

"Probably not," said Blackie while returning from the kitchen after checking on the Chef's untypically slow progress.

"It's sorted," said Steadman. "I've jammed a crow bar across it. Harry Houdini would struggle to break in now."

"That's good," said the Chef. "You can rest a bit easier

now Hewlett. Are you ready for something to eat?"
"I've never been looking forward to one of your breakfasts more," said Hewlett.
"Do you think you're going to be up to helping us search for the missing engine driver?" said Steadman.
"Not just yet," said Hewlett. "I've got a really bad headache. Let me see how I feel a bit later."
"The missing train driver's dead," said Blackie.
"How would you know that?" said Hewlett.
"Gut instinct," replied Blackie.
"You can sod off with your gut instinct," said Steadman. "You're getting like Hulmey for your negativity. I like to believe the man's still alive. And I'm going out again as soon as that bastard wind dies down. Which reminds me-has the weather improved or is it just my imagination?"
"What do you mean?" said Hewlett.
"I haven't noticed the train rocking for a while," said Steadman.
"That's a point," said Hewlett. "Neither have I."
"Which means it'll almost certainly happen now you've decided to mention it," said Blackie before snatching a magazine from the seat of an empty chair and settling back down.
"And I suppose that also means, it'll be my fault for mentioning it if we go hurtling down the side of the bridge later tonight," said Steadman. "Is that what you're saying Blackie?"
"You shouldn't tempt providence," said Blackie.
"You need to take someone with you if you're going outside," said the Chef.
"I intend to," said Steadman.
"Why don't you ask Hamill," said the Chef. "He seems to be the only one who's had a decent night's sleep."
"You couldn't be more wrong," said the Professor. "He was diligently patrolling the corridors most of the night."
"And it wasn't even his shift," said Blackie.
"I actually slept like a baby," said Steadman. "Although I did have a funny dream."

"How funny?" said the Chef while donning a clean apron. "Is it worth sharing? Come on Steadman-we could all do with a good laugh."
"I don't mean funny in the humorous sense," said Steadman.
"What do you mean then?" said Hewlett.
"It was strange," said Steadman.
"Whereabouts were you in this dream?" said the Professor.
"Back home in our attic bedroom in Ilford Avenue," said Steadman. "We were planning a tip run. I was going through a box of junk and family keepsakes. I remember looking at some old school photos and cringing at the way I had my hair. I looked a right tart. Then, all of a sudden, I found myself transported back in time."
"To when?" said the Chef.
"It must have been about 1973," said Steadman. "My last year at school. It was raining and miserable as usual. It always seemed to be raining and miserable when I was at school. I hated bloody school. I didn't see the point of it........ I was behind the bike sheds with two of my mates. We were smoking. I already smoked like a chimney by then. I'd actually been smoking for three years by then."
"Was this the time somebody threw a load of bangers inside the bike shed and one of your mates peed his kecks?" said the Chef.
"No," said Steadman. "This was another time. This was when we found someone snooping on us."
"Who was it?" said the Chef.
"This lick arse third year pupil," said Steadman. "You know the sort. Every school seems to have one or two of them. The type that hangs round the caretaker and takes messages from classroom to classroom."
"Did he blow you up to the head?" said the Chef.
"He didn't get the chance," said Steadman. "Me and me mates grabbed him and ensured he didn't."
"How did you manage that?" said the Chef.
"We made him smoke the rest of our ciggies," said

Steadman.

"I hope you're proud of yourself," said Blackie. "That sort of thing's considered bullying nowadays."

"It serves the little bastard right for spying," said the Chef.

"I'd say so too ordinarily," said Steadman. "But the poor bugger suffered an asthma attack shortly after and nearly died."

"Bloody hell!" said the Chef.

"He couldn't get his breath," said Steadman. "We didn't know what to do. It was terrible. It was bloody terrible. The next day, we were ordered to the headmaster's room to explain ourselves to his mother. She was frail and looked really old compared to my mum. She seemed more scared of us than we were of her."

"Why do you think that was?" said the Chef.

"Because of our size, I imagine," said a teary eyed Steadman. "Me and me mates were all well over 6 foot by then. She was almost apologising for having us summoned. I remember staring at the hem of her coat."

"Why's that?" said the Chef.

"Because I couldn't look her in the eyes," said Steadman. "I couldn't bring myself to. It was an old tatty looking coat. The lining was hanging down in places. It was made of something resembling tartan. But I don't imagine for one second, it was real tartan. And she was wearing these huge boots. She was wearing these huge boots...she was wearing these.....these huge, great big boots."

"I think you've established what she had on her feet," said Blackie.

"Shut up Blackie," said the Chef. "The man's struggling."

"They were men's work boots," said Steadman. "They were much too big for her. She had newspaper stuffed inside them."

"What would that be for?" said Hewlett.

"To make them fit better or keep water out," said the

[508]

Chef. "It's what very poor people used to do Hewlett.
Did her son recover?"
"He did yes," said Steadman.
"Were you caned?" said Hewlett.
"She wouldn't have it," said Steadman. "She told us
that our punishment would be the guilt we would carry
during the next couple of weeks or more. But she was
wrong. She was so bloody wrong. I still carry that
burden of guilt with me today. I can't help seeing the
tatty coat and the ill fitting boots."
"Is this a recurring dream?" said the Professor.
"That part is," said Steadman. "But last night's dream
had an extra instalment."
"What do you mean?" said the Professor.
"I was carried off at the end of last night's dream," said
Steadman. "The lad had died in last night's dream and I
was carried off."
"Carried off by who?" said the Chef.
"I don't know for certain," said Steadman. "They were
shadowy figures."
"What do you mean, 'shadowy figures'?" said the
Professor.
"They're hard to describe," said Steadman. "You'd
have had to have seen the movie 'Ghost'."
"'Ghost', did you say?" said the Professor.
"I've seen it," said the Chef.
"Was that the one with Patrick Swayze?" said Hewlett.
"And Demi something or other," said the Chef. "She
was really fit."
"Demi Moore," said Steadman. "It's me and my wife's
favourite film. We've watched it hundreds of times. It's
the only film that's ever made me cry. I just can't help it.
Especially when he's led away at the end to the
accompaniment of that haunting soundtrack."
"And that happened to you in your dream, did it?" said
the Chef.
"Not exactly," said Steadman. "The likeable Swayze
was taken away by the good spirits. I was dragged away
kicking and screaming by the nasty, menacing ones. The

same ones who had taken away the villain in the movie."
"Do you fear the same thing will happen to you?" said
the Professor. "Is that what this is all about?"
"I think there's a part of me that feels I was never
punished enough for what I did to that unfortunate boy,"
said Steadman.
"That's interesting," said the Professor.
"Maybe you should stop watching the bloody film," said
Blackie. "I don't understand people like you Steadman.
Why do people do that? Why do people keep watching
something if it keeps making them whinge?"
"I have my reasons," said Steadman.
"Explain them," said Blackie. "I'm all ears."
"It reminds me of my old fella, for one thing" said
Steadman before reaching into his trouser pocket and
retrieving an old but well preserved coin. "He bought
me the video one Christmas as a stocking filler. 1993, I
think it was."
"What's the coin?" said Hewlett.
"It's his golf ball marker," said the Chef. "Or should I
say-it's what Steadman uses as a golf ball marker."
"It's probably illegal," said Blackie. "It probably
infringes some long established rule or other."
"It infringes no rules," said Steadman.
"It's American, isn't it?" said the Professor after leaning
forward to examine the item with the left and stronger
lens of his spectacles.
"It's a one dollar coin," said Blackie. "I should
know-I've had to pick the thing up for him often
enough."
"I don't understand," said the Professor.
"You need to partake in match play golf to understand
what that means," said Blackie.
"Where did you get it?" said Hewlett.
"I'm coming to that," said Steadman.
"It's not exactly rare," said the Professor.
"I never claimed it was," said Steadman. "It belonged to
my dad."
"Did he leave it to you?" said the Chef.

"It was slipped under my bedroom door, the night he died," said Steadman.

"Really?" said the Chef. "By who?"

"To this day, I honestly don't know," said Steadman.

"It must have been your dad," said Blackie. "Why would it be anyone else?"

"My father had died almost two hours earlier," said Steadman.

"I'm sorry," said Blackie.

"Could your mum have done it?" said the Chef.

"She might have done," said Steadman. "But she's always claimed otherwise whenever pressed on the subject. And my mother's never been one for telling fibs."

"You're close to your mum aren't you?" said the Chef.

"That would be an understatement," said Steadman. "I worship the ground she walks on. She's the typical slippers by the fire, doting mum with classic old fashioned values. Do you know, during the 25 years I lived with her, prior to marrying Barnie, she never once allowed me to leave the house before making sure of two things."

"What were they?" said the Chef.

"I had a good breakfast inside me and we'd hugged and made up if we'd had one of our rare disagreements," said Steadman.

"What about other members of your family," said Hewlett. "Is it possible one of them slipped the coin under your door?"

"Nobody else was in the house," said Steadman. "There was just me and my mum. My dad had been gravely ill for some time. He'd been in and out of hospital. We had a feeling he was going to go that night. That's why I'd locked myself in my bedroom. I didn't want to be there at the precise moment he drew his last breath. I don't think I could have coped with witnessing something like that."

"Are you sure you didn't imagine the coin thing?" said the Chef. "Are you sure your dad hadn't just dropped

the thing in your room at some point? I say that
because-didn't something similar happen in that film
you've just been talking about?"

"It did yes," said Steadman. "Something very similar."

"What was that?" said the Professor. "And what was
this film about?"

"A ghost," said Blackie. "The clue was in the title."

"Take no notice Professor," said the Chef. "He's still
on one. I'll tell you what happened...It's a love story
with a difference. The main character, Sam Wheat is
murdered by a drug fuelled thief within the first twenty
minutes of the film."

"But for some reason, he was able to return as a ghost,"
said Hewlett. "Nobody really knows why. It's probably
not that important to know why."

"It's because he wasn't ready for the afterlife," said
Steadman.

"And he wanted to protect his lovely wife from the man
who had murdered her husband," said the Chef. "A
man that was still on the scene."

"I see," said the Professor.

"The problem was Professor-even though Sam had
returned in the guise of a ghost, his wife couldn't see
him," said the Chef. "Only this whacky black medium
called Oda Mae Brown could see him. And try as hard as
she could, she couldn't convince his wife that her
husband had come back to help her."

"So Sam had to find a way to make his wife believe the
woman," said Hewlett.

"That's where the coin thing comes in," said the Chef.
"Because, in the movie, Sam Wheat, the ghost
eventually manages to slide a coin under his wife's front
door."

"An Indian Head penny, to be precise," said Steadman.

"What was the significance of the coin?" said the
Professor.

"It belonged to the main man-the man who'd been
murdered-Sam Wheat-her husband," said the Chef. "He
and his wife had found it in a jar while they were

[512]

renovating their new home."

"That particular coin was quite rare as well," said Steadman.

"I get you," said the Professor. "At least, I think I do."

"You have to appreciate something Professor," said Steadman. "Every member of my family, firmly believe in the concept of reincarnation. My auntie was a locally renowned spiritualist. She used to conduct monthly séances in her living room. They were always well attended, I can tell you. My old man had often told me that if he should ever pass away unexpectedly, he'd do his best to make contact with me from the other side."

"Is that what you think the appearance of the coin signified?" said the Professor.

"I like to think so," said Steadman. "I'm going to try to do the same when I eventually pass away."

"And I'm going to haunt and torment the lot of you," said Blackie.

"I thought you'd already started," said the Chef.

"Started what?" said a suspicious and unusually dishevelled looking Hamill after entering the room and heading over to the serving hatch.

"We've been talking about a strange dream that Steadman had last night," said the Chef.

"Lucky for Steadman," said Hamill. "I've not slept a bloody wink. I've been up all night patrolling those freezing cold corridors."

"We know that," said the Chef.

"And don't think for one minute your diligence went unnoticed," said Steadman.

"That's right," said the Chef. "Would you like a bit of breakfast sir?"

"I'd like a lot of breakfast," said Hamill while scanning the room with a very definite air of suspicion. "Have the rest of you eaten?"

"We're just about to," said Steadman.

"You've just usurped the wounded Hewlett in the original pecking order," said the Chef.

"I should think so too," said Hamill before taking his

customary chair. "It's about time I got some credit from you lot. Did the lads get away alright?"

"As well as can be expected," said the Chef.

"What was the weather like for them?" said Hamill.

"Favourable for once," said the Chef.

"Favourable!" said Blackie. "You've got to be having a laugh Chef. It was minus 10 degrees when those poor buggers set out."

"I know that," said the Chef. "But at least the wind had dropped and made getting down off the bridge so much easier."

"And they were in good spirits were they?" said Hamill.

"I wouldn't go as far as to say that," said the Chef. "Our kid was close to fouling his trousers. He'd been off and on the khazi for almost an hour before they set off. I thought he was going to withdraw from the venture at one time. He must have thrown up half a dozen times during the early hours."

"How long do you think it's going to be before we can expect to hear something?" said Hamill while meticulously arranging his cutlery.

"I've no idea," said the Chef. "What do you think Professor?"

"It's hard to say," said the Professor. "If everything goes well and the weather holds, and they don't encounter any hostile gypsy robbers and they don't fall into any frozen ponds and they don't get lost and they don't come across any packs of ferocious hounds or get eaten by a starving big cat or bear."

"How long Professor?" said the Chef after sighing impatiently.

"I'm sorry," said the Professor. "That was very rude and flippant of me. Let me see.....I suppose, if things fall into place and all those potentially problematic things remain inconsequential, we might get a welcome little knock on the door some time tomorrow afternoon."

"No earlier?" said Steadman.

"I wouldn't have thought so," said the Professor.

"Never mind," said Steadman before rising to stretch his

back. "It'll give me time to go looking for that missing train driver."

"You're going nowhere until you've had a decent breakfast down you," said the Chef.

"Alright mum," said Steadman.

"And don't be going out there alone," said Hamill. "As the Professor just alluded to-there are dangerous people and animals out there. Wait until Tommy gets up. Take that mad bastard with you. Where is the lazy bugger, by the way? He's usually shaved, showered and talking shed loads of shite by now."

"Tommy's gone," said the Chef.

"Gone!" said Hamill. "What do you mean, 'gone'?"

"Tommy went with the others," said Steadman. "Didn't you know?"

"Of course I didn't know," said Hamill. "I wouldn't be enquiring as to his whereabouts if I knew he'd gone. When was all this arranged?"

"Some time last night," said the Chef. "I genuinely thought you knew."

"He said he couldn't allow a couple of lightweights like Hulmey and Hilly to make such an arduous journey alone," said Steadman while watching a wide eyed and crimson faced Hamill head slowly over to the window with his left hand clamped firmly over his mouth.

"I've got to be honest Hamill-I'm delighted Tommy's gone with them," said the Chef. "He was absolutely right. Hilly and our kid wouldn't have been able to cope on their own. They'd have been back here within a heartbeat if anything snarled at them."

"Or pulled faces or called them a pair of sissies," said Blackie.

"Sod off you," said the Chef.

"Did they happen to say which way they were planning on heading?" said Hamill.

"Why?" said Steadman. "You're not thinking of going after them are you?"

"I just want to know which way they were intending to go," said Hamill.

[515]

"Is that important?" said the Chef.

"I'd say it's very important," raged Hamill before spinning round and hammering his fists against the nearest table. "Which fucking way did they go?"

"That way," said the confused and momentarily rattled Chef while pointing to the window and beyond. "They were heading east towards a small bay of some sort. They reckon there'll be houses dotted around it. They think there'll be a little fishing community there. What's the problem Hamill?"

"Yes, what's up Hamill?" said Steadman. "Only yesterday, you couldn't wait for them to set off."

"I've had a change of mind since," said Hamill before returning to his chair and cradling his head between his hands. "For fucks sake! I don't believe this."

"What's the matter Hamill?" said the Chef. "Do you know something we don't?"

"I know loads of things you lot don't," said Hamill. "Bloody hell! I suppose that's what being decent and caring does for you."

"What do you mean?" said Hewlett.

"What do I mean?" said Hamill. "What do I fucking well mean! I'll tell you what I mean Hewlett. If I hadn't been up all night making sure the likes of you were safe, I'd have been able to spend a bit of time in here with those three lads. Which means, I'd have known what they were up to and which direction they were intending to go."

"But you knew what direction they were intending to go," said Steadman.

"I knew no such thing," said Hamill. "I knew what direction young Anthony was intending to go."

"What's the matter Hamill?" said the Chef. "You've got me worried now. Have you got something you want to share with us? Did those gypsies tell you something?"

"Yes-I mean no-I mean yes.....Not in as many words," said Hamill.

"What did they say?" said the Chef. "I'm sorry to press you like this Hamill-but something simply doesn't add

[516]

up here. Not so long ago, you told us those gypsies had fled with their tails between their legs. Now, it seems they're still a live danger."

"They are still a danger," said Hamill. "They're very much a danger. But not necessarily to us. I think they're going to go after the lads."

"Why would you think that?" said the Chef.

"Because I saw them pointing east and making gestures," said Hamill.

"When was this?" said Steadman.

"When was this Hamill?" said the Chef.

"When they eventually reached the bottom of the bridge and came back into view," said Hamill. "I imagine they must have felt safe then."

"Could you recognise any of the gestures they were making?" said the Chef.

"Only the one," replied Hamill.

"Which was what?" said the Chef.

"The all too familiar back handed, slit throat gesture," said Hamill.

"Oh Christ!" said the Chef before making his way to the window.

"Well let's just be thankful Tommy Mac's gone along," said Steadman.

"Yes, let's do that," said Hamill. "Let's do that shall we. In the meantime, if anyone wants me, I'll be in my room catching up on some much needed lost sleep."

"Don't you think you should be helping us look for the missing train driver?" said Steadman.

"It's not my shift," said Hamill. "I did the graveyard shift."

"You did that voluntarily," said the Chef. "What if we insist upon you helping?"

"That's right," said Steadman. "What if we all make you come along?"

"Keep dreaming Steadman," said the exiting Hamill. "I'm still to meet the man who can successfully enforce his will on me."

CHAPTER TWENTY ONE
DEAD IN THE WATER

Despite the highly encouraging fact the temperature had risen by just over ten degrees, the journey across the narrow bridge had been every bit as difficult as was initially predicted. That was because nature had damned the three man party with the most dreadful visibility imaginable and a violent and unpredictable wind that would arrive in gusts which resembled mini explosions. It meant that within no time at all, after releasing the rope which had been their umbilical cord since alighting the train, the trio of wary adventurers had become separated, disorientated and ultimately, one man short.

"Is he dead?" said the slowly retreating Chairman upon watching Tommy Mac drop to his knees and rest an ear on the stricken Club Secretary's chest. "I don't think so," replied Tommy. "But he soon will be if we don't get him out of his soaking wet clothes." "Bloody hell Tommy," said the Chairman. "He must have plunged right through the ice. How the hell did he manage that? Look at it. That ice must be at least ten inches thick."

"He fell from about a hundred feet," said the breathless Tommy while easing the first of the unconscious Club Secretary's arms out of his coat sleeve. "I'm surprised he's still in one piece to be honest."

"He's going to be a cripple isn't he?" said the Chairman. "He's going to be a cripple for the rest of his life, isn't he Tommy?"

"We don't know that yet," said Tommy. "Did you see him slip?"

"I did yes," replied the Chairman. "I was right next to him. I couldn't hold him. It all happened so quick. One second I had him, the next I was grasping thin air. I just heard a scuffle and a yell. He's not going to die is he? He's not going to die is he Tommy?"

[518]

"I don't know," said Tommy while continuing to undress the Club Secretary. "But he'd probably have more chance of surviving if you pulled your shit together and helped instead of standing around discussing his life expectancy."

"I'm sorry," said the Chairman before drawing an enormous breath. "I'm sorry Tommy. What do you want me to do? Do you want me to help you undress him?"

"I want you to look for somewhere we can shelter," said Tommy.

"Like where?" said the Chairman while struggling to peer through a thick, pea soup-like mist that was almost strangulating.

"Like a line of trees or bushes," said Tommy.

"A line of trees or bushes!" said the Chairman. "Why would there be trees and bushes here?"

"Because we're in the fucking countryside," said Tommy. "Just head away from the bridge. You should still be able to see it above the mist. And for fuck's sake-don't you go falling through the ice."

"Oh Christ yes," said the Chairman. "I forgot we were standing on ice."

"Find somewhere Hulmey," pleaded Tommy. "Find somewhere and find somewhere quick or your mate will be dead or in a coma within no time at all. This is your time to shine fella. This is the hour."

For the next thirty minutes, the Chairman searched frantically for something that would provide shelter and although much of that period had been spent turning small circles and trying to regain his feet, he eventually came across the remains of a small boathouse which, through a lack of any natural protection and years of violent gales, had developed a pronounced lean to its left. Reaching it while carrying a dead weight had been a massive endeavour however and as a result, both bearers were physically shattered by the time they had propped the stricken and barely conscious Club Secretary up against the most stable of the four remaining walls.

[519]

"How is he?" said the Chairman after finally regaining enough strength to speak.

"Barely conscious but alive," said Tommy. "Pretty much the same as us. Now then-when you've got your breath back, try to find something that'll burn."

"Like what?" said the Chairman.

"I've always found dry wood works," said Tommy. "You could start by dismantling what's left of that old jetty. Use the driest stuff. Use the stuff that hasn't been under water for years. And watch it doesn't collapse from under you. I don't want to be nursing the two of you. Have you brought any spirits?"

"What do you mean, spirits?" said the Chairman.

"Alcohol," said Tommy.

"I've got a flask of brandy," said the Chairman. "Do you want me to give Hilly a drink?"

"I want you to pour it over one of your spare shirts," said Tommy.

"I've only brought one extra one," said the Chairman.

"Pour the brandy over the fucking shirt," said the exasperated Tommy. "Then cover it with the smallest bits of tinder. The stuff that's dry but rotten. Have you got any paper by any chance?"

"I haven't-but....." said the Chairman.

"But what?" said Tommy.

"There's Hilly's ledger," said the Chairman.

"What!" said Tommy. "Are you telling me Hilly brought his club ledger with him?"

"I did," said the Chairman.

"What the hell for?" said Tommy.

"Because, as Chairman, it's my responsibility to look after all the books at the close of every active club day," said the Chairman.

"Jesus!" said Tommy. "You committee members never cease to amaze me. How could bringing that ledger be a priority at such a pig of a time in our lives? Get it torn up. Use every single page if you have to. Particularly the page that proves I'm behind with me subscriptions. Now, shape yourself Hulmey. This isn't a game of football. You can't go off at half time if you're feeling your hamstring. Your mate's in serious trouble here."

The Chef had been absolutely right in his remark to Hamill during breakfast. The two original members of the expedition had indeed needed Tommy Mac, somebody who wouldn't flinch when faced with an extreme dilemma. In reality, his ability to remain calm under pressure had not only saved the Club Secretary's life, but had probably saved his own and the Chairman's too. However, unlike his best friend Hamill, Tommy wasn't the type to bask in his newly found importance and use it as a means to demean his only fully conscious fellow traveller.

"How did you manage that?" said the Chairman while edging closer to the welcome blue and red flames. "It wasn't happening for me. I was about to throw in the towel."

"A fire needs oxygen," said Tommy. "You were actually starving it. That's ironic really isn't it?"

"What is?" said the Chairman.

"The fact that the fire and Hilly were in need of oxygen almost at the same time," said Tommy.

"I suppose it is," said the Chairman. "Have you ever done that before?"

"Done what before?" said Tommy.

"Administered CPR to someone," said the Chairman.

"Is that what it's called?" said Tommy.

"Do you mean you don't know?" said the Chairman.

"I don't," said Tommy.

"How did you know what to do then?" said the Chairman.

"I saw somebody doing it on one of those TV hospital programmes," said Tommy. "I forget what the show was called now. It'll come to me in a minute."

"It's not important," said the Chairman. "The important thing is-you knew what to do. Do you think he'd been under the water long?"

"It depends what you mean by long," said Tommy while proceeding to massage the Club Secretary's purple, slab-like feet. "I wouldn't have thought so. I know this much though-he did well to pull himself up and out. I wouldn't have thought he had that sort of strength."

"It's just another notch on my fuck up belt," said the Chairman before tossing another couple of handfuls of dry twigs on the fire.

"What makes you say that?" said Tommy.

"Because I should have made contingency for one of us slipping," said the Chairman.

"You weren't to know the wind was going to suddenly pick up as violently as it did," said Tommy.

"Maybe not," said the Chairman. "But I should have insisted on the three of us being roped together."

"We'd probably all be dead if you had," said Tommy. "Now stop beating yourself up. You're beginning to bore me."

"I can't help it," said the Chairman. "I've hardly put a foot right since Tommy Weir died and I was forced to take over the reins. I either dither too long or make decisions that result in fiasco. I'm a complete waste of space."

"I wouldn't exactly say that," said Tommy while pointing to the doorway. "You got that washing line up in no time at all and you're doing a fine job of keeping most of that freezing cold wind off me and Hilly. Anyway-let's talk about our failings some other time shall we. We're going to have to get our positive heads on. We're going to have to live by our wits from now on."

"Well that won't be a problem for you," said the Chairman while emptying the last of the water from his injured friend's left shoe. "I couldn't have done what you did in a month of Sundays."

"It was nothing," said Tommy. "It wasn't exactly a heart bypass procedure. All I did was resuscitate a breathless man."

"You did more than that," said the Chairman. "You took control of the situation and saved the day. I, on the other

[522]

hand, bottled it. I completely froze. While I froze, you sprang into action. I couldn't move. I was paralysed with fear. It was as if both my feet had been nailed to the ground. I couldn't do anything. I'm afraid to say, your mate Hamill's been right about me all along. I'm a shithouse when it comes to a crisis of any sort. I always have been. Jesus Christ Tommy-Jesus bloody Christ Tommy, think about it this way. Imagine the mess I'd be in now if you hadn't decided to come along. The chances are, I wouldn't have even found Hilly, let alone revive him."

"If it makes you feel any better-I couldn't organise things the way you and Hilly do," said Tommy. "I wouldn't know where to start when organising a trip. I wouldn't even know how to block book a hotel or an overseas flight. We all have things we do well and we all have things we don't do quite as well. For instance-I've never been able to make a decent cup of tea over an open fire while in an old boathouse in the middle of nowhere. Did you know that?"

"Is that what you'd like?" said the Chairman upon reaching for his bag.

"More than the Crown Jewels right now," said Tommy. "And another thing Hulmey-you're not the only one here who's got a reason to feel ashamed."

"What do you mean?" said the Chairman.

"I smuggled a gun on board the train," said Tommy.

"Was that you was it?" said the Chairman while carefully arranging the thicker burning embers in preparation to support his small tin pot.

"You knew about the gun, did you?" said Tommy.

"I've known for a couple of days," said the Chairman.

"And I was actually there when the bloody thing was fired."

"Fired!" said Tommy. "When was this? I didn't know the gun had been fired."

"You wouldn't do," said the Chairman.

"Who was it?" said Tommy. "Who fired it Hulmey?"

"Does it really matter?" said the Chairman.

[523]

"Probably not," replied Tommy. "But I'd still like to know."

"You'll no doubt find out in time," said the Chairman. "If you're still interested that is."

"It was Hamill wasn't it Hulmey?" said Tommy. "I know it was. I can tell by the way you're refusing to look me in the eyes. Just say nothing if I'm right."

"Do you take sugar?" said the Chairman.

"Just the one," said Tommy. "Bloody hell! What a clown I've been. That stupid bastard plagued me for that gun. I wanted to get rid of it you know. I told him I wanted to get rid of the thing. What did he fire at? Do you happen to know?"

"I do but I'd rather not say," said the Chairman.

"Fair enough," said Tommy. "Unless.....Oh Christ! He didn't did he? He didn't did he Hulmey? He didn't shoot that mountain rescue bloke did he?"

"He apparently mistook him for a bear," said the Chairman after dropping another fistful of snow into the simmering pot. "And, by the way Tommy-in fairness to your mate-the man did look remarkably like a bear in all that fur. Even Hilly thought he was a bear and he's got 20-20 vision."

"Why didn't you say anything to the rest of them?" said Tommy.

"I couldn't afford to," said the Chairman. "Hamill detests me as it already is. I'd have been in fear of my life."

"Are you going to tell the police?" said Tommy.

"Tell them what?" said the Chairman. "I didn't actually see the gun being fired. I just heard what sounded like firecrackers going off."

"But you do know it was Hamill who pulled the trigger?" said Tommy. "You knew that much didn't you?"

"Hamill shot a bear," said the Chairman. "Now I think we should change the subject before I start tying myself in knots."

"Alright," said Tommy. "What do you want to talk

[524]

about?"

"How about anything other than Hamill, bears and guns," said the Chairman.

"Very well," said Tommy. "Why don't we discuss the reason why you denied me membership of the club for so long. Was there a reason?"

"I'd heard you were trigger happy," said the Chairman.

"Very funny," laughed Tommy. "What was the real reason?"

"You had a terrible reputation as a kick off merchant," said the Chairman.

"I know I did," said Tommy. "But that was before I got married and settled down. That was during a bit of a mad phase in my life when I knocked around with a load of moronic football hooligans."

"Mud has a tendency to stick," said the Chairman.

"You can say that again," said Tommy. "I don't think I'll ever be accepted within certain Crosby circles."

"And I don't think I'll ever be known as anything other than the man who brought our club to its knees," said the Chairman. "As I've said a thousand times before. I was never cut out to lead. I'd prefer to take orders rather than hand them out."

"Well why don't you collect a bit more firewood while I try to make your mate a bit more comfy," said Tommy. "And be quick about it."

"Very well sir," said the Chairman. "Right away sir."

The incident on the lake had cost the trio an irretrievable amount of time and had therefore left the Chairman in little doubt as to what his next move should be. However, he was well aware that such a course of action, to return to the train with his slowly recovering friend as soon as the wind dropped, would almost certainly shatter the morale of his expectant club members almost beyond repair. That is why, for the next hour, he had toyed with the idea of asking the much stronger and far more resilient Tommy Mac to take the Club Secretary back to the train while he continued on towards the coast. And that was the way he was leaning, until the constantly alert and wary builder shattered his train of thought by easing his trousers to his knees and urinating over his right shoulder.

"What the hell Tommy!" said the Chairman after successfully completing an undignified somersault. "What do you think you're doing lad? Have we already gone native have we?"

"I reckon I know what you're thinking Hulmey," said Tommy. "You want to go back don't you?"

"We've got no choice Tommy," said the Chairman. "We've got to get Hilly back to the train. We've got to get him to the Professor. Look at him. He's in shock."

"So what are you saying?" said Tommy. "Are you suggesting we all go back? Is that it? Is that what you want to do Hulmey-less than a quarter of a mile into the journey, we all head back to the train like three daft lemons?"

"Not all of us," said the Chairman. "Just you and Hilly."

"Just me and Hilly!" scoffed Tommy. "What are you talking about? You're not thinking of going on alone are you?"

"I don't think I've got any choice," said the Chairman. "I can't carry Hilly. I can barely wade through this snow on my own as it is. And if we all go back, those lads on the train are going to be in bits. They're depending on us Tommy. We're their very last hope."

"I'm not going back Hulmey," said Tommy after kicking a displaced cigar shaped ember back onto the fire. "You can go back if you want to. I'm pressing on."

"But that's the point I've been trying to make," said the Chairman. "I won't be able to get Hilly back to the train without your help."

"Then we push on," said Tommy. "We push on when Hilly comes round. And if it comes to it-I'll make some sort of sled out of this shack and I'll drag the dozy fucker the rest of the way."

"And what if he doesn't come round?" said the Chairman.

[526]

"We bury him where he lies," said Tommy. "But let's be honest Hulmey-nothing has to be decided until first thing tomorrow."

"Why not?" said the Chairman.

"Didn't you hear that rumble?" said Tommy.

"What rumble?" said the Chairman.

"There's one hell of a storm brewing," said Tommy. "We need to batten down the hatches for the night."

"Jesus!" said the Chairman. "You're right. Look at that bloody sky. Have you ever seen anything more menacing? And there's another rumble. How far off do you think it is?"

"I've no idea," said Tommy. "But I wouldn't waste any time fetching some more wood and blocking up that doorway."

"Is there going to be enough wood?" said the Chairman.

"Use your nous if there isn't Hulmey," said Tommy. "Build a wall of bricks out of snow like the Eskimos do."

"Wouldn't you be better doing that?" said the Chairman. "After all, you're the master builder."

"Not anymore I'm not," said Tommy. "I've moved on. I'm in the business of saving lives now. I've moved into the insurance profession now."

"Have you really," said the Chairman. "Would you mind passing me some snow?"

"I would, as it happens," said Tommy. "You're the bricklayer. If you want a hod carrier, pay for the services of one."

"Thanks for thinking about it," said the Chairman. "Would pouring me another cup of tea be too much trouble for the newly qualified broker?"

"Far too much trouble," said Tommy. "If you need an apprentice, I suggest you hire one. Now hurry up with that wall. I've got a feeling, that storm's just around the corner."

It would be another three hours before the Club Secretary opened his eyes and although he hadn't uttered a word, his approving nod in the direction of his rescuer Tommy Mac, demonstrated that he was beginning to regain at least some of his faculties. That gesture had been warmly received by both his travelling companions and had given rise to a welcome period of calm and contentment. It wasn't long therefore, before the fumes of the fire had penetrated the eyes of the other two men inducing an almost trance like state that had them thinking about their very different domestic situations.

"When was the last time you told your wife you love her Hulmey?" said Tommy while trying to form his overstuffed bag into something resembling a pillow.

"The last time I saw her," said the Chairman. "That would be the morning we all departed for London. Why do you ask?"

"Because I can't remember the last time I said it to Cathy," said Tommy.

"Some blokes never say it," said the Chairman. "It doesn't mean they feel any less affection for their partners. They just can't put their feelings into words."

"I think I've lost her you know," said Tommy.

"Don't be daft," said the Chairman.

"It's true," said Tommy. "I've lost her Hulmey."

"Well, win her back," said the Chairman. "You won her once didn't you?"

"I suppose so," said Tommy. "I remember asking her out for the first time. I was a gibbering wreck. I couldn't form a coherent sentence. Everything I tried to say was coming out as if it was in another language. She was just staring at me with this confused and sympathetic look on her face. She told me a few weeks later, she thought I had some sort of mental disability."

"It's not easy chatting someone up," said the Chairman. "Most fellas find it hard to talk to the gentler sex, never mind asking one of them out on a date."

"Some people seem to manage it alright," said Tommy.

"I know," said the Chairman. "Salesmen are generally good. They just go in all guns blazing and to hell with the consequences."

[528]

"Why do you think that is?" said Tommy.

"Probably because they've had the door slammed in their face so many times," said the Chairman. "They've become hardened to rejection. What's the matter Tommy? Are you going through a sticky patch or something?"

"I stormed out of the house about a fortnight ago," said Tommy. "We'd had a blazing row. It was over next to nothing, to be honest."

"Most husband and wife arguments are," said the Chairman. "They're often just a way of clearing the air. Where have you been staying?"

"In the back of the firm's van outside our house," said Tommy. "I've rigged an extension lead up to it. I've got a portable tele in there, a mini fridge and I can charge me phone and things like that."

"It sounds as if you've it mad," said the Chairman. "You want to get the Radfords in to slap a bit of paint around. What does Cathy think about your new living arrangement?"

"She doesn't seem too worried," said Tommy. "She still brings me a bacon butty and the paper every morning. And she's got the Sky remote control to herself now. That's always been very important to Cathy."

"Well, as you say-it sounds like it's all been about nothing," said the Chairman. "Just bury the hatchet lad. Go and speak to her. Take her some flowers. Tell her you're sorry."

"I can't," said Tommy. "I can't bring myself to. I'm worried she'll give me the elbow."

"She won't," said the Chairman. "It sounds to me as if she's finding the whole thing hilarious. Unless there's a bit more to all this. Is there more to it Tommy?"

"I forgot her birthday," said Tommy.

"Oh shit!" said the Chairman. "That explains it then. That's a bad one that is. I've got mates who've never been forgiven for doing that."

"Don't say that Hulmey," said Tommy. "For God's sake, don't say that. I'm close to phoning the

[529]

Samaritans as it is."

"It's true, I'm afraid," said the Chairman. "Forgetting your partner's birthday is bad shit."

"I'm nothing but a selfish, uncaring bastard," said Tommy.

"I don't know about that," said the Chairman. "A couple of hours ago you saved my best friend's life. Not *your* best friend, I might add. My best friend. And what's more, you risked your own life in the process. That probably makes you the least selfish person I've ever shared a boathouse with. Now drink that lovely tea I've made for you."

"I will when it cools down," said Tommy.

"Blow on it," said the Chairman.

"That's what the missus always tells me to do," said Tommy. "Especially when we have soup and I'm sitting looking at it through the haze. I like to tear me bread into little pieces and drop it in. That helps cool it down a bit too. And then I eat it from around the edge. That was one of the first things my mum taught me. Would *you* talk to Cathy for me Hulmey?"

"You're her husband Tommy-there's only you can do that," said the Chairman. "It's got to come from the heart."

"Would you put a letter together for me?" said Tommy.

"I've got no paper," said the Chairman before pulling his coat over his head and closing his eyes. "And don't you dare ask me why not."

"There's plenty on the train," said Tommy. "Why don't you sneak back and get some while they're all asleep. It'll only take you five minutes."

"Go to hell Tommy," said the Chairman. "That's not even remotely funny. I know we haven't made anything like the expected progress, but there's no need to rub it in."

"I'm sorry," said the highly amused McShane before jamming a knuckle between his teeth. "Oh and by the way Hulmey-I love what you've done with the old place. That washing line was a great idea. Has anyone ever told you, you'd make somebody a lovely wife?"

"I'll never be your wife," said the Chairman.

"Why the hell not?" said Tommy.

"I need to be told I'm loved on a regular basis," said the Chairman.

"You bitch!" laughed Tommy after immediately sitting bolt upright. "You absolute horror bag. Bloody hell Hulmey-you don't miss much do you? I bet you even know how much back subscriptions I owe."

"£84, as at the first of December," said the Chairman.

"Enough said," said Tommy. "Do I get a discount for saving the Club Secretary's life?"

"Only if he lives," replied the Chairman before disappearing under his assortment of loose clothing.

The Club Secretary would be the last to get to sleep that night and not just because of the eerie atmosphere provided by the electric storm or the possibility that something savage and menacing might be lurking nearby. It had been because, for the first time in his life, he had become, what is sometimes referred to as 'a burden'. He had listened in a state of utter exasperation, as his two travelling companions discussed the possibility of carrying him back to the train and never before in his life had he wanted to put forward his own input more. In fact, never before in his life had he felt so utterly and frustratingly helpless. He had tried to talk several times since being propped up against the flimsy boathouse wall. He had tried to ask for a drink. He had tried to remind Tommy that he hated brandy. And he had tried to talk again when a small burning branch fell out of the fire and settled perilously close to the hem of the Chairman's coat. Yet, once again, nothing audible came out of his mouth. Not even a cough, a wheeze or a whimper. In the days that would follow, his two companions would put his condition down to one thing-he had stared death in the face and it had scarred him terribly and very possibly permanently. It was as simple as that, as far as they were concerned. At that point however, only the Club Secretary knew the real reason why he had gone into extreme shock and had subsequently lost the ability to talk. Only the Club Secretary could appreciate what it had been like to suddenly plunge through ice into freezing cold water and then find himself wrestling with the body of a man who had drowned a week or so earlier. And not a stranger, by the way. A relatively familiar individual who, very curiously, had still been clutching his Health and safety manual tightly to his severely bloated chest.

Back in the dining room, the hero of the frozen lake, Tommy Mac, was receiving anything but plaudits, acclaim and congratulatory pats on his powerful back. In fact, his decision to join the Chairman and the Club Secretary in their quest to find some sort of community was being viewed by one particular individual as something akin to treason.

"The bloody imbecile," said Hamill who, after a couple of hours of trying every strategy known to himself and the Professor, including dropping a ridiculous amount of Triazolam, had found it impossible to get to sleep. "Why Tommy Mac of all people? Why not one of you lot? After all-apart from the Professor and Little Lord Fauntleroy, you lot are Hilly and Hulmey's mates. What was the soft sod thinking? I just don't get it. I really don't."

"What don't you get?" said the Chef.

"Why Tommy would want to tag along with your hand rag of a brother and the other over officious ball bag," said Hamill. "It just doesn't make sense. He's usually got no time for them."

"Maybe he wanted to give them a better chance of making it," said the Chef. "Let's be honest-he's stronger than our kid and Hilly put together."

"That makes perfect sense to me," said Blackie. "What difference does it make anyway? He's trying to help us isn't he."

[532]

"Help us!" scoffed Hamill. "It's Tommy that's going to need help. He's going to be stuck with two permanent millstones around his neck."

"He'll be alright," said the Chef.

"I think I know what's going on here," said Steadman.

"What's that?" said Hamill.

"You're worried the expedition might succeed and Hulmey will be seen as the hero of the piece," said Steadman.

"Rubbish!" said Hamill. "I'm not worried about that at all. Good luck to them if they save the day. But let's be fair and honest here-if they do succeed, it'll be down to Tommy McShane, not that streak of piss, poor excuse for a Chairman. I just don't understand why I wasn't asked."

"You'd gone absent without being granted leave," said the Chef.

"You mind your mouth," said Hamill. "I've never run away or hid from a challenge in my life. I'd been on patrol and you know it Chef. You all knew where I was."

"Would you have gone with them if they'd have asked?" said Steadman.

"In less than a heartbeat," said Hamill. "And I'll tell you this much-we'd have definitely made it to a town or something, if I'd have tagged along."

"I think they'll make it anyway," said the Chef.

"They won't," said Hamill. "Not unless Tommy decides to push on alone."

"Well I very much doubt if he'll be pushing on any time soon," said the Professor.

"Why not?" said Hamill.

"Have you heard it out there?" said the Professor, who at that particular time had been the closest to the window. "Can you hear that rumbling in the distance?"

"There's another bloody storm coming," said Steadman.

"Nice one," said the Chef. "Another night of hanging on to our mattresses for dear life."

"And hoping we make it to the morning," said Blackie.

[533]

"Put the kettle on Chef," said Hamill. "Your kid will be on his way back after hearing that. He's going to want a steaming cup of something and a bowl of hot water to soak his aching feet."

"Our kid will have settled in for the evening," said the Chef. "He might not be most people's idea of a modern day Shackleton, Hamill-but he's nobody's fool."

"That's a matter of opinion," said Hamill. "You might as well put the kettle on anyway Chef. I'm beginning to spit feathers."

"I told you before Hamill," said the Chef. "As far as the kitchen and cooking duties go, it's every man for himself now."

"Do as you're told," said Hamill. "Just be a good boy and do as you're bloody well told."

"I've hung up my apron," said the Chef.

"Make the fucking tea," said Hamill.

"I'll make it," said Hewlett. "If it helps stave off another murder, I'll make it. Do you all want tea?"

"I'll have coffee if you don't mind," said Hamill. "The last pot of tea you made tasted like cat piss."

"I don't actually think it was a bad effort considering I'd never made tea before," said Hewlett.

"What!" said a stupefied Steadman after dropping his magazine and spinning around in his chair. "What did you just say Hewlett? Did you just say you've never made tea before?"

"I've never had to," said Hewlett. "It's not my job to make tea. Waggers and Mrs Barlow make and serve the liquid refreshments in our home. And they get more than adequately paid for doing so."

"I should think so too," said Steadman.

"Can you make coffee?" said Blackie.

"I can learn," said Hewlett. "Does the process require the crushing of beans?"

"It normally requires the opening of a jar and the use of a teaspoon," said Steadman. "For crying out loud. I think you're going to need to come out of self imposed retirement Chef."

[534]

Just less than three quarters of an hour later, a period during which he had made numerous polite coffee-making related enquiries to the remarkably patient and congenial Chef, Hewlett emerged from the kitchen carrying a tray bearing a pot of steaming hot tea and two slightly overfilled mugs containing what looked like a pair of passable creamy white coffees. In doing so, he had not just proved he was prepared to roll up his sleeves and do a bit of menial work, he had also changed the dynamic within the dining carriage because he had unwittingly become the focal point of the next few conversations and associated witticisms. That wasn't to last long however because, within seconds of the last remnants of the teapot being drained, the conversation inevitably returned to the remaining men's most worrying and pressing concerns.

"What are their chances Professor?" said the Chef after joining the old man at his isolated table near the window. "And I want you to be brutally honest with me."

"I can't really say," said the Professor. "Why are you asking me?"

"Because you're intelligent, rational and impartial," said the Chef. "And your answer's not likely to be prejudiced by any dislike of any of the expedition members."

"I think you'll find that was a poorly disguised dig at yours truly," said Hamill while holding out his empty mug for the beleaguered and highly annoyed Hewlett to collect. "But, as it happens, I'd like to know that too. What are their chances Professor? Would you say they're better than fifty-fifty?"

"I'd certainly like to think so," said the Professor. "I've got a very important steam locomotive convention to attend on Christmas Eve."

"Bloody hell!" said Steadman. "I never thought of that. It's getting dangerously close to Christmas isn't it?"

"It's the 20th of December," said Hewlett while struggling to remove his apron strings.

[535]

"What!" said the Chef. "The 20th? Is it really? Oh God. We're not going to make it are we?"

"Make what?" said the Professor.

"We're going to miss Christmas Day with our families," said Steadman.

"Not necessarily," said the Professor. "We've still got a few days to play with."

"It'll suit me if I arrive back at around 7 o'clock on Christmas Eve," said Hamill. "I'll be able to get showered and changed and go straight to the pub. I can't stand the hassle of Christmas. My missus can't cope. That's the only time of the year we have anything resembling a harsh word. She has this habit of leaving everything to the last bloody minute. And you want to see the amount of food she buys. You'd think there was going to be a nuclear explosion. You'd think we were going to have to go underground for a year until the dust from the fallout settled."

"My one's the same," said the Chef. "And there's only the two of us at home now."

"Where's your Mark?" said Blackie.

"He's found love again," said the Chef.

"Oh dear," said Blackie.

"I've never missed a Christmas day with my girls," said Steadman. "Even when I was working away."

"Which reminds me Steadman-try not to be late this year," said Blackie.

"Late for what?" said Hewlett.

"We play nine holes of high intensity golf at West Lancs on Christmas Day," said Steadman. "It enables me to recoup some of my Christmas shopping money."

"You don't always win," said Blackie. "You didn't win last year."

"We didn't play last year," said Steadman. "I had the flu, if you remember right."

"I'll take you to the cleaners and back this year," said Blackie.

"I can't make it this year," said Steadman.

"Why not?" said Blackie.

"Remind me to tell you later," said Steadman.
"Me and Angela are having our Christmas dinner out this year," said the Chef. "I've had enough of slaving over a hot stove when under the influence. We're going to the Royal Hotel in Waterloo."
"It's nice there," said Steadman.
"What do you do Hewlett-are you at Balmoral or somewhere like that?" said Hamill.
"I have dinner at home," said Hewlett. "It's one of the highlights of the family year. And then my brothers and I ride for an hour or two. We ride particularly hard on Christmas Day. We sometimes latch onto the Cheshire hunt if everything is done and dusted early enough."
"I wouldn't broadcast that if I was you," said Steadman. "Particularly now that Facebook is so popular."
"What do you do Blackie?" said the Chef. "Where do you go for your Christmas dinner?"
"Kenny Biddo's house," said Blackie. "Although, I don't think it's going to be quite the same this year after I've told his wife that her husband and favourite son are dead."
"There'll be a lot more spuds and turkey to go round," said Hamill. "You'll probably get seconds."
"Fuck off Hamill," said Blackie. "That's way below the belt even for you. Poor Anne's going to be inconsolable."
"Are *you* going to tell her?" said Steadman.
"I suppose I'm going to have to," said Blackie.
"No you're not," said Hamill. "That should be the new Chairman's responsibility."
"Don't start Hamill," said the Chef. "Things are bad enough as they are."
"It's all such a mess," said Hewlett while returning from the kitchen with a jug of water and a plate of chocolate digestive biscuits. "And by the way gentlemen-are you aware that we're almost out of bread?"
"What!" said Hamill.
"We're down to the last loaf," said Hewlett.
"We can't be," said Hamill. "I counted five loaves only

yesterday evening. Is there any in the freezers?"

"I don't know," said Hewlett. "Do you know Chef?"

"As far as I'm aware, what you see is all there is," said the Chef.

"You're joking aren't you," said Hamill. "For fuck's sake. What's everybody been doing with it?"

"Eating it I imagine," said Blackie. "The Chef's no longer cooking hot meals. So people have just been making toast and sandwiches."

"And then there was the carry out," said Steadman.

"What bloody carry out?" said Hamill.

"Hulmey and the others had to have a carry out," said Steadman.

"And we had to make sure they had enough," said the Chef.

"Had enough!" said Hamill. "Fucking hell! 5 loaves. You've provided enough butties for a battalion. How long did you think they were going for?"

"We didn't know," said the Chef. "We just had to make sure they had plenty."

"What was wrong with giving them tinned goods and a can opener?" said Hamill.

"The extra weight they'd have to carry," said the Chef. "And the fact they might sometimes struggle to light a fire."

"I still think it was excessive," said Hamill. "5 loaves worth of sandwiches! The caterers never used that much bread at my wedding reception."

"I think you'll find their need exceeds ours by some distance," said the Professor.

"Why's that?" said Hamill.

"Because they're going to be burning up more calories than us," said the Professor.

"That's right," said the Chef.

"Well from now on, I'm going to be keeping a keen eye on our provisions," said Hamill. "I personally think what the Chef's done is diabolical."

"And I think we should be concentrating on counting bodies rather than loaves of bread," said the Chef. "Has anyone made a recent body count? Does anyone know how many men we've lost?"

"It depends what you mean by lost," said Steadman. "I know Tommy Weir and Alec Morris are dead.

"And I know for a fact Kenny Biddo's dead," said Blackie.

"And there's poor Woody," said Hamill.

"And Davey Larko and Alty," said the Chef.

"And young Anthony Biddo," said Blackie.

"We haven't had confirmation of that yet," said the Chef. "I think we should just consider him missing until we do."

"Well, while we're on the subject of missing persons- Eddie Meehan is also one of those unaccounted for," said Hewlett.

"Of course he is, yes," said Steadman. "He was actually the first to go missing."

"Which means he can safely be added to the list of fatalities," said Hamill.

"Why can he?" said Hewlett.

"You work it out Hewlett," said Hamill. "He's been missing for the best part of a week during the worst Winter in living memory. Let's be honest-if he'd have made it to a town, we'd have almost certainly heard something by now."

"And you have to consider what was in that mountain rescuer's diary," said Blackie. "He came across the body of a young man. It had to have been young Anthony."

"I'd have thought so too," said the Chef. "Who else could it have been?"

"That's right," said Steadman. "Jesus Christ! That's 8 dead or missing isn't it? That's 8 good men we've lost."

"You've actually lost 9," said the Professor.

"It's 8," said Steadman. "It's definitely 8 Professor. We've just named them all."

"You failed to include your friend Mr Matthews," said the Professor.

"That's because he's on the sick list," said the Chef.

[539]

"Unless you're going to tell us his condition has suddenly become terminal."

"Mr Matthews passed away some time yesterday afternoon," said the Professor.

"Oh no!" said Steadman. "Oh no, no, no. Not Matthews."

"But you said the disease wasn't going to kill anyone," said Hamill. "You told us the disease wasn't life threatening and would pass in time."

"That particular disease *would* pass in time," said the Professor. "But the late and soon to be lamented Mr Matthews was suffering from something quite different. He was suffering from something very similar to the Ebola virus."

"Ebola!" said Steadman. "That's a bad one isn't it?"

"It's an appalling disease," said the Professor. "It's one of the worst diseases known to afflict man. And for that reason, we need to get that unfortunate man's body off this train as quickly as possible."

"How are we going to do that?" said Hamill.

"We're going to have to carry him," said the Professor.

"Carry him!" said Hamill. "You must be out of your considerable mind Professor. Are you sure you're not running a fever too? I'm not touching that bloody thing. In fact, I'm not going anywhere near the diseased fucker."

"I'd rather not handle the body either," said the Chef.

"It'll be alright," said the Professor. "I've put his body into a plastic suit bag. It's zipped tight shut. Which means, provided the person who assists me wears disposable clothes, one of my face masks and a pair of latex gloves, they should be fine."

"Should be fine!" said Hewlett. "I'm sorry Professor-that's not nearly reassuring enough for me. You can count me out too."

"That body needs to be incinerated right away," said Hamill. "We should just torch his bed."

"Don't be bloody stupid," said Steadman. "The whole carriage could go up."

[540]

"The whole train could go up," said the Chef.

"I agree," said the Professor. "Which means, our only alternative is to discard it."

"Which in turn, means touching it," said Hamill.

"It doesn't," said the Professor. "I've just told you. The body's sealed inside a bag. The disease has therefore been contained. It just needs discarding."

"What do you mean discarding?" said Steadman. "Do you mean, removing it from the train?"

"I do yes," said the Professor. "But I don't think we should take any chances. I think we should throw it over the side of the bridge."

"Why's that?" said the Chef.

"Because there's a lake beneath us," said the Professor. "And by my calculations, the weight of the body should almost certainly break the ice. In this temperature, it'll be completely sealed within an icy tomb in a matter of seconds. The virus will no longer have anywhere to go and will consequently die. Now will somebody help me please?"

"I think you're on your own Professor," said Hamill. "Me and the lads have just told you-we're going nowhere near the thing."

"That's a pity," said the old man. "That really is a pity."

"I'll help you Professor," said Steadman.

"What!" said Blackie.

"I'll dump the body with you," said Steadman.

"That's very kind of you," said the old man.

"Don't be a bloody fool Steadman," said Blackie.

"I'm not being a fool," said Steadman. "I'm just doing the sensible and decent thing. Mine and the Matthews's families go back a long way. Did you know Brian Matthews's mother was one of those 'wise women' people went to see whenever they had problems? They didn't bother going to the doctors. She was better than any doctor. She must have saved more people's lives and more people's sanity than Mother Theresa and a thousand psychiatrists put together. That's why I'm going to do something for her. I'm going to make sure her son doesn't become a pariah. I'm going to ensure her son doesn't become famous for creating a national health crisis."

"But you'll be risking your life," said Blackie.

"I won't," said Steadman. "My life's as good as over."

"What!" said Blackie.

"What are you talking about?" said the Chef.

"My life's as good as over Chef," said Steadman.

"How come?" said Blackie.

"A fortnight ago, I was diagnosed with cancer of the oesophagus," said Steadman. "Unfortunately, my symptoms weren't recognised until far too late."

"Bollocks!" said Blackie. "You look fine. You look absolutely brand new. Is this a joke Steadman?"

"If it was a joke, it would be in extremely poor taste," said Steadman. "I'm sorry you had to hear it like this, but that's the way it is."

"How long have you got?" said Blackie.

"Not long," said Steadman. "There are signs the cancer's already beginning to spread upwards towards my brain."

"Which means what in terms of days and weeks?" said Blackie.

"I've got anything between a fortnight and a month," said Steadman.

"Jesus Christ!" said the Chef.

"That's why I'm the perfect candidate to handle that body," said Steadman. "You can consider it my last Christmas present to you all."

"When were you planning to tell us?" said Blackie.

"After Christmas, if I'd managed to survive that long," said Steadman.

"How's Barney taken it?" said the Chef.

"She's being strong for the sake of the kids," said Steadman.

"Do the kids know?" said the Chef.

"I informed them a couple of days ago," said Steadman.

"That couldn't have been easy," said the Chef.

[542]

"It wasn't," said Steadman. "It was the singular most difficult thing I've ever had to do in my life."

"I don't believe what I'm hearing," said Blackie while proceeding to pace the floor. "I'm going to struggle to get my head around this."

"I don't think I'll ever be able to get my head around it," said the Chef.

"It's alright," said Steadman. "I'm alright lads. I've already come to terms with it. I'm more than ready for the off."

"You might very well be," said Blackie. "But I'm not. I'm not remotely ready for you pissing off. None of us are ready. Bloody hell Steadman-you can't drop something like that on our toes and expect us to be ready."

"I'm sorry if I've inconvenienced you," said Steadman. "That was never my intention. Now then-I'm going to get my winter woollies on, dump our poor mate's body over the side of the bridge and set off in the general direction of home. You never know, if you're all rescued in time, and I make better than expected progress, we might still be able to have one last drink in the Bug."

"You need to make your way to the nearest hospital and declare your condition," said the Professor.

"I will do," said Steadman while heading to the door.

"Is this likely to be the last time we'll ever see you?" said Blackie.

"It might very well be yes," said Steadman.

"It's a crock of shit," said Blackie.

"It's just the way it is," said Steadman. "It's the way the cookie crumbles, as they say."

"Why don't you just spend your last few remaining days with us," said Blackie. "To hell with the body. Just leave the rotten thing there. It's doing nobody any harm where it is."

"That body has to be removed as quickly as possible," said the Professor.

"Why's that?" said Hamill.

"Because the disease will already be trying to find a way out," said the old man.

"Arc the rest of us in any danger Professor?" said Hewlett. "Could one or more of us fall foul of what Brian Matthews died of?"

"It's possible," said the Professor.

"How possible?" said Hewlett.

"Very possible," said the Professor.

"Oh my God!" said Hewlett.

"Is it final letter writing time?" said the Chef.

"What do you mean, 'final letter writing time'?" said the Professor.

"Has the time come when we should be writing a last letter to our loved ones?" said the Chef.

"Behave yourself Chef," said Hamill. "Don't be so bloody melodramatic."

"For what it's worth, I've already written mine," said the Professor.

"What!" said Hamill.

"I actually penned my letter within a few minutes of sealing up your friend," said the Professor.

"Oh shit!" said the Chef before slumping into the nearest available chair and placing his head between his knees. "Oh dear God. Please God-don't do this to us."

"Calm down gentlemen," said the Professor before taking Steadman by the left arm and leading him to the door. "I wrote the letter only as a precautionary measure. "I've included details of the disease and things like that. The chances are, as long as we dispose of this body right away, everybody else will be fine. Now come along my brave Madame Comtesse. Your guillotine awaits."

"Don't do it Steadman," said Blackie. "Stay here and wait for the others to return. Hulmey will probably be knocking on some unwary fisherman's door as we speak Stay here and let's have one last drink."

"I've got to go," said Steadman. "I've got to go and do one last really good thing. Good luck boys. I'll see you on the other side for 18 holes and a shit load of banter

[544]

and lager. And bring plenty of money Blackie. It's a rollover, don't forget."

That was the last time the men saw anything of the remarkable and extremely colourful character who had come to be known in respectable and fun loving Crosby circles as 'Steadman Hamilton-Swan' but in the years that followed, several people local to where the train had become stranded, would occasionally talk of a tall, thin man who, on misty, autumnal evenings, could be seen wandering through the valley swishing a long, thin branch of a sycamore tree as if it was a pitching wedge.

When the Professor eventually returned after showering for almost an hour, the only sounds that were heard in the near empty and sombre dining carriage were the clearing of throats, the nervous rearrangement of squeaking leather clad feet and the odd unstifled sob. That same evening, the devastated Blackie and the equally distraught Chef returned to their rooms to find a one silver dollar piece lying on the centre of each of their pillows. That signalled the moment of terrible realisation. That was when they began to realise the events of earlier had not just been a series of nightmares. That was when they began to mourn the loss of their golfing partner, the big brother they had so often longed for and the greatest of all their many friends.

CHAPTER TWENTY TWO
DOGGED

When the first evidence of morning sunlight began to filter through a cluster of five small knotholes in the boathouse roof, the extremely weary Chairman took a deep breath, closed his eyes and began to tremble violently. This time however, his trembling hadn't been perpetrated by a fear of monsters or villains-this time he was trembling due to enormous relief because, despite all that had gone wrong the previous day, which included almost losing his best friend to hypothermia, his small band of adventurers had survived the night and the bitterly cold early hours that had followed. That had been because of three significant things. The incredibly fortunate, almost miraculous discovery of the boathouse while visibility was at its worst, the unselfish care and consideration that Tommy Mac had afforded the Club Secretary from the moment he had discovered him clambering out of the icy lake, and the Chairman's dedication to the painstaking and vital task of keeping the fire going during an eight hour period when the temperature had plummeted to almost minus 20 degrees Fahrenheit and the temptation to lie back and go to sleep had been almost impossible to resist.

"Where did you find the posh toasting fork?" said the wincing Tommy Mac while stretching out his back. "I made it out of the window latch," said the Chairman. "I reckon it's solid brass. Do you want to buy it as a stocking filler for your missus?"

"Not really," said Tommy. "But listen Hulmey-I am prepared to give you a couple of bob for whatever you've got cooking. It smells fantastic. What is it?"

"Cheese and onion on toast," replied the Chairman before handing his yawning travelling companion a mug of piping hot tea. "It's actually one of 2000 cheese butties I found at the bottom of my bag."

"There's even more at the bottom of mine," said
Tommy. "Your kid certainly wasn't going to allow us to
starve was he?"
"He's always been very protective of me," said the
Chairman. "Are you ready to eat now, or are you going
to take a shower first?"
"I'll eat, thank you very much," said Tommy. "What do
I owe you?"
"I'll work it out when we get home," said the Chairman
before handing his eager companion the hot cheese slice.
"Do you want me to put it on your tab?"
"If you don't mind," said Tommy before slipping a
corner of the slice between his lips and immediately
howling. "Jesus Christ Hulmey-What are you trying to
do to me?"
"What's the matter?" said the smiling Chairman.
"That bloody sandwich is the matter," replied Tommy.
"It should have come with a government health warning.
I've gone and burnt me bloody mouth."
"Did you forget to blow on it?" said the Chairman while
doing his utmost to hide his amusement.
"What do you mean, 'blow on it'?" said Tommy. "You
don't blow on cheese on toast."
"You do," said the Chairman. "Or at least, wait for it to
cool down. Just shove a bit of snow in your hungry gob.
Unless you'd prefer water."
"You can stick your water up your arse," said Tommy.
"And stop trying to appear sympathetic. I can see you.
giggling. Did you manage to get any sleep, by the
way?"
"Not an awful lot," said the Chairman. "I was too busy
watching the fire. That was actually quite stressful that
was."
"I've no doubt it was," said Tommy. "You know what
you've done don't you?"
"What have I done?" said the Chairman. "Apart from
rendering you almost dumb."
"You've probably kept the three of us alive," said
Tommy.

[547]

"What makes you say that?" said the Chairman.

"You kept that fire going Hulmey," said Tommy.

"Without that fire, we' might have all dropped off to sleep and died right here. I've read quite a lot about trying to survive in the extreme cold. That's how it happens. The body shuts down after a while. You just don't wake up."

"Did *you* manage to get any sleep?" said the Chairman.

"I slept quite well as it happens," said Tommy. "At least until those bloody hounds kicked off howling. Did you hear them?"

"They were at it all night," said the Chairman.

"Why do you reckon they howl like that Hulmey?" said Tommy.

"I don't really know," said the Chairman. "Maybe they're calling a mate."

"Have you heard anything from them this morning?" said Tommy.

"Not a dickey bird," said the Chairman. "I've seen no sign of them either."

"You've been outside have you?" said Tommy.

"I needed to stretch my legs," said the Chairman.

"More cramp?" said Tommy.

"It's bloody murder," said the Chairman. "It's my own fault Tommy. I've done no real exercise for ages. How's your mouth?"

"It's on the mend, no thanks to you," said Tommy.

"I noticed you managed to eat the rest of your cheese on toast," said the Chairman.

"I did yes," said Tommy. "It was nice. I'd happily have that for every meal."

"That's not going to happen I'm afraid," said the Chairman. "We're only going to be eating cold food from now on."

"Why's that?" said Tommy.

"Because the smell of food cooking is likely to attract those dogs," said the Chairman.

"Dogs are meat eaters aren't they," said Tommy.

"Surely they're more likely to eat one of us than one of

your cheese toasties."

"I don't know about that," said the Chairman. "I reckon a starving mutt will eat just about anything. Let's be honest Tommy-they're not patrolling this area for nothing. They must think they're on to something."

"That's true," said Tommy. "Maybe they've got designs on the occupants of the train."

"Don't say that," said the Chairman. "Our kid's terrified of dogs."

"Why's that?" said Tommy.

"He was badly bitten by one when he was three," said the Chairman.

"How come?" said Tommy.

"He made the classic schoolboy mistake," said the Chairman. "He tried to pet a bad tempered corgi while it was eating. He should be alright on the train though. As long as the doors stay secure, that is."

"Have they ever been secure?" said Tommy.

"Good question," said the Chairman. "I used to check those doors time and time again and yet they still somehow kept coming open. I don't get it."

"I don't get a lot of things that happened on board that train," said Tommy. "That's why I was grateful for the chance to get away from the bloody thing. Have you tried to wake Hilly yet? I say that because it's usually about this time he takes his early morning plunge."

"He's already been up, done 20 lengths and gone back to bed," said the Chairman.

"Really!" said Tommy.

"He's still not said anything mind-but at least he's proved he's capable of walking unaided," said the Chairman. "He certainly seems to have plenty of energy."

"He will have," said Tommy. "He's hardly walked a fucking yard yet."

"That's a point," said the Chairman. "By the way-have you noticed how much the wind has dropped?"

"I was thinking that," said Tommy while peering through one of the larger holes in the boathouse roof.

[549]

"And there's a fair bit of sun too. Perhaps our luck's beginning to change."

"It wouldn't be before time," said the Chairman. "Why don't you give Mark Spitz a nudge while I go out and get some bearings. And try to get some food down the ignorant bugger. He's going to need it. He's likely to be carrying me this afternoon."

The only low point during an unusually upbeat and bright start to the day was that, for some reason, and despite much cajoling, the Club Secretary had refused to eat. He h*ad* taken on plenty of water though and had demonstrated a very definite enthusiasm for the journey, firstly by insisting he packed his own things and then by attempting to lead the group off. However, that was a change in the prearranged order that lasted just under half an hour, at which point the Chairman politely ushered his friend to the rear, corrected the group's direction and urged them forward with a flamboyant wave of his right hand.

At that time, they had heard nothing at all from the hounds, but it wasn't long before the trio were coming across plenty of visual evidence to remind them the pack wasn't too far away; piles of fresh, steaming faeces and huge globules of hot porridge like saliva, being some of the most obvious of all the physical indications. That was something which had caused the men to become wary and extremely hesitant and as a consequence, for the next couple of hours, progress had ranged between slow and even slower. Nevertheless, to the men's immense credit, and despite their constant fear of ambush, they continued on and for the next hour they began to make a more acceptable amount of ground.

The welcome sense of achievement provided by that improved rate of progress, wasn't to last long however, because within an hour another potentially far reaching problem had been identified by the exasperated Chairman.

"Something's wrong lads," he said after bringing his confused and frustrated companions to a

[550]

halt.

"What do you mean?" said Tommy.

"I can't seem to be able to keep us on our intended course," said the Chairman. "I don't understand it. I keep setting us off in an easterly direction and then, within minutes, we're all over the place."

"What do you mean, 'all over the place'?" said Tommy. "As far as I'm concerned, we're still going the same way we set off."

"We're not," said the Chairman. "We're now heading in a direction that's more like north-east."

"Would that be a problem?" said Tommy.

"It could be a massive problem," said the Chairman. "It could mean us missing the bay. It could also result in us going round in circles for hours and hours. It could even mean us getting lost completely."

"Is the compass working?" said Tommy.

"I assume so," said the Chairman. "There's not that much to a compass. Which means, there's not much that can go wrong."

"Do you think the needle's getting stuck?" said Tommy. "Let's be honest, that thing was probably designed for much warmer places like the Amazon Basin not the Antarctic."

"The needle seems free," said the Chairman.

"Have you tried tapping or shaking the thing?" said Tommy.

"Of course I have," said the Chairman.

"Breathe on it then," said Tommy. "Or put it down your kecks to warm it up for a few minutes. Do something Hulmey. Get the thing working because, unless I'm mistaken, there's another storm about to hit us and if it does, it'll cover our tracks and we won't know our arses from our elbows, never mind what's east and what's west."

"Oh Christ yes," said the Chairman before removing his haversack and dropping to his knees. "I didn't see that. We need to dig in. We need to build some sort of windbreak and wrap ourselves up in everything we've

[551]

got."

The storm actually lasted three and a half hours, a period during which the men's hastily and poorly constructed igloo type structure had needed rebuilding at least a dozen times and the Chairman had suffered the most appallingly painful cramp spasms to both calves. When the three eventually emerged to the sound of a conscientious, nesting bird, each was emotionally and physically drained but although they had lost so much time and none of them had the slightest clue which way they were now facing, they all looked upwards in unison as if to offer thanks to some unseen benefactor for helping them survive their latest ordeal. That is when something caught the attention of the ever alert and eagle eyed Tommy Mac.

"Are my eyes deceiving me or is that some sort of manmade structure almost to the left and ahead of us?" he asked while pointing at what appeared to be just a thin grey line in the distance.

"Where are we looking?" said the excited Chairman after arriving at his companion's left shoulder.

"Over there," said Tommy.

"Over where?" said the Chairman. "I can't see anything. All I can see is white."

"You're going to have to follow me then," said Tommy.

"Follow you where?" said the Chairman.

"Just do as you're told," said Tommy.

"But that's more like north east," said the Chairman. "That's way off our original route. What is it you've seen Tommy?"

"A wall, unless I'm mistaken," replied Tommy.

"A wall!" said the Chairman. "Do you mean like somebody's garden wall?"

"That would be my dearest hope," said Tommy. "Are you coming, or do you want to stay where you are and play Eskimos with Hilly?"

What the remarkably observant Tommy Mac had actually spotted, just less than five hundred yards in the distance, was what remained of a dry sandstone wall which at one time had fully enclosed an ancient cemetery consisting of around thirty reasonably well kept graves that were marked by unpretentious headstones and a variety of simple wooden crosses. Entry to the cemetery and access to those graves was by means of an elaborately carved oak lichgate, the slated roof of which appeared to be about to collapse due to rotten under timbers and the weight of heavy snow. Nevertheless, despite the obvious danger, both men paid the cemetery and the people interred beneath it the fullest respect by entering through the dangerous gateway rather than vaulting the wall which at one time appeared to have been the more attractive and safest proposition.

"This place could have been our camp if we'd seen it an hour earlier," said Tommy.

"I've got news for you Tommy," said the Chairman. "It's still going to be."

"Are you kidding me?" said Tommy. "Shouldn't we be trying to claw back a bit of lost time?"

"It's nearly four o'clock," said the Chairman. "We've got less than an hour before it's pitch black again."

"Bloody hell!" said Tommy. "How's that happened? Where's all the bloody time gone?"

"We started out quite late," said the Chairman while heading towards the near angle of the wall. "We'll rig up some sort of shelter over here where the wind won't affect us as much. Do you want to help me gather some wood and I'll get a fire going."

"Get Hilly to help you," said Tommy before slumping onto his bag. "He might have lost his voice but he hasn't lost the ability to move his arms and legs. Don't baby him Hulmey. Keep giving him things to do. And keep his mind active. Meanwhile, if you give me your bags, I'll start setting up our camp."

Compared to his disappointing showing not long after his little group had taken up residence in the dilapidated boathouse, getting the fire going had been little trouble at all for the Chairman because whoever

[553]

had tended the graveyard had left a large bale of dry kindling wrapped in a tarpaulin just to the left of the latch gate.

"I can't believe we didn't spot this place earlier," said Tommy. "We were so close. It reminds me of what happened to Captain Scott."

"He died didn't he?" said the Chairman.

"He died just 11 miles from his next supply depot," said Tommy. "11 miles from fuel, heat and food Hulmey. I was told that story by my favourite teacher Mr Jones, during a history lesson when I was 9. That was the part that upset me most. That intrigued me that did. It intrigued and saddened me. 11 bloody miles! That's about the distance from my house in Crosby to Formby Village. It's nothing is it?"

"That depends upon the conditions and what gear you're wearing," said the Chairman before handing Tommy a slightly damp and wrinkled piece of paper. "Take a look at that."

"What is it?" said Tommy.

"It's a map the Professor drew for me shortly before we set off," said the Chairman. "Take a look at it. Tell me what you think."

"I think it's everything you claim it to be," said Tommy after a few minutes serious consideration. "It's a roughly drawn map. What do you want me to think?"

"What do you reckon the little shaded area marked with a cross is?" said the Chairman.

"I was just wondering that myself," said Tommy. "I don't know. But I would have thought that series of dashes leading to and from the shaded area is some sort of path or narrow road."

"I would too," said the Chairman. "What about the big house-shaped thing marked OBI. What do you think that might be?"

"I really haven't got the foggiest," said Tommy. "Have you?"

"What if the little shaded area marked with a cross represented this cemetery," said the Chairman. "Do you think that would be encouraging?"

"I don't know," said Tommy. "You've lost me here
Hulmey. You're talking in riddles."

"I'm not," said the Chairman. "Didn't you do any map
reading when you were at school?"

"A little bit," said Tommy. "I think we did a bit about
Ordnance Survey maps."

"That's what I did too," said the Chairman. "And if I
remember right, on every Ordnance Survey map, a cross
represented a church. That's right isn't it?"

"If you say so," said Tommy. "But this isn't a church.
What we find ourselves camped in now, isn't a church.
This is a cemetery."

"I know it is," said the Chairman. "But it's still got a
religious connection. Or am I just getting a bit carried
away?"

"I think you are," said Tommy. "And by the way-have
you stopped to wonder how and why the Professor could
have been familiar with this part of the country?"

"I don't think he was," said the Chairman. "He had a
diary with a load of very old maps of Britain at the back
of it. I think he drew that map from one of them. He's
even included a simple scale."

"Is that when inches represent yards?" said Tommy.

"Something like that," said the Chairman. "If I've read
it right, every inch on this map represents 3 miles."

"Which means what?" said Tommy.

"It means we're here," said the Chairman.

"What do you mean 'here'?" said Tommy.

"It puts us right here Tommy," said the Chairman while
pointing down. "About 3 miles from where we set off."

"3 miles!" said the mortified Tommy. "3 measly miles!
For God's sake Hulmey-we must have walked more than
3 bloody miles. Most men can walk that in less than an
hour."

"In normal conditions they might," said the Chairman.
"But we've been wading through knee deep snow
against a ferocious wind while stopping to look around
every two minutes for hungry dogs that might just want

[555]

to make us their next meal. And don't forget Tommy-we hardly made any ground at all the first day because of Hilly's accident on the lake."

"I still think we've travelled further than that," said Tommy. "That map's wrong, I tell you. In fact-that old windbag Professor's wrong. I think you'll find he's full of shit."

"Why's that?" said the Chairman.

"Because he is," said Tommy. "No man alive could possibly know as much as he claims to. He knows everything about everything. Everything you ask him, he's got an answer for. He's meant to be a scientist but he knows things about steam engines, the weather, cures for diseases and everything. He was even giving Hewlett advice about what laptop to buy the other day."

"He's the nearest thing to a genius I've ever come across," said the Chairman.

"He might very well be," said Tommy. "But don't they say, there's a fine line between genius and madness? For all we know, this map might lead us to Timbuktu."

"I'd be the first to applaud him if it did," said the Chairman. "I've heard Timbuktu's lovely this time of year. But let's get back to the map. Let's agree to differ regarding the amount of ground we've covered. Let's concentrate instead on the long house-shaped thing marked OBI-what do you think that might be?"

"I've no idea," said Tommy. "I've really no idea. Although...could it be...could it be an inn? Could it be the Old something Inn?"

"Possibly," said the Chairman. "Inns were often used as landmarks in days gone by. But I'm wondering if the letters could stand for, 'something, something institution'. I'm wondering if it might be a school or a college."

"That's possible too," said Tommy. "But according to this map, it seems to be in the middle of nowhere. There's no catchment area. There are certainly no houses drawn around it. Where would it draw its pupils from?"

"I'm not suggesting the place would still be open for educational purposes," said the Chairman. "It could have originally been built in the 18th or 19th centuries to educate the children of railway workers. Those men would have lived in tented villages. And the school wouldn't have been needed after the work on the railway was completed. The workers would have moved on to their next project. The building's probably derelict now."

"So why would the old boy bother drawing it on the map?" said Tommy.

"Because it's a notable landmark," said the Chairman. "It doesn't have to exist as a viable business anymore. Think about the old sausage factory in Litherland. That's been gone for God knows how many years, but people still direct others by it to this day."

"That's very true," said Tommy. "Is the bay we're meant to be heading for marked on the map?"

"It is yes," said the Chairman. "It's marked 'POINT B' in large capital letters."

"Might I assume the bridge where we set off from is marked point A?" said Tommy.

"You might," said the Chairman.

"And how many inches is that bay from the bridge?" said Tommy.

"Without a ruler-I'd say about 5," said the Chairman.

"Fucking nice one!" said Tommy before angrily kicking off his right boot.

"What's wrong?" said the Chairman.

"That's not exactly what I wanted to hear," said Tommy.

"Why's that?" said the Chairman.

"Because that would mean your map's a fair and accurate representation of this area," said Tommy. "That would mean you've been right all along. That would mean we've only covered 3 bastard, stinking miles."

"We'll make some of the lost time up tomorrow," said the Chairman. "We'll have a good supper and get up and get moving immediately at first light. Now let's get this fire roaring and make sure we've got plenty more timber on hand. Then, if it docs go out, it won't take very long to revive."

As it happened, keeping the fire lit wasn't to be the only concern during the hours that followed because just after midnight, the Chairman was awoken by an extremely uneasy Tommy Mac who, after kneeling down and placing a hand over his mouth to urge him to be silent, pointed towards the far side of the cemetery.

"Listen," he whispered while at pains to ensure his travelling companion didn't jump up or make any sudden moves.

"Listen to what?" whispered the bemused Chairman.

"Just wait a second," whispered Tommy. "You'll hear it yourself soon."

"Hear what?" whispered the Chairman.

"People talking," whispered Tommy. "I swear it Hulmey. I swear it on my kid's lives."

"I can't hear anything," whispered the Chairman. "Apart from dead leaves rustling in the wind and the fire hissing and crackling from time to time."

"I'm telling you Hulmey-there's someone or something here with us," whispered Tommy. "I told you we should have moved on. This place gives me the creeps."

"That's because it's full of dead people," whispered the Chairman. "I think you'll find it's just your imagination Tommy. We're in an old graveyard and there's a hell of a mist descending. It doesn't get much more spooky than that. All we need is a full moon, an owl to hoot and a bat to fly over us. Now try to get back to sleep, or me and Hilly will end up carrying you tomorrow."

"There's somebody here," said Tommy upon releasing his companion and instantaneously reaching for one of the longer and thicker lengths of timber. And I intend finding out who."

Despite all the Chairman's powers of persuasion, it was another two hours before the

[558]

genuinely unnerved Tommy returned to his bed and another hour before he managed to fall back asleep. Within a few minutes however, he was back on his feet and more agitated and animated than ever.

"What the hell!" he said after one of the larger headstones had come crashing down within inches of his toes. "Did you see that Hulmey? Did you see that? I told you something strange was going on."

"Nothing strange is going on," said the exasperated Chairman before throwing off his covers and rubbing his eyes. "It was just the wind Tommy. It's picked up a hell of a lot over the last half hour. It's got to be close to hurricane force right now. I'm surprised there's still a headstone standing, to be honest."

"I am too," said Tommy. "But why now Hulmey? Why now? That stone must have stood there for something like a hundred years. It could even be more, for all we know. Why has it decided to fall over now? And why has it chosen to fall over, the very night we decide to set up camp here?"

"I don't know," said the Chairman while continuing to rise unsteadily. "Maybe our presence has disturbed the ground. Now move your backside and give me a hand."

"To do what?" said Tommy.

"To stand it up," said the Chairman.

"You're having a laugh aren't you," said Tommy. "That thing must weigh nigh on half a ton."

"I don't care what it weighs," said the Chairman. "It needs to be stood up."

"Why does it?" said Tommy.

"Because it represents somebody's life," said the Chairman.

"So what," said Tommy. "What difference does it make to you? You've never met who's lying under it. Let the family of the deceased stand the thing up when they next come to lay flowers. It's certainly not your responsibility Hulmey."

"I don't care," said the Chairman. "It's the moral and decent thing to do. If that was my mother or father's

headstone, I'd want somebody to put it right for me."
"Just leave it," said Tommy. "You're going to do your
back in. And if you do, and you cost us any more time,
me and you are going to fall out good style. Just leave
the fucking thing and go back to bed."
"I want it sorted now," said the Chairman while leaning
over to grab his steam engulfed gloves that had been
drying by the fire. "I want it done before we go back to
bed. And I'm not going to rest until it is."
"Why, for crying out loud?" said Tommy.
"I've just told you," said the Chairman. "It's the right
and decent thing to do."
"It's none of your business," said Tommy. "And
anyway-what if the person buried in that grave wasn't
particularly nice."
"What do you mean?" said the Chairman.
"What if he was a mass murderer or child molester," said
Tommy. "And what if the person laid to rest in that
grave just tried to crush the life out of me. You didn't
think of that, did you Hulmey."
"I didn't," said the Chairman. "It's not in my nature to
think like that. But it is in your nature Tommy. Because
you've been around that bad minded and twisted Hamill
far too long. You've grown like him. You see the very
worst in people rather than the good. The possibility
that the person related to that headstone might have
actually just saved your life has probably never entered
your head has it."
"Saved my life!" scoffed Tommy.
"That's right," said the Chairman. "Think about it
Tommy. Just prior to that headstone falling over, you
heard a strange whispering. Nobody else heard
anything. You heard whispering and for some reason, it
caused you to get up. Now think about where you'd
made your bed earlier."
"I'd made it right here," said Tommy. "I'd made it right
here where I am now."
"No you didn't," said the Chairman. "You originally
made your bed in the shadow of that fallen headstone.

You've moved back several feet since you first heard
those whispers. I know that because, where that stone
has settled, is where you were lying when I handed you
your tea just after we'd made camp."

"No it's not," said Tommy.

"Oh yes it is," said the Chairman. "Where's your mug
Tommy?"

"It's here," said Tommy while scanning the immediate
ground. "It's round here somewhere."

"I think you'll find it's under the headstone," said the
Chairman. "Exactly where you'd have been had you not
moved. Whether you were aware of it or not Tommy,
you moved back out of range of the fallen headstone.
You moved back to safety."

"Those voices were very definitely human," said
Tommy.

"They probably were," said the Chairman. "But a firm
believer in the supernatural could make a case for the
voices being from beyond that grave. A believer in
ghosts and the afterlife might suggest someone's been
watching over you Tommy."

"Bollocks!" said Tommy before returning to his bed,
wrapping himself in his blanket and curling up into a
tight ball. "If anyone was watching over me, we
wouldn't be in the mess we're in now. We'd have
certainly covered more than three fucking miles in a day.
Go to bed Hulmey. And just remember what I said
about your back. Don't go doing anything silly. Because
make no mistake-I'll leave you here in agony if I have
to. We've already got one sodding invalid we can well
do without."

CHAPTER TWENTY THREE
THE STONE

Although the feral dogs had howled almost continuously and the wind had reached speeds in excess of anything it had achieved during the previous week, the period after the last of the men had turned in for the night, had passed without incident or any fresh concerns. Getting to sleep had proved extremely difficult however but that problem had at least ensured there was always somebody to tend the fire and keep a lookout for intruders or opportunistic night prowlers. That didn't mean everything within the camp had been good spirited though. In fact, after Tommy's outburst regarding the carrying of 'passengers', he and the Chairman had not exchanged a single word. At least, not until around 6 o'clock when the Club Secretary and the aforementioned belligerent became aware of the powerful and alluring aroma of simmering coffee.

"Has that piece of shit compass dried out yet?" said Tommy after joining the preoccupied Chairman by the fire.

"I don't think it was ever damp," said the Chairman. "I'll take a look at it in a minute. Do you want coffee with your rat poison?"

"Have you got a spare mug?" said Tommy.

"I've got your mug," said the Chairman while pointing towards the place where the fallen headstone had landed. "It's a bit like you Tommy. It survived its brush with death relatively unscathed. The soft ground must have saved it."

"It must have done," said Tommy. "By the way bugger lugs-I see you defied me. How the hell did you manage that?"

"Manage what?" said the Chairman.

"To stand the headstone back up," said Tommy.

"Don't be at it," said the Chairman. "You helped me lift it."

"Did I hell as like," said Tommy. "I told you yesterday, in no uncertain terms-that headstone was a potential backbreaker. I wanted nothing to do with the bloody thing."

"Are you having me on?" said the Chairman.

"Not at all," said Tommy. "I didn't help you. It must have been Hilly."

"It must have been," said the Chairman while scratching his head and doing his best to peer through the dense early morning mist that was showing little sign of lifting. "I definitely couldn't have done it on my own. I kept getting it most of the way up and then having to let it go. I did that about half a dozen times until I felt some very welcome assistance. I was on my knees gasping for breath by then. I didn't even have the energy to look round and say 'thanks'. I just naturally assumed it was you."

"It wasn't," said Tommy. "Where is Hilly, by the way?"

"He's gone for another leak, I would guess" said the Chairman. "I've never known anyone pass water like him."

"Do you think that's got something to do with what happened to him on the lake?" said Tommy. "Do you think he's still pissing himself through fright?"

"It's possible," said the Chairman.

"I wouldn't have bothered me arse getting up," said Tommy.

"What do you mean?" said the Chairman.

"I'd have stayed where I was and pissed myself," said Tommy.

"No you wouldn't," said the Chairman.

"I would," said Tommy. "I did it yesterday when we were inside the igloo. It's quite pleasant to be honest. It warms you up."

"It's a disgusting thing to do," said the Chairman.

"I couldn't care less," said Tommy. "I saw a BBC documentary about the R A F once. One of their pilots, a really well spoken bloke, admitted doing it while

[563]

returning from a bombing raid over Dresden. It's just
one of those unsavoury things you have to do at certain
times. There's no shame in it. I'm certainly not going to
make any apologies for doing it."

"Are you going to apologise to Hilly?" said the
Chairman.

"What the hell for?" said Tommy.

"You offended him," said the Chairman.

"How did I manage that?" said Tommy.

"You inferred he was a burden to us," said the
Chairman.

"No I didn't," said Tommy.

"You did Tommy," said the Chairman before removing
a burning log from the fire and rising to his feet. "I saw
the look on his face when you referred to him as an
'invalid'. He wasn't best pleased, I can tell you."

"I was jarred off," said Tommy. "I was on one. The fact
we'd only marched something like 3 miles in a day, had
really hacked me off. I'll give him a big sloppy kiss and
make it up with him when he gets back."

"Well, make sure you do," said the Chairman before
settling back down and picking up his mug. "That man's
not too well. He needs all the encouragement he can
get."

"He needs a kick up the arse," said Tommy. "He's cost
us vital time. And if he's gone and got himself lost
again, he's going to cost us even more. When did you
first realise he was missing?"

"I didn't even consider it until just now," said the
Chairman before placing his half full mug to the side of
the fire and climbing back to his feet. "He's actually
been missing for some time."

"Are his things still there?" said Tommy.

"Everything's here except him," replied the Chairman.

"This is bad this is Tommy. This is very, very bad."

"Just calm yourself down," said Tommy. "He'll be here
somewhere. As you said before-he's got a cob on. He's
probably sitting somewhere feeling sorry for himself.
Can you see any footprints?"

[564]

"Not as yet," said the Chairman upon returning from the fire with a much longer and brighter torch. "But there should be plenty. There's been no overnight snow. His footprints are going to stand out a mile. Hang on a minute...What's that over there to your left? Is that the daft bugger? Is that him Tommy?"

"It's not, I'm afraid," said Tommy after quickly vaulting three successive graves and landing in front of a life size memorial of a British infantryman. "It's just a statue. It's a statue of a young soldier. It's in remembrance of 4 brothers who fought and died in the Second World War. Jesus Christ-the oldest brother was only 24."

"And they each died on the same day," said the Chairman. "Bloody hell! What must their poor parents have thought?"

"That statue must have cost a pretty penny in its day," said Tommy. "It's solid bronze isn't it?"

"I think you'll probably find it's some kind of wood that's been stained to look like metal," said the Chairman. "It probably cost nothing but a talented carpenter's time and effort. I don't like this Tommy. I don't like this one little bit. I'm beginning to think you were right."

"About Hilly taking the hump?" said Tommy.

"About the whispering you heard," said the Chairman. "Maybe there *were* people here last night."

"What are you saying?" said Tommy. "You're not suggesting Hilly's been abducted or murdered are you?"

"Not at all," said the Chairman. "He could even be better off than us "

"How do you mean?" said Tommy.

"Those voices could have been travellers," said the Chairman. "And if they were, Hilly's likely to be in safe hands."

"What makes you think that?" said Tommy.

"Why wouldn't he be safe?" said the Chairman.

"Gypsies aren't mindless thugs. They wouldn't have harmed a dumb mute just for the sake of it. They'd have probably taken pity on him."

"It's possible," said Tommy. "But if they were travellers, why didn't they come over and introduce themselves?"

"They probably didn't realise we were here," said the Chairman. "Why would they? Right now, with this mist the way it is,-you could hide a small army in this cemetery. Hilly might have got up to take a leak and stumbled over something in the dark. And anyone coming across him, would have assumed he was on his own. He wouldn't have been able to explain his situation. Come on Tommy-let's get packed up and get back to the train."

"Back to the train!" said Tommy.

"That's right," said the Chairman while quickly gathering the cooking utensils. "Grab your things and put that fire out."

"Why go back to the train?" said Tommy.

"Because that's where they'll be taking him," said the Chairman. "That's where he'll have pointed to while trying to explain where he came from. Hurry up Tommy.

"Why didn't he try to show the travellers where we were?" said Tommy.

"He mightn't have wanted to risk betraying us," said the Chairman. "He was probably wary of them. Come on-let's try to latch onto their tracks before it starts snowing again."

"You latch onto their tracks if you want to," said Tommy after slinging his bag onto his right shoulder.

"I beg your pardon," said the Chairman.

"I'm pushing on," said Tommy. "I'm heading for the bay. Just leave me the map."

"I'm going to need it," said the Chairman.

"Give it here," said Tommy. "You can follow the traveller's tracks."

"This is wrong," said the Chairman after reluctantly handing over the map and angrily kicking out at a small mound of disturbed snow. "You owe it to your fellow member to help him."

"I'm going to help him," said Tommy. "I'm going to get to that bay and send back help. I'm going to do what we originally set out to do. You never cease to amaze me Hulmey. You're the most negative fucker I've ever come across. You've been itching for the chance to turn back, ever since I dragged Hilly from that lake." "We need to know for certain he's safe," said the Chairman. "That's not exactly true is it?" said Tommy. "It's just you that needs to know he's safe. I'm content to believe he's being taken care of by decent, considerate people. And guess who taught me to think like that Hulmey." "But what if he's not being cared for?" said the Chairman. "What if he's been kidnapped. What if he's being beaten to a pulp or skinned alive as we speak." "You tell me," said Tommy. "You tell me what you're going to do if you find he's being mistreated Hulmey. You tell me what you're going to do if you catch up with Hilly's so-called kidnappers. You need to get real lad. If he is in the hands of nasty people who want to do him harm, there's very little you and I are going to be able to do about it. Let's be honest-if they are kidnappers, they're likely to be of the hardnosed gypsy type. They'll fuck you and me over in the time it takes a human heart to beat. And that's supposing we were able to catch up with them. They'll know this part of the country far better than we do. They'll know it like the back of their hands. They'll know it blindfolded. Don't forget-they'll have found this cemetery by choice. We found it by pure chance."

For some time after, the massively concerned Chairman continued to search the cemetery for clues as to the whereabouts of his closest friend and even though he had been joined on a number of occasions by the far more pragmatic and considerably less sympathetic and enthusiastic Tommy Mac, he had found absolutely nothing-not even a patch of discoloured snow where the Club Secretary might have relieved himself earlier. However, finding no blood or any evidence that a violent

[567]

struggle had in fact taken place, had, to a certain degree, persuaded him that his fellow club member was not necessarily in any imminent danger and as a result, he had not chosen to head back to the train as threatened, but had instead tagged onto the determined Tommy Mac who, for the next three hours, never once uttered a word and never at any point, looked back to acknowledge his one remaining companion's presence. At least, not until the Chairman suddenly slipped and let out a pitiful and almost pathetic, puppy-like yelp.

"Oh, for fucks sake," said Tommy. "Here we go. Here we fucking well go. The human sick note strikes again. Nice one Hulmey. Give yourself a big round of applause lad. That's great that is. That's just fucking great. You've gone and done it haven't you."

"What do you mean, 'gone and done it'?" said the Chairman through tightly clenched teeth while very tentatively easing down his right sock.

"You've incapacitated yourself haven't you," said Tommy. "You've finally gone and scuppered our mission."

"I didn't mean to," said the grimacing Chairman. "I tripped."

"What do you mean, 'tripped'?" said Tommy. "We've been wading through waist deep snow for the past hour. How could you possibly manage to trip and hurt yourself?"

"The ground got firmer," said the Chairman.

"What do you mean?" said Tommy.

"The ground suddenly got firmer," said the Chairman.

"I don't understand what you mean," said Tommy.

"It's hard over here Tommy," said the Chairman. "The ground's harder here and the snow's not anything like as deep. And I don't think that's a coincidence. I think I might have found something of significance."

"Like what exactly?" said Tommy after quickly removing his bag and dropping to his haunches.

"I'm not sure yet," said the Chairman while proceeding to dig. "I'm wondering if it's that path."

"What path's that?" said Tommy.

"The path that was marked on the map with a load of dashes," said the Chairman.

"I doubt it," said Tommy. "It wouldn't be our bloody luck."

"Now who's being negative?" said the Chairman while continuing to create an ever widening hole in the snow.

"It's the path I tell you. Look Tommy. That's a cobble. I'm sure of it. Look.....There's two cobbles-four cobbles-8 cobbles...We've done it Tommy. I don't know exactly how and I couldn't care less why. But we're back on course."

"On course for what?" said Tommy.

"The inn or the institution or whatever it is," said the Chairman. "The house marked OBI. And look at those two rows of hedges ahead in the distance."

"Oh bloody hell!" said Tommy. "Where did they come from?"

"The mist must be lifting at long last," said the Chairman.

"Well thank God for that," said Tommy. "We're finally going to get some cover from that living bastard of a wind."

"Those hedges represent far more than cover," said the Chairman. "I think they're likely to be running either side of the path. They're showing us which way to go. Why don't you check the map for scale. See how long that path actually is."

"I will," said Tommy. "After I've taken a look at your ankle and decided whether or not you're going to need to be shot."

Tommy needn't have worried however, because the only thing that had been irreparably damaged when his companion had taken his tumble had been one of his plastic water bottles and the only significant time that had been lost had been due to his own inability to make sense of a wringing wet map that was looking more like a damp dishcloth by the second. It was little wonder therefore, that what happened three

[569]

quarters of an hour later, had left the Chairman smiling wryly and suppressing the urge to roar with laughter.

"There's no need to use language like that," he said after rushing to the aid of his foul mouthed companion who was lying flat on his back with his hands over his face. "My convent educated mother could have been passing by."

"I couldn't give a shite if Mother Theresa and the pope were passing," said a fist clenched and crimson faced Tommy before reaching under his backside to reveal a rectangular sheet of metal, the back of which was coated in a dark red film of wet rust. "What the hell's that I've just slipped on?"

"I've no idea," said the Chairman.

"Have a look at the bloody thing," roared Tommy.

"I don't want to touch it," said the Chairman

"Why not?" said the incensed Tommy.

"It's just been up your bottom," said the Chairman.

"Only half of it," said the grimacing Tommy. "What the hell is it Hulmey?"

"It's a warning sign," said the Chairman .

"What does it say?" said the impatient Tommy.

"It says, 'CAREFUL-SLIPPERY SURFACE'," said the Chairman.

"Very fucking funny," said the stern faced Tommy while struggling vainly to climb back to his feet. "This isn't the time for jokes. I'm in agony here. I may never walk again. What does it really say, dick brain?"

"I'm not sure you're going to want to know," said the Chairman while scanning the horizon suspiciously.

"Let me be the judge of that," said Tommy.

"Why don't you read it for yourself," said the Chairman before returning the sign to his companion and taking a long, nervous look around. The sign read as follows:

**ALL VISITORS MUST REPORT TO THE
GATEKEEPER'S COTTAGE
IN THE EVENT OF YOUR VEHICLE
BREAKING DOWN, YOU ARE STRONGLY
ADVISED TO WAIT FOR THE ASSISTANCE
OF AN ARMED GAME WARDEN.
DO NOT, UNDER ANY CIRCUMSTANCES,
OPEN YOUR WINDOWS OR LEAVE YOUR
VEHICLE.**

Because they had immediately turned their attention to anything that might be approaching from behind or any of their many blind spots, it was some time before the increasingly wary pair turned to face each other to try to make sense of their situation.

"What do you make of it?" asked Tommy after once again handing the sign to his anxious and equally suspicious looking companion.

"I don't know," said the Chairman.

"I think you can do a bit better than that," said Tommy. "What do you make of the bloody thing Hulmey?"

"I'm not sure," said the Chairman. "I don't like it though."

"I don't either," said Tommy. "Because, unless I'm very much mistaken, that's the sort of sign you'd normally see on the approach to a safari park."

"That's exactly what I was thinking," said the Chairman. "Although it could also have something to do with them."

"What do you mean 'them'?" said Tommy.

"I mean those over there," said the Chairman while encouraging Tommy to turn around and follow his outstretched right arm which was pointing towards a large pack of slathering dogs that had gathered in a huge arc no more than 70 yards to the men's rear.

Without so much as another word or a gesture of any sort, the two men discreetly buckled up their bags and after locating what appeared to be the parameters of the cobbled path the Chairman had discovered when slipping, they headed off in the general direction of the two lines of hedges at a speed that even under normal circumstances would have been regarded as acceptable. It meant that for the next hour, as each member of the expedition sought to put as much distance as possible between themselves and the starving dogs, the leadership changed hands no less than a dozen times. That was the reason they had been able to reach the two rows of hedges far sooner than might have been expected and also why they had little energy left in reserve on their eventual arrival.

"Can you see them?" said the shattered and almost breathless Chairman before slumping to his knees and rolling onto his stitch affected left side. "Have they gone? Have we lost the bastards yet?"

"I wouldn't have thought so," said the ever watchful Tommy. "Let's be honest, we're a meal waiting to happen. They've stopped yapping though. That's at least one good thing."

"Is there any way we can block up this end of the hedgerow?" said the Chairman.

"Only with lots of packed snow," said Tommy. "But that's not going to hold them for long. How many sandwiches have you got left?"

"Not enough to build a decent wall," replied the Chairman. "Why?"

"I'm wondering if we threw them a load, it might distract them and give us enough time to find somewhere a bit less exposed," said Tommy.

"It's worth a go," said the Chairman. "But where are they? They seem to have gone to ground."

"With any luck, they've found something more attractive to stalk," said Tommy while struggling to release the soaking wet straps on his bag.

It soon became clear however, that there was to be no immediate respite for the exhausted duo because, immediately after Tommy had hurled two large handfuls of tuna sandwiches in the general direction from whence they had travelled, the dogs resurfaced like

ants from a recently disturbed hill. An almighty
commotion then ensued. A commotion that had caused
both men to jam their eyes shut and place their hands
over their ears.

"Jesus Christ-have you ever heard anything like that in
your life?" said Tommy while retreating crab-like to his
companion's position. "The poor bastards must be close
to death."

"They're tearing each other apart," said the Chairman.

"I hope to Christ you're right," said Tommy. "Because,
the fewer numbers we have to contend with, the better
chance we've got of getting out of this mess alive."

"I couldn't agree more," said the Chairman. "How
much more protection from these hedges have we got
left?"

"No more than 30 feet," said Tommy after tossing
another clutch of sandwiches away and skywards.
"That's providing they don't realise there's another way
in."

"Bloody hell," said the Chairman. "I never thought of
that. Can you see anything ahead of us yet?"

"Nothing as yet," said Tommy while urging his
companion forward. "Just the usual grey wall of mist.
Unless....."

"Unless what?" said the Chairman.

"Unless that *is* a wall," said Tommy. "Is that a wall
Hulmey?"

"I don't know," said the Chairman. "But I might just be
able to see a bit better if you let go of my bloody collar."

"Sorry lad," said Tommy. "I didn't even realise I was
doing that."

      The keen eyed and ever alert Tommy Mac had
once again been right. He *had* seen a wall. An
extremely high and sturdy looking wall which was no
more than 30 feet directly ahead of them. A wall built
into which, was a badly weathered but solid oak door
which was hanging precariously from one bent and
rusted hinge. However, because the two lines of hedges
that had been affording the men a certain amount of

[573]

cover and protection for just under an hour, terminated about 20 yards from that inviting point of entry, getting to that door was going to require a monumental leap of faith and a massive amount of courage.

"I think I'm going to be sick," said the Chairman after despatching his penultimate pack of sandwiches as far to the rear as possible. "I'm not sure I'm going to be able to do this Tommy."

"You can and you will," insisted Tommy.

"But listen to them," said the Chairman. "Listen to those jaws grinding together. They're like eating machines. They've almost gone insane. Mother of God...Have you ever heard anything like it? We're not going to get out of this Tommy. You mark my words—we're going to be eaten alive."

"We're not," said Tommy. "At least, not without a fight."

"A fight!" said the Chairman. "We can't fight that lot Tommy. There's too many of them. Jesus! Have you seen the size of some of those things? I've seen smaller donkeys on Brighton beach."

"What's the alternative?" said Tommy.

"We bury ourselves," said the Chairman. "We bury ourselves as deep as we can and we leave a breathing outlet and wait for them to lose interest."

"And what if they don't lose interest," said Tommy. "What if we bury ourselves and are then forced to listen while they slowly dig us out. Can you imagine that Hulmey? Can you imagine hearing them getting closer and closer? Can you imagine them becoming more and more frantic as they begin to recognise our scent? You bury yourself if you want. I'll even help you. But I won't be staying here. I'm going to toss the last of my sandwiches to the hungry bastards and make a run for it."

"Do you reckon you can beat them in a race?" said the Chairman.

"I'm going to have to beat them if I want to stay alive," said Tommy. "And even if they do catch me, I'm going

[574]

to go down fighting. What do you reckon?"

"I hate the idea," said the Chairman. "I'd rather stay where I am and wait for them to leave."

"You could be waiting for days," said Tommy.

"Then, so be it," said the Chairman.

"But what about the weather," said Tommy. "It's going to be something like minus 10 degrees again tonight. How long do you think you'll last in that sort of temperature without the benefit of a fire? I'd give you no more than 12 hours."

"Then I'll fall asleep and die from the effects of the cold," said the Chairman.

"That would be ironic wouldn't it," said Tommy. "Considering the way you've always hated the cold."

"I do hate the cold," said the Chairman. "I despise the cold. But not as much as I despise pain."

"Do you want to drop a load of painkillers?" said Tommy.

"What for?" said the Chairman.

"To numb the pain should you be discovered," said Tommy.

"Have you got any?" said the Chairman.

"Not a single one," replied Tommy. "That's why I offered you some."

"What have you got?" said the Chairman.

"Naproxen," said Tommy.

"Are they any good?" said the Chairman.

"I've no idea," replied Tommy. "I bought them off this fella at the gym when I was returning from injury. He told me they were steroids. They should be alright. You'll know if they're any good as soon as the first set of gnashers lock onto your meat and two veg."

"Go to hell!" said the Chairman. "How are we going to do this?"

"Do what?" said Tommy.

"The running for our lives thing," said the Chairman.

"That's more like it," said Tommy.

For the next few uncertain, heart pounding minutes, Tommy Mac did his level best to motivate his persistently hesitant companion in preparation for their forthcoming 20 yard life or death sprint to the swinging door-a merit worthy effort that appeared to be getting results until the enormous steam belching Alpha male and his equally imposing blood spattered mate suddenly appeared to the left side of the hedge. Their arrivals had undermined pretty much everything Tommy had been trying to achieve but even more damaging, as far as morale was concerned, was a hideous air piercing screech that followed soon after. A sound which had rocked both men back onto their heels and one that had brought every other living thing within the immediate vicinity to a complete and utter standstill.

"What in God's name was that?" whispered the Chairman after another ear bursting and massively disconcerting whoop-like screech had boomed across the canopy beyond the confines of the wall.

"I don't know," whispered Tommy. "But I think it might have been our cue to make a run for that door."

"I can't," whispered the Chairman while yanking at his companion's coat tail. "I can't move Tommy."

"You fucking well can," whispered Tommy while moving aside to allow the Chairman to get a better view of things. "Take a look at those dogs Hulmey. Look at them. They're scared to death. They're cowering. Some of them are even beginning to skulk away. Something beyond that wall's scared them. Something's got those bloody things worried shitless."

"It's had a similar effect on me," whispered the Chairman.

"And me," whispered Tommy while slowly inching forward and urging his colourless, fear wrapt companion to follow suit. "But let's just take full advantage of the first bit of good luck we've had for days and get ready to run for our lives."

CHAPTER TWENTY FOUR
SIGNS

The wall that was now separating the two men from the increasingly impatient and frustrated pack of starving hounds, was about twelve feet high and made up of numerous lime mortar bound, grey granite slabs each about the size and shape of a full sack of common building cement. It had been capped with a single course of roughly moulded dark red coping stones in the shape of waves while protruding from each of those was a barley twisted twelve inch wrought iron spike, many of which were now in the considerable and remorseless grip of ivy. The door by which the two men had gratefully gained entry to the garden had been one of twenty four that were dotted around the perimeter and although closing it over and securing its two obstinate rusty bolts had given the men a very welcome sense of security and relief, it wasn't long before their focus shifted to potential threats within the grounds and in particular, large creatures that could fly or extremely agile animals that could dwell comfortably within the canopy above. The fear of something swooping down and attacking them, had therefore soon usurped all of their previous concerns and it had affected their rate of progress to such an extent, it wasn't long before the two men were once again bickering like two old mother hens. That had been the reason the pair had reluctantly made the decision to go back to the door and skirt the wall in the hope it would eventually bring them to a main driveway and that was how they eventually came across two very tall and imposing looking forged iron gates, above which was a metal framed archway, welded to which were the following words:

THE OLD BUDLAM INSTITUTE FOR THE
INCURABLY INSANE EST.1758
QUI AUTEM INTRAT NON RELINQUIT.

"I'd have to assume these are the gates which at one time would have led to the main house," said the Chairman.

"And despite desperately wanting to strangle you, I'd have to agree," said Tommy.

"And that also explains the letters 'OBI' on the map I've been referring to," said the Chairman.

"It does yes," said Tommy. "You said it might be an institution of some sort."

"I didn't expect it to be a nuthouse," said the Chairman. "I thought it would be a school."

"Is there any difference?" said Tommy.

"None that I can think of," said the Chairman.

"Does it really matter?" said Tommy. "It's a type of hospital isn't it? That means if it's still housing even one last nutcase, it should have a phone."

"I suppose so," said the Chairman.

"There's no supposing about it," said Tommy. "It'll have a phone, I'm telling you."

"Only if it's still standing," said the Chairman.

"Oh for crying out loud!" said Tommy. "Will you listen to yourself."

"What's the matter?" said the Chairman.

"You," said Tommy. "You're what's the matter. You and your bloody negativity. How does your poor wife cope with it? Why do you even bother getting out of bed in the morning Hulmey?"

"I'm just trying to be realistic," said the Chairman. "I'm trying to prepare you for a fall."

"I don't need preparing," said Tommy. "I'm very used to falling by now. And I've still got the bruises to prove it. Now can we get moving. Because if we don't, I'm likely to become an ice version of one of those bloody statues."

The statues that Tommy had been referring to numbered hundreds and were replicated at perfectly spaced intervals along every stretch of every paved garden path. For instance, along one route, there were four life size Chinese warriors, one of whom was in the process of hurling a spear, one of whom was brandishing a long sword, another readying a cross bow and the shortest and youngest looking of the four, loading a handful of shot into a sling. Between them were three statues of elegant Chinese women wearing mandarin gowns and bearing heavy bindles and ceremonial daggers. Few of them had escaped the ravages of time and inclement weather and as a result, their plinths had become extremely unstable giving the illusion they were supporting something animate and therefore something capable of mischief. That hadn't concerned the two men to any great degree however-on the contrary-arriving at the conclusion they had been walking round in a circle for just over an hour had ultimately done that.

"We need to stop and think this out," said the Chairman after drop kicking his bag and slamming his hands onto his hips. "Something's wrong here Tommy."
"I'll tell you what's wrong," said Tommy. "You've just blindly led us into some sort of impossible to get out of maze.""I didn't mean to," said the Chairman. "I just headed away from the wall down the first path I saw. I'll get us on the right track shortly. I just need to work this out systematically."
"Well, I'd get a move on if I was you," said Tommy. "Because that garden door's not going to hold those dogs forever."
"I know it's not," said the Chairman.
"I'd have thought we'd have seen a sign of some sort," said Tommy.
"That's what I've been thinking," said the Chairman.
"A simple arrow would have helped. Unless."
"Unless what?" said Tommy.
"Unless we're literally being led along the wrong garden path," said the Chairman.
"Nobody's been leading us anywhere," said Tommy.
"I wouldn't be too sure of that," said the Chairman.
"Because I'm beginning to suspect we've been the victims of a clever trick. I'm beginning to suspect there *are* signs around us but we've just not been aware of them."

[579]

"That's a bit too deep for me," said Tommy.

"Well let me explain it this way," said the Chairman. "I think it's just possible that, instead of being led to the house, the signs are constantly leading us the wrong way."

"What signs are they?" said an open armed and unimpressed Tommy. "As far as I'm concerned, there are no signs."

"Not in the conventional sense," said the Chairman.

"I still don't get you," said Tommy while helping himself to a quick drink.

"Alright," said the Chairman. "Which way have we been going Tommy?"

"Every bloody way," replied Tommy.

"Are you sure about that?" said the Chairman.

"I'm certain," said Tommy.

"I'm not," said the Chairman. "I think we've always been going the wrong way."

"I wouldn't argue with that," said Tommy. "Why don't you tell me something I don't know."

"Alright," said the Chairman. "I don't think we've been going the wrong way by accident. I think there's a bit more to it than that."

"Like what?" said Tommy.

"I think we've unconsciously been encouraged to go the wrong way," said the Chairman.

"By who?" said Tommy.

"The statues," said the Chairman.

"Oh for fucks sake," said Tommy. "You've either been hitting the ale too hard or watching too many fantasy films. I think you need to go somewhere quiet and have a nice lie down. You're not serious are you Hulmey? Are you? Are you serious?"

"I'm perfectly serious," said the Chairman while leading his companion to the edge of the nearest path. "Think about it this way Tommy. I once visited a medieval castle that was regarded as impossible to take."

"Why was that?" said Tommy.

"Because of the way it was made," said the Chairman.

"It was designed in such a way that if the invaders even managed to scale the outer wall, they would soon find themselves in an area without any protection at all. The occupants of the castle would be waiting thirty feet above them to pick them off or drop oil on them. It would be the classic fish in a barrel scenario. The attackers had very deliberately been funnelled there."

"What's that got to do with our situation?" said Tommy.

"Very possibly nothing," said the Chairman. "But look at those statues Tommy. Look at the way the spears, bows and swords are pointing. I don't think that's a coincidence. And look at the statues of the women. Look at the way their heads are slightly cocked to one side. Look at their free hands. They're beckoning us. They're encouraging us to follow. They're persuading us to go a certain way. And every path we've taken has the same group of statues pointing the very same way. And like a complete and utter gobshite, I've fallen for it. That's the way I've been going. That's the way I've felt compelled to go. I did that instinctively and was powerless to stop myself. I'm telling you Tommy. These statues are all about suggestion. I've got a funny feeling it's a clever security ploy designed to keep unwanted visitors away from the house."

"If it is, it's very effective," said Tommy. "It's certainly keeping us away. What do you suggest we do?"

"We take a lateral approach to the problem," said the Chairman.

"Meaning what?" said Tommy.

"We need to defy our natural urge to conform," said the Chairman.

"Would you mind putting that in plain English," said Tommy.

"We have to think laterally," said the Chairman. "We need to go against the flow."

"I see," said Tommy. "Against the flow hey. That should be right up my street. I'm a defiant bastard. I've done nothing but go against the flow most of my life. What are we waiting for?"

[581]

"Nothing in particular," said the Chairman.

"Well let's get going then," said Tommy.

"Let's just take five," said the Chairman while twitching nervously. "There's no reason to hurry is there?"

"I'd have thought there was every reason," said Tommy. "Come on-let's go."

"Just wait a minute," said the Chairman.

"Why, for God's sake?" said Tommy. "What the hell's going on Hulmey?"

"Nothing's going on," whispered the Chairman. "But it might be a good idea if you kept perfectly still for the time being."

"What for?" said Tommy. "Why?"

"Just for your own sake, do as I say Tommy," whispered the Chairman.

"But I need to know what for," said Tommy.

"Keep your voice down," whispered the Chairman.

"Why?" said Tommy.

"There's something directly above you that might just be ready to pounce," whispered the Chairman.

"What sort of something?" whispered Tommy.

"I'm not sure," whispered the Chairman. "But let's just say this-it's far too big to be a domesticated cat or an owl."

By the time Tommy had fully grasped what the Chairman had said, another terrifying screech was already reverberating from the treetops above and when that had been followed by the sound of parting and splintering branches, the two men, regardless of all that had just been said about going against the flow and doing things methodically, had quickly scooped up their bags, and sped off in a direction that by then had become only too familiar. It meant that, for the next few minutes they were in a state of extreme and uncontrollable panic with only one intention-to put as much distance between themselves and whatever was roaming the canopy above.

With the mist still thickening and the underfoot conditions like that of an ice rink, it therefore wasn't long before the inevitable occurred.

"That's it," said Tommy while trying to extricate himself from a thick confusion of razor sharp thorns. "This is ridiculous. I've had enough. Starving dogs or no starving dogs, as soon as I manage to get myself free, I'm going back to that door and I'm heading for the bay."

"Wouldn't you like to investigate that first?" said the breathless Chairman upon dropping to his knees.

"Investigate what?" said a wincing Tommy.

"There's something that looks like a garden shed about 20 feet beyond your left shoulder," said the Chairman. "It's unlikely to be up to the standards of the Ritz Hotel, but it might just provide us with a bit of shelter for the night."

"How do you know it's a shed?" said Tommy.

"It appears to have a window and a roof," said the Chairman.

"It couldn't be the main house could it?" said Tommy.

"It's nowhere near big enough to be the main house," said the Chairman.

"That's a shame," said Tommy. "Because, whether you believe that house still exists or not, that's what we're really meant to be looking for isn't it?"

"It is yes," said the Chairman. "But I don't think that's going to happen any time soon. This garden's vast. You could lose ten Wembley Stadiums in here. I think we should get inside that shed and wait until the morning. Everything will look a lot different then."

"That's as long as I haven't bled to death," said Tommy.

"Are you badly injured?" said the Chairman after joining his companion on the other side of the hedge.

"I'm bleeding from places me mother didn't even get to wash," said Tommy before slowly climbing to his feet and proceeding to flick the snow from his shoulders.

"I've got some sticking plasters in my bag," said the Chairman.

"You won't have nearly enough," said Tommy. "Now

[583]

let's get to that shed before Tarzan's demented uncle returns."

The old shed the Chairman had spotted while the luckless Tommy was trying to free himself from the thorny bush, was about twelve feet long by ten feet across and had been constructed almost entirely from six inch wide tongued and grooved spruce panels and as well as being used to store fertilizer and a large variety of antiquated garden tools, it had been the place where a variety of unwanted household artefacts had been despatched after becoming surplus to requirements. To the two most recent occupants, the residual smell was very familiar and reasonably pleasant and welcoming-it was that of the old high street chandlers, a mix of creosote, fire-lighters, Methylated spirits and strong disinfectant. Nevertheless, there was a distinctive overriding musty odour which was almost certainly coming from any number of old fabrics including a pile of badly mildewed velvet curtains and a couple of woven rugs which had been rolled up like huge cigars. As the Chairman had suggested moments earlier amid Tommy's muted cries of anguish, the structure wasn't remotely of the five star quality but it was perfectly dry, had a sealed roof, four sturdy walls and, most importantly, a solid door that could be bolted from the inside.

Within minutes of securing that door, the beaver-like Tommy had discovered a number of essential items including an adequately fuelled industrial paraffin heater which he had managed to light first time and a pair of battered and bruised hurricane lanterns which, when eventually lit, illuminated places previously unseen such as the far corner where two stuffed animals, a wing-spread Golden Eagle and a coiled King Cobra, were balancing precariously on top of a tired Welsh Dresser. In fact, the shed was crammed to bursting point

[584]

with interesting artefacts from several bygone ages
which was probably the reason the discovery of a
recently discarded chocolate bar wrapper and a couple of
home rolled cigarette butts had attracted the men's
attention and provoked the first debate. However, the
'should we stay or should we go', discussion that almost
immediately followed, only lasted until an enormous
gust of wind had threatened to turn the shed on its side.
At which point, the Chairman, after quickly removing
his hat and gloves, headed over to the far side of the
building, unveiled a badly split green leather
Chesterfield armchair and sat down.
"This had my name on it from the moment we arrived,"
he said before closing his eyes and taking a deep breath.
"This is a real chair. This is a man's chair."
"Why are you sitting on it then?" said Tommy.
"That's not nice," said the Chairman. "You can be very
hurtful at times you know Tommy. You need to be
looking for something to sit on yourself. I'm sure I saw
a nice, comfy looking rocking chair over there."
"Over where?" said Tommy.
"There," said the Chairman. "Under that pile of striped
bedding. I was going to nab it for myself but I often get
dizzy on rocking chairs."
"That doesn't surprise me in the least," said Tommy.
"What do you make of the cigarette butts?"
"I don't know," said the Chairman.
"Who do you think they belonged to?" said Tommy.
"It's impossible to say," said the Chairman. "A passing
tramp, possibly."
"Do you think they might belong to somebody who
works in the garden?" said Tommy.
"It's possible," said the Chairman. "But they look years
old."
"The chocolate wrapper isn't years old," said Tommy.
"That looks brand new to me. By the way-what did you
see in the trees Hulmey?"
"I'm not sure," said the Chairman. "It was an animal of
some sort. Quite a large one too. It was very interested

in you."

"It must have been female then," said Tommy.

"You're beginning to sound like Blackie," said the Chairman. "Do you think they're alright?"

"Who?" said Tommy.

"The lads back on the train," replied the Chairman.

"I imagine so," said Tommy. "They're certainly a lot better off than us."

The conversation continued pretty much in that vein for another hour, covering topics such as what their partners might be feeling, how long it would be before the railway company realised their first rescue team had failed, the whereabouts of the badly traumatised Club Secretary and what had scared the pack of starving dogs into a condition resembling paralysis. Those things and many more had been discussed at considerable length until, just after 8.30, when the Chairman suddenly realised he was not only talking to himself but had probably been doing so for some considerable time. However, less than half an hour later, he was unwittingly doing so again.

'What the hell was that?' he said after hearing a dull thud on the shed door. And when that was followed by another slightly louder thud less than a minute later, he rose from his chair and after taking a few very ponderous steps back, he began to consider a number of possibilities. Who the hell could that be? What the hell could that be? Had those knocks simply been caused by a sudden and violent gust of wind? Had the noises therefore been made by the swinging limb of a nearby tree? Or, had he imagined the whole thing as a result of sleep deprivation and stress. As far as he was concerned, any one of those possibilities would have been more palatable than opening the door and being confronted by the creature that had recently been watching Tommy McShane.

And then there was another thud on the door. A noticeably much louder thud like that of a big bass drum. And then there were another two thuds. And then another three in quick succession that not only demonstrated a very definite rhythm but appeared to suggest growing impatience.

"Tommy," he whispered while gently and surreptitiously kicking his companion's exposed left shin. "You need to wake up Tommy. We've got a situation here."

The oblivious Tommy continued to sleep however. In fact, after appearing to hear the Chairman's last desperate plea, he had grunted, turned over and drawn his coat over his face.

"For God's sake Tommy," whispered the Chairman while continuing to slowly and ever so quietly back away from the door. "I think there's someone outside." And still Tommy slept and still the Chairman could do little more than whisper his impassioned pleas. That was until he heard another powerful knock on the door. A knock that had caused him to recoil like a fired cannon and slam his head against the base of the old Welsh dresser.

"Can I help you?" said the scrambling Chairman while discreetly looking for something club-like to defend himself with. "If you're looking for the main house, you're not too far away. Just follow the path with the Chinese statues running along it."

He would make several more polite enquiries over the next five or six minutes, each of which had gone unanswered but just as he was about to settle back down, he heard a much louder thud that had clearly come from a badly dipping portion of the roof.

"Hang on a minute," he said after breathing an audible sigh of relief and patting his heaving chest. "Hang on a damn minute Hulmey. That was snow. That was just a big clump of snow landing on the roof. That's what I must have been hearing. It was just snow falling. That's it. The tree branches can't cope with the weight of the snow. That's what it was. And that's why that part of the roof is on the verge of collapse. What a bloody idiot I am."

However, despite his obvious relief, and despite his desire to believe the thuds had been natural in origin, he had still been unable to settle back down because there was another possibility that was beginning to gnaw away at him. Another possibility that was just as feasible as the snow-related one. A possibility he just couldn't ignore and wasn't prepared to rule out. The possibility that the knocks on the door had been made by his missing friend the Club Secretary who, after getting lost, had somehow managed to find and follow his and his only remaining companion's tracks. That made sense too. That made good sense. That actually made perfect sense because that same badly traumatised and dumbstruck friend wouldn't have been able to respond to his many enquiries. 'It couldn't be could it?' he had asked himself before carefully unhooking the nearest lamp and making his way to the window. "Is that you out there Hilly?" That is when the noises ceased.

For the next uncertain hour that followed, and while his travelling companion continued to look more comatose than asleep and at times, more dead than alive, the Chairman stood mumbling to himself with his arms spanning the window frame and his forehead resting against the condensated glass pane. By the end of that horribly intense and time confused period, and despite remaining hopeful that his best friend had managed to find him, he had resigned himself to one of his initial and more convenient theories-the knocks on the door had just been falling heavy clumps of snow. That was until he heard a pitiful whimpering like that of something or someone seriously distressed or somebody or something in terrible pain.

Those incredibly distressing cries had disturbed the Chairman more than anything else that had gone before and as a result he began to view his oblivious companion with utter contempt-a contempt made all the worse after he had been struck on the nose by a flailing arm while once again attempting to rouse him from his deep slumber. It was an incident that had brought about a short period of self pity during which he wondered whether the best cause of action would be to return to the comfort of his leather bound chair, draw his coat over his head and simply hope the problem would go away. That was until he heard another pitiful moan that was all too clear and all too close and all too human-sounding to ignore. Nevertheless, despite resigning himself to the fact he needed to respond quickly, it would still be another fifteen minutes before the deeply troubled Chairman could bring himself to act.

"I don't bloody well need this," he said to himself while trying to ease his right foot into his steaming, damp left shoe. "Why me? Why me of all people?"

From the moment he eventually climbed back to his feet, everything the tormented Chairman did was pronounced and to the accompaniment of his mumbled complaints. He snatched the hanging lamp from the rafter, jammed his woolly hat over his head, wrenched his zip tight shut, stomped his feet on his way to the door and tore the bolts from their hasps as if he was discarding defective parts from a cheap toy production line conveyer belt. And still, to his utter dismay, Tommy didn't move a muscle or utter a single sound. At least not until his companion had taken half a dozen tenuous steps outside and the terrible cold hit him as effectively as a bucket of icy water over his head.

"What the hell!" he said after hearing the door slam closed and the two shed bolts slide back into place in rapid succession. "I don't believe this. Is he for real? Is that bloody imbecile for real? He's just locked me out. I do not believe this."

The Chairman's dire situation was compounded almost immediately because in his desperation to get back to the shed door to alert his companion that he was stranded outside, he had lost his footing and hit his forehead on the gnarly base of a dying Sycamore tree. That fall had left him badly dazed, disorientated and unable to appeal to his companion for help but worse of all, was a sudden all

[589]

consuming fear he might never be able to get back to his feet again. That however, was when he learnt something that chilled his spine far more effectively than the patch of marble like snow he was lying on. That was when he realised the yelping noises he had come out to investigate weren't coming from his exhausted or injured friend but were in fact, coming from an animal. In fact, to be even more precise, they were coming from a large number of animals.

Nevertheless, at that point, he still had no idea as to the species of the creatures and whether they constituted any sort of danger. All he knew was that they seemed to have the ability to communicate with one another, were just at home on the ground as they were up in the treetops and had huge amber coloured eyes that never seemed to blink, not even when a large, dislocated branch from the aforementioned Sycamore tree came thumping to the ground close by or when an incredibly ferocious gust of wind suddenly tore through the trees like a low flying rogue missile.

The Chairman had blinked though. In fact, the heavy, falling branch had acted like an army drill instructor's wakey, wakey call. Nevertheless, once up, he was faced with yet another dilemma because, to his horror, there was now another set of amber eyes between himself and the shed door which meant that, in order to avoid crossing the imposing creature's path, he had no choice but to make his way to the shed window and hope he could illicit his companion's attention before he fell back into one of his notoriously long and deep sleeps. Of course, that undertaking would have been far easier had he not landed on his lamp when he fell-a lamp which was now lying in the snow beyond repair and haemorrhaging the last of its fuel.

However, there was some compensation in knowing he hadn't slipped too far from the shed, so finding the window, despite the coal mine-like darkness and despite the treacherous underfoot conditions, wasn't likely to be too much of a problem. That was providing one very important thing. That was providing the animals didn't attack or cut him off at some stage of his relatively short journey. And to the Chairman's enormous relief, they hadn't. They had hardly moved at all. In fact, for some reason, the closer he came to the window, the quieter and more settled those animals became. And yet, they were still very much there and still watching his every move. He knew that because, although they had ceased their previous energetic activities, he could see their steaming breath. He could see up to ten small clouds of that steaming hot breath. One slow rising cloud for every curious observer.

And curious observers is what and how the creatures remained, at least until the Chairman turned to face the window and saw the reflection of what appeared to be a primate of immense proportion.

"What the hell!" he said after quickly spinning around and thrusting out his palms to protect his face. But, like a flash, the creature was already gone. Like a flash, there was nothing before him but misty air.

"What's going on?" he muttered to himself before turning back around and proceeding to pound the window pane with the soft, fleshy portion of his right fist. And then his muttering became louder and more appealing. And then he started shouting louder and hysterically. "For God's sake Tommy-open the bloody door. There are things out here that want to hurt me. Open the bloody door."

That is when the panic stricken Tommy suddenly appeared at the window and pandemonium broke out inside and outside the shed simultaneously. That was the moment the Chairman realised that what he had just seen was not in fact a reflection, but the real thing. The real thing but on the other side of the window.

For the next ten minutes or more, the interior of the shed resembled a Dodge City wild west saloon on pay day with furniture continually crashing and violence alternating from one wall to another and from one corner to the opposite one without any pause whatsoever. It

[591]

had all been performed to the beat of the Chairman's fist and the accompaniment of an ear pounding chorus of whoops and howls from the troop of creatures that for some reason had finally found their voices and it ended when the shed door burst open and a breathless and bloodied Tommy Mac emerged holding the back of his neck.

"Mother fucker!" he said before spitting out one of his lower front teeth. "That cheeky mother fucker!"

"What the hell was that all about?" said the highly confused, mightily relieved and desperately cold Chairman while following his seething companion back into the shed.

"Don't ask," said Tommy while wiping his mouth with his sleeve.

"What do you mean, don't ask?" said the Chairman. "What was all the commotion Tommy? It sounded like World War Three had broken out."

"I was attacked by a huge goblin or something," said Tommy. "That's what all the commotion was."

"A goblin," said the Chairman. "It didn't look like a goblin to me."

"What do you mean?" said Tommy. "Are you telling me you knew that thing was in here."

"I saw it through the window," said the Chairman.

"What were you doing looking through the window?" said Tommy.

"Trying to get your attention," said the Chairman. "You'd gone and locked me out."

"What were you doing outside?" said Tommy.

"I thought I heard Hilly," said the Chairman. "Where is it? Where is this so-called goblin?"

"In that old coffin shaped thing there," said Tommy.

"This?" said the Chairman. "This Ottoman?"

"Yes," said Tommy.

"Is it dead?" said the Chairman.

"I don't think so," said Tommy. "I think it's just unconscious. Don't let it out. Don't let it out Hulmey. It's fucking mental."

"I've no intention of letting it out," said the Chairman while struggling to relight the remaining lamp. "And by the way Tommy-you could be helping me here. Where's your flashlight?"

"The batteries gave out just before I stumbled into that bitch of a hedge," said Tommy. "I ditched the case. Is that a problem?"

"I suppose not," said the Chairman while slipping off his right boot. "I'll use this lamp."

"For what?" said Tommy.

"I want to take a close look at this creature you've just battered half to death," said the Chairman.

"What the hell for?" said Tommy.

"I want to know if it's in any pain," said the Chairman.

"In any pain!" said Tommy. "Have you thought of asking me how I am? I went toe to toe with that angry fucker. There were no Marques of Queensbury rules with that bastard thing. It bit, it spat and it scratched. The dirty bugger even shit in its hand and threw it at me at one point."

"I'm surprised you didn't do the same back," said the Chairman.

"What makes you think I didn't?" said Tommy.

"How did you manage to overpower it?" said the Chairman.

"I hit it over the head with a poker," said Tommy.

"That's nice," said the Chairman. "The old Marques would have been proud of you."

"I couldn't give a shite about the old Marques," said Tommy. "It's not coming into my home and calling the shots."

"Your home!" said the Chairman. "How do you know this isn't the animal's home?"

"Because, unless I'm mistaken, wild creatures such as goblins, usually live in the jungle," said Tommy. "And by the way-they don't eat Mars Bars and smoke rollies either. Do you really want to take a look? Have a look Hulmey. But be careful. It's lightning quick. Move that pile of old books. I'll be honest-I've never seen

[593]

anything like it. Not even at Chester Zoo."

"It's a baboon," said the Chairman before urging his companion to lower and add some weight to the Ottoman lid. "They can be vicious buggers those things."

"I know that," said Tommy. "I've just gone three hard rounds with it."

"Did you antagonise it in any way?" said the Chairman.

"What do you mean antagonise it?" said Tommy. "I didn't do a thing to it. I was lying on me chair minding my own business. I turned over to make myself a bit more comfy and saw the thing going through me bag. I wasn't having that."

"Is that when you hit it with the poker?" said the Chairman.

"That's when I told it to do one," said Tommy.

"How did you manage that?" said the Chairman. "Are you conversant with monkey lingo?"

"I just said, 'gertcha'," said Tommy.

"Well that explains why it went for you," said the Chairman.

"Why does it?" said Tommy.

"Because in Swahili, 'gertcha' means, 'Stand still while I put this rope around your neck.'," said the Chairman.

"That's not even remotely funny," said Tommy while very deliberately securing the bolts on the shed door. "Now follow me closely with that lamp. We're going to need to find out where the sneaky bastard got in."

"And then we're going to have to let it go," said the Chairman.

"Let it go!" said Tommy. "Are you out of your fucking mind? Why would you want to let the bastard thing go?"

"Because it's the right and proper thing to do," said the Chairman. "And its friends are already out there campaigning for its release."

"What friends?" said Tommy.

"There's about another 12 of those things outside," said the Chairman. "And judging by the level of their eyes,

some of them are almost as tall as you and me. It might
be a good idea if you go outside and talk to them."
"What do you mean, 'talk to them'?" said Tommy.
"Apologise for your behaviour," said the Chairman.
"Like hell I will," said Tommy. "I wasn't the one in the
wrong. I've just told you. I was minding my own
business. I didn't start anything. I owe those nasty
bastards nothing. Anyway-more to the point-what are
they doing here Hulmey?"
"They're a feature of this park I suppose," said the
Chairman. "You saw that warning sign."
"Do you think they're the reason the dogs didn't follow
us?" said Tommy.
"That would be my guess," said the Chairman before
taking one of the large books that Tommy had used to
hold down the Ottoman lid and settling down. "I don't
think there's a dog alive that would stand a chance
against one of those things."
"Mine would," said Tommy. "My pure white American
Pit Bull, Buster would. He's on the dangerous dogs list."
"You said that as if it's some sort of noteworthy
achievement," said the Chairman. "Has it killed anyone
yet?"
"Not killed," said Tommy. "But he did severely injure
a piece of shit drug dealer who thought he could start
doing business at the end of our street."
"How do you mean 'severely injure'?" said the
Chairman.
"He tore one of his calf muscles out and ate it," said
Tommy.
"That's lovely, that is," said the Chairman.
"It made a right mess of the hall, stairs and landing
carpet when it came back in," said Tommy. "Cathy was
livid."
"I bet she was," said the Chairman. "Did you have to
have him put down?"
"The authorities wanted to," said Tommy. "But I was
having none of it. He was a hero as far as I'm
concerned. He'd rid our street of vermin. He's probably

[595]

saved numerous kid's lives. I just wrapped him in a blanket and got him out of the way."

"Where to?" said the Chairman.

"I got our kid to mind him for a few months until the whole thing blew over," said Tommy. "He lives over the water in Birkenhead. He's back now. He's as happy as Lassie, as they say this side of the Mersey. I don't know what I'd do without him."

"Aren't you worried he'll get recognised and they'll come back for him?" said the Chairman.

"Not now he's been painted," said Tommy.

"Painted!" said the Chairman.

"Me and me missus dyed him," said Tommy.

"You did what?" said the Chairman.

"We dyed him chocolate brown," said Tommy. "It took us ages to get the tone right. The place was a right fucking mess. The dye was up the wall, on the ceiling, on the furniture and everywhere. I think there was eventually more dye on me and her than the dog. We looked like Ike and Tina Turner by the time we'd finished. 72 bottles of Garnier at nearly a fiver a bottle we used."

"Bloody hell!" said the Chairman. "Which one of you daft buggers footed the bill for that?"

"Neither of us," said Tommy. "We got a crisis loan from the Social Security."

"What!" said the Chairman.

"We told the Social Security we'd had a chip pan fire," said Tommy.

"Nice!" said the mortified Chairman. "It's innovative thinking like that, that makes me proud to be British. Why did you need so much dye?"

"The soft bugger kept licking the stuff off," said Tommy. "It must have thought it was gravy. It had the shits for a month. What's that you've got there?"

"It's an old photo album," said the Chairman. "It's full of pictures of steam trains. Take a look for yourself. Look at the large photo on or around the fifth page. Come to think of it, there's a couple of angry looking dogs on that."

"Do you mean the photo entitled, 'The Mallard'?" said Tommy.

"The next one," said the Chairman. "The one on the next page. Tell me what you think."

"It's just a train as far as I'm concerned," said Tommy after a short deliberation. "It's actually the last sort of photograph I want to be looking at after what we've just been through. Haven't you got any Polaroid snaps of your missus in her skimpy drawers?"

"Don't be at it," said the Chairman. "They're for my eyes only. Look at the photo Tommy. What's the first thing that takes your eye?"

"The dogs I suppose," said Tommy. "They're German Shepherds aren't they? Or are they Alsatians? I've never been able to tell the difference.""Neither have I," said the Chairman. "But that's not what I'm getting at. Look at the caption at the bottom. Read it out to me."

"A two cylinder...a two cylinder DRB Class 52?" said Tommy.

"That's right," said the Chairman. "Now look at the photo again Tommy. What would you say is the main subject matter?"

"The main subject matter?" said Tommy. "The train I suppose. The DRB 50 something or other."

"Why's that?" asked the Chairman.

"Because that's what the caption says," said Tommy.

"Try to forget the caption," said the Chairman. "Put that to the back of your mind for a minute or so. Explain what's happening on that photo?"

"An old lady's being set upon by a group of soldiers," said Tommy.

"That's right," said the Chairman. "The main subject of that photo is a terrified old lady being abused by two big burly German officers, while two laughing soldiers in the foreground are struggling to restrain their snarling dogs."

"Well there's that as well I suppose," said Tommy. "What of it?"

"Well don't you find that strange?" said the Chairman.

"Why should I?" said Tommy.

"Because, surely the more interesting and most sensational thing about that photograph is the cruel and brutal attack on the poor old woman-not what sort of steam engine she's just been dragged from," said the Chairman.

"I suppose it depends what your interests are," said Tommy.

"I think it's perverse," said the Chairman. "I find it extremely hard to stomach. I'll go even further than that. I think the person who added that caption in fountain pen is an unfeeling freak who probably achieved his first hard on by pulling the legs off a spider. I just hope to Christ I never meet the heartless bastard."

"I think most train spotters are freaks," said Tommy. "Now are we going to try and get some sleep or are you planning to go for another moonlight walk?"

"Are we all secure for the night?" said the Chairman. "Is that hole where King Kong got in, blocked up?"

"I've put a heavy fireguard and a piece of marble top against it," said Tommy. "But it might be an idea to leave the lamp on. That thing didn't get in here until you went walkabout and left the shed in complete darkness."

"I think you might be right for once," said the Chairman. "Did it eat the last of your butties by any chance?"

"It took a little bite out of each," said Tommy before cramming the shredded remains of a beef and mustard sandwich into his gaping mouth. "Do you want one?"

"I'll pass if it's all the same to you," said the disgusted Chairman.

CHAPTER TWENTY FIVE
ARRIVAL

For what remained of the evening and the six and a half hours before the two men rose, stretched out their aching backs and began to make preparations for what they hoped would be the last and most rewarding stage of their journey, the baboons, although remaining curious and watchful, never once attempted to breach the shed's defences. They had been far less vocal too and instead of whooping loudly as they had while the frantic Chairman was trying to gain his sleeping companion's attention, they had taken it in turns to hum a mournful, almost haunting lament as if to reassure their captured friend and family member, help was not too far away. However, within seconds of the revitalised and crudely patched up Tommy Mac releasing the bolts from the shed door and signalling his companion to follow, every one of them had returned to their homes high up in the treetops and each had become invisible and completely silent.

Another encouraging and welcome aspect of the morning was the absence of the heavy mist which meant for the first time since entering the grounds, the two men were able to appreciate the size, splendour and incredible diversity of the garden. That had also reduced the sense of menace, because whereas during the previous evening when visibility was almost zero, and so many of the cleverly sculpted bushes had appeared to be monstrous predators ready to pounce at any given moment, now they were just how nature had intended them to be-harmless, quivering snow capped parts of the flora. They had been guilty of persistently obscuring the men's view however-at least until they reached a crossroads and a beaming Tommy took his startled and indignant companion by the right sleeve. "I spy a smoking chimney," he said before dropping to one knee to refasten his left bootlace.

It would still nevertheless be almost three

hours before the men caught their first glimpse of the old house, a period during which both men's self control had been tested beyond any previous limits. In fact, at one point, and despite knowing the building lay so tantalisingly close, both men had been on the verge of aborting their mission and heading back to the little door to resume their originally planned route. That was until they discovered and then crossed a previously unseen rickety bamboo bridge and made their way through a long and seemingly endless tunnel of Laburnum.

"Bloody hell!" said the breathless Tommy before dropping his bag and following it to the ground. "There it is. We've found the house Hulmey."

"Are you sure it's the right one?" said the Chairman.

"Sod off, you sarcastic bastard," said Tommy.

"I was only asking," said the smiling Chairman.

"You were trying to be funny," said Tommy. "I'm just glad we didn't stumble across this place last night. I think I'd still be running away now. It looks like something from a Gothic horror movie."

"Those gargoyles certainly are," said the Chairman. "But at least that's a little bit more encouraging."

"What is?" said Tommy.

"That upper stained glass window to the left," said the Chairman. "The one directly above the large downstairs bay."

"What do you mean?" said Tommy. "Why's that encouraging?"

"Because it's one of the few windows not boarded up," said the Chairman.

"It is isn't it," said Tommy. "Why do you think that is?"

"It might have something to do with money," said the Chairman. "Or the lack of it."

"How do you mean?" said Tommy.

"People can't afford to heat these big homes anymore," said the Chairman. "They're just too big. It'd cost the earth. There must be hundreds of rooms in this place. The owners sometimes throw dust sheets over their furniture, close off most of the house and live in just one wing. In its day, this place would have had an army of maids and servants. Now there's probably just the owner and a tiny skeleton staff living here."

"And is that who you think might be on the other side of that window?" said Tommy.

"I don't know, " said the Chairman while pointing towards the tall, elaborately conceived chimney stack. "But somebody must have lit that fire. I just hope they're going to hear us knock."

The Chairman needn't have worried, because upon arriving at the impressive and hugely imposing front porch and raising a heavy bronze knocker in the shape of a snarling wolf's head, the heavy oak door slowly creaked open.

"What's the problem?" he said upon noticing his companion's reluctance to follow him inside.

"I don't know," said an uncharacteristically edgy Tommy while scanning a section of open land just beyond the nearest row of unkempt hedges. "I just get the feeling we're being watched."

"We are being watched," said the Chairman before taking his companion by the upper arm. "That's why I'd like to get inside as soon as possible. And for your information, we've been getting watched since we exited that archway."

"Who by?" said Tommy.

"I've no idea," said the Chairman. "But I do know this-he's not the friendly or talkative type."

"Do you think he might be a gardener or something like that?" said Tommy.

"It's possible," said the Chairman.

"Maybe it's someone who's lost like us," said Tommy.

"We're not lost," said the Chairman. "This place was clearly marked on our little map and whether it was by skill or good fortune, we managed to find it."

"That's true," said Tommy. "Who do you think he is then? It couldn't be Hilly could it?"

"I wouldn't have thought so," said the Chairman. "Unless he's gained about 12 stone and grown 3 feet in height since we last saw him."

Within seconds, Tommy had glided past the club Chairman into the vestibule and after hanging his bag on an impressively carved but badly distressed mirrored hall stand, he kicked the snow from the soles of his shoes and awaited his companion.

"What's the matter Hulmey?" he asked. "Has he spotted us?"

"I don't think so," said the Chairman. "He's up to something though."

"What do you mean?" said Tommy.

"He's staring up at the treetops," said the Chairman. "He seems to be calling something to him. Listen. Can you hear him?"

"I can't hear a thing for that bloody wind," said Tommy.

"He's calling something," said the Chairman.

"Maybe he's got a cat," said Tommy. "It might have got stuck up a tree."

"It's possible," said the Chairman while heaving the huge door over. "And, by the way, now might be a good time to put a match to your lamp. I've got a feeling there's going to be a lack of electricity in this place."

"I was thinking the very same thing," said Tommy. "And I was also wondering why there's no vestibule door."

"No door!" said the Chairman.

"There's no door," said Tommy. "At least, none that I can see. It's the same panelling all the way around."

"That's odd," said the Chairman. "Are you sure?"

"I'm positive," said Tommy. "There's no sign of any knobs or hinges either."

"Have a look at the floor," said the Chairman. "See if there's any footprints or signs of wear."

"There's nothing," said Tommy. "To be honest, there's no part of the floor that doesn't look scuffed."

"There's got to be some way in," said the Chairman.

"Try pressing some of those wooden panels."

"Which ones?" said Tommy.

"I'd start with the ones you can reach," said the Chairman. "And press them as hard as you can. If they were designed for that big bastard out there to get in, the panel probably needs hitting with the force of a two ton truck."

For the next thirty minutes, while the Chairman searched feverishly for some sort of secret latch or hidden lever, Tommy proceeded to press as many of the identical wooden panels as he possibly could. He pressed individual panels, he pressed pairs of panels and he pressed panels in sequences across, down and diagonally. And yet, nothing happened. Nothing happened at all. That was until he kicked out in frustration, lost his balance and stumbled against his startled companion's shins.

"What was that?" said the slowly retreating Chairman upon hearing a series of loud clicks followed by what appeared to be the whirring of heavy machinery.

"Bloody hell!" said Tommy after quickly scrambling to his feet and staring at the ground as if it was about to gobble him up. "Have we found it? Have we found the way in?"

"I thought we had," said the Chairman. "But it's all gone quiet now. What did you do? What exactly did you do Tommy?"

"I didn't do anything," said Tommy.

"You did," said the Chairman. "You lost your rag and kicked out in frustration. Which panel did you kick Tommy?"

"I'm not sure," said Tommy. "One of those lower ones over there."

"Try kicking it again," said the Chairman. "Let's be honest. Unless you've recently taken up ballet dancing or gymnastics, there's only so many of those panels you can reach. As far as I recall, you were definitely in the far corner. Try kicking them one at a time and waiting a bit for a response."

And that's what Tommy did. He kicked a panel and waited. And then he kicked another panel and

waited and another and another and another. And yet,
nothing happened. Nothing happened at all. "I don't get
it," said the Chairman. "I distinctly heard the sound of
machinery."

"I did too," said Tommy. "But for some reason it's
stopped. Why did it stop? Help me here Hulmey-you're
meant to be the one with the engineering nous."

"I'm not sure I can help you," said the Chairman. "Why
don't we try to retrace your steps."

"Alright," said Tommy. "Where do you want me?"

"Back in the corner facing the wall," said the Chairman.

"And then what?" said Tommy.

"Choose a panel and kick it," said the Chairman.

"Which one?" said Tommy.

"It doesn't really matter," said the Chairman. "It's going
to have to be trial and error until you hit the jackpot."

"Alright," said Tommy after kicking the very corner
panel. "Now what?"

"Count to ten with me," said the Chairman. "One-two-
three-four."

"Now what?" said Tommy.

"Try kicking the panel next to it," said the Chairman.
"And wait again."

"Nothing's happening," said Tommy after counting
another slow ten. "Now what? Do you want me to kick
the next panel?"

"I want you to try to do everything you did before," said
the Chairman.

"That's what I've been doing," said Tommy.

"That might not be entirely the case," said the
Chairman. "If I remember right, you kicked the panel
and then pinned me to the hallstand."

"That's because I lost my balance," said Tommy.

"That doesn't matter," said the Chairman. "Just kick
the panel and get back to me as quick as you can."

"This is bullshit," said Tommy after kicking another
three panels, stepping back each time and joining the
Chairman. "I'm sure you're winding me up Hulmey.
You're not filming this are you?"

"Just wait a minute," said the Chairman upon hearing the faintest click.

"What was that?" said Tommy. "What was that Hulmey?"

"Don't you move a muscle," said the Chairman after pulling his companion close. "It's starting again. I think we might have cracked it Tommy."

It was actually another thirty seconds before something significant happened. This time, there were four loud clicks in quick succession and an even louder whirring of machinery followed by what seemed to be the releasing of a large industrial chain.

"There you go," said the Chairman while watching a portion of the wall directly opposite the main door slowly begin to slide open bringing what had previously been a magnificent central hallway into full view.

"Bloody hell!" said Tommy.

"What did I tell you?" said an immensely satisfied looking Chairman after picking up his bag and heading towards one of a pair of beautifully carved newel posts that were standing like sentries at either side of a grand staircase. "We're in."

"Thanks to me," said Tommy.

"No thanks to you," said the Chairman.

"I beg to differ," said Tommy. "I did all the spade work. I literally did all the panel beating, if you'll pardon the pun."

"The problem needed thinking out," said the Chairman upon stepping into the hall. "It's brilliant when you come to think of it."

"What makes you say that?" said Tommy. "It's just a sliding bloody door?"

"The security aspect of it's genius," said the Chairman. "Think about it Tommy-to enter this house, you've got to locate and apply pressure to a particular wall panel, and after doing that, retire and stand in a particular spot."

"Do you think standing by the hallstand made all the difference?" said Tommy.

"I most certainly do yes," said the Chairman. "I reckon,

in order to gain entry here, you've either got to be the same weight as the big fella we saw earlier."

"It's a pity you didn't bring your missus along then," said Tommy. "It might have saved us a lot of time and effort."

"I'll pretend I didn't hear that," said the Chairman.

Before they had begun their ascent of the hugely impressive, albeit cobweb draped and dust coated staircase, the Chairman had briefed his companion as to how the two of them might be perceived by any occupants of the old house. He had reminded him that, as far as the law was concerned, and regardless of the fact the front door had been open to allow them unchallenged access, they were still in fact trespassers and were therefore likely to be viewed with a certain amount of suspicion. It was advice that Tommy had listened to intently and appeared to have taken on board, at least until he lost patience with the painfully hesitant Chairman and bounded past him with the effervescence of a playful three year old. That change in the recently established order wasn't to last too long however, because within seconds, he was back at the bottom of the stairs clawing at the seams of the vestibule panel through which he and his companion had just gained entry to the hallway.

"That's just great isn't it!" he said while pounding the partition with his two fists. "That's just typical of our bloody luck."

"What's the matter?" said the Chairman.

"You know damn well what's the matter," said Tommy. "The bloody door has shut on us. We're trapped. How the hell are we going to get out?"

"Get out!" said the Chairman. "Bloody hell Tommy! Are you for real? A few minutes ago you were desperate to get in."

"I know I was," said Tommy. "But that door remaining open would have left us with a definite way out should things go tits up."

[606]

"There will be a way out," said the Chairman. "But let's address that problem when the time comes for us to leave."

"I'd prefer to address it now," said Tommy. "I want to be sure we can escape if we have to. I don't like this Hulmey. I don't like this one little bit."

"This building used to be an asylum," said the Chairman calmly. "It's got to have security measures in place. It would have housed all sorts of crazy bastards and psychopaths at one time or another."

"What if it still does," said Tommy.

"That's the chance we're going to have to take," said the Chairman. "But let's be honest Tommy-no asylum manager worth his or her salt is going to allow their inmates to roam about unsupervised. They'll be safely locked up somewhere. And if there are still lunatics being held here, we'd be hearing them screaming and shouting by now. And there'd be a receptionist to greet us and all sorts of orderlies and doctors walking about. No, I'm not having it Tommy. This house is far too quiet to still be housing the mentally ill. I think you'll find it's reverted to its original status as a national heritage building."

"What does that mean in terms of the place having a telephone we can use?" said Tommy. "Is it a good thing or a bad thing?"

"It doesn't bode well to be perfectly honest," said the Chairman.

"Why's that?" said Tommy.

"Largely because of the unsightly wiring they require," replied the Chairman. "The National Heritage people would probably frown upon it. Modern wiring just doesn't go with the existing old fashioned fixtures and fittings. But I'd have thought by being a builder, you'd have known all that. Have you never worked on any National Heritage sites?"

"None that I'm aware of," said Tommy.

"Have you ever been to look around one?" said the Chairman.

[607]

"Look around what?" said Tommy.

"A stately home," replied the Chairman.

"You're joking aren't you Hulmey," said Tommy. "It's me you're talking to. I can think of hundreds of better ways to waste my hard earned money. Have you? Is that the sort of thing you like to do?"

"On occasions yes," said the Chairman. "I've visited loads of stately homes. And I've actually stayed in quite a few too."

"Really!" said Tommy.

"Yes, really," said the Chairman. "I stayed in one only this year. I booked it as an anniversary present for the wife. A place called Borley Rectory in Essex. It was advertised on line as the most haunted house in England. Me missus loves anything like that. She's right into the supernatural and spiritualists and tarot card readings. She's like that cute little American kid. She's convinced she sees dead people."

"And does she?" said Tommy.

"She claims she does," said the Chairman. "It's living people she struggles to see. People who come calling at the house for money such as the milkman, the insurance agent and Davie Larko, who does her MOT and car services. She rather conveniently fails to see any of them. Charlie Muggings here is the only one who sees and takes care of them. I don't know how she does it. I really don't. Do you know what Tommy-in all the time we've been married, she's never once been around when any of those people have called to be paid. It's uncanny. It really is uncanny."

"Maybe she's got a sixth sense," said Tommy.

"If that was meant to be a pun, let me be the first to congratulate you," said the Chairman.

"Thank you," said Tommy. "Did *you* see any ghosts?"

"I didn't," said the Chairman. "But it was actually me who got the biggest fright."

"Why's that?" said Tommy.

"Because I thought the price was £180 for a three night stay," said the Chairman. "It turned out to be £180 for a night."

"A night!" said Tommy. "Fuck me! I wouldn't have needed to have seen any ghosts. The bill alone would have been enough to scare the shit out of me. But by the way Hulmey-while we're on the subject of scary things-whatever you do-don't suddenly look up."

"Sod off Tommy," said the Chairman. "Do you think I'm stupid? Do you think I'm going to fall for that old trick?"

"I'm not messing Hulmey," said Tommy. "Don't make any sudden movements."

"Why not?" said the Chairman.

"Because there's a great big, fuck off rat the size of a dog about to pounce on you," said Tommy.

"Where?" said the Chairman after snatching his companion's lamp and thrusting it upwards. "I can't see anything."

"It's up there somewhere," said Tommy. "It must have gone into hiding.....or maybe it hasn't. Oh Christ! There it is again. Can you see it now?"

"I can yes," said the Chairman while slowly and cautiously continuing to climb.

"What are you going to do?" said Tommy. "Have you got anything to squish it with?"

"I like to hope it doesn't have to come to that," said the Chairman.

"And I hope it does," said Tommy. "Oh God! There it is again. The horrible thing's eyeballing me now."

"It's a big bastard isn't it?" said the Chairman.

"It's about the biggest I've ever seen," said Tommy. "And I've worked inside some shit dumps I can tell you. If you get the chance, kill it stone dead Hulmey. Whatever you do, don't let it bite you. You'll end up getting Sepsis and losing your hand or something. I hate the filthy things. They've got no right to be in people's houses."

"This animal might choose to disagree with you there," said the Chairman.

"Why's that?" said Tommy.

[609]

"It's been domesticated," said the Chairman.

"Domesticated!" said Tommy.

"That's right," said the Chairman while urging his companion to keep pace. "This one's likely to have a name and a comfy bed."

"Why's that?" said Tommy.

"Because it's actually a cat," said the Chairman.

"A cat!" said Tommy.

"That's right," said the Chairman. "A well nourished and well cared for one too."

"But I could have sworn it was a rat," said the squinting Tommy while scratching his head.

"It's an easy mistake to make," said the Chairman. "Particularly for someone who confuses goblins with baboons. It was the fake diamond collar and the bell around its neck that convinced me in the end. No self respecting rat would be seen dead in a Gangsta rap outfit

"Piss off Hulmey," said Tommy after pushing past his companion and almost knocking him off his feet. "This place isn't exactly lit up like Blackpool promenade."

"It's not, to be fair" said the Chairman after arriving on the landing. "As I just said-it's a mistake anyone could have made. Now then David Attenborough-which way do you suggest we go?"

In an effort to hide his embarrassment, Tommy hadn't bothered to respond to the Chairman's question but instead had chosen to follow the slightly better lit of two sparsely furnished corridors, upon the upper walls of which were mounted a vast array of wild animal head trophies and a huge collection of weapons which ranged from the medieval to the comparatively modern. By half way along, he had not been challenged by any proprietor or member of staff and was therefore a bit confused and more than a little annoyed when he turned around to discover his companion hadn't been keeping up with his moderate pace.

"What the hell's the matter now Hulmey?" he asked after dropping his bag and throwing out his arms remonstratively.

"Listen," whispered the Chairman.

"Listen to what?" whispered Tommy.

"It's that sound of grinding machinery again," whispered the Chairman. "And you know what that means don't you?"

"What?" whispered the impatient Tommy.

"It means someone's not too far behind us," whispered the Chairman.

"Is that necessarily a bad thing?" whispered Tommy.

"I don't know," whispered the Chairman. "I suppose it depends who that someone is and how we're perceived."

"We're just a couple of people who got lost in the snow," whispered Tommy before lashing out with his right foot as the very same cat he had earlier mistaken for a rodent, tried to make its way through his legs to get to a ball of fluff that had just taken to the air.

"Behave yourself Tommy," whispered the Chairman.

"The flea ridden thing's getting right up my nose," whispered Tommy. "It's going to do me a mischief if I'm not careful."

"It was just being playful," whispered the Chairman upon arriving at his companion's shoulder. "It's what cats do. Did you see which way it went?"

"That way," whispered Tommy. "Straight ahead."

"That's good," whispered the Chairman. "Now, don't take your eyes off it whatever you do."

"Why's that?" whispered Tommy.

"Because it might just be heading for its owner," whispered the Chairman.

"What makes you think that?" whispered Tommy.

"Because you've hurt the poor thing," whispered the Chairman. "It needs comforting. Didn't you see it limping?"

"It deserves to be limping," whispered Tommy. "I could have tripped and broken me neck. And by the way Hulmey-what makes you think it's got an owner? For all you know, it might just be a mangy old stray that's sneaked in through a damaged vent or something."

"It's wearing an expensive looking collar," whispered

the Chairman. "Which means, at one time or other, somebody loved, cared and shopped for it. And that somebody might be the very person we're about to ask for help. Let's just hope you haven't broken the little thing's leg. Because if you have, and the owner puts two and two together, we're not likely to get the warm reception we're hoping for."

"I hardly touched the filthy thing," whispered Tommy. "I just helped it on its way."

"Shush!" whispered the Chairman.

"I won't shush," said Tommy.

"Just be quiet a minute Tommy," whispered the Chairman. "Listen."

"Listen to what?" whispered Tommy before reaching over and taking hold of his companion's coat tail.

"Listen," whispered the Chairman.

"What the hell to?" whispered Tommy.

"Didn't *you* hear that?" whispered the Chairman.

"Hear what?" whispered Tommy. "Hear what Hulmey?"

"It sounded like someone giggling," whispered the Chairman.

"Giggling!" whispered Tommy.

"That's right," whispered the Chairman. "Almost like a naughty child."

"A child!" whispered Tommy.

"Like a child," whispered the Chairman while taking a couple of steps back. "But it's not a child."

"What do you mean?" whispered Tommy.

"It's not a child," whispered the Chairman. "It's too tall to be a child. It's actually an adult. A woman, I think. An old woman. She's just around that corner."

"When did you develop the ability to see round corners?" whispered Tommy.

"I can see her reflection in that old shield on the wall," whispered the Chairman.

"What's she doing?" whispered Tommy.

"She's just standing there giggling to herself," whispered the Chairman. "She's clutching something to her chest."

"Clutching what?" whispered Tommy. "It's not a knife is it? She's not clutching a fucking weapon is she Hulmey?"

"Relax," whispered the Chairman while repositioning his lamp. "It's just something soft and furry. I think it's a teddy bear."

"Who do you think she is?" whispered Tommy. "Do you think she's the owner?"

"She could be," whispered the Chairman.

"What do you think she's up to?" whispered Tommy. "And even more importantly-why do you think she hasn't introduced herself?"

"I don't know," whispered the Chairman. "She's too interested in her...."

"In her what?" whispered Tommy. "Too interested in her what Hulmey? Her teddy bear?"

"It's not a teddy bear," whispered the Chairman. "It's moving. It's alive. It's wriggling. It's a small animal of some sort. She's kissing it on the nose now. I think it's some sort of pet. It's either a rat or a ferret. See for yourself. Come here. You'll be able to see what's going on if you adjust your position slightly."

"I don't want to see her, thank you very much," whispered Tommy. "This is freaking me out. Let's go and find another way. I don't like this Hulmey. In fact, let's just get the hell out of here."

"Just wait a minute," whispered the Chairman.

"Wait for what?" whispered Tommy. "Wait for her to jump out on us? Why is it you always want to wait?"

"Because waiting, instead of acting on impulse, gives me time to think," whispered the Chairman.

"I've already thought," whispered Tommy. "Come on, let's go the other way. It's obvious the woman doesn't want anything to do with us."

"Just give me a minute," whispered the Chairman before suddenly going completely rigid, clamping his hand over his open mouth and slowly sliding down the wall.

"What's the matter?" whispered Tommy after dropping

to his haunches. "What's going on Hulmey?"

"Nothing," whispered the Chairman after lowering his head.

"Never mind nothing," whispered Tommy. "You've turned as white as a sheet. What's going on Hulmey? Talk to me lad. Talk to me, will you. What's happening lad?"

"You wouldn't believe me if I told you," whispered the Chairman.

"Try me," whispered Tommy. "For fuck's sake, try me Hulmey."

"She ate it," whispered the Chairman after flicking away a short length of white foamy phlegm that had been dangling from the corner of his mouth since the very moment he hit the floor.

"She did what?" whispered Tommy.

"She just ate a living creature," whispered the badly shaken Chairman. "She held it up by its tail and dropped it down her throat."

"Jesus Christ!" whispered Tommy before immediately retreating to the wall as an extremely haggard, pallid and grey haired old woman slowly and almost surreally emerged from around the corner and began to dance a foxtrot with a non-existent partner.

"That's her," said the Chairman.

"What the fuck!" whispered the horrified Tommy while trying unsuccessfully to help the baulking Chairman to get back to his feet. "What's going on here Hulmey?"

"I don't know," whispered the Chairman. "I can only assume she's one of the inmates. I must have been wrong. This place must still be operating as an asylum."

"Do you mean to say there's likely to be more like her?" whispered Tommy while watching the phantom-like woman pirouette before dancing away to her own softly hummed tune. "What do you think Hulmey?"

"I think it's extremely unlikely she's going to be a one off," whispered the Chairman. "And with that in mind, I think we've got a very important decision to make."

"If it's to stay or get the hell out of here as fast as we

can, I've already made my decision," whispered
Tommy. "Let's be honest Hulmey-if the mentally
unhinged are allowed to roam around unsupervised, this
isn't the place for the likes of you and me."

"I couldn't agree more," whispered the Chairman before
grabbing his companion's belt and hauling himself back
to his feet. "But wouldn't you like to find out where that
cable leads first?"

"What cable?" whispered Tommy.

"The white one running along the top of the skirting
board," whispered the Chairman. "Because that looks
very much like telephone cable to me."

"It does to me too," whispered Tommy. "And it looks
quite recently laid too. How about I go and investigate
while you keep watch from the top of the stairs."

"How about I go and investigate and you keep watch,"
whispered the Chairman.

"Why would you want to do that?" whispered Tommy.
"Don't tell me you've suddenly grown a pair."

"I think there's someone coming up the stairs,"
whispered the Chairman while pointing towards the
previously trodden part of the landing. "In fact, I'm
certain there is."

"And once again, is that necessarily a bad thing?"
whispered Tommy before picking up the lamp and
slinging his bag over his shoulder. "It could be the
owner of the place for all you know."

"It very well could be," whispered the Chairman. "But it
could be another inmate. And don't forget, someone
residing here thinks it's acceptable to have a troop of
baboons roaming around the grounds. Which reminds
me.....Oh bloody hell! Oh no. Oh damn it!"

"What's the matter?" whispered Tommy.

"The baboon," whispered the Chairman.

"What about the baboon?" whispered Tommy.

"We forgot to release it," whispered the Chairman. "It's
still inside the Ottoman. Bloody hell Tommy. The poor
bugger's going to suffocate or starve."

"It won't," whispered Tommy. "It'll break its way out

when it comes round or gets hungry. Did you see the teeth and claws on that thing? They're like hedge cutters. It's probably back with its mates already. Anyway-we can check up on it when we go back to the shed"

"Go back to the shed!" whispered the Chairman while cautiously inching around the corner. "When did that become part of our plan?"

"When I realised I'd left my wallet," whispered Tommy.

"How did you manage that?" said the Chairman.

"It must have fallen out of my trouser pocket when I was fighting the gorilla," said Tommy.

"It was a baboon," whispered the Chairman. "Was there much in it?"

"Not really," whispered Tommy. "About thirty quid, a couple of cash cards and a photo of me and the missus when we were in Marrakesh a few years ago. One of those street photographers took it of the two of us. He had a monkey, funnily enough."

"They often do," whispered the Chairman.

"Cute monkeys attract tourists. Particularly kids and animal lovers.....But listen.....What do you make of that?"

"Make of what?" said Tommy.

"Is that music I can hear?" said the Chairman. "Is that somebody playing a piano?"

"I wouldn't exactly say that," whispered Tommy while pointing to the gap at the bottom of a large four panelled door about twenty feet ahead. "But someone seems to be occupying that room. Is that a fire I can hear crackling?"

"That's what I was thinking," said the Chairman.

What the Chairman had actually heard was not music as such but a mish mash of non conforming and random notes played on a piano that was either missing keys or badly in need of tuning. It was resounding from a room at the far end of another long, dark corridor, upon the walls of which were hanging a succession of ornately framed prints of surly looking gentlemen dressed in all manner of military attire.

"I wouldn't have liked to have met this gnarly old bugger on the battlefield," whispered Tommy after pausing opposite a portrait of a formidable looking Bavarian Cavalry officer.

"He's got a look of Hamill about him," whispered the Chairman.

"He's certainly got his frown and furrowed brow," whispered Tommy.

"There's no doubt about that," whispered the Chairman before pulling his companion to one side. "But listen Tommy...let's get serious for a moment. If there are people on the other side of that door, they're going to get one hell of a shock when we walk in. They'll probably become extremely agitated. Let me do all the talking. Allow me to put them at ease. Let's just be as polite as possible, see if they've got a phone we can use and take it from there."

"What if they call the police and have us arrested for trespassing," whispered Tommy.

"That would be absolutely fantastic," whispered the Chairman. "That would be my wildest dream come true."

"Who goes there?" came a gruff and very authoritative sounding voice from somewhere just beyond the half open door. "Advance and identify yourselves this very minute or risk immediate arrest."

"We're sorry to bother you," said the Chairman after tentatively inching open the door and stepping inside a large living room. "Our train got stranded not too far from here."

"Your train!" said the taller of two elderly men who were sitting either end of an enormous, highly polished dining table.

"What train would that be? As far as I'm aware, there aren't any trains running through these parts. There haven't been for some time. That's right isn't it Major."

"It is indeed Colonel," said the stern faced Major while

struggling to release the complicated brake on his massively outdated wheelchair. "I think you'll find you're being lied to."

"It's the truth," said the Chairman while slowly approaching the more vociferous of the men who was in the process of picking up the injured cat. "The line has recently been reopened by a private rail company."

"God blimey Charlie!" said the Colonel. "Did you hear that Major? That is a bit of filth. That's the last thing I wanted to hear."

"I'm sorry to be the bearer of bad news," said the Chairman.

"Don't worry yourself," said the Colonel. "I've heard far worse. In fact, I've heard a hundred times worse. Tell me young man-is this rail line you've just referred to, going to be carrying one of those characterless, electricity powered things?"

"It's going to be carrying a reproduction steam train," said the Chairman. "It's a really impressive looking bit of kit to be honest. The company want it to emulate the old Orient Express for luxury and service."

"Do they really?" said the Colonel. "They've got their work cut out. That old train was a thing of rare beauty and engineering excellence almost second to none."

"Have you travelled on it?" said the Chairman.

"I travelled on it several times during the 1930s and early '50s," said the Colonel. "I once had afternoon tea with the great Marlene Dietrich. She was another thing of rare beauty. She even autographed the train menu for me. I've still got it somewhere. I was offered a lot of money for it."

"I bet you were," said the Chairman.

"And listen to this," said the Colonel before looking right and left and gradually lowering his tone as if afraid of being overheard. "I even saw a man murdered while I was on board the old thing."

"Really?" said the Chairman.

"I watched a man get pushed from it at high speed," said the Colonel. "An American chap he was. Somewhere

near Salzburg, I think we were. The authorities claimed
it had been an accident. They said there was a fault with
one of the doors. But it was no accident, I can assure
you. He was very definitely pushed. I saw it happen
with my own eyes. I think the unfortunate victim might
have been a Navy boy."

"Did you report what you'd seen?" said the Chairman.

"Did I hell as like," said the Colonel. "Everything was
very cloak and dagger during that delicate political era.
People were going missing all the time. You were often
scared to blink in case someone thought you were
communicating in code. By the way-what do you
think?"

"Think about what?" said the Chairman.

"Was your mode of transportation up to scratch?" said
the Colonel. "Did it cut the mustard?"

"Accommodation wise yes," said the Chairman. "It was
just a shame the engine wasn't up to the rigours of the
journey."

"Where exactly were you meant to be heading?" said the
Colonel.

"Scotland," said the Chairman while encouraging his
sheepish looking companion to join him. The Scottish
Borders. Selkirk, to be exact. It was only for a short
overnight stay. It was just meant to be a test run to
establish costs. Unfortunately, this is as far as we got."

"Are there just the two of you?" said the Colonel.

"There are now," said the Chairman.

"What do you mean?" said the Colonel.

"There were originally three of us," said the Chairman.
"We volunteered to go looking for help. But we became
separated from our Club Secretary last evening."

"Oh dear!" said the Colonel. "That's not good is it.
This isn't the time of year for getting lost. Might I
assume the others are still on board the train?"

"You might," said the Chairman. "There's another 12
or so members, including my brother."

"Members of what, might I enquire?" said the Colonel.

"We're a Veteran Football Club from Merseyside," said

the Chairman.

"That's a relief," laughed the Colonel while watching his beloved cat limp over to the fireplace. "For a moment I thought you were going to tell me you're all members of a new branch of the constabulary. The last thing I want is busy body people like that sniffing round this place."

"But that doesn't stop you inviting the buggers over for drinks," said the Major.

"I know," said the Colonel. "But I like to keep my enemies close. And I often get bored with the same old conversations."

"Why did you refer to the police as your 'enemies' Colonel?" said the Chairman.

"Because some of the blaggards are constantly trying to have me closed down," said the Colonel.

"I see," said the Chairman. "Well, you can rest assured my friends aren't policemen."

"That's good," said the Colonel. "You should have brought them with you. Aren't you concerned they'll all freeze or starve to death."

"They're alright in that respect as far as we know," said the Chairman. "There's still plenty of food and the heating system's still holding up."

"That's good," said the Colonel. "And I assume they're being well looked after are they?"

"What do you mean?" said the Chairman.

"I assume the stewards are making a real fuss of them," said the Colonel.

"There are no stewards," said the Chairman. "The train took off without them."

"Goodness me!" said the Colonel. "What a calamity."

"We've been catering for ourselves," said Tommy. "Our new Chairman's brother's an excellent chef."

"Is he really," said the Colonel. "Well that's at least one thing in your favour. And it'll be an even bigger blessing if your missing friend manages to turn up here. I'm going to ask my manservant Albert to keep an eye out for him."

"Would he be the very large, powerfully built chap we
saw in the garden?" said the Chairman.
"Probably," said the Colonel. "He takes his morning
walk about now."
"He's not very talkative is he?" said Tommy after
coming to his companion's side.
"He didn't see you," said the Colonel.
"He did," said Tommy. "He'd been watching us for
some time."
"He did not," said the Colonel. "Trust me young man.
He didn't see you."
"Does Albert look after the garden?" said the Chairman.
"He does what he can," said the Colonel. "It's become
an enormous burden to be perfectly honest. There was a
time when we had enough staff to keep on top of it. That
was when the property was in its heyday. It used to be
awash with colour then. There were flowers and exotic
plants everywhere. Now it's overgrown and almost
impossible to manage."
"It's still very impressive though," said the Chairman.
"Some of those statues are amazing."
"What statues?" said the old man.
"The statues," said the Chairman. "The statues along
some of your paths. The life size statues of the Chinese
or Japanese warriors."
"I know nothing of any statues," said the Colonel.
"But I saw them," said the Chairman. "There must have
been hundreds of them."
"You must be mistaken," said the Colonel.
"I know what he saw," said the Major.
"Well you can keep that to yourself for the time being
Major," said the Colonel. "The last thing our guests
want to listen to are tales of things that go bump in the
night. In fact, I think the time's come for me to
commence with the obligatory pleasantries. So let me
introduce my companion and myself. I am Colonel
Maurice Cavanagh formerly of the Welsh Expeditionary
Force and that far less mobile and evidently less genial
individual sitting some distance opposite me is Major

[621]

Henry Howser, also of the aforementioned force. And for the record, that rather disillusioned looking cat you see enjoying the warmth of my hearth is Mr Spriggs. He is arguably more human and more civilized than either of your hosts."

"He's a bloody nuisance," said the Major.

"You leave him alone," said the Colonel. "I'm a little bit worried about him to be honest."

"Why's that?" said the Chairman.

"He seems to have picked up an injury of late and I have absolutely no idea how or why," said the Colonel. "It's not like him. It's not like him at all. He's a hardy little fellow. Would either of you chaps be able to shed any light on the matter?"

"I'm afraid not," said the Chairman.

"What about you," said the Colonel after turning his attention to the obviously uneasy Tommy.

"I ask you that because, Mr Spriggs appears to be looking at you in a rather accusing and disdainful manner."

"I've never seen him before in my life," said Tommy. "I do love cats though. Me and the wife own several. We breed them, as it happens."

"How marvellous," said the Colonel. "Have you been doing it long?"

"About 30 years," said Tommy.

"By Jove!" said the Colonel. "I bet there's not much I can teach you about felis catus. What are they?"

"Sorry?" said Tommy.

"What breed are they?" said the Colonel. "Are they Siamese...Burmese...Iranian?"

"I'm not sure," said Tommy. "I know they're not Iranian. They're definitely not Iranian. I think they might be Persian."

"You've got your one in remarkable condition," said the Chairman.

"Mr Spriggs is only ever fed live food," said the Colonel. "That's the secret to a cat's perfect health and longevity. He's 43 years of age you know."

"Wow!" said the Chairman. "That is impressive."

"I know," said the Colonel. "And if I had my way, he'd live for another 43 years. That's why I don't like to see him in pain. It distresses me terribly. I can only assume he's been fighting with Matilda again. I thought all that had stopped after I'd spoken to them both."

"Who's Matilda?" said the Chairman.

"A bloody lunatic who should have been taken out and shot many moons ago," said the Major before turning to face the window.

"Take no notice," said the Colonel. "The Major lacks compassion. Matilda's a darling. To be honest, I'm surprised you haven't already met her. She rarely misses an opportunity to embrace our visitors."

"Would she be the long grey haired old lady that likes to dance?" said the Chairman.

"That's her," said the Colonel. "I think the waltz is her favourite. She's 104 years of age you know."

"Bloody hell!" said the Chairman. "She's aged remarkably well. I'll have to ask her what her secret is. Was she a patient here?"

"She's family," said the Colonel indignantly. "She's Mr Spriggs's grandmother."

"What!" said the Chairman. "Sorry Colonel-what was that?"

"She's Mr Spriggs's grandmother," said the Colonel. "She didn't scare you did she?"

"Not at all," said the momentarily confused Chairman. "By the way, I'm Ken. Ken Hulme. I'm the recently appointed Chairman of the men's club I alluded to before. And this is my expedition partner, Tommy. He's done his bit for his country Colonel. He was once part of the British armed forces himself."

"Was he really?" said the beaming Colonel. "Oh my days! So he was. So he was. I thought he looked familiar."

"He'll have got you mistaken for someone else," said the Major while continuing to adjust his position. "He does that frequently. So you better hope that particular

[623]

someone didn't do him a disservice or owe him any
money."

"You be quiet," said the Colonel. "Now then
gentlemen. Take your wet things off and go and warm
yourselves by the fire. Then, come and join me and old
misery guts at our table. It seems ages since we last had
visitors. I want you to tell me what's been happening in
the big wide world."

The living room, just like the main staircase,
had at one time been extremely grand but although there
was still evidence of that previous grandeur such as the
dark panelling, the huge statuary marble fireplace and an
elaborate ceiling made up of 64 coloured and gilded
octagons, it was now showing very definite signs of
neglect and decline-particularly on the inside of the
external elevation, where short lengths of the intricately
moulded cornice where now perilously close to collapse.
It was warm and intimate nevertheless, and even though
there was no immediate evidence of any telephone, it
appeared to be, at the very least, a more than acceptable
temporary stopping off point.

"Sit yourselves down," said the Colonel after
finally giving up on his attempt to gain his injured cat's
attention. "And tell me how you managed to cheat all
my clever security measures and break into my
property."

"We didn't break in sir," said the Chairman after taking
a chair directly opposite the Colonel and urging his
companion to join him. "Your front door was wide
open."

"Again?" said the Colonel. "That big lump Albert's
getting worse. I've lost count of the times I've told him
to make sure he locks up when he goes out. But tell me
this-how did you manage to get into the hallway?"

"By sheer chance really," said the Chairman. "We
slipped over on the wet floor and I think our combined
weight did the rest."

"I see," said the Colonel. "I might have to do
something about that. Tell me more about your friends

back on the train. Do you think they'll follow you here?"

"I very much doubt it," said the Chairman.

"Why's that?" said the Colonel.

"Because we took the only worthwhile equipment and the best of the outdoor Winter clothing," said the Chairman.

"And one or two of the lads are sick and in need of looking after," said Tommy.

"Sick!" said the Colonel before turning to his companion.

"It was nothing serious," said the Chairman. "Just a 24 hour bug. Vomiting and diarrhoea-that sort of thing. Bugs are always rife at this time of year. I blame the extra people on the streets. The last minute Christmas shoppers, for example."

"I sincerely hope it *was* a 24 hour thing," said the Colonel. "I can't afford to be catching anything nasty at my time of life. Neither can any of my staff for that matter."

"Staff!" said the Chairman.

"I was referring to my security staff," said the Colonel. "Although I'm beginning to wonder what I pay them for. By rights, you shouldn't have made it past the main gate. You certainly wouldn't have done so in days gone by. I'm beginning to wonder whether our Mr Bimoko's still fit for purpose."

"Mr Bimoko!" said the Chairman.

"He's my long serving head of security," said the Colonel.

"Head of security!" scoffed the Major.

"You be nice," said the Colonel. "Bimoko's a good man. He's the reason you continue to sleep soundly in your bed at night."

"He sounds foreign," said the Chairman.

"He hails from darkest Africa," said the Colonel. "Some part of Guinea to be more precise. He's been part of my staff since he was a young rapscallion."

"He's another bloody nuisance," said the Major.

"Take no notice of that miserable old crow," said the Colonel. "He has no time for Bimoko because he once induced him to shit his bed."

"Really!" said the Chairman.

"His feather mattress was ruined," said the Colonel.

"He came dancing into my room in the early hours sporting an enormous erection," said the Major.

"Only the once," said the Colonel.

"Once is once too often," said the Major.

"He didn't mean anything by it," said the Colonel. "It's the African in him. They're very passionate and tactile people the blacks. And it's not happened since has it?"

"It's not going to," said the Major. "I'll strangle the bastard if he ever does it again."

"You won't touch him," said the Colonel. "I've told you before, Bimoko's like a son to me. So if there's any punishment to be dished out, I alone will be the one to administer it. For goodness sake, why don't you just take him to one side, pour a couple of brandies and talk the matter over like men?"

"I'll just avoid him and keep my bedroom door locked, if it's all the same to you," said the Major.

"Then keep your door locked," said the Colonel.

The Colonel, the more talkative, genial and dominant of the two men was very tall and thin with medium length, grey wavy hair which was damped down and parted at the centre. He had deep blue eyes which would widen whenever his passion for a particular subject intensified, thick bushy sideburns, a long almost white handlebar moustache and a small scar in the centre of his left cheek in the shape of a letter 'T'. He was dressed very similarly to his companion in a faded red British Army Mess Dress jacket and red single striped trousers but even without the uniform it was clear by his general demeanour and poise that he hailed from military stock. The other man was far less pleasant and accommodating and was sitting sideways on to the table in an old Victorian three wheeled Bath chair that had not just seen better days but had struggled through many thousands of them. Because of his disability, it was impossible to say just how tall he had been in his pomp but he was very heavily lined, almost completely bald, had deep set almost lifeless brown eyes and sported a long grey beard that, just like the once magnificent garden, was in desperate need of cultivation.

"So how long did you journey from your train?" said the Colonel while struggling to prise open a small well worn tin marked 'Capstan Full Strength'.

"It's hard to say," said the Chairman. "The weather was horrendous. We had to do it in short stages. I suppose it was about 12 hours in all. We actually arrived here last night."

"Did you really," said the Colonel.

"We took refuge in one of your sheds," said Tommy.

"How did you manage that?" said the Colonel. "Those sheds are meant to be locked at all times."

"This one wasn't," said Tommy.

"There you go," said the Major. "So much for your super efficient head of security."

"You, be nice," said the Colonel. "Which shed was it?"

"I couldn't tell you," said the Chairman. "I'm not familiar with the layout of your garden."

"Well what exactly was stored in it?" said the Colonel.

"A load of old tat," said Tommy.

"Old tat!" said the Colonel indignantly.

"It wasn't old tat," said the Chairman. "There were a lot of quality items in there."

"Like what?" said the Colonel.

"Like.....like several stuffed animals," said the Chairman.

"That's right," said Tommy. "I forgot about them. They were cool."

"Was one of them a King cobra by any chance?" said the Major.

"I think so," said the Chairman. "It was definitely a snake of some sort. And there was this magnificent wingspread eagle."

"They were mine," said the Major.

[627]

"And there were a load of old photo albums and encyclopaedias," said Tommy.

"I know where you were now," said the Colonel. "You were in sector 173B. That wouldn't be too far from the boundary wall. And it was unlocked, you say?"

"It was yes," said Tommy.

"It wasn't actually," said the Chairman. "I broke in."

"You broke in!" said the Colonel. "Well why did your companion just suggest otherwise?"

"Because I arrived at the shed a few minutes before him," said the Chairman. "He'd suffered a nasty fall and had got caught in a thorn bush. I'm sorry Colonel. I'll pay for any damages. It was just that we were so desperate. We needed a place to hide."

"From what?" said the Major.

"A pack of starving hounds," said Tommy.

"They'd been tracking us for hours," said the Chairman.

"They'd followed us into the garden," said Tommy.

"I don't think so," said the Major while easing back in his chair.

"They had," said Tommy. "Honestly, they had."

"They did no such thing," said the Colonel before placing his pencil thin, newly rolled cigarette behind his right ear. "I'm familiar with that pack. They never enter these grounds. At least, not anymore."

"And why would that be Colonel?" said the Chairman.

"Let's call it 'the self preservation instinct', shall we," said the Colonel before reaching across the table with his bone handled cane and carefully drawing a tall crystal decanter towards him. "They know better. Now then. Would you two gentlemen like to join me for a snifter?"

"Gentlemen!" scoffed the Major. "One of them has just admitted wilful damage while the other scoundrel has lied to you through his eye teeth."

"We needed somewhere to shelter," said the Chairman.

"I can probably excuse that," said the Major. "But there's no excuse for telling bare faced lies."

"Be a good gentleman Major Howser," said the Colonel. "Have you never told a lie when you've felt

[628]

under pressure?"

"As a prisoner of war I have," said the Major. "But only to mislead my enemy captors."

"Well maybe that's what our guest has done in a sort of way," said the Colonel. "Perhaps he saw us as the enemy. Because, let's be honest Major-you in particular, haven't exactly welcomed him with open arms, have you?"

"He's not welcome," said the Major. "Neither is that irresponsible vandal friend of his. I don't trust them and I don't like them. You should insist they leave post-haste."

"You forget yourself sir," said the Colonel.

"I rarely forget anything," snarled the Major.

"And I roundly say you do," said the Colonel. "You're forgetting all those times we arrived cap in hand at a native village hoping desperately to be received with warmth and kindness. And receive these men with warmth and kindness, is what I intend doing. And by the way Major-that's whether you like it or not."

For the next thirty minutes, after the disgruntled Major had made his way to an old French writing bureau that was situated at the far end of the room, the Colonel listened intently as the Chairman told him more about the new computerised train. He then went on to talk about the latest mobile phones, the internet phenomenon, social media and cars that would soon be able to run off electricity as well as traditional fuel, but shortly after the subject had shifted to global conflict, and in particular which countries were currently at war with each other, the Colonel cupped his hands around his mouth, leaned forward and issued the following, chilling warning.

"You and your friend must be extremely wary of the Major. He clearly hasn't taken kindly to your presence. He's a very sick and disturbed individual. His mood can swing alarmingly and without warning or provocation. Whatever you and your companion do-don't ever make the mistake of getting too close to him."

"Do you mean emotionally Colonel?" whispered the Chairman.

"I mean, don't get too close to him in any way at all," whispered the Colonel.

"Thank you Colonel," whispered the Chairman. "I appreciate that."

"Appreciate what?" said the returning and suspicious looking Major.

"You mind your business," said the Colonel.

"I've had my wrists slapped Major," said the Chairman. "I've had to promise not to go near any of your garden sheds again."

"Not even to fix the lock on the shed door?" said the Major.

"I'll get Albert to do it," said the Colonel.

"Albert didn't break it," said the Major.

"I'll gladly fix it if you provide me with a few tools," said the Chairman.

"And so you should," said the Major.

"And I say he shouldn't," roared the Colonel after slamming his cane down on the table. "That man is our guest. And that's the last I want to hear of the matter."

For some time after the Colonel's outburst, there had been an awkward period of silence during which the two guests sat fidgeting nervously, the Major ground his teeth horribly while reducing his embroidered handkerchief to a tiny silk ball and the master of the house stared intently at the sleeping and murmuring Mr Spriggs. That was almost certainly why the Chairman and his agitated travelling companion had reacted with such disproportionate enthusiasm when a large sheet of snow suddenly cascaded from the rooftop and exploded on the saturated wooden sill beneath.

"Oh my God! Did you see that?" said the Chairman while pointing towards the window.

"I did yes," said the excited Tommy. "The whole room seemed to shake."

"My word-it doesn't take much to get you boys erect does it?" said the Major.

"Now, now Major," said the Colonel. "There's no need to be facetious. The boys were just making polite conversation."

"They need to be making tracks, not polite conversation," said the Major.

"And they no doubt will do when the weather picks up," said the Colonel. "But in the meantime, instead of tormenting them and making them feel unwelcome, why don't you try to get to know them. You never know, you might find you have a few things in common."

"I very much doubt it," said the red faced Major while trying to persuade his unresponsive wheelchair to move a few degrees to the left. "But I'll humour you, if you insist Colonel.....What do you do gentlemen? What do you do, to provide for your wives and associated litters?"

"I'm an engineer for quite a large car wash company," said the Chairman.

"And I'm a self employed builder," replied Tommy.

"That's no doubt why the weather's of so much interest to him," said the Colonel.

"That's right," said Tommy. "I wouldn't earn a bean while the weather's like this."

"Is that the currency you choose to be paid in?" said the Major.

"What do you mean?" said Tommy.

"You just inferred you normally get paid in beans," said the Major. "Tell me-if I was to give you a cup full of haricots, would you venture out into the bleak mid Winter and fix the lock on that shed door?"

"I wouldn't hesitate to repair the lock for free," said Tommy.

"The beans referral was just a figure of speech Major," said the Colonel. "But while we're still on the subject of monetary payment-what does a builder do for money during long spells of inclement weather Tommy? Do you make some sort of provision for periods like that?"

"I try to," said Tommy. "But it doesn't always work out like that."

"What happens when you get out of bed, open the

[631]

curtains and find that it's snowing or raining heavily?" said the Major.

"I'm generally pissed off for the rest of the day," said Tommy.

"What do you do with yourself?" said the Major.

"Nothing," said Tommy. "I just mooch about the house and get on my wife's nerves. Although I have been known to kick the cat in frustration on a number of occasions."

"Kick the cat," said the Colonel. "You didn't happen to kick my cat in frustration did you?"

"Of course not," said Tommy. "It was just another figure of speech. I use expressions like that all the time. To be honest, I don't even own a cat."

"But you said you had three," said the Colonel.

"I have," said the increasingly flustered Tommy. "At least, in a manner of speaking I have. I bought the wife three beautiful Persians to celebrate our diamond wedding anniversary."

"Diamond anniversary?" said the puzzled Major.

"That's right," said Tommy.

"He means crystal," said the Chairman. "You mean crystal anniversary, don't you Tommy?"

"I do yes," said Tommy. "I always get those two mixed up."

"I bet your wife doesn't," said the Major.

"Do your Persians need much encouragement to breed?" said the Colonel.

"Ours don't," replied Tommy. "Ours just get right down to business."

"But you always insist on them doing it naturally, don't you Tommy?" said the Chairman. "You and your missus never force the issue do you?"

"Never," said Tommy. "If they don't want to shag, they don't have to shag, is our policy."

"That's good to know," said the Colonel. "I loathe people who force animals to do things against their will. That's why I've always hated certain circus proprietors."

"I'm right with you there," said Tommy.

"Why don't you tell them what your gypsy friends do to people who abuse animals," said the Major.

"Not now," said the Colonel.

"Why not?" said the Major.

"Because it wouldn't be a suitable subject for the dining table," said the Colonel.

"Tell them," said the Major. "They're not children. They're grown men. And we're not eating at this particular moment in time. Nobody's going to throw up on your old Axminster. Tell them what your gypsy friends do to wicked people."

"What do they do Colonel?" said the Chairman.

"Do they torture them?" said Tommy.

"They do far more than that," said the Major.

"What do they do?" said the Chairman.

"They punish them in a most grotesque and imaginative way," said the Colonel.

"How grotesque?" said the Chairman.

"They make them wear a mask for the rest of their lives," said the Major.

"Wear a mask!" said the Chairman. "That doesn't sound too grotesque to me."

"What sort of mask?" said Tommy.

"A pig mask," said the Colonel. "It's quite a complicated procedure, to be honest."

"Well, we're unlikely to be going anywhere soon," said the Chairman while pointing towards the window which now a resembled a pure white cinema screen. "Tell us Colonel. You've got me intrigued now. How can somebody be made to wear a mask as a punishment?"

"By welding it to their heads," said the Colonel.

"What!" said the Chairman.

"The men responsible for carrying out the punishment, buy a large pig's head from a butcher and remove the brain, the eyes and skull," said the Colonel while making himself more comfortable. "That leaves them with what is, to all intent and purpose, a floppy pig's head mask. They then seize the animal accused and after shaving his scalp and binding his hands and feet, they place the mask over his head and secure it with chicken wire."

"My God!" said the Chairman.

"They then take a pair of tin snips and slice off the offender's two thumbs and all his fingers up to his first knuckle," said the Colonel.

"What for?" said Tommy.

"So he can never peel the mask off," said the Major.

"That's right," said the Colonel.

"Jesus Christ!" said the Chairman. "And he's banished then, is he?"

"When they've finished with him he is," said the Major.

"Finished with him!" said Tommy. "So there's more to this punishment is there?"

"There's the best and juiciest bit," said the Major.

"Which entails what?" said the Chairman.

"They dangle their prisoner's head over an open fire and allow the boiling hot fat to slowly weld the mask to his face," said the Colonel.

"Mother of God! said the Chairman.

"I did warn you the story wasn't appropriate for the dining table," said the Colonel.

"You did yes," said the Chairman. "I should have listened to you Colonel. I don't think I'll ever be able to eat bacon again. But listen Colonel-I want to assure you of something. Neither of us hurt your cat. To be honest, the first time we laid eyes on Mr Scripps, was when we entered your room and saw you stroking him."

"It's Spriggs," said the Colonel. "The cat's name is Mr Spriggs."

"I'm sorry," said the Chairman.

"That's alright old boy," said the Colonel. "I get people's names mixed up all the time. I get lots of things mixed up for that matter. I think I must have received one too many blows on the back of my head."

"Do you get phone numbers mixed up?" said the Chairman.

"Indubitably," said the Colonel. "I'm dyscalculic. That's number blindness, by the way. Although, the remarkable thing is-I've never once failed to recall my full army service number."

"Neither have I, come to think of it," said Tommy.

"What was it?" said the wide eyed Colonel.

"I'd rather not say if you don't mind," said Tommy.

"Fair enough," said the Colonel. "That's your prerogative. Where did you serve?"

"Belfast, Bosnia and Yugoslavia mainly," replied Tommy.

"Did you manage to rise through the ranks at all?" said the Colonel.

"I made Sergeant," replied Tommy proudly.

"Bravo," said the Colonel. "Or should I have said, 'bravo sergeant'?"

"Did you go out on manoeuvres when it was snowing?" said the Major. "Or did you remain in your tent annoying the hell out of your subordinates?"

"Very funny Major," said Tommy.

"He's not funny at all," said the Colonel. "He's being downright rude. Now then-would anyone care for a top up while I've still got the top off this bottle?"

Despite the Chairman's persistent attempts to interrupt and steer the conversation towards something potentially less explosive, for the next hour, the Major continued to bate and badger his increasingly agitated travelling companion and that is why he had felt such enormous relief when, after tending to his drying garments, he turned around to discover the two old men had drifted off into a really heavy sleep.

"What happened there?" he whispered while slowly tiptoeing back to his chair.

"They just nodded off as if hit by a couple of tranquilizer darts," said Tommy.

"Well, thank God they did," whispered the Chairman.

"Because for one heart thumping minute, I thought you were going to lose it and give that Major what for."

"I did too," whispered Tommy. "He's one cantankerous old twat. My blood's boiling."

"I can see that," whispered the Chairman. "You've got

a face like thunder. But don't underestimate him
Tommy. The Colonel tipped me the wink about him
earlier."

"What did he say?" whispered Tommy.

"He told me to keep a safe distance from him,"
whispered the Chairman. "He more or less told me the
man's not mentally stable."

"He's in the right place then," whispered Tommy.
"Have you looked into his eyes by any chance. I've
never seen a look of wickedness like that in all my life."

"Me neither," whispered the Chairman. "So let's not
take it for granted the miserable old buzzard's genuinely
asleep."

"Do you think we should slip away while we can?"
whispered Tommy. "Because there's no phone here, is
there? I certainly can't see one."

"That doesn't mean there isn't one," whispered the
Chairman. "The Colonel's as keen as mustard on all
things technological. He must have some way of
communicating with the outside world. But listen
Tommy-even if we do choose to leave, let's at least
make sure we're both thoroughly dried out and ready for
the next stage of our journey. Don't forget-we've no
food now. What do you think?"

"I think you're probably right as usual," whispered
Tommy. "But I don't want to stay here too long. I don't
mind admitting this Hulmey-I'm scared almost shitless."

"You don't do scared," said the Chairman.

"It's true," said Tommy. "In fact, I've never been so
scared. I don't know what it is. This place is all wrong.
This place reeks of something-but for the life of me, I'm
still struggling to work out exactly what."

"It's not bacon is it?" said the Chairman.

"I sincerely hope not," said Tommy. "What a story that
was."

"It was sick," said the Chairman. "By the way-do you
know what the moral of that tale was?"

"Only too well," replied Tommy while watching the
limping and forlorn looking Mr Spriggs make his long

and ponderous way to his basket.

It was just over an hour before the Colonel woke and after coughing, spluttering and muttering something incomprehensible, he rubbed his eyes, slid back his chair and began pointing accusingly at the startled and hopelessly confused Chairman.

"God's holy trousers," he yelled before snatching up a letter opener and brandishing it dagger fashion. "Who in damnation are you and what are you doing at my table?"

"It's me Colonel," protested the Chairman after raising his hands above his head. "It's just me and my companion. We got lost remember."

"Got lost!" said the Colonel.

"That's right," said the Chairman while rising very slowly and deliberately. "I told you earlier, just before you nodded off. Our train broke down a few miles from here."

"Your train!" said the Colonel. "What train was that?"

"Our train," said the Chairman. "The one I told you about. The one that's a bit like the original Orient Express."

"Has it arrived?" said the Colonel. "Should I be preparing to embark?"

"No Colonel," said the Chairman. "You're at home. You're in the living room of your home. Look around you. You've just woken up. There's the Major. I'm a visitor. Me and my friend called at your house for help."

"Help! You called here for help! Oh, my dear boy, do forgive me," said the Colonel before placing the letter opener on the table and urging his two anxious visitors to be seated again. "So you did. So you did. I'm so very sorry. You'll have to forgive me gentlemen. I sleep so heavily. I often wake up and wonder where the hell I am. The Major will vouch for that. When he's fully compos mentis, that is."

"That's alright," said the Chairman. "I'm the same when I first rise."

"To be honest, I don't even remember finishing my last

[637]

brandy," said the Colonel.

"You didn't," said the Chairman. "Mr Spriggs finished it for you."

"Did he really," said the Colonel. "Of all the blooming cheek. Where is the little bounder?"

"He left the room about half an hour ago," said Tommy.

"How did he seem?" said the Colonel.

"He was fine," said Tommy. "He was walking great. He was walking alright, wasn't he Hulmey?"

"He was yes," said the Chairman.

"What sort of mood was the little bugger in?" said the Colonel.

"I don't really know," said Tommy. "I suppose he was a little bit subdued."

"It's probably because you've got unfamiliar guests," said the Chairman. "Why do you ask Colonel?"

"Because he can be a little bastard in drink," said the Colonel. "He gets all obnoxious and opinionated."

"Opinionated!" said Tommy. "I didn't know cats had opinions."

"Try bathing one and feeding it something it doesn't fancy," said the Colonel. "But you don't really know cats do you. For instance, you don't know the difference between a Persian and an Iranian."

"I do," said Tommy.

"A Persian *is* an Iranian," said the Colonel. "They're the same breed."

"That's what I was thinking," said the Chairman. "I think poor Tommy's still suffering a little concussion from the fall he had in your garden."

"Maybe that's it," said the Colonel. "Now why don't you tell me some more about that train of yours. Does this mean there's going to be a regular rail service near here?"

"I think so," said the Chairman. "We were told it might develop into a once weekly service for affluent sightseers. But I wouldn't worry too much if I was you Colonel. The nearest station will be something like fifty miles away. You're unlikely to be plagued with tourists f that's what you're concerned about. Unless you want visitors, that is."

"It wouldn't be the worst idea," said the Colonel. "It might bring some much needed coffers in. I might even open up as some sort of half way house or inn. Albert's developed into quite an accomplished cook. Nobody sets a better table, I can tell you. Which reminds me-are you gentlemen hungry at all?"

"I'm fine," said Tommy before leaving his chair to examine one of the old sepia prints that was hanging on the far wall beneath a brass wall lamp that, for some reason, had turned upside down. "I wouldn't say no to a cup of tea and a biscuit though."

"He's got a ticklish stomach," said the Chairman. "That story about the pig's head mask and the gypsies has probably put him off food for the rest of his life."

"What about you," said the Colonel. "Has it put you off food?"

"I' could eat almost anything right now," said the Chairman.

"Very well," said the Colonel. "Almost anything it is then. Now let me prepare you both for meeting the aforementioned Albert."

"You say that as if he's some sort of badly behaved dog," said Tommy.

"That wouldn't be the worst analogy I've ever heard used," said the Colonel. "He's certainly as loyal and protective as any dog."

The Colonel then went on to explain that Albert was the last remaining inmate from when the house was operating as the Old Budlam Institute for the Incurably Insane and how he had arrived at the home with his elderly Yorkshire Terrier and a battered old suitcase on the 31st of October 1973 after his parents had reached the point when they could no longer control his steadily increasing bouts of rage.

"How old would he have been Colonel?" asked the Chairman.

"He'd just turned 15," replied the Colonel. "He

weighed just under 280 pounds and was already just under 7 feet tall."

"Bloody hell!" said the Chairman. "No wonder his parents were concerned. He must have taken some handling."

"It took up to 7 burly orderlies to control him at times," said the Colonel. "He put two in the infirmary during his first week here. One of them remains affected to this day."

"That's awful," said the Chairman. "Did you ever get to know what triggered his outbursts?"

"I did, as it happens," said the Colonel. "That was a condition of people being accepted here. I never allowed anyone to take up residence here without knowing the underlying reason for their problem."

"Had he been abused by any chance?" said the Chairman.

"He'd been systematically sexually abused by his politician father and Justice of the Peace grandfather since the age of 2," said the Colonel. "I discovered that by means of a tip off from his older sister shortly after he'd arrived here."

"Were the offenders ever prosecuted?" said Tommy.

"Not in the conventional sense," said the Colonel.

"What do you mean?" said Tommy.

"They got their comeuppances," said the Colonel while refilling his and the Chairman's glasses.

"How is Albert now?" said the Chairman. "Has he ever tried to attack you?"

"He lashed out quite a few times during the early days," said the Colonel. "But he's not done for some time."

"Why's that?" said Tommy.

"Because I wasn't prepared to tolerate that sort of behaviour," said the Colonel.

"How did you deal with him?" said Tommy.

"That's not really any of our business," said the Chairman.

"He was beaten severely and deprived of light and food," said the Colonel. "Just like every other inmate

who stepped out of line. But unlike most, he responded
to his punishment positively. He sees me as his
surrogate father now. He worships me."
"What do you think he'd do if anyone went to attack
you?" said Tommy.
"Why do you ask?" said the suspicious Colonel.
"I was just wondering," said Tommy.
"I think in a roundabout way, my companion was
seeking reassurance regarding our safety," said the
Chairman.
"You're perfectly safe as long as you follow two very
important rules," said the Colonel.
"I'm all ears," said Tommy. "What are they?"
"Don't ever approach me in any way that might be
construed as threatening, and make sure you never raise
your voice in anger when talking to me," said the
Colonel.
"What would happen then?" said Tommy.
"Nothing that you're likely to remember," said the
Major after yawning loudly.
"Decided to join us, have you Major?" said the Colonel.
"I have indeed," replied the Major. "And not a moment
too soon it seems. Which one of these two vagabonds
did it sir?"
"Did what?" said the Colonel.
"Approached you with malicious intent," said the
Major.
"We didn't," said the Chairman. "We were talking
hypothetically. We were wondering what Albert would
do if anyone looked like attacking the Colonel."
"I've been preparing them for their first meeting with my
devoted manservant," said the Colonel.
"Why did you even bother?" said the Major. "They're
going to be leaving soon aren't they?"
"We are yes," said the Chairman.
"Well don't let me get in your way gentlemen," said the
Major.
"I let him down you know," said the Colonel while
replenishing his glass. "I let the poor bugger down

[641]

badly."

"In what way?" said the Chairman.

"I made a massive error of judgement," said the Colonel. "By rights. I should have been charged with gross misconduct and had my licence revoked."

"Why's what?" said the Chairman.

"I allowed him to leave these premises unsupervised," said the Colonel. "Can you believe that? What a stupid, idiotic and reckless thing to do. I'll never forgive myself. Not even if I live for another hundred years."

"When was this?" said the Chairman.

"About two years into his stay," replied the Colonel.

"Did he try to run away or something?" said the Chairman.

"It wasn't like that," said the Colonel. "He was happy here. He would never have run away."

"Did he attack someone?" said the Chairman.

"He blinded somebody," said the Major.

"My God!" said the Chairman.

"You keep your nose out of this, you nosey old buzzard," said the Colonel. "You don't even know the full story. You've only learnt snippets of it by snooping and listening to rumour mongers like that no good, sex obsessed Wop in the basement."

"It's true though," said the Major after turning to face the window.

"Is it Colonel?" said the Chairman. "Is that what he did? Did Albert blind somebody?"

"He did yes," said the Colonel while running his index finger around the rim of his glass. "He was a veterinary surgeon of some note. Ronnie Jenkins, his name was. He'd been a very good friend of mine. I'd known him for about 30 years."

"He left a young receptionist in a coma as well," said the Major.

"You shut your stinking interfering trap," roared the Colonel after hurling his glass into the fireplace. "I've just told you. You don't know all the facts. And don't forget-Albert's been very good to you over the years. If

[642]

it wasn't for him, you'd spend all day with a dirty arse and would have to sleep in that ridiculous chair. You think about that mister. You think long and hard about that."

It was clear by the way the Major raised his right hand submissively that he knew he had been very close to stepping over the imaginary dividing line which determined what the Colonel would tolerate and what he would not and that might well have been the last the fascinated Chairman would have heard of the account had he not leant over, slid the Colonel a replacement glass and poured him another drink. "You were saying Colonel."

"I was saying what?" said the old man. "What was I saying?"

"You were telling me about Albert blinding the vet," said the Chairman.

"The vet!" said the Colonel. "That's right-the vet. Is he here? Is Jenkins here? Is it already that time of the month. I only paid the bloody man last week. God blimey Charlie. Where's the time gone?"

"I think I might have confused you Colonel," said the Chairman. "Before the Major interrupted you, you were telling me about Albert blinding the vet."

"Of course I was," said the Colonel after taking a long sip of his drink. "He did yes. He did indeed. But it wasn't really his fault, I assure you. There were extenuating circumstances."

"I've no doubt there were," said the Chairman. "What were they?"

"He killed Chip," said the Colonel.

"Chip!" said the Chairman. "Who's Chip?"

"Albert's dog," said the Colonel. "His little Yorkshire Terrier. Chip was Albert's dog."

"Do you mean, he put him to sleep?" said the Chairman.

"That's right," said the Colonel. "At least he gave the instruction to put him down. He later claimed it was the only decent thing he could do. He said the poor dog was suffering horribly. It had kidney disease apparently He said he had to put it out of its misery."

"Well it sounds as if he did the ethical thing," said the Chairman. "That's what vets do. It's not fair to let an animal suffer unnecessarily."

"I know," said the Colonel. "You don't have to tell me that. Jenkins was perfectly within his rights. But poor Albert didn't see it like that. As far as he was concerned, he walked into the surgery with a note from me and a reasonably fit animal and then stood by while someone in a white coat ended its life with a syringe. There's no way someone like Albert could have understood the concept of euthanasia. I certainly couldn't explain it to him. He was too naive and backward in those days. He couldn't even string a cohesive sentence together."

"And that's why he blinded the man," said the Chairman.

"Apparently so," said the Colonel. "According to the only witness, he went berserk and after wrestling the syringe from the vet, he stuck it in both his eyes."

"Jesus Christ!" said the Chairman.

"They were my very words when I was first informed of the incident," said the Colonel. "And if you're wondering why Albert's still here under my roof after committing such an awful crime, the answer's far more simple than you might imagine."

"That's exactly what I was wondering," said the Chairman.

"No other institution would take him," said the Colonel. "None of them could control him. I eventually received what almost constituted a king's ransom to take him back."

"From who?" said the Chairman.

"Some department of the Home Office," said the Colonel. "At least I think it was the Home Office. I know it was some government department or other. Anyway-the cheques they keep sending me have been instrumental in keeping this place running."

"Did you ever replace Chip?" said Tommy.

"I thought about it," said the Colonel. "But it wasn't really necessary in the end."

"Why not?" said the Chairman.

"Because Albert soon found a new best friend in Mr Bimoko," said the Colonel before tugging at a rope that was dangling from the ceiling a couple of feet above his position. "He and Albert are pretty much inseparable these days. They're like brothers. You'd be well advised never to make the mistake of coming between them."

"I'll take that on board," said the Chairman. "By the way Colonel-I thought the way the Major spoke to you earlier on was bang out of order."

"Did you really?" said the Colonel.

"I did," said the Chairman. "Considering all you do for him."

"All I do for him!" said the Colonel after sitting bolt upright and folding his arms. "That man saved my life on countless occasions. I'm only here affording you hospitality and pleasant conversation because of him."

"I'm sorry Colonel, that was very rude and intrusive of me," said the Chairman.

"It certainly was," said the Colonel. "Just make sure it never happens again or you'll find yourself in the back of the next stagecoach out of here with a sore neck and a flea in your ear."

There then followed a period of relative calm during which the Colonel continued to drink heavily while contemplating silently, the Major scowled and at times appeared to be arguing with himself and the Chairman became more and more concerned regarding his travelling companion's restlessness. However, to his enormous relief, it wasn't long before his host and his long time live in friend were once again fast asleep and snoring loudly.

"Bloody hell! What do you make of these two loonies?" whispered Tommy while surreptitiously heading over to the far end of the room. "Are these not the wackiest pair of old codgers you've ever met in your life?"

"They might very well be," whispered the Chairman.

[645]

"But don't you go offending them. "

"Why?" whispered Tommy.

"Have you taken a look outside?" whispered the
Chairman. "Do you want to be told to leave?"

"Of course not," whispered Tommy. "But I don't want
to stay here either. Have you got round to asking the old
boy about a phone yet?"

"Not in so many words," whispered the Chairman. "But
I'm becoming more convinced by the minute there is
one somewhere."

"Why's that?" whispered Tommy.

"The Colonel's just threatened to put me in a
stagecoach," whispered the Chairman.

"A stagecoach!" said Tommy.

"I think he might have been referring to a taxi," said the
Chairman. "So, just be patient Tommy. And don't
forget-these men exist in a very different world to ours.
Time means very little to them. They're in no hurry to
do anything. They don't share our sense of urgency."

"What sense of urgency's that?" whispered Tommy.

"You haven't even asked them where the nearest town or
village is yet. Why is that Hulmey?"

"Because the opportunity hasn't arisen," whispered the
Chairman. "I'm biding my time."

"Well I'm biding my time by having a look around,"
whispered Tommy. "This place is fantastic. It's like a
museum. Have you seen this musket Hulmey? It must
be well over a hundred years old. It's probably worth a
fortune. Do you reckon I could sneak it out under my
coat?"

"Just put it back," whispered the Chairman while all the
time keeping one wary eye on the snoozing old men.
"Put it back and get your arse back here."

"I will in a minute," whispered Tommy before drawing
back a heavy black velvet dividing curtain to reveal two
tailor's dummies, one dressed in a rather bland khaki
Chinese Republican Army uniform of the mid 20th
century, and the other, wearing a bright red tunic
complete with white cross belts and a faded sun helmet

[646]

befit with gilt and silver plate badge.

At that point, what the Chairman had been privy to was Tommy Mac at his most playful, reckless and belligerent. It meant that there was no talking to him and no way of getting him to do as he was advised and it therefore wasn't long before he had stripped the second dummy and was marching from one side of the room to the other in perfect time to his own unvoiced commands.

"Oh, for crying out loud," whispered the exasperated Chairman. "What's the matter with you Tommy? Get that bloody thing off. Are you completely off your tree? You're going to get us both kicked out into the freezing cold."

"This is the dog's bollocks this is," whispered Tommy while holding out his arms to examine the superbly embroidered silver buttoned cuffs. "I think this is what the British wore at the Battle of Rorke's Drift. What do you think Hulmey-do you think I look a bit like Stanley Baker in this?"

"I couldn't care less who you look like," whispered the mortified Chairman. "And you can put that down too. If they wake up and see you brandishing a rifle, they'll think we're here to rob them."

"It's a single shot, hinged, falling block, Martini-Henry," whispered Tommy. "Or so it says on this little plaque."

"I couldn't give a shit if it's a Goblin Teasmade," whispered the Chairman. "Get that bloody uniform off and get back here now."

"I will in a minute," whispered Tommy. "I've just got this uncontrollable urge to play soldiers. Is it true our regiments wore red coats to disguise bloodstains?"

"I don't know," whispered the Chairman. "I suppose it's possible. But for Christ's sake Tommy-take my advice-get back here or it might be your blood it's having to disguise."

"Chill out will you Hulmey," whispered Tommy before stepping in front of a full length mirror and adopting a series of firing stances. "Can't you see I'm having fun for the first time in days?"

"I can see that yes," roared the Chairman. "But I'm not going to lct you have it at my fucking expense. Get back here now or me and you are finished."

"What! What!" said the startled and barely conscious Colonel while fumbling aimlessly for his cane. "What's going on? Is there a problem? I thought I heard raised voices. Do I need to call out the guard?"

"Everything's fine," replied the Chairman. "I'm sorry sir. I stubbed my big toe on the table leg and yelled out in pain. It's........"

"It's Carruthers," said the Colonel before slapping his hand on the table and waving the highly confused Tommy towards him. "As I live and breathe, it's my old mucker Sergeant Carruthers. How was your leave young man? Did you manage to get any bottom action?"

"I beg your pardon," said Tommy. "Are you talking to me Colonel?"

"You know damn well I'm talking to you," said the Colonel. "What's the matter with you man?"

"I don't understand," said Tommy.

"I bet you don't," said the Colonel while turning to the Chairman. "This is what happens when they take an extended leave of absence. They find it hard to readjust."

"But he's....." said the Chairman.

"He's a damn nuisance-that's what Carruthers is," said the Colonel. "And a barrack room lawyer to boot. But a fine soldier nevertheless. By the way Sergeant-I've got some good news for you. Your telephone arrived back from the menders yesterday morning via courier. But I'm going to advise you this and I'm going to advise you for the very last time. Get control of that infamous temper of yours. It's going to be the ruination of you. You'll find the receipt for the repair in the top drawer of the Major's writing bureau."

"What was the matter with the phone?" said the Chairman.

"It's component parts had become separated," said the

Colonel.

"Sorry!" said the Chairman. "I'm not with you Colonel."

"Sergeant Carruthers threw it out of his bedroom window in a fit of pique," said the Colonel. "I think Mr Bimoko had been rummaging through his things again. In about fifteen bloody pieces it was. Anyway Sergeant-welcome back and all that. Why don't you put your weapon down and come over here and meet our visitor. He's the er...He's the President of a Veterinary Club from somewhere or other. I thought he'd arrived with another of his members, but I must have been mistaken."

"I'm pleased to meet you Sergeant," said the Chairman after quickly standing up and thrusting out his right hand to greet his seriously confused companion. "Good news about the telephone hey Carruthers?"

"The telephone!" said Tommy.

"The Colonel's had it repaired for you," said the imploring Chairman. "That's good isn't it? That's got be good news hasn't it Carruthers."

"It has yes," said Tommy before taking his chair.

"Aren't you forgetting yourself Sergeant?" said the Colonel before turning to face the window.

"Forgetting what?" said Tommy.

"Your tunic," said the Colonel almost in a whisper. "We have company. Button up your tunic man. And be quick about it."

"I'm sorry sir," said a fumbling Tommy.

"I should think you are," said the Colonel.

"How was your break?" said the Chairman.

"My break!" said Tommy.

"Your leave of absence," said the Chairman. "How was it?"

"Erm.....fine," said Tommy. "It was good. I got quite a lot done. I had lots of days out and things like that. And I was able to catch up with the kids."

"Kids!" said the Colonel. "What kids are these Carruthers? I always thought you were a confirmed bum bandit."

[649]

"He's probably talking about his nephews and nieces," said the Chairman.

"I am yes," said Tommy. "I was talking about my sister's kids. Chantelle, Britney and Zak."

"Jack hey," mused the Colonel. "I used to have a batman called Jack. A magnificent fellow. He was a great one with the ladies. I've never known anyone pull the birds like him. The poor man was riddled with all sorts of sexually transmitted diseases at one point. The last time I saw him, he was stretched out buck naked over an anthill somewhere near Damascus. I have to assume he'd stepped over the mark and shagged the wrong man's wife. I had to put a bullet through his head. That's about the time I met Carruthers. He took over his duties then. We served more than a hundred campaigns together you know. He saved my life on at least three occasions. I'd do anything for that man. That's why I gave him such an extensive leave. You were on the verge of a nervous breakdown weren't you Carruthers?"

"I think I still am," replied Tommy after burying his face in his hands.

"I'm sorry Carruthers-I didn't quite catch that," said the Colonel. "Take your hands away from your face for goodness sake."

"Sorry sir," said Tommy. "I said, I'm feeling a lot better now."

"You could have fooled me," said the Colonel before pouring another glass of brandy and sliding it across the table to where Tommy was seated. "You look dreadful. You're a shadow of your former self. Now why don't you play the game and explain why you're so terribly on edge."

"I'm not on edge," said Tommy. "I mean, I'm not on edge sir. I'm just struggling to readapt."

"What's the matter Carruthers?" said the Colonel.

"Nothing sir," said Tommy.

"You're lying to me," said the Colonel. "I know that because the first thing you did on your return, was

retrieve and load your faithful rifle. What's the matter
man? What's got you so agitated? What have you seen?
Are the Chinese finally on the move? Are we in
trouble? Speak to me mans."

"It was those wild dogs wasn't it?" said the Chairman.

"What wild dogs?" said the Colonel.

"I was stalked and chased by a pack of starving hounds
sir," said Tommy. "I thought my time had come. I
really did."

"Oh dear," said the Colonel. "How far did they follow
you?"

"Right to your front door," said Tommy.

"What!" said the Colonel. "My front door! But that's
almost unheard of. Those animals haven't entered my
grounds for ages."

"This was a different pack," said Tommy. "These
didn't exhibit any fear whatsoever."

"My word!" said the Colonel.

"I didn't want to say anything because I felt guilty," said
Tommy. "After all, I led them here. I should have done
the decent thing and led them away from the house. I
feel awful now."

"Are you hurt at all?" said the Colonel.

"I've just sustained a few minor scrapes and bruises,"
replied Tommy.

"Oh dear!" said the Colonel. "We need to get those
sorted out. Dog bites can turn really nasty. And I think
I'm going to have to call Mr Bimoko in to clarify the
situation."

"Is there anything I can do?" said the Chairman.

"Like what?" said the Colonel.

"Have you got a vehicle of any sort?" said the
Chairman. "I could drive the Sergeant into town to get
his wounds looked at and dressed."

"I've got a 1938 Leichter Panza Wagon," said the
Colonel.

"What's that?" said the Chairman.

"It's a German armoured car," said the Colonel. "I
acquired it at an army surplus auction in Cardiff a few

years after the second great war ended."

"Does it still work?" said the Chairman while slowly edging forward in his seat.

"Does it still work!" said the wide eyed Colonel. 'Does it still work?' he asks. It's got a Horch V8 engine. Why wouldn't it work, for goodness sake?"

"I'm sorry," said the Chairman. "You'll have to forgive my ignorance Colonel. I'm not familiar with the old Horch V8. Would you mind if I turned it over?"

"Not at all," said the Colonel. "You'll find the keys just outside the door on a hook. But watch it doesn't slip off its blocks when it first fires up."

"What blocks?" said the Chairman.

"It's on four stacks of masonry bricks," said the Colonel. "Albert went and removed all the wheels. He likes to roll them around the garden. I suppose that's the playful child coming out in him. They're probably all out there somewhere but God only knows where. The MG 34 works though."

"The what?" said the Chairman.

"The machine gun," replied the Colonel. "You could always man that if push comes to shove."

"I'll do that Colonel," said the disgruntled Chairman before knocking back the last of his brandy and exhaling loudly.

It was then that the Major woke and once again, despite the atmosphere around the table being reasonably cordial, he was in a typically foul mood and seemingly keen to make at least one of the visitors feel uncomfortable.

"Would you look at the state of you," he sneered while pointing towards the wary and tired looking Tommy. "Tell me-what have you come to the fancy dress party as?"

"It's Carruthers," said the beaming Colonel. "It's good old Sergeant Carruthers. Didn't you recognise him Major? I must admit, I had to look twice myself. He's got rid of the fuzz and the sideburns and shed a stone or two."

"He certainly looks younger," said the Major without averting his eyes from his tobacco tin. "Carruthers hey. That is a turn up for the books. I could have sworn I attended his funeral the August before last."
"Nonsense," said the Colonel. "That would have been one of his brothers. I think he's arrived not a day too soon."
"Why's that?" said the Major.
"The Chinese are on the move," said the Colonel. "Our friend here Mr....Mr...I'm sorry. What do you call yourself again?"
"Field Marshal Bernard Montgomery," said the Major.
"You be quiet," said the Colonel.
"I'm Mr Hulme," said the Chairman.
"That's right-Mr Hulme," said the Colonel. "Our friend here Mr Hulme came across a Chinky patrol late last evening. That's right, isn't it sir?"
"I can't say for certain," said the Chairman. "It was very dark."
"But you told us you'd seen them," said the Colonel.
"With all respect sir-I actually said they were statues," said the Chairman.
"That's what they wanted you to think," said the Colonel. "They were Ninja warriors. They can stand still for days if they have to. I once saw one of them stand perfectly still for three months. The defiant little beggar died of malnutrition in the end. They're Chinese assassins. Professional, ruthless, cold blooded killers. They've been massing outside the perimeter wall for some time now. You were extremely lucky."
"Why's that?" said the Chairman.
"Because at the time you came across them, you and your absent friend were just considered to be a couple of lost souls," said the Colonel. "You had no affiliation with me or this house. And it's me they're after. It's very much me they've got it in for."
"Why's that Colonel?" said the Chairman.
"I can't really say for absolute certain," said the Colonel. "But it's more than likely because of some sort of

atrocity I committed while I was serving in East Asia."
"What sort of atrocity?" said the Chairman.
"The usual thing," said the Colonel. "We burnt villages, plundered sacred temples and took young women."
"Took women!" said the Chairman. "What do you mean?"
"Would you like me to draw you a picture?" said the Colonel. "We did the same sort of thing in India. I got lucky there. I just about escaped by the skin of my teeth. I had an ancient curse put on me, would you believe."
"What sort of curse?" said the Chairman.
"Something to do with a giant bandicoot," said the Colonel.
"What's a giant Bandicoot," said the Chairman.
"It's a rat the size of an adult man," said the Colonel. "I was warned by an irate village elder that one was going to visit me and take away my spirit. It's never happened, mind you. And to be honest-I don't think it ever will now. Not with the lovely and no nonsense Matilda patrolling the corridors night and day."
"I suppose not," said the Chairman.
"A lot of those Ninja warriors are women you know," said the Colonel. "Stunningly beautiful things they are. They're the deadliest. They've got tiny feet. Their unfortunate victims never hear them coming."
"You're going to have to search all the anterooms," said the Major. "There's every chance the Chinese have made a nest in one."
"You make an excellent observation Major," said the Colonel. "I'll get Bimoko onto that right away."
"What about your visitor," said the Major.
"What about him?" said the Colonel.
"Don't you think you should get him out of the way before it all goes off?" said the Major. "Let's be honest-he's not the fighting type. He'll be no good to man nor beast if the excrement hits the fan. In fact, he'll just get in the bloody way. Why don't you get Albert to sneak him out the back?"

"I might just do that," said the Colonel before slipping an open barrel key off a busy fob and sliding it to the Chairman. "But I want him to help us load the rifles first. He'll be alright for now. As you know, the Chinese are sneak thieves. They never attack in broad daylight. Carruthers can show him how to load. Can't you Sergeant?...Can't you Sergeant? Saints preserve us.....I'm talking to you Carruthers."

"Sorry Colonel," said Tommy. "I was miles away sir."

"I was just saying, you'll teach our guest Mr Holmes how to load the rifles," said the Colonel. "Wake up man will you. We're about to do battle, for goodness sake."

"Right you are sir," mumbled Tommy. "Right away sir. Three bags bloody well full sir."

"I'm sorry!" said the Colonel. "Did you say something Carruthers?"

"I was just reciting a defensive drill sir," said Tommy.

"I assume the rifles are.....?"

"The rifles are where they always are," said the Colonel. "Oh my days Carruthers-what's happened to you since you've been away? It's as if your brains have been scrambled. You haven't been water tortured have you?"

"No sir," said Tommy. "It's just that you told me you were going to store the rifles in a new hiding place."

"Did I?" said the Colonel. "I don't remember that. Is that what I said? Anyway-that doesn't matter right now. They're still in the last cupboard on the right. To the left of those mannequins. Pretty much where they've always been stored. You can lay them out on this table for examination."

"And then you can take me to the shitter," said the Major.

"I beg your pardon!" said Tommy.

"I need to go to the bathroom," said the Major. "All this excitement has been a bit too much for me. I think I might have had another little accident."

"Can't you wait?" said Tommy. "After all, there's a battle about to commence."

"Take him now," said the Colonel. "And get him back here as quick as you can. He's probably our best shot."

"But aren't I needed here sir?" said Tommy. "Shouldn't I be getting the rifles ready?"

"You should yes," said the Colonel. "But you're going to take the Major to the toilet first. What's the matter with you man? It's not as if you haven't cleaned the man's bottom before."

"Can't your guest do the honours while I press on?" said Tommy.

"Who me?" said the Chairman.

"Yes you," said Tommy. "Couldn't *you* take the Major to the toilet while I attend to the guns? After all, didn't you once tell me you had aspirations to become a doctor?"

"Really!" said the Colonel. "A doctor hey! That is interesting."

"I took a basic first aid course while I was at college," said the Chairman.

"And you worked at the Royal Liverpool Hospital for five years," said Tommy.

"Did he really?" said the Colonel. "How marvellous."

"Only as a fitter," said the Chairman.

"He supervised the work on the cardiology department Colonel," said Tommy.

"As a......" said the Chairman.

"By Jove!" said the Colonel. "Did you hear that Major? We've got a budding heart surgeon here Major. God blimey Charley! What a huge slice of luck. A surgeon hey. We've got a surgeon at our disposal Major. That actually changes things enormously. Do you know what Mr Holmes-instead of being surplus to our requirements, you're going to find yourself a vital cog in our war machine. In fact, I'm going to put you on the payroll hence with and afford you the rank of senior army-physician. And don't you dare argue with me mister-because I won't have it any other way. Do you hear me, Mr Holmes?"

"I hear you," said the Chairman.

"Are you sure?" said the Colonel. "Because I'd have thought a 'thank you' would have been in order at this particular juncture."

"Thank you very much Colonel," said the Chairman.

"Don't mention it old bean," said the Colonel. "Now get to work."

"Doing what exactly?" said the Chairman.

"You could start by sorting the poor Major out," said Tommy.

"He most certainly will not," said the Colonel. "Damn and blast you Carruthers! The man's a qualified surgeon not a nappy changer. He left cleaning dirty bottoms behind him many moons ago."

"That's exactly what I was about to say," said the Chairman.

"Is there anything you require doctor? " asked the Colonel. "Will you want to examine any of us before the battle commences?"

"I'd like to establish your Sergeant's level of fitness," replied the Chairman.

"Would you really?" said Tommy. "And how do you propose you're going to do that?"

"You could drop down and give me ten," said the Chairman.

"You what!" said Tommy.

"I'd like you to drop down and give me ten," said the Chairman. "Although, on second thoughts, don't bother. You'd better see to the Major. He's starting to turn purple."

"He is isn't he," said the Colonel. "So you need to move yourself Carruthers."

"But Colonel!" protested Tommy.

"Don't argue with me man," said the Colonel. "Just get on with it. Can't you see-the poor man's in considerable distress. Get him to the lavatory right away before he explodes."

"But sir," said Tommy.

"Get him to the shithouse now or I'll call Albert and have you dealt with," said the Colonel.

[657]

"As you like sir," said Tommy before kneeling down beside his highly amused travelling companion and unfastening his bootlace.

"Can you hear me Hulmey? he whispered through the very tightest of pursed lips.

"You're coming over loud and clear," whispered the Chairman from behind his splayed right hand. "You're playing a blinder Tommy lad. Just remain Sergeant Carruthers until we get use of that phone. And by the way-I want you to know I fully appreciate what you're about to do."

"I very much doubt it," whispered Tommy. "And you better hope for your sake, the old bastard doesn't want to take a crap."

"I think you'll find he already has," whispered the Chairman while pinching his nose. "He's going to need cleaning up. Just close your eyes and think of the lads back on the train."

"It's your eyes that are going to be closed," whispered Tommy after quickly switching feet. "You've surprised me Hulmey. I thought you were one of the straight guys. You're actually one conniving twat. Do you realise I'm likely to be at your beck and call from now on?"

"I realised that immediately upon my promotion to the position of senior army physician," whispered the Chairman while proceeding to lean back in his chair and stretch his arms above his head. "Now get to work...the poor Major looks as if he's about to give birth."

"You fucking arsehole," whispered Tommy before taking a deep breath and rising in the manner of somebody preparing to go to the gallows. "I won't forget you for this Hulmey. You watch your back lad. Especially when those rifles are being loaded."

"And you watch yours," whispered the Chairman. "Especially when the Major's loading his underpants."

"Fuck you," said Tommy.

"And this is me being serious, Tommy," said the Chairman. . "Remember what the Colonel told me about the Major. He's not right in the head. So for God's sake-whatever you do-don't get his John Thomas caught in his zip."

Tommy was to be gone just under thirty minutes, a period during which the Colonel had been keen to discuss his many physical ailments and the harassed Chairman had been just as keen to change the subject to just about anything else, and that was the reason he had left his chair to take a tour of the remarkably cluttered but fascinating living room.

"Is this you on this picture Colonel?" he asked after stopping to consider an old 12 by 8 sepia print which had slipped from its corner mounts and had come to rest at something like 45 degrees.

"Which one is it?" asked the Colonel who, at that point, had been busy rearranging the men's empty glasses into a triangular table centre piece.

"The one where the three men are standing behind an enormous dead elephant," said the Chairman.

"I know it now," said the Colonel. "I'm the good looking one on the left. That's my old mate Arnie Sykes in the centre. And the big stocky bugger on the right was our South African guide. He was one incredibly tough hombre that man. He was nicknamed 'the bull' by all and sundry. By Jove, you wouldn't want to get on the wrong side of him for love nor Krugerrands. I forget his name now. But bear with me-it'll come to me in a minute. I once saw him wrestle two silverbacks just for the price of a stein of Guinness."

"Why two?" said the Chairman.

"It was meant to be a tag team bout," said the Colonel. "But his boozy Irish tag partner took flight when he saw the size of the gorillas. He was black and blue and looked just like a bundle of bloody, tattered rags by the time the scrap was over."

"I bet he was," said the Chairman. "How did he get on?"

"He went five rounds," said the Colonel. "If I remember right, he lost three teeth and part of his left

ear. Van something his name was Van Bullens. That's
right. Van Bullens, his name was. That's the
fellow...Jaco Van Bullens."

"And was it you that bagged the elephant Colonel?" said
the Chairman.

"No it wasn't," said the Colonel. "That beautiful and
majestic creature was killed by heartless poachers. The
scum of the Earth they are. The scourge of Africa. I did
bag myself one of those though."

"A poacher?" said the Chairman.

"That's right," said the Colonel. "If you look closely
enough at the right hand top corner, you can just make
the bastard out. He's hanging by his feet from the branch
of an old fever tree."

"My God!" said the Chairman after moving closer to
take a better look. "Is he dead?"

"At that time, he was only wishing he was," said the
Colonel. "But he did eventually die. We didn't kill him
though. We made sure of that. That would have
brought the wrath of the local tribes people down on us.
We'd have had witch doctors and all sorts of machete
wielding vigilantes after us. We didn't have to kill him."

"What do you mean?" said the Chairman.

"We let the wildlife do it for us," said the Colonel.

"Did you throw him to the lions?" said the Chairman.

"Not exactly," said the Colonel. "We shot a badly
injured baby impala and smeared its blood and guts all
over the lad's private parts. We then backed off and
waited."

"For what?" said the Chairman.

"For something to pick up the scent," said the Colonel.
"It didn't take long before the first interested party came
calling. A young leopard it was. A beautiful thing. Very
elegant. We were amazed, to be honest."

"Why's that Colonel?" said the Chairman.

"Because, all it did was lick the blood off the hysterical
bastard's body," said the Colonel. "We had to send Van
Bullens back with the bloodied impala carcass to give
him another dowsing. Make no mistake, it was still

fantastic to see the bastard writhing and begging for mercy. A couple of mature lions did for him in the end. Magnificent creatures they were. They were brilliant because you would expect them to go berserk and compete with each other for the spoils. That would have ended it all too quickly in my opinion. But they didn't. They just tore away little chunks of the bastard's flesh at their leisure. A bit like you and I would do in an Indian Restaurant. We hung another 3 poachers that day. I wanted to mount their heads on the wall of my lodge but Van Bullens talked me out of it."

"What ever happened to him?" said the Chairman.

"He was hacked to death by poachers one Christmas Eve," replied the Colonel.

"My God!" said the Chairman.

"It came as no surprise to be honest," said the Colonel. "He was extremely outspoken and used to end his drinking binges by singing a song which mocked the victims of Tsavo."

"What's Tsavo?" said the Chairman.

"Have you not heard of Tsavo?" said the Colonel while angling his chair in order to face his visitor directly. "Have you never heard of the Tsavo massacre?"

"No," said the Chairman. "What was it? In fact-where is it?"

"It's a region of Kenya," said the Colonel. "It became famous when a couple of man-eating lions killed about 100 construction workers during the late 1800s."

"100!" said the Chairman.

"About that yes," said the Colonel. "Figures differ depending on who's telling the story and how drunk, trustworthy or historically knowledgeable that story teller was."

"Over what sort of period did the killings take place?" said the Chairman.

"Just less than a year, I think" said the Colonel.

"Bloody hell!" said the Chairman. "That's two a week."

"It was unprecedented," said the Colonel.

[661]

"I bet it was," said the Chairman. "Did they ever find out why the animals acted that way?"

"There are several theories," said the Colonel. "I personally think it was something to do with an injury the two lions had sustained while hunting large prey."

"I don't get you," said the Chairman.

"It's not that difficult," said the Colonel. "Lions usually hunt creatures much bigger than themselves, like zebra and water buffalo. They stalk, they chase and they bring them down. That takes a hell of a lot of effort. Which begs the question-what does a lion do if it's unable to chase something down?"

"It would starve to death, I suppose," said the Chairman.

"I believe so too," said the Colonel. "Unless it could find carrion, road kill or other easy prey. And that's exactly what those two lions did as far as I'm concerned. They discovered the bridge worker's camp. They found hundreds of men who, at some time or other, would have to sleep or rest. At that time, Tsavo must have looked like a royal banquet to those beautiful creatures."

"Have you been to Tsavo?" said the Chairman.

"Only the once," said the Colonel. "During my steam locomotive enthusiast days. I imagine it's changed somewhat since. I've got a photograph album somewhere. I took photos of trains wherever I visited. It's here somewhere. Where in damnation is it now?"

"I think there was a photo album something like the one you're describing in the shed we slept in," said the Chairman.

"Was there really?" said the Colonel. "What in the name of Jupiter is it doing there, I wonder. That album contains some of my fondest memories. What do you think doctor. Do you think you could retrieve it for me when things have settled down?"

"I'd be only too happy to," said the Chairman before leaning over and topping up the old man's glass.

It wasn't long before the Colonel was asleep and snoring loudly again but this time his sleep wasn't of the previous deep and satisfying level-this time his sleep was far lighter and punctuated with disturbingly real images which, on a number of occasions, had brought the old man, not only to his feet, but to the verge of panic.

"Double up on the south wall-take every man in three from the north. Concentrate your fire on the smoke from their rifle fire," he had yelled at one time, to some none existent subordinate. And that was a pattern that might have continued indefinitely had it not been for the bathroom door suddenly bursting open and a livid and swollen eyed Tommy Mac emerging behind the Major's outdated wheelchair.

"What happened?" said the Chairman after watching his companion apply the brake and quickly head over to the window.

"I've no idea," said the Major before removing his tobacco tin from his trouser pocket and placing it on the table. "He claims to have got something in his eye."

"Really?" said the Chairman. "Are you alright Tommy? I mean-are you alright Carruthers?"

"I will be," said a wincing and extremely irate Tommy while dabbing his reddening eyes with a lower portion of the curtain. "Just give me a minute."

"What's going on?" said the waking Colonel. "Has it started? Has the fighting begun?"

"Your Sergeant's sustained a nasty eye injury," said the Major.

"My word!" said the Colonel while swivelling in his chair. "That's not good. A powder burn, was it?"

"A powder burn yes," said the rueful and unamused Tommy while glaring almost pleadingly in the direction of the Chairman.

"You need to be more careful Carruthers," said the Colonel. "I'm afraid you're becoming sloppy in your old age. If that's what a long leave of absence does to you, don't ever bother handing in a request for another."

"The man's no longer fit for purpose," said the Major.

"I'll be the judge of that," said the Colonel. "You need

to be more patient with people Major."

"And you need to start listening to me," said the Major.
"That man's become error strewn. I can tell you this
much-he's not going to get his hands on my rifle."

"Why not?" said the Colonel.

"Because I want to make sure mine's going to
discharge," said the Major. "I'm not going into battle
with an untried firearm. Look at him for Pete's sake.
He's a mess. There's nothing in his eyes. He's crying.
He's having a breakdown of some kind. He's become an
absolute liability. That's not the cast iron individual
we've grown to respect and admire. He's nothing like
the man I used to admire. Why don't you let him go?
Why don't you do the decent thing, give him a few bob
to retire on and turn him out?"

"I can't," said the Colonel.

"Why not?" said the Major.

"Because I owe him more than that," said the Colonel.
"That man's been extremely loyal to me over the years."

"Loyal!" said the Major. "Don't talk nonsense Colonel.
The man I just shared the bathroom with has no loyalty
towards you whatsoever. He did nothing but slate you."

"He did what?" said the Colonel.

"You twisted old bastard," said Tommy.

"Easy Tommy," whispered the Chairman.

"There you have it," said the Major. "The old
Carruthers wouldn't have dared speak to me like that."

"I was thinking the very same thing," said the Colonel.
"And I assure you Major-I intend dealing harshly with
the blighter. But right now, we need to be recruiting not
reducing our numbers. We're going to need the extra
fire power he can offer."

"Fire power!" said the Major. "The man's returned here
a blinking shambles. I doubt if he could hold a knife and
fork steady, never mind a Martini Henry rifle. You said
so yourself Colonel. The man doesn't seem to know
what bloody day it is."

"He's just struggling to readjust," said the Colonel.

"I'm not," said Tommy. "The Major's right. I am a

mess. My soldiering days are over. When it all goes off here, I'm going to be neither use nor ornament. With your permission Colonel, I'll hand in my uniform and get my things and go. All I ask is, you allow me to use the telephone to arrange somewhere else to stay."

"Telephone!" said the Colonel. "What telephone would that be?"

"The one you had repaired for me while I was on leave," said Tommy. "The one I stupidly tossed out the window during my 'fit of pique', as you called it."

"I don't know what you're talking about," said the Colonel. "But even if I had a telephone, I couldn't possibly allow you to use it."

"Why not?" said Tommy.

"Because of the impending threat of the Chinese," said the Colonel. "They're very cunning people. They've probably already taken over the telephone exchange. In all honesty, we should already be talking in code. Now cease all this nonsense about leaving and go and fetch those trifles and mullets."

"Trifles and mullets!" said Tommy.

"I'm talking in code," whispered the Colonel while tapping the side of his nose.

"I see," said Tommy. "That's clever that is Colonel. I didn't quite get what you meant at first."

"I don't doubt you," said the smiling Colonel. "And you're an English speaking British subject. Imagine how long it's going to take the Chinks to work my code out. And remember Carruthers-walls don't just have four corners-they have ears too."

"Would you like me to give him a hand?" said the Chairman.

"If you wouldn't mind," said the Colonel while watching his disillusioned 'sergeant' trudge off. "But keep an eye on the poor beggar. Watch him closely. Monitor his state of mind. It's just possible, he's now under the influence of the communists. Shoot him if you think it's necessary."

"Shoot him!" said the Chairman.

"That's right," said the Colonel. "You are capable of doing something like that aren't you doctor?"

"I am yes," said the Chairman. "I'm more than capable sir. Where would you like me to do it?"

"Between his eyes," said the Colonel. "Put a round between his eyes. No more than one though."

"Very well sir," said the Chairman. "When the time comes, I'll do exactly that."

When the two guests returned from the weapon cupboard with the last two cases of ammunition, about twenty minutes later, they were relieved to find the Major fast asleep at his desk. The Colonel, on the other hand was wide awake and in the process of reassembling one of his vast and impressive collection of old rifles. "48 seconds," he said after laying the weapon down on the table and immediately halting his old stopwatch with his left thumb. "48.2 seconds. That's not too shabby. Not too shabby at all for a man of my advanced years."

"Is that anywhere near your personal best?" said the Chairman.

"It's not a million miles away," said the Colonel. "42 seconds is my best. But that was before the osteoarthritis set in. It's a bugger of a thing. And while we're on the subject of buggers-what's our current situation Carruthers?"

"It's highly promising sir," said Tommy. "I'm pleased to report our men have driven the first wave back as far as the boundary wall."

"That's excellent," said the Colonel. "Have there been any casualties?"

"None, as far as I'm aware of," said Tommy.

"Bravo," said the Colonel. "Good work Carruthers. Now stand to and help yourself to a snifter. You can pour me and the good doctor one while you're at it. I've got a feeling we're going to need it. I've just received some rather disturbing news about Mr Spriggs."

"Mr Spriggs!" said the Chairman.

"My faithful cat," said the Colonel. "Or should I say, 'my former, faithful cat'."

"What do you mean your, 'former cat'?" said the Chairman while doing his utmost to avert his eyes from his equally unsettled companion. "Nothing's happened to the poor thing has it? Has something happened to him Colonel?"

"I've had to turn him out," said the Colonel.

"Turn him out!" said the Chairman. "Do you mean evict him?"

"That's right," said the Colonel. "I've very reluctantly decided to sever our long association."

"Why's that?" said the Chairman.

"Albert caught him fraternising with the Chinese," said the Colonel.

"Oh dear!" said the hugely relieved Chairman. "That's awful."

"It is isn't it," said the Colonel. "It's diabolical to be fair. It constitutes a disturbing breach of trust. I blame his heavy drinking."

"Where will he go?" said the Chairman.

"He'll live with Mr Bimoko," said the Colonel. "He'll take care of him now. Although, I might get Albert to put a spade over his head later."

"Why would you want to do that?" said the Chairman. "I thought you loved him."

"There's only so much love you can afford a traitor," said the Colonel. "I despise treachery. Give me a good old fashioned murderer any day of the week. You know where you stand with a murderer. You'll meet Bimoko soon. You're going to like and enjoy him. You're going to like him a lot. You've actually got a look of him. By the way-you've just missed Albert."

"Is that what the smell is?" said the Chairman.

"I beg your pardon," said the Colonel.

"I'm talking about that lot," said the Chairman while pointing to the hearth where a large stack of damp logs were beginning to give off a slightly putrid stench. "Would you like me to throw a few of them on the fire?"

"For goodness sake doctor-why would you want to own a perfectly capable dog and bark yourself?" said the

[667]

Colonel. "You need to keep those precious hands of yours sterilised and undamaged. Carruthers will sort the fire out. And by the way Sergeant-that should have been done first thing this morning."

"I wasn't actually here this mor..." said Tommy.

"Sorry!" said the Colonel.

"Just get on with it Carruthers," said the Chairman. "I think the Colonel's had enough of your nonsense for one morning, don't you?"

"I do indeed sir," said Tommy before placing four of the wettest logs on the fire and wiping the sap from his hands on his trousers. "Is there anything else sir?"

"Not as yet," said the old man. "Just put your back to that fire and stand to for the time being."

"Right here sir?" said Tommy.

"Right there yes," said the Colonel. "Keep your ears pricked and your eyes on that window. I'll call you if I need anything else. Is there anything you need doctor?"

"There is actually," said the Chairman. "My eyes are beginning to sting. It must have something to do with those freshly cut pine logs. Would you ask Carruthers to fetch me a damp flannel please."

"Certainly," said the Colonel. "See to it will you Carruthers. And bring a clean one for goodness sake. Not one the Major's had around his filthy private bits."

"Right away sir," muttered Tommy before saluting and heading to the bathroom. "Right, away sir."

When the pan faced Tommy returned with the flannel a good five minutes later, he was surprised to see the famously non smoking Chairman with a large Cuban cigar clenched between his teeth.

'Oh will you look at the cut of that ball bag,' he muttered to himself before handing the item to his highly amused companion. 'They must be filming the sequel to *Gone With the* Wind. Clark Gable's arrived on the set.'

"I'm sorry-I missed that Carruthers," said the Colonel. "What was that about the table?"

"I was just commenting on the quality of this one sir,"

said Tommy. "I was wondering whether you'd recently had it French polished. By the way sir-while I'm here-is there anything else I can get you and your guest?"

"I'm fine," said the Colonel. "What about you doctor. Would you like my man to fetch you anything else?"

"I'm alright for now, thank you Carruthers," said the Chairman. "But I don't think he should go too far."

"That's exactly what I was about to tell you," whispered Tommy from behind his open left hand. "Don't push your luck Hulmey. As you know-my patience has very definite limits."

"You need to stand to," said the Chairman before hearing a loud pop and watching his gaping mouthed travelling companion immediately drop to the ground.

"Oh dear mother of God!" yelled Tommy.

"What's happened?" said the bemused Chairman after drawing back his chair.

"It's that damp bastard wood," replied Tommy through gritted teeth. "One of those burning embers has exploded and shot right up me back passage. Mother of God, the pain!"

"Report Carruthers," said the Colonel after snatching his rifle and hitting the floor just under the window. "Report man will you. Are they inside the boundary wall? Have they penetrated our outer defences? What's happening Major?"

"I don't know as yet," said the Major upon releasing his brake and making his way behind one of the fireside chairs. "I *can* confirm there have been shots fired though."

"I think poor old Carruthers has bought one," said the Colonel.

"Where abouts?" said the Major.

"In the arsehole," said the Colonel before pointing towards his Sergeant who by then was writhing around the floor with his two hands clenched around his exposed buttock cheeks. "See what you can do for him doctor."

"Right away sir," said the Chairman.

Within seconds, another burning pine ember had exploded and hit one of the badly frayed velvet curtains setting it alight almost immediately.

"They're playing that cowardly game are they," said the Colonel before handing the Chairman his ice bucket. "The bastards are trying to smoke us out. Put that fire out will you doctor."

"What fire?" said the Chairman. "What fire where?"

"The one above your head," said the Colonel before opening the window and firing two shots into the nearest tree. "And when you've done that, see what you can do for Carruthers."

"Can you see anything?" said the Major after arriving at the window. "How many are there?"

"Hundreds," said the Colonel before taking careful aim, firing and removing the lower limb from a nearby Sycamore tree. "Don't wait for me Major. Commence firing man. Fire at will. We're going to be overrun."

"Help me Hulmey," pleaded Tommy after grabbing the Chairman's right ankle. "For the love of God, help me. Do something will you. I'm burning away from the inside here. For pity's sake, do something will you. I'm going to have no fucking insides left."

"Do what?" said the Chairman. "What exactly do you want me to do Tommy? Tell me."

"Do the necessary," said the Colonel while just about managing to avoid another speeding projectile that had burst from the fire. "Just do the necessary and get back to this wall."

"What do you mean, 'do the necessary' Colonel?" said the Chairman. "What does that even mean? I'm not a soldier. I didn't even play soldiers when I was a kid. Tell me what that means will you Colonel."

"Shoot him," said the Colonel. "Put the pathetic bugger out of his misery. His constant whining is beginning to drain the men's morale. Here-move aside-I'll do it."

"That won't be necessary," said the Chairman after quickly placing himself between the Colonel and his wounded companion.

[670]

"Move aside," roared the Colonel.

"I'm sorry Colonel," said the Chairman. "I can't do
that. He's not ready to give up the ghost just yet. I know
this man."

"You know him!" said the Colonel.

"Instinctively I do," said the Chairman. "I know the
sort of person he is. He's still very much in the fight.
Just leave him with me. I'll have him as right as rain in
no time at all."

"Very well," said the Colonel. "But I want to see that
bullet. I want to know what weapons those Commy
bastards are firing."

Tommy's treatment had begun twenty minutes
after the last red hot, speeding projectile had shattered
one of the coloured leaded lights at the top left hand
corner of the large bay window. It consisted of a half
filled freezing cold bath containing a considerable
amount of ice collected from the living room window
ledge, a rubber tube, normally used for rinsing hair and a
lavish amount of Petroleum jelly.

"There you go," said the Chairman after despatching
what was left of Tommy's badly charred underpants into
the bin next to the lavatory pan. "I couldn't save your
briefs though. You're going to have to go commando
from now on. I think that's actually quite appropriate
seeing as you were injured in the line of fire."

"Go to hell," said a wincing and badly shaken Tommy
while gingerly rising from the ledge of the bath. "Just
go to hell Hulmey. And, by the way I've got some news
that's going to wipe that smirk from your face for good."

"What's that?" said the Chairman.

"The Major somehow knows I was the one who kicked
Mr Spriggs," said Tommy.

"What!" said the Chairman.

"He knows I was the one that injured the Colonel's cat,"
said a still grimacing and hobbling Tommy while
proceeding to make his ponderous and painful way to
the towel rail.

"How?" said the Chairman.

"I've no idea," said Tommy. "I don't know how and I don't know why. But he bloody well knows. He also knows I'm an imposter."

"How do you mean?" said the Chairman.

"He knows I'm not Sergeant Carruthers," said Tommy.

"You what!" said the Chairman.

"He knows I'm not Carruthers," said Tommy. "He told me when I took him to the bathroom. He's insane Hulmey."

"He's just very old and confused," said the Chairman. "Just try to ignore him."

"He's insane, I tell you," said Tommy. "He tried to blind me."

"He what!" laughed the Chairman.

"It's not a laughing matter Hulmey," said Tommy. "He threw bleach in my eyes. He made out it had been an accident-but it wasn't. He did it deliberately. We need to get out of here and we need to get out of here fast. The man's completely unhinged Hulmey."

"Maybe so, but he's not the one who runs the show," said the Chairman. "The Colonel calls the shots in this house. You've seen the way it is. The Major's rarely allowed to get a word in edgeways. And right now, for whatever reason, the Colonel and I are on reasonably good terms."

"I'm not," said Tommy. "I'm not on good terms with the silly old fool. I'm his fucking dogsbody. And don't forget Hulmey-whether the Colonel calls the shots or not, the Major outranks me by some way. So if he decides to tell his old mucker I was the one that hurt his beloved cat, he's very likely to accept his word. He could do anything. Come to think of it-the bastard could have me court marshalled and shot. He could even send for his gypsy friends to punish me. Fucking hell Hulmey. I could end up wearing the head of a pig for the rest of my fucking days. I'm telling you Hulmey-we need to get out of here."

"I know," said the Chairman. "You're absolutely right. But what about the phone."

[672]

"There is no bloody phone," said Tommy. "You heard the old boy."

"I think there's still a good chance there is," said the Chairman. "I think he's just forgotten about it temporarily. Consider how many times he's already forgotten my name Tommy."

"He's more than forgotten mine," said Tommy. "He thinks I'm someone from his past. And by the way- you're milking that like a good un."

"I just find it hilarious, that's all," said the Chairman. "Now let's go back and be as nice and polite as possible. And if you get the chance, have a look in the writing bureau drawer."

"What for?" said Tommy.

"The receipt for the telephone repair job," said the Chairman.

"Of course," said Tommy. "I forgot about that."

"And if you can, try to snaffle a couple of those rifles when nobody's looking," said the Chairman. "Make sure they're loaded and put them somewhere within easy reach."

"Now you're talking my language," said Tommy. "Are the rest of our clothes dry by any chance?"

"I should think so," said the Chairman. "Why do you ask?"

"Because I'd like to get out of this stupid bloody uniform and become Tommy McShane, the builder again," said Tommy.

"And I for one would strongly recommend you leave it on," said the Chairman.

"Why's that?" said Tommy.

"Because that uniform, regardless of how unfairly you think you've been treated since you've been wearing it, gives you a certain standing within this home," said the Chairman. "And more importantly, it affords you the sort of freedom of movement, I'm not necessarily going to be granted. Promise me you won't take it off Tommy. Promise me you won't take it off until we're on our way out of here."

"Alright," said Tommy.

"Promise me on your kid's lives Tommy," said the Chairman.

"I promise," said Tommy. "But once we're out of here, that uniform's history and me and you are going to have one serious discussion."

When the two visitors eventually re-emerged from the bathroom, they were delighted to find the Major so utterly engrossed in whatever he was composing at his writing desk, he hadn't even bothered to shake his head or utter one of his typically offensive comments. The Colonel on the other hand, was in celebratory mood. He was standing next to the central bay window, holding his half full brandy glass at arm's length while beaming with delight.

"All hail my conquering heroes," he said before taking a quick look outside and drawing over what was left of the right hand curtain. "You'll no doubt be glad to learn, our spineless bastard enemy have fled almost to a man."

"That is good news," said the Chairman.

"They've got no bloody backbone those Chinks," said the Colonel. "They never did have. If it wasn't for their considerable numerical advantage, they wouldn't represent any threat at all. Now then. How is my brave Sergeant faring?"

"He's on the mend and ready to report back for duty-aren't you Carruthers?" said the Chairman.

"I am sir, yes," said Tommy.

"That's excellent news," said the Colonel. "I thought we'd lost you. I really did. I thought we'd lost him doctor. Did you manage to remove the offending shell?"

"Unfortunately not," said the Chairman. "It's still lodged up his rear end. But I don't think there's any real cause for concern. It's unlikely to do any further damage where it is."

"Are you sure?" said the Colonel.

"I'm as sure as I can be, under the circumstances," said the Chairman.

[674]

"Would you like me to try to remove it?" said the
Colonel, to the consternation of his anxious Sergeant'.
"I've carried out such a procedure before, you know.
The same thing happened to an old sapper friend of mine
called Ginger Harris. He took a sly bullet from an
Afghan sniper while flushing out insurgents in
Kandahar. The man was in mortal agony. I've never
heard screams like them in my life. Pitiful, it was. It's a
very tender part of the anatomy, the anal passage."
"You're telling me," said Tommy.
"We ended up tearing off Ginger's strides and bending
him over a cannon," said the Colonel. "It wasn't
exactly surgery of the Harley Street calibre, but we did
eventually manage to extract the offending missile."
"How exactly?" said Tommy.
"With some Vaseline and a pair of fire tongues," said the
Colonel. "Just like those buggers in the hearth. In fact,
they might be the very fellows. I have a habit of never
throwing anything old and useful out. I suppose that's
why the Major's lasted here so long. What do you think
Carruthers-would you like me to go ahead with the
procedure? Would you like me to sort your bottom out
for you?"
"I'm absolutely fine," said Tommy while tightening his
belt. "I'm in no discomfort at all now. I'll probably just
shit the bullet out when it's ready to move on."
"That's true," said the Colonel. "That's the natural way,
to be fair. I do that a lot with splinters. Unfortunately,
leaving it where it is, will leave me wondering."
"What do you mean?" said the Chairman.
"I'm desperate to know what those Commy bastards
have been using for ammo," said the Colonel. "You can
almost guarantee the Ruskies have some involvement.
Anyway-never mind. What about infection doctor. Do
you think there's any danger the wound might become
septic?"
"It's possible," said the Chairman. "We'll just have to
wait and see."
"Waiting can be a very dangerous game," said the

Colonel. "That's how limbs are lost. What about cauterising the wound doctor. Would you recommend that? Would you like me to put an iron in the fire for you?"

"An iron!" said the Chairman.

"That's right," said the Colonel. "I'll heat up a poker and you or I can ram it up the Sergeant's jacksie. It'll all be done and dusted in a matter of seconds."

"Would that work?" said the Chairman.

"It's not going to happen," said Tommy. "I'm fine. I've taken a load of strong painkillers."

"You're fine because of one thing and one thing alone," said the Colonel before offering his free hand to the Chairman. "It's because of this accomplished man of medicine here. It's because of his expertise and ability to perform under intense pressure. Well done doctor. I'm going to mention you in despatches."

"That's very kind of you Colonel," said the Chairman. "What do you think Carruthers?"

"I'm a little too overwhelmed to think," said the seething Tommy.

"Are you too overwhelmed to fetch your saviour a celebratory drink?" said the Colonel.

"Not at all sir," mumbled Tommy while heading to the well stocked drinks cabinet. "Right away sir. Should I make it a large one sir?"

"Indeed you should," said the Colonel. "And then you can go and make up the man's bed."

"I'm sorry!" said the Chairman.

"I want you to stay the night," said the Colonel. "In fact, I must insist upon it. It's too dangerous to move on now. By the morning, the Chinese will be in complete retreat and you can safely be on your way again."

"It makes sense, I suppose," said the Chairman. "And to be honest, a warm bed sounds very appealing right now. But listen Colonel-I wonder if your generosity and common decency could stretch just that little bit further?"

"What is it old bean?" said the Colonel before settling

back down. "You name it, and I'll see what I can do for you. As long as you don't want to share my bed, that is."

"It's not that Colonel," laughed the Chairman while gently tapping the table top. "I was just wondering if you'd allow Carruthers to go with me?"

"Go with you!" said the Colonel.

"Just as a guide until I'm out of danger," said the Chairman. "As you know, I'm not wholly familiar with this part of the country."

"That's not a bad idea as it happens" said the Colonel while proceeding to hold his brandy bottle up to the light. "In fact, it's a very good idea. I'll get Albert to fix you both something for your journey."

"That's very kind of you sir," said the Chairman. "What sort of night do you think we're in for?"

"A very stormy one," said the Major upon arriving at the table. "I wonder how Mr Spriggs is going to fare beyond the range and comfort of your fire."

"Not very well I imagine," said the Colonel ruefully before reaching over and retrieving an old muslin bag from the top of the piano and clutching it to his chest.

"This is where he slept for over 40 years doctor."

"Is it really," said the Chairman.

"He loved the piano," said the Colonel. "He liked to prance across the keys and make sounds. But he was never a natural musician like the multitalented Bimoko."

"He could sense trouble though," said the Major. "He could sense trouble like no animal I've ever come across. He was better than any guard dog or peacock."

"What do you mean Major?" said the Chairman.

"He'd be the first to hear something," said the Major. "And then his back would arch and he'd stare intently in the general direction of that something until whatever it was or whoever it was materialised. That's how I knew you were on the way here Mr Hulme."

"You seem to be inferring I'm trouble Major," said the Chairman.

"I'm doing nothing of the sort," said the Major while

[677]

angling his skeletal frame to enable him to stare directly into the uneasy Tommy Mac's eyes. "I'm just extolling the virtues of poor Mr Spriggs, our recently injured cat."

CHAPTER TWENTY SIX
HARSH WORDS

Tommy Mac had been as good as his word for once and unbeknown to his deeply concerned travelling companion, had not only added the red striped trousers to his existing uniform but had even slept in the entire outfit in case he had been summoned in the early hours by the house proprietor. He had been allocated a nicely decorated and sparsely furnished bedroom a few doors down from the Colonel's modest sleeping quarters and within earshot of the Major's far more lavish room, and upon rising at around 7.30 am, had been tasked with finding the Chairman and escorting him back to the main room. He was to find his companion in no mood for the usual banter however-in fact, he was to find him in no mood for dialogue of any sort.

"What the hell was all that about?" he roared immediately upon entering the living room.

"I beg your pardon!" said the startled Colonel.

"You heard me-what was all that crazy palaver about?" said the Chairman.

"My boy!" said the Colonel. "My boy, my boy, my boy. "What is it? What on earth's come over you? What happened for pity's sake?"

"You know damn well what's happened," said the Chairman.

"I'm afraid you have the advantage over me doctor," said the Colonel before turning to face his equally confused 'Sergeant'. "Do you know what's happened Carruthers?"

"I've no idea sir," said Tommy.

"You had me locked up Colonel," said the Chairman.

"Only for your own safety old fellow," said the Colonel while urging the Chairman to take his seat.

"Own safety!" said the Chairman. "I wasn't safe. I wasn't remotely safe. I was violently assaulted."

"You were what?" said the Colonel.

"I was dragged from my room by that lunatic manservant of yours and nearly drowned," said the Chairman.

"What do you mean, 'nearly drowned'?" said Tommy.

"You forget yourself Carruthers," said the Colonel. "This is house business. You just concentrate on producing and delivering palatable tea."

"I'm sorry sir," said Tommy. "I'm just concerned, that's all. The doctor was very kind to me yesterday. I just don't like the idea of him being upset."

"That's perfectly understandable," said the Colonel. "After all, the man probably saved your life in all fairness. "Do you want milk and sugar doctor?"

"I want milk, sugar and lashings of explanation," said the Chairman. "But first of all, I want you to explain how and why I ended up in that filthy cell when you've got so many far more comfortable rooms at your disposal."

"What do you mean by, 'filthy cell'?" said the Colonel.

"I woke up and found myself locked in a dingy cell, which the vast majority of civilized human beings would consider unfit for pigs to be kept in," said the Chairman. "To be honest, I don't even know how I got there."

"Albert conveyed you," said the Colonel. "You'd crashed out much the worse for drink. You'd had a few too many. You were talking utter balderdash by the end of the night. You were telling me how you were able to talk face to face with a family member in Australia by means of a little box with a screen."

"It's called Skype," said the Chairman. "But that's not important right now. I want to know what I was doing in that cell."

"I can't help you," said the Colonel. "It certainly wasn't my idea. I had a nicely appointed room prepared for you. Carruthers will tell you. He'd made up your bed at my behest. That's right, isn't it Sergeant?"

"It is yes," replied a genuinely concerned Tommy while carefully lifting the teapot lid. "It was a nice little room as far as I'm concerned. It was definitely no pig sty."

"I slept in a prison cell," said the Chairman. "It didn't even have a light or a window."

"I know what's happened," said the impish looking Major before returning his fountain pen to its jar, freeing his brake and turning to face the table. "Albert's gone and confused your visitor with one of your new intake. Tell me doctor-did you enjoy your ice bath?"

"Enjoy it Major!" said the Chairman. "The ice was about 3 inches thick in places. I doubt if an industrial jackhammer could have penetrated it. I'm now black and a variety of shades of blue. In fact, a Dulux paint chart is unlikely to contain more shades of blue."

"I'm so sorry doctor," said the Colonel.

"Not as sorry as I am," said the Chairman. "That ice had to be broken and my spine was the tool of choice. My spine was used in the same way a toffee hammer is. And when the ice did eventually break, I couldn't breathe. I was fighting to get my head above the water. And all the time, that fucking lunatic servant of yours was forcing me back under."

"That's because you need to be fully immersed to get the full benefit from an ice bath," said the Colonel.

"Full benefit!" said the Chairman before quickly rolling up his sleeves and holding out his bared and purple arms. "Look at that Colonel. Look at the state of me. I've still got goose pimples. All that happened about 8 hours ago, and I'm still shivering like a leaf in a force ten gale."

"We're you deloused?" said the Major.

"Oh yes," said the Chairman. "I was deloused alright. That happened just as I was beginning to think the worst was over. I had a load of white powder thrown over me indiscriminately. It stung to high hell and I couldn't see a thing. I must have been blind for about 30 minutes. My eyes are still stinging now, if the truth be known. What was that horrible stuff?"

"Insecticide," said the Major.

"Insecticide!" said the Chairman. "Fucking insecticide! That's nice isn't it. That's lovely that is. Jesus Christ!

[681]

One minute I'm being hailed as a hero for saving a man's life, the next I'm being treated like a common garden slug. I'm surprised I didn't have salt poured all over me. Explain that will you Colonel. Try to explain what the hell's been going on."

"I'll do that gladly if you'll let me get a word in," said the Colonel. "I'm afraid the Major's right. Albert must have confused you with a new inmate. It appears you've had the full treatment doctor. I'm dreadfully sorry. I can only apologise."

"You can do more than that," said the Major. "You can charge him."

"Charge me for what?" said the Chairman.

"Your hydro-treatment and your overnight stay," said the Major.

"You can go to hell," said the Chairman while making his way to the fire. "I'm paying you nothing. I've never endured a night like that in my life. And by the way Colonel. What's with all the howling and whooping during the early hours? Those baboons can't get in here can they?"

"An elite group can," said the Colonel.

"What do you mean, 'elite group'?" said the Chairman.

"The brighter ones," said the Colonel. "The leaders. They watch the upstairs corridors for me. They arrive about midnight and patrol until Albert rises at around 6 am."

"They do what?" said the Chairman.

"They work the graveyard shift," said the Colonel. "They work a seven day week. And before you go accusing me of unkindness or worker exploitation, just remember this—those animals were lost before I took them on and trained them up. They had no structure to their lives whatsoever."

"I'm sorry sir-are we talking about baboons here?" said the Chairman.

"Very much so," replied the Colonel. "They're a vital part of my security staff. They love working here. They particularly love working nights. They actually prefer nights to days. And they're far more reliable than humans because humans are constantly taking sick leave and expecting bank holidays off. Which reminds me doctor-do you realise it's Christmas Eve?"

"I didn't actually," said the befuddled Chairman before turning to his companion. "Did you know that Carruthers?"

"I didn't," said Tommy. "Bloody hell! It's Christmas Eve! Oh bloody hell."

"What's wrong Sergeant?" said the Colonel. "You've suddenly gone all glassy eyed. What's the matter?"

"Nothing sir," said Tommy. "I think some of that delousing powder's still in the air. I hate the horrible stuff. I can't stand getting anything in my eyes."

"I know what's the matter with him," said the Major. "He's forgotten my Christmas present."

"That's it," said Tommy.

"Is it too late to get a letter off to Santa?" said the Chairman.

"To ask him for what?" said the Colonel.

"A ride home on his sleigh for one thing," said the Chairman. "And some warm clothes would be nice. This candy striped nightshirt just isn't me. By the way Colonel-where are my clothes? Where are the clothes I had torn from my back?"

"They'll be in the wash," said the Colonel. "They'll be repaired and ready for you tomorrow."

"Tomorrow!" said the Chairman. "I'm hoping not to be here tomorrow Colonel. I've got a wife and kids to see and a turkey to carve."

"Take the Leichter Panzerspahwagen for goodness sake," said the Colonel. "The keys are on a hook outside the door."

"It's got no wheels," said the Chairman.

"What!" said the Colonel. "No blooming wheels! Of all the.....That'll be the Chinese. That'll be those bastard gooks. Of all the off handed, four flushing stunts to pull. By Jove...Is there no limit to the devious nature of those dirty Commy bastards? Did you hear that Major-the Chinese have sabotaged our only means of escape."

"That's dreadful," said the Major. "I hope they haven't cut off our water supply and sabotaged our means of getting a wash."

"So do I," said the Colonel. "See to that will you Carruthers. Take the Major for his morning ablutions. Chop, chop. And let's not make it hard for the man or I'll be forced to have Albert resume the duty. You don't want to go back to those days of bruised testicles and a painful bottom crack do you?"

"I most certainly do not," said the Major.

"Well behave yourself then," said the Colonel.

A few minutes later, almost immediately after the bathroom door had been closed and bolted, the Colonel topped up his cup, added a small drop of milk and beckoned the Chairman to sit by his side.

"How are you doing doctor?" he said after taking his guest by the left wrist.

"I've had much better nights," replied the Chairman.

"I don't doubt it old bean," said the Colonel.

"Why was I locked up Colonel?" said the Chairman.

"It was nothing personal, I assure you," said the Colonel. "I insist on all my guests being locked in their rooms after lights out. The last thing I want is for them to be walking the corridors late at night or during the early hours of the morning."

"Why's that?" said the Chairman.

"Because I don't want any harm to come to them," said the Colonel. "This is a former asylum Mr Holmes. If Albert sees anyone unfamiliar walking along my corridors, he'll assume they are escaped inmates and deal with them harshly. Trust me doctor-it wouldn't be the first time he's made that mistake."

"But I wasn't wandering the corridors," whispered the Chairman.

"I know that," whispered the Colonel. "And once again, I offer my most genuine and wholehearted apologies. He's a heavy handed oaf isn't he?"

"You can say that again," whispered the Chairman. "He picked me up between his right finger and thumb as if I was a rolled up newspaper. Bloody hell Colonel. I couldn't have felt more helpless if I'd been scooped up by a JCB. Are you absolutely sure I'm safe here? What if he sees me sitting at your table and suddenly goes ape."

"He won't," said the Colonel. "Not while I'm here."

"I hope you're right," whispered the Chairman. "What about the Major. If you don't mind me saying so, he doesn't take kindly to strangers does he?"

"He's become embittered," whispered the Colonel.

"Regarding what?" whispered the Chairman.

"All sorts of things," whispered the Colonel while quickly glancing towards the bathroom door. "But it was the loss of his only son that impacted most. He took that very badly. He took that very badly indeed."

"I would myself," whispered the Chairman. "I don't know what I'd do if I lost mine. What happened Colonel-was he another casualty of one of those God-awful wars?"

"Was he heckaslike," whispered the Colonel. "It was nothing like that. He lost him here."

"Here?" whispered the Chairman.

"So he claims," whispered the Colonel.

"I don't understand," whispered the Chairman. "What are you saying Colonel."

"I'm not sure the lad ever existed," whispered the Colonel.

"What!" whispered the Chairman.

"Nobody but the Major ever got to meet him," whispered the Colonel. "Nobody but Major Hauser ever laid eyes on him. On the day he was supposed to have called and subsequently disappeared, the majority of my staff had been working in the garden. Me, Albert and Carruthers had been erecting some newly made scarecrows near the west wall. The crows had been driving me nuts that Summer. If I remember right, I'd just about run out of ammunition. I'd shot hundreds of the bloody nuisances. It was only when we returned to the house at the end of the day, we noticed the Major pacing the hall and looking distraught."

"And that's when he told you his son was missing was it?" said the Chairman.

"He told us he'd sent him to fetch a bottle of wine from the cellar and he hadn't returned," said the Colonel.

"How long had he allegedly been missing?" whispered the Chairman.

"About 3 or 4 hours, according to the Major," whispered the Colonel. "But I've got to be honest with you doctor. The whole thing didn't seem to make sense as far as I was concerned."

"Why not?" whispered the Chairman.

"Because, in all the years I'd known the Major, including those years prior to him coming to live with me, he'd never once mentioned a son," whispered the Colonel. "And to this day, I'm still not convinced he had one. I know he'd never been married. I know that much. As far as I was concerned, the only real love in his life was the army. He'd always been completely dedicated to his profession."

"Did he tell you anything about the lad?" whispered the Chairman. "Did he describe him at all?"

"He told me quite a lot, to be fair," whispered the Colonel. "And in a certain amount of detail too. He said he was very pleasant, athletically built, articulate and good looking. He said he'd gained a first class honours degree at Balliol College, Cambridge and played second eleven cricket for Surrey. He said he'd done very well for himself and owned a lot of property. He sounded a bit too good to be true if the truth be known."

"Did he say why he'd called?" whispered the Chairman.

"Not as far as I can remember," whispered the Colonel before once again turning to face the bathroom where voices had been raised momentarily. "Tell me doctor- how trustworthy are you?"

"I'd say I'm up there with the best," whispered the Chairman. "Why do you ask Colonel?"

"Because, if I was to tell you something, would you promise never to reveal it to a living soul?" whispered the Colonel.

"I think you can safely stake what's left of your life on it," whispered the Chairman. "What is it Colonel?"

"The Major remains convinced his son's still here," whispered the Colonel.

"Still here!" whispered the Chairman.

"He believes the lad is still wandering the basement corridors," whispered the Colonel.

"Oh dear!" whispered the Chairman. "How sad. How very sad. How long has he allegedly been missing?"

"40 years," whispered the Colonel.

"40 years!" whispered the Chairman. "Bloody hell! 40 years! That's insane that is. That really is insane."

"It is isn't it?" whispered the Colonel.

"Which means his son's visit must have been a figment of the Major's imagination," whispered the Chairman.

"I've no doubt about it," whispered the Colonel. "Until some bright sleuth proves otherwise that is."

"And that's not going to happen," whispered the Chairman.

"That would be my conclusion too," whispered the Colonel. "Particularly when you consider how many discrepancies the police found in his original statement."

"Like what?" whispered the Chairman.

"Like the fact Balliol College is part of Oxford University and not Cambridge," whispered the Colonel. "And the fact Surrey County Cricket Club have no record of the lad ever being registered with them. I was forced to bring a psychologist out eventually. Although, when I say forced, I mean advised."

"What did he make of it all?" whispered the Chairman.

"He classified the Major as a pathological liar," whispered the Colonel. "He espoused the notion the old boy had fabricated the whole thing because he harboured a subconscious yearning to have a son. The 'Father Complex', I think he called it. He said it was quite a common phenomenon among men who had never married or had never had any children."

"That's quite tragic, when you come to think of it," whispered the Chairman. "I almost feel sorry for the poor old bugger now."

"How do you think I felt?" whispered the Colonel. "I'd known him and served with him for the best part of my adult life. It was extremely hard to bear. For years, I'd suddenly realise he was missing-then I'd find him, candle or lantern in hand, in some remote part of the house, calling out for his boy. Whether it's a load of old bull or true, he'll never get over it doctor. To this day, he'll stop a conversation in mid sentence, believing he can hear the lad crying out for him. It was an obsession which ultimately cost him the use of his legs."

"What do you mean?" whispered the Chairman.

"He suffered a terrible and almost fatal fall," whispered the Colonel while continuing to watch the bathroom door at more regular intervals. "I warned him. I did warn the silly old fool. But he wouldn't listen. As was often the case, he thought he knew best. Eventually, Albert found him early one morning at the bottom of the east tower. He'd tumbled down 72 concrete steps. The marvellous Nigerian surgeon that operated on him said that the injuries he'd sustained, resembled those of someone who'd been flattened by a stampeding herd of water buffalo."

"Bloody hell!" whispered the Chairman.

"He'd broken just about every bone in his body," whispered the Colonel.

"Would that include his spine?" whispered the Chairman. "Can I assume by the very fact that he's now wheelchair bound, he'd damaged his spine too?"

"No doctor," whispered the Colonel. "You may not. Albert was responsible for that."

"What!" whispered the Chairman.

"It wasn't Albert's fault to be fair and honest," whispered the Colonel. He was only trying to help. The Major shouldn't have been moved. He should have been treated where he lay. He's not walked a single yard from that day onwards."

"My God!" whispered the Chairman. "I'm beginning to appreciate why he's got such a bad attitude now."

"But that's not all," said the Colonel.

"No!" whispered the Chairman.

"A few months after he'd returned from hospital, I started receiving letters," whispered the Colonel.

"From who?" said the Chairman.

"His daughter Hope," said the Colonel.

"His daughter!" whispered the Chairman. "Bloody hell! This story gets more fantastic by the minute. That must have got you thinking Colonel."

"It most certainly did," whispered the Colonel.

"What did she want?" whispered the Chairman.

"She wanted to know if I knew the whereabouts of her missing brother," whispered the Colonel. "She claimed she'd tracked him down to here through a missing persons organisation based in Camden. She also said she'd had help from an eminent spiritualist who was convinced the lad was still alive. She implored me to resume the search. Her letters contained some of the most evocative lines I've ever read doctor. They were heart wrenching and almost poetic. Some of them would put many of the World War One poets in the shade."

"And did you resume the search?" whispered the Chairman.

"Of course I did," whispered the Colonel. "I saw it as a moral obligation. I even brought a couple of sniffer dogs in. But once again, we found absolutely nothing. Not a footprint, not a hair fibre, not a hand mark on a wall, not a cigarette butt on the ground or a drop of blood."

"Did this Hope girl ever call here," whispered the Chairman.

"The girl didn't exist," whispered the Colonel.

"She didn't exist?" whispered the Chairman.

"She was another contrivance doctor," whispered the Colonel. "I came to realise the Major had been writing the letters himself. He still does it to this day. He waits until I'm not around and then tucks them inside my usual bundle of mail. He still writes at least one a week and signs them in the girl's name."

"Even now-even now after 40 years or more?" whispered the Chairman.

"That's what he's doing while he's at his desk," whispered the Colonel. "And to try to disguise the fact he's the one compiling them, he writes them with his left hand. He's ambidextrous you see doctor."

"He's more than ambidextrous, if you'll forgive me for saying so Colonel" whispered the Chairman just as the bathroom door slowly began to creak open. "He's a time wasting fantasist. He should be writing fiction, not anonymous letters to thoroughly decent old men."

As if choreographed, the Major's return coincided perfectly with the giant manservant Albert's entrance and for some time after, both Tommy and the Chairman didn't utter a word or move any one of their tension bound muscles. That was until the Colonel introduced the big man but even then, even after the apprehensive Chairman had risen to offer his slightly trembling hand, the servant had remained completely still and as emotionless as stone.

"Albert's going to cook us a fine breakfast," said the Colonel after closing the door behind his departing member of staff. "It's not going to be anything too fancy mind. He's just going to do some fried eggs, sausages, bacon and one or two loaves of buttered toast. How does that sound doctor?"

"It sounds fantastic," said the Chairman.

"What about you Carruthers-are you going to join us?" said the Colonel while checking the level of the teapot. "Or are you still struggling to put weight on that tender rear of yours?"

"I think I can manage to sit down for the duration of a breakfast," said Tommy.

"That's good," said the Colonel. "And tell me Sergeant-have you managed to complete a decent evacuation since the unfortunate incident?"

"Sorry!" said Tommy.

"Have you had a good dump since you were shot?" said the Chairman.

"Not yet," said Tommy.

"Well let me know as soon as you have," said the Colonel. "I'm desperate to get into your waste and examine that bullet. Aren't you doctor?"

"Very much so," said the Chairman. "But I'm even more desperate to change the subject before Albert's bacon and eggs arrive. Which leads me nicely to something I've been meaning to ask Colonel."

"What's that old bean?" said the Colonel.

"I was wondering where you get your fresh produce," said the Chairman.

"We grow a lot of it ourselves," said the old man. "We've got a large heated greenhouse near the south wall. It was the Summer house at one time. But we never really used it as such."

"What about the bacon and sausage and things like that," said the Chairman. "Where do they come from?"

"The market," said the Colonel.

"Market!" said the Chairman. "How often do you go there?"

"We don't," said the Colonel. "My gypsy friends bring the market to us."

"How often do they call?" said the Chairman.

"They don't," said the Colonel. "They set up a makeshift stall a few hundred yards from the main gate. They rob me blind, if the truth be known."

"What do you mean?" said the Chairman.

"They demand double what the legitimate market traders charge," said the Colonel. "But they bring the mail and the fresh milk too, so I suppose I can't complain too much."

"Don't you have a postman?" said the Chairman.

"We used to have one," said the Colonel. "In fact, we've had quite a few over the years. They just stopped coming after a while."

"Why do you think that is?" said the Chairman. "They

didn't go missing did they?"

"Not as far as I know," said the Colonel. "If that had been the case, I'd have had the bloody constabulary snooping around making enquiries. They just stopped delivering the mail and that's about the size of it. You'd make a good detective doctor. I say that because you seem to be asking an awful lot of questions this morning."

"I'm just interested in how you're able to run and maintain such a magnificent home," said the Chairman. "And being a doctor, I always take a keen interest in people's dietary habits. I think you're remarkable to be honest."

"Thank you doctor," said the Colonel. "And I think you're remarkable too. What you did for Carruthers yesterday was nothing short of miraculous. But on the subject of running the home doctor-I have to admit, Albert deserves much of the credit for that. He cooks and he washes and every fortnight, I give him a huge shopping list and an envelope stuffed with money and he hands them to my gypsy friends. And hey presto, before you know it, my larder's full again."

"Does Albert understand money?" said the Chairman.

"The gypsies understand Albert," said the Colonel. "They understand that what he gives them is all they're going to get and what they give him has to be fresh and completely faithful to my grocery list."

"I like that," said the Chairman. "Do you ever go into town Colonel?"

"Not anymore," said the Colonel. "I don't need to. I don't even need to go to the bank."

"Why's that Colonel?" said the Chairman.

"My money gets delivered biannually by a security firm," said the Colonel. "You don't want to know where I hide it do you?"

"Of course not," replied the Chairman.

"Would you like some more tea doctor?" said the Colonel.

"I'd love some more tea," said the Chairman. "But in

the meantime Colonel-I've got one more question I'd
like to ask, if I might be so bold?"

"Fire away," said the Colonel. "What is it young man?"

"It's to do with something that caught my eye when I
was passing your window yesterday afternoon," said the
Chairman. "It intrigued me to be honest."

"What was it?" said the Colonel after sliding his guest a
cup of fresh tea.

"I saw what appeared to be a long row of camera tripods
about 70 yards in the distance," said the Chairman. "I
wouldn't have noticed them if they hadn't been
glistening in the late afternoon sun."

"They belong to the bastard Chinese," said the Colonel.
"They're Soviet built machine gun mounts. But don't
worry doctor-it's very unlikely you'll ever see weapons
mounted on them."

"Why not?" said the Chairman.

"Because they're bluffing," said the Colonel after
retrieving an old pair of field glasses from under the
table and making his way to the window. "They want us
to believe they're better armed and equipped than they
actually are. It's all like an elaborate game of chess, you
see doctor."

"And you don't strike me as the type of person who'd
deliberately knock over his king," said the Chairman.

"That's very good doctor," said the Colonel. "Do you
play? Do you play chess at all?"

"Only at a very basic level," said the Chairman.

The answers to the plethora of questions the
Chairman had felt the need to ask had only served to
make him want to know more and he might well have
asked more had the door not suddenly and abruptly
opened to reveal the enormous Albert holding a large
silver plated tray across each of his massive palms.

"I think that's our cue to retake our seats doctor," said
the Colonel before slipping his binoculars under the
table and settling back down.

"I've been looking forward to this since you teased me
with the mention of a sandwich last evening," said the

[693]

Chairman before spearing two rashers of smoked bacon and carefully delivering them to the right of his plate.

"Teased you!" said the Colonel. "Did you not get the sandwich?"

"Unfortunately not," said the Chairman.

"You should have said something old boy," said the Colonel. "It's little wonder you were blazing this morning. There are few things that affect the mood as profoundly as hunger."

"I couldn't agree more," said the Chairman while finding his attention drawn to the impressive moulded ceiling. "Has this place always been an asylum Colonel?"

"It's been a few things," said the Colonel while struggling to pin his sausage to his last portion of fried egg. "It was a military hospital during the second world war. A lot of servicemen were treated here. Many of them are buried in nearby cemeteries. I believe this area has more graveyards per square acre than any other in the country. I often wonder whether that was the reason the place was chosen to house so many gravely ill men."

"It would make a lot of sense," said the Chairman.

"When the place was in its pomp, you would have fully appreciated why it was considered," said the Colonel. "Recuperation wise, it was as good as any of the acclaimed English spa towns."

"Did you oversee things during that time?" said the Chairman.

"I was abroad," said the old man. "I was needed by my regiment. One of my good friends and neighbours handled the day to day running of the place in my absence. Pinkie Fairclough, his name was. He couldn't serve in the forces because of some long standing medical condition. The job killed him in the end."

"Why's that Colonel?" said the Chairman.

"He shagged himself to death," said the Colonel.

"Really!" said the Chairman.

"He was a right handsome bastard was Pinkie," said the Colonel. He had a rare old time with those young nurses

from what I've heard. He must have knocked up scores
of the beauties. He was still sporting an impressive
erection when he was found dead in his mother in law's
bed."

"So when did the old place become a lunatic asylum
Colonel?" said the Chairman.

"Two or three years after the war had ended," said the
Colonel. "Don't ask me to be any more accurate than
that because basic maths is beyond me at my time of life.
Quite a few of the men who'd suffered badly during the
construction of the Burma Railway were looked after
here. They experienced the sort of nightmares a top
horror writer would baulk at. As I just said, some of
them ended their days here. They died out in Burma, if
the truth be told. The Japs treated them appallingly. We
had one here you know."

"Had what?" said the Chairman.

"A Jap," said the Colonel after swilling his mouth. "The
Home Office arranged it. A young pilot. Takeshi, I
think his name was."

"They sent a Japanese pilot here!" said the Chairman.
"That doesn't make sense. Why would they do that
Colonel? Why would they do such a provocative thing,
when they knew you had British servicemen here who
had been victims of Japanese atrocities?"

"Because I agreed to take him," said the Colonel.

"Why?" said the Chairman.

"I needed the money doctor," said the Colonel while
straightening his moustache. "It was as simple as that. I
got to the point when I didn't care less who we took in.
The dregs of the Earth and scum of the planet were
admitted here at some time or other. I agreed to house
the sort of people no other asylums would tolerate. Our
place became like an enormous lavatory and I became
the man whose job it was to decide which shite was to be
disinfected and which was to be flushed away never to
be seen again. The house was crumbling, you see
doctor. And I got thirty times the usual rate for housing
those sort of people. What I made from having them

[695]

here, helped rebuild the west wing, repair much of the roof and fully carpet and tile the first floor."

"Did you ever get to know why the lunatics were sent here?" said the Chairman.

"I insisted upon knowing," said the Colonel. "In the Jap's case, it was mass murder. His file was the most concise I've ever read. The Japanese are a very meticulous people doctor. Their attention to detail is second only to the Germans."

"Might I assume his poor victims were British?" said the Chairman.

"They were Japanese," said the Colonel.

"Japanese!" said the Chairman.

"He'd murdered six of them," said the Colonel.

"Over what sort of time frame?" said the Chairman.

"Less than an hour," replied the Colonel.

"My God!" said the Chairman. "Did you ever learn how?"

"He drowned them all," said the Colonel.

"Jesus Christ!" said the Chairman. "The fucking nutcase. What the hell possessed the man?"

"The love of his Emperor apparently," said the Colonel. "And the fact that he wanted to die for his country. He was an aspiring Kamikaze pilot you see doctor. It was to be his job to fly his bomb laden plane into an enemy battleship or aircraft carrier. His file is full of testimonies from men he served under. One of them said something I found extremely ironic."

"What was that?" said the Chairman.

"He said, 'dying for his Emperor is what Takeshi lived for'," said the Colonel. "But he was to be sorely disappointed."

"What do you mean?" said the Chairman.

"His superiors wouldn't allow him to fly a mission," said the Colonel.

"Why's that?" said the Chairman.

"Because he had a young family," said the Colonel. "And at that point, the Japanese were only allowing single men to take part in their Kamikaze

programme. They told him he could keep applying
though. They told him that sooner or later, if the worst
came to the worst, they would run out of single,
unattached young men and would therefore be forced to
change their selection process and admission criteria.
They weren't all wicked you know doctor. I've met
scores of thoroughly decent Japanese people during my
travels and I've always found them delightful."
"And that decision turned him insane did it?" said the
Chairman. "Is that what you think?"
"I think we can safely say it took him to the brink," said
the Colonel. "Because, within 24 hours of shaking hands
with the six member selection panel that had denied him
his greatest wish, he'd....."
"He'd murdered them," said the Chairman.
"No doctor," said the Colonel. "He'd murdered his wife
and children."
"What!" said the Chairman.
"He'd murdered his entire family," said the Colonel.
"My God!" said the Chairman.
"He'd returned home and brutally removed the six
impediments that had been stifling his aspirations," said
the Colonel. "He reported for duty the following
morning and informed his superior officer that his
circumstances had changed and that he was now a single
man with no dependents and therefore a legitimate
candidate for the next Kamikaze missions."
"Oh my God!" said the Chairman. "Oh my God! that's
awful. I've never heard anything so sick in my life.
How in the name of God, can any so-called civilized
family man murder his entire family?"
"That's what I kept asking myself," said the Colonel.
"But that's not necessarily how many thousands of
Japanese zealots viewed his crime."
"What do you mean?" said the Chairman.
"Many considered Takeshi to be a national hero," said
the Colonel.
"A hero!" said the Chairman.
"That's right," said the Colonel. "Don't forget doctor-

[697]

what Takeshi had originally hoped to do as a Kamikaze pilot would have ordinarily made him something of a martyr and legend. He'd been prepared to give up his life for his country, his Emperor and his people. And listen to this doctor-he was only sent to Britain because angry mobs were demanding his release from his Japanese prison."

"And he ended up here because nobody else would take him," said the Chairman.

"That's right," said the Colonel.

"Bloody hell!" said the Chairman. "What a harrowing story. Did he survive here long?"

"I haven't the foggiest," said the Colonel. "That's a good question. I can't remember the last time I saw him. What year is it now?"

"2007," said the Chairman.

"2007 hey," said the Colonel. "And I think he came here at the age of 25 in the winter of 1947 or 1948. That should be easy enough to work out shouldn't it?"

"I reckon he'd be about 85," said the Chairman.

"He'll be a long time dead in that case," said the Colonel. "But don't tell anyone from the Home Office that."

"Why not?" said the Chairman.

"They'll withdraw the bastard's funding," laughed the Colonel while checking the level of the teapot. "And that wouldn't be good. That wouldn't be good at all."

"Do the Home Office people ever call to carry out inspections?" asked the Chairman.

"Just once a year," said the Colonel. "I think they're due any time now as it happens."

"Once a year suggests they must be content with the way you run things," said the Chairman. "But I'll tell you this much Colonel...if I was one of those inspectors, I'd be calling here every week."

"Why's that?" said the Colonel.

"Because of the quality of food you provide," said the Chairman.

"You enjoyed it did you?" said the Colonel.

"Very much so," said the Chairman.

"It'll be a different story altogether when you're presented with the bill," said the Major before nudging his wheelchair brake free and setting off towards his desk. "A different story altogether."

"I was hoping you were going to treat me Major," said the Chairman before winking at his highly amused host.

"You can hope all you like," said the Major without glancing back. "You're going to have to pay it yourself. In fact, there are quite a few things you're going to have to pay for before you leave this house."

"Like what?" said the Chairman.

"Ignore him doctor," whispered the Colonel. "There's no charge, I assure you. Your company is payment enough as far as I'm concerned. Having you here has been like a breath of fresh mountain air."

"He needs to be moving on," said the Major. "Did you see the way he wolfed down his food. He's going to eat us out of house and home if he stays any longer."

"I'll move on as soon as the blizzard passes," said the Chairman.

"You're welcome to stay as long as you want," said the Colonel. "Take no notice of the Major. He's often like this when he's struggling with writer's block."

"I'm like this because I know an imposter when I see one," said the Major.

"And I know a true gentleman when I see one," said the Colonel. "Now then-collect another bucket of ice will you Carruthers. And, for God's sake, keep your fat arse to the wall this time."

###

The blizzard continued relentlessly for the next three and a half hours, a period during which Tommy attended to the fire and took care of drinks, the increasingly irate Major despatched more than a dozen screwed up balls of paper into his waste bin and the Colonel listened intently while the Chairman explained the concept behind a large variety of new fangled innovations. That was until a heavily perspiring and highly agitated Albert burst into the room and beckoned his master towards him.

"What is it?" said the Colonel after rising and taking his servant by the shoulders. "What's the matter old fellow?"

"It's Mr Bimoko," said the big man before heading over to the window and placing his hands on the top of his head.

"What about Bimoko?" said the Colonel after picking up his cane and hobbling to the big man's side. "Speak up man for goodness sake. "Has something happened to him? Was he injured during the fighting?"

"He dead," said Albert.

"He's what?" said the Colonel while taking a few paces back and almost stumbling over his chair.

"He dead," said Albert.

"Dead!" said the Colonel.

"He no breathe," said Albert.

"Oh no-please no!" said the Colonel.

"Are you absolutely sure Albert?" said the Major while making his slow way to the table. "He couldn't just be sleeping heavily could he?"

"He dead," said Albert. "No wake him. No wake him. Albert tried to wake him. And Shook him. Albert shook hard. Bimoko not speak. Bimoko not moving."

"Where is he?" said the Colonel while fumbling with the top button of his tunic. "Is he in his room? Take me to him Albert. Take me to him right this very minute. I must see my boy. Where is he?"

"In big box," said Albert.

"What big box?" said the Major.

"That's what he sometimes calls the panelled vestibule," said the Colonel. "Would you bring him to me please Albert. I don't think my legs are strong enough to cope with this."

"I will," replied the big man before handing Tommy's wallet to the Colonel. "Found this near Bimoko."

"Let me see that Colonel," said the Major. "This could

be a significant find."

"Take a look, by all means," said the trembling Colonel. "But I think it's just something I've recently thrown out for one reason or another."

"How old was Mr Bimoko?" said the Chairman.

"Not yet old enough to succumb to old age, if that's what you're implying," said the Colonel. "If anything, he was in his prime. I reckon a sniper must have done for him. He was a lethargic bugger, at the best of times."

"Do you mind if I keep this wallet Colonel?" said the Major while proceeding to regard the photograph of Tommy and his wife. "Mine's showing definite signs of wear and tear."

"You're welcome to it old bean," said the Colonel. "Unless it belongs to the doctor."

"It's not mine," said the Chairman. "Mine's safely tucked away in my inside pocket."

"I think it might be mine," said Tommy.

"Yours Carruthers?" said the Colonel. "How can it be yours? The initials on this wallet are TM. Unless it is yours and for some unknown reason you've been masquerading as somebody you're not."

"It's not yours Sergeant," said the Chairman. "It's got a look of yours but I think yours is in slightly better condition."

"That's what I was thinking," said the Major. "There's a photograph inside and it's definitely not you Carruthers. Unless of course, you've suddenly developed an attraction towards the female of the species."

"Do you think it might have been Mr Bimoko's?" said the Chairman.

"It could have been," said the Colonel. "The damn fool was always losing things. I taught him to play chess, you know doctor. It always amazed me how quickly the Africans could pick things up."

"Did you teach him to speak English?" said the Chairman.

"Don't be ridiculous," replied the Colonel.

"But he could understand it perfectly well. I find that

[701]

with all our African brothers and sisters."

"When did you last see him?" said the Chairman.

"Late last night," replied the Colonel. "Just before I turned in. Do you know what-you've got me thinking now doctor."

"About what?" said the Chairman.

"About what I said before about Bimoko being hit by a sniper during the battle," said the Colonel. "Although that couldn't have happened in hindsight. The Chinese would have been well in retreat by then."

"You'll know more when you examine his body," said the Major.

"That's true," said the Colonel. "I think I'll go and see him now. I don't want to put it off. Why don't you pour some more drinks Carruthers. I'll be no more than fifteen minutes or so."

The Colonel had been gone nearly an hour, an hour during which the three remaining occupants of the living room never uttered a single word, never blinked and only moved to raise their respective glasses to their lips. However, just after the recently disgraced Mr Spriggs had limped into the room, arched his back and hissed loudly, Tommy rose very deliberately and gestured to his companion to follow him to the bathroom.

"I'm out of my mind with worry Hulmey," he whispered after a quick glance towards the Major.

"Why's that?" whispered the Chairman.

"Because, as crazy as it might sound, I've got a feeling the unfortunate Mr Bimoko was the baboon I left locked in the Ottoman," whispered Tommy.

"I was thinking the very same thing," whispered the Chairman. "At least, until the Colonel said he'd spoken to him late last night."

"What difference would that make?" said Tommy.

"It would mean he'd managed to escape and make his way here," whispered the Chairman. "And that would mean you're off the hook."

"Oh God, yes," whispered Tommy. "Bloody hell

Hulmey-what would I do without you to sort my
paranoia out?"
"That's what a highly qualified doctor's for," whispered
the Chairman. "And your Mr Spriggs is still hanging on
in there too."
"I know he is," whispered Tommy. "But he hates me.
You can see it in his eyes. He's certainly not the
forgiving type."
"He's not the obedient type either," said the Chairman.
"I thought he'd been given his marching orders for
fraternising with the enemy."
"I thought so too," said Tommy. "Maybe he's a double
agent. Say nothing to the little fucker. Do you want to
use this bathroom while we're here?"
"I'll pass," whispered the Chairman. "I once had a bad
experience in a bathroom. You go if you want. I'll get
back to my seat. I think I can hear the Colonel returning.
        The Chairman hadn't been wrong and by the
time he had arrived at his chair, the Colonel, after
issuing some instructions to Albert, was already making
himself comfortable.
"Are you alright Colonel?" he asked while pouring the
teary eyed old man a large brandy. "Would you like me
to fetch you a towel to dry your hair."
"It's alright," said the Colonel. "It's only snow. It'll dry
of its own accord."
"Is it true?" said the Chairman. "Is Mr Bimoko dead?"
"It is, I'm afraid," said the extremely gaunt looking
Colonel.
"Where is he?" said the Major.
"I've left him where he was found," said the Colonel.
"He's nice and dry there."
"In the vestibule?" said the Major.
"In one of the sheds not too far from the north boundary
wall," said the Colonel.
"Which one?" said the Major.
"I'm not entirely sure yet," said the Colonel. "You
can't see a thing through that driving snow. I just kept
my head down and followed the big man."

"Could you tell if the lock had been tampered with?" said the Major.

"I didn't stop to look, to be honest," said the Colonel. "I'll have to ask Albert. Is that important?"

"It could be," replied the Major. "If the lock was broken, it could be the shed where the doctor sheltered for the night."

"Is that relevant?" said the Colonel.

"Possibly," said the Major. "Where exactly was he found Colonel?"

"Inside a battered old Ottoman," said the Colonel.

"Oh Christ!" mumbled Tommy before once again, turning his attention to the fading fire.

"That's odd," said the Major.

"I know," said the Colonel. "I've pondered long and hard about that. Perhaps he knew he was dying and wanted seclusion."

"It's possible," said the Major. "But I think it's just as likely somebody locked the poor bugger in."

"For what reason?" said the Colonel.

"Bimoko might have attacked them," said the Major.

"He didn't attack me, if that's what you're implying" said the Chairman. "As God is my judge, he didn't. I've got a feeling there were baboons in the vicinity of that shed, but none of them approached me."

"And I didn't know Ottomans could be locked," said the Colonel.

"Me neither," said the Chairman. "They're just blanket chests aren't they?"

"They are yes," said the Colonel.

"Very well-have it your own way gentlemen," said the Major. "But I intend getting to the bottom of this distasteful business. I don't think Bimoko was inside that Ottoman of his own free will and I'll not rest until I've proved it."

"How are you going to go about that?" said the Colonel.

"By examining the inside of the chest," said the Major. "If he did indeed die of natural causes, there'll be no signs of a struggle. There'll be no gouges or claw marks on the Ottoman door."

"That's very true," said the Colonel. "But you're going to have to wait until he's buried. Nobody's moving my boy until then."

"Fair enough," said the Major while very deliberately and accusingly eyeballing the Chairman.

"There wasn't a mark on him,," said the Colonel.

"That's at least some tiny crumb of comfort I suppose. I'd have hated to think of him spending his last living moments in agony. There's likely to be all out civil war now."

"Why's that Colonel?" said the Chairman. "Because Bimoko's troop haven't got a leader," said the Colonel. "They've been weakened considerably."

"Do you mean to say there's more than one troop Colonel?" said the Chairman.

"Oh yes," said the Major.

"There are two identifiable troops," said the Colonel before removing a silk handkerchief from his trouser pocket and dabbing the corner of his left eye. "A magnificent beast called Kazimir's in charge of the other lot-but you very rarely see them. You don't want to see them, to be honest. They're a nasty bunch. A very nasty bunch."

"Why's that?" said the Chairman.

"They attack indiscriminately," said the Colonel. "Unlike Bimoko's troop, they can't differentiate between who's welcome here and who needs to be chased off. For instance, Kazimir once dragged an old Corporal friend of mine from his car and hauled him the length and breadth of the garden for over an hour. The man was in a right old state when it was all over. You've never heard such a din. There was no arse in his kecks and no skin on his elbows when he was eventually released."

"I bet there wasn't," said the Chairman. "I hope *I* never run into this Kazimir."

"Don't worry. When it's time for you to leave, just go the way I direct you and you'll be fine," said the

Colonel. "Now what about this drink. Do the honours will you Carruthers. Go and replenish our supplies. I think you'll find one of our empty crates in the hall. And watch those cellar steps. They'll be treacherously slippy right now. Albert will have walked a lot of snow in with him."

"Do you want me to help him," said the Chairman.

"Why would I?" said the suspicious looking Colonel after exchanging glances with the Major.

"In case he gets lost," said the Chairman. "You don't want him getting lost do you Colonel?"

"Carruthers knows this house like the back of his hand," said the Colonel.

"Of course he does," said the Chairman before rising and yawning loudly. "What the hell was I thinking? That's what sleep deprivation does to you."

"What exactly do you want Colonel-do you want brandy, whiskey and that sort of thing?" said Tommy.

"He wants a bottle of Dandelion and Burdock," said the Major.

"Shut up you," said the Colonel. "Bring a large variety please Sergeant. Surprise me if you want. What do you want doctor?"

"I'll have what you're having," said the Chairman. "And I want Carruthers to get some fresh air flowing through his lungs too."

"What!" said Tommy.

"Get some fresh air," said the Chairman. "It'll enable you to clear your head and think better. In fact, I'm going to make that an order. If you get the chance-get some fresh air. Get lots of it. Do you hear me Carruthers?"

"I hear you," said Tommy.

"Do you Tommy?" whispered the Chairman after discreetly coming to his companion's shoulder. "Do you understand me Tommy?"

"I think so," replied Tommy.

"That's not good enough," whispered the Chairman. "Do you understand what I'm saying Tommy?"

"I do yes," whispered Tommy. "But what about you?
Are you going to be alright?"
"Let me worry about me," whispered the Chairman.
"Come with me," whispered Tommy.
"I can't," whispered the Chairman. "Somebody's got to
keep these two distracted."
"I feel a twat leaving you here," whispered Tommy.
"That's because you are a twat," smiled the Chairman.
"Now fuck off."
"What's the holdup Carruthers?" said the Colonel.
"I was thinking the very same thing Colonel," said the
Chairman while watching his companion hasten away.
"No wonder the dozy bugger got shot. Would you mind
if I took a chair by the fire sir? I think last night's
exertions are beginning to take effect."
"Maybe you need another ice bath," said the Major.
"Take no notice doctor," said the Colonel. "Why don't
you go to your room?"
"My room!" said the Chairman.
"The one I originally had prepared for you," said the
Colonel. "The bed's still turned back and ready. Have a
couple of hours rest and I'll wake you when the
blizzard's past."
"That's very decent of you Colonel," said the Chairman.
"But if it's all the same to you sir, I think I'll just take a
nap by the fire. This is a rare opportunity for me. I've
never been able to resist a real log fire."
"Very well doctor," said the Colonel. "As you wish.
You make yourself nice and comfortable. In the
meantime, I'm going to start making the funeral
arrangements."
"Whose funeral arrangements?" said the Chairman.
"My former long serving head of security," said the
Colonel.
"Of course," said the mightily relieved Chairman.

CHAPTER TWENTY SEVEN
MIXED TIDINGS

The Chairman awoke slightly confused and just a little heavy headed to the sound of the Colonel playing something unfamiliar on his stunning Bluthner rosewood piano, the alluring aroma of simmering breakfast ingredients and an unfettered scowl of disapproval from the Major who, for the past hour, had been putting some finishing touches to his latest letter of appeal. At that point, as had become the norm since arriving at the peculiar old house, he had no idea who he was meant to be and therefore what his credentials were expected to be, but he did know where he wanted to be and who he desperately wanted to be there with.

"Merry Christmas doctor," said the Colonel before very precisely closing the piano lid and cracking his knuckles. "What do you think?"

"Think about what Colonel?" said the Chairman.

"My rendition," said the Colonel.

"It was very impressive," said the Chairman. "What was it you were playing?"

"I'd have thought you'd have known," said the Colonel. "I could have sworn you bought me the sheet music for the piece. It was Joplin, just for the record. Is that a name you're familiar with doctor?"

"It is as it happens," said the Chairman. "She died of a heroin overdose, didn't she?"

"The Joplin I'm referring to was a man," said the Colonel. "You have slept heavily haven't you doctor."

"What time is it?" said the Chairman while scanning the walls for a working clock.

"It's about 8.30," said the Colonel.

"8.30! said the Chairman. "Forgive me Colonel, but would that be morning or evening?"

"Morning," laughed the Colonel. "I'd have woken you a lot earlier but I appreciate how much sleep you must have lost the previous evening."

"Is it still snowing?" said the Chairman.

"It is unfortunately," said the Colonel. "And the winds picked up again. But don't be too disheartened doctor. That means we can enjoy an extremely rare white Christmas day. And while we're on the subject of Yuletide and peace on Earth and good will to all decent men, there's a little gift for you by your left foot."

"A gift!" said the slightly bemused and somewhat suspicious Chairman before leaning forward and recovering a small box wrapped in pre-used, wrinkled blue and silver paper. "Is this for me Colonel?"

"Open it," said the Colonel.

"Santa didn't stop for me," said the approaching Major.

"Really Major," said the Chairman almost inaudibly. "I wonder why that is."

"Maybe he's been on the wrong end of one of your deeply offensive insults," said the beaming Colonel. "Anyway doctor-take no notice of that miserable old buzzard-what do you think?"

"I don't know what to think," said the Chairman after allowing the remnants of the wrapping paper to flutter to the floor. "I'm actually a little lost for words. I think you might have made a mistake sir."

"What sort of mistake?" said the Colonel.

"I think you might have given me somebody else's gift," said the Chairman.

"Why on Earth would you think that?" said the Colonel upon arriving at his familiar place at the table.

"Because this is a genuine Rolex watch sir," said the Chairman.

"I'm fully aware of that," said the Colonel.

"But this is too much sir," said the Chairman. "This is probably worth more than my car. This has got to be worth thousands."

"That's of no importance to me," said the Colonel before tugging on the servant's rope. "It's been an absolute pleasure having you here. I'm just showing my appreciation, that's all. I've got a few other things for you in my room. You're going to need them when you leave."

"Like what?" said the Chairman.

"A far more practical winter coat, for one thing," said the Colonel. "And a pair of wellingtons. They're an absolute must for this sort of weather. Oh, and I'm going to give you my old Cambridge University scarf."

"Cambridge!" said the Chairman. "Did you attend Cambridge sir?"

"Only on a regimental recruitment drive," said the Colonel. "Those clever Dick types always tended to make good officers."

"Where did *you* study doctor?" said the Major.

"Liverpool," replied the Chairman.

"Liverpool University?" said the Colonel.

"That's right," said the Chairman.

"What did you achieve?" said the Major.

"Quite a lot," replied the Chairman.

"What degree did you get?" said the Major.

"A very good one," said the Chairman.

"Meaning what?" said the Major. "Did you get a first, a second-did you get a pass?"

"I got a pass yes," said the Chairman.

"That's interesting," said the Major.

"Why is it?" said the Chairman.

"Because I've never heard of anyone achieving just a pass and going on to become a fully fledged doctor," said the Major. "I imagine that's almost unheard of."

"It was yes," said the Chairman. "It was a one off. I made the front page of my local paper."

"Will you be making tracks after your breakfast?" said the Major.

"I will be yes Major," said the Chairman. "Unless you want me to stay."

"Very droll doctor," said the Colonel while gently rapping the table with his incredibly long and bony fingers. "Now come and join us. I think I can hear Albert arranging his plates and trays. By the way-you'll be pleased to know, your clothes are dry."

"That's a relief," said the Chairman.

"They're on the hallstand along the corridor," said the Colonel. "I'm afraid you're going to have to excuse the creases. Albert's never really mastered ironing."

"That's alright," said the Chairman. "I'm just grateful to have them back. I look like an old granddad in this gown."

"Aren't you going to tell him about the incident?" said the Major.

"What incident is this?" said the Chairman before slipping his newly acquired timepiece onto his right wrist and drawing back his chair. "What's happened Colonel?"

"We were burgled some time during the early hours of the morning," said the Colonel.

"Burgled!" said the Chairman.

"It means we've had certain articles stolen," said the Major.

"I know what 'burgled' means," said the Chairman.

"It's the fallout from Mr Bimoko's sad demise," said the Colonel. "I haven't had the chance to train his successor yet."

"Never mind his successor, you need to get his body out of that shed and into the basement," said the Major. "Or it won't be long before something picks up his scent and makes the poor beggar their next meal."

"That's true," said the Colonel. "I'll get Albert onto it right away."

"Did the thief manage to get away with much?" said the Chairman.

"Just some food, one of my old trench coats and a couple of Lee Enfield rifles," said the Colonel. "And they did something that's got me and the Major not a little bit baffled."

"Done what?" said Chairman.

"They've stripped a length of cable from the top of the hall skirting board," said the Colonel.

"That's odd," said the Chairman. "Have you any idea why?"

"I've boiled it down to three possibilities," said the

Colonel. "One-the intruder simply tripped in the dark and inadvertently pulled the cable from its clips. Two-the intruder was going to use the cable to strangle my good self and three-the sneaky beggar was deliberately trying to cut off our only means of communicating with the outside world."

"I think you've got all possible bases covered there Colonel," said the Chairman.

"Which of them would you favour doctor?" said the Colonel.

"I'd plump for the third one," said the Chairman. "Do you happen to know if Carruthers saw anything?"

"Carruthers is in disgrace," said the Colonel.

"Why's that?" said the Chairman.

"Because he went and did what I warned him not to do and fell down the bloody cellar steps," said the Colonel.

"Oh dear," said the Chairman. "Is he alright? Is he alright Colonel?"

"He'll probably be in a wheelchair for the rest of his life," said the Major.

"What!" said the Chairman.

"Take no notice," said the Colonel. "He's just a bit bruised, dizzy and embarrassed. "But he's made a right Horlicks of his tunic."

"Where is he now?" said the Chairman.

"Laundering the thing and trying to keep out of my way, I would imagine" said the Colonel. "I should have taken the Major's advice and got rid of the silly ass. He's no longer fit for service. You saw him yourself doctor. How long did the blighter last when the Chinese opened up on us? I reckon it was no more than five seconds."

"I reckon it was no more than three," said the Major.

"It's a shame," said the Chairman.

"It's a crying shame," said the Colonel. "But I'm not going to discharge him today doctor. I couldn't let the man go on a Christmas Day, could I? I'd be the talk of the barracks. I'd have windows opened on me."

"What does that mean?" said the Chairman.

"It's an old fashioned military slight," said the Colonel.

[712]

"The window is opened in the presence of somebody whose behaviour has been considered unacceptable."
"Would that be to release the stench of betrayal or cowardice?" said the Chairman.
"That's exactly it," said the Colonel. "For instance doctor, if I had good reason to believe you'd betrayed me or the Major in some way, I'd go over to the nearest window, open it and expect you to leave post haste."
"And I'd go and fetch my rifle," said the Major.
"I bet you would," said the Chairman. "Have either of you two gentlemen ever suffered that window opening indignity?"
"Never," said the Colonel. "Never once doctor. Me and the good Major have never let anyone down. That's right isn't it Major?"
"It was until quite recently," replied the Major.
"What!" said the Colonel abruptly. "I beg your pardon Major. Explain yourself sir. Explain yourself this very minute."
"I'm afraid I've gone and let our esteemed guest down," said the Major.
"In what way?" said the Colonel.
"I've no Christmas present for him," said the Major.
"What!" said the Colonel.
"That's alright Major," said the Chairman.
"It's not alright at all," said the Colonel. "It's very far from being alright. The Major's known for months you'd be coming over to join us for the festive period."
"I *have* got him a card though Maurice," said the Major before slipping the Chairman a previously used but tightly sealed business envelope. "I actually made it myself."
"That's very nice of you Major," said the slightly suspicious Chairman. "Should I open it now sir?"
"I'd wait until Easter Sunday," said the Major. "I think that's what people usually do with those sort of things...Of course you should open it now...it's a bloody Christmas card, for the love of God."
"Of course it is," said the Chairman. "How foolish of

me."

"The Major's quite an accomplished artist," said the Colonel. "He's received considerable local acclaim for his amusing caricatures. He's often been compared to the great postcard artist, Donald McGill."

"I can see why," said the Chairman after carefully teasing open the envelope and removing a postcard size vanilla coloured card. "This is meant to be me isn't it Major?"

"It is indeed," said the Major before placing his clasped hands across his chest.

"How's he portrayed you doctor?" said the Colonel.

"As a snowman," said the Chairman. "A snowman who's wearing a dunce's hat and carrying a white stick. I don't get it."

"Then I suggest you keep studying it," said the Major. "Read the sentiments on the back page."

"I've read them," said the Chairman. "I've read them twice. They're delightful."

"Thank you very much," said the Major.

"You're welcome," said the Chairman.

"Do you fancy reading them out?" said the Colonel.

"I'd rather not, if it's all the same to you ," said the Chairman.

"It's personal," said the Major.

"I bet it is," said the Colonel. "I hope it's not offensive Major."

"It's not offensive at all," said the Chairman. "To coin your previously used phrase Colonel-the Major's just making sport with me. It's just a bit of fun, that's all."

"I sincerely hope you're right," said the Colonel. "It wouldn't be the first time the Major's been rude to one of my visitors. I've had people stomp out of here, eyes bulging and red in the face, many a time."

Despite his admirable attempt to make light of the situation, the card had made the Chairman feel more afraid and vulnerable than at any time since he had entered the old house and for some time after his breakfast had been served, he had found himself without appetite and in a state of mental neutrality. The beautifully hand written message on the back of the card read as follows;

Dear New Inmate,
This is not just a Christmas card, this is a welcome to your new home card. Please enjoy your last hours of freedom because tomorrow you start learning the harsh realities regarding this institution. You weren't deloused and ice bathed by accident Mr Hulme. You were deloused and ice bathed because you are a new inmate and new inmates must be devoid of germs. And by the way, I've had your number since the moment you arrived. You are an imposter and within the next couple of hours, the Colonel will be alerted to that highly disconcerting fact. And just one more thing Mr Hulme-do not make the mistake of showing this card to your host or I'll see he has immediate possession of your friend's wallet. (By the way-that's the friend who killed Mr Bimoko.)
Have a lovely day and welcome to the Old Budlam Institute for the Incurably Insane.
Major Henry Howser.

In a very short period of time, the Chairman had been the beneficiary of an incredibly generous gift worth several thousands of pounds and the recipient of a

Christmas card containing the most chilling and unsettling message imaginable. It was no wonder therefore, that as a result, and despite everything he had already been through, he had never felt so utterly helpless and alone in his life.

"Have you little hunger doctor?" said the Colonel.

"I'm sorry Colonel," said the Chairman while fumbling for his cutlery. "I was miles away."

"Where exactly?" said the Colonel.

"In my home in Crosby," said the Chairman. "I was thinking about my wife and kids. This is the first time we'll have been apart on Christmas Day."

"Have you never had to work during the festive period?" said the Colonel.

"Before I was married I did," said the Chairman. "But never as a father and husband. I'm sorry Colonel-I'm not feeling very good. Would you mind if I left the table and went to get a bit of fresh air?"

"Not at all," said the Colonel. "But you don't want to be going outside. Just stick your head out of the far window. And, for goodness sake, watch out for snipers."

"I was thinking of putting my coat on and going for a little walk," said the Chairman.

"What!" said the Colonel. "A little walk! In this weather! Are you out of your mind doctor? Do you want to catch your death of cold?"

"The Colonel's right," said the Major. "You don't want to do that. Where are we going to find another doctor if you take ill?"

"Shut up Major," said the Colonel. "The man's not feeling too good."

"Well, would you mind if I went to my room?" said the Chairman.

"*Your* room!" said the Major.

"The room the Colonel so kindly had prepared for me yesterday?" said the Chairman while turning to face his host. "Would you mind too much if I did that sir?"

"Of course not," said the Colonel. "Of course not old bean. But don't go wasting that excellent food. Get it down you man. Get it down you while you're fit and able. You know the old adage doctor. A soldier should never pass up the opportunity to eat."

"It'd probably be best if he took a nap here," said the smirking Major while vigorously rubbing his hands. "I've just rejuvenated the fire."

"I think I'd prefer to go to my room," said the Chairman.

"And I think you're better off here," said the Major while watching the torn up Christmas card burst into flames, quickly transform into ash before whooshing up the chimney in four separate triangular pieces. "Don't forget Colonel-we still haven't established how and where that interloper entered the building."

"That's right Henry," said the Colonel. "Perhaps we're all safer here for the time being."

"And we're right next door to our considerable arsenal," said the Major.

"That's true," said the Colonel. "That's very true. Now listen doctor. Enough of that Greta Garbo, 'I want to be alone' stuff. Finish that delightful breakfast and I'll get Albert to fetch you a nice thick blanket from my room. We'll all have a nice cosy after-breakfast sleep."

For the next hour, after giving up all hope of getting to his prepared sleeping quarters and possibly beyond, the Chairman sat staring into the fire while trying to fathom out a way to evade the ever watchful glare of the menacing Major. He had seen both old men doze off several times during that period but each time he was about to slip off his blanket and make for the door, at least one of them would rear up like a startled rabbit and scan the room suspiciously. It was a pattern that continued until the fire began to show very definite signs of failure, at which point, the Major drew his wheelchair alongside the hearth, tossed another couple of logs on the fire and leant back and closed his eyes.

Believing the move to be a charade, a

deliberate ploy to catch him in the act of trying to escape, the Chairman remained cautious however, and as a result, even when the old man turned and began to snore ridiculously loudly, he resisted the temptation to make good his escape. However, in turning around, the Major's jacket had bagged up exposing his inside pocket and in particular the top edge of Tommy Mac's wallet. 'Jesus!' said the Chairman to himself. 'If that scheming old bastard stays still for a minute, I might just be able to reach that thing.'

For the next few minutes, while keeping one eye fixed on the other restless old man, the Chairman edged to his left millimetre by millimetre while every now and then freezing whenever the Major sighed, muttered something meaningless or simply twitched. And then it was backwards ever so slowly, millimetre by millimetre whenever the old man turned to make himself more comfortable.

Just under an hour later, on what was his umpteenth foray forward, he at last found himself in reaching distance of the wallet and almost ready to make the decisive grab. That however, to the Chairman's consternation, was when the old man suddenly sat bolt upright as if consumed by mortal dread.

"It's you!" he said while staring pleadingly into the Chairman's eyes. "It's you. It's you, it's you, it's you. It's you Casper. It's you my boy. You clever so and so. You've found your way back."

"I'm afraid you're mistaken," said the confused and extremely unnerved Chairman while ever so gently trying to prise the old man's talon-like fingers from the neck of his gown.

"You've made it back," whispered the Major after a quick glance towards the Colonel. "Well done young man. That's the spirit. That's the famous Howser spirit in you."

"But I'm not...." whispered the Chairman.

"What you are and what you're not isn't important right now," whispered the Major. "Listen to me and listen very carefully. You're in grave danger here. You need to get out while you've got the chance. But do not, under any circumstances, try to leave via the front door. Albert and Bimoko's men have that area under constant surveillance. They'll cut you down in no time at all. The only safe way for you to get out is through the basement. Promise me you'll do that. Promise me Casper."

"Alright, I promise," whispered the Chairman after a quick glance towards his slowly rousing host.

"But I don't know the way. I don't know the way to the basement."

"Of course you don't," whispered the Major. "How foolish of me.....How very foolish of me. Anyway-it's not too difficult. Just go out of the door and proceed as far as the corridor allows you. Then turn left and take the second corridor on your right and look out for another door marked, 'DANGER-NO ADMITTANCE', in crudely painted black letters. That particular door is different from the others. You'll find it far heavier. Look above it. There should be a long rusty key hanging from a length of tatty orange string. Here-take my spare matches. You'll need them. It's very dark in that basement. Now run my Casper. Run for your life. Run, and despite anything you might hear, don't look back. You'll find some clothes on the hallstand. Take them. You won't survive in those corridors for long without those. Don't forget now. And don't forget this son.....I love you and always will."

"I love you too dad," whispered the Chairman after another glance towards the Colonel.

###

Whether the Major had been delirious, suffering the adverse effects of the previous night's heavy drinking bout or demonstrating evidence of senility, it hadn't affected his ability to provide accurate and easy to follow directions. Therefore, it wasn't long before the Chairman arrived at the bottom of the perilously steep and poorly lit basement steps and was having to decide whether to go right or left. It was a

[719]

choice which could have been made with the toss of a coin until, after ever so cautiously venturing right for about twenty yards, he became aware of a strange, almost haunting melodic sound like that of a young child humming a lullaby. In normal circumstances, the sound might not have warranted any attention at all but within a diabolically gloomy and oppressive setting where enormous rats outnumbered the human population at a ratio of around twenty to one, it was anything but pleasant. In fact, it was so deeply unsettling and so extremely unpleasant, he was soon fighting the urge to relieve his bladder right where he stood. Nevertheless he had not yet reached the point where turning around and heading back up the basement steps became a viable consideration and for some time after bracing himself against the basement wall, he found himself mentally running through a list of possibilities. Was the music being made by the seriously mentally disturbed Matilda?, being his first. Was the noise being made by one of the many house dwelling animals?, was the next. Or was the noise in any way supernatural in derivation? As far as he was concerned, each possibility deserved credence and couldn't be completely dismissed but one thing was for certain-the Chairman was more afraid than at any time in his life including the time he was mistakenly dragged from the dingy cell during his first night under the Colonel's roof.

And then something dawned on him which almost immediately turned his fear to anger and had him gnashing his teeth and wanting to tear his hair out strand by strand.

'The bastard!' he said to himself. 'The fucking evil bastard. That twisted Major's done me up like a kipper.' That was when he heard what he assumed to be the door at the top of the basement steps creak open and almost immediately slam shut. And that was when he realised he not only needed to hide, but needed to hide as quickly and as effectively possible.

The footsteps that immediately ensued could

have only been made by one occupant of the strange and intimidating old house. They were loud and pronounced as if made by somebody who not only desired to be heard but very definitely wanted to strike fear in those within reasonable hearing distance. It was the classic, Nazi Storm Trooper stomp and the louder it became, the less inclined the Chairman had been to move. However, that was until Albert, after reaching the bottom of the basement steps and putting a match to his spirit lamp, dispatched what appeared to be a dirty, soaking wet sack into one of the empty cells.

'That's got to be the unfortunate Mr Bimoko,' he said to himself after quickly and discreetly slipping behind the nearest of two wicker laundry baskets that had been berthed about ten feet from the cell door.

However, it wasn't long before the Chairman was being tormented by the possibility the sack contained something other than the much loved baboon and that was despite him being present when the Colonel and Major had discussed putting the dead animal in the basement to prevent a nasty stench occurring. The reason for that doubt was the condition of the sack. The sack had been soaking wet and dirty. The sack which had contained a much loved friend had been soaking wet and dirty. That just didn't add up as far as the Chairman was concerned because Albert and Bimoko were supposedly inseparable and the animal loving Colonel considered the creature to be like a son.

'Why would they put someone or something they love in a filthy old sack?' the Chairman kept asking himself repeatedly.

It was a question which had plagued him to such an extent that immediately after the big man had reached the top of the basement steps, he had made his tentative way over to where the suspicious item had been delivered, and the chances are, if he had continued instead of pausing on the threshold to contemplate the whys, wherefores and possible horrors, he might well have learned the truth much quicker. Instead, he had

[721]

remained loyal to type. He had dallied and dithered and, in doing so, had allowed a succession of negative possibilities to affect his thinking. 'What's it got to do with me?' he asked himself before stepping from the doorway and yanking up his collar aggressively. But then he countered that almost immediately by responding, 'maybe it's got a lot to do with me'.

In fairness to him, the life size bundle of rags that the Chairman had initially examined and recoiled from, had felt so genuinely and incredibly human. It appeared to have had two perfectly formed arms, two equally authentic muscular legs, two feet and a solid torso. It had even come to rest on the floor of the cell with one leg shooting forward and the other shaped like the familiar 'A' frame. The head however, which he hadn't got round to examining initially, was the one thing that gave lie to his original assumption. The head, on further inspection, was decidedly disproportionate because the head had been made from a pumpkin befit with huge round eyes, a triangular nose and a large crescent shaped smile. It now all made perfect sense as far as the mightily relieved Chairman was concerned. It all made sense because he could recall the Colonel telling him about his massive crow problem and how he had had to design and create deterrents which looked as real and as scary as possible. "Bloody hell!" he said to himself after exiting the room and driving his fingers through his hair. "I thought for a while, that bundle of sacking was going to contain Hilly. A scarecrow! A bloody scarecrow! What a strange and mysterious house this is. It has you believing anything. What the hell next?"

That was when the humming started again, but this time the area it appeared to be coming from was far easier to pin point. That was because the room it was resounding from had a gap at the bottom of the door and that gap was enabling a narrow slither of light to escape and reflect against the adjacent wall.

Once again, the Chairman found himself in a

quandary. After all, despite finding the light and the humming in some strange way alluring, it was impossible to lose sight of the fact that he was in the pitch black basement of a notorious lunatic asylum and could therefore be within yards of somebody who was completely deranged. And yet, for some inexplicable reason, and despite the danger and the alarm bells that were ringing in his ears, he still continued to press forward inch by cautious inch towards that thin slither of light and pleasant tune.

"Is that you Pirrip?" came a voice like that of a strict headmistress.

"I beg your pardon," said the Chairman politely.

"Is that you Pip?" asked the woman. "Are you Mr Pumblechook's boy?"

"I'm a visitor," said the Chairman before gently pushing open the cell door, and finding himself in the presence of an old woman wearing what looked like a yellowing and grubby wedding dress and a black veil covering her entire head and shoulders. "I'm sorry to be a nuisance. I'm a very good friend of the Colonel. I've been visiting him and seem to have got myself lost on my way out. I wonder if you'd be so kind as to point me in the direction of the nearest exit."

"You need to talk to Jaggers," said the woman abruptly while making her way behind a tall and oil paint spattered easel.

"Who's Jaggers?" said the Chairman.

"He's an enormous great monstrosity of a man," said the woman before reaching for a length of rope that was hanging from the ceiling. "I could call him if you'd like."

"That won't be necessary," said the Chairman. "Don't bother the man-he's probably busy. Just show me the quickest or best way out of here and I'll leave you to get on with your project."

"How dare you be so impertinent as to command your hostess," said the woman. "You forget yourself Pip. You're nothing but a common labourer's boy. Now bring yourself nearer to me. Let me take a closer look at you."

"I'd rather remain here, if you don't mind," said the Chairman while ensuring the toes of his right foot remained firmly wedged under the open door. "I'm sorry to have inconvenienced you. Maybe I should move on."

"Come here-let me look at you," said the woman.

"I'd rather not if it's all the same to you," said the Chairman.

"Come here Pip," said the woman. "Come hither this very minute. You're not afraid of a frail old woman who has never set eyes on the sun since the day you were born are you?"

"Of course not," said the Chairman before taking the tiniest step forward. "I'm sorry erm......I'm sorry Miss-or should I call you madam?"

"You've forgotten my name haven't you Pip?" said the woman. "How unfeeling and inconsiderate of you. Has it really been that long since we last conversed at Satis House? Has it really? It's Havisham, if you must know. And you can address me as Miss Havisham, as was initially agreed. Now close that door and sit yourself down."

"I'm sorry Miss Havisham, but I'm in a bit of a hurry," said the Chairman after taking a quick look around the room. "I can't stop. I'm going to have to be on my way."

"Then, be on your way," said the woman with a dismissive and derisory flick of her left hand. "And good riddance to you boy. But let me ask you something first-do you intend going right upon exiting my room or left?"

"I'll erm....I'll take a right I suppose," said the Chairman.

"That's unfortunate," said the woman.

"Why is it?" said the Chairman.

"Because if you go right you'll probably get lost," said the woman.

"I'll go left then," said the Chairman.

"Which in turn will guarantee you'll get lost," said the old woman.

"I'll just keep looking until I find my way out," said the Chairman.

"That's commendably bold of you," said the woman.

"But let me warn you first young Pip. You're likely to die or go mad trying. Many already have. Hundreds in fact."

"Do you know the way out of here?" said the Chairman.

"Of course I do," said the old lady while shaking her head indignantly. "Do you think I'm an imbecile?"

"Not at all," said the Chairman. "I'm sorry if I gave you that impression. I just found myself in the dark and was beginning to think I'd never find my way out."

"You'll get out," said the old woman.

"How exactly?" said the Chairman. "Would you draw me a map?"

"I can't do that," said the woman. "But I will provide you with directions."

"That would be great," said the Chairman.

It was at that very moment, while the old woman appeared to be searching through a large pile of papers that were lying close to her feet, that the Chairman became aware that there was somebody or rather something else in the room. Something that was to take his uneasiness to a new height.

"Who's your friend?" he asked after taking a discreet backward step towards the door.

"That's Estella," replied the old woman. "She's my adopted daughter."

"Is she really," said the Chairman.

"Yes really," said the old woman. "Do you doubt me? You do don't you? You have the temerity to doubt me, don't you boy?"

"She's a baboon," said the Chairman. "She's actually a baboon who's wearing a dress, to be even more precise."

"I know that," said the old woman. "Do you think I'd allow the girl to walk around this den of iniquity stark naked?"

"Of course not," said the Chairman before turning his attention to one of the many wall clocks. "Is that the time? Bloody hell! I'll have to be making tracks."

"I thought you wanted me to provide you with directions," said the old woman.

"I do," said the Chairman. "But you appear to be an extremely busy woman."

"Nonsense," said the woman. "I can spare you twenty minutes. Stay and talk awhile Pip. Conversation is good for the soul. Tell me about your school and your new acquaintances and things. Why don't you give it until the clocks strike 9?"

"The clocks aren't going to strike 9," said the increasingly suspicious Chairman. "All your clocks have stopped at 8.40. Why's that? Why is that Miss Havisham?"

"Because that's the very point in time my life ended," said the woman.

"What do you mean, 'ended'?" said the Chairman.

"That's when I received the news that my beloved Compeyson wasn't going to meet me at the altar," said the woman. "Tarry a while Pip. I have a sick fancy that I want to see some play."

"A sick fancy!" said the Chairman.

"I want to watch you play cards with my Estella," said the woman. "What can you play Pip?"

"My name's not Pip," said the Chairman while nervously scanning the room.

"Alright-what can Philip play?" said the woman.

"Philip!" said the Chairman.

"Philip Pirrip. That's your full title," said the woman. "Don't worry boy. I've met scores of young lads who wilt and can do little more than stutter and stammer whilst in my presence."

"I'm sorry Miss Havisham but I'm not one of them," said the Chairman. "I have to be going. I'm a very busy man."

"Then take this," said the woman.

"Take what?" said the Chairman before eagerly
stepping forward to accept a tightly folded piece of
quality notepaper. "Are they...are they the directions I
asked you for Miss Havisham?"

"They're directions of a sort, yes," said the woman. "It's
up to you to interpret them."

"Bloody hell!" said the Chairman. "Thank you Miss
Havisham. Thank you ever so much. I feel so bloody
guilty now. I've been so rude to you . I don't know
what to do or say to make it up to you."

"You could stay and play cards with Estella," said the
woman. "That would be fair recompense-don't you
agree?"

"I'd love to, but I'm in a bit of a rush," said the
Chairman before turning around to discover the door
was now shut and not only shut but firmly locked.

"What the hell! How the hell have you managed that?"

"Managed what?" said the woman.

"Managed to lock the door without moving from your
position," said the Chairman.

"I have my means," said the woman. "Play cards with
Estella Pip. Humour a tired old lady and I promise I'll
open the door and let you out. What can you play?"

"Not much," said the Chairman before grudgingly
taking a seat on the only available chair. "I'm not one
for playing cards. Snap and Happy Families are the only
two card games I know."

"I'm going to teach you another," said the woman
before beckoning the excited baboon over. "You'll
enjoy it. You'll enjoy it immensely. There's a 'cruelty'
element within the game that excites and intrigues me
greatly."

"What's it called?" said the Chairman.

"Bugger my Neighbour," replied the woman.

"I beg your pardon!" said the Chairman.

"Bugger my Neighbour," said the confused old woman
after watching the Chairman quickly head over and put
his back to the door. "What's the matter boy? You
appear to have come over all pale and sheep-like."

[727]

"Do you blame me?" said the Chairman. "I'm sorry Miss Havisham. I don't like the sound of that game."
"Why not Pip?" said the woman. "Has London altered you so much? Is it now beneath you to beg?"
"Beg!" said the Chairman.
"It's what the game's all about," said the woman. "That's why it's called, 'Beggar my Neighbour'."
"Beggar?" said the Chairman.
"That' right," said the woman. "What's the matter with you boy?"
"I thought you said something else," said the Chairman.
"I clearly enunciated, 'beggar'," said the woman. "Is there something wrong with your hearing boy?"
"Not at all," said the Chairman. "I'm afraid I'm still half asleep Miss Havisham. Beggar my Neighbour, it is then. I'm looking forward to it already What are the rules?"
"I'm coming to that Pip," said the woman. "Be patient boy."
"I'm trying to be patient," said the Chairman. "But I need to be moving on. I've got people to see. And by the way Miss Havisham-whether you like it or not-I'm only playing the one round."
"As you please," said the woman. "Let's put a time limit on the game then. Let's say you play for twenty minutes shall we? Let's say you play until the clocks strike 9."
"That sounds reasonable," said the smiling Chairman while rolling up his coat sleeve to reveal his newly acquired watch. "But we're going to use my watch to time the event. Twenty minutes and that's it. Twenty minutes and you're going to have to let me go. Although.....What the hell! That's odd."
"What's odd?" said the old woman.
"My new watch," said the Chairman while vigorously tapping the dial. "My new watch the Colonel gave me for Christmas. It's stopped. For some reason it's stopped dead."
"It stopped at 8.40, didn't it?" said the woman. "I know

that because everything stops at 8.40."

"It's just a coincidence," said the Chairman.

"Be nice and play cards Pip," said the woman.

"I'm not Pip," said the Chairman.

"Don't argue with me boy," said the woman.

"I will argue with you," said the Chairman before taking a poker from the fireplace and heading back to the door. "I think I've had enough of this nonsense. What are you up to Miss Havisham?"

"I'm not up to anything," said the woman. "But I suspect you might be. Maybe I should call Albert."

"Please don't do that," said the Chairman before placing the poker on the floor and raising his hands. "Let's just sort this out politely between the two of us Miss Havisham."

"It's too late for that," said the woman after theatrically placing one hand on her brow. "You've slighted me. It's remarkable. It's uncanny. It constitutes the cruellest possible irony. You've slighted me at the precise time Compeyson did. There was no call for it. I feel faint. I'm going to have to call Albert."

"Please don't do that," said the Chairman. "Please don't do that Miss Havisham. He'll lock me up. He'll think I'm an escaping prisoner."

"Isn't that what you are?" said the woman.

"My God, no," said the Chairman. "I'm a very good friend of the Colonel. I'm a visitor. For God's sake, believe me Miss Havisham-I'm a respected and welcome visitor."

"I know that," said the woman. "I'm just sporting with you. I know exactly who you are. You're my visitor. Why all the histrionics? You're Phillip Pirrip. I arranged your visit. I watched you arrive with Mr Pumblechook through my telescope. That's right isn't it?"

"It is yes," said the Chairman.

"Why did you turn on me then Pip?" said the woman.

"Because I've not been well Miss Havisham," said the Chairman. "I lost a lot of sleep the other night and haven't been myself since. That's why I don't feel up to playing cards right now. My concentration levels are down to below zero."

"That's perfectly understandable," said the woman while urging the baboon back to its perch. "So let me give you something a little less demanding to do."

"Like what?" said the massively relieved Chairman.

"I want you to take a look at a piece of my art and evaluate it," said the woman. "Do you think you can do that?"

"I'll give it a go," said the Chairman. "Is it that one-is it the one that's resting on your easel?"

"It is indeed," said the woman. "It's a full length painting of you."

"Of me?" said the suspicious, amused and slightly self conscious Chairman.

"That's right," said the woman.

"Why me?" said the Chairman.

"Because you fascinate me," said the woman. "You always have. You've grown dashingly good looking Pip. And you're beautifully formed too. Tell me-have you ever posed nude for an artist before?"

"Before!" smiled the Chairman. "I've never posed nude in my life. Is that what you've done Miss Havisham? Have you by any chance, painted me with no clothes on?"

"I have as it happens," said the woman.

"You've got a nerve, if you don't mind me saying so" said the Chairman. "And some imagination too, by the way."

"Imagination didn't enter into it," said the woman. "I've seen you entirely naked."

"I very much doubt it," said the Chairman. "You might have seen your imaginary Pip fellow without clothes, but you've never seen me without any."

"I've seen you utterly and completely naked," said the old woman.

"When was this?" said the Chairman.

"I watched you getting ice bathed and deloused," said

the woman.

"You what!" said the Chairman.

"You made a right commotion," said the woman. "The Alpha baboons were going berserk. They must have thought one of their troop was being tormented. What happened Pip? Has the Colonel implemented a new admittance procedure? Has he started bathing and delousing the visitors now?"

"Albert had mistaken me for an inmate," said the Chairman.

"Never!" said the woman.

"It's true," said the Chairman. "Go and ask the Colonel if you don't believe me. He'll vouch for what I've just told you. He played merry hell with Albert for what he'd done. Go on. Go and ask the Colonel Miss Havisham."

"I don't need to," said the old woman before turning her easel to reveal her recently completed painting of the dripping wet and naked Chairman. "I know you're not an inmate. You're Pip. You're Philip Pirrip. You're my visitor. What do you think?"

"I don't know what to think to be honest," said the Chairman upon snatching the painting in order to view it under a better light. "Look at me. Look at the state of me. I'm all wrinkled and purple like a dried raisin."

"What do you think of the proportions?" said the woman.

"I'm not happy with them to be perfectly honest," said the Chairman.

"Why not?" asked the woman.

"Because I'm not," said the Chairman. "And don't bother asking me to explain why, because I'm not prepared to say."

"Is it your legs?" said the woman. "Have I got your legs all wrong?"

"It's not the legs," said the Chairman. "The legs are fine."

"Is it the torso?" said the woman. "Have I made you look too bulky?"

[731]

"The torso's fine too," said the Chairman. "It's quite complimentary, to be perfectly honest. I've never had much of a six pack. Now just drop the subject will you and let me out. It must have turned 9 o'clock by now."
"It's the penis isn't it?" said the woman. "I've made it too big haven't I?"
"Too big!" said the Chairman. "Too fucking big! It's almost nonexistent. What happened Miss Havisham-did you run out of penis coloured paint?"
"Not at all," said the woman. "I paint things exactly as I see them at the time."
"I don't doubt it," said the Chairman. "But I'd just stepped out of a freezing cold ice bath. And as far as I'm concerned, and as far as the rest of the male population of the civilized world is concerned, that's the worst possible time to be having our dicks applied to canvas."
"What do you suggest I do then?" said the woman. "Do you want to sit again?"
"No I don't," said the Chairman.
"Would you like me to extend your penis to some degree?" said the woman.
"I don't want you to go anywhere near my penis," said the Chairman. "I just want to go home. By the way-where exactly were you when you saw me being violated?"
"In one of the ventilation shafts," said the woman.
"That's nice," said the Chairman. "That's lovely that is. That's very lady like that is. That's what's known as an invasion of someone's privacy. You could go to jail for that you know Miss Havisham."
"That's what happened to my mother," said the woman.
"Was she a peeping Tom too?" said the Chairman.
"She was a Romany whore," said the woman.
"A what!" said the Chairman.
"A Romany whore," said the woman. "She died of pneumonia when I was five. That's her picture above my bed. She was beautiful wasn't she?"
"There's no doubt about that," said the Chairman. "Now

will you kindly open the door and let me out. And would
it be too much trouble for you to provide me with a
candle or a lantern so that I can read what you've
written. That corridor is so dark. You can hardly see to
the end of your own nose."

"Why don't you just read the directions and apply them
to memory?" said the woman before retiring behind her
easel. "Let's be honest Pip, that's what most intelligent
boys would do."

"I'll do just that," said the Chairman. "I was going to
do that anyway Miss Havisham. I'll do that right
away..........I'll do that right now.....Oh for fuck's
sake.....you twisted old bitch."

"What the devil's the matter?" said the woman.

"You know damn well what's the matter," said the
Chairman before picking up the poker.

"I don't," said the woman. "You asked me for directions
and I kindly accommodated you."

"You gave me sweet bugger all," said the Chairman.
"You've just been messing with my head. You've
written, 'up, down, right, left, across, under, over,
sideways, forward and back'."

"They're directions aren't they?" said the woman.

"They're meaningless as far as my exit goes and you
know it," said the Chairman. "My suspicions have been
right about you Miss Havisham. You're a fucking
nutcase. Although, now I come to think of it-you
wouldn't know, would you?"

"Wouldn't know what?" said the old woman.

"How to get out of here," said the Chairman. "You
wouldn't have any idea."

"Why wouldn't I?" said the woman.

"Because you're an inmate yourself," said the
Chairman. "You're as deranged as any of the fucking
loonies locked up here."

"I'm perfectly sane," said the woman.

"You're not," said the Chairman. "You're delusional.
You seem to think it's acceptable to dress monkeys in
clothes. And you even believe they're capable of

playing parlour games and things like that."
"I'm down here because I choose to reside down here,"
said the woman.
"You choose to!" said the Chairman. "That confirms
your insanity then."
"It confirms nothing of the sort," said the old woman.
"I'm family. Take a look around you Pip. Does this look
like a typical prison cell? Look at the lavish furnishings
young man. Feel the quality of the carpet and
bedspread. I bet this cell's every bit as luxurious as the
London apartment you share with your old pal Herbert."
"It's very impressive, to be fair," said the Chairman.
"But I know where I'd rather live. I want to be amongst
normal human beings. And I'd want to see the sky from
time to time."
"And I don't," said the old woman while angrily
shoving her easel aside. "That's where we differ Pip.
I'm not interested in seeing the sky. As far as I'm
concerned, perpetual darkness is an appropriate
backdrop for my pathetic and increasingly depressing
existence."
"Is it really!" said the Chairman. "What about company
Miss Havisham. Don't you crave that?"
"I can have company whenever I want it," said the
woman. "I can eat with the Colonel and Major if I
choose to. But that's no longer something that interests
me. I'm bored with all that. I don't want to have to
continually listen to tales of derring do and heroism from
old has beens. I'm content to be here, right next door to
my neighbour, the remarkable Mr Cripples."
"Who the hell's Mr Cripples-a mountain gorilla?" said
the Chairman.
"He's my former tutor," said the woman. "And anyway
Pip-even if he was a mountain gorilla, I'd still respect
and admire him. It certainly wouldn't worry me."
"It'd scare the crap out of me," said the Chairman.
"It wouldn't prejudice me one iota," said the woman. "I
would actually consider it a privilege to have a friend
like that."

"A privilege!" said the Chairman.

"Very much so," said the woman. "The vast majority of animals are massively superior to humans."

"Not intellectually they're not," said the Chairman.

"I'll grant you that," said the woman. "But moralistically they are. They'll never cheat on you, they'll never lie to you, they'll never steal from you and they'll never do you a dirty trick."

"I get your point but I wouldn't entirely agree," said the Chairman. "My dad's tabby cat Mogsy used to pinch his slippers and hide them on him. It used to drive him nuts."

"That's called play," said the woman.

"What's your tutor's story?" said the Chairman.

"What do you mean?" said the woman.

"Why is he here?" said the Chairman. "Did he poison a classroom full of students or something?"

"His story's arguably more tragic than mine," said the woman. "But that's for him to tell. He tells it best and I tend to tell my story best."

"Tell it then," said the Chairman.

"It would take too long," said the woman. "But I will tell you this much. Before I moved into this room, I was spending up to 80 hours a week with Mr Cripples."

"Why was that?" said the Chairman. "Had you fallen in love?"

"I have an unquenchable thirst for knowledge," said the woman. "It made perfect sense to pack my things and settle down here next to a true academic. I'm not an inmate. I'm as free as a bird. I can go wherever I want in this house. You were right about one thing though."

"What's that?" said the Chairman.

"I am a little bit insane," said the woman.

"Dangerously so?" said the Chairman.

"Only if I'm pushed too far," said the woman.

"How far would you say I've pushed you?" said the Chairman.

"You had me close to the point where I wanted to use vulgar language," said the woman. "And while we're

[735]

on the subject of vulgarity-have you ever considered taking some polish to your boots?"

"Have you ever considered your attire?" said the Chairman. "That's a wedding dress you're wearing isn't it Miss Havisham?"

"It is, and it won't be long before it becomes my burial gown," said the woman.

"Aren't you afraid of it catching fire?" said the Chairman after noticing a couple of dark brown scorch marks on the item's hem.

"I would welcome that," said the woman. "That would be a fitting end to my meaningless and appalling life. I often fear Mr Cripples will catch light one of these days."

"Why's that?" said the Chairman.

"Because he's made of paper," said the woman.

"Is he really!" said the Chairman before folding his arms and shaking his head. "Do you know what Miss Havisham-I'm trying to have a sensible conversation with you and you're making it very difficult."

"I'm not making it difficult at all," said the woman.

"Then lift up your veil and let me look you in the eyes," said the Chairman.

"I can't do that," said the woman. "I only ever lift my veil in order to eat and drink."

"Why's that?" said the Chairman.

"Because I have to constantly be on my guard," said the woman.

"From what?" said the Chairman.

"I suffer seizures from time to time," said the woman.

"What sort of seizures?" said the Chairman.

"An extremely disconcerting type," said the woman. "The type where you're conscious of everything that's going on around you but you can't move a muscle until the fit passes. It's scary. It's really scary. Particularly when you consider the sort of angry and opportunistic creatures that we have to share this place with. It means I live in constant fear of having my eyeballs eaten away while unable to do a thing about it. Can you imagine what that would be like?"

"I'd rather not," said the Chairman. "What else do you fear Miss Havisham? For instance, do you fear Albert at all?"

"Albert wouldn't dare lay a hand on me," said the woman. "I'm the Colonel's blue eyed darling. I used to sing and play the piano for him before I moved down here."

"He seems to be a decent old stick," said the Chairman. "But that Major's hard work."

"In what way?" said the woman.

"He's got some serious anger issues," said the Chairman.

"That's the pixies," said the woman.

"The pixies!" said the Chairman.

"They torment the life out of the poor man," said the woman.

"What do you mean 'pixies'?" said the Chairman. "Do you mean baboons?"

"I mean pixies," said the woman. "Do you not know what a pixie is young man?"

"I think so," said the Chairman. "It's a supernatural or mythical creature isn't it?"

"These aren't supernatural," said the woman. "These beings are as real as you and I. Whatever you do, don't ever leave anything lying around. Only the other day, I saw one of them frolicking around the garden in a pair of the Colonel's old long Johns. That's what I hate most about them. They seem to think the garden belongs to them and them alone. They're the main reason there are no flowers anymore."

"Isn't it more to do with the lack of qualified garden staff?" said the Chairman.

"Not at all," said the woman. "It's because the pixies took all the flowers to make necklaces and bracelets. They're consumed with hate you know Pip. But they hate me most of all."

"Why's that?" said the Chairman.

"I don't really know," said the woman. "They often

[737]

accuse me of acting all superior."

"And do you act superior?" said the Chairman.

"It's not an act," said the woman. "I am superior to them. They're groundlings. They're vermin. They're no better than slugs or greenfly. They need exterminating. They're the reason I decided to take Estella in."

"I don't understand," said the Chairman.

"They were bullying her relentlessly," said the woman. "Which reminds me. Did you happen to come across that other evil bully Bimoko when you were making your way here?"

"I might have done," said the Chairman.

"Did you?" said the woman.

"I did yes," said the Chairman after some considerable thought.

"Did he bother you?" said the woman.

"He attacked my companion," said the Chairman.

"The incorrigible rogue!" said the woman. "Is he alright?" Is your friend alright?"

"He's fine," said the Chairman. "He was just a bit shaken up and badly bruised."

"It's just not right," said the woman. "I swear I'll swing for that unruly piece of work one of these days."

"You won't need to," said the Chairman.

"Why not?" said the woman.

"Bimoko's dead," said the Chairman.

"Pardon!" said the woman.

"My companion killed him," said the Chairman. "But to be fair Miss Havisham, it was an unfortunate accident."

"Embellish me, for goodness sake," said the excited woman before abandoning her easel and settling down on her immaculately dressed single bed. "Pray tell me more."

"He attacked my friend Tommy not long after we'd taken refuge in one of the garden sheds," said the Chairman. "But Tommy's very strong. He does a lot of heavy weights and a bit of boxing. He managed to overpower him and lock him in a cupboard."

"Good for him," said the woman.

"I wanted to go back and let the creature out, but one thing led to another and I think he ended up suffocating," said the Chairman. "I felt awful. I still do to be honest."

"Don't you dare recriminate yourself," said the old woman. "That Bimoko was a contemptible fiend. He persecuted so many decent people. He made peoples' lives an absolute misery. He dragged a poor man around the garden once. Good for your friend Tommy, I say. That's splendid. That really is splendid news. I must tell Mr Cripples. Where is he now? Where is this remarkable Tommy chap?"

"He escaped some time during the early hours of the morning," said the Chairman. "He was terrified the Colonel would find out what he'd done to Bimoko and punish him."

"He had every right to be terrified," said the woman. "The Colonel adored Bimoko. He reared him from a baby. He used to allow the filthy creature to eat at his table and sleep in his bed. The very thought of it makes me feel bilious. I've seen Bimoko foul himself during lunch and not even bat an eyelid."

"Oh God!" said the Chairman. "I think I'd have thrown my lunch up. Do you think my mate Tommy would have made it Miss Havisham?"

"Made it?" said the woman.

"Do you think it's possible for someone to get out of this place?" said the Chairman.

"I do as it happens," said the woman. "But there are many hidden dangers here. They'd have to be armed. Was your friend Tommy armed?"

"I think so," said the Chairman. "He'd stashed a couple of the Colonel's rifles."

"That's good," said the woman. "That was very good thinking. Now let me make you some tea. I assume you still take tea do you Pip?"

It soon became clear to the Chairman that the woman had at least two different, interwoven identities, the more dominant and prevalent being the bitter and unpredictable Miss Havisham, who called him Pip and had the ability to make him feel like a nervous pupil on his first day of a new school. The other identity, was no less complex but nevertheless, more pleasant and amenable. She was an aged spinster who craved social interaction and someone who might or might not have been related to the Colonel. She had provided a lot of information regarding the old house and its peculiar residents and he was therefore relieved when she and not the former mentioned character handed him an empty floral designed china cup about ten minutes later.

"It's not too hot is it?" she asked a few minutes later after noticing her guest hadn't begun to drink. "Would you like me to add a little cold water?" "It's fine," said the Chairman after pretending to take the politest of sips.

"Did you want sugar?" said the woman.

"I don't take it, thank you," said the Chairman. "This is nice as it is. This is exactly how I make my tea. Can I ask you something Miss Havisham."

"Go ahead," said the woman. "As long as it's not to do with the value of my estate. That subject's no longer open to discussion. I refuse to discuss that matter with anyone but Mr Pumblechook. I had Camilla and the other toadies and humbugs here last week. My estate and what I might be worth is all they ever want to talk about."

"Who are they?" said the Chairman. "Are they more garden dwelling creatures?"

"They're distant relatives of mine," said the woman. "They're related to the Pocket family. For some indemonstrable reason, they're convinced they're in line for a share of my considerable wealth. What do you want to ask me Pip?"

"I think you've already answered me," said the Chairman. "I was going to ask you about visitors and such. What about this place Miss Havisham. Does it still house any lunatics?"

"I don't think so," said the woman. "But I wouldn't

really know for sure. I rarely venture beyond this
corridor anymore. There is the Italian, of course."
"Who's the Italian?" said the Chairman.
"He's a loathsome, cunning individual who occupies a
cell about twenty feet from this very room," said the
woman while edging slightly closer to her guest. "He
goes by the name of Gino, but he has been known to use
other names. For some inexplicable reason, he's
allowed visitors too. But do you know what's strange
young man-do you know what's really strange?"
"Tell me," said the Chairman.
"They are always attractive young women and you
rarely see the same woman twice," said the woman.
"Why do you think that is?" said the Chairman.
"He does bad things to them," said the woman. "I've
watched them leave his room in the most frightful states.
I've seen them pass my door nursing broken noses, black
eyes and burst lips. A few of them could barely walk.
Heaven knows why that was. "
"Does the Colonel know about this arrangement?" said
the Chairman.
"I don't know," said the woman. "I like to think not.
Mr Cripples, who knows everything about everything by
the way, told me the Italian was formerly a notorious
gangster who twice survived being shot and buried
alive."
"It sounds like sensationalistic gossip to me," said the
Chairman.
"It's not gossip at all," said the woman. "The Italian
told him."
"It must be true then," said the Chairman. "What does
your Mr Cripples think of the Italian?"
"He hates him but finds aspects of his character
fascinating," said the woman. "He told me the Italian
once showed him a case stuffed with money."
"That'll be how he pays for the girls," said the
Chairman.
"Possibly," said the woman. "He's evil. There may be
other inmates here, but there are none that I'm aware of.

But on the previous subject of visitors, there was a time when I received them quite regularly."

"Like who for instance?" said the Chairman.

"People who'd got lost during bad weather," said the woman. "Or people who'd been found trespassing on the Colonel's property. The Colonel would have them brought to this room to stay with me."

"With the greatest respect Miss Havisham," said the Chairman. "They wouldn't have been visitors in the conventional sense. They sound more like detainees to me."

"That's what I eventually deduced," said the woman. "I suppose I was kidding myself. They were more than often in a sorry old state."

"Why didn't they just make a run for it?" said the Chairman.

"Many did," said the woman. "But then they started arriving here with their wings clipped."

"What do you mean, 'wings clipped'?" said the Chairman.

"They'd had one or two of their feet severely crushed in a vice," said the woman.

"What!" said the Chairman.

"They could do nothing but hobble by the time they'd been introduced to me," said the woman.

"I've seen some of them crawl on their stomachs to the far end of this corridor in an effort to escape."

"My God!" said the Chairman. "Who do you think was responsible for the atrocity?"

"It could have been any number of people," said the woman. "But I'll wager it was the Ukrainian brothers."

"Who were they?" said the Chairman.

"A couple of sick and twisted orderlies," said the woman. "They were fiends. They seemed to live to be wicked and to strike fear into people. It was widely rumoured they'd been reared in a Nazi death camp in Poland. I think it was Treblinka. They showed Albert how to stomp. They even taught him how to make bird distracters out of living people. They terrified those

[742]

poor devils who had been captured."

"I bet they did," said the Chairman. "Were you able to help any of them?"

"Not really," said the woman. "They were often too hysterical. They were past helping. They were certainly beyond reasoning with. They'd carry on and scream and shout and threaten to do awful things to the poor Colonel."

"Do you know what happened to them?" said the Chairman.

"I don't know for sure," said the woman. "All I can tell you is that whenever the ranting and raving reached a certain pitch, a laundry basket would arrive outside my door."

"A laundry basket!" said the Chairman. "Was that to take their clothes and personal affects away?"

"It was to take them away," said the woman. "Albert would bear hug them into unconsciousness and then toss their limp carcasses into the basket. The sick bugger would hide in it sometimes and jump out on them. It was horrific, but quite exhilarating too. That would be the last I'd ever see of them."

"My God!" said the Chairman. "Do you know what Miss Havisham-I hid behind what might have been a laundry basket while I was making my way here."

"That might be the very one," said the woman. "So no ranting and raving hey Pip."

"You can count on it," said the Chairman.

"I insist on it," said the woman while wagging a finger. "Tell me Pip. How far from here would you say that aforementioned linen basket was?"

"I'm not sure," said the Chairman. "Although, come to think about it-it wasn't too far from the stairs. That's the only reason I could see anything."

"Oh dear," said the woman.

"What's the matter?" said the Chairman.

"I think that's where poor Mr Pumblechook is being held," said the woman.

"Why would you think that?" said the Chairman.

[743]

"He hasn't been to see me," said the woman. "And the fact that I watched somebody being thrown into one of the cells a couple of days ago. I like to enjoy a pipe you see Pip. I love the aroma of strong tobacco. But rather than allow my abode to become tainted with unpleasant fumes and stains, I always stand in the doorway to appreciate it. I see quite a lot from that particular vantage point. I wonder what's happened. I can only assume Mr Pumblechook has done the Colonel some sort of disservice."

"I've got to be honest Miss Havisham-I don't think there was anyone there," said the Chairman. "I was hovering around that vicinity for about fifteen minutes and didn't hear so much as a murmur or the rattle of a cell door."

"You wouldn't have done," said the woman before leaving her position and heading to her dressing table. "Mr Pumblechook's a very proud and dignified individual. He's a man of very few words and he's not prone to gestures of the hysterical or extravagant sort. He would never make a fuss, regardless of his situation. By the way Pip. You seem to be taking an age drinking your tea. Hurry up will you boy. Hurry up. I've just had something of a brainwave."

"Regarding what?" said the Chairman.

"Regarding the unfortunate Mr Pumblechook," said the woman. "I want you to do something for me."

"Like what?" said the Chairman.

"Procure his freedom," said the woman.

"I beg your pardon!" said the Chairman.

"Put that cup down and I'll tell you more," said the woman.

"I haven't finished," said the Chairman.

"Nonsense!" said the woman. "Your cup's been empty for some time. Now stop stalling and tighten your britches boy. There's no time to lose."

"Why me?" said the Chairman.

"It's what is sometimes referred to as 'quid pro quo'," said the woman. "You do something for me and I'll do something for you in return."

"What do you propose doing for me?" said the
Chairman.

"Make sure you get out of here," said the woman.
"Does that sound reasonable?"

"It sounds more than reasonable," said the Chairman.
"But I don't want to be putting my life at risk any more
than it already is. And besides-that Pumblechook
character's locked in a cell isn't he? How the hell am I
going to get him out?"

"There'll be a key in a small gap between the bricks
above the lintel," said the woman.

"A key!" said the now heavily perspiring Chairman.

"There's a key above all the holding cells," said the
woman. "Only Albert can reach them. I certainly
wouldn't be able to. But you're tall and beautifully put
together. By standing on the basket, you just might."

"Jesus Christ!" mumbled the Chairman before rising
and running his fingers through his hair. "Beautifully put
together! I'm not together at all. I'm in bits. I'm falling
apart."

CHAPTER TWENTY EIGHT
ESCAPE

B ack in the main room, there was much confusion and not just because two men in the pay of the master of the house had gone missing, but because Albert had found two loaded rifles and a box of .577 cartridges next to a half open kitchen window. It was a discovery that had sent the Colonel's paranoia into overdrive and it therefore wasn't long before the Chinese were bearing the brunt of the old man's notorious rage. The Major had not been anything like convinced however but although initially presenting a forceful and reasonable case that Carruthers might have simply stationed the rifles at each of the upstairs windows in preparation for the next Communist attack, he had, as was nearly always the case, been forced to back down and accept the head of the household's conviction. Nevertheless, in some regards, the situation had improved for the Major because things were now back to the way they were prior to the two club member's arrival. Those who he considered to be imposters and therefore a threat to his and his old friend's lives had moved on like many before them. The weather had improved too and it was therefore possible to gaze upon the snow glazed garden which now resembled a massive and spectacular Winter grotto. Had the Colonel done so just as it was coming to midday, he would have witnessed something quite remarkable and extremely moving. He would have seen Bimoko's entire mournful troop sitting in a dignified circle around the disturbed area where Albert had recently put their leader into the ground.

In the meantime, the Chairman was making his cautious and ponderous way along the corridor towards the cell where the old woman suspected her good friend and adviser Mr Pumblechook was being held but because the door leading to the basement steps had blown closed after a severe and sudden gust, he no longer had the advantage of the staircase light to help him find his way. That meant that he was now having to do something completely alien to him and navigate like a blind man-by feel and instinct. That didn't mean he hadn't applied a method to his intention though. In fact, he had refused to leave the old woman's room until he had mentally retraced just about every one of his previous 117 steps and had gauged how long the venture was likely to take him. However, he had failed to take into consideration the amount of times he would find himself spinning fully 360 degrees, the amount of times he would take a couple of backward steps and the amount of times he would freeze in terror after hearing something suspicious and potentially menacing. That meant that he had soon reached a point in his punctuated and harrowing journey, when he couldn't tell whether he was going away from where he had initially set off or whether he was heading back towards it.

Becoming completely disorientated was probably the least of his many fears however. Being captured by the menacing Albert and being severely punished for trying to escape ranked very high on his list too. He was also worried about being collared and beaten senseless by the infamous Italian, but the one thing he feared most and the one thing that had played most heavily on his mind since he had drummed up the courage to set off, was to open the cell door that was supposedly housing the luckless Mr Pumblechook and find himself confronted by a homicidal maniac or any number of savage creatures.

It wasn't long before he began to question just about everything the old woman had told him, particularly after he realised the thin slither of light that had been emanating from under her door had suddenly vanished. There was no reason for that, as far as he was concerned. That just didn't make any sense. That slither of light was vital to him because that slither of light could have been used as a sort of homing beacon. That is when his fear suddenly turned to extreme anger. That was when he realised how foolish he had been to put his trust and faith in someone who was not only a complete stranger but more importantly, somebody who was residing within a lunatic asylum. That was when he decided it was time to abandon the rescue and run and keep on running until he found his way out of the house or collapsed due to exhaustion in the process. He would, in fact, manage to run only 87 yards.

The Chairman had never attended an opera and had never once sat and listened to an opera either on vinyl, cassette or compact disc, but like most reasonably intelligent adults, he could recognise something that was operatic in style. He could also recognise the language it was being sung in. It was that bouncy, biting and beguiling language uttered by millions of Italians. "Mama Mia!" came a distinctive and concerned sounding voice from the far end of the room. "Guarda la dimensione di quel grumo sulla tua testa."

"Oh my God!" muttered the Chairman to himself after suddenly realising he was bound to the frame of a bed. "Oh no, no, no. What the hell have I done?"

"Tu chi sei?" said the man.

"I'm sorry, I don't understand," said the Chairman.

"Who the Dickens are you?" snapped the man.

"I'm.....I'm erm.....I'm Henry," said the Chairman. "Henry Stalling."

"Henry Stalling!" said the man while propelling himself over to where the Chairman was laying by means of a three wheeled office chair. "And who might Henry Stalling be?"

"I'm a travelling businessman," said the still badly dazed Chairman while trying unsuccessfully to rise from his position. "I've got a proposal for you."

"Una proposta!" said the man while proceeding to examine a golf ball sized lump on the centre of the Chairman's forehead. "Una proposta per me?"

"I can you get you women," said the Chairman.

"Women!" said the man.

"I run a top class escort agency," said the Chairman. "I have the best and most beautiful looking women imaginable on my books."

"Chi ti ha mandato?" said the man.

"I'm sorry, I don't understand," said the Chairman while continuing to try to raise his head above the level of his pillow.

"Who sent you here?" said the man.

"The Colonel." said the Chairman. "The Colonel sent me. He wants you to have a more classy type of bed partner."

"Questo e molto buono da parte sua," said the man.

"Oh, mi displace. I'm sorry signore....that means, 'that's very decent of him'. Now tell me the truth or I will put my stiletto through your left ear and scramble your brains into something resembling a mushroom omelette mix."

"I'm telling the God's honest truth," said the fear stricken and almost hysterical Chairman. "I can get you women. I can get you them by the bus load if you want."

"I don't want them by the bus load," said the man. "I've only ever craved the one."

"Then I'll get you one, if that's your poison," said the Chairman. "How do you want her? Do you want her slim? Do you want her big? Do you want her black or Asian? Just say the word and I'll oblige you."

"You're talking nonsense," said the man. "You're no businessman-you're just another escapee."

"I'm not-I'm a respected businessman," said the Chairman.

"You're an escapee," said the man. "I know that because you still reek of delousing powder."

"That was a mistake," said the Chairman. "Albert mistook me for someone else. For God's sake, will you listen to me. I'm trying to do you a favour."

"Then do me one," said the man. "Tell me about my choice in music. Evaluate it. And be as cruel or as kind as you like."

[749]

"I love it," said the Chairman. "I've always loved classical music. What is it? I might try and see if it's available on line."

"It's Or tutto o chiaro," said the man while proceeding to wave his hands in the manner of an overzealous orchestral conductor. "It's from Tosca. That's the world renowned soprano Renata Tebaldi singing now. You'll hear the highly acclaimed baritone Tito Gobbi engage her soon. There he is now. They complement each other beautifully, don't you agree?"

"I couldn't agree more," said the Chairman. "My wife sings."

"Does she really," said the man. "What does she sing?"

"Karaoke mainly," said the Chairman.

"What's that?" said the man.

"It's like a sort of solo singing with words to follow," said the Chairman. "She's very good. She's sung just about everywhere."

"Has she ever performed at Carnegie Hall?" said the man.

"No, but she's performed an open mike event in a bar in Carnegie Avenue," said the Chairman. "She's a domestic cleaner you know."

"A cleaner!" said the man while simultaneously terminating his performance. "Why would you think that would be of interest to me?"

"No reason," said the Chairman.

"You're not suggesting my room's in need of a visit from your Mrs Mop are you?" said the man.

"Not at all," said the Chairman. "I like the way you've got your room. I've always preferred a cluttered room. I'm a traditionalist. I hate all that modern minimalist stuff."

"It's a mess," said the man. "But that's the way I like it. Let's start again shall we. Who are you really? And be absolutely honest this time, or I'll make your stay even more unpleasant than is necessary."

"Alright," said the Chairman after taking a deep breath. "I'm Ken Hulme. I'm the Chairman of a veteran men's club from Crosby in Merseyside. We do a lot of charity work for the elderly and mentally unstable. Our train broke down not too far from here."

"Your train!" said the man.

"A friend of ours arranged what should have been a 10 day trip with his company," said the Chairman.

"Have you thought of having him certified?" said the man.

"Of course not," said the Chairman. "What makes you ask that?"

"Because it sounds as if your friend's stark raving mad," said the man. "Who in their right mind organises an all male excursion at this time of the year?"

"We set off on the 7th December," said the Chairman. "We were scheduled to be well back in time for the Christmas festivities. We've been waiting for a rescue team to find us ever since."

"That actually sounds reasonably plausible," said the man. "Perhaps you're not the level 5 lunatic I initially took your for."

"Thanks very much," said the Chairman.

"You're welcome," said the man. "So while you're on a roll, tell me something else Mr Hulme. What do you imagine you're doing in my room? Or to put it another way-how would you assess your current predicament? And once again, I urge and advise complete honesty."

"I've got a feeling I'm your prisoner," said the Chairman after struggling to clear his throat.

"What brings you to that assumption?" said the man.

"It's obvious isn't it?" said the Chairman. "I'm dressed in a bright yellow boiler suit with OBI stamped on the breast pocket and I'm tied to a bed with a massive lump in the centre of my head. I can only assume you or an associate of yours, knocked me out and dragged me here."

"You stumbled in here," said the man. "You came in here of your own volition. You were badly dazed and performing an enormous amount of arm waving. I had no choice but to restrain you. But I didn't strike you.

Using violence to illicit a response has never been my way. You simply passed out. As for your injury-you must have slipped and banged your head somewhere along the corridor. Your clothes were torn and covered in rat droppings. I had to get you out of them before you stunk my room out. That boiler suit is asylum issue and has never been worn. Your personal effects including your watch are on my dresser."

"Does that mean I'm free to leave?" said the Chairman.

"You can leave whenever you want," said the man while slowly removing the first of the Chairman's four restraints. "But if I was you, I'd give it about an hour. You might be suffering a concussion. In the meantime, would you like a cup of tea?"

"I'd like to see your door open first," said the Chairman.

"Then open it," said the man upon removing the final tie. "Be my guest."

"You're Mr Cripples, aren't you?" said the mightily relieved Chairman after successfully opening the door and placing his restraints on top of a pile of old leather bound books.

"You could say that," replied the occupant.

"Bloody hell!" said the Chairman. "Thank God for that. I thought you were the Italian."

"If I was Gino, you'd be without a fully functioning throat by now," said the man. "Do you want that aforementioned tea?"

"I'd love that tea," said the Chairman before settling back down on the bed and proceeding to massage his darkening lump. "I'm sorry If I've been offhand in any way."

"Apology accepted," said the man. "I think I can safely assume you've met my quirky neighbour."

"Miss Havisham you mean?" said the Chairman.

"Is that who she is today?" said the man.

"What do you mean?" said the Chairman.

"She's in character," said the man. "She's currently reading Great Expectations by Charles Dickens. Are you familiar with that particular literary masterpiece Mr

Hulme?"

"I'm familiar with the author," said the Chairman. "I studied 'Tom Brown's School Days' for my English G.C.S.E."

"What did you think of it?" said the man.

"It was alright," said the Chairman. "I know it might sound strange, but I thought that Harry Flashman character was fantastic."

"You want to apply for a job here," said the man.

"In what capacity?" said the Chairman.

"As a cleaner," said the man. "In fact, any position but teacher of classic literature."

"Why's that?" said the Chairman.

"Flashman wasn't one of Charles Dickens's many inventions," said the man.

"Really?" said the Chairman.

"A talented Rugby School old boy named Thomas Hughes wrote Tom Brown's School Days," said the man. "You've been missing out Mr Hulme. You should try and read some Dickens. Judging by your enthusiasm for the Hughes work, I think you'd like him. He was arguably the greatest writer of the Victorian era. He created almost 1000 characters. Funnily enough, I actually consider Miss Havisham to be his most fascinating and compelling invention."

"She was left at the altar wasn't she?" said the Chairman.

"She didn't get as far as the altar," said the man. "Which leads me to point out the fact -you certainly picked the wrong time to enter that particular room."

"Why's that?" said the Chairman.

"Because Miss Havisham lives to persecute the male of the species," said the man. "Who did she cast you as Mr Hulme?"

"How do you mean?" said the Chairman.

"What did she call you?" said the man.

"Erm.....Pip or Phillip," said the Chairman.

"That figures," said the man after carefully removing a blackened, steaming kettle from a single ring gas stove

[753]

and placing it on a badly scorched heart shaped bread board. "He's the protagonist. He comes into a lot of money in the end, so you might want to hang about."

"Where did she acquire the wedding dress?" said the Chairman.

"There's a room full of theatrical props and costumes somewhere in the house," said the man. "During much happier climates, the old Colonel used to get his waiting and kitchen staff to stage monthly shows for him and his friends. I used to write and adapt the scripts."

"Are you in the employ of the Colonel?" said the Chairman.

"In a manner of speaking," said the man before handing the Chairman a mug of piping hot tea and wheeling himself back to his previous position. "I get full board and all the books and materials I want in exchange for answering his mail and sorting out his accounts."

"Do you get paid anything for tutoring," said the Chairman.

"I do that because it's my passion," said the man. "Teaching stimulates me and enables me to increase my own depth of knowledge. It keeps my brain ticking over. I've taught quite a few people here over the years."

"Like who?" said the Chairman.

"Like the person currently going by the name of Miss Havisham," said the man. "She's got an IQ of 196."

"Is that good?" said the Chairman.

"It puts her very firmly in the 'genius' bracket," said the man. "Particularly when you consider the fact Einstein's IQ was said to be between 160 and 190."

"That's impressive," said the Chairman.

"I reckon the top universities in the country would roll out the red carpet for her tomorrow morning if she cared to apply," said the man. "Although, I'm going to be honest. She was already very bright when she was first brought to my attention. Teaching Albert to read and write was nevertheless my greatest achievement."

"Do you still teach him?" said the Chairman.

"He's not turned up for a class for nigh on 8 years," said

the man.

"Why do you think that is?" said the Chairman.

"He couldn't accept being told he was wrong," said the man. "He became extremely difficult. I began to fear for my life. I resorted to giving him ticks instead of crosses in order to avoid confrontations. I've got to be honest-I wasn't too displeased when he started skipping class and knocking around with Bimoko instead. That was 'addio' Albert."

"Where did you learn to speak Italian," said the Chairman.

"I taught myself right here in this very room," said the man.

"How did you manage that?" said the Chairman.

"Through the Linguaphone system mainly," said the man. "As part of our agreement to do his admin and keep his books, the Colonel provides me with any teaching aids I ask for. At least he used to before the postman stopped calling. I speak 11 languages including Mandarin Chinese. I actually learnt that before I arrived here."

"Is that the hardest language to pick up?" said the Chairman.

"It's commonly regarded to be," said the man. "But it's also the most widely spoken native language too. It's an interesting fact that isn't it?"

"It is yes," said the Chairman.

"Do you love your wife Mr Hulme?" said the man.

"I worship her," said the Chairman.

"Then, when you see her again, whisper this phrase into her ear," said the man. "'Ni hai you bie de'."

"What does it mean?" said the Chairman.

"It means, 'you are something else'," said the man. "It's something I used to say to my wife quite frequently. And it never failed to bring a smile to her face."

"I'll try to remember that," said the Chairman.

"I'll write it down for you," said the man. "In fact, I'll write it down phonetically. Don't forget.....Knee hay yo bee ay dar. Knee hay yo bee ay dar'."

"Do you mind me asking you something?" said the Chairman after repeating the expression several times and receiving his host's approval. "Feel free," said the man. "I love being asked questions. I live to be asked questions. Questions are like food and drink to me. I have to have them. Without them, I'll just wither and die like an unwatered Aspidistra. What is it you want to know Mr Hulme?"

"Your real name would do for a start," said the Chairman. "Because I can't believe for one minute, it's really Mr Cripples."

"Mr Cripples is a minor character from *Little Dorrit*," said the man. "He runs an evening academy. My constant neighbour hit upon the idea of calling me it after she'd read an abridged version of the novel. The name works on a number of levels. I think I might just be stuck with it forever. It's certainly stuck with our Miss Havisham. She's appalled if she hears me being called anything else."

"Is she crazy?" said the Chairman.

"Everyone within these walls is crazy to some degree," said the man. "You have to be a bit crazy in order to survive. It's the law of the jungle in here, if you'll excuse the tired and well worn cliché. You live by your wits from minute to cliff hanging minute. What made you want to escape?"

"I began to fear for my life," said the Chairman.

"Why's that?" said the man.

"Because my companion had killed the baboon formerly known as Mr Bimoko," said the Chairman. "I'm sorry if you were fond of him."

"I loathed him," said the man. "But that was an accident wasn't it?"

"It was yes," said the Chairman. "How could you possibly know that?"

"News travels fast in here Mr Hulme," said the man. "Were you close to your companion?"

"We were never the best of friends," said the Chairman.

"But we'd certainly grown close. I think that's because we'd survived a few close scrapes together. And we'd had quite a bit of fun until things turned sour. I wouldn't have got this far without Tommy. I'm just not the outdoor or adventurous type."

"Did he have any dependents?" said the man.

"He's got a wife and two kids in their late teens," said the slightly confused Chairman. "What do you mean, 'did he'?"

"It's not important," said the man before turning his attention to a bulging box file that was teetering on the brink of sliding behind his desk.

"It is important," said the Chairman. "You've just referred to my friend in the past tense."

"It was a mistake," said the man.

"But not one an accomplished teacher of English would make," said the Chairman. "What's going on sir? What did you use the past tense for when referring to my friend ?"

"Because he's gone," said the man almost inaudibly.

"I know he's gone," said the Chairman. "He's gone to get help."

"He's dead Mr Hulme," said the man.

"He's what?" said the Chairman.

"Your companion Tommy's dead," said the man upon lowering his head. "He was brutally murdered by Albert during the early hours of this morning."

"That's rubbish!" said the Chairman after a short delay.

"I watched it happen from my doorstep," said the man.

"I'll tell you this much Mr Hulme-your friend put up one hell of a fight."

"You've got to be mistaken," said the Chairman. "Tommy will be well gone by now."

"Your friend's lifeless body is in a cell that's situated almost opposite the basement steps," said the man.

"He can't be," said the Chairman after placing his mug on the floor and striding purposely towards the door. "I'm not having it Mr Cripples. I've never known anyone get the better of Tommy Mac."

"Albert did," said the man. "He snapped his spine as though it was a twig. Go and see for yourself if you don't believe me. You'll recognise him by his striped and muddied army surplus trousers."

"I'll recognise him by his face," said the Chairman. "Give me a lantern or a candle please Mr Cripples."

"He won't have a face," said the man after wheeling himself to the Chairman's side and taking him firmly by the wrists. "He won't even have a head or any internal organs. He's a human scarecrow now. He'll have a pumpkin for a head."

"A pumpkin!" said the Chairman after a short and agonising period when thinking clearly and uttering even the simplest words seemed impossible. "Oh Jesus Christ no. Oh no! Oh mother of God no! That's right.....the Colonel said he'd fallen down some steps. He'd taken his tunic off to clean it. I told him not to do that Mr Cripples. I specifically told him not to remove his uniform."

The Chairman sobbed unashamedly and uncontrollably for just short of an hour, a period during which the room's only other occupant sat motionless and respectful with his left hand over his mouth. Unlike the curious and unpredictable 'Miss Havisham', there had been nothing insincere or peculiar about him, although his long mousey hair looked as if it should have been attached to the head of a much younger person rather than someone who appeared to be in his late seventies or early eighties.

"Would you like me to make you another mug of tea?" he said after watching the Chairman slowly raise his head, open his moist and reddened eyes and glare upwards as if to admonish some treacherous overseer.

"Tea would be nice," replied the Chairman after gathering himself and pinching his running nose.

"Tea it is then," said the man before tapping the Chairman on his left knee and wheeling himself back to his tiny and cluttered kitchen area. "And then I'm going to tell you a story that'll blow your mind."

"I very much doubt it," said the Chairman. "I think I've already seen and heard just about everything."

"But not quite everything," said the man. "I bet you've never heard of a disorder called Species Dysphoria."

"You're absolutely right," said the Chairman. "I wouldn't begin to try to guess what that is."

"It's not a perfect fit Mr Hulme, but the symptoms exhibited by a Species Dysphoria sufferer are the closest I've come across to those exhibited by my sick wife," said the man. "Are you with me so far Mr Hulme?"

"Just about," said the Chairman. "But try to keep the pace nice and slow and the language relatively simple Mr Cripples."

"Very well," said the man. "Let me ask you this Mr Hulme. Would you ever consider having full blown sex with an animal?"

"Of course not," said the indignant Chairman.

"Why not?" said the man.

"Because I wouldn't," said the Chairman. "I consider myself to be a normal human being with normal needs, normal desires and normal moral standards. The very idea of having sex with an animal disgusts me."

"Why do you think that is Mr Hulme?" said the man.

"I've just told you," said the Chairman. "It disgusts me. It's wrong. Doesn't it disgust you?"

"It most certainly does," said the man. "But the concept doesn't disgust everyone."

"It should do," said the Chairman.

"But the fact remains, it doesn't," said the man. "Have you never heard of people who enjoy having sex with animals Mr Hulme?"

"I have yes, as it happens," said the Chairman. "It's called bestiality isn't it? But people who do that sort of thing have got to be freaks."

"I couldn't agree more," said the man. "But consider this. How freaky would you consider their behaviour to be if that particular human being who had sex with, for instance, a wolf, actually believed they were a wolf themselves?"

[759]

"That's a good one," said the Chairman. "Do such people exist?"

"Very much so," said the man. "They consider having sex with a wolf, the same as you having sex with your wife."

"Is that why you're in here Mr Cripples?" said the Chairman. "Have you had sex with an animal?"

"In a manner of speaking, I suppose I have," said the man.

"For fuck's sake," said the Chairman while nervously shifting position. "I thought you were a bit too good to be true."

"The animal I was referring to was my wife," said the man.

"You've lost me," said the Chairman. "I told you to keep the pace slow Mr Cripples."

"Do you know Hightown at all Mr Hulme?" said the man.

"I know it well," said the Chairman. "Our football team used to play their home games there every other Sunday."

"You must know the Hightown bends then?" said the man.

"I know them well," said the Chairman. "Why do you ask?"

"Because I once crashed my car along those bends Mr Hulme," said the man. "And in doing so, I inadvertently killed a stray cat."

"Shit like that happens I'm afraid," said the Chairman.

"I know it does," said the man. "But the crude philosophy, 'shit happens' wasn't going to be enough to placate, comfort and reassure my devastated wife. She was never the same person again."

"How do you mean, 'never the same'?" said the Chairman.

"From that day forward, she started to behave like a cat," said the man.

"She what!" said the Chairman.

"She started to sleep in a cardboard box rather than the

marital bed. She would only eat fresh fish and would only empty her bowels into a cat lit tray," said the man.

"You've got to be joking," said the Chairman.

"I wish I was joking," said the man.

"How long was she like that?" said the Chairman.

"She's still like that to this day," said the man. "I don't think she'll ever change."

"Why not?" said the Chairman.

"Because nobody can do anything for her," said the man. "I tried everything. I took her to 5 different countries and visited over 200 so-called mind experts. I saw mystics, faith healers, witch doctors, renowned hypnotists and the world's leading psychologists. I even sought out a highly regarded young gentleman who lived in Crosby. That's where you live isn't it Mr Hulme?"

"That's where I've lived for most of my adult life," said the Chairman. "Who was he? Who was he Mr Cripples? I might just know him."

"A teacher friend of mine referred me to him," said the man. "He said he'd done amazing things with women who had suffered years of domestic abuse and psychological coercion. He could dramatically alter their mindset apparently."

"What was his name?" said the Chairman. "It wasn't Matthews was it by any chance?"

"That's the very fellow," said the man.

"Bloody hell!" said the Chairman. "I know Matthews very well. As a matter of fact, he's a member of our club. He's actually back on that train I've come from. And, come to think of it, he used to do a bit of agony aunt stuff back in the day. If I remember right, he caused a hell of a lot of trouble. Bloody hell-what a tiny world we live in Mr Cripples."

"It's not that tiny Mr Hulme," said the man. "I used to live no more than thirty minutes from Crosby. Me and the wife used to shop there quite often. You and I have probably passed on the street lots of times without knowing it. I think his first name was Ryan."

"It was more likely to be Brian," said the Chairman.

"Was he able to help in any way?"

"He wouldn't see me," said the man. "He wouldn't even answer his door."

"That's not like the Brian Matthews I know," said the Chairman. "He's normally only too glad to help people."

"He wouldn't help me," said the man.

"I don't understand that," said the Chairman. "I really don't. Maybe he was scared."

"Scared of what?" said the man.

"Scared of all the bad feeling rearing its ugly head again," said the Chairman. "If I remember right-he'd had a few nasty run ins with some angry, abandoned husbands and a couple of them had set about him and left him for dead. I hate to admit it, but they were actually relatives of mine. They did a right job on the poor bugger. They did a fair bit of time for it. I think he was forced to leave the country at one point."

"I didn't know that," said the man. "Maybe that explains his reluctance to help. Would you happen to know his close friend Seymour by any chance?"

"Seymour!" said the Chairman. "That's some name isn't it. I don't think so."

"He's the Colonel's cousin," said the man. "He's responsible for the admittance procedure here at the asylum. He and your friend Matthews had travelled around India together apparently. He's a doctor of something or other. I think it might be tropical medicine. He was visiting your friend when I was waiting to be granted a clinic. Funnily enough, he was the one that told me about this place. He was the one who persuaded me to bring my wife here."

"Why didn't you just book her into a legitimate psychiatric clinic?" said the Chairman.

"Because, the chances are, she'd have been locked away for the rest of her life and my access to her and visiting rights would have been restricted," said the man. "I didn't want that. I wanted as much contact with her as possible. This asylum became my best bet because it was so much more relaxed and roomy than any of the others I'd visited. I was even encouraged to take up residency here."

"When was this Mr Cripples?" said the Chairman.

"When did you hit the cat on the Hightown bends?"

"Around the beginning of the nineteen eighties," said the man.

"What!" said the Chairman.

"I think it was 1981," said the man. "But it could have been 82. In fact, it was 82, because that's when my basement journal begins. That's the year I took ill too."

"With what?" said the Chairman.

"That's still a point for conjecture," said the man. "I just woke up one morning in a lather of sweat and noticed my legs were dark red and swollen like tree trunks."

"What was it?" said the Chairman.

"A very serious bacterial infection," said the man. "At least according to the specialist the Colonel had brought in it was. He told me I'd been bitten by something of tropical origin."

"That could have been nasty," said the Chairman. "That happened to a good friend of mine while he was working in Sri Lanka and he lost a leg."

"I lost both of mine," said the man.

"You what!" said the Chairman.

"These are prosthetic limbs," said the man before turning in his chair and tapping his left and right knees with the knuckles of each hand. "They're not the best made things, but they're better than nothing. They enable me to get around my room and that's pretty much all I need."

"That's awful," said the Chairman.

"It was devastating at the time," said the man. "I was relatively young then. I still had aspirations to see more of the world. But it doesn't really worry me now. I've had my life. Apart from a compos mentis wife, I've got everything I need right here in this room."

"How long were you hospitalised?" said the Chairman.

"I wasn't," said the man. "The operation was carried out here in this very asylum's infirmary."

"That's a bit unusual isn't it?" said the Chairman.

"That's how most people have reacted when I've told them," said the man.

"Have you any idea who carried out the procedure?" said the Chairman.

"I know exactly who operated," said the man. "An army surgeon friend of the Colonel called Dawkins. Aided and abetted by the same man who advised me to bring my wife here."

"Matthews's travelling friend Seymour, you mean?" said the Chairman.

"That's the chap," said the man.

"Was your wife aware of all this?" said the Chairman.

"I've not seen my wife from that day forward Mr Hulme," said the man. "I was almost immediately transferred down here."

"Did nobody ever think to bring her to see you?" said the Chairman.

"Apparently not," said the man. "Anyway, she'd gone feral by then. She probably wouldn't have known me. As far as I know, she still has the run of the house. I'm surprised you haven't come across her."

"I've hardly come across anyone other than those within the Colonel's inner sanctum," said the Chairman.

"Oh....apart from some haggard old woman who likes to dance and eat live rats."

"That's her," said the man before breaking into a wry smile.

"What!" said the Chairman.

"That's my wife," said the man. "That's my darling Tilly."

"It can't be," said the Chairman. "I'm sorry Mr Cripples. I don't want to come across as antagonistic, but the woman I saw, must have been close to receiving her hundredth birthday letter from the queen. I've never seen so many lines on a person's face in my life. And she definitely wasn't called Tilly. I think she was called

Matilda."

"It was Tilly, I tell you," said the man. "Tilly's just a shortened version of Matilda. And she's yet to celebrate her fiftieth birthday."

"Jesus Christ!" said the Chairman. "I'm so sorry Mr Cripples. That's terrible. That is so awful. You haven't had a lot of luck have you? I don't know how to respond to all that."

"You can start by calling me Gabriel," said the man upon thrusting out his right hand. "I'm Gabriel Spendlove."

"And I'm completely and utterly dumfounded," said the Chairman. "I thought I'd heard it all while sitting with the Colonel and that other bad tempered bastard."

"Are you talking about Albert?" said Spendlove.

"I'm talking about the Major," said the Chairman.

"The Major's more to be pitied," said Spendlove.

"I've no pity for him at all," said the Chairman. "He made my stay an absolute misery."

"Why do you think that was Mr Hulme?" said Spendlove.

"Because he's a senile old bastard that resents outsiders," said the Chairman.

"You've got him wrong Mr Hulme," said Spendlove. "The Major's just about the kindest and most considerate man I've ever met."

"You've got to be kidding," said the Chairman. "Are we talking about the same person here Mr Spendlove? I've never been made to feel more uncomfortable in all my life."

"That man's the only reason I've remained sane over the past 25 years," said Spendlove. "Shall I give you an example of his kindness Mr Hulme?"

"Go right ahead," said the Chairman. "He didn't send you flowers on your birthday did he?"

"He sent me love letters," said Spendlove.

"Love letters!" scoffed the Chairman.

"He sent me love letters supposedly written to me by my beloved Tilly," said Spendlove. "Of course, I didn't

[765]

know that at the time. I just thought her psychologist or counsellor or whatever you want to call him or her, had somehow managed to get her head right for a short time. I suppose I was subconsciously clutching at straws. Nevertheless, a letter a week for just over three years, that lovely man wrote me Mr Hulme."

"Do you still receive them?" said the Chairman.

"They stopped abruptly some time ago," said Spendlove.

"Did you ever ask why?" said the Chairman.

"The last one was mistakenly signed, 'Major Henry Howser'," said Spendlove. "I assume he must have made the mistake of writing it while he was more drunk than he usually managed to get. You've been privileged Mr Hulme. You've been in the presence of a great man."

"I've been in the presence of madness," said the Chairman. "That man couldn't have made me feel more uncomfortable if he'd strapped me to a rack and stuck red hot needles in my eye balls."

"Why do you think that was Mr Hulme," said Spendlove.

"Because he's bitter, twisted and cantankerous," said the Chairman.

"He wanted to get you to leave," said Spendlove. "He knew the danger you were in. He was trying to save your life."

"Then why didn't he just tell me to leave?" said the Chairman.

"Because he hasn't got the authority to order people to leave," said Spendlove. "You've spent long enough here to notice how he pussyfoots around the Colonel. You've noticed that haven't you Mr Hulme?"

"I have yes," said the Chairman. "Why is that? Is that just to do with rank and seniority?"

"There's a bit more to it than that," said Spendlove. "It's actually to do with his son."

"His son!" said the Chairman.

"The Major had a son Mr Hulme," said Spendlove.

"Were you not aware of that?"

"I was made aware that he had an imaginary son," said the Chairman. "But as far as I can recall, nobody could prove his existence."

"Casper was as real as you and me," said Spendlove. "He'd done very well for himself apparently. He'd graduated from Nuremberg University with a first class degree and after making a rapid rise to the top within a massively successful advertising company, he'd returned home and bought some property around the west of England and parts of North Wales."

"Are you talking about the lad that was meant to have gone missing?" said the Chairman.

"I'm talking about the lad that very definitely went missing," said Spendlove. "I'm talking about the Major's only son and heir. I'm talking about the young man the Colonel had locked away."

"Locked away!" said the Chairman. "But I was led to believe the authorities searched high and low for the lad."

"They did," said Spendlove. "But this place is massive Mr Hulme. It's like an iceberg. There's far more beneath the surface than above it. You could hide a herd of elephants down here and never see them more than twice a year."

"I don't get it," said the Chairman. "What had the lad done wrong? What had the lad done to deserve being locked up?"

"He'd wanted to take the Major away with him," said Spendlove. "And the Colonel was having none of it."

"I see," said the Chairman while scratching his head. "But how would you know this Mr Spendlove? Where's your proof? Where's your evidence that proves the young lad actually existed?"

"On the floor of a cell, a few hundred yards from this very room," said Spendlove while frantically rooting through the top drawer of his desk. "At least his skeletal remains and the last remnants of his clothes are. I should have some of the other evidence here."

"Like what?" said the Chairman.

"His wallet and some other personal effects," said Spendlove.

"Bloody hell!" said the Chairman. "Have you any idea who originally found them?"

"I did," said Spendlove.

"You did!" said the Chairman.

"That's right," said Spendlove.

"You managed to walk a few hundred yards?" said the Chairman.

"Of course not," said Spendlove. "I'd hitched a ride in the laundry basket."

"You did what?" said the Chairman.

"As became something of a tradition, my neighbour used to take me for a spin around the block to celebrate the end of a school term," said Spendlove. "I've got a wheelchair somewhere, but I've been forbidden from using it. I was in the laundry basket when I came across the poor lad's remains."

"I see," said the Chairman. "Have you any idea how he died?"

"I can't say for certain Mr Hulme," said Spendlove. "All I can tell you is that his suit was crimson where once it was a shade of light grey, and what was left of his frame could have comfortably fitted into an average size gymnasium bag."

"Jesus Christ!" said the Chairman. "That's so sad. Did the Major ever find out?"

"About his son's death?" said Spendlove.

"About his son's imprisonment," said the Chairman.

"He did yes," said Spendlove.

"How?" said the Chairman.

"He'd heard him crying," said Spendlove.

"How come?" said the Chairman.

"The lad had been moved to a cell next to the main internal ventilation shaft," said Spendlove. "The staff used to do that when the cells became intolerable due to the volume of human waste."

"What happened?" said the Chairman. "What happened

when the Major realised his son was being held?"

"The two men exchanged blows," said Spendlove.

"They really went for it by all accounts. At least until Albert took the Major by the throat and shook him into unconsciousness."

"How did the Colonel explain it all?" said the Chairman.

"He told the Major he'd caught his son going through his safe," said Spendlove.

"Which I imagine was nonsense," said the Chairman.

"I'd have thought so too," said Spendlove. "The lad was very comfortably off. He didn't need money. But the Colonel claimed he had a number of witnesses to the alleged crime. Including a local magistrate, I might add."

"The shady bastard!" said the Chairman.

"The poor Major had nobody to fight his corner," said Spendlove. "That's why he was eventually forced to accept the Colonel's cruel ultimatum."

"Which was what?" said the Chairman.

"Allow his son to remain where he was or let the police sort the matter out," said Spendlove. "And by the way Mr Hulme-the Colonel's got the local police in his back pocket and has had for several decades."

"Jesus!" said the Chairman. "What a scheming, manipulative old bastard."

"What he did next will appal you even more," said Spendlove.

"What was that?" said the Chairman.

"He used the young lad as a method of control," said Spendlove.

"What do you mean?" said the Chairman.

"He had the lad savagely beaten," said Spendlove. "The Major told me he'd never heard screams like them. The screams had resonated through the dining room. And the lad would get a similar beating whenever the Major stepped over a particular mark."

"Like mentioning his son?" said the Chairman.

"That's right," said Spendlove.

[769]

"Have you ever been tempted to let the Major know that his son's now dead?" said the Chairman.

"I'd have to be out of my mind to do that," said Spendlove. "I can't begin to think what state I'd be left in if that particular letter got intercepted."

"Who delivers your letters?" said the Chairman.

"My neighbour," said Spendlove. "But me and the Major haven't corresponded for some time. Funnily enough, it was last Christmas. I wondered if he was dying."

"Why's that?" said the Chairman.

"Because for the very first time since we'd been corresponding, he took a massive risk," said Spendlove.

"Took a risk to do what?" said the Chairman.

"To tell me how he lost the use of his legs," said Spendlove.

"I know how he lost the use of his legs," said the Chairman. "He fell down the cellar steps while looking for his son. I thought that was common knowledge."

"It's certainly what I'd been led to believe," said Spendlove. "But it's not what I subscribe to now. It was certainly no accident Mr Hulme. The Major was the victim of a most heinous and despicable act. The Major was punished."

"For doing what?" said the Chairman.

"For continuing to search for his son," said Spendlove. "And more importantly, for threatening to contact the investigative press."

"Did the Colonel have him beaten?" said the Chairman.

"He had him more than beaten," said Spendlove. "He had him paralysed."

"What!" said the Chairman.

"He had the man's spinal cord severed," said Spendlove. "The Major explained that, after a massive bust up with the Colonel, he had retired to his room and that while he was slipping on his nightshirt, the two Ukrainian thugs, who you might or might not already be familiar with, burst into his bedroom and pinned him to the bed. He then went on to explain how he heard somebody else enter the room and how he awoke a few days later paralysed from the waist down."

"That's sick!" said the Chairman. "The evil bastards. Did he ever find out who the mystery man was?"

"Not as far as I know," said Spendlove.

"Who do *you* think it was?" said the Chairman. "Who do *you* think entered the room and made the incision Mr Spendlove? Do you suspect it was the Colonel?"

"I did at first," said Spendlove. "He seemed to be the obvious suspect. But then I thought about it for while and came to the conclusion that it must have been somebody with considerable surgical prowess. Somebody capable of maiming the old boy while ensuring they didn't kill him outright."

"Wouldn't that have been easier?" said the Chairman. "Wouldn't it have been easier for the Colonel to have the Major silenced for good and claim he'd died of old age or something?"

"I've no doubt it would have," said Spendlove. "But the Colonel genuinely loves and respects the old boy."

"Loves and respects him!" said the Chairman.

"He's his best friend," said Spendlove. "They've been through so much together. It's a common known fact, the Major saved the Colonel's life on at least three occasions. His life wouldn't be worth living without old Major Howser in it."

"I see," said the Chairman. "But how does that relate to your situation?"

"It relates perfectly," said Spendlove. "Because, before I was operated on, I'd argued night and day with the Colonel just like the Major had. I'd seen things going on here that just weren't right. Not necessarily regarding Tilly, but with other unfortunate inmates. I'd seen that mad bastard Colonel use some of the inmates to pull pony carts full of logs from one end of the garden to the other on a baking hot Summer's day. Make no mistake Mr Hulme-Albert and the Ukrainians and one or two other dubious characters, carried out most of the atrocities but the ideas were all of the Colonel's making.

[771]

And just like the Major did before he lost the use of his legs, I made the mistake of warning that old bastard that if he didn't put things right, I'd contact the national press to expose his vile misdemeanours."

"Do you ever regret making that threat?" said the Chairman.

"Only every second of every day," said Spendlove. "As I said before, the Major tried to save your life Mr Hulme. Trust me-he's a very good man."

"I realise that now," said the Chairman. "Bloody hell!, Mr Spendlove. He actually guided me towards you."

"There you are then," said Spendlove. "You're safe."

"Am I really?" said the Chairman.

"Of course you are," said Spendlove. "Why do I sense doubt Mr Hulme?"

"Because something's just not right," said the Chairman.

"Like what?" said Spendlove.

"Lots of things," said the Chairman before rising, snatching the hot kettle and slowly making his way to the door. "For instance-where are your old friends and colleagues Mr Spendlove? And more importantly-why in 25 years, have none of your visitors exposed this place for the medieval torture chamber it really is?"

"My friends and colleagues don't know I'm here," said Spendlove.

"What!" said the Chairman.

"I faked my death Mr Hulme," said Spendlove.

"You did what?" said the Chairman.

"I faked my suicide and Tilly's associated death," said Spendlove.

"Fucking hell-you are mad aren't you?" said the Chairman.

"I was utterly disillusioned," said Spendlove. "Nothing I'd tried had worked. I decided to shut myself off from the rest of the world. Mr Hulme-I want you to consider this. For the last few months while I was still residing at my beautiful Cheshire home, I'd been inundated with visitors. Make no mistake, a few of them had been genuinely concerned about Tilly's mental state and the affect it was having on me. But the vast majority of them had only called to see a freak show. They'd called to see the remarkable young woman who had somehow turned into a cat. Tilly had become like a circus sideshow. We were only short of a couple of clowns, a trapeze artist and a ringmaster. That's one of the reasons I chose this old place. It's out of the way, it's in the middle of nowhere and consequently nobody ever bothers me or her. You can lose yourself here Mr Hulme."

"I've no doubt about it," said the Chairman before returning the kettle to its rightful place and settling back down. "You'll have to forgive my rude outburst, Mr Spendlove. My nerves are shot. I'm very close to losing my mind completely."

"That's perfectly understandable under the circumstances," said Spendlove. "So why don't you allow me to reprogram you Mr Hulme."

"Meaning what?" said the Chairman.

"Let me get you into a more positive frame of mind," said Spendlove.

"The only way you're going to do that is to give me one or two examples of people who've managed to escape from here," said the Chairman.

"I'm afraid I can't do that," said Spendlove.

"Why not?" said the Chairman.

"Because nobody's ever returned to boast about their successful escape," said Spendlove.

"Of course," ," said the Chairman. "Alright then-how many do you think have tried? Or more importantly, how many people have you tried to help?"

"Off the record?" said Spendlove.

"Absolutely," replied the Chairman.

"A considerable amount," said Spendlove after a short period where he had stared deeply into his highly agitated visitor's eye."

"What does 'a considerable amount' equate to?" said the Chairman after taking a deep breath.

"You don't want to know," said Spendlove.

"I do want to know," said the Chairman. "It's in my

bloody interest to know. How many people have you helped escape from here Mr Spendlove. You don't have to be accurate. Just give me a rough estimate."

"Between eighty and a hundred," said Spendlove. "I can't be any more accurate than that."

"Between eighty and a hundred!" said the mortified Chairman.

"About that," said Spendlove

"Jesus Christ!" said the Chairman while running his fingers through his hair. "And you definitely have no any idea how many have been able to make it out successfully?"

"The Colonel claims it's zero," said Spendlove. "He never gets tired of boasting that alarming and remarkable statistic. "

"Do you believe him?" said the Chairman.

"I do his books," said Spendlove. "When the escapees are recaptured, they're recorded as new inmates and given serial numbers. But don't forget Mr Hulme-between eighty and a hundred might seem a lot, but those break outs took place over a 20 year period."

"It's still not the answer I was desperately hoping for!" said the Chairman. "In fact it's devastating news. Oh Jesus Christ! I'm going to die here. I'm going to die in a dingy cell. I'm never going to see my wife and kids again."

"Calm down," said Spendlove.

"I won't calm down," said the Chairman after rising to his feet. "I can't bloody well calm down. I told you before-I'm not the heroic type. I'm going to have to find a phone and ring the police. You're going to have to scan your memory banks and direct me to the phone Mr Spendlove. I've seen the cable running along the upstairs corridors. Where is it Mr Spendlove? Where does the Colonel keep his phone?"

"There is no phone," said Spendlove.

"What!" said the Chairman.

"There hasn't been a phone here for a long time. said Spendlove. " But I *can* offer you something Mr Hulme. I can offer you something I've never been able to offer the other escapees."

"What's that, a helicopter?" said the Chairman.

"A guaranteed way out of here and a free run to the boundary wall," said Spendlove.

"A free run!" said the Chairman. "Bloody hell Mr Spendlove. 50 or so people have died or have been recaptured during that supposed 'free run' to the boundary wall."

"I know that," said Spendlove. "But you're forgetting something Mr Hulme."

"Forgetting what?" said the Chairman while dabbing his eyes with his sleeve.

"You're forgetting the fact your mate Tommy has paved the way for you," said Spendlove.

"My friend Tommy's dead," said the Chairman.

"I know that-but don't forget-before he passed on, he managed to kill Bimoko," said Spendlove. "And Bimoko would have represented your greatest obstacle in your pursuit of freedom. Very little ever got past Bimoko. That's one of the reasons the Colonel worshipped him so much. Nothing phased Bimoko, not even fire. The other baboons can be fended off if necessary."

"Fended off with what?" said the Chairman. "Have you got a machine gun?"

"I can do better than that," said Spendlove. "I can provide you with fireworks."

"Fireworks!" said the Chairman.

The Colonel always demands a firework display to let the New Year in," said Spendlove. "He stores them somewhere along this corridor. The baboons are terrified of them. They'll run a mile at the sight of a Roman Candle or the sound of a Banger going off. How does that sound Mr Hulme?"

"It'd sound a lot better if you were coming with me," said the Chairman.

"I can't Mr Hulme," said Spendlove. "These legs wouldn't cope in the snow."

"Why not?" said the Chairman.

"They're made of papier-mâché, reinforced with wire," said Spendlove. "They'll go to mush in the wet and cold. There *was* an old wheelchair knocking around but it seems to have gone missing."

"For God's sake," said the Chairman. "That bastard Colonel thinks of everything. Made of paper hey-bloody hell! That's what Miss Havisham must have meant when she said she was worried about you catching fire."

"It sounds like you're beginning to think coherently again," said Spendlove.

"I sincerely hope so," said the Chairman. "Which way do you suggest I go after leaving these grounds?"

"That's better," said Spendlove. "I'll draw you a map. I suggest you leave via the main drains. You'll surface half way up the garden on an avenue flanked by a number of Chinese warrior statues."

"I've seen them," said the Chairman. "I've actually walked along that avenue. I failed to find it the second time though."

"That's because the garden's cleverly designed to confuse anyone unwelcome or unfamiliar," said Spendlove. "If you follow your instincts like any normal human being, you can find yourself lost in those grounds forever. The secret to escaping these gardens is to defy your instincts and not be governed by them."

"I actually worked that out shortly after arriving here," said the Chairman. "That seems an awful long time ago now. I think I've aged thirty years since then. Are you sure you don't want to give it a go Mr Spendlove? Maybe we can do something to reinforce or protect those legs of yours."

"I'm absolutely sure," said Spendlove after recovering a thick, brown, leather bound book from the top drawer of his desk and pressing it into the hand of his visitor. "Just make sure a member of the national press gets this."

"Great Expectations?" said the slightly bewildered Chairman.

"That's subterfuge," said Spendlove. "That's only the

cover. Inside, you'll find a list of all the atrocities I've
witnessed and catalogued since I've been in residence
here. It's also proof of my absolute faith in you."
"What do you mean?" said the Chairman.
"You're the only person I've ever trusted with that
highly damaging information Mr Hulme," said
Spendlove.
"Why's that?" said the Chairman.
"Because you're the only person I've ever fully believed
can make it out of here," said Spendlove. "I know you
can do it Mr Hulme. For God's sake, get that book to
the press. Do it for your friend Tommy if not for me.
Get this awful place shut down as soon as you can."
"And do you think this little book will do the trick?" said
the Chairman.
"Not necessarily in itself," said Spendlove. "That's
why I'd like you to do something else for me, if you
don't mind."
"What's that?" said the Chairman.
"I want you to wheel me to where the body of young
Casper is," said Spendlove.
"What for?" said the Chairman.
"I want you to take a lock of the young lad's hair and
bag it," said Spendlove. "His DNA can be identified
with that. That should be enough to convince the
authorities to open up a fresh investigation. We'll pick
up the fireworks on the way."
"Do you know how long the lad's been dead?" said the
Chairman.
"Not really," said Spendlove. "I know it was some time
before I arrived here with Tilly."
"What about madam next door," said the Chairman.
"Do you think she'd like to get out of here?"
"I'd rather you not ask Mr Hulme," said Spendlove.
"My good neighbour's pretty much all I've got now."
"Of course," said the Chairman. "Forgive me Mr
Spendlove. That was very insensitive of me. You two
must keep each other sane. Does *she* ever go out?"
"Quite frequently," said Spendlove. "She went out the

[777]

other night as it happens. She sometimes goes for long walks with Albert during the early hours. They get all wrapped up in their furs and off they go like daddy and baby Sasquatch. God knows where they went this time. She brought me back that razor the last time she ventured out."

"This one here?" said the rapidly paling Chairman while heading over to the mantelpiece.

"You can have it if you want it," said Spendlove.

"With the greatest respect Mr Spendlove-it's not yours to give," said the Chairman.

"I beg your pardon!" said Spendlove.

"It's mine," said the Chairman almost apologetically before placing his right hand over his mouth.

"Yours!" said Spendlove.

"It's my travelling razor," said the Chairman. "The wife bought it for me last Christmas."

"Oh dear!" said Spendlove. "I am sorry Mr Hulme. How embarrassing. She must have found it upstairs and snaffled it."

"I never brought it with me," said the trembling Chairman. "Oh Jesus Christ, Mr Spendlove....she and Albert must have somehow managed to board our train."

CHAPTER TWENTY NINE
THE BANDICOOT

The discovery of the razor and more importantly, the potentially disastrous implications of that discovery had affected the Chairman to such an extent that from the moment he had left Gabriel Spendlove's room until the precise time he arrived at the cell where the remains of young Casper were said to be lying, he had not uttered an audible word, not even when he was helping his equally subdued conspirator out of the laundry basket which for about 300 yards and seventeen minutes had been his peculiar conveyance. It was ironic therefore, that the first thing uttered after the ultra cautious Spendlove had tentatively teased open the cell door with the fingertips of his right hand, was a muted request for silence.

"What's the matter?" whispered the Chairman.

"We're going to have to keep our voices down," whispered Spendlove while pointing to a cobweb covered black enamelled air vent cover which was located on the opposite wall about shoulder height.

"Why's that?" whispered the Chairman. "I thought you were allowed the freedom to move around this place."

"I am," whispered Spendlove after putting his right ear as close as possible to the grating and urging the Chairman to join him. "But I'm not allowed to come this far. This area's out of bounds for the likes of me and my neighbours."

"What's the old onion sack for?" whispered the Chairman.

"I'm going to gather the poor lad's remains," whispered Spendlove. "I'm going to get my neighbour to give him a decent burial. Unless you want to do it Mr Hulme."

"I don't, to be brutally honest Mr Spendlove," whispered the Chairman. "But I will, nevertheless."

"That's very decent of you," whispered Spendlove before placing his right index finger across his lips. "Listen.....somebody's just entered the dining room above us."

"Bloody hell!" whispered the Chairman. "That is clear."

"I know," whispered Spendlove. "So keep your voice down Mr Hulme, and whatever you do, don't talk directly into the vent."

"It's as if they're standing right next to us," whispered the Chairman.

"I know," whispered Spendlove while slowly easing himself to the ground. "So imagine what it must have been like for the Major when his son was pleading for mercy. The poor man must have heard every blow."

"And every splintering bone," whispered the Chairman.

"Hang on a minute Mr Spendlove....can you stop what you're doing for a second please. That voice sounds familiar."

"That's the Major," whispered Spendlove. "He's having one of his regular coughing fits."

"Not that one," whispered the Chairman. "Wait a second...Wait a second....That one. The slightly higher pitched voice of the two. There it is now. He's just mentioned something about brandy. He's just said, 'bottoms up'."

"That's the Colonel's oddball cousin," whispered Spendlove.

"Cousin!" whispered the Chairman.

"That's his cousin Seymour," whispered Spendlove. "Didn't you know the Colonel had living family?"

"He never mentioned any to me," whispered the Chairman.

"Why would he?" whispered Spendlove. "It's not as if you and he were long lost buddies."

"He told me just about everything else regarding his life," whispered the Chairman.

"I very much doubt it Mr Hulme," whispered Spendlove. "He'd have only told you certain carefully chosen and favourable segments. It's the Colonel's cousin, I'm telling you. Who did you think it was?"

"It sounded a bit like this quirky old gentleman who was

on our train," whispered the Chairman while helping his companion back to his feet.

"Was he a member of your club?" said Spendlove.

"No-he was just a train spotter who'd slipped and banged his head on our platform," whispered the Chairman. "We took care of him. He was awesome. He probably belongs in the genius category along with your neighbour. He did so much for us. Nothing was too much trouble for the old boy. I don't know what we'd have done without him to be honest. Anyway-whoever the Colonel's visitor is, he's certainly full of the Christmas spirit."

Within seconds however, and just as Gabriel Spendlove was beginning to tighten the drawstrings on his little sack, the atmosphere within the upstairs room changed dramatically and instead of contesting for a closer position to the air vent, both occupants of the cell found themselves wincing and backing away.

"What the hell!" whispered the Chairman.

"You bastard," yelled a wringing wet and shivering Brian Matthews before peeling off the first of his saturated socks and hurling it into the hearth. "You absolute monster of a man. Are you nice and warm beside that fire Professor? Are you comfortable enough?"

"More than enough, thank you very much " said the Professor. "Why don't you pour yourself a little drink and come and join me."

"I wouldn't drink with you if you were the last person on the planet," said Matthews. "You tried to murder me."

"I did nothing of the sort," said the Professor after breaking off from poking the fire. "What an audacious and malicious thing to say."

"It's the truth," said Matthews while continuing to peel off his dripping wet outer garments.

"You were pronounced dead by one of your committee members," said the Professor.

"That's a lie and you know it," said Matthews. "The only person on board that train, qualified to pronounce

[781]

people dead was you."

"That maybe so but I'd been relieved of all my duties by the time you were confirmed dead," said the Professor. "I'd been put out to pasture like a sick old mule."

"I don't believe that," said Matthews. "Those men were hanging on to every word you said. Some of them weren't prepared to take a painkiller without consulting you first. Whose idea was it to zip me into a suit bag and throw me over the side of the bridge Professor?"

"Mine," said the Professor.

"There you go," said Matthews.

"According to your friends, you were stone cold dead Brian," said the Professor. "You had to go somewhere. We'd tried to store bodies in the remote carriages before but they were attracting starving animals. You should actually be thanking me."

"Thanking you!" said Matthews.

"That's right," said the Professor. "That watertight suit bag probably saved your life."

"You hard faced bastard," said Matthews. "Do you realise the magnitude of what you've done Professor?"

"Pray tell me Brian-what exactly have I done?" said the Professor.

"You're responsible for the deaths of at least 4 of our club members," said Matthews.

"My word!" said the Professor while pretending to go weak at the knees. "I have been a busy boy haven't I. How exactly have you concluded that Brian? And don't forget-the ill fated trip was all your idea. You invited me along. It was you that had the gripe with all their family members."

"What gripe was this?" said the Major.

"Do you want to tell him Brian?" said the Professor. "Do you want to explain your long established grudge? Do you want to tell the Major how you'd been hounded out of your home by the fathers, nephews and cousins of the current members of your club? Do you want to explain what that was like for your mum and dad and how they'd eventually been forced to leave their home of

fifty years? And by the way Brian-don't you dare play
the role of innocent victim. It was you that concocted
the plan in the first place. It was you that wanted those
people punished."

"I know it was," said Matthews. "But you told me you
were just going to torment them and make them feel
uncomfortable."

"And that's exactly what I did," said the Professor. "It
wasn't me who locked that imbecile in the far carriage."

"I know it wasn't," said Matthews. "But it was you that
brought the engine to a halt. It was you that allowed
Alec Morris to take the blame for the train setting off
before it should have. It was you that made him the
most detested person on the train. It was you that
therefore got him beaten half to death. How did you stop
the train, by the way Professor? I ask you that because,
at the time the train came to a halt, you were at the rear
resting your injured head."

"I used a special computer console," said the Professor.
"It's the size of a cigarette case. I could have started and
stopped that train if I was sitting in a bar in Timbuktu.
It's an amazing thing. It can do just about anything."

"Can it bring people back to life?" said Matthews.

"Not as yet," said the Professor.

"It just helps kill them," said Matthews.

"Are you going to blame me for the murders in the mail
room?" said the Professor.

"I am yes," said Matthews. "Because if the train had
kept moving, no bear, wolf or psychopath would have
been able to board the fucking thing."

"A psychopath might have already been on board," said
the Professor. "Am I to blame for your alcoholic friend
Beedo's death?"

"His name was Biddo," said Matthews. "His name was
Kenny Biddo. He was a proud father of two and a
highly regarded electrician."

"Highly regarded electrician!" said the Professor.
"Don't make me laugh Brian. I heard he'd brought
down just about every company he'd ever worked for

including the likes of Rolls Royce and Marconi. He
didn't have anything to do with the iceberg early
warning system on the Titanic did he?"

"Of course not," said Matthews. "How old do you
think he was? And by the way Professor-Marconi and
Rolls Royce were already in a financial mess before
Biddo was taken on. He certainly didn't contribute to
their closure."

"You haven't answered my question Brian," said the
Professor. "Am I getting the blame for Beedo's death
too?"

"Absolutely," said Matthews. "You mightn't have shot
him and you mightn't have put a knife in his back, but
you as good as killed him. You created and nurtured an
atmosphere of terror, the poor bastard couldn't cope
within."

"That's outrageous," said the Professor. "The man
clearly had underlying mental health issues. He
shouldn't have been let out of his bed never mind
allowed to go on a 10 day stag affair. A stag affair, I
might add, with a load of reckless, incompetent morons
and where alcohol was in abundance and free to all and
sundry."

"He'd have been fine under normal circumstances," said
Matthews. "He'd have paced himself. He could hold
his drink as well as any man."

"He was seriously mentally disturbed," said the
Professor. "Bloody Nora Brian. He tried to set fire to
one of your fellow members."

"By Jove" said the Major.

"That was an accident," said Matthews. "That's already
been explained and you know it."

"Can you explain his homophobia and deep rooted
paranoia?" said the Professor. "Bloody hell Brian-some
of his accusations were farcical. He had to be locked up
for his own safety in the end. For Heaven's sake-his own
son chose to leave the train because of his increasingly
erratic behaviour. His son Brian! Even his own son had
lost patience with him."

"You need to wipe your face Brian," said the Major before wheeling himself over and handing Matthews his handkerchief. "You appear to have been the victim of an extremely cruel prank."

"I know all about my face Major," said Matthews. Apparently I'm meant to be a weasel. But do you know what I really am Major.....I'm a rat. I'm a two faced scheming, shithouse rat."

"You're a thoroughly good man," said the Major. "You're one of the most decent and honest people I know. You've done a hell of lot for these poor devils here. In fact, you and Spendlove have done more than anyone. Take Matilda as an example. You've done wonders with her."

"But she still thinks she's a cat," said Matthews.

"I know she does," said the Major. "But at least you've got her walking on two feet and using a conventional toilet again."

"I'm in trouble Major," said Matthews while fidgeting nervously with his top button. "I'm in very serious trouble. Oh God! What's Rose going to think? What are my kids going to think? What am I going to tell them?"

"Go home and talk to them," said the Major.

"I can't do that," said Matthews. "I can't do that Major. It would mean me bumping into the Altys and the Larkins and the Woodhouses. Jesus Christ! What have I done? "What was I thinking?"

"You were angry," said the Major. "You wanted some recompense for what you'd been put through. It's human nature to want some sort of payback Brian."

"I'm finished Major," said Matthews. "I can't ever return home now. I can't face those devastated families. I can't go home and continue as if nothing happened."

"Then stay here," said the Major. "Go and prepare a room next to Spendlove and the queer one. I'll get Albert to fetch you some decent furniture and carpet from one of the outhouses. You've seen the way those rooms can be made cosy. Settle here. We can resume

[785]

our chess series."

"I would Major," said Matthews. "I'd gladly move down there. But how would I sleep at night Major? How would I ever sleep properly again?"

"You could get yourself some sleeping tablets," said the Major. "I might even have some myself."

"That's the last thing I want Major," said Matthews. "I wouldn't want to sleep for fear of being paid a visit like you and Gabriel were. I can't imagine what it would be like to wake up without any legs. No Major...There's no alternative-I'm going to have to go to the police and admit everything."

"Are you sure that's wise?" said the Major.

"It's the decent thing to do under the circumstances," said Matthews. "Why don't you tell the Major about the disease Professor."

"The disease!" said the Major.

"He pretended there was a contagious disease on board the train," said Matthews.

"Really," said the Major.

"That wasn't actually planned," said the Professor. "That was just a by-product of the previous Chairman passing away."

"What did you do Seymour?" said the Major.

"I incubated the notion that the Chairman of the club, instead of dying from a massive heart attack, as was the case, had died through contracting a most despicable disease," said the Professor. "A highly contagious disease that would ultimately turn the sufferer insane through mortal dread. In fairness, it was a disease entirely of my own invention. I made most of the symptoms and ramifications up as I went along. It was remarkable. People would keep asking me questions about the condition and every time, I'd find myself responding with the worst possible scenario."

"And from that moment on, he played God," said Matthews.

"What do you mean?" said the Major.

"He pretended to have an antidote," said Matthews.

"An antidote for a disease that didn't exist?" said the Major.

"Genius wasn't it?" said the Professor. "But I have to wholeheartedly deny that accusation. I didn't tell them I had an antidote. I told them I had something that would significantly reduce their suffering until the disease passed."

"I see," said the Major. "And did it ease their concerns?"

"To a certain degree," said the Professor. "It definitely eased mine."

"What do you mean?" said the Major.

"The passengers had become volcanic," said the Professor. "They were ready to erupt at any time. They'd already as good as killed one decent man. A postman, I think they said he was. I was a stranger. I had no standing among those people. I was convinced I was next in line for the chop or the next to be consigned to the ice room. Pretending I had that medication proved to be a masterstroke. It was like having a suit of impregnable armour. Nobody would say 'boo' to me after that for fear of being denied the vital medication. I've never had so many friends. I've never had so much attention. I had people coming to my sleeping carriage offering me all sorts of inducements."

"I was never ill was I Professor?" said Matthews.

"Never for one minute," said the Professor. "You were just becoming a pain in the backside for me."

"That's because I thought you were going too far," said Matthews. "What did you do Professor? How did you manage to knock me out for that length of time?"

"I just kept dosing you up with Temazepam and something to unsettle your stomach," said the Professor. "I slipped your first dose into your night time drink after you'd plagued me to ease off for the best part of our second evening on board. I couldn't let you blow my cover. I'd have been lynched."

"I wouldn't have blown your cover," said Matthews. "That's not my way Professor. Are you going to do the

decent thing and admit your part in all that went on?"
"Is that what you'd like?" said the Professor.
"It would be the honourable thing to do," said
Matthews. "We could hand ourselves into the police
together."
"What if I wrote a letter addressed to the Chief
Constable of Merseyside admitting full responsibility
and exonerating you?" said the Professor. "I could get
the Major to witness it to give it more clout. Would that
satisfy you Brian?"
"Not really," said Matthews.
"Why not?" said the Professor.
"Because you're not solely to blame," said Matthews.
"I've got to shoulder at least some of the blame."
"Take his offer Brian and don't be so bloody pig
headed," said the Major. "Live out the rest of your life.
Have holidays with the wife. Play with your
grandchildren. For goodness sake-think about what
you've done for so many others."
"The Major's right Brian," said the Professor. "Let's be
honest-you were out of the game for so long while the
train was stranded. And for that reason alone, you've
got every right to be considered completely blameless."
"Don't ruin your life Brian," said the Major. "Just bury
your infamous pride for a short while. Will you please
do that Brian? I'm begging you as your long standing
friend."
"I don't want the Professor punished," said Matthews.
"We go back too far."
"I won't be punished," said the Professor. "By this time
tomorrow, I'll be on my way to South America never to
be seen on these old shores again."
"Is that a promise?" said Matthews.
"I've never promised anyone anything in my life," said
the Professor. "But because it's you and because I hold
you in such high regard, I'm prepared to tread new
ground. You've got my solemn oath Brian."
"Take the deal Brian," said the Major. "Take it for
goodness sake. And think about it this way. When you

get back to Merseyside, you're going to be the go to guy
as far as those unfortunate widows and young daughters
are concerned. You'll be able to make amends for some
of what went on. You'll be able to help them cope with
their grief."
"That's a very good point," said the Professor.
"Alright," said Matthews. "I'll go along with what
you've just suggested Seymour. But only as long as I
can have a signed and witnessed copy of your
admission."
"You can have as many copies as you like ,old boy,"
said the Professor. "But I also have one very important
stipulation."
"What's that?" said Matthews.
"I want to be the one who tells Maurice and I want to be
the one who breaks the news to my boys when they
eventually arrive," said the Professor.
"Break the news about what?" said the preoccupied
Colonel while making his way into the room with a
recently assembled rifle under his right armpit. "Can
someone help me here. I think I've dropped a shell."
"I think there's one by the middle leg of the table," said
the Major. "Not far from your left foot."
"I need to talk to you Colonel," said the Professor after
leaving his chair and taking his cousin by the shoulders.
"About what old boy?" said the Colonel while
continuing to search around his feet for the missing
bullet.
"I've got a confession to make," said the Professor.
"A confession!" said the Colonel.
"I've done a very bad thing Maurice," said the teary
eyed Professor.
"Haven't we all," said the Colonel.
"This was a heinous act of betrayal," said the Professor.
"How heinous?" said the Colonel.
"I've brought trouble to your home," said the Professor.
"Trouble in the form of what exactly?" said the Colonel.
"In the form of this grotesque creature here," said the
Professor before slowly stepping aside and pointing at

[789]

the unsuspecting Matthews. "I'm afraid I've unwittingly brought the Indian mystic's curse upon you."

"God's holy trousers!" said the Colonel. "Upon my soul! Is that what I think it is?"

"It's me Colonel," pleaded the almost dumfounded and open armed Matthews.

"Answer me Seymour-is that what I think it is?" said the Colonel.

"It's the giant bandicoot of Hindustani legend," said the Professor. "Oh dear God! Can you ever forgive me Maurice?"

"Don't listen to him Colonel," pleaded Matthews. "Look at me closely. It's me. I'm your friend Brian. I counsel some of your mental patients. My face has been painted to make me look like a rodent. I do a lot of work here for you."

"The Indian mystic must have been bang on the ball," said the Professor. "If I remember right, he told you the giant bandicoot would visit you in the guise of someone familiar."

"That's right," said the Colonel. "That's exactly what he told me."

"It's nonsense," pleaded Matthews. "I'm not a monstrous rat-I'm a human being. For goodness sake, it's me Colonel."

"Don't listen to it Colonel," said the frantic Professor before snatching a candlestick from the top of the piano. "It's trying to get into your head. It's trying to possess your mind. Save yourself Maurice. Make a run for it and I'll do what I can to stall the horrible thing."

"I've never run away from a scrap in my life," said the Colonel before raising his rifle and firing two successive shells into Brian Matthews's bewildered face. "There you go gentlemen. That's how you deal with the giant bandicoot of Hindustani legend. Now then-who's going to pour me a celebration brandy?"

"Oh my God!" whispered the Chairman while sliding down the wall of the abandoned cell with his hands over his eyes. "Oh mother of God!"

[790]

"Come on," whispered Spendlove. "We can't stay here.
We need to get out of here and we need to get out of
here fast."

"I'm not sure I'm going to be able to move my legs,"
whispered the Chairman.

"You will and you must," whispered the ashen faced
Spendlove. "You're just in the first stage of shock."

"I can't move," said the Chairman.

"You can move," said Spendlove. "Now for God's sake
pull yourself together and get me back to my bloody
room."

"Alright," whispered the Chairman while gingerly
climbing back to his feet with the aid of the wall. "Take
it easy fella."

"I'll start taking it easy when I'm back in my bloody
room," whispered Spendlove.

"Alright," whispered the Chairman. "I'm on my way.
Are you alright Gabriel?"

"I'm fine now you're back on your feet," whispered
Spendlove.

"You're not fine at all," whispered the Chairman. "I've
just heard you swear for the first time and you've
suddenly lost the ability to look me straight in the eyes.
What's the matter Gabriel?"

"Nothing," whispered Spendlove. "It's just that
distressing incident in the dining room. It's shaken me
up badly."

"I'd have thought you'd seen or heard far worse than
that over the years," whispered the Chairman.

"Something's the matter isn't it Gabriel? What is it?
What's turned your face grey and got you trembling all
of a sudden? Answer me or you'll end up stranded here
like poor Casper. What the hell's the matter Mr
Spendlove?"

"The Professor's boys are on their way," whispered
Spendlove while peering along the corridor.

"His boys!" whispered the Chairman. "Where have
they suddenly popped up from?"

"They've been working here on and off for some years

Mr Hulme," whispered Spendlove.

"Are they his sons?" whispered the Chairman.

"They're his henchmen," whispered Spendlove.

"Why haven't you mentioned them before?" whispered the Chairman.

"I thought I had," whispered Spendlove after hoisting his little sack over his shoulder. "Although I might have referred to them somewhat differently."

"What do you mean?" whispered the Chairman.

"I might have referred to them as the Ukrainians," whispered Spendlove. "They consider an unlocked cell door a legitimate reason to trash, kill or maim. Now, do you understand my urgency and sudden change in demeanour Mr Hulme?"

There was no doubt that at the moment he shook Gabriel Spendlove's silky smooth hand and took possession of an old bicycle lamp and a canvass bag stuffed with the remains of Casper, a clump of Roman Candles, a travel blanket and a small amount of provisions, the Chairman had been hell bent on one thing-to get into the main drain as quickly as possible and make his escape without ever looking back. And that had still been his sole intention had it not been for him suddenly tripping on a loose cobble in the area adjacent to the basement stairway. That had been his one and only aim until he found himself staring at the macabre silhouette that was the slowly decomposing body of the recently mutilated Tommy Mac.

That stumble had not just caused him considerable pain and cost him valuable minutes, it had given him time to evaluate his situation from a responsibility and ethical perspective. As he sat gently massaging his rapidly swelling left knee, he began to look back at certain episodes which had shaped and defined his and his fellow member's ill fated journey. For example, the look of bewilderment on his missing best friend's face at the precise moment the train moved off unexpectedly. The look of dread on his brother in law Alec Morris's face at the moment of his arrest. The look on the heartbroken Blackie's face after he had announced the passing of his deeply troubled but much loved uncle, Kenny Biddo. The look of incredulity on his brother's face after he had returned to the dining carriage after visiting the blood and guts spattered mail room. None of those faces however evocative, had affected him like the face he was now flashing his torch upon. A face carved into a large, scooped out pumpkin. It just didn't seem fair. It just didn't seem fair to the Chairman that some callous, unfeeling monster, had thought it acceptable to replace the head of the bravest man he had ever known, with an overgrown vegetable. It wasn't right. It just wasn't right. It was outrageous and disrespectful. And that is why, instead of continuing on as advised by the well meaning Gabriel Spendlove, the Chairman had instead, dusted himself down, taken a couple of deep breaths and made his way sideways in the direction of the very place where Brian Matthews had so recently been murdered and where trouble was almost inevitable. However, instead of being greeted by a blood drenched crime scene as he had expected, the room was sanitised, the atmosphere within that room was chilled and there was nothing to suggest anything untoward had recently taken place.

"Look what Matilda's dragged in Major," said the Professor before returning his gaze to the roaring fire. "She hasn't bitten you has she Mr Hulme?"

"Why would you think that?" said the Chairman before snatching an empty wine bottle, breaking it against the edge of the table and heading towards the hearth.

"Because you're limping dear boy," said the Professor. "I'd keep an eye on that if I was you. If that flea riddled thing has bitten you, you could quite conceivably end up losing a limb."

"I fell," said the Chairman.

"You need to be more careful," said the Professor. "You're not getting any younger you know Mr Hulme."

"I'm just becoming more bitter like the rest of you," said the Chairman. "Are you satisfied now Professor?"

"Satisfied!" said the Professor. "What do you mean?"

"Have you achieved everything you set out to achieve?" said the Chairman.

"I've no idea what you're talking about," said the Professor.

"You've been a naughty boy Professor," said the Chairman.

"I realise that," said the Professor before placing his brandy glass on the floor and slipping his hand inside his jacket. "How much do I owe you?"

"What are you talking about?" said the Chairman.

"What do I owe you Mr Hulme?" said the Professor. "What do I owe you for the train ticket? And by the way-I'm not paying for the return leg of the journey."

"Is that why you think I'm here Professor?" said the Chairman. "Do you think I'm here to recover your lousy ticket money?"

"I can't think of any other reason," said the Professor.

"I can think of plenty," said the Chairman. "Why did you do it Professor?"

"Do what old bean?" said the Professor.

"Why did you kill my men?" said the Chairman.

"Your men!" scoffed the Professor.

"Alright-why did you murder my fellow members?" said the Chairman.

"I haven't murdered anybody," said the Professor.

"Well, let's put it another way shall we," said the Chairman. "How many deaths were you responsible for while you were on board that train?"

"None whatsoever," said the Professor.

"Bullshit!" said the Chairman.

"It's the truth," said the Professor. "But I suppose you could mark me up for one if you want to be pedantic and petty minded."

"What do you mean?" said the Chairman.

"I watched one of your men fall to his death and did nothing to help him," said the Professor.

"Jesus Christ!" said the Chairman while shaking his head.

"That's what he was yelling," said the Professor.

"Who was it?" said the Chairman. "Was it Tony Biddo by any chance?"

"It was your highly efficient Health and Safety Officer," said the Professor.

"Eddie Meehan?" said the Chairman.

"I assume so," said the Professor. "We were never formerly introduced."

"What happened?" said the Chairman.

"He slipped and fell over the side of the bridge," said the Professor.

"Slipped?" said the Chairman.

"That's right," said the Professor. "Do you doubt me?"

"I most certainly do," said the Chairman. "It's Eddie Meehan we're talking about here Professor. Eddie Meehan didn't have accidents...Eddie Meehan prevented them. You'd argued with him hadn't you Professor?"

"You're a lot more astute than you were ever given credit for Mr Hulme," said the Professor.

"Answer the question Professor," said the Chairman. "You'd argued with Eddie hadn't you?"

"We'd disagreed on certain technical points," said the Professor.

"I bet you had," said the Chairman. "I reckon he'd worked you out."

"Nonsense," said the Professor. "He hadn't worked me out at all. Nobody's ever been able to get inside my head Mr Hulme."

"Maybe not, but I reckon he'd worked the train out," said the Chairman. "He'd discovered the train could still run hadn't he Professor? And I reckon he discovered that very early. I know that because he went missing very early. He almost scuppered your plans to cause mayhem didn't he Professor? That's why you didn't help him."

"I didn't help him because I might have fallen myself," said the Professor. "There's no law that compels a man to help someone who's dying."

"There's a moral duty," said the Chairman. "I couldn't have just stood by and watched a man die. For that matter, I couldn't have stood by and watched my worst enemy die."

"Good for you," said the Professor. "If I had a lollipop right now, I'd give it to you and pat you on the head for being a good boy."

"You sarcastic bastard," said the Chairman. "Was it you that was persistently opening the train doors?"

"The place needed airing," said the Professor. "It stunk like a badly managed abattoir at one time."

"Then why didn't you just open the carriage windows?" said the Chairman. "Can't you see what you did Professor-by leaving those doors open, you invited anything wild, hungry and inquisitive to climb on board the train. You mightn't have butchered Alty and Larkin Professor, but you played a major role in their deaths. Do you want to explain how you stopped the train?"

"The same way I started it," said the Professor. "With a simple computer console. I helped build that train Mr Hulme. I invested quite a sum in it. Me and my cousin Maurice love trains. I'll have to show you our photograph albums some time. I reckon we've got the largest collection of railway-related prints in the country."

"I think I came across one of your albums while taking shelter in one of the garden sheds," said the Chairman. "Was that before you killed Bimoko?" said the Professor.

"I didn't kill him," said the Chairman. "But I've got to be honest-I probably could have done a bit more to save him. But let's get back to the subject of photography Professor."

"Yes, let's do that," said the Professor. "Did you happen to see my collection of prints up to and including the Mallard's 1938 world record breaking run at Stoke Bank?"

"I didn't actually," said the Chairman. "But I did see a

particularly evocative image that still makes me shudder."

"Which one was that?" said the increasingly interested Professor while moving to the edge of his seat. "Was it taken pre war or some point after the war?"

"I think it was taken some time during the war," said the Chairman. "It depicts a terrified old lady being abused by a large group of Nazi guards."

"That must have been taken in Southern Poland," said the Professor. "The train was probably the Deutsche Reichsbahn's Class 52. It was, now I come to think of it. I remember taking that photograph now. That hysterical old cow just wouldn't stay out of the frame."

"Hysterical old cow!" said the Chairman. "She was probably on her way to the gas chamber. Her husband was probably lying face down in a ditch with a bullet in the back of his head. You're one heartless bastard Professor.

"I'm heartless!" said the Professor. "What about that tragic young lad."

"What tragic young lad?" said the Chairman.

"The son of the drunken father," said the Professor.

"Young Anthony," said the Chairman. "What about him?"

"You as good as killed him," said the Professor. "What a ridiculous thing to do Mr Hulme. Of all the idiotic, reckless things to do! There was nothing of that lad. How do you suppose he was going to survive outside in weather like that? Did you see the clothes he had on? The poor boy was already shivering before he set off."

"He volunteered to go," said the Chairman. "He actually insisted on going. And he only went because he'd had enough of the shenanigans that were going on inside the train. The train, I might add, that you stopped for your own amusement. Do you realise-if he's never seen again, it'll be your fault?"

"Do you realise I don't give a hoot?" said the Professor.

"You're completely and utterly insane aren't you Professor?" said the Chairman.

[797]

"Funnily enough, that's the conclusion my new
therapist arrived at towards the end of my first session."
said the Professor. "And we'd only exchanged names,
established my level of stress and discussed my many
demons."

"You should have shown her the photo of the terrified
old lady outside Auschwitz," said the Chairman. "And
of course, pointed out the inappropriate caption
underneath. That might have saved her a lot of time and
effort."

"I didn't think of that," said the Professor. "I did tell
her about my long held fascination with steam trains
though. We talked a lot about that."

"Was that because she liked choo choo trains like you?"
said the Chairman.

"It was because she was appalled, as it happens," said
the Professor. "Or maybe not appalled-let's say, she was
fascinated."

"Why was that?" said the Chairman.

"Because she said that, after what I'd been through, I
should hate trains and all they stood for," said the
Professor.

"Why's that?" said the Chairman. "Had you been
thrown from one or something?"

"My mother was crushed to death to make way for one,"
said the Professor.

"Really!" said the Chairman. "How did that happen?"

"She'd been bed ridden Mr Hulme," said the Professor.
"My father had passed away a couple of years earlier
from tuberculosis, and my two older brothers had
decided to go off to join the Communists somewhere in
Eastern Europe. That left me as the man of the house at
the tender age of 14. That meant I had to feed, wash and
change my diseased and incapacitated mother."

"What was wrong with her?" said the Chairman.

"She had some form of cancer," said the Professor.

"Do you mean to say you don't know exactly what form
of cancer your mother had?" said the Chairman.

"I wasn't really interested," said the Professor. "I don't

mind admitting it-I resented her being ill. I hated her for being ill. None of my neighbour's mothers were ill. I used to watch the other boys playing football and cricket from my bedroom window. I used to mentally hit and kick every ball."

"Why didn't you just sneak out and join them for half an hour like any normal boy would have done?" said the Chairman.

"I wouldn't have been welcome," said the Professor.

"Why's that?" said the Chairman.

"I was universally despised," said the Professor.

"Why?" said the Chairman.

"I electrocuted the school hamster during a science experiment when I was 9," said the Professor.

"Fucking hell!" said the Chairman. "Why, for Christ's sake? Why kill an innocent little creature?"

"It was an accident Mr Hulme," said the Professor. "All the other boys had been content to administer electric shocks to dead frogs. That wasn't enough for me. I wanted to experiment on something living and breathing."

"Such as the hamster," said the Chairman.

"That's right," said the Professor. "Our Science teacher had been off sick that day, so we had our history teacher covering two classrooms. It enabled me to remove the hamster and test it."

"What do you mean, 'test it'?" said the Chairman.

"I wanted to see what level of electric shock it could take," said the Professor. "I thought it had died several times before it actually did. But it kept coming back to life. I loved that. I did a similar thing with my mother Mr Hulme."

"You administered electric shocks to her?" said the Chairman.

"I fed her chicken broth," said the Professor. "I sometimes found her choking while I was feeding her chicken broth. She had this repulsive habit of nearly choking on chicken broth."

"Why feed it to her then?" said the Chairman.

[799]

"Because I enjoyed watching her choke," said the Professor. "I enjoyed watching her writhe and turn purple. I enjoyed watching her back arch like a cornered stray cat. It was great. That used to be the highlight of my day. She'd turn the colour of ripe beetroot and howl like a dog. The incontinence was the lowlight. I hated that. I sometimes found myself up to my elbow in her disgusting excrement. I hated having to change her. I'd scrub myself for hours to get rid of the stench and stains."

"I imagine she changed your dirty arse when you were a baby," said the Chairman.

"I've no doubt she did," said the Professor. "But I hadn't been blessed with the maternal instinct. I was a boy. I wasn't cut out to do something like that. And then one day-one beautiful rainy and windswept day-one glorious life changing November day-my prayers were finally answered."

"Had the poor woman passed away?" said the Chairman.

"It wasn't that good a day Mr Hulme," said the Professor. "We received a letter from a railway company informing us they had bought the right to lay tracks across our property. We were given 3 months and a certain amount of money to seek alternative accommodation."

"What's so good about that?" said the Chairman. "That would have meant disrupting your poor mum while she was in pain. Did she protest or apply for a stay of execution?"

"I didn't tell her," said the Professor.

"Didn't tell her!" said the Chairman.

"I didn't see the point," said the Professor. "She was a virtual vegetable by then. She couldn't construct a cohesive sentence."

"She was still entitled to have a say in affairs," said the Chairman. "She must have been able to nod or shake her head."

"She was as it happens," said the Professor. "She was

actually quite good at nodding. But I still opted not to tell her."

"What happened?" said the Chairman.

For the first time since the Chairman had entered the room, the Professor rose from his armchair and after giving the fire a quick poke, he moved to the dining table, poured himself a large drink and took a seat directly opposite his accuser

"Mr Hulme, did you ever get excited about the prospect of Christmas?" he asked while meticulously flattening the creases in his trousers.

"I still do," said the Chairman. "Why do you ask?"

"Because, as a child, I never experienced that sort of excitement," said the Professor. "I never received any presents as a child. What I know about Christmas, Santa Claus and presents and good will to all men, I've read in books or magazines. I can therefore only imagine what that Christmas Eve feeling of excitement and anticipation is like. Tell me what it was like Mr Hulme."

"It was great," said the Chairman. "It was the best time of the year. It was almost impossible to get to sleep."

"What was your sense of anticipation like?" said the Professor.

"Incredible," said the Chairman. "But what's this got to do with you Professor?"

"Quite a lot, I believe," said the Professor. "I think I experienced something like that level of excitement the night before the bulldozers were due to arrive at our old house."

"You hated your house that much did you?" said the Chairman.

"I despised it," said the Professor. "I was desperate to see it raised to the ground."

"You didn't allow your mother to see that did you?" said the Chairman.

"Of course not," said the Professor. "I tried to keep everything hush hush. I didn't even tell her nurse."

"What nurse was this?" said the Chairman.

[801]

"A local District nurse," said the Professor. "She'd
been designated the task of driving my mother to a half
way house not far from where we lived. She was to
come back for me later that day."
"That makes sense," said the Chairman. "How did the
demolition go? Was it all you'd ever dreamed about?"
"It was much better than that," said the Professor.
"How long had your mother lived there?" said the
Chairman.
"Over forty years," said the Professor. "It had belonged
to her mother before that."
"Bloody hell," said the Chairman. "God love the poor
woman. It's a blessing she didn't see it come down
then."
"She did see it come down," said the Professor.
"She what!" said the Chairman. "You didn't let her
stand by and watch that sorry spectacle did you
Professor?"
"Of course not," said the Professor. "I gave her the best
seat in the house."
"What do you mean?" said the Chairman.
"Mother was still inside the place," said the Professor.
"She was what!" said the Chairman.
"Shc was still in it," said the Professor.
"Still in it!" said the Chairman. "I don't understand.
Why would she still be in it? How's that possible
Professor? Surely the demolition team checked your
home before they began work."
"I told them the house was empty," said the Professor.
"Empty!" said the Chairman. "And they swallowed that
did they?"
"After I'd told them my mother had died from a new and
deadly strain of Smallpox, they did" said the Professor.
"They ran like a disturbed army of ants after I'd told
them that. Then I sat back on a nearby tor with a ham
and pickle sandwich and watched an enormous red
bulldozer marked S T R C, level our family home in the
time it usually takes to soft boil a medium size egg."
"Fucking hell!" said the Chairman. "I don't know what

[802]

to say. I really don't know what to say. That's got to be
the sickest thing I've ever heard. I'm just glad your
mother was virtually unconscious at the time."
"She wasn't unconscious Mr Hulme," said the
Professor. "She was wide awake. She must have come
to after the bulldozer's first shove. My last
remembrance was of her hammering on her bedroom
window with this look of abject terror on her face. Your
Health and Safety Officer had a very similar look on his
face seconds before he plummeted to his death."
"Oh, for the love of God!" said the Chairman. "Oh, for
the love of God! That's unreal. That's almost beyond
belief. You absolute nutcase. You complete and utter
nutcase. Please tell me you served a considerable
amount of time in prison."
"I didn't serve a day in prison Mr Hulme," said the
Professor. "I was awarded £2,000,000 in punitive
damages."
"What!" said the Chairman.
"My wealthy uncle sued the railway company for
negligence," said the Professor."That doesn't make any
sense," said the Chairman. "It wasn't their fault. You'd
told them the place was empty."
"I know I did," said the Professor. "And I admitted I
did. But I was a minor at the time Mr Hulme. The judge
told the director of the company that they shouldn't have
taken the word of one so young. Particularly one who
had suffered such high levels of stress by having to nurse
his sick and failing mother. That's how me and cousin
Maurice were eventually able to afford this old shack
and how I was able to travel the world and see wondrous
things."
"I'm lost for words," said the Chairman. "I'm
completely lost for words. I can't believe you sat by and
watched your poor mother die in such a horrible way."
"I didn't just sit by Mr Hulme," said the Professor. "I
finished my sandwich and then masturbated for a good
half hour."
"My God!" said the Chairman. "You're deranged."

[803]

"Why's that Mr Hulme?" said the Professor.

"Because you repeatedly cause people's deaths and then plead innocence," said the Chairman.

"I am innocent," said the Professor. "I didn't drive the bulldozer. I didn't neglect to carry out the essential inspection of the condemned property prior to its demolition."

"Are you prepared to admit it was you that caused most of the trouble on the train?" said the Chairman.

"Do you mean the root cause?" said the Professor.

"I suppose I do yes," said the Chairman.

"In that case, your predecessor must take the blame," said the Professor.

"My predecessor," said the Chairman. "Do you mean Tommy Weir?"

"The rather imposing grey haired chap," said the Professor.

"That's nonsense," said the Chairman. "That's utter nonsense. Tommy Weir was dead before most of the problems started."

"Tommy Weir ordered your men to carry me on board the train after I'd fallen," said the Professor. "Had he not done that, there would have been no little old me. There would have been no fly in the ointment or tormentor in chief, so to speak."

"And therefore, no phantom disease and so on and so on," said the Chairman.

"And don't forget this Mr Hulme," said the Professor. "Your previous Chairman Tommy Weir was the first to suggest your much lamented friend Morris might be to blame for stopping the train. He and he alone came up with that supposition. Think about that Mr Hulme. Think about the sequence of events that took place after he'd planted that seed in the minds of your members. If he'd dropped a hand grenade in the middle of the dining carriage, he wouldn't have caused any more chaos."

"I don't believe you," said the Chairman. "I just don't believe you. I've never known anyone manipulate the truth like you."

"Thank you very much," said the Professor.

"That wasn't meant as praise," said the Chairman. "But while we're on the subject of the dining carriage, would you mind updating me on the condition of the surviving passengers."

"You mean your brother don't you?" said the Professor.

"I mean all of them," said the Chairman.

"I bet you do," said the smirking Professor. "They're absolutely fine, if you must know."

"Are you sure Professor?" said the Chairman.

"I'm positive," said the Professor. "They were playing gin rummy when I decided to do my emotional impression of the much vaunted Captain Oates."

"Thank God for that," said the Chairman before lowering his head.

"But I think it's only fair to warn you, they'll probably all be dead within the next 12 hours," said the Professor.

"What!" said the advancing Chairman before suddenly becoming aware of Albert's presence. "What's wrong with them Professor?"

"I've had to euthanize them," said the Professor.

"You've had to do what?" said the Chairman.

"I've put them out of their misery," said the Professor. "They'd run out of food you see Mr Hulme. There was nothing but a tiny pork joint left."

"I thought there was plenty of food," said the Chairman.

"There was until the last of it became contaminated," said the Professor.

"Contaminated!" said the Chairman. "Contaminated with what?"

"The disease," said the Professor. "They couldn't dump the food quick enough after I'd alerted them to that possibility."

"You evil bastard," said the Chairman. "What about tinned produce."

"There was no tinned produce," said the Professor. "If I remember right, your intrepid band of plucky volunteers took the last of the canned goods. That's right isn't it Mr Hulme?"

[805]

"It is unfortunately," said the Chairman. "Did none of them think about doing the obvious thing and following me, Tommy and Hilly?"

"That had been their plan until I provided them with some vital life extending sustenance," said the Professor. "What sort of sustenance?" said the Chairman.

"Some very special Champagne," said the Professor.

"Champagne!" said the Chairman. "What was so very special about it?"

"It contains ten times the calorie content of normal Champagne," said the Professor. "In other words, if an egg cup full of normal Champagne could sustain a man for a day, an egg cup full of my special Champagne would easily keep that same man going for 10."

"What else was special about it?" said the Chairman.

"It was laced with toxic chemicals under the guise of a sleep component," said the Professor. "I had to mention the sleep component to all and sundry in case the other passengers began to suspect something was untoward after watching the first recipient of the formula nod off. The oblivious Mr Hewlett helped me mix it."

"And the poor buggers fell for it hook, line and sinker," said the Chairman.

"As was always the case," said the Professor. "They're going to toast their families and lost friends and drink the stuff together at midnight."

"You evil, cold, calculated man," said the Chairman. "You twisted old fucker. You murderous bastard."

"Murderous!" said the Professor. "How dare you. Don't you dare intimate such a horrible thing. Where on earth have you got that idea from Mr Hulme?"

"From you," said the Chairman. "I got it straight from the lunatic's mouth. You've just told me you've poisoned the last of my fellow club members."

"I know I did," said the Professor. "But I haven't killed them Mr Hulme. That would be callous of me. I've just put them to sleep for a time. The starving wild animals, that will inevitably come calling will ultimately finish them off."

"I strongly recommend you leave Mr Hulme," said the Major. "I think you've already offended my friend the Professor enough."

"It's alright Henry," said the Professor. "It must be hard for the man. After all, it's not every day you realise you no longer have any friends."

"I'd rather have none than count you as one," said the Chairman.

"That's not nice," said the Professor.

"Do you know your way out Mr Hulme?" said the Major.

"I'll find it," said the Chairman.

"Why don't you wait and tell your sorry tale to the police," said the Professor.

"What police?" said the Chairman.

"Just leave Mr Hulme," said the Major.

"I will Major," said the Chairman. "I just want to know what the Professor's talking about first. What police are you referring to Professor."

"For goodness sake, will you just go," said the Major.

"I'm talking about the Colonel's dinner guests," said the Professor.

"And they're police officers are they?" said the Chairman.

"One's an Inspector, the other's his Sergeant," said the Professor. "Listen.....that's them arriving now. It sounds like they've already been hitting the booze quite hard."

"Mr Hulme, I strongly recommend you leave now," said the Major.

"I'm going nowhere," said the Chairman before removing a dining chair and heading over to the area of the writing desk. "I think the next half hour is going to prove interesting."

"Those men will have been drinking Mr Hulme," said the Major. "Why don't you leave and make arrangements to contact their office tomorrow?"

"I don't want to," said the Chairman. "I want to sort this situation out now. By the way Major, did you know

[807]

my good friend Brian Matthews has been murdered."

"Murdered!" said the Professor. "Goodness me Mr Hulme. You seem to have murder constantly on your mind. Are you sure you haven't been reading too much Agatha Christie?"

"I heard it happen through the downstairs vent," said the Chairman. "I heard the voices and I heard the shots."

"Did somebody mention shots?" said a smiling, well dressed bean pole of a man before heading over to the Professor and shaking him warmly by the hand. "Nice to see you Major. How are the haemorrhoids?"

"They're in retreat, as we speak Inspector," said the Major.

"That's excellent," said the Inspector. "You've met young Joe Hayes haven't you?"

"I think so," said the Major while slowly approaching the table. "Did you drive here gentlemen?"

"We were chauffeured," said the Inspector.

"Chauffeured!" said the Major. "Which unlucky sod pulled that filthy beggar of a duty?"

"One of our new female recruits," said the Inspector.

"Wait until you see the chassis on her Major."

"Do you think she'd run me into town Inspector?" said the Chairman.

"I very much doubt it," said the Inspector while proceeding to regard the Chairman with a certain amount of suspicion.

"Why not?" said the Chairman. "I'm a citizen in trouble and I'm appealing to the police for help."

"You're likely to be a citizen in trouble with me if you don't hush your mouth," said the Inspector.

"Did I hear raised voices?" said the late arriving Colonel before taking his familiar chair.

"It's one of your lags Colonel," said the Inspector. "The audacious rapscallion wants a ride out of here."

"I imagine they all do," said the confused looking Colonel while fidgeting with his right sleeve.

"Is there a problem Maurice?" said the Inspector.

"I appear to have mislaid my timepiece," said the

Colonel.

"You're always losing things," said the Major. "It'll turn up somewhere."

"My spectacles have vanished too," said the Colonel.

"They're on your head," said the Major.

"So they are," said the Colonel.

"Tell me Inspector-are you still on good terms with our local environmental health officer?" said the Professor.

"I'm on reasonable terms with the man," said the Inspector. "I'm on better terms with his comely and buxom young wife. Why do you ask?"

"We had a distasteful incident earlier," said the Professor.

"What sort of incident?" said the Inspector.

"We found a rat running amok," said the Colonel. "A huge bloody great thing it was. It was about the size of a grown man."

"It was the size of a grown man because it *was* a grown man," said the Chairman.

"A man!" said the Sergeant while very obviously stifling the urge to laugh.

"He was a good friend of mine," said the Chairman.

"The rat was?" said the Inspector.

"He was a man," said the Chairman. "His face had been painted to make him look like a rat. The Colonel mistook him for the mythical giant bandicoot. That's why he shot him."

"Is that right Colonel?" said the Inspector while helping himself to a brandy. "Did you get the dirty, diseased thing?"

"I got him right between the eyes," said the Colonel.

"Good for you," said the Inspector. "You don't want vermin infesting your lovely, palatial home."

"You couldn't be more right," said the Professor.

"We suffered a tragic loss the other day," said the Colonel while urging his guests to help themselves to drinks.

"Oh dear," said the Inspector. "Was it anyone I knew?"

"It was Mr Bimoko," said the Chairman. "The

Colonel's much vaunted head of security."

"Head of what?" said the Inspector.

"He was the Colonel's much loved and respected head of security," said the Chairman.

"Are you talking about 'the' Bimoko?" said the smiling Inspector while holding his glass up to the light.

"That's right," said the Chairman.

"And are you aware that Bimoko's a baboon?" said the Inspector.

"To you he is," said the Chairman.

"To the rest of the sane and rational world he is," said the Inspector. "Now go and do a piano or cello recital or something. I assume that's why you're here. Why is he here Colonel? Why is this man here? What's his function?"

"I'm not sure," said the Colonel. "He looks vaguely familiar though."

"He will look familiar-he's one of your recent loony intake," said the Inspector.

"I look familiar because for the last few days, me and the Colonel have drunk copious brandies and shared stories together," said the Chairman. "Look at me Colonel. Try to remember me. I sat right there where Sergeant Hayes is now. You told me about safaris and poachers and all sort of things."

"That's right," said the Colonel after a brief hesitation. "I've got you now. You're my old doctor."

"Doctor!" said the Inspector.

"I'm not a doctor," said the exasperated Chairman.

"He's being modest," said the Colonel. "He's one of the finest field doctors I've ever seen operate. He recently removed a bullet from the back passage of one of my men while we were under heavy fire. But for the life of me, I can't remember who that individual was now. Help me here doctor. Who was it? Tell the Inspector."

"It wasn't really...." said the Chairman.

"Just tell the Inspector," said the Colonel after hammering his fist against the table. "Who was it damn you?"

"Sergeant Carruthers," mumbled the Chairman.

"That's him," said the Colonel. "That's the very chap."

"When was this?" said the Inspector.

"A couple of days ago," said the Chairman.

"A couple of days!" said the Inspector.

"Yes," said the Colonel.

"But that's not possible," said the Inspector.

"Carruthers passed away about 3 years ago, didn't he?
I'm pretty damn sure I attended the man's funeral."

"That's what I thought," said the Colonel. "But a
couple of days ago, that man over there, claimed he'd
removed a bullet from Caruthers's rear passage."

"I didn't," said the increasingly flustered Chairman. "It
was....Oh God in Heaven!"

"Tell me something doctor-are you qualified to perform
surgery," said the Inspector.

"Of course not," said the Chairman. "I've never
claimed to be a doctor. Come on Inspector-you know
the Colonel better than me. He's a very old man. He's
getting confused."

"And so am I," said the Inspector. "Why don't you start
from the beginning and tell me how you got here."

"I'd be only too pleased to," said the Chairman. "It's
probably the only way we're going to get to the truth.
I'm a visitor Inspector. I'm a visitor that came across
this house by chance. I'm the Chairman of a veteran
amateur football club from Merseyside. Our train
stopped not too far from here."

"What train was that?" said the Inspector. "And
Sergeant-it might be an idea if you start taking a few
notes."

"Right away sir," said the Sergeant.

"He claims he came on the Orient Express," said the
Professor.

"Really!" said the Inspector. "That is interesting.
Would that be the Venice Simplon Orient Express?"

"I think so," said the Chairman. "I don't really know."

"Do you realise what you're saying-I'm sorry-what's

[811]

your name again?" said the Inspector.

"Hulme," said the Chairman. "My full name's Kenny Hulme."

"Really!" said the Inspector.

"Yes, really," said the Chairman. "What's the problem?"

"Denny Hulme's dead," said the Inspector. "I was a massive fan of the flying Kiwi. I watched him beaten a second by Jack Brabham at Brands Hatch in the late sixties. Denny Hulme hey. This is an unexpected pleasure indeed."

"For me too," said the Professor. "I'm a big fan of motor racing."

"You misheard me Inspector," said the Chairman. "I said, 'Kenny Hulme'."

"That's what I thought he said," said the Sergeant.

"You carry on with your notes," said the Inspector. "And try to make them legible for once. Anyway, Denny-I mean Kenny....let me get back to the point. Are you claiming to have travelled here aboard the Orient Express?"

"I'd swear to it on my two children's lives," said the Chairman.

"Where did you depart from?" said the Inspector.

"London," said the Chairman.

"Alright," said the Inspector. "That would make sense. And where were you bound?"

"Selkirk," said the Chairman.

"Selkirk!" said the Inspector. "And would that be Selkirk in Scotland?"

"That's right," said the Chairman. "But we got stranded not far from here."

"That's a shame," said the Inspector. "That really is a crying shame. I want you to listen to me very carefully Mr Hulme. I've actually travelled on the Orient Express a fair number of times. Which means I'm more than a little familiar with the route it follows. But while I agree you can board the train in London, I assure you, the Orient Express never has and probably never will, head north to Scotland."

"Maybe the driver took a wrong turn," said the Professor while attending to the fire.

"We didn't have a driver," said the Chairman.

"I beg your pardon!" said the Inspector.

"We didn't have a driver," said the Chairman. "The Professor controlled the train from a console."

"A console!" said the Inspector. "What exactly is a console?"

"It's like a little box," said the Chairman. "It has buttons and things you have to press."

"Is this right Seymour?" said the Inspector.

"It's absolute balderdash," said the Professor. "He must be talking about my new Bakelite cigarette case. That's got a couple of buttons. I'll say this for the man. He's got one hell of an imagination. His mind must never stop. He must be mentally exhausted."

"It's a shame isn't it," said the Inspector. "Such a bloody awful shame."

"The only shame here, is in the fact that you're allowing certain people to distort the truth Inspector," said the Chairman. "Why don't you come with me to the basement and I'll show you something that might be of interest to you."

"Show me what?" said the Inspector.

"Some human remains," said the Chairman.

"Human remains!" said the Sergeant.

"That's right," said the Chairman.

"Do you happen to know who they belonged to?" said the Inspector.

"I do but I'd rather not reveal that at this point," said the Chairman.

"And I must insist you do," said the Inspector.

"Otherwise, I'm not interested in your claim. Whose remains are they Mr Hulme?"

"Can we step outside the door and I'll tell you?" said the Chairman.

"No we certainly cannot," said the Inspector. "You can tell me here, where I'm among friends and feel relatively

safe. Whose remains do you think they are?"
"The Major's son," whispered the Chairman after
drawing a deep breath.
"Whose son?" said the Inspector.
"The Major's," said the Chairman after lowering his
head. "They belong to his son Casper."
"Casper!" said the Inspector.
"I think you'll find he's talking about Casper Howser,"
said the Professor.
"That's right," said the increasingly excited Chairman
upon leaving his chair. "You know about them. You
know about those remains don't you Professor?"
"I know about Kasper Hauser," said the Professor. "But
why don't you begin first Mr Hulme. Why don't you
tell us what you know about our mysterious Mr Hauser."
"There's not much to tell," said the Chairman. "I know
he came here to visit the Major and was never seen
again. I know he'd done very well for himself prior to
his visit. I know he'd bought property. I know he'd
studied in Germany for a time."
"Where about in Germany?" said the Professor.
"Nuremberg I think," said the Chairman. "Why don't
you ask the Major."
"I want nothing to do with this," said the Major before
wheeling away to his desk.
"I do," said the Professor. "Because I know what's
going on."
"And what's that exactly?" said the Inspector.
"Mr Hulme is a fantasist of the highest order," said the
Professor. "That's probably why he was brought here
in the first place. Tell me Inspector-are you a cowboy?"
"Of course not," said the bemused Inspector.
"Where you ever a cowboy?" said the Professor.
"Never," said the Inspector. "I've been a member of the
constabulary all my adult life. I did play at being a
cowboy when I was a kid."
"Can you remember how it felt to be a cowboy?" said
the Professor.
"Now you're asking," said the Inspector. "I suppose it

was exciting. It was certainly a lot of fun."

"Who was your cowboy of choice?" said the Professor.

"The Lone Ranger," said the Inspector. "Every time. I was in awe of the man. "

"When did you cease being the Lone Ranger Inspector?" said the Professor.

"At the end of each game," said the Inspector.

"Like most normal people," said the Professor.

"But not like the supreme fantasist Mr Hulme. Did you ever read a Marvel comic and imagine you had superpowers Inspector?"

"I suppose I did yes," said the Inspector. "Didn't most young boys?"

"I'd presume so," said the Professor. "I used to imagine I was Superman. I used to imagine I could fly. But the thing is Inspector, unlike our Mr Hulme-I knew being Superman was only a temporary guise and not reality."

"I knew that too," said the Chairman.

"I don't believe you did," said the Professor. "I'll bet you a pound to a penny, you've read the Agatha Christie novel about the murder on the famous Venice Simplon train."

"I haven't," said the Chairman.

"You must have seen the film then," said the Professor.

"I have yes," said the Chairman.

"Of course you have," said the Professor. "That's why you're convinced you've travelled on the Orient Express."

"I have travelled on it," said the Chairman.

"Only in your mind Mr Hulme," said the Professor.

"What part did you play Mr Hulme?"

"I played myself," said the Chairman.

"I very much doubt it," said the Professor. "I bet you cast yourself as the famous crime solving detective, Hercule Poirot? I imagine you'd have had to be him. He's the only one that does anything remotely heroic. That's what the supreme fantasist does Inspector. They attach themselves to their heroes in much the same way a limpet attaches itself to a rock."

[815]

"Is that why you think he's fabricated the story about the human remains?" said the Inspector. "Do you think that's got its roots in something he's seen or read?"
"I've no doubt it has," said the Professor. "Let's be honest Inspector-the story about that so-called friend of his who turned into a rat could well have its origins in the classic Robert Louis Stevenson novel, where the doctor turns into a sort of wild animal."
"That would be Doctor Jekyll and Mr Hyde," said the Inspector. "That's the one," said the Professor. "Or even one of those trite and ubiquitous werewolf movies."
"What about the human remains he claims he's found?" said the Inspector. "What are their origin? Where's he mustered that story from?"
"I haven't mustered it from anywhere," said the Chairman. "They very definitely exist. They're lying waiting to be discovered in one of those basement cells."
"You're lying Mr Hulme," said the Professor. "Those remains are a product of your over fertile imagination. That story could have derived from any number of Gothic Horror books or films. Although, I'm now beginning to think it runs a little deeper than that."
"What do you mean?" said the Inspector.
"I think our Mr Hulme might have progressed to more factual and intellectual stuff," said the Professor.
"What makes you think that?" said the Inspector.
"Because, in referring to a young lad who once turned up here out of the blue, he was almost certainly talking about somebody who did actually exist," said the Professor.
"The Major's son did exist," said the Chairman.
"You be quiet Mr Hulme," said the Inspector. "Who was he Professor?"
"A young chap called Kasper Hauser," said the Professor. "That's Casper with a 'K', by the way Sergeant. He's a well known figure in German and Hungarian history. He had links with Nuremberg too. And funnily enough he was a confirmed histrionic and

fantasist himself."

"I've never heard that story," said the Chairman.

"And I beg to differ," said the Professor.

"I do too," said the Inspector. "I'm beginning to wonder whether Hulme's his real name."

"It's not his real name," said the Colonel.

"Oh Jesus Christ!" said the Chairman.

"I beg your pardon Colonel," said the Inspector.

"That man you're referring to is called Holmes," said the Colonel. "I recall him introducing himself to me now. He's Mr Holmes."

"Oh for God's sake!" said the Chairman to himself before turning to face the window.

"Did you say 'Mr Holmes' Colonel?" said the Inspector.

"That's right," said the Colonel.

"We're back in the world of best selling fiction," said the Professor.

"We're back in the world of insanity," said the Chairman.

"Are we talking about Holmes, as in the famous detective Sherlock Holmes?" said the Inspector.

"I'd have certainly thought so," said the Professor.

"Bloody hell," said the Inspector while scratching his head. "I think I'm going to have to take one of my tablets."

"I seem to recall him telling me about a gigantic hound that had stalked him as far as the boundary wall," said the Colonel.

"It was a pack of hounds," said the Chairman.

"They must have been the Hounds of the Baskervilles!" laughed the Inspector while clutching his chest. "Did he say whether they were covered in phosphorous?"

"I think he might have done," said the Colonel.

"Oh God!" said the Chairman under his breath.

"I wonder where his sidekick Watson is," said the Professor.

"Watson arrived with him," said the Colonel. "He's gone missing since. An ex army chap he was. Built like a brick outhouse. You wouldn't want to mess with that particular fellow."

"Albert had little trouble putting him away," said the Chairman while approaching the table with a scrap of paper. "Phone my wife please Sergeant. Take this number down. Take it down very carefully. Just ask her to confirm my name, departure point and where I was meant to be heading. In fact, ask her to confirm my middle name."

"Why's that?" said the Inspector.

"Because only me, her and my big brother know what it is," said the Chairman.

"What's *her* name-Mary Poppins?" said the Professor.

"That's a good one," laughed the Inspector.

"Her name's Ruth," said the Chairman. "Phone her please Sergeant. And please hurry."

"I'm on to it," said the Sergeant.

"She'll confirm everything I've told you," said the Chairman. "Unless you want to go and talk to Mr Spendlove and Miss Havisham."

"And ask them what exactly?" said the Inspector.

"Whether I'm a visitor or not," said the Chairman.

"Are they the best you can do as regard character witnesses?" said the Inspector.

"They are as it happens," said the Chairman. "I trust them implicitly."

"Jesus Christ!" said the Inspector. "Trust them implicitly! The last time I was here, the queer one was inconsolable. She'd been left standing at the aisle."

"She must have been reading Great Expectations," said the Professor.

"Go and ask Mr Spendlove to vouch for me then," said the Chairman. "He'll even tell you the name of the town I've come from."

"He's no better than the literature weirdo who lives next to him," said the Inspector.

"He's a great man," said the Chairman. "He gave up everything he had to be here close to his wife."

"A wife he insists has turned into a cat," said the Inspector. "He's not credible Mr Hulme."

[818]

"He's more than credible," said the Chairman. "His wife does think she's a cat. I've seen her swallow a live rat whole. That man's the nearest thing to a living Angel I've ever come across."

"Which would make him the Angel Gabriel," laughed the Professor.

"That's very good Seymour," said the Inspector. "And on Christmas Day too. We only need a few wise men, a number of shepherds and we've got ourselves a nativity play."

"I could be Joseph," said the Sergeant. "After all-that is actually my name."

"You can be Joseph then," said the Inspector. "Have you had any success with that phone call Sergeant?"

"In a manner of speaking, yes," said the Sergeant while scribbling frantically.

"Did you speak to his wife?" said the Inspector.

"I spoke to his ex wife," said the Sergeant.

"What do you mean, 'ex wife'?" said the Chairman.

"She said she's no longer got a husband," said the Sergeant. "She said her husband's dead."

"He's dead?" said the Inspector.

"That's what she told me," said the Sergeant.

"Oh deary, deary me," said the Professor.

"She's angry," said the Chairman. "The woman's angry because I'm not there for Christmas dinner and I haven't been in touch to explain why. Did she know my middle name?"

"She did yes," said the Sergeant. "She said it was Scott."

"Thank God for that," said the Chairman. "Take a look for yourself Inspector. Take a look at that scrap of paper and tell me what I've written."

"I've already looked," said the Inspector. "But I've got to be honest-I'm no less confused."

"Why's that?" said the Chairman.

"Because Scott was Sherlock Holmes's middle name," said the Inspector.

"No way!" said the Chairman. "No bloody way.

You've made that up."

"It's a fact," said the Professor. "Not a well known one, but a fact nevertheless."

"Who exactly are you?" said the Inspector.

"I've told you who I am," said the Chairman. "And if you wait around long enough, the Colonel will start to recall things."

"I'm already recalling things," said the Colonel. "You got yourself lost didn't you?"

"I did yes," said the Chairman.

"I've got you now," said the Colonel. "You're the commodore of a club of some sort."

"Oh thank God," said the Chairman before punching the air. "I'm the Chairman actually. What else can you remember Colonel? Can you remember me sitting at this table as your welcome guest?"

"I can remember that vividly," said the Colonel. "I think you complemented me on my piano playing."

"That's right," said the Chairman. "It was very impressive."

"We had a fair old drink together, didn't we?" said the Colonel.

"You drank me under the table," said the Chairman.

"That's right, I did," said the Colonel. "I had to get Albert to put you to bed. I think he put you in the wrong room, if I remember right. They were smashing times. It's just a pity things turned sour between us."

"In what way Colonel?" said the Inspector.

"He wasn't the respectable gentleman he first appeared to be," said the Colonel.

"What do you mean Colonel?" said the Professor.

"He started doing bad things," said the Colonel.

"I beg your pardon Colonel!" said the Chairman.

"What sort of bad things?" said the Inspector.

"He shouted at me and used all manner of profanities," said the Colonel.

"Did he really," said the Inspector. "What for?"

"Because Albert had fucked up," said the Chairman. "He'd mistaken me for an inmate and ice bathed and

[820]

deloused me without so much as a by your leave. I was
livid. I'd never been so livid. Wouldn't any innocent
man be?"

"I suppose so," said the Inspector.

"I certainly would be," said the Sergeant.

"But we'd shaken hands after that," said the Chairman.

"We had yes," said the Colonel. "But then you started
stealing from me."

"What!" said the Chairman.

"Stealing what exactly?" said the Inspector.

"My silver," said the Colonel.

"I'd taken one knife," said the Chairman. "You've seen
that garden Inspector. It's like an East African nature
reserve. It's a whole world of trouble. I had to have
some sort of protection if I was going to head into it
again."

"What else did he take?" said the Inspector.

"A pair of old rifles," said the Colonel. "And then one
of my coats. And I'd actually turned a blind eye to that.
But the watch was something quite different."

"Are you saying he stole your watch?" said the
Inspector.

"Absolutely," said the Colonel upon baring his right
forearm.

"I did not steal your watch," said the Chairman.

"But you do admit to stealing the rifles?" said the
Inspector.

"Me and my companion stashed a pair of rifles to aid our
escape," said the Chairman. "For the same reason I felt
the need to take the knife."

"What about the watch?" said the Inspector.

"I don't know what he's talking about," said the
Chairman.

"You guttersnipe!" said the Colonel. "How dare you lie
to my face. I've just seen the watch face shimmer when
your sleeve flicked up."

"You probably did," said the Chairman. "But I didn't
steal it Colonel. I didn't steal the thing. You gave it to
me. As God is my judge, you gave me it as a Christmas

present. Here-have it back if it means that much to you."
"A Christmas present, you say!" said the Inspector upon
moving forward and slipping the watch from the
Chairman's wrist. "This is some Christmas present.
Have you any idea how much a watch like this is worth
Mr Holmes?"
"I've got a reasonable idea," said the Chairman. "I
know it's worth thousands rather than hundreds."
"And are you still claiming you were given it?" said the
Inspector.
"I *was* given it," said the Chairman. "Why do you
doubt me Inspector?"
"Because it doesn't make sense," said the Inspector. "It
makes no sense at all. How long have you known the
Colonel?"
"A few days," sighed the Chairman.
"A few days!" said the Inspector. "That was some act
of generosity then, wasn't it."
"I know it was," said the Chairman. "But what was I
meant to do?"
"Give it back," said the Inspector.
"I tried to," said the Chairman. "I tried to give it back."
"Is that right Colonel?" said the Inspector.
"It's stuff and nonsense," said the Colonel while helping
himself to another drink. "That man's nothing but a
mountebank and hoodwinker. And I'll tell you
something else that might interest you Inspector."
"What's that?" said the Inspector.
"He tried to swipe the Major's wallet while he was fast
asleep," said the Colonel.
"Is that true Mr Hulme?" said the Inspector."
"It is and it isn't," said the Chairman.
"Which is it then?" said the Inspector.
"The wallet belonged to my friend Tommy," said the
Chairman. "But don't ask me to produce Tommy as a
witness to that statement because he's dead. In fact, he's
a bit more than dead. He's been turned into a
scarecrow."
"A scarecrow!" said the Sergeant.

[822]

"Don't bother asking him to explain," said the
Inspector. "I've heard enough. The man's a complete
and utter nutcase."
"That's what I've concluded too," said the Professor.
"Why doesn't that surprise me?" said the Chairman.
"What are you going to do now Professor-sit on a hill
with an egg butty and masturbate to your heart's
content?"
"I'm going to enjoy my Christmas dinner," said the
Professor. "And by the way, thank you Mr Hulme."
"For what?" said the Chairman.
"For entertaining us," said the Professor. "We normally
have to listen to Matilda sing carols or that freak
Spendlove play his boring cello. Your performance has
been the best ever."
"Was it deserving of a reward?" said the visibly
trembling Chairman.
"Most definitely," said the Professor.
"Then allow me to leave," said the Chairman.
"You can leave any time you want," said the Professor.
"Really?" said the Chairman.
"Yes, really," said the Professor. "You're a supreme
fantasist Mr Hulme. You can enter a different world or
dimension at the blink of an eye. You can be anyone you
want to be and any place you want to be. It's called
escapism."
"That's not what I meant?" said the Chairman. "Can I
leave please Professor?"
"I wouldn't have thought so," said the Inspector before
seizing the Chairman and twisting his right arm behind
his back. "At least not for a good few years. Is there
anything you want to say to this miscreant before we
take him down to your cells Colonel?"
"Not really," said the Colonel. "I'll just open a
window."
"Open a window!" said the Inspector.
"It means he's disgusted with me to the point of wanting
to throw up," said the Chairman.
"He's not alone," said the Inspector. "What about you

[823]

Professor? You must feel betrayed too."

"I do as it happens," said the Professor. "But I'm not one to hold a grudge. To be honest, I'm more interested in looking at the poor man's legs."

"Why's that?" said the Inspector.

"He took a really heavy fall earlier while in the basement," said the Professor after slowly dropping to his knees and rolling up the Chairman's trouser leg. "And I don't like the look of this redness and swelling."

"It doesn't look swollen to me," said the Inspector.

"You need a trained eye," said the Professor.

"Oh my God!" said the Chairman after being forced to the floor. "For pity's sake, Inspector. The evil bastard's going to take my legs. Stop him Inspector. This is madness. For pity's sake, stop him. I'm a visitor, I'm telling you. Phone my wife again Sergeant. Let me speak to her. Will you listen to me. My train got stuck not far from here. As God is my witness, I'm a visitor."

END OF BOOK ONE

AVAILABLE SOON FROM K.D.P.

IN THE PRESENCE OF MADNESS

BOOK TWO

Printed in Great Britain
by Amazon

49387529R00470